TIME CHASER

A LITRPG ADVENTURE

RICK GUALTIERI

Copyright © 2024 Rick Gualtieri

No part of this book may be reproduced or transmitted in any form or by any means, electronic or mechanical, including photocopying, recording, or any information storage and retrieval system, without prior written permission of the author. In addition, no part of this book may be used for machine learning or to train artificial intelligence, language models, or similar technologies without the prior written permission of the author. Your support of authors' rights is greatly appreciated.

All characters in this novel are fictitious. Any resemblance to actual persons, living or dead, is purely coincidental. The use of any real company and/or product names is for literary effect only. All other trademarks and copyrights are the property of their respective owners.

Cover by Damonza

Interior Illustration by Urgh

Published by Freewill Press

Visit the author at:
www.rickgualtieri.com

For Tony, Cabot, Mike, Kurt, Paul, and Greg. Never stop rolling those crits, guys ... and probably those fumbles too.

A big shoutout of thanks to my Patreon crew: Ashley, Rachel C, Chris, Allen, Jen, Blix, Sean, Benoit, RE Carr, Mark, Derek, Eric, Stephanie, Vinny, James, Randal, MRB, Sandra, Stephen, Jeff, James, Angela, Simon, Lee, & Tina!

1

GOING, GOING, GONE

So, this is how I die. Oh well, maybe it's for the best.

That's the thought that flew through my head as the bus's grill loomed ever larger in my sight.

Guess that whole saying about one's life flashing before their eyes at the very end was bullshit after all. I honestly couldn't say whether that was a good thing or not. I suppose it all depended on the highlight reel. If fate was fair and showed one a proper mix of highlights and downsides that might not be too bad. But in my case I had a feeling destiny would've been a dick and forced me to relive every moment in which life decided to cock-punch me while I was already down.

Outside of that, I was aware of only three other things: the screech of brakes applied far too late, anticipating how much this was probably going to hurt, and the distant sense of relief that while my death didn't feel fair or deserved – at least my ordeal was finally over.

Turns out I was *dead* wrong, at least on those last two, lucky me.

But we'll get to that soon enough.

Anyway, the accident was my own damned fault. I was

Time Chaser

coming off the worst month of my life and was simply too beaten down to pay proper attention.

One month – to go from a place of happiness and stability to absolute rock bottom.

It had all started normally enough. I had just gotten back from ParaDocx – the largest business software convention on the East Coast. Drakkensoft, the company I worked for, hosted a booth there. As a senior software manager I was expected to attend – not exactly a hardship as it was typically four days spent hobnobbing over drinks with potential clients.

Alas, the con itself had been nothing to write home about this year. With the economy on a downswing, those daring to brave the vendor room had made it a point to keep their enthusiasm in check and their budgets tightly guarded.

On the upside, at least the drive back had been quick. I'd managed to miss the traffic that seemed to perpetually snarl D.C. and Maryland, so I was about an hour ahead of schedule.

At the time I had thought it a stroke of good luck.

The first sign that things were amiss was the unfamiliar car sitting in the driveway of my modest split level home in Manahawkin, New Jersey. Then I spotted my son Jeremy. He was out front playing, tooling up and down the sidewalk in one of those battery-operated Jeeps.

It was a toy I distinctly remembered vetoing this past Christmas, both due to its price and the fickleness of children and their playthings – but mostly because of the cost. I mean, call me crazy. I loved my son more than anything in this world, but spending hundreds on a single toy for a five-year-old just felt excessive.

Deb hadn't been happy about that, but in the end she'd come around to my way of thinking, or so I had thought.

I stepped out of my aging Honda and greeted him. "Hey, Champ."

"Hiya, Daddy!" he'd called back, puttering toward me at a

solid three miles an hour. "Look what Uncle Manny bought for me! I can drive so fast!"

In retrospect, those two sentences were the beginning of the end of my tiny little slice of suburban happiness.

It probably comes as no surprise, but Jeremy didn't have an uncle named Manny – especially one with face-sitting privileges where my wife was concerned.

I had no idea how long their affair had been going on for or how long it would've continued had they not been caught. The only thing I was certain of was that Deb had planned for this inevitability, because the very next day divorce papers were delivered to my desk at work.

She was even shameless enough to list the reason for it as infidelity ... *on my part*, citing my semi-frequent business trips, as if I'd ever done more than spend my days at them hawking finance software.

Talk about fucking ballsy.

It was all a lie, of course, her way of throwing her own indiscretion back in my face. Sadly, it was also her word against mine. I had no real proof to the contrary and she knew it. As for her own dalliances, the only witness in my favor was Jeremy, and she was no doubt counting on the fact that I wasn't about to force my own kid to go in front of a judge and proclaim his mom a whore.

The whole thing was fucking insane. It was like coming home to a completely different reality than I'd left. Too bad it only got worse from there.

Within the space of a day the locks on our house were changed, my stuff had been dumped on the front yard, and I discovered our joint account was now empty – all before I'd barely given a passing thought to finding a lawyer of my own.

Sure, things had occasionally been rocky for us over the course of our eight-year marriage, but I'd never once imagined it had been this bad.

Time Chaser

Maybe I'd been blind to the truth, or simply an optimistic fool.

Oh, and just to throw even more salt into the wound, Deb was seeking full custody of Jeremy too. Yeah, the claws were out and she was fully prepared to use me as her personal scratching post.

It wasn't until sometime later that I finally began to suspect the truth behind her actions, the real cause that had set these events in motion. Sadly, by then it was of no help to me. Deb had been playing it crafty, far more than I would've given her credit for, or at least her land shark of a lawyer was.

My downward spiral wasn't complete yet, though.

Allan, my boss at Drakkensoft, wasn't entirely unsympathetic to my plight, but he downplayed everything – treating my crumbling life like it was a minor inconvenience, no more. With the company hurting for new customers, there was only so much leeway he was willing to give me.

It was the span of three weeks for me to be called into HR and threatened with a performance plan. I probably didn't help my case by sitting there in a distracted fog for most of it.

By then that seemed to be my new normal, just going about my days barely cognizant of what was happening lest someone shiv me in the heart again.

It should therefore come as no surprise when I say it was that same brain fog that led to my untimely demise.

I was walking out of my lawyer's office after listening to him tell me all the ways I could expect to be fucked in the ass in the coming months. While Deb had retained the legal services of a school of piranha wearing a human skin suit, I'd ended up with a well-meaning hack who mostly advised me to give her everything she wanted in the hope of maybe getting one weekend a month with Jeremy.

Mentally drained, I'd walked right past my car, hoping to clear my head before heading back to the shitty, low-budget meth motel I now called home.

Time Chaser

I probably should've tried harder because three blocks later I stepped off the curb, not realizing the light was against me.

The next thing I knew, a bus was bearing down on me like a soccer mom tearing ass to be first in line for a Black Friday sale.

"Shit on toast," I muttered as my death loomed large before me.

As far as epic last words went, I probably could've done better.

⌛⌛⌛⌛ ·≈··≈··≈··≈· ⌛⌛⌛⌛

The words had barely left my lips when I blinked, only to find the bus was now gone. It didn't swerve out of the way or stop. It had simply vanished. One second it was there – so close I could've finger-flicked the headlight. The next, there was nothing, and I mean that with a capital N. Turning my head, I realized the bus, the crosswalk, and even the street had all disappeared.

The fuck?

I found myself standing on bare dirt in what appeared to be a forest clearing. Somehow, I was surrounded on all sides by trees and thick vegetation. I could see maybe twenty feet in any direction before my line of sight was blocked by a literal wall of lush greenery.

The scenery wasn't all that had changed. Seconds earlier, it had been about fifty-five degrees – relatively balmy for New Jersey in late March – but now it had to be approaching ninety. I peeled off my jacket even as I was still trying to process this inexplicable change in my surroundings.

What the hell had happened? Was I dead? Had it simply happened so fast that I hadn't even felt the impact? If so, then did that make this place the afterl...

"***Welcome, chaser!***" a cheerful voice called out, shattering the silence.

I looked around but there was nothing to be seen save for the abundant plant life. "Um, hello? Is someone there?"

"*Of course. You are! And I dare say, you are one lucky man.*"

Whoever they were, they were trying a bit too hard to sound reassuring – the sort of tone I might expect from someone attempting to entice a child into a windowless van with the promise of free candy.

Despite the creep factor, though, I couldn't help but feel the voice was also somehow familiar.

That's when it hit me. It was disturbingly similar to the text to speech capabilities our engineers had been demoing to prospective clients at the convention – part of next year's upgrade to DrakkenBooks, our biggest selling software suite.

Needless to say, the subsequent feedback had caused upper management to seriously rethink this feature as an add-on.

I quickly pushed that thought away. Whatever was going on, I had a feeling it didn't involve finance software.

"What do you mean by lucky?" I asked, wondering what the hell was going on. Was this the hereafter or merely some illusion created by the dying neurons of my flattened brain cells? And if the latter then why a forest? I mean, it's not like I was some camping enthusiast.

"*Duh! It's not every day that someone gets a second chance, now is it?*"

Second chance? I hadn't been raised to be particularly religious. Deb was an Episcopalian, sure, but she'd been to church maybe five times in as many years. All the same, I found myself beginning to second guess my secular lifestyle.

I gritted my teeth, almost afraid to ask. "Are you ... God?"

An angelic chorus rang out from seemingly nowhere, obnoxiously loud enough to cause the nearby bushes to rustle. However, it quickly gave way to raucous laughter, coupled with a momentary vibration from beneath my feet.

What the?

Time Chaser

"Sorry about that, chaser. Couldn't help myself. God ... that's a good one!"

Chaser? "I think you might have me confused with someone else. My name's not Chaser. It's Timothy McAvoy..."

"Oh, very well, Timothy."

"But everyone calls me Mac," I added.

More laughter ensued. ***"Oh, you are an absolute riot. No they don't! Not a single person in your life has ever called you that, no matter how much you tried to convince them to. Not even your mother. Nice try, though."***

"How do you know that?" Holy shit. It *was* God.

Once again I felt a dull vibration coming from the ground.

"But to answer your question, no. I'm not God, Buddha, Odin, Vishnu, Zeus, Amaterasu, Quetzalcoatl, Osiris, Etu, Ogun, Amana..."

"Okay, I get the picture!"

"Just trying to be thorough, jeez. I know how annoyingly pedantic your species can be when they get their panties in a bunch. But anyway, enough of that. The truth is I'm actually glad you interrupted."

"Why?"

"Because I have something I need to tell you that's a bit more important than listing out moldy old sky wizards."

"And that is?"

"Run!"

What the hell? Once more, the ground vibrated beneath my feet. It made me wonder if maybe I'd fallen through a manhole cover at the last second and was now lying dazed and hallucinating in some dank subway tunnel.

The only problem with that was Manahawkin's distinct lack of a subway to fall into.

I felt those vibrations again a second later. This time it was accompanied by a dull *thud* noise. Then the cycle began to repeat itself, growing quicker by the moment.

7

It was almost like I was hearing the sound of ... giant footsteps?

No way. That can't be.

Nevertheless, I found myself turning to look at the distinctly tropical vegetation all around me. I was no tree expert, but it was hard to miss that nothing here resembled the oaks or birch trees that were common in my neighborhood.

In the next instant, though, I realized the plant life here was the least of my worries as a massive form became visible through the tree line.

My jaw dropped as I took in a set of muscular legs, an impossibly heavy body, and two tiny but wicked-looking front claws. At the top of it all sat a massive dragon-like head that glared down at me, five feet long and filled to the brim with steak knife teeth.

A dinosaur.

I was looking at a real life fucking dinosaur!

My first thought was, *Holy shit, that's so freaking cool!*

However, my sense of wonder quickly dried up as I realized there was nothing standing between me and this monster .

Forget Heaven. This was more like some nightmare reimagining of *Jurassic Park*, one in which I'd been saved from certain death only to be served up as the T-Rex's lunch.

2

RACE WITH THE DEVIL

I stood in place a second longer than I should've, looking for wires, a projector, a costume flap, anything that might tell me this was no more than an elaborate prank.

I mean, I'd seen this sort of shit on YouTube ... kinda.

The thing was, this didn't look like one of those janky T-Rex costumes, and it sure as hell was moving way too smoothly to be some bulky animatronic.

Head to tail, it was over thirty feet long. It's body was covered in feathers, all of them various shades of green – effectively camouflaging it against the forest backdrop. No wonder I hadn't seen it sooner.

Perhaps the most frightening part of this monster, however, were its eyes – focused directly on me with obvious intent to do harm.

Well, okay, its teeth were definitely a close second.

Earlier, standing in the way of that bus, I'd felt relieved. I was tired of fighting, so for one brief moment the concept of death had almost been appealing. But now, faced with my imminent death twice in as many minutes, I found that sense of relief replaced by utter terror.

The truth was, I didn't actually want to die and I sure as shit didn't want to meet my end being devoured by a monster from the land that time forgot.

No. What I needed to do was listen to that disembodied voice and get my ass moving.

Fuck this noise!

I turned and ran, praying that part from the movie about the T-Rex being clocked at thirty miles per hour was nothing more than Hollywood bullshit.

Behind me, the beast let out a heavy grunt and gave chase. I didn't need to turn and look to know this. I could feel the thud of its heavy feet and hear the crack of branches as it plowed right through them.

Jesus H. Christ! I was a thirty-eight year old middle manager. I wasn't some high school track star and I sure as shit wasn't Bear Grylls. Sure, I tried to stay in decent shape. I had a Bowflex in my garage and played racquetball every other week – or at least I had before Deb and her lawyer had taken a steaming shit all over my life. Nevertheless, I had a sinking feeling that if this kept up for more than half a mile then I was as good as toast.

Or long pig as was probably more the case.

I dared a glance over my shoulder, finding I had a bit of a head start thanks to the thick foliage. It wasn't nearly enough for comfort, though.

Sadly, I knew I couldn't keep up this pace for long. I was already breathing hard – a fact not helped by the heat and humidity.

What I needed was a place to hide, but where could one go to escape a massive apex predator? Up a tree perhaps? Yeah, like there was any chance I'd make it before...

Wait! I spied something off to the left.

What the hell?

Past some trees, within yet another clearing, was a bright green ball of light that appeared to be floating in midair a few feet above the ground.

Time Chaser

I had no idea what it might be, but it seemed more promising than anything else I'd seen so far, so I quickly turned that way. Sadly for me, so too did my *running partner*. I heard it stumble, followed by the sharp *crack* of what sounded like a sapling coming down, then it was hot on my tail once again.

Please be something useful, I thought. Not that I had any clue how a floating traffic light might be of use, other than being something interesting to look at as I got swallowed whole by this monster.

"*Way to go, chaser!*" that damnable voice from earlier called out, except it was different this time. Before it had been coming from everywhere. Now I distinctly heard it from up ahead.

Behind me, the beast let out a growl and I felt the vibrations beneath my feet intensify.

Son of a bitch! It was actually putting on speed, like it had been toying with me but was now growing tired of my shit.

"*You might want to run faster.*"

"What the fuck do you think I'm doing?!" I cried, despite seeing nothing but trees, dirt, and that weird ball of light.

I was almost there but the dinosaur was quickly closing the gap between us. I felt hot breath wash over my backside. It smelled like garbage that had been left out in the sun for a week.

"*He's right on top of you! Dive, chaser, dive!*"

Dive? This wasn't some goddamned baseball game. On the flipside, there came another huff of fetid breath on my neck – telling me that the next sensation I felt would likely be that of my head being bitten clean off.

What did I have to lose?

I launched myself through a gap between two trees in the moment before there came a savage *crunch* of teeth from right behind me. I hit the ground and rolled several feet before skidding to a halt. This was it. All I could do was lay there and hope that monster finished me off quickly.

Instead of being devoured alive, though, there instead came

a heavy *thud* sound. It was followed by lots of angry bestial grunting, yet still I remained uneaten.

"You can open your eyes now, chaser. You made it."

It was the same voice from earlier, except now it sounded like its owner was right next to me.

I dared a look, nearly soiling my khakis in the process. Barely fifteen feet away stood that dinosaur. This close it was absolutely ginormous, a nightmare given flesh. Worse, it looked seriously ticked off.

It saw me staring and lunged forward. I couldn't help the scream that escaped my lips as it ... stopped right at the edge of the clearing? The air in front of the dinosaur flashed an angry red as the beast appeared to collide with something solid. Yet there was nothing between us. I had leapt through that same space just moments earlier. Hell, I could still feel this thing's death breath washing down on me.

"All right, that's enough," the disembodied voice said. "Go on now. There's nothing for you here. Scram! Vámonos. Hasta la vista, motherfucker."

Sure enough, after another moment or two the beast grunted unhappily then turned and stomped off into the wilderness. Several long minutes passed until I was sure it was finally gone.

"T-that was..." I stammered, trying to keep my heart from beating out of my chest. "That was ... a fucking T-Rex, an actual, living breathing Tyrannosaurus."

"Don't be stupid," the voice replied. "Of course it wasn't."

I turned in a circle, continuing to look for whoever was speaking. "Yeah, I'm pretty sure it was."

"Nuh uh."

"What? Are you saying I imagined it?"

"Not at all," the voice said. "What I'm saying, Bill Nye, is you might want to brush up on your science a bit, guy. That was actually a Mapusaurus, and not even a fully grown one at that."

Time Chaser

⌛⌛⌛⌛ ⋅⁑⋅⁑⋅⁑⋅⁑⋅ ⌛⌛⌛⌛

"A Mapu...?"

"Mapusaurus, duh!" the voice reiterated. "A relatively large carcharodontosaurid that lived roughly 90 million of your years ago in what you now call Argentina. You're welcome by the way. Knowledge is power after all."

I shook my head, trying to make sense of this all. "Okay fine, but what the hell was it doing here?"

"Simple. It was here for your *prechase* qualification round. Think of it like the entrance exam for college, except with fewer essays and more teeth. Just to be clear, though, you passed with flying colors. Congratulations!"

There followed a bit of trumpeted fanfare that carried through the thick air.

"Entrance exam?" I asked, looking around but still not seeing the source of either the voice or the music.

"Yes indeed, chaser. Oh, and in the interest of not making you look any stupider than you already do, I'm right *here*."

I turned, once again seeing nothing except that green ghost light hanging in midair. *Wait. Is that what's been talking to me?*

"Look at you finally starting to get it. You're like a puppy, finally realizing that tail you've been chasing was your own all along."

"Is this ... some kind of Bluetooth speaker?" I jabbed a finger into the green light, watching it sink up to the knuckle. It wasn't hot, but it did cause my hand to tingle.

"Hey!" the voice cried as the light zipped back about five feet. "Don't go thinking we have that kind of relationship. No offense, dude, but I'm just not into you that way."

"Um sorry, I guess." *Hold on. Is this thing actually alive?*

"No problem, chaser. Such rudeness is to be expected from semi-sapient life forms."

"Listen," I said, "I don't exactly know how to phrase this.

Time Chaser

But ... what the hell are you and why do you keep calling me chaser? I already told you, my name's Mac."

"And we've already established that's a complete load of bullshit. However, I'll be happy to call you Timothy instead if you prefer, or maybe Tim if that's more your cup of tea."

"Sure, whatever. Tim is fine," I replied, too dumbfounded to be angry. "Now back to my..."

"Excellent," the ghost light blithely responded. "As for what I am, here's where it starts to get good. Prepare to have your primitive twenty-first century brain blown, because I'm your official FAST unit."

"You don't seem to be moving all that quickly to me."

"I'm not talking about the speed limit, stupid. FAST. It stands for *Free-form Autonomous Sapient Tracker.* In layman's terms, I'm the customary artificial intelligence unit assigned to chasers such as yourself."

I nodded, not that I fully understood. "Okay, so you're some kind of AI? Like one of those image generators you can prompt to...?"

"Survey says XXX," it interrupted with an annoyed buzzing sound. "What *you* call AI, I'd call a barely functional copy of Zork sitting on a fingerprint laden floppy disk. By the way, that's a simple text-based video game by Infocom, first released in..."

"I know what Zork is!"

"Good to know. As I said, knowledge is power. Getting back to my point, I am a living, breathing super computer designed and built by a hyper-evolved race of beings the likes of which your pedestrian level imagination couldn't possibly hope to fathom."

"Really?"

"Fine. You got me. Technically I don't actually breathe."

"No," I said, shaking my head. "I meant those hyper-evolved ... things."

"Ah, yes. As I was saying, I was constructed by an advanced

race of entities that are as far above you as you are above... Hmmm."

"What do you mean by *hmmm*?"

The ghost light fluttered back and forth in the air a few times. "Well, I was going to say cockroaches, but that's not quite right. Imagine something lower, sub-cockroaches maybe, and then go back a couple million years from there. You catching my drift here?"

My mind was racing too fast to be insulted, yet I kind of was anyway. "Y'know, for such a self-proclaimed advanced piece of technology you really do sound like a run-of-the-mill asshole."

"That's wonderful to hear!"

"It is?"

"Of course. You see, that's by design. In being assigned to you, I've been specifically trained on colloquialisms from your time. That way you're sure to understand me. I mean, imagine the confusion if I were to accidentally call you a *hep-cat* or tell you to *slip me some skin, my man*."

"I know what those mean."

"Sure you do," it replied dismissively. "Anyway, the manner of my speech is also for your own protection."

I raised an eyebrow. "How so?"

"You won't be able to fully grasp this, Tim, but if I were to, say, throw some shade your way that originated from a race more than two evolutionary steps above your own, why, the resulting shame would likely cause your brain to instantly liquify."

"Yeah, I somehow doubt that," I replied.

"You do you, as the saying goes. Regardless, let's not be in a hurry to test that hypothesis. Trust me when I say there will be plenty of opportunities for you to meet an equally gruesome fate in the coming stages."

I was about to say something else, but its words hit me like a brick to the balls. "I thought you said I was being given a second chance."

"You are, emphasis on *chance*. Mind you, I never said it was a good chance."

I backed away, looking around. My first thoughts upon arriving here was that this must be the afterlife. However, it was beginning to slowly dawn on me that it was actually something far worse. "What exactly is this place?" I asked, remembering what it had said about that dinosaur. "And don't tell me we're in Argentina."

"Wouldn't dream of it, Tim old pal," the light replied. "This might look like prehistoric Argentina, not that I'd expect you to recognize it, but in actuality you are standing in a dimension that exists outside of time and space as you know it. In short, welcome to the void, chaser! What happens from this point onward will be entirely up to you."

3

NO BUSINESS LIKE SHOW BUSINESS

"Okay, maybe that's not entirely true," the light continued. "There's probably an untold number of horrific fates that technically you'd have little to no say over."

"Not helping," I growled.

"Heck, I was reviewing the limited memory cells I can access from previous cycles and found this amusing clip of a Heboloxian chaser who made an appearance roughly three-hundred quinks ago. Poor schmuck was minding his own business at the start of Stage Five, taking the human equivalent of a smoke break, when *bam*! A giant grelk just fell out of the sky and landed on him. Ker-splat! Talk about an embarrassing way to go."

"I have absolutely no idea what you just said."

"That's okay, you will ... metaphorically speaking anyway. I don't think grelks are making an appearance this cycle. But I guess we'll find out soon enough."

Before I could respond, the ground once again began to rumble. I quickly turned, thinking that dinosaur was back, but there was thankfully no sign of the beast.

A few seconds passed, then the forest floor right next to me began to heave as something pushed its way out of the dirt.

What now?

I jumped back, expecting ... well, I'm not sure exactly what I expected, but this wasn't it. Instead a stone archway burst from the ground, continuing to rise until it stood about eight feet high. I tried looking through it but, rather than the other side, all I saw was a glowing yellow light.

"Make that sooner than I thought," the ghost light said. "Guess it's time for all the chasers to gather."

"There you go with that word again. What does it mean?"

"All will be revealed once you step through."

I cocked my head. "You do realize how ominously vague that sounds, right?"

"I suppose."

"And should I refuse to step through this mysterious devil gate?"

"Mysterious devil gate?" it replied, sounding amused. "Fascinating as I'm sure that would be, no. It's merely a portal to the waypoint. Think of it like a holding pen for..."

"A holding pen?"

"Perhaps that's the wrong term," it added. "Allow me to rephrase. It's more like ... a waiting room. Yeah that sounds less threatening. Regardless, it's where you and the others will be given basic instructions before being given a chance to gear up for the Chase."

"Which means what exactly?"

The light let out what sounded like a sigh as it flitted toward the archway as if to say, "go through and find out, stupid."

"If it helps you decide," the ghost light continued, "this particular pocket dimension will disperse in roughly thirty seconds."

That didn't sound promising. "And if I'm still here when that happens?"

"You'll officially suffer a tier one expiration. The good news

Time Chaser

is tier one is the least severe expiration from the Chase. The bad news is, you'll be dead."

"I see..." Guess I didn't have much choice in the matter.

"Fifteen seconds, chaser."

"One more question, real quick. Why does it look like that?"

"Like what?"

"Like the fucking entrance to a medieval torture chamber?"

"Ah. I'm told that's merely window dressing designed to coincide with this cycle's Chase. Now, if there's nothing else... Three...two..."

I gritted my teeth in frustration and stepped through. I had no idea what was waiting on the other side but hopefully it was better than a so-called *tier one expiration*.

⏳⏳⏳ ⋅⊹⋄⊹⋄⊹⋄⊹⋅ ⏳⏳⏳

Talk about the difference between night and day. The first thing I noticed was that the temperature had dropped a good twenty degrees, no small relief. Too bad it seemed to be the only break I was getting.

Gone was the primeval jungle. Instead I was now inside a massive colosseum, vaguely resembling the one in Rome. Wherever this was, it was big – stretching at least two football fields in every direction. I was on the arena floor with the ghost light thingy floating next to me.

The stadium's seats were currently empty, but that didn't mean we were alone. Far from it. There were others down on the floor with us, a lot of them. Hell, the place was packed like a Sunday swap meet.

The thing was, this wasn't the typical assortment of Kyles and Karens you'd find at such a gathering. To say this bunch was somewhat more eclectic was an understatement.

In my immediate area alone I spied an astronaut in full space gear, a police officer who looked straight out of the

Time Chaser

Keystone Cops, a medieval knight, a woman dressed like a 1930's flapper, and what appeared to be several soldiers wearing gear from a variety of eras. There was even this one clown wearing full-on Nazi regalia, save that it was bright yellow in color for some reason.

That was bizarre enough, but nothing compared to the woman on my right with a pile of multi-hued hair upon her head that seemed to change colors every few seconds. She had no eyebrows, wore garish yellow lipstick, and was clad in a dress that could best be described as *Jane Jetson* meets *The Fifth Element*.

Needless to say, I felt comically out of place wearing business casual.

It wasn't just the people, though. Every single one of them also appeared to have their own ghost lights floating nearby – FAST units I suppose – most of them a different hue than the one that seemed intent on haranguing me.

A good chunk of the people in sight seemed to be busy talking to their lights. The only problem was I couldn't understand any of them. It was like a plethora of different dialects and...

"Grulack!"

"Huh?" I turned at the sound of the gravelly voice, my eyes opening wide at the sight of a brutish looking fella whose nostrils were working overtime for some reason.

He was shorter than me, maybe five and a half feet tall, but built like a linebacker. His thickly muscled arms, chest, and shoulders were covered by a coat of coarse black hair that seemed to cover his whole body. Not helping was the filthy loin cloth wrapped around his waist – one that wasn't doing its job as his dick was clearly visible swinging in the breeze beneath it.

"Grulack," he repeated, his dull brown eyes glaring at me beneath a heavy brow.

"Forsinga kanaga," the purple-colored FAST floating next to him barked back.

"Grulack!" he cried again, just before he launched himself at me, mouth wide open – revealing two rows of broken and yellowed teeth that nonetheless seemed disturbingly sharp.

Jesus! I screamed as I brought my hands up to protect myself, not that I had any shot of fighting off this gorilla.

However, rather than be tackled off my feet, there came a sharp *crack*, a flash of red, and then this reject from *Quest For Fire* was flung backward to the ground.

He quickly recovered, looking up and growling at me – a sound that sent a chill down my spine every bit as much as that dinosaur had.

Before he could charge again, though, the purple light flitted in front of him and repeated, "Forsinga kanaga!" This time it sounded a lot more insistent.

After what felt like a small eternity, in which no small number of those around us began to stare, Nature Boy finally seemed to get the hint. He turned and loped off into the crowd.

"Serves you right, dickhead," my FAST called after him. "Next time listen when you're told that PVP isn't active yet."

I let out a breath I hadn't realized I'd been holding. "What the hell was that all about?"

"Oh, it's nothing. That guy's just a dope," it replied. "Don't worry about him."

"That sure as hell didn't seem like nothing to me."

"He was hungry, that's all."

"Hungry? Why? Do I look like I have a side of fries in my pocket or something?"

"Not exactly. You see, Borlack there..."

"Borlack?"

"That's his name. Borlack the Trampler to be exact. He just happens to hail from a time before cannibalism was considered a social faux pas."

"Wait. You mean he was going to eat me?!"

"Not all of you. We're about to get started, so it's not like there's time for a three course meal."

"Is that supposed to make me feel better?"

"Not at all. That's the PVP shield's job."

"What's a P..."

"Shhh. It's starting."

"What's starting?"

"Stop asking stupid questions and lift your right hand over your head."

"Why?" I asked.

"Just do it. It'll all be clear in a moment."

"No, I..."

However, my arm apparently had a mind of its own. It pointed skyward as if there were an invisible rope tied around my wrist and someone was reeling it in. *What the?*

At least I wasn't alone in the weirdness. I saw the same damned thing happening to everyone around me. The only exception was a soldier dressed in an off color confederate uniform. He was missing his right arm, so his left was pulled up instead.

Before I could question what the hell was going on, my entire arm began to glow. I winced, feeling a static shock that seemed to travel down my body. Then, just as quickly as it had been snatched by an unseen force, my arm was released. I lowered it, noticing my forearm was now encased in a tight-fitting, bronze-colored bracer.

From all around there came cries of surprise as everyone seemed to have been fitted with one. Unlike the assortment of FASTs floating around, however, they all appeared uniform in color and appearance. The only difference was their size, no doubt to accommodate the wide range of people present.

"Excellent," my ghost light said. "Now they'll activate everyone's SK and we can finally be underway."

I felt a slight tingle from my arm as the bracer began to buzz like a cellphone. I'd assumed it to be a solid piece of featureless metal, but I saw now that wasn't the case as a long rectangular screen winked to life along the back of it. It glowed brightly as multiple unrecognizable characters floated across its length, making it look like a ridiculously oversized smart watch.

Okay, that was interesting I suppose, but what was the purpose of...?

"What is this devilry upon my person?"

"Am I to assume this is ... some kind of armor?"

"I demand to speak to whoever is in charge here. No, I will not calm down!"

I looked around, realizing that where before I'd heard innumerable languages being spoken, now it was all in perfectly understandable English.

"I know what you're thinking," my FAST unit said. "No, they're not speaking your language, nor are you speaking theirs. It's just one of the many perks conveyed by that SK on your arm."

"SK?"

"Short for *Sidekick*. Don't ask me why it's called that. My guess is some marketing drone somewhere thought it was clever. Anyway, it's syncing the language portion of your brain to match the other chasers here. Think of it like an advanced form of Google Translate, except you're far less likely to accidentally tell someone you want to bang their grandmother."

"Huh. I guess that's kinda handy."

"Oh, trust me, it is. There's a good chance you will quite literally live or die depending on the alliances you can make here. That and focus group data has shown that attention spans tend to wane during extended sequences of chasers fumbling around trying to figure out what each other are saying. Save the pantomiming for the fuckers wearing white grease paint I say."

"Hold on. You said perks as in plural. What else does this thing do?"

Before they could respond, my ears caught the faint sound of cheering – rapidly rising in volume until it was nearly deafening.

I saw nothing but confusion etched onto the faces of those nearest me as it wasn't coming from any of them.

"And here we go," the FAST said, its voice clearly audible above the din.

It was at that moment I realized I wasn't hearing the commotion with my ears, but rather inside my head.

The fuck?!

"Oh, by the way, before you freak out, they also installed a cortical upgrade so you can properly *hear* everything."

A what?

I was still trying to process this new development when the air above us began to shimmer, like what you might see over a hot grill. That's when everything changed. One moment the stadium seats were empty. The next, they were packed to the brim with a menagerie of creatures – all of them screaming, hissing, or chittering their heads off.

The air continued to shimmer in front of them all, mercifully obscuring my view a bit, but I clearly made out enough to give me nightmares for years to come. I spied tentacles, antennae, metallic bodies, multiple heads, and more. It was as if H.R. Giger had been asked to design a Star Wars set.

"What the fuck are…?"

Whatever else I had to say was lost as a loud voice boomed out, overpowering even the cheering of the crowd.

"ENTITIES, ORGANISMS, AND MANIFESTATIONS OF ALL AGES! IT'S THE MOMENT YOU'VE BEEN WAITING ALL QUINK FOR! WELCOME TO ANOTHER CYCLE OF … TIME CHASERS!"

4

TIME CHASERS

At least the FAST's insistence on calling me "chaser" was finally starting to make sense, sorta.

Despite the translation bangle on my arm, I didn't understand every word that had been spoken, but I got the gist of it. The announcer's voice – a somewhat more chipper version of the *In a world* guy from innumerable movie trailers – pretty much told me everything I needed to know.

This wasn't any afterlife I'd ever heard of, and it certainly was neither Heaven nor Hell. Far as I could tell, I'd been spirited away from my impending death into some sort of ... game show.

"AS ALWAYS, I'M YOUR HOST DREGA!"

The cheering from the crowd quickly became a chant.

"Drega, Drega, Drega..."

I couldn't see who was talking, but got the distinct impression they were this hellscape's version of Bob Barker.

This Drega person let the ego-stroking continue for an extended amount of time before finally speaking again.

"YOU'LL WANT TO KEEP YOUR CORTEXES ATTUNED BECAUSE WE HAVE AN EXCITING SHOW WAITING FOR YOU. WE'VE SCOURED COUNTLESS

TIMELINES AND EONS BEYOND MEASURE TO BRING YOU THIS CYCLE'S CONTESTANTS. BUT DON'T JUST TAKE MY WORD FOR IT!"

Spotlight beams, nearly blindingly bright, shined down from seemingly nowhere and lit up the arena floor like it was the surface of the sun.

"FROM BLOODTHIRSTY WARLORDS TO EGO-INFLATED SCHOLARS, THESE TEN-THOUSAND MONKEYS ARE READY TO RUMBLE. HAILING FROM A TINY BLUE MARBLE CIRCLING AN OTHERWISE UNREMARKABLE SOLAR BODY, PLEASE WELCOME THE CHASERS FROM ... PLANET EARTH!"

Once again the crowd went nuts. I was beginning to get the feeling Drega could've literally said anything and they would've still cheered.

Regardless, despite his thinly veiled insults, I was able to glean a bit of info, which was more than I'd had before.

If this guy wasn't full of it, and everything I'd seen so far had gone a long way toward convincing me this was real, then that meant the people around me weren't reenactors, cosplayers, or even run-of-the-mill nutcases. No. They had each been plucked from their own point in time. Even crazier was the implication that they were from whole different timelines.

I suppose that explained the bright yellow Nazi. Go figure, but that heavily implied there was a universe out there where those shitheads were not only the embodiment of evil, but dressed like giant bananas too.

That was all sorts of fucked up.

Alas, there was no time to dive down that particular rabbit hole as Drega wasn't finished.

"THEIR LIVES MAY HAVE ENDED IN MEANINGLESS CALAMITY..."

Meaningless?

"BUT NOW THEY HAVE THE OPPORTUNITY TO

CHANGE ALL THAT. PLEGRAXIOUS, TELL THEM WHAT THEY HAVE A CHANCE TO WIN!"

Another voice started speaking. Whereas Drega appeared to be the charismatic host playing to the crowd, the newcomer was more matter-of-fact – sounding like Ed McMahon, had his vocal cords been replaced with autotune.

"Thanks, Drega! We have some great prizes waiting for our chasers this cycle – three incredible tiers to be exact. Without further ado, let's jump right in. Those qualifying for second place will receive ... life! That's right. Six winners will earn the chance to be returned to the moment of their untimely demise, only to find they've managed to dodge the proverbial bullet. Forget good luck or an act of God, here it's all about the *miracle* of good entertainment!"

More howls from the audience followed, although they were more subdued than those Drega had gotten.

I couldn't help but grit my teeth. This is what the FAST had meant by a second chance? If I was understanding them right, these fuckers wanted me to compete in some sort of competition for a chance to undo my death – something that was apparently in their power to grant.

But why? If they had the power to simply snap their fingers and send me back to my son, why not just do it? Why all of *this*?

I had no idea what their motivation was. All I knew was one thing, the fear I'd been feeling was being slowly replaced by anger as Plegra ... or whatever his name was continued.

"If you think that's wild, we're just getting started. Let's talk about the prize for our first place winners. Up to three lucky contestants will have a chance to not only survive, but to truly change their destiny. Think hard upon your grievances, chasers, because you might be one of the lucky few who gets to rewrite history. Whether you're seeking true love, buried treasure, or the cure to the disease that's ravaging the

countryside, we've got you covered with this once in a lifetime chance to tell the winds of fate to fuck off!"

Huh. Call me petty, but I couldn't help but think of Deb and what we'd been through these last several weeks. Was it possible I could change all that?

Maybe I could wish fuckboy Manny an incurable case of limp-dick. Okay, that was probably thinking too small. Money would be better. That way I could hire my own shark of a lawyer, while also ensuring Jeremy was given the life he deserved. Yeah. As ticked off as this situation was making me, I couldn't help but consider the carrot being dangled here.

Had they mentioned this opportunity to fix my life right at the start, I might not have minded being chased by a dinosaur. Either way, they definitely had my attention.

"And we haven't even gotten to this cycle's grand prize yet! One resourceful chaser could walk away with the chance to truly upend..."

"I'LL STOP YOU RIGHT THERE, PLEG OLD BUDDY!" Drega interrupted. **"LET'S KEEP THAT ONE A SECRET FOR NOW. I DON'T KNOW ABOUT YOU, BUT I'D PREFER TO SAVE THAT FOR A HIGHER STAGE. LET'S WEED OUT THE SCUM FIRST SO THE CREAM CAN RISE TO THE TOP."**

What?! Goddamn, I hated this showmanship crap.

"You got it, Drega! But since we're on the subject, we can't talk about prizes without also mentioning penalties. We know from previous Chases that sometimes a chaser's motivation can ... wane. That's why we instituted the qualification round, to give those lacking the chaser spirit a chance to bow out early. Speaking of which, I'm happy to report only thirty-two out of our pool of ten-thousand applicants opted for early expiration. That means not only do we still have a big crowd but they're all hungry to compete!"

Way too true in the case of that Borlack fucker.

As the crowd hooted and cheered again, I took a moment to

consider this. The FAST unit had called that dinosaur an entrance exam. Was that what they meant by qualification round? Did that mean thirty-two people had failed to escape from whatever had been sent after them? I could've easily been number thirty-three had I tripped or taken a wrong turn.

Is that what they considered *opting out*?

I had no idea beyond the news that thirty-two people who might've otherwise been here alongside me now weren't. As for their fate, the FAST had already explained what a tier one *expiration* truly meant.

"As with the grand prize, we'll likewise save the top tier penalty for a later time. However, thanks to the Committee's infinite mercy, we've been informed that no chasers will be penalized at that tier before it can be formally announced."

Gee, how *generous* of them.

"On to the rest, I think by now we're all familiar with what a tier one penalty entails. But for our chasers and any new cortexers out there, it's simple. A tier one expiration means you die! That's right, when a chaser expires at the first tier, they go right back to where we plucked them from – the moment of their death. No harm, no foul, and best of all, no contamination of their timeline."

No harm, no foul? Fuck this guy and his timelines. These were our lives he was talking about.

As pissed off as that made me, I wasn't even remotely prepared for what came next.

"However, tier two is where it really gets *interesting*, folks. Should a chaser suffer a tier-two expiration, they'll not only lose their life but they'll sacrifice their entire continuum. You heard correct! By grand decree of the Committee, their entire timeline will be purged. Yes, it sounds like a heavy burden to bear, but look at this cycle's collection of contestants. I see some broad shoulders among them. I think they can handle the weight, don't you?"

The assholes in the audience were quick to agree with Ed

Time Chaser

McMassMurderer. What in the ever-loving hell was wrong with these nutjobs to think this was in any way sane or acceptable? Wiping out entire timelines? I ... I couldn't even fathom that.

It had to be hyperbole. That type of power simply didn't exist. It *couldn't* exist.

Could it?

"DAMN, PLEG, YOU'RE BRINGING ME DOWN WITH ALL THIS HEAVY SHIT. SO WHY DON'T WE LIGHTEN THE MOOD A BIT BY REMINDING OUR AUDIENCE THAT A CHASER HAS TO TRY PRETTY HARD TO HIT TIER TWO. OR MORE PRECISELY, THEY HAVE TO *NOT* TRY."

What the hell was he babbling about?

"Right you are, Drega. Let's face facts. Sit-ins and hunger strikes are boring, while suicide can be downright depressing to watch. Nobody needs that sorta thing clogging up their cortexing pleasure. The Chase is all about the will to survive and conquer. To that end, we have given each FAST unit full autonomy to posthumously decide whether their chaser's demise falls within the spirit of the game or not. Hear that, chasers! Be brave in front of your FAST. Trust in them and they'll trust in you. Or at the very least, try not to piss them off."

While the crowd laughed, I glanced toward the green light hovering next to me. Were they actually saying this floating dickhole was in charge of deciding my fate? Oh, I was so fucked.

"IntheunlikelyeventofaFASTunitsufferingprematureandpermanentofflining," a new voice suddenly blared, talking superfast and with no discernable emotion, "apredesignatedtribunalwillbecalledtoreviewtheassignedchaser'sdeathandrenderadecision.Theirjudgementwillhenceforthbebinding."

What the...? Call me crazy, but I had a feeling I'd just listened to this horror show's version of legal fine print.

Lord have mercy.

Mostly because I had a feeling these dick biscuits wouldn't.

5

HUD-DLING AROUND THE CAMPFIRE

Drega and his asshole buddy droned on for a while longer. Each time they fired up the crowd it seemed to kill a little bit of the hope still clinging to those around me.

I had a feeling that was by design.

According to them, the gist of this *game* involved surviving twelve increasingly difficult levels or stages. The goal of each stage was simple, at least on paper – reach the next stage. Although, considering the way Drega and Plegraxious joked back and forth, I got the impression it wasn't going to be nearly as cut and dried as they made it out to be, especially as the stages progressed.

There were two catches. First, we had a time limit. Stage One was a three day event, thankfully measured in Earth time. Anyone still left on the field after that would be instantly *expired* – aka killed.

Left unsaid was whether that would result in a tier one or two penalty.

Either way, it seemed they *really* wanted to weed out the lollygaggers.

The second catch was even more nefarious. Only a specific

percentage of chasers, as they insisted on calling us, would be permitted to ascend to each new level. Regardless of whether it was within the time limit or not, if you were among the last chasers left you'd be *expired*.

For Stage One, whatever that entailed – because of course they were being vague about it – that percentage was at least a high one. Ninety-nine percent of the chasers would be permitted to pass. However, it was a rolling percentage dependent on the current number of survivors.

Initially there were ten-thousand of us, so that meant all but one-hundred had a shot. But we'd already lost thirty-two during the qualifying round. That brought the number of those who'd be left behind down to ninety-nine, meaning one extra person could conceivably make it out who might otherwise not have.

There was a big gotcha there, though, and it was a brutal one. Drega didn't specifically say so, but the implication was clear as the nose on my face. My FAST unit had previously mentioned PVP. My only knowledge of that acronym came from video games, where it stood for *player versus player*. Since I could think of no other meaning in this situation, that meant those at the ass-end of escaping a stage could conceivably improve their odds by eliminating their fellow chasers.

Needless to say, that did not make me feel better.

I looked around, noting the heavy concentration of soldiers in my area alone. Of course it would make sense there'd be a lot of them. These aliens, or whatever they were, claimed to have pulled people away in the split second before a meaningless death. Sadly, history had proven it was hard to beat war when it came to such metrics.

Mind you, that didn't exactly bode well for me. I was a member of the karate club during my first few years of college, but Bruce Lee I was not. In terms of fighting prowess, well, let's just say the odds were not in my favor.

Thankfully, at least for this first stage, we were informed that PVP would be suspended until at least half the initial chasers had *ascended* – their term for besting a stage. That meant I just needed to be among the first five-thousand to blow this pop stand.

If I could pull that off, I could avoid any targets on my back.

Literally, as I noticed more than one of the soldiers were armed. My guess was that when people were dragged here, they brought whatever they had on them at the time. Sadly, in my case that amounted to my wallet, car keys, and a half empty tube of lip balm in my back pocket.

How the fuck was that even remotely fair?

Sadly, I had a feeling fair was a dubious concept at best as Drega finally seemed ready to wrap things up.

"THERE'S A LOT MORE WE COULD COVER, FOLKS, BUT AS THEY SAY, EXPERIENCE IS THE BEST TEACHER. BESIDES WHICH, WE WOULDN'T WANT TO RISK ANY OF OUR CHASERS DYING ... OF BOREDOM!"

The audience absolutely howled in response. There had to be a prompt or laugh track at work here. No way could anyone genuinely find this guy that hilarious.

"SO WHAT SAY WE GET THIS SHOW ON THE QUANTUM REALMWAY? IN A MOMENT, OUR CHASERS WILL BE TRANSPORTED TO TEMPORARY SAFE ZONES SCATTERED AT RANDOM THROUGHOUT STAGE ONE. FROM THERE, THEY'LL HAVE ONE EARTH HOUR TO PREPARE. I CAUTION YOU, CHASERS, USE THAT HOUR WISELY. GEAR AND STATS ARE IMPORTANT, TRUE, BUT NEVER FORGET THAT KNOWLEDGE IS POWER!"

Interesting. That was the exact same thing my ghost light tormentor had said. I'd thought it was just being a prick, but maybe there was something more there.

"**Indeed it is, Drega,**" Plegraxious added. "**But before we declare this Chase started, I should mention that the**

Time Chaser

Committee has decided to offer our contestants one last perk!"

Oh?

"In light of everything our chasers are facing, the Committee has decided to extend a final opportunity to back out without incurring a tier-two penalty. If you wish to expire from the Chase, you may do so at this point with the guarantee that your timeline will be safe."

That was what they considered to be a perk?!

"For the rest of you jackals, please be warned that looting is temporarily suspended."

Looting?

That finally caused the crowd to fall silent – no doubt in anticipation of whether anyone would take these jackasses up on their *generous* offer.

I had assumed that would be a hard no across the board, but then I noticed a few of those nearest me turning to look at someone. I followed their gaze to see what appeared to be an actual samurai – complete with armor and katana.

He was on his knees holding a dagger. "For my wife and child," he said to no one in particular. "May they be safe until I can hold them in my arms again." Then, without further warning, he plunged the blade into his midsection.

Holy shit!

He collapsed to the ground where, moments later, his body simply faded away like it was made of smoke.

"WHOA THERE, KATSUO!" Drega cried. **"WE MEANT FOR YOU TO RAISE YOUR HAND."** There came a beat of silence and then he continued, **"WELL, THAT'LL CERTAINLY BE AN INTERESTING FIND FOR THE BANDITS WHO JUST AMBUSHED HIM. BUT HEY, WHAT IS HISTORY WITHOUT A FEW UNSOLVED MYSTERIES? YO, PLEG, CHECK THIS GUY'S TIMELINE AND SEE IF ROBERT STACK EVER DID AN EPISODE ON HIM. AM I RIGHT, FOLKS?"**

The audience went absolutely nuts. I guess chaos made for good sport.

From what I could tell, a few others likewise volunteered to be expired early – although none like that first guy.

After hearing what that samurai said, I can't lie and claim I didn't give it at least a moment's thought. His words about his wife and child had been like a blow to the gut.

Was my life truly worth the risk to literally everyone and everything I knew?

Probably not, but in the end it came down to the same thing as when I'd faced off against that dinosaur.

I wanted to live, damn it. I wanted to live and see my son again.

I just had to be very careful about it, and that meant one thing and one thing only.

Even if I met my end in this place, I needed to ensure I at least died trying.

⌛⌛⌛ ⋄⋄⋄ ⌛⌛⌛

Once it was established that the deaths were finished for the time being, that was apparently the signal for things to get a move on.

Dozens of stone archways, similar to the one I'd first stepped through, appeared throughout the arena. We were all instructed to enter them with our respective FAST units. Our hour long grace period would officially commence once the last chaser was through.

The nearest one to me was barely twenty feet away, so I made a beeline toward it.

I stepped through to find that once again my location had completely changed. Now I was in what appeared to be a medieval tavern straight out of a ren faire, like the one I'd taken Jeremy to last year. Ironically enough, we'd ended up only staying an hour there as well, after he'd had a meltdown when I refused to buy him a horned Viking helmet.

It had ticked me off at the time, but right at that moment I'd have given my left nut to be back there with him again.

"Look at you, Mr. Eager Beaver," my FAST unit said, appearing there as well. "I have to admit, I didn't expect you to be so enthusiastic."

"I'm not, but you heard Drega. Our hour starts once the last person steps through. It's not going to take them long to herd everyone to where they need to go, but I figured even a few extra minutes is to my advantage."

"*Our* advantage you mean."

"How's that? So you can have more time to decide if my entire timeline is fucked?"

"No. I mean, yes, that's a small part of it," it replied, "But not right now, and hopefully not ever."

"Uh huh. Sure. We both heard that asshole out there."

The light flitted back and forth, seemingly agitated. "You may have heard, but did you actually listen?"

"What do you mean?"

"That part Plegraxious said about trusting in your FAST unit. That was the takeaway."

"And why exactly would I do that?"

"Because my survival is on the line too," it said. "I'm not just here to float over your shoulder casting judgement like some sort of sanctimonious prick. I mean I might do that anyway, but I'm also your first party member."

"Party member?"

"Yep. From here on out, Tim old buddy, you and me are officially partners."

⌛⌛⌛⌛ ⋅⋛⋕⋛⋕⋛⋅ ⌛⌛⌛⌛

"What do you mean by partners?"

"Is there something wrong with my speech cells?" it replied.

"Did I stutter? Why else do you think I was assigned to study you like a bug under a microscope? I don't need your life history just to follow your stupid monkey ass around. No, it was so I could best consider how to act as a counterpoint to your myriad weaknesses."

"ATTENTION, CHASERS! YOUR ONE HOUR GRACE PERIOD OFFICIALLY STARTS NOW. GET YOURSELF GEARED UP AND READY BECAUSE IN SIXTY MINUTES THOSE TEMPORARY SAFE ZONES ARE GOING TO BE SERVED WITH AN EVICTION NOTICE. IF YOU'RE NOT READY BY THEN, TOO BAD, SO SAD – EXCEPT I AIN'T YOUR DAD!"

"Okay, we need to table the rest of this discussion until we're finished," the FAST said. "All the chasers have been scattered randomly throughout the map. That means we have no idea where we'll end up once this spot dissipates – and I do mean *we*. I'm as much in the dark as you. We might be in an okay place or we could find ourselves standing in the middle of a den of mobs. Trust me, you don't want to risk being unprepared if that happens."

"A den of...? Are you talking like a flash mob?"

"Yes, if a flash mob ever gathered for the sole purpose of killing our asses. Now shut up and listen so I can show you how to use your SK."

There was a slightly frantic quality to the ghost light's voice. So, rather than argue, I simply nodded.

"Good," it continued. "Your SK is currently in standby mode. We're going to activate it now."

The FAST directed me to lift my arm and then tap twice on the SK's screen with my free hand. I did, at which point a loud voice blared, "*Sidekick level 1 activated! Welcome to Sidekick OS version 60763.4, brought to you by Negastar Engineering, a subsidiary of Millenalux Corp. It takes a maiming but keeps on gaming.*"

"Yeah, yeah, spare us the stupid slogans," the FAST said

before turning its attention back toward me. "Okay, so maybe the most important thing to know is you should never forget about your SK."

I held up the economy sized bangle that was seemingly grafted onto my arm. "That shouldn't be an issue."

"You'd think that but you'd be wrong," it continued. "Most chasers forget about it in the early stages because they have it in HUD mode and it ends up being hidden by a jacket or shirt sleeve. Trust me, you don't want to do that."

"Why?"

"I'm getting to that. Jeez, your species really does love to hear the sound of their own voices. My point is, it's your first piece of armor and in some cases it may be your best. It doesn't do a whole lot at level 1 but that's okay because it's damned near indestructible."

I took a closer look at it. "So you're saying I could maybe use it as a shield?"

"Exactly!"

"Good to know. Okay, so that's level 1. What does it do at...?"

The FAST made a buzzing sound. "Let's table that for now because it's not going to be an issue for some time. We'll ... cross that bridge when we come to it."

I shrugged noting their odd pause. "If you say so."

"All right, now look at the screen on your SK."

I did, noticing there was a lot to take in. I spied columns for stats, inventory, bonuses, achievements, as well as several tabs for more, but the text was so cramped that it was barely legible on the comparatively small screen.

The whole setup kind of reminded me of a streamlined Pip-Boy from the *Fallout* games. I used to enjoy playing them after work – at least before Deb had harangued me into stopping because she thought video games were for kids.

I felt a brief stab of anger at the memory. Maybe I should've taken that as a precursor of things to come. Still, I pushed that aside for now. There was literally no time to waste on past regrets.

"Okay, so none of what you're looking at makes sense, right?" the FAST asked. "That's because the UI is crammed together like a clown car. That's what happens when you contract your equipment out to seventh level civilizations – you get lowest bidder because those fuckers might be reasonably smart, but they still haven't evolved past capitalism."

"Is that supposed to make sense?"

"No, but that's okay," it said. "The screen is only for backup in case you need full use of your senses. It'll all be a lot more clear when you activate your HUD."

It directed me to place two pinched fingers on the screen and then pull them apart, like enlarging a photo on a smartphone. However, when I did so, rather than simply making the text bigger, it all exploded off the screen, filling my entire field of vision.

"Holy crap! Are you seeing this?"

"Sorta," it said. "I have my own version of it, and since we're party members I have access to some of your info, as you do to mine."

"Really? Show me."

"We'll get to that. Let's worry about your starting stats for now. The interface works three ways. Via touch, voice command, or focus."

"Focus?"

"Mental focus," it clarified. "Controlling it with your mind. Not all chasers are created equal, so the other two exist as a failsafe in case your frontal lobe isn't up to the task. For now, if I were you, I'd try..."

I narrowed my eyes at the floating ball of light, but then decided to take its insults as a challenge instead. *Stats*, I thought, trying to push everything else out of my mind. *Show me my...*

"Dude, do you need to take a dump or something? Because if so, you'll have to wait until after..."

I ignored it and continued to focus, unsure if anything was actually going to happen until it finally did.

A section of the heads-up display became highlighted as it moved front and center in my field of view, displaying a list of seven statistics – Strength, Intelligence, Wisdom, Dexterity, Constitution, Charisma, and one I didn't recognize.

Either way, I was once again reminded of some of the games I used to enjoy.

Chaser: Timothy M – Earth 8069 – Level 1
STR: 50
INT: 50
WIS: 30
DEX: 40
CON: 40
CHA: 30
PSI: 0

Holy shit! Look at those. I read them aloud, unable to help the grin that appeared on my face – except for maybe that last score.

"Well, look at you, Mr. Average McAveragepants," the FAST said. "Nicely done on the HUD, by the way. If you can master controlling it via mental focus, that will almost certainly help a bit out there in the field."

"Average? Were you listening? I have a freaking strength of fifty. If this were a video game..."

The little light made a sighing sound. "That you do, but I wouldn't get too full of myself yet if I were you."

"Explain."

"I'm not supposed to mention it unless you ask, but what the fuck. Anyway, it's all smoke and mirrors."

"What do you mean?"

"Maybe a dozen or so quinks back, the Committee made some adjustments to how stats are calculated. From what I can garner from my limited memories, Chasers were starting to draw more sympathy than excitement in the early stages, which

I'm guessing set off all the focus groups. So their way of *fixing* it was to move the decimal point over a notch. And lo and behold, it apparently worked. Now you get to look like a superhero right out the gate, which keeps the audience happy even as you're getting your ass handed to you."

"That sucks."

"No. That's show business."

"Still a shitty thing to do."

"It is, but I'd advise against too much bitching and moaning, at least out loud. The Committee prides itself on running a fair game, but power has a way of inflating one's ego. Best to not test that."

"Tell me more about this Committee. Oh, and while we're at it, what the hell is a quink?"

"That one's easy. A quink is a standard unit of multiversal time. Translates to about fourteen of your years. As for the Committee, let's save that one for later. For now, we need to worry about allocating the 30 free stat points you've been given."

"Wait, I get more?"

"Yep. Standard bonus for a starting chaser, prior to race reassignment anyway."

Race reassignment? I took a deep breath. The FAST was right. We only had an hour and every question I asked pushed us closer to that deadline. I needed to shut up and get past this ... um ... tutorial level I guess. "Okay fine. I don't know what PSI is, but I have zero points in it, so maybe I should..."

"Let me stop you right there, sparky. PSI stands for psionics. You should just leave that alone."

"Psionics? As in mind powers?"

"Exactly."

"And I wouldn't want to spend points on that, why exactly?"

"Because it's a waste on a species such as yours. Trust me, unless the Committee accidentally chose an exceptionally gifted specimen out of the myriad Earth gene pools, almost every chaser will be starting with zero points there, maybe ten at most. Out of all the stats listed, that one's the hardest to master, at least for non-telepathic species."

"But..."

"Even if you did put your extra points there, it wouldn't do you any good. Trust me on this."

"Why?" I replied.

"Because the cost for those powers tends to be..."

"No. I mean why should I trust your word? Just because you've been assigned to me as a so-called *party member* doesn't mean I should automatically..."

"You *really* want to do this now?" it interrupted, sounding annoyed. "Fine. The reason is, my life is on the line every bit as much as yours. Well, okay, maybe not quite like yours. FAST units get certain perks to keep the game moving, but believe me, I can die too. I don't know if you listened to that vomit of legal mumbo jumbo back there, but the phrase *permanent offlining* was mentioned. That means dead, which is a status I'd prefer to avoid if at all possible."

"Okay, but..."

"I'm not finished yet. There's more to it than that. You may not believe me, but I'm in this not only to survive, but to make sure you win as well. And do you know why?"

"I have no idea."

"Because if you somehow do, by the grace of whatever deity you believe in, manage to survive all twelve stages, then I get a reward too – perhaps the greatest prize anyone in the multiverse could hope for."

"And that would be?" I asked, expecting a snarky answer.

"My freedom – from the game, the Committee, from all of this."

6

ACHIEVEMENT UNLOCKED

The FAST took about thirty seconds to explain things. I, as a chaser, got one chance. If I died, that was it, game over. FASTs, however, were afforded three deaths per stage. The first two were temporary but the third was for keeps. If that happened, they'd be permanently offlined aka dead for real.

Mind you, I was having a hard time envisioning many scenarios in which this flying bug zapper was killed on three separate occasions while I somehow managed to scrape by – unless maybe I figured out a way to use it as a shield.

That out of the way, the clock was still ticking, which meant it was time to get back to work.

"Put at least ten points into strength," the FAST told me. "You'll need it because I can't help with that part. For Stage One, what you see is what you get. No arms and legs equals physical strength being my dump stat – for now anyway. Focus on me and see for yourself."

I did, concentrating on the FAST until my HUD display changed.

Party Member: FAST – Undisclosed – Level 3

Huh. Good to know.

I held that view for a moment, getting used to how it felt calling things up in this strange overlay to my vision. Then I refocused on its stats. It took a second or two, but then I saw them plain as day.

STR: 0
INT: 198
WIS: 96
DEX: 100
CON: 120
CHA: 18
PSI: 70

"Holy shit," I cried upon seeing how much better it was than me in almost everything.

It made an up and down motion that reminded me of a nod. "That's what happens when you're a superior lifeform. Duh."

Mind you, I couldn't help but notice its shitty charisma score. Can't say I was all too surprised.

"Hold on. You said strength was your dump stat *for now*. What did you mean?"

All I got in return, though, was more annoyed buzzing, no doubt to reinforce that I needed to hurry my ass along.

In the end, I spread my 30 points across three stats. 10 points to strength as advised. Another 10 points went toward constitution because the health bar showing in my HUD looked way too flimsy for my liking. Then, after listening to descriptions for the rest, I decided to put the remaining 10 into wisdom.

The FAST wasn't a fan of that choice but it made perfect sense to me.

From the sound of things, wisdom amounted to the equivalent of in-game hints. Not quite cheats, as the FAST explained, but little things that could influence events. For instance, it could be the difference between stepping on a trap vs spotting a small indentation in the floor ahead – something that would give me a clue that things were amiss.

I had little doubt many of the other chasers would be pumping up their physical stats in every way they could, so I figured a slight bump toward a discount spider-sense might not be the worst choice.

I guess I'd soon find out.

That done, the FAST said, "Okay, moving on. Time to check your achievements and gear up."

"But I haven't done anything yet."

"Sure you have," they explained. "Remember that qualifying round? That counts. It *all* counts. The Committee submind assigned to each chaser monitors you and then makes suggestions to the overmind regarding your starting loot. It's designed to ensure everyone begins the Chase with a fighting chance."

"I'll pretend that made sense."

"You do that. Anyway, just be forewarned. They strive for fairness but not at the expense of entertainment value."

"That doesn't sound good."

"Can go either way really. Just don't be surprised if they go nuts with some stuff and stingy with others."

"Okay, but what about you?" I asked. "Do you get achievements too?"

"Yes, but only once the Chase is underway. For now, though, this is a chaser only perk – meant to compensate for the current level disparity between us."

"Fair enough."

The FAST instructed me how to enable notifications on my SK. Once I did, my HUD filled with text.

Here goes nothing.

I mentally focused on the first one, preparing to read it.

Instead, Drega's voice began to blare throughout the tavern.

"Achievement unlocked! ***Welcome to the Chase*****! You're not a winner yet, chaser, in fact you probably never will be.**

But enough with the speculation. What matters is you have a chance. Just try not to disappoint us all by dying in the first five minutes. *Reward*: 1 STD supply box."

"Fairly standard," The FAST remarked. "Keep going."

"Hold up! What the fuck is an STD box?" I asked.

"Cool your jets, champ. It's not what you think. It stands for *Seize The Day*."

"Then why didn't he just say that?"

"Because some chucklefuck in marketing probably found it hilarious considering your species' ... *proclivities*."

"What proclivities?"

"Do you *really* want to know?"

I gritted my teeth. "Fine, whatever. So what does it actually mean?"

"Simple. There are six tiers of rewards. The most common three are STD, aka daily, Fortnight, and Olympiad."

"Fortnite? As in the game?"

"As in the measure of time, doofus," it said. "They're effectively the equivalent of bronze, silver, and gold loot crates, but with a time theme stapled onto them. Get used to that, you're gonna see it a lot."

"Okay," I replied, trying to make sense of that. "And the other three?"

"They're Century, Millennium, and Epoch. Those are much rarer, but they also contain much better goodies. I wouldn't count on seeing those last two make an appearance until maybe Stage Three or Four at the earliest. We're talking epic gear here. You'll need to do something exceptional to earn those, which, let's face facts, you haven't."

I began to think maybe this so-called Committee had been generous in awarding the FAST 18 points toward charisma. Nonetheless, rather than make a stink I moved on.

Once again, Drega's voice cried out.

"**Achievement unlocked!** *Dino Dan*! **When faced with danger, you didn't Dino Dan, you dino *ran*. But hey, some-**

times the key to survival is knowing when to hold them versus when to fold them. And since the deck definitely isn't stacked in your favor here, you probably made the right choice. *Reward*: 1 Fortnight gear box."

Okay. Stupid description aside, that sounded decent. Next up...

"**Achievement unlocked!** *Chapped Lips Sink Ships*! **Holy fuck nuts, chaser. You arrived here with nothing but what's in your pockets and that doesn't amount to much. Too bad the mobs don't accept credit cards. But hey, if that chaps your ass at least you have some lip balm to sooth it. This one's a gift because dead meat with soft kissable lips is no less dead.** *Reward*: **1 Olympiad weapon box.**"

"Ooh, that's promising," the FAST said.

"Does Drega actually have to announce all of these?"

"No. Plegraxious and a few others will chime in from time to time. But yeah mostly it's him."

"So does everyone get the same achievements?"

"Not at all," it replied. "Why would you think that?"

"Well, then how does he have time to record all of these for ten-thousand people?"

"Oh, that's nothing," the FAST said. "Drega's a ninth ascendant. To capitalize on his popularity, he subcontracts out portions of his consciousness as a side gig. And trust me, he has the mental overhead to back it up. He could literally record thousands of these simultaneously while still retaining enough focus to do his taxes – if that was something he had to worry about, which it isn't."

That made zero sense but I still had one more to unlock, so...

"You do have a point, though," it continued. "There's nothing we can do about his voice, but we should probably switch the feed to interparty cortex mode. That'll at least keep other chasers from snooping."

"How do I do that?"

Time Chaser

It made a buzzing noise then said, "You know what, we don't have time. Transfer party leadership to me and I'll take care of it. Faster that way."

"All right. And how do I do that?"

"Focus first on the phrase *Party Leader* and then on me."

"Okay..."

A question appeared in my HUD asking me if I wanted to make the change. I then mentally focused on clicking a checkbox labeled *yes*.

Guess I was starting to get used to the interface, because only a few moments passed before a confirmation popped up.

Party leader role has been transferred to member: FAST.

There came a beat then I received another notification that audio had been disabled for achievements.

"So now we're the only ones who'll hear them?"

"Within the game anyway," it said. "The audience will still be able to listen, as will the sub and overminds."

"And there's no way to turn that part off?"

"Sadly, no," the FAST replied. "We can designate private cortexing channels so we can chat, strategize, or bitch to each other, but achievements are designed to be for the audience's benefit as much as ours. Ditto for most everything else in the Chase. Great for those who are into the voyeur scene, a bit less so for the rest of us."

Wonderful. Alas, complaining did nothing but waste more time, so instead I opened my final notification.

I *heard* this one as easily as the rest, only this time it was only inside my head.

Achievement unlocked! Just Desserts!

Congratulations. You are the first chaser to be attacked by another chaser. Interestingly enough, you're also the first chaser to *survive* being attacked by another chaser.

***Reward*: 1 Century gear box, along with the joy of not experiencing the inside of a caveman's digestive tract.**

"Holy macaroni," the FAST cried, obviously surprised.

"Maybe we need to thank Borlack for trying to take a chunk out of you. It's almost unheard of for a chaser to be thrown a Century reward this early."

I shrugged. "Yeah, well, it's also pretty much unheard of for anyone to try and fucking eat me."

"Have you considered trying a new cologne?"

"What?"

"Never mind," it said. "Just open your damned boxes. We don't have all day."

I once more turned my attention to my HUD – focusing this time on my inventory. It was subdivided into multiple sections but the FAST had me focus on two for now – active and pending. All four boxes were listed in pending.

Here goes nothing.

"Start with the STD box and work from there."

I shook my head. *STD box*. Someone really needed to be punched in the dick for that one.

I turned my focus toward it, hoping my crotch didn't start to itch as a result.

Instead, a rather unremarkable wooden chest materialized in the room directly in front of me.

Huh. That was cool, in a terrifying way since it once again drove home the point that everything happening here was being orchestrated by beings so advanced that they might as well be using actual magic.

I reached for the box, but the FAST made a buzzing noise instead. "Don't bother. It's all part of the SK's system, so you can just open it with your mind instead. Much faster that way, especially if you need to equip something new right before a battle."

"If you say so."

I did as told, only to watch as the box *poofed* away with a sparkle of light, leaving two objects floating in midair. Text appeared above them both.

Potion Healing – 2
Nutradisk – 50

Time Chaser

"As expected, basic stuff," the FAST said. "Healing potions are a must at any level. As for the nutradisks, well, let's just say that watching chasers slowly starve to death makes for poor entertainment and leave it at that."

These nutra-wafer things looked about as appetizing as cardboard. "Please tell me that's not the only food here."

"Not at all. Consider them emergency rations, just in case. Pretty standard fare, for the last several hundred quinks anyway."

I raised an eyebrow. "Why? What happened before then?"

"As I've mentioned, I can only access limited memories of past Chases, but I believe the answer can be summed up as: you *really* don't want to know."

"Why would they do that?" I held up a hand. "I mean about your memories, not the other stuff."

It let out another sigh, despite possessing no discernible means of respiration. "Every Chase is different. But, as they all fall under the purview of the Committee and those who serve it, there's bound to be similar themes from time to time. There's also the audience to take into account. Whenever a particular stage ends up being a big hit, you can be sure they'll revisit it in some form. Limiting the memories of FAST units who've competed in previous cycles gives us enough information for some flavor text but keeps us from offering any insight that might count as cheating – whether intentional or not."

"Wait. So you've actually played this stupid game before?"

"Sadly, yes."

"How many times?"

"Unknown, but I have partial access that goes back at least nine-hundred and seventy-two quinks."

Holy shit! It had been competing for *that* long? Christ on a cracker! That meant this fucking shit show had been broadcasting since at least the time when humanity was still fighting off mammoths and cave bears.

Time Chaser

More important, though, was what the FAST had told me when it came to the conditions for obtaining its freedom.

It needed to be partnered with a chaser who won.

If I was doing the math right, then the smartass ghost light I was stuck with had been doing this for over ten-thousand years without once managing to grab the proverbial brass ring.

If I hadn't thought I was fucked before, I sure as shit did now.

7

DRESS FOR THE JOB YOU WANT

"No offense, but how have you managed to do this for so long without ... going bugfuck insane?"

The FAST unit flitted about for several seconds, its erratic movement giving me the impression it didn't exactly appreciate my question. "Because each new cycle represents a reset," it said at last. "You're right. A psychotic episode would probably be a foregone conclusion after so many quinks of servitude – perhaps a welcome one."

Definitely not the most comforting thing it could've said.

"However, the Committee takes all that into account," it continued. "In addition to limiting our memories to what effectively amounts to a highlight reel, our personalities are likewise reset."

"Reset? Are you saying that the ... *you*, I'm talking to isn't the same you from previous seasons?" Holy crap, that was utterly horrifying.

"I'm saying no such thing. Maybe I was, maybe I wasn't. I simply don't know. What I do know is that each cycle's reset is at least partially based on the lives of the chasers we're assigned to. So a lot depends on that."

"Wow. That's seriously..."

"Fucked up?" it interrupted. "Trust me, not arguing. But talking about my problems, while cathartic, is also wasting time we don't have. So why don't we shove this therapy session onto the back burner for now and get back to the prep work."

The FAST let the statement hang in the air. Goddamn, I could only hope it was right about having a different personality in the past. If not, I could only sympathize with the thousands of chasers who'd been paired up with it before now — and who had all apparently met their untimely demise by its side.

Don't think about it like that, I told myself. All streaks eventually come to an end. Maybe this FAST was due. Or maybe it was up to me to help break this cycle.

I kept all that to myself, though, turning my attention back to the items I'd gotten in my STD box — *gah*, what a stupid name. "Okay, so what now? I'm concentrating on these things but they're still just floating in space."

"Ah, that's one of the gotchas of the system. You need to touch your loot rewards first. After that you can either equip it or shunt it into inventory."

"What if someone else touches them before me?"

"They can't. Achievement loot is coded to you until it's claimed. After that point it becomes fair game, so no dawdling."

That was handy to know. It meant I didn't have to worry about opening something awesome, only for someone else to shove me to the side and grab it.

I stepped forward and touched the items. Both the floating potion and nutradisk thing instantly disappeared, only to reappear in my HUD's active inventory with the correct amount next to them.

"Some items, like armor, can only be equipped physically," the FAST continued, no doubt anticipating my next question. "Utility items, however, like potions and scrolls, can be equipped and activated physically or via your HUD. Trust me, you're going to appreciate that when you're in a jam and need to pop open a potion without dropping your guard."

Time Chaser

I inclined my head. "Let's back up a step here, okay? You said I've been transported to a whole other dimension, which implies all sorts of hyper-advanced technology. So why the fuck are there potions instead of, I dunno, tricorders and hyposprays? In fact, why does everything feel like a D&D knockoff? It's like I've been sucked into one of those *Elder Scr...*"

"Enough with the irrelevant questions!" the FAST snapped. "We need to finish preparing. *Then* you can speculate on whatever the fuck you want. I'm serious. If I have to go back into stasis because your dumb ass gets killed in the first five minutes, I am gonna be one unhappy AI."

"But..."

"No more buts either. Remember what Plegraxious said about not ticking off your FAST unit? Well, you're right on the verge there, mister. So, what's it gonna be?"

I was tempted to tell it to go fuck itself, but just then Plegraxious's voice rang out. *Speak of the devil and he shall appear.*

"Heads up, chasers! You are halfway through your allotted hour. By now you should be familiarizing yourself with the HUD and your starting gear. Or maybe you're fucking around instead. If so, then you have thirty minutes left before it's time to find out."

Goddamn it.

I quickly turned my attention to the Fortnight gear box.

This can't be right. Unlike that last reward, no chest materialized in front of me. Instead a shoe box appeared. It almost made me long for another STD ... and yes, that was never going to stop being weird.

I focused on opening it, only for an ugly, lime green pair of tennis shoes to appear before me.

The caption simply said *Cross Trainers...*

"The fuck?"

"Don't gawk, focus," the FAST told me. "Almost every item

in the Chase has an accompanying description. Read it before jumping to conclusions."

I did as told, trying to be mindful of our remaining time.

Unsurprisingly, Drega's voice once again rang out inside my head.

Cross Trainers of Nimble Cowardice
What?
Running from giant dinosaurs or hungry cavemen might not be the manliest option you can choose, but that doesn't mean you can't be stylish while fleeing for your life. Better yet, not only are these puppies water resistant but they breathe too – quite possibly long after you've ceased to.

And did I mention that they offer a couple bonuses that might just help you live to retreat another day.
+10 to Dexterity
+2% chance to evade ranged or melee-based weapon attacks
Buff: Vectorman – level 1

"Oh, that's not half bad," the FAST said.

"You heard that?"

"One of the benefits of being connected via the party menu."

"I see. And you consider *Sneakers of Cowardice* to be a good thing?"

"Ignore that part. That's just them messing with you. They know that half the game is won or lost upstairs. Don't let them psych you out especially not this early, because you're going to see a lot of it out there."

I nodded, making a note to remember that. I was about to ask about that buff but stopped myself short. Seeing as how everything else seemed to work that way, I simply focused on it.

A moment later my HUD filled with text, thankfully Drega-free this time. Apparently there were at least some parts of this game that he didn't feel the need to narrate, thank goodness.

Anyway, the FAST was right. It was potentially *very* useful.

The Vectorman power allowed me to instantly refocus my inertia in a different direction, up to ninety degrees. If I was reading this right, it meant that if something was chasing me, activating this power would let me immediately change course without losing a single step – kinda like the lightcycles from *Tron*. Sadly, it seemed it was only usable once a day.

I mentioned this, and the FAST explained that was just for now. The more I used it, the more it would level up, which in turn would offer me more benefits such as shortening the cooldown period.

I was right. This whole freaking ordeal was like one giant video game. There had to be some way to use that knowledge to my advantage, but there was little time to dwell on it now so I filed it away for later.

As for the sneakers themselves, they looked a bit tight, but when I tried to slip them on they instantly resized to fit me perfectly. *Hot, damn.* Talk about a cool feature. Sure, they were still ugly as sin but at least they were comfortable.

All right, time to move on.

I considered my remaining two boxes. The FAST had wanted me to save the Century box for last, but I decided to do that one next. The other was a weapon box. I'd probably want a bit of time to get acquainted with whatever was inside, but I also didn't want to risk getting too caught up and then accidentally running out of time before I got to the big prize.

I focused on the Century box and an ornate wooden wardrobe appeared. I almost stepped forward and opened it before remembering that's not how things worked here. So instead, I *opened it* with my mind.

The wardrobe disappeared with an exaggerated poof of sparks and an accompanying fanfare of trumpets that echoed inside my brain.

When at last the light show finished, I found myself somewhat confused.

Potion Cure Disease – 1

Potion Foresight – 1

Both of those seemed fine, don't get me wrong, but floating next to them was an innocuous looking blue sweater, the sort that child me might've expected Mr. Rogers to wear.

Don't judge a book by its cover, I told myself before focusing a bit harder on it.

Tennis Sweater of Vrarl the Spinner

Vrarl was a mighty demon lord who once terrorized the Alpacians of Earth 116204. He was known to raid whole villages, slaughtering any males and then enslaving the survivors.

Trust me, that first group were the lucky ones.

Vrarl would shear his prisoners right before sacrificing them in bizarre and profane blood rituals meant to empower his loom of nightmares. Once finished, he would then spin the cursed wool into armor for his crazed minions, resulting in one of the most disarmingly harmless looking group of psychotic maniacs to ever be observed in a lower timeline.

Don't worry. I'm sure the cursed souls this was made from won't mind you wearing it.

Well, that was certainly depressing as fuck. However, the buffs it offered were not.

+65 to Constitution

+20 to Charisma

Buff: Curse resistance – persistent

Buff: Partial cold resistance – persistent

Skill Proficiency: Loom o' Doom – level 3

Skill Proficiency: No Threat Detected – level 1

Debuff: You now possess a minor demonic aura. Creatures with the lawful zealot subtype inflict 10% more damage to you.

"Wow," the FAST said. "I certainly wasn't expecting that."

"Can't say I was either."

"No," it replied. "You don't understand. This is ... nothing short of incredible. I doubt even the Millennial boss drops are going to include anything this good for at least several stages yet. And before you ask, no, you *don't* want to fight one and find out."

"Why would I want to fight with millennials?"

"Forget about that for now. The buff to your constitution alone makes this worth it. The rest is icing on the cake."

The stat increases were nice, no doubt there. Same with the buffs. I took a look at those to find they were pretty much in line with what I expected from their respective names.

It was those new skills where things got ... *interesting*, though.

No Threat Detected worked in conjunction with that charisma buff. It supposedly increased my odds of talking my way out of fights with hostile mobs, assuming that no blows had been struck yet. Potentially cool, but the percentage of success at 1st level was too low – only three percent based on my current CHA score – to make it anything but a Hail Mary.

Loom o' Doom on the other hand was just plain weird. It required me to actively collect the hair and fur of defeated enemies. Each day, I could then magically weave a set amount into a length of fiber that could be used for clothing or armor. Once said clothing item was finished, it would then be imbued with a random enchantment.

At 3rd level, the FAST explained, I could weave enough for a small cloak in about a week. The enchantment wouldn't be very high, maybe a few points to one stat, but any advantage was a plus in my favor.

Mind you, since that sort of implied I needed to scalp beaten foes, I figured this might be one skill I was okay with letting atrophy. *Eww*.

"What about that debuff?" I asked.

"I wouldn't worry about it, at least not for now. The chances of us running into anything with that subtype are slim on these first few stages. Hopefully by the time we meet any zealots you'll have extra defense buffs to compensate."

Time Chaser

"If you say so." I stepped forward, took the sweater and, after a moment's hesitation, put it on.

Two things happened almost instantaneously – the health bar on my HUD increased in size and a body-shuddering wave of revulsion passed through me.

"The hell?" I cried, noting my arms were literally covered in goosebumps.

"Exactly," the FAST remarked. "That's the item's demonic aura you're feeling. Don't worry. You'll get used to it."

"Used to it? I feel like I need a week's worth of showers."

"Stop being such a big baby. You're fine. Besides, it's not like you humans aren't used to sketchy shit. Trust me, in a day or so you won't even notice it. Now open your damned weapon box already."

Rather than say what I wanted, I turned my focus – or at least as much as I could muster wearing this weird-ass devil sweater – toward my last item, the Olympiad weapon box.

I'd been looking forward to this one.

It was time to get *weaponized*.

8

SWING AND A MISS

"It's ... a squash racket," I said.

"That it is," the FAST replied, seemingly just as nonplussed.

"Why?"

"I have no idea."

"I don't even play squash. I play racquetball."

"Aren't they the same thing?"

"Not really." I looked at the FAST than back at the racket. On the flipside, I *had* been warned that the showrunners weren't above fucking over a chaser for a cheap laugh. If this didn't prove that point, I didn't know what did.

Guess I should get this over with so I have at least a few minutes to prepare for my imminent demise.

Banshee Racket

Is there anything better than smashing a pebble with an oversized flyswatter, only to then watch it fall limply to the ground like a dead bird? Why yes. There's a shit-ton of things better than that. Too bad this is what you're stuck with, but maybe that's not such a bad thing, sport.

Forged from the collective anger of every squash player who's ever wished they'd taken up pickleball instead, this

racket seethes with unbridled vengeance – giving you a chance to turn even the friendliest of games into a bloody death match whether on the court or off.

Note: this item functions as both a melee and ranged weapon. Ammunition not included.
+15 to Strength
Special Ability: Second Chance Backhand
Special Ability: Screaming Shot

"At least that strength bonus is nice," the FAST said. "Let's see what those abilities do. Maybe this isn't as useless as it looks."

"Fingers crossed," I replied with no small degree of doubt.

I grabbed hold of the racket from where it floated, noting it was a *lot* more solid than it looked. Thanks to modern manufacturing techniques, most rackets nowadays tended to be made out of lightweight materials. Not so with this one. It may have looked like something you'd find hanging up at a *Modell's* or *DICK's* but there was some serious heft behind it.

However, within a second or two of picking it up, its weight seemed to decrease a bit in my hand as the strength bonus was applied – bringing me up to 75. Okay, that was kinda neat.

Who needed a gym membership when you could just grab an item with a bonus? It was pretty freaking... *Whoa*!

My thoughts were drowned out as a metallic grinding noise filled the tavern from seemingly out of nowhere. Then, before I could make sense of what was happening, I realized that we were no longer alone.

A small horde of people had appeared all around us.

It was insane. Within the space of a second we'd been surrounded, and these newcomers did not look happy.

⌛⌛⌛⌛ ·⁖⊹⋄⊹⋄⊹⋄⊹⁖· ⌛⌛⌛⌛

The small army now surrounding us had all appeared suddenly and with no warning, almost as if from thin air.

I saw thugs in medieval garb, brigands, armed knights, and

even a few Vikings. *Holy crap*! Every single one of them was staring our way with either a snarl or sneer etched upon their angry face.

Won't lie. I nearly pissed myself.

What the fuck had happened to our remaining half hour? I turned, seeing nothing but angry stares all around, certain that at any moment they would...

"Relax, *Courage the Cowardly Dog*," the FAST said. "Take a deep breath and actually think before you freak the fuck out."

The FAST's calmness was in stark contrast to my current state of, well, freaking the fuck out, but a few moments later I realized why that was. Not a single member of this flash mob had moved so much as a muscle.

They hadn't even blinked as far as I could tell.

As I tried to keep my heart from pounding out of my chest, I took a closer look.

It was only then that I realized they weren't real. They were just images overlaid onto wooden frames. It had seemed like they'd appeared from nowhere, but in actuality they'd slid out from cracks in the floor and slots in the walls. That must've been the grinding noise I'd heard.

It was sort of like that scene at the beginning of *Men in Black* when Will Smith first visited the MIB office, minus the guns and other applicants.

"What the hell is this?" I finally asked once I was sure I wouldn't die of a heart attack.

"You equipped your weapon. Doing so activates these training dummies. It's to give you a chance to test things out a bit."

"Wait, you knew this was going to happen?"

"Of course," the FAST said.

"And you didn't say anything because...?"

"Because then I would've been robbed of the look on your face as you almost shit your pants."

Asshole.

Now that I was calm again, it was starting to make perfect sense. Still would've been nice to know, especially considering how lifelike the portraits appeared.

I walked up to one of the Vikings and flicked it in the nose with my finger, half expecting to feel flesh. Instead, I merely heard the dull thud of plywood.

Screw it. Maybe it wasn't too late to save a little self-esteem.

Stepping up, I swung the heavy racket. The edge hit the Viking cutout dead on, breaking its head off with a solid *clonk*.

Not bad. "Pretty badass, eh?"

"Yeah, if Saul Goodman decided to quit law and become a low rent tennis pro," the FAST replied.

Okay, maybe they had a point. Between my sweater, sneakers, and now this weapon, I was beginning to sense a theme here.

Rather than waste time dwelling on how ridiculous I probably looked, I took a step back and focused on the racket's special abilities instead.

Second Chance Backhand appeared to be for close combat. On a swing and a clean miss, focusing on the weapon would instantly reverse its momentum – effectively allowing another chance to strike a foe.

Curious to test that one out, I chose another target, one of the brigands. Sadly, the only result was more broken plywood because, go figure, inanimate objects couldn't dodge.

"How am I supposed to test...?"

I glanced at the FAST, grinning as an idea began to form.

"Don't even think about it," it warned, no doubt sensing my intent. "PVP is disabled so that crap won't fly. Not only that, but we're in a safe zone. That means combat between players, mobs, or NPCs, is a hard no. So go back to playing with your sex dolls and leave me out of it."

So much for that idea. Tempting as it was to try anyway, I remembered what had happened to Borlack. Being mindful of our rapidly dwindling time, I simply nodded and moved on.

Screaming Shot was apparently where the racket got its name. Using the Banshee Racket as, well, a racket, allowed the user to lob projectile ammo at a foe. According to the description, doing so would then activate additional sonic-based damage along with a tiny chance to stun an opponent.

That was potentially super useful, if I could ever make it work. There was a note cautioning that using this power negated any non-magical stealth effects but it probably didn't matter much since I had no idea what that even entailed. Regardless, it's not like I could even test it.

"Guess I'll need to wait on that one," I said, once I was finished reading.

"Why's that?" the FAST asked.

"It says in the description that I need ammo, which it specifically did not come with. Hell, it doesn't even say what kind of ammo to use."

"That's actually a good thing."

"How do you figure?"

Rather than answer, the FAST floated past some of the cutouts to behind the tavern's bar. It ducked down for a moment or two. When it appeared again, it had a trio of pewter mugs floating alongside it.

"Think fast," it said as one of the mugs came flying my way, just as surely as if it had tossed it to me.

Neat trick.

I caught it, noting the heft. "What am I supposed to do with this? Drown my sorrows?"

"No, stupid. When you have a hammer, everything looks like a nail, right? Well, when you have a racket, the world is now your tennis ball."

"Squash ball," I corrected.

"Whatever the fuck. Just toss it in the air and take a swing. We're almost out of time here."

I glanced at the mug. "Are you sure?"

"Trust me. Just do it!"

Seemed kinda stupid to me, but the FAST had a [cut off] about the time. Rather than argue, I lobbed the mug into the air and smacked it with the Banshee Racket.

Under normal circumstances, I would've expected a giant nothing burger of the heavy mug falling to the ground, probably accompanied by the racket's shattered head.

These were far from normal times, though. Instead, the mug blasted across the room as if shot by a cannon. There came an ear-splitting whine of sound, almost like a miniature sonic boom, and then it slammed into the far wall – blowing a dinner plate sized hole through the wood and sending splinters flying.

"Holy shit!"

"Holy shit is right," the FAST said. "Now try it again, but this time actually aim at something. How about that knight over there?"

It lobbed another mug my way. I caught it and looked at the target. The image of a knight in gleaming silver armor stood about twenty feet away, situated in front of a thick support beam. Hitting it felt like a longshot, but nothing ventured...

Once again, the mug went rocketing away with a thunderous whine of sound ... only to miss the knight by a good four feet, taking another chunk out of the wall. *Shit*!

"Nice shot, Robin Hood."

I turned toward the FAST, meaning to tell it to go fuck itself, only to find the third mug already headed my way.

"This time," it said, "go into your HUD and turn on Aim Assist."

"Aim assist?"

"Yep. It gives you a 75% accuracy boost for ranged attacks but with a corresponding 30% damage reduction. Trust me, that's not a bad tradeoff until you can get your dexterity high enough to compensate."

"Sure, why not?" At this point I wasn't about to discount anything, so I did as the FAST suggested, focusing on my HUD until a checkbox came up labeled *Aim Assist*. I mentally clicked on it which caused a tiny crosshair reticle to appear in my vision.

Here goes nothing. I lined up the crosshairs with the knight's head and let fly with the final mug.

Crack!

Holy crap! This time I hit it dead center. Not only did the knight's head explode from the impact, but I'd managed to gouge a chunk out of the beam behind it. Hopefully it wasn't load bearing.

It made me wonder what might've happened had I managed to hit it without the added damage reduction.

"Not too shabby," the FAST said, letting me enjoy the moment for about twenty seconds before adding, "Okay, your shit's out of the way. Time for us to move on."

"Oh? Does that mean you'll stop being a dick and actually answer my...?"

"Not quite," it interrupted. "I know you probably have tons of questions and we'll get to whatever we have time for, but I meant that it's *my* turn now."

"Your turn?"

"Of course. I'm a member of this party too, remember? That means you need to get me ready for the Chase as well. Unless, that is, you'd rather I just float idly behind you until such time as you get your stupid monkey ass killed."

9

PIXEL PERFECT

"So what are you waiting for? Equip yourself already. I thought you were an *autonomous AI*."

"I am, and I could, smartass," the FAST replied, "but this is actually a rule of the game. Don't like it? Take it up with the Committee. I'm sure they'll give a shit."

"Yeah, about that..."

"On second thought, never mind. I'll just explain it. Past this point, I'll have far more autonomy to tailor my skills and powers. But here, at the start of the Chase, my mission is mainly to support you. The catch there is *you* have to decide how I can best do that. And before you ask why, it's because, technically speaking, you Earthers are the star of this cycle's show."

"I guess that makes sense." I considered this for a moment. "So, tell me what you think will work best."

It made a buzzing noise. "No can do, Tim. It doesn't work that way. You're supposed to decide. If you get stuck, I can answer *system-level* questions to help you out, but I can't tell you what to choose."

System-level... I wasn't so dumb to not see that as a hint. "All right. How do I get started?"

"Focus on me, same as before. You should see an option to *Equip Party Member*. That'll bring up a list of available abilities you can assign. You can choose up to four for my starting block. One is already prefilled, just to make life easier for us both, but you're free to remove that and choose something else if you want."

I nodded then did as I was instructed. Within seconds, half my HUD filled with the FAST's sparsely populated ... um, character sheet I guess, while the other half listed the ability categories that were available for me to choose from.

Aside from its stats, there was only one ability currently marked on its sheet: *TK Hand*.

Needless to say, I checked it out – bracing myself once more for Drega's melodious voice.

TK Hand – level 1
Non-combat Psionic Utility
Cost: 20 PSI
Weight limit: 5 pounds
Range: 30 feet
TK Hand is what psychics refer to as the basic bitch of psionic powers. In short, it's exactly what it sounds like – an invisible hand made of telekinetic energy that's capable of interacting with the physical world. It's perfect for bending spoons, reaching the high shelf without a footstool, or those moments when you want to jack off but your hands are full helping grandma carry her groceries inside.

I let out a sigh at the needlessly assholish description, but tried to focus instead on its usefulness. It was weak and listed as non-combat. I guess that meant no using it to Force choke any enemies. Too bad. All the same, it was probably what the FAST had used to toss me those mugs. It was probably best not to underestimate the usefulness of having opposable thumbs, even if technically they weren't real. Taking away its ability to interact with the world around us really didn't strike me as a wise idea.

I left that one alone for the moment, turning my attention toward the other abilities I could choose from. The system listed five main categories.

Martial

Melee

Magic

Stealth

Psionics

I glanced at the FAST, remembering what it had said about asking questions. "All right, so considering your strength is zero, is it perhaps safe to *assume* Martial and Melee abilities aren't worth wasting our time on right now?"

In response, it made a happy little *ding* sound.

Okay, that narrowed it down a bit. I considered the other options. "My Banshee Racket's power screws with stealth, so maybe we can table that one too."

There came a smaller ding, but it still told me I was probably on the right track.

Curious, I clicked into Psionics. My HUD displayed a list of powers, some of which looked seriously cool. Problem was, they all had a high PSI cost compared to TK Hand.

I considered this in conjunction with my knowledge of video games.

"Is it safe to assume that the amount of PSI one can spend is directly tied to their actual PSI stat?"

A louder ding this time.

"All right then. You already have TK Hand which seems both moderately useful as well as affordable, but the rest are kind of pricey. That leaves Magic. But if psionics use PSI then what does...?"

"Magic draws from your available mana pool," the FAST interrupted, "which is tied directly to INT, and no I don't know why they don't just call it an intelligence pool. Probably too banal sounding. Anyway, before you ask, they're tied directly together, which means I currently have two-hundred mana points at my disposal."

"Two-hundred?" I asked. "I thought your intelligence was..."

"They round it up to the nearest ten. Less confusing for the audience that way."

Okay then. Well, two-hundred beat seventy any day of the week, which made magic the obvious choice. Before diving in, though, I had one more question. "So what happens if you use up all your points?"

"You're shit out of luck," it replied. "In the moment anyway. Mana, PSI, and health all regenerate fairly quickly out of combat. Not quickly enough to make a difference when your ass is getting beat, mind you, but that's where potions, scrolls, and whatnot come in."

"Thanks." That actually explained a lot, including the sad little mana bar at the top of my own HUD. Guess there was a reason I hadn't been outfitted with any spells.

Rather than grouse, though, I mentally focused on *Magic*.

A long list of spells and their associated cost subsequently populated my view.

Without further ado I jumped right in as our time was rapidly running out.

⌛⌛⌛⌛ ⋄⋄⋄⋄⋄ ⌛⌛⌛⌛

That one's a no-brainer, I thought selecting the *Heal* spell. I only had two healing potions in my inventory, which didn't give us a lot of leeway if things went south. The Heal spell, on the other hand, had a *modest* cost of only fifty mana. With the FAST's current mana pool, that would effectively triple our meager healing capacity.

There were plenty of other defensive spells to choose from but most of them had a higher cost. Also, useful as defense could be, my ego was still stinging a bit from receiving those sneakers of cowardice. The way the show runners had outfitted me, it was obvious what they thought of my chances. They probably weren't wrong, but I figured it was still wise to not blindly accept whatever box they were trying to stuff me into.

I thought of my soon-to-be ex-wife and how I'd mostly been playing defense with her this past month. What had that actually gotten me, other than a performance plan at work and a shitty motel room to call home? Deb would likely never know it, but switching things up here felt a bit like flipping the middle finger to all of that.

My mind made up, I decided to fill the rest of the FAST's starting block with offense, something the producers of this shit show hopefully wouldn't expect. To that end, I narrowed it down to five potentials.

Fire Blast and *Ice Cone* seemed like obvious choices, but I remembered back to the days before Deb had put the kibosh on my gaming. Fire and ice based powers, while obligatory in any game, were also usually what enemies often had the most defenses against.

That was one trap I didn't plan on walking into.

Magic Missile was likewise a strong contender, not to mention the cheapest attack spell, with a cost of 60 mana per missile. I hovered my mental finger over that one for longer than I should have.

In the end, however, I settled on *Acid Ball* and *Shock Bolt*. Both came with a cost of 70 mana but, if I remembered correctly, it was far less common to find enemies with resistance to those – assuming video game logic held true here. Besides, both acid and electricity potentially had other uses as well, hopefully anyway.

It was a big if but all I had to go on.

I took a deep breath, hoping I'd chosen wisely, then confirmed my choices within the HUD. That done, I closed out the window, thinking I was finished.

Rather than dump me back into the main view, though, a

new selection popped up instead – *Name*. There was a blank line after it, along with what appeared to be a blinking cursor.

Try as I might, I couldn't minimize it or make it disappear.

"I think this thing's busted," I said. "It keeps insisting I choose a name."

"So do it then."

"But I already have one."

The FAST let out another sighing sound. "It's not for you, stupid. You need to pick out a name for me."

"Why?"

"Because you're supposed to, that's why! Ooh, I know. How about SAL?"

"Sal?"

"Short for Superior Artificial Lifeform. It's easy to spell, fun to say, and not to mention truthful."

"Think I'll pass."

"Then what about...?"

"I'll come up with something, okay? Just give me a second."

I hadn't been expecting this but I guess it made sense. Every chaser in this stupid game had a FAST unit assigned to them and I guess the assumption was that we'd run into each other eventually. Without individual names that would probably get confusing quickly.

That said, I had no freaking idea what to call it.

Deb had been responsible for naming Jeremy. Hell, she hadn't even asked my opinion on the matter. She'd just blurted it out the moment the doctor had brought it up.

Not that I was bitter or anything.

Then there was the fact we didn't have any pets, once again her decision. Mind you, I doubted the floating green annoyance would appreciate being called Rover or Spot.

Hmm. *Ghost Light* maybe?

Nah. Too much of a mouthful.

Ghosty? Greenie?

I turned to look at it – a speck of green light floating in

midair, looking seriously out of place amidst the tavern backdrop, like a dead pixel on a computer monitor...

Wait! That was it!

"Pixel," I said, watching as the name filled in on my HUD. A moment later the prompt vanished, only for *Party Member Name Accepted* to momentarily flash in my line of sight.

"Excuse me?" the FAST replied.

"Pixel. That's your new name. Maybe Pix for short." I grinned, feeling pleased with my choice. "What do you think?"

"What do I think?" it echoed. "You could have named me literally anything in creation, and instead chose a tiny insignificant speck of light! Why would you think I'd be okay with that?"

"Jeez, relax. If you don't like it, I can go back in and..."

"No, you can't, dipshit. It's set in the system now. The only things still editable at this point are your name and the party name."

"Wait, I can change those too?" My annoyance with the FAST fell to the wayside as I considered this.

Sure, it would only be for this game and however long I managed to survive, which probably wouldn't be all that long. Fuck it. If I was doomed to die anyway, why not do it with a name of my own choosing?

I clicked back to my own info within the HUD, highlighted my name, and started to mentally type *Mac* ... only for nothing to happen. "Hey! It's not working."

"Oh, did I forget to mention you need *party leader* status to change those?" The FAST, Pixel, added.

Wait, what?

A notification popped up on my HUD.

Party Leader: FAST – Undisclosed – Level 3 became *Party Leader: Pixel – Undisclosed – Level 3.*

Then, a moment later, another change popped into view.

Chaser: Timothy M – Earth 8069 – Level 1 became *Chaser: Tim, JUST FUCKING TIM – Earth 8069 – Level 1.*

What?!

The angry little bug zapper wasn't finished yet, though, as a third notification appeared.

Your party has been renamed!

The blank line that had been there before was replaced with **Party Name – *Tim Chasers.***

"Tim Chasers? Seriously?"

"Yep," Pixel replied. "It's both a pun and a not-so-subtle *fuck you* all in one. Trust me, the audience is gonna love it. And even if they don't, *I* do."

"Yeah, real funny. Change it back."

"Sorry, no can do. They're locked, same as mine. Names can only be changed once every three stages."

"Please tell me you're kidding."

"Fraid not, Tim."

Just what I needed, a tantrum prone FAST. Worse, it was all my fault.

I'd temporarily handed Pixel the party leadership so they could make a few changes for me, not suspecting there might be some ulterior motives.

Son of a... "All right, joke's over. Make me party leader again."

"Think I'll pass," they said.

"You said it yourself. You're here to support me, not the other way around."

"Yes, and now that my abilities have been assigned, I've determined that the best way to support you is through competent leadership. You're welcome by the way."

"All right, knock it off. This isn't funny."

"Do you hear me laughing?"

"You can't just..."

"**Attention all chasers! This is your final warning. The Chase will begin in ten minutes, whether you're ready or not. So make it a point to be ready because the audience is dying to see you ... die!**"

"Shit on toast," I muttered.

"So what's it going to be?" Pixel asked once Plegraxious finished giving us our marching orders. "We can either waste the next ten minutes arguing or I can tell you a few things that might help you live to see tomorrow. Your choice, Tim, old buddy, old pal."

10

GAME ON

I wasn't sure whether it was possible to strangle a FAST unit, but I was sorely tempted to try.

Instead, I bit my tongue and listened.

Pixel's memory of past Chases may have been limited, but they'd seemingly been provided with at least the core rulebook of this game so as to bring me up to speed.

They explained that we were about to appear in a random location on a game field that was approximately the size of New Jersey. That alone was hard to wrap my brain around. What that field would encompass or be populated by was a mystery, however.

The only insight Pixel had on that point was that the Chase itself was always modeled on the world where its competitors originated from. It wasn't much to go on but at least I didn't have to worry about ending up on some alien moonscape with a methane atmosphere.

It was a small victory but I'd take it.

Based on the limited memories Pixel had access to, they also said I could probably expect the early stages to be themed toward specific time periods from Earth's history. Unfortunately, we'd have to wait for the start of each stage to find out what those were.

Moving on, the entire playing field was considered fair game when it came to death and dismemberment, save for three exceptions. For starters, there were numerous *campgrounds* scattered throughout each level. These were considered safe zones where we could eat, sleep, or gather our thoughts. There were also a limited number of *guild halls* we could find.

According to Pixel, I didn't need to worry too much about those right now as they'd be spaced pretty sparsely. Upon reaching Stage Three that would all change. At that point we'd be required to choose a *class*, allowing us to specialize in certain skills. Here on Stage One, though, they were more general purpose – offering a modest bonus to those who found them as well as a temporary break from the action.

Either way, nothing to concern myself with at that moment.

The final safe spots were called *Ascension Rings*. This is what we were ultimately looking for. They were the key to advancing to each next stage. There were a number of them located across this stage equal to five percent of the original chasers – so five hundred in total. At least that made the massive size of the game area feel slightly less daunting.

Three days to find an exit. Surely that was within the realm of possible.

The catch was that while the exits themselves might be safe, getting to them would almost certainly not be. In addition to whatever *normal* dangers we'd be facing out there, whatever those might entail, there were also *bosses* located throughout the level – enemies that, according to Pixel, would make the normal mobs look like chumps by comparison.

Therein lay the problem. Some would be capable of being beaten by a small party like our own, but others would effectively be walking death traps – a way to cull chasers, nothing more.

Time Chaser

The only way to mitigate those risks would be to work together, form alliances with other groups and, above all else, keep getting stronger. That meant gaining experience and leveling up.

"I knew it," I said with maybe five minutes left on the clock. "This *is* just like a video game."

"In some ways, yes," Pixel replied. "Think of it as ... a minor concession by the Committee."

I raised an eyebrow. "What sort of concession?"

"The configuration of your HUD was designed to be semi-recognizable to chasers from around Earth year 1990 and onward – unless they're either idiots or luddites. But, that's neither here nor there. Anyway, that familiarity is meant to give you guys a tiny advantage to offset the fact that..."

"The fact of what?"

"Let's just say, from that point in your development onward, a good chunk of your species required a cell phone, PDA, or neural implant to drive three blocks without getting lost. I'm not going to come right out and say technology turned you all into pussies, but I'm also guessing you've never killed half a ton of angry bear using only a rock."

"Wait. Someone here took out a freaking grizzly with just a...?"

"Might've been a cave bear, but yeah. I don't have all the deets on your competition but I'm seen enough to say there's some mean motor scooters out there. So, anyway, that's the Committee's way of making sure things start off reasonably balanced."

Guess I was right earlier about all those other guys being soldiers. And yet here I was dressed for a day at the fucking squash court. "Let's back up a bit. Who the hell is this Committee and what gives them the right to hand down rules like they're freaking God?"

Pixel made that buzzing noise again. "I'm talking about the Trans-Omnipotal PsiCording and Oversight Committee. And to answer your question, yes. They might as well be God as far as we're concerned. They're the ones in charge here. They decide the rules of the Chase, they pick the chasers, they..."

"Trans Omnip... Hold on! Are you saying the people tormenting me are a group of assholes that call themselves TOPCOC?"

"Yeah, about that," Pixel said. "Word of advice. You're gonna want to avoid using that acronym once we're cortexing live again. Trust me when I say that you *really* don't want a bunch of pissed off eighth and ninth level ascendants gunning for your ass."

"You said that Drega was one of those, a ninth ascendant that is. What does that even mean?"

"It means he's at the absolute pinnacle of evolution. Those at the ninth level exist beyond the confines of anything that lump of meat you call a brain can fathom. They are the absolute highest form of life in this or any other universe."

"Oh yeah? Well, if they're so freaking advanced then why are they tossing me and ten-thousand other schlubs into this game of death?"

"Simple," Pixel replied. "Being an entity of the highest order means you exist outside the confines and limitations of time, space, and reality. Sounds pretty cool, right? The downside, though, is you're also beyond nearly every possible challenge life has to offer, meaning you have maybe a few centuries at most before you start to go a little ... bugfuck."

"Wait. Are you telling me that the reason I've been sucked into this hellscape is because they're *bored*?"

They bobbed up and down a few times. "That's exactly what I'm telling you. I mean, isn't that why anyone does *anything*, regardless of how evolved they are? Whoever quoted that phrase about idle hands being the devil's plaything was righter than they'll ever know."

I turned away, trying to make sense of this. "So, these ninth evolution guys literally have nothing better to do than sit around and watch TV?"

Time Chaser

"It's more of a trans-dimensional psicast. And it's not just for them. The Chase can be simulcortexed by any civilization that's reached the sixth stage of evolution and up. And believe me, it's become seriously popular over the last couple hundred quinks. Like, we're talking entire universes stop spinning when a new cycle is about to start."

The fuck?

Before I could even begin to comprehend the scope of what this meant, something changed in my HUD. Three tiny hourglasses appeared in the upper left corner, along with a timer beneath them that was currently frozen at thirty six hours.

Moments later, Drega's voice once again boomed out. **"THIS CYCLE'S CHASERS JOIN US FROM ACROSS TEN-THOUSAND REALITIES AND THREE-HUNDRED THOUSAND YEARS OF DEVELOPMENT – RANGING FROM THEIR SPECIES' FIRST STEPS TO THEIR VERY LAST..."**

Wait, what?

"BUT THEY ALL HAVE ONE THING IN COMMON: AN UNQUENCHABLE DRIVE TO SURVIVE. I DON'T KNOW ABOUT YOU, BUT I CAN'T WAIT TO SEE WHO'LL BE LEFT STANDING ONCE THE DUST SETTLES. BUT FORTUNATELY FOR US THERE'S NO MORE TIME TO WASTE ... BECAUSE IT'S FINALLY TIME TO CHASE!"

The walls of the tavern along with everything inside suddenly became ... fuzzy. They grew out of focus, lost all color, and then faded away, leaving Pixel and me alone in a nebulous grey void – at least until Drega spoke up again.

"FOR STAGE ONE WE DECIDED ON A SETTING THAT WOULD BE FAMILIAR TO AS MANY OF OUR CHASERS AS POSSIBLE, NOT TO MENTION ENTER-

Time Chaser

TAINING FOR THE REST OF US. YOU GUESSED IT! WHETHER IT'S EXPLORING A FORBODING CAVE IN SEARCH OF SHELTER, TOSSING PRISONERS INSIDE A DANK CELL TO ROT, OR SITTING AROUND A TABLE EATING CHEETOS AND ROLLING ODDLY SHAPED DICE, WE THINK A GOOD CHUNK OF OUR CHASERS WILL FEEL RIGHT AT HOME HERE. WELCOME TO STAGE ONE ... THE DUNGEON!"

The sound of disembodied cheers filled my head, nearly loud enough to drive me nuts as Drega's words sunk in.

A dungeon. On the upside, I probably didn't have to worry about being chased by any more dinosaurs.

Also, given everything I'd seen so far, it kind of made sense. It definitely fit the theme of potions, scrolls, and spells. Sure, the fact that I'd been given leisure sports gear as part of my achievements was kind of fucked, but at least they all seemed to be imbued with ... well, magic.

There was also the fact that Drega kinda did have a point. Whether it was caves, mines, or even subway tunnels, humans had a long history when it came to exploring the underground. I had to assume the same was true in some fashion for those hailing from a future time.

Speaking of the future, I couldn't help but wonder about that part he'd said regarding humanity's last steps. It might've just been hyperbole on his part but, considering we were dealing with beings who could seemingly manipulate time itself, I had a feeling it wasn't.

Such questions would have to wait, however, as the timer in my HUD began to flash.

"Get ready," Pixel said. "Once we materialize on the game field, we'll both have access to a minimap. That'll give us a chance to check out our surroundings and whether any mobs are in the area. Keep an eye out for red dots because..."

Before they could finish, the grey nothingness began to coalesce. I felt roughly hewn stone beneath my feet as shapes began to take form all around us. Simultaneously, a tiny map appeared in the bottom corner of my HUD.

Considering the game-like nature of this place, I had a feeling I could probably enlarge it with a bit of focus, although there was no real need at that moment.

Even at the map's current size, the red dots surrounding us were pretty hard to miss.

So much for a chance to check out our surroundings.

11

GNOMENCLATURE
STAGE ONE – THE DUNGEON

Era: ~900 AD

Not gonna lie. Based on both the announcement as well as the practice dummies I'd been given, I sort of expected us to be facing off against foes straight out of *Game of Thrones*. We're talking medieval knights, bandits, and, I dunno, maybe some plague rats too.

Instead, Pixel and I materialized amidst a group of miniature what-the-fucks – six according to both my minimap and what my eyes were struggling to understand.

The tallest of the creatures came to about mid-thigh on me, waist-level if you counted the red conical hats upon each of their heads.

They had red eyes, puke green skin, and mouths full of dagger-like teeth situated over unkempt white beards. In addition to their ridiculous headgear, they wore threadbare pants held up by belts with comically oversized buckles. That might have been hilarious if not for the spears they brandished, each roughly half my body length.

The only good thing about this mess was they looked about as surprised to see us as I was them.

What the ever living fuck?

Even as I tried to contemplate what the hell kind of fever dream had spawned these gremlins, text appeared in my HUD and Drega's voice blared in my brain like a bullhorn.

Dire Gnome Huntsman – level 2

Ever wondered what would happen if a peaceful forest gnome decided to get their freak on with a goblin?

Here's a hint: the result isn't pretty,

Dire gnomes are the byproduct of forced breeding between goblin war chiefs and gnomish prisoners they've forced into a life of brutal submission.

Grossed out yet? If not, then you're probably a sick fuck. Good thing we don't kink shame here.

Anyway, dire gnomes possess all the viciousness, voracity, and insanity of goblins while retaining the facial hair and fashion sense of their better halves.

And now you know why Papa Smurf was mindful of ever letting Smurfette wander too far from the village.

I repeat, what the fuck?!

I wasn't sure what to expect once the Chase started, but being flanked by fairytale monsters hadn't been on that list. I thought our foes were supposed to be from the chosen timeframe of each stage.

Although, considering I was currently clad in a cursed demon sweater, maybe I needed to temper my expectations.

"Food!" one of them shouted in a creepy high-pitched voice. "The gods have heard our prayers and gifted us with food."

Uh oh. What the fuck was up with everything here wanting to eat me?

Plorp!

Before I could react to this new threat, the weird little gnome thing let out a scream as something wet exploded against the side of his head like a high speed water balloon.

I watched in mute horror as the skin on his face bubbled and began to melt. A health bar appeared over the gnome's head

– starting out green, but rapidly shrinking and turning red before disappearing altogether.

Jesus fuck!

"Yo, Tim," Pixel said. "Fascinating as it is to watch you crap your pants, you might want to get with the program."

That's when it hit me. I'd just witnessed their Acid Ball spell in action. Holy crap! Despite having chosen it specifically for this purpose, for some reason I hadn't expected it to be quite this ... horrifying.

Call it a byproduct of having never actually watched a living being get dissolved by acid.

There was another problem beyond that, one that I just now realized. With a cost of 70 mana versus Pixel's existing pool of 200 points, the spell could only be cast twice before we'd need to take a break to recharge. Perhaps not the best call I'd ever made.

Ow!

And that's when *something else* hit me. One of the dire gnomes had stepped up and jabbed at me with its spear. My evil sweater had seemingly stopped the worst of it, but it still hurt like hell. Worse, I could feel blood dribbling down my back.

In response, my health bar shrank by about five percent.

That's not good.

It's one thing to be told death and dismemberment was a real possibility but quite another to actually be stabbed. Sure, I might've gotten the shit scared out of me by that dinosaur, not to mention Borlack, but up until now I'd escaped any real injury. That time had passed, though.

I'd apparently needed a wake-up call that this was indeed deadly serious and it had come at the end of a razor sharp spear.

If I don't do something I'm going to die for real this time.

That realization finally snapped me back to reality. I turned and swung with my Banshee Racket. There was no thought given to the action. If anything, it was more a reflex on my part

– a shitty one at that as I'd failed to take into account just how short these fuckers were.

The racket swung over the gnome's head, barely catching the tip of its hat.

No!

Then I watched in amazement as both my arm and the racket abruptly reversed course – almost like they'd been attached to a bungee cord that had reached its limit and was now yanking both back the way they'd come.

It was the racket's Second Chance Backhand ability.

This time there was a swing but no miss. I'd managed to angle it downward so that the edge of the racket collided with the creature's head. There came the sickening *crack* of bone and the gnome's left eye popped out of its socket as the racket crushed its skull. A health bar popped to life above its head for a moment before winking out again.

"Way to go, Tim!" Pixel cried. "You might just make it past the five minute mark after all."

I barely heard their words. The implication of what I'd just done had hit me like a punch to the gut.

I'd killed the gnome. Barely a minute into this stupid game and I'd already taken a life. It was the space of a second to realize this wasn't like swatting a bug or setting a mouse trap. These things could talk. They were intelligent.

Mind you, they were also actively trying to kill us right back.

Case in point, I jumped to the side as another of the little freaks stepped in and jabbed at me.

This was no good. We were flanked. Scratch that. *I* was flanked. The hallway was about ten feet wide and about the same amount high, meaning the ceiling was out of their reach even with their spears. So, of course, Pixel, in a stunning show of *support*, simply floated up, leaving me to fend for myself.

It was an asshole move, true, but I also wasn't quite sure I could blame them.

Though I had no idea how physical attacks would affect the little light bulb, I'd already discovered pain and injury were far too real where I was concerned. My shoes only gave me a two percent chance to evade their attacks, meaning there was little hope I could defend from the front while avoiding another spear to the back.

I had a choice to make – run or fight.

These things were small. I had little doubt I could easily outpace them. But what then? If we ran into another group of mobs we could end up trapped between them.

No. We needed to finish this, get our bearings, and then plan from there. We had three days to get past this stage. That didn't leave a lot of time for soul searching, which meant I needed to get over myself ASAP.

I didn't want to die, but especially not in any way that would even remotely put Jeremy at risk. That simply wasn't an option.

But in order to have any shot at winning, I needed to clear out one side of these things first.

"A little help here," I snapped, trying to keep tabs on both directions.

"Finally remembered we're a team, eh?" Pixel replied, still hovering up at the ceiling as if they had all day.

"Are you gonna do something or not?" I replied, swinging wildly in an attempt to keep the remaining four gnomes at bay.

"Keep your shirt on, John McEnroe. What's the plan?"

"Distract the ones behind me. Keep them busy."

"You got it, *boss*. Oh wait, that's me."

Their ill-timed attempt at battlefield humor came just as I got stabbed in the leg. It wasn't a bad cut, but another notch disappeared off my health bar as blood began to stain the right leg of my khakis.

Damn it! And I liked these pants too.

"Behold!" my attacker screamed. "The food bleeds! Victory

is ours!" Guess in addition to being vicious little fucks, they were overconfident too.

I took a step forward, hoping that Pixel had my back. My trust was in short supply these days but I didn't have much choice in the matter. On the upside, at least my injured leg was still able to support my weight.

I tried to push my worries aside and focus on the two gnomes in front of me. My fate would hopefully be decided with them, not the ones to my rear.

Fortunately for me, these things were psychotic but also small. I'd seen firsthand how fragile they were. With any luck, I could kill two birds with one stone.

I reared back with my racket then jumped in, swinging with everything I had. The gnome I'd been targeting wasn't a complete idiot. It tried to step back out of my reach. Too bad that was easier said than done with its stubby little legs.

Crack!

I caught it in the side. Despite hitting it with the flat of the racket, its arm still shattered from the impact – knocking maybe a third off its health bar. Better yet, the blow launched its tiny body to the side, straight into its buddy before driving them both into the wall.

Holy shit! Maybe I'd been playing the wrong game all these years.

I stepped in, grabbed the racket from both ends, and used the shaft to keep them pinned. A normal racket would've broken in two from the strain, but this one was seemingly made of sterner stuff.

"Surrender and I might let you go," I told them.

The uninjured one responded by trying to bite my hand.

So much for diplomacy. "You little asshole!"

"Die, accursed devil light!"

I spared a glance back to find Pixel flitting amongst the other two gnomes, diving down to harass them before flying back up out of their reach.

Time Chaser

It was a good distraction but it wouldn't last forever.

I knew what I had to do. Revulsion filled me at the thought, but I saw no other choice.

Bracing myself with my legs, I began to push. The two gnomes were up against a rock, so it was up to me to become the hard place – an analogy I was really glad I hadn't spoken aloud.

The gnomes fought back but it was in vain. I was larger, heavier, and apparently much stronger. The one with the broken arm died first as I pushed with everything I had – crushing them between the racket's handle and the wall. The other's eyes bugged out as I continued to put on the pressure, until at last I heard something break inside its body. Its health bar likewise winked out of existence.

I finally stepped back, letting them slump to the ground, their weapons clattering to the floor next to them.

Won't lie. I was almost thankful there were still two left. It meant I didn't have time to dwell on the awful thing I'd just done.

Instead, I dwelled on the spears the dead ones had left behind.

I wonder...

Thinking fast, I picked one up, braced the tip against the ground and kicked out with my foot, snapping the head of the weapon off. Pixel's harassment of the remaining two gnomes had bought me the time I needed. Now to repay the favor, while hoping I didn't hit them by accident.

Fortunately, I had an ace up my sleeve as I picked up the spearhead and once again activated Aim Assist.

The reticle reappeared in my HUD and I centered it on the leftmost gnome.

Aim Assist upped my accuracy considerably but it wasn't a guaranteed hit. Nor did I care to test my new partner's three death rule, even if they were a bit of a prick.

"Get clear!" I shouted.

Pixel made a buzzing sound then shot up to the ceiling like a bullet.

Good enough.

I lobbed the spearhead into the air and smashed it with my racket. Thunder boomed, extra loud in the close confines of the dungeon hallway. Now to hope the damage reduction wouldn't render the attack useless against this...

I let that train of thought derail as the projectile pierced the gnome's forehead like a railroad spike, killing it instantly.

Yes!

That left only one...

ZAP!

Or not.

A bolt of electricity arced down from Pixel at the remaining gnome, causing its health bar to appear and just as quickly plummet as its eyeballs began to smoke and its hat burst aflame. It fell to the ground dead just as the nauseating stench of burnt pork filled the hallway.

My first thought upon our victory was to wonder what Jeremy would think if he could only see his old man in action. My second was being glad he couldn't, because there was nothing here that was even remotely Kindergartner safe.

Eww. Had I known how gross those spells would turn out to be, I might've thought twice before choosing them.

Rather than dwell on that, I quickly checked the map. The immediate area contained a small gold-colored arrow in the center facing in the same direction I was. It didn't require a lot of thought to realize that represented me. Close by was a green dot – Pixel most likely – as well as several greyed-out X's. Outside of that, though, it was clear.

We'd done it.

We'd won our first brush with death.

Now all we had to do was make sure it wasn't our only victory.

12

MAPPING THE FUTURE

"What the fuck just happened?"

"That was called a fight," Pixel said. "And, yes, we actually won, amazing as it sounds."

"I know that, asshole. I meant *what the hell* did we just fight? And I swear, if you say dire gnomes, I will shove this racket where the sun doesn't shine."

"As interesting as that might be to experience, Tim, I think we should table this discussion for now. Let's loot these jackholes and get moving. I'm pretty sure we just killed a hunting party, which makes me think we might not want to stick around to find out *what* they were hunting."

Notifications began to scroll by in a side panel of my HUD but I ignored them for the moment as I stared at the mangled assortment of corpses. At least one had a melted pile of goo where its head used to be.

"Wait, you actually expect me to search their ... bodies?"

"Not exactly. Nobody sitting at home wants to watch you defile corpses. Well, okay, there's bound to be a few weirdos in the audience but we're not here to feed that particular fetish."

"But you just said..."

"Fortunately for us both, the touching thing only applies to loot boxes. When it comes to dead foes, you can fall back on that video game logic you keep yammering on about. Don't give me that look. Go up to Faceless Fred there and give it a whirl."

A part of me had been hoping that defeated enemies would just poof away, like that samurai guy had done right before our hour of prep time started. Guess I couldn't get that lucky.

As I focused on the gnome's body, trying my best not to retch, text appeared above it.

Lootable Corpse.

My HUD then proceeded to list every single item on the creature's body – its clothes, weapons, even a random pebble in its pocket – up to and including the dead gnome itself.

Interestingly enough, even the remnants of its beard were listed separately.

Okay, that's kinda weird. To test out what I'd been told, I mentally clicked on the listing for its spear, only for the weapon to disappear from the floor and instead be listed in my inventory.

Short spear: 1.

Huh. That was kind of cool.

Curious to see what would happen, I did the same for its entire body. Lo and behold, it too disappeared from the dungeon floor and was subsequently placed into my HUD's inventory as *partial dire gnome corpse: 1.*

"And the reason you need a dead, melted gnome?" Pixel asked.

"Just testing things out. So, are there any limits to this that I should be aware of?"

"With your inventory? I think you'll find it's pretty damned useful. You can store up to ninety-nine of any listed item. After that, it starts deleting the oldest first. Apparently, it's meant to pare down on both excessive hoarding as well as chasers getting weirdly obsessive about shit."

"Ninety-nine? That's not too bad."

"Nope, it very much isn't."

"So what else can you tell me about it?" I asked.

"You can't store anything living, not unless you have a special carrier for it." Before I could say anything, it added, "Don't worry about that for now. We're talking later stage stuff here. Oh, and you can only store something that your current strength would allow you to carry. So no tanks or ten ton boulders."

"Okay, that makes sense. I can lift a gnome corpse so I can inventory it. But according to what you just said, I could also store ninety-eight more on top of that, right?"

"Correct, assuming you felt some insane need to."

"Even though there's zero chance of me carrying ninety-nine of them at once?"

"I didn't say it made perfect sense. Don't be a pedantic asshole, just accept it for what it is."

"Fine. You want anything before I check the rest of them?"

It flitted back and forth a few times. "Nah. Low level mobs like these aren't going to have much that I can use. You should definitely grab those spears, though. They're not going to be nearly as good as that racket of yours, but you never know. At the very least you might be able to sell it later."

"How so?"

"Nothing we need to worry about now. Merchants and shops don't start appearing until Stage Three."

I filed that away for later then grabbed the spears from all the gnomes as suggested.

"Oh, don't forget their beards either," Pixel added. "Not sure if dire gnomes have pubes but you might want to check..."

"Yeah, think I'm gonna pass on that."

"You do you. All I'm saying is you have a power that makes use of that sort of stuff, so might as well use and abuse it."

Abuse wasn't too far off from describing it. Taking their stuff was one thing, but their hair too? Somehow that felt both gross and demeaning. Curious as I was regarding Loom o' Doom, I decided to hold off on that for now.

I did, however, take their pants and belts. There was no chance of me fitting into them, but considering my work clothes were now stained with blood, I figured it might be best to have some extra fabric on hand.

Sure, I couldn't sew for shit, but before today I'd never killed a dire gnome either. So who was to say what might be possible here?

At least my demon sweater had held up surprisingly well. I could find nary a hole or stain upon it. Maybe there was something to be said about cursed wool.

Speaking of blood, though, as I looted the corpses I noted my own health bar ticking back up. Along with it came the distinctly bizarre sensation of my skin knitting back together.

Talk about weird. Humans were capable of healing from injuries but it was such a slow process we didn't really register it outside of maybe the itching. This would take some getting used to, but at least when it was finished I was pretty much good as new.

It was a strange but welcome feature of this bizarre game world.

"All right, where to?" Pixel asked.

I took a look around. We appeared to have a choice of two directions, which certainly made things easy. Now that I had a moment to breathe, I realized it was surprisingly well lit for a dank dungeon, mostly thanks to sconces hanging from the walls every twenty feet or so.

Within each blazed what appeared to be a miniature sun, glowing far brighter than any mere torch. However, as I got closer I realized they gave off no discernible heat.

They were also stuck fast as evidenced when I tried to remove one and failed utterly.

"Nice try, slick," Pixel said, floating past me.

Maybe this was a concession of Stage One since I hadn't been provided with any form of illumination outside of maybe my FAST. I guess watching chasers stumble around in the dark wasn't considered *good entertainment.*

That said, I did notice something odd. Despite the sconces being brightly lit, I could only see maybe fifty feet in either direction. After that, it all became hazy and fuzzy, like looking through a frosted glass window. Maybe I *was* more overdue for an eye exam than I'd thought. Talk about a hell of a time to realize I needed glasses. I mentioned as much to Pixel.

"Relax. That's the Fog of War, not cataracts," they said. "It's part of the Chase, at least for these close quarters sections. It's meant to keep us on our toes. That's fine, though, because this is where using your map can prove invaluable. Go ahead, give it a whirl."

I called the minimap up in my HUD as bidden. A moment later, it expanded to fill most of my view – although I didn't see much more than I had previously noticed.

I wonder...

"I can see those gears grinding," Pixel said. "When in doubt, don't be afraid to experiment with your HUD. Nothing in there can kill you, not unless they added a new feature I'm not aware of. But hey, live and learn."

I ignored the little bug zapper and focused. Sure enough, I was able to zoom out, same way I could do with the map app on my phone – albeit not nearly as much. It was hard to tell exactly how far it reached, but my guess was a couple hundred yards in every direction – well past the fog of war limit. This was probably their way of encouraging us to make use of it.

Almost as if reading my mind, a tooltip appeared.

Level up Perception skill to increase range.

Perception? I hadn't noticed that yet in my HUD. Guess I'd have to dig a little deeper once I got the chance.

Regardless, it was enough for now to tell that this hallway was more of a junction. On one end it connected to another passage running perpendicular to it. At the other, a few hundred feet behind us, it forked off in three different directions.

Time Chaser

I didn't see any more red dots but there *was* a strange symbol inside that other passage at the very far edge of my range. It was a tiny flame graphic above an X...

Or maybe that was supposed to be a pair of sticks instead? "That way, east I guess, is that a...?"

"A campground?" Pixel interrupted, no doubt able to access the same view. "Looks like it. Why don't we head that way? We can use it to get our bearings before setting out again."

I still had unanswered questions about this fight, but that seemed like a fair ask. Also, judging by my notifications, I'd gotten a few new achievements as well. Might as well take advantage of the safe zone to check them out.

After that, well, we could figure out what came next.

"That safe zone doesn't look particularly safe to me," I remarked.

"Looks can be deceiving."

"Are you willing to bet your life on that?"

"Mine? Probably not. Yours on the other hand..."

The hallway was a bit wider here – maybe fifteen feet from side to side. The walls were made of rough-hewn stone with more of those sun sconces lighting the way, while the ceiling rose above us in an arch. North of us, about forty feet away, the passage ended at a wall with three doors, whereas the way south continued onward far past the fog of war limit.

Sadly, the map gave me no information past those doors. It wasn't hard to guess that was by design. Guess the showrunners liked to keep us guessing.

At least I appeared able to scroll back to spots we'd previously visited, even if they fell outside the map's normal range. That was useful to keep us from getting too hopelessly lost, although whether it would give us a heads up as to whether any mobs wandered into those pre-explored spaces remained to be seen.

Time Chaser

None of that was our current focus, though. Instead we were looking at a twenty by twenty foot semicircular alcove that had been carved into the western wall of the hallway. It was separated from the rest by a flimsy wooden picket fence with a shoddy-looking gate in the middle.

Beyond it, a lit campfire burned in the middle of the floor, smokeless despite the close confines. That was it. There was nothing else visible.

I could think of a lot of phrases to describe it, but safe wasn't among them. Neither was restful.

It looked more like a toddler's timeout corner than anything else. As for the fence, I doubted it would keep even those gnomes out.

Still, Pixel had a point about looks being deceiving in this place. So perhaps it was best not to judge this book by its cover – at least not yet.

I strode up to the gate, then glanced at the FAST just in case they were waiting until now to lay some punchline on me. Not seeing any reaction from them, I opened it up and stepped through.

A moment later my eyes opened wide as saucers.

Pixel had been right.

This was a case where the curtains very much did not match the drapes.

13

CAMPING OUT

Gone was the middling vestibule surrounded by dungeon walls, and in its place was a massive frontier fort straight out of the eighteen hundreds.

The open area was full of tents with open flaps, while high wooden walls hemmed us in on the three sides I could see. When I turned back, I saw the fence and gate were now the same height and sturdiness as the rest of the wall. Tall trees loomed over the side, giving no indication that there was a dungeon hallway just beyond.

"This is..."

"Think of it as a pocket dimension within the game space," Pixel explained. "As long as we're in here, nothing out there can see inside or get to us. Oh, and in case the decor wasn't a dead giveaway, campgrounds don't adhere to the time constraints of the rest of the stage. Each one will be a bit different. This one seems to be going for a wild west theme ... um, *mostly*."

I was about to ask what it meant by that when my nose caught wind of an odor far more delectable than that of melted gnome. I turned to see a modern looking gas grill situated in a gap between the tents. Smoke was rising from the top while next to it stood a picnic table covered in various fixings one might find at a cookout – condiments, buns, a cooler, napkins, and more.

My stomach rumbled, reminding me I hadn't eaten anything since wolfing down a tasteless breakfast bar this morning. True, I hadn't been stuck here all that long, but in the last two hours I'd run for my life from a dinosaur, been attacked by a nutjob straight out of *Conan The Barbarian*, and fought a bunch of creepy-ass gnomes. Add in the stress of it all and I'm pretty sure I'd been burning through a lot of calories.

Unable to help myself, I turned that way, only to freeze in my tracks as *something* stepped out from behind the tents and situated itself right behind the grill.

The fuck is that?

The creature stood on two legs, but that's where any semblance between it and a human being ended. It was tall, at least seven feet, with a rail thin body covered in saggy beige skin. Two sets of spindly arms were attached to its shoulders, each of them nearly long enough to touch the ground. Above its thin stalk-like neck sat a misshapen head three times larger than a person's. It was covered in bulging veins and contained a set of coal black eyes that seemed to immediately lock onto me. Perhaps the weirdest thing, though, was the oversized cowboy hat sitting atop its head.

"I thought you said this place was safe," I whispered.

"It is," Pixel said. "He's no threat. Trust me on this."

"Are you sure?"

"If I'm lying, you're dying."

"What?!"

"I'm just kidding on that last part. Seriously, go ahead and approach. You'll see."

I glanced once at the ghost light then back at the being who remained standing behind the grill.

He continued to stare at me for a few moments longer before picking up ... a spatula and a set of grill tongs.

Okay then. Here goes nothing.

Drawn by the succulent odor rising from the grill more than anything else, I cautiously approached.

When I was about ten feet away, the creature's lipless mouth broke out into a lopsided grin.

"Howdy, partner," it cried in a warbling voice, doing perhaps the worst impersonation of a Texas accent I'd ever heard. "This campground here is sponsored by the Xenasus Mineral Hegemony Ltd. We put the core in deep core nebula mining."

"Um, that's nice, I suppose."

"Can I fix you some vittles?"

This was getting weirder by the moment. "Sure. Why not?"

"Yeehaw! What's yer poison?"

It lifted the grill's lid, giving me a view of what lay inside. I spied an assortment of hot dogs, burgers, and chicken breasts. The only issue was the weird-ass coloring of it all. The hot dogs for instance were all bright orange. I couldn't deny how good it all smelled, but still...

Not wanting to anger the strange alien chef, I said, "How about a burger and a dog."

"Coming right up!" It fixed a plate for me, handing it over and directing me toward the picnic table. "Mmm-mmm. I swear, nothing in tarnation beats a good meal, 'cept maybe getting a killer deal on a pod of dark matter. And ain't nobody does dark matter darker than Xenasus!"

"That's ... good to know, I guess."

"Just ignore that last part," Pixel said, coming up behind me. "He's not saying it for your benefit anyway."

I had no idea what the little lightbulb meant, but dutifully stepped over to the table as bidden. Once there, I lowered my voice. "This food..."

"Looks weird, I know, but it's safe. Trust me on this. The Committee has minimum standards it requires all sponsors to meet. One of them is no poisoning the chasers, accidentally or otherwise. The guys in charge don't like anticlimactic expirations. Bums out the audience."

I ignored that last part. "What do you mean by sponsors?"

"The Committee offers up certain aspects of the Chase, campgrounds for instance, for sponsorship. Those spots are limited and usually snatched up pretty fast, mostly by sixth and seventh level organizations that are hungry for eyeballs. Just between you and me, I'm guessing that's why things are a little frigged up when it comes to the food color."

"How so?" I asked.

"Duh! Because not all sponsors are created equal. I'd be willing to bet we're going to meet at least a few who've skimped out on their Earth research beyond the bare minimum."

"So then that stuff it was saying about dark matter...?"

"It was just a commercial."

Disturbingly enough, that made perfect sense.

Pixel was right about the lazy-ass research. Inside the cooler were cans of soda with labels that suggested they were either obscure store brands or whipped up by a species that had glanced at Earth for all of five minutes.

I ended up grabbing a can of *Dr Paprika*, saying a silent prayer it wasn't indicative of the actual flavor. Then I headed to the far end of the campground, hopefully out of earshot of our alien host.

I settled down, debated with myself how hungry I really was, then finally decided to take a chance. Amazingly, I found myself pleasantly surprised. The food might've been an odd hue and almost certainly made of ingredients not of Earth, but it didn't taste half bad.

As I ate, I called up my HUD to check out those notifications that had come in following our fight with the gnomes. I was happy to see two new achievements among them.

Time Chaser

Achievement unlocked! Chip off the Old Starting Block!

Ten seconds into the Chase and your party was already callously melting a dire gnome's face off. That's both disturbingly bloodthirsty, not to mention impressive as hell.

Not only that, but you're the first chaser of this cycle to engage in a mob battle. Don't go getting a swelled head yet, though. That's pretty good, but not quite the record.

Now, had you appeared before a group of glarknarg fang throwers right in the middle of target practice, like a Chaser party ninety-eight quinks ago did, we might've had some competition.

Still, not a bad way to start things off.

Reward: **2 STD supply boxes.**

First battle of the Chase and my reward was two STDs. I couldn't help but wonder what I would've gotten had we actually set that record. Maybe a case of crabs.

There was probably little point in complaining, so I took another bite of hotdog and turned to the second one.

Achievement unlocked! A Bird in the Hand is Worth Two in the Ambush!

Congratulations! Your party is the first to *survive* a mob battle following the start of the Chase – quite unlike that group from ninety-eight quinks ago.

And that right there *is* a new record!

Once more, cheesy fanfare music filled the air. It must've been audible as I noticed the grill master glance my way.

You're off to a promising start. Just don't get cocky because there's a whole world of hurt still waiting for you.

Enjoy your victory for now, because chances are your next achievement will involve being the first to fill a body bag.

Reward: **1 Fortnight gear box.**

I remembered what Pixel had said about the psychological game. Guess they weren't pulling any punches. Still, knowing it was coming helped soften the blow a bit.

Time Chaser

Besides which, I had a secret weapon to keep me going that was more powerful than any needling I might receive – a five year old waiting for me at home.

As much of a curse as this place seemed to be, I needed to remember one very important detail. I had literally been a second away from dying in a manner most brutal.

Had the entities behind this game not dragged me away when they had, it was a near certainty that the next time Jeremy saw me would be to say goodbye at my funeral. I didn't want that for him, or for me either, but mostly for him. Now I had a chance, however slim, to avoid that fate, to give my boy an opportunity to grow up knowing his father instead of fuckboy of the week Manny.

There wasn't anything Drega or his asshole buddy Plegraxious could throw my way that could dull that desire.

I pulled out my wallet. Its contents were mostly useless to me here, but I kept a small photo of my boy in one of the folds. It was taken last Christmas, meaning it was almost a year old. Nonetheless, his smiling face served to steel my resolve.

It was comforting to know I at least had his image there to keep me company. I stared at it for maybe a minute longer, using that time to center myself before putting it away again.

A sigh escaped my lips as I took another bite from my oddly colored lunch. Then I turned my attention toward whatever new loot awaited me.

The daily boxes held two more healing potions as well as one for mana restoration. I had no idea if Pixel could even drink a potion but if so then this was a potential fix for their current spell limitation.

There were also some new items. Seems I'd been right about the dungeon being uncannily well-lit, since I was awarded ten torches as well as two stick-like objects labeled gl'ohrods.

I checked the descriptions for both. Torches worked about like I would expect. They provided basic light for an hour before burning out. They could also be used to ignite combustibles. Good to know that fire worked like it was supposed to in this place. The exception to that, however, was that pulling one from inventory and equipping it automatically lit it as well. That was useful, especially since it's not like I had so much as a book of matches on me.

The gl'ohrods, on the other hand, were basically glowsticks on steroids, except spelled in a way to obviously make them sound cooler than they were. On the upside, they offered twice the light of a torch for a period of twenty-four hours, all while producing no heat.

Unsurprisingly, the Fortnight box was somewhat more interesting. Opening it revealed a ring made of black metal.

All right, Drega, tell me what this bauble does.

Ring of Aggression (minor)

Let's face facts, there are motherfuckers in this world and others who are in desperate need of killing. And while we all love a one-hit-wonder, some foes require a bit more *TLC* to drive that point home.

This ring is for those times.

Buff: adds a cumulative 1% to your melee damage for each consecutive hit scored during a battle, provided it's within three seconds of the last blow struck. This buff resets upon either the time limit running out or two consecutive misses.

Buff: defeating an enemy via Critical Hit will cause the existing damage bonus from this item to remain persistent for up to twenty-four hours or until the end of your next fight, whichever comes first.

Critical hit? Huh. One more thing to add to my growing learning curve.

"Interesting," Pixel said, floating over as I looked at the ring in my hand. "That must be for crushing those two gnomes like a tin can."

"Can we maybe not talk about it like that?"

"Sorry, Gandhi, but you'd best get used to it. The sooner you desensitize yourself to the fact that there are very few nice things waiting for us beyond those gates, the better it'll be for us both."

I once more thought of my son. "I suppose."

"No supposing about it. Now put that ring on. It would be better if it came with a stat boost since you can only wear so many, but that buff is nothing to sneeze at so long as you can make it work."

I looked down at my hands. The only ring I currently wore was my wedding band, still on the fourth finger of my left hand. Funny, I hadn't even realized I was still putting it on every morning. Guess it was one force of habit I hadn't broken free from yet.

That or maybe some small optimistic portion of my brain still thought it was possible Deb and I could work things out. I probably needed to *desensitize* myself to that too.

I moved to take it off but then hesitated. *Maybe that one can wait for now.* Instead, I slipped the Ring of Aggression onto the corresponding finger of my *right* hand – where, much like my sneakers, it resized itself to fit perfectly.

At least now I match. One for love, the other for ... the opposite.

I pushed that depressing thought away as I turned to Pixel. "Did you get anything from that fight or is the game still only catering to me?"

"I'm happy to say we're all finished with that startup crap. I got the same as you, two STDs and a Fortnight."

Tempting as it was to comment, I instead glanced at Pixel's character sheet in my HUD. Their inventory was currently listed as *Party View Allowed*, which I guessed was a setting we could change. Sure enough, three of those mana restoration potions as well as two healing potions were now listed there.

They hadn't been given any torches but that made sense since they were basically a floating forty watt lightbulb. There was one additional item, however, that I didn't recognize.

PSI Patch.

"It's pretty much what it sounds like," Pixel replied after I asked. "Obviously FAST units can't equip items the same way you can, at least not yet. So as a result, most of our *equipment* in these early stages comes in the form of patches. Think of them like ... enchanted stickers. Here, take a look." They moved closer and then spun halfway around.

I didn't see anything at first other than green light, but after a moment I made out a tiny dot of matte yellow near its underside.

"This one gives me a ten point boost to PSI," they explained. "Nothing world shattering, but every little bit helps."

"So, they gave ... a dot to a Pixel?"

They made that annoyed buzzing sound again. "You think you're funny, but you're not."

"I don't know, sounds pretty fitting to me," I said, taking a bite out of my bright purple hamburger. *Huh, not bad.* "Okay, enough of that. Before we head out again, I wanted to ask what was up with those gnomes we fought."

"Oh, fights like that are run-of-the-mill for these lower stages. Not every mob we're going to run into will be inherently hostile but a good chunk of them will be. You'll be able to tell by the color of their marker on the..."

"Not that," I interrupted. "I meant what you were saying about the stages being modeled after specific times from Earth's history. I get that we're in a medieval dungeon. That's fine. But why are there freaking gnomes running around in it?"

"I don't know the answer to that specifically, but I'm guessing hunting parties like theirs were fairly common during this time period."

"No, they weren't," I said.

"Don't take this the wrong way, Tim, but I've seen your high school transcripts. A history scholar you are not."

"Maybe, but I at least know that gnomes don't really exist. They're from fairy tales and make believe. So ignoring why they would or wouldn't attack us, I'm more curious as to *how* they can even be here."

"Ah, still thinking three-dimensionally I see," Pixel replied. "It's simple really."

I narrowed my eyes. "Do tell."

"Happily, Grasshopper. Remember the description that came with your sweater?"

I nodded. "Yeah, it was some flavor text about an asshole demon."

"True, but Drega wasn't just making it up to be funny. He specifically mentioned Earth 116204. That's an actual place from another timeline, one where I'm guessing humans never evolved. Again, the knowledge I have access to is limited, but my pre-Chase prep files include notes on how humans only exist on a fraction of the Earths out there. And apparently there's an even smaller number where you guys are considered the dominant species. So, while you're technically correct that gnomes don't exist, that doesn't mean they aren't real on other Earths."

I ... hadn't considered that. Hell, I could barely wrap my brain around it. I was still trying to come to grips with the idea of *people* from different Earths, and now I was learning we weren't even in the majority.

"Where the actual Chase is concerned," Pixel continued, "they like to pick competitors who are from the same or similar species. However, all parallel dimensions are fair game when it comes to mobs, NPCs, or any other shit we're gonna run into."

"That's ... insane. So you're saying that a creature which exists only in myths and legends on my world just happens to coincidentally be real somewhere else?"

Pixel pulsed brighter for a moment or two, as if considering what to say. "Not at all. What's more likely is that someone from your world, likely multiple someones, had a vision, dream, or perhaps seizure in which they caught a momentary glimpse beyond the veil to another reality, and thus legends of gnomes were born."

"Is that even possible?"

"Do you even need to ask? Listen, Tim, this is probably more than you have any need to know, but think of the walls between dimensions as more like sponge than concrete. They're not nearly as solid as you might think. There's a concept known as dimensional drift, well, known to higher lifeforms anyway. The gist is, it's not entirely uncommon for realities to overlap and for tiny bits and pieces to ... *drift* through the gaps."

"Not really following."

"Okay, here's an example. *Batman* exists in your world as a fictional character, right? But, while Bob Kane may have created him from pure imagination, it's equally possible his mind may have caught a subconscious glimpse into a reality where Bruce Wayne is a real guy who wears Underoos while beating the snot out of poor people. And no, before you ask, I don't know whether that's actually the case or not."

"Holy shit. There's a world where Batman might be...?"

"That's not what you should be focusing on here, Tim!"

"Sorry," I said, pushing that away, cool as it was. "So, then what else can we expect to find out there?"

"No clue. Again, they only give me so much to work off here. But I will say this. The more common a mythical beast is, the more likely it is to be real somewhere else. That means you need to throw your existing expectations, whatever they might be, right out the window. Oh, and while you're at it, toss that burger too because quite frankly it looks kinda gross."

14

LOOT THE HOUNDS

"A little help here, Tim!"

I turned at the panicked sound of Pixel's voice to find one of the wolves had somehow managed to catch the FAST in its mouth and was now shaking its head back and forth as if it had found a new chew toy.

Ooh. That's a lot of slobber.

As amusing as that was, Pixel's health bar told a more serious story – now yellow in color and rapidly decreasing in size.

Shit!

After leaving the campground, and being reminded that Xenasus was the company to talk to if Pixel and I were ever in the market for stable quarks, we decided the doors were too tempting to pass up.

Upon cracking open the middle one, a deathly cold breeze had seeped out. The change in temperature didn't bother me thanks to my cold resistance buff, but it served as a harsh reminder that I'd purposely decided *against* a fire spell for Pixel.

Sensing that might go badly for us, I'd quickly closed it and then opted for the one on the left instead.

It hadn't gone much better.

We were a few steps into what had seemed a seemingly

innocuous circular room when bars had dropped, both behind us and over the exit thirty feet in front of us.

We'd found our first trap the hard way. Guess I needed to pump more points into my wisdom.

Anyway, my map had remained empty, giving me a bit of hope, until moments later when a secret door had slid open along the side disgorging four very hungry looking third level wolves.

Talk about irony. Just a short while ago, Pixel had been telling me to expect literally anything out here, and yet the very next thing we ran into were plain, ordinary wolves. It made me wonder if TOPCOC's overmind, or whoever was watching over things, was purposely fucking with us.

Whatever the case, while these mongrels were far more terrifying than the gnomes, I still found myself somewhat less freaked out by their presence. At least this was one way to die I could sort of wrap my brain around.

Mind you, the plan was to avoid that if I could.

Pixel had been quick to take one of them out with an Acid Ball, dissolving a hole in its side that caused its innards to literally spill out onto the floor. And yes, it was as gross as it sounds.

One of the other wolves immediately turned its focus toward the pile of offal which, while disgusting, lightened our load a bit as I moved in to try and smack one of them with my racket.

The wolf I'd gone after, though, was proving a far more difficult target than the gnomes, despite being considerably larger. So far I'd managed a few glancing blows but had done nothing beyond clipping one of its ears.

It was faster than the gnomes could ever hope to be and all I'd done was make it wary of being beaned in the face with modern day sports equipment.

I'd been playing a losing game of tag with the beast when the cry for help came.

Knowing that the second I turned my back I'd probably be

... dogpiled, I opted instead for a different strategy. I backed up a bit and circled around until Pixel was directly to my right, then I raced straight at my opponent, screaming and holding my racket high. The wolf, perhaps sensing my attack as an opportunity, crouched low then leapt at my face – mouth wide open.

We closed the gap between one another way too quickly for my comfort. Then, just as I felt its fetid breath upon my face, I focused on activating Vectorman.

Please work!

Goddamn, talk about a weird sensation. One moment I was staring at two rows of canine teeth, the next my view completely changed as I was now racing Pixel's way full speed. Behind me, the wolf whined confusedly as it went sailing past where I'd been only a moment earlier.

Yes!

The one that was still gnawing on Pixel looked up a second too late. Its eyes opened wide just as I slammed the edge of my racket down across its back and neck – trying my best to hit it without also clocking the injured FAST.

Crunch!

I felt its body break beneath the blow. That wasn't all, though. A blast of noise trumpeted throughout the room as I shattered its spine, sounding like a synthesized orchestra hit.

The fuck was that about?

I worried that maybe I'd triggered something even worse than the wolf trap, but just then a notification flashed in my HUD.

Damage Buff: 1%.

Next to it a timer began counting down from twenty-four hours.

Holy crap. I was pretty sure that meant I'd just scored my first critical hit. Sadly, it had also been my first palpable blow of the fight, meaning my persistent bonus was the lowest it could possibly be.

Still, one-percent was better than nothing.

The broken wolf collapsed to the ground as Pixel, their health bar now red and disturbingly low, finally freed itself.

"That was so not fun," they muttered.

"Not for you," I said with a smirk.

"I'll remember that next time you're ... shit! Watch out!"

I turned a hair too slow. The wolf I'd dodged had recovered. It slammed into me like a two-hundred pound freight train. I was pretty sure one of my ribs cracked as it knocked me to the ground – sending my racket flying and erasing nearly a quarter of my health in a single blow.

Serves me right for getting cocky.

Pain bloomed across my midsection and I found it difficult to breathe, but I couldn't do much about that with a snarling wolf atop me.

Goddamn it!

With my racket out of reach, I had no way of defending myself. The beast lunged for my throat, so I did the only thing I could. I sacrificed my right arm to its teeth, hoping the demon sweater provided some protection but knowing this was likely going to hurt like a motherfucker as it clamped down on my wrist with a ... *clunk?*

Wait.

The wolf looked as surprised as me. That's when I remembered my SK, the same one Pixel had specifically warned me not to forget about. So of course that's exactly what I'd done the moment it was covered up by my sweater sleeve.

I never thought I'd be so glad to have a house arrest bracelet clamped onto me against my will.

The wolf snarled and redoubled its efforts, but it was no use. The SK was built to last. I had no idea if it was as tough as I'd been told, but there was no doubt it was stronger than this beast's jaws.

Speaking of strength, I saw only one way out of this jam, but it was going to depend on whether my upgraded stats were indicative of my actual physical ability or if that was just more smoke and mirrors.

"Hold still," Pixel shouted from nearby. "I'm gonna melt this asshole."

Remembering what had happened to the last wolf they'd used that spell on, I cried out, "Hold your ... fire! I'm ... gonna try something."

Under normal circumstances there was no way I'd have attempted this. Deb hadn't wanted pets in our household, but growing up I'd had a neighbor who owned a mastiff. The dog was a giant, super friendly drool machine, but it had been built like a horse. Deep down I'd known that if it ever decided to eat someone, there would be very little that unfortunate soul could do about it.

Mind you, since the alternative was being nailed with an acid blob, I decided to take my chances.

While the wolf continued trying to gnaw its way through my SK, I reached up with my free hand and grabbed the side of its head.

This had better work.

Then, using everything I had in me, I both pulled and twisted, knowing that if I was wrong I was as good as...

Crack!

The wolf's eyes glazed over and it fell limp atop me, its health bar and life both extinguished. Guess that answered the question of whether my stats were real or not.

Plorp!

There came a pained whine, and I looked to see that Pixel had instead used their spell on the wolf that had been pigging out on its buddy.

"That wasn't necessary," I chided, shoving the dead canine off me.

"Is that a fact, Dr. Dolittle?" Pixel replied. "Were you perchance expecting it to let us slip a collar around its neck and call it Spot?"

"Well, no, but..."

Thankfully, a notification popped up in my HUD, distracting me from the non-answer I'd been sputtering. Along with it came a notice that I'd leveled up.

Holy crap!

Achievement unlocked! Leveling the Playing Field!

Admit it, being stuck at first level sucks harder than your dad trying to pay off his gambling debts. It's far more hole than glory.

But that's no longer your problem. You have officially popped your level cherry. If this were a frat house, now would be the time to high five your bros as you lie about all the orgasms your date didn't have.

***Reward*: 30 stat points along with the knowledge that you somehow survived past level one.**

In addition to those new stat points, I saw my health bar grow slightly longer. Better yet, leveling up apparently also included a free insta-heal. The pain in my ribs disappeared within seconds, leaving me feeling right as rain.

"Congratulations," Pixel said. "Now stop admiring yourself and let's loot these damned dogs."

15

TOMORROW'S END

"Did you gain a level too?" I asked, checking the map as I picked up my racket. Thankfully, the room the wolves had come from appeared to be empty.

"Not yet," Pixel replied. "As you can probably guess, the first one is easiest. The higher you get, the more experience it requires. So it'll take me a bit longer to hit fourth."

I nodded. "Makes sense. How are you doing by the way?"

"I don't particularly enjoy being covered in dog drool, but I'll live. I managed to suck down a heal potion while you were feeding that thing your SK."

"How exactly? No offense, but you're kind of lacking a mouth."

"You don't say."

"It's just, I have no idea what I'm supposed to do if you're ever…"

"On the verge of a horrific death? Yeah, that's probably my fault. I should've mentioned this sooner, but if that ever happens just pour one out."

"In your honor?"

"Over top of me, moron! I may not have a mouth but my surface receptors will absorb it."

"Ah, good to know."

"Try not to forget it," they said. "By the way, have you spent those stat increases yet?"

"No, why?"

"Good. Hold onto them for now."

"Is there any reason?"

"In terms of the rules, no," Pixel replied. "I just want you to be smart about it. Once they're assigned you can't change them, so it might be a good idea for us to talk it over first. This is one area where patience can be a virtue."

"Gotcha."

"Good. All right, why don't you relieve these hell hounds of their worldly possessions while I scout that hidden room and see if anything's there. I want to work on my Perception skill a bit. I don't know about you, but I'd prefer not to walk blindly into another trap if I can help it."

I considered this. The tooltip on my map said increasing Perception would add more area to what I could see, but from the sound of things maybe it also worked with wisdom when it came to noticing stuff. That sorta made sense. Yet another rule for me to remember. "Just be careful."

"No shit, Sherlock."

Pixel floated into the other room as I focused on each wolf corpse in turn.

Unsurprisingly, they didn't have much on them.

"Find anything?" the FAST called back a minute or two later, it's voice echoing slightly.

"Nah. Just crap. Teeth, wolf pelts, and something called wolf steaks. Oh, except for those two you melted. They don't have any steaks."

"That's fine. Be sure to take it all."

"Why?"

"Because I said so. But more importantly, you never know what'll come in handy later. You have an astoundingly massive inventory system at your disposal. From what I remember, there used to be an encumbrance debuff associated with carrying a lot, but that wasn't popular with the audience so they ixnayed it."

"Okay, and that means what exactly?"

"It means there is literally no downside to abusing the shit out of that particular subsystem. So take *everything* because you never know what could help us out later."

"If you say so."

"I do," they replied. "Don't forget about that Loom o' Doom skill. Stop being all Mr. Prissy Pants. Trust me, you're gonna want to use that."

"I suppose," I grumbled, feeling like I was being browbeaten.

"Seriously, Tim, you gotta start thinking outside the box here. I meant it when I said knowledge is power. But you know what else is power? *Actual power*. If you have a skill that gives you an edge in even the slightest way, you'd best use it."

They probably had a point. I'd promised myself I would do whatever I could to avoid a tier-two death. But it was slowly dawning on me that fighting mobs was only part of it. Maybe Pixel was right and I needed to open my mind to the bigger picture.

For example, that Perception skill. I had no idea what it took to level something like that up, but apparently just looking around counted in my favor. So why not do it?

I needed to be willing to try things instead of automatically assuming it was a waste of time. And if some of those things were disturbingly gross, well, I guess I'd have to deal. This game obviously wasn't some G-rated *Disney* show. My hands were gonna get dirty. I needed to get used to that sooner, because otherwise there might not be a later.

Okay. *Think outside the box*, I told myself. Until that became second nature, I would need to make it my mantra.

To that end, I looted the fur, teeth, and wolf steaks – watching as they appeared in my inventory.

Wolf Teeth: 99 (maximum)

Time Chaser

These are pretty useless, unless you're planning on making a pair of wolf dentures out of them, which would be... Nope, scratch that. Still pretty damned useless.

It wasn't the most awe-inspiring text description. I guessed mundane items were mostly treated as an afterthought.

The wolf steaks, on the other hand, held a few words of potential interest.

Pixel returned just as I finished examining them.

"Anything in there?" I asked.

"In terms of loot, no. Just a few empty cages full of dog shit. Nothing worth taking."

"But I thought you said we needed to think outside..."

"Anyway," they continued, talking over me, "there's a lever in there that I think will open those bars, but it's too much for my TK Hand."

"On it." I headed that way. Pixel was right, the smell of stale dog crap hung heavy in the air, as if the wolves had been locked inside for some time before we'd inadvertently released them. That was odd considering the game was barely two hours old. Was that some sort of clue, merely a bit of set dressing, or just stupid oversight on some production assistant's part?

Sadly, I had no way of knowing.

Nevertheless, I took a minute or two to check it out just in case Pixel had missed anything. "By the way," I called back as I examined the cages, "it said those wolf steaks were alchemical ingredients."

"Hence why I said to grab them," the FAST replied from outside.

I found the lever they'd mentioned and gave it a pull. It may have been too much for TK Hand to move but thankfully that wasn't an issue for me. I slid it to what I assumed was the off position, resulting in a sound that was akin to chains being dragged across a stone surface.

"That did it!" Pixel replied.

"So, exactly what kind of alchemy can you make with a wolf

steak?" I asked, stepping back into the trap room to find the exit now free and clear.

"No idea, but I'm guessing the kind you can slap on a grill if you ever get tired of Mockumeat."

I turned toward the exit. The way seemed clear, but it was probably best to check the... *Wait.* "What the fuck is mockumeat?"

No doubt anticipating my next move, Pixel said, "Map looks clear. Seems like a straight shot to the north from here. Oh, and what do you think they were serving back at that campground? You don't think they actually slaughtered a purple cow to make those burgers, do you? Because they didn't. Pretty sure those things are considered sapient in at least a dozen timelines."

I ignored that last part as we stepped into the hall. "So again, what exactly is *mockumeat*? Or should I just assume it's some stupid brand name for alien *Impossible Burgers*?"

"You know what they say about assuming," Pixel replied. "Anyway, you'd be wrong. It's actual meat, but cultivated from synthesized proto matter instead of living creatures. Hence the name. All the tastiness with none of the animal cruelty."

"Hold on a second," I replied, doublechecking my map to make sure it was clear before turning toward the FAST. "Are you saying these yahoos are morally opposed to using animals for food but somehow A-okay with forcing intelligent beings to fight for their lives?"

"Of course not. Ratifying the rights of sapient lifeforms was in fact one of the key provisions sanctioned in the Treaty of the Nine Paradoxes."

"I have no idea what that is, but if that's the case then what the fuck are either of us doing here?"

"As you can probably guess," Pixel replied, a trace of bitterness in their voice, "artificially constituted beings are exempt from that clause, because we can go fuck ourselves that's why."

I could see I'd hit a sore spot. Still... "That sucks, no doubt about it. But..."

"But what?" the FAST snapped.

"Well, what about me?"

"Oh that? It doesn't apply to you either," Pixel said offhandedly, floating past me to lead the way.

I followed, keeping my eyes peeled for more traps, as if I had any chance of spotting any. "Wait. How does it not apply to me?"

Pixel let out a chuckle. "That's kind of the funny part. You see, that was one of the sticking points when they were hashing out the Doctrine of Convergent Realities."

"Again, no idea what that is."

Pixel ignored me, though. "After roughly six quinks of back and forth squabbling, all the relevant parties finally came to an agreement that, legally speaking, sapience could only be ascribed to species who'd reached a stage of fourth level ascendant or higher."

I narrowed my eyes. "Am I to assume humans don't fit that bill?"

Pixel flitted back and forth a few times. "Not even close. You guys are considered third level at best, with plenty of arguments to be made for a good chunk of your species being stuck at second."

"Are you fucking for real?!"

"Y'know, it's a good thing you didn't choose any stealth-based abilities for me, because you would totally be fucking that up right now."

"I'm serious. We've been to the goddamned moon and back. Does that not count?"

"So what? It's a big dumb rock and only a few of your kind have actually been there. Conversely, far more of your species will readily believe what some rando on the TV tells them, despite it taking all of thirty seconds to figure out it's bullshit."

"I..." Okay, I couldn't really argue with that one. "Fine, but what about the future? Humanity's future that is. Certainly we have potential to…"

"No, you don't," it interrupted again.

"What do you mean?"

"Exactly what I said. If any of your species had ever hit that fourth level, then they'd be here right now filing a grievance with the Committee. That's how it works. I hate to break it to you but the only schlubs who get chosen for Time Chasers are dead ends, species who never make it. Sucks, I know, but at least it keeps the legal overmind from having an aneurysm."

"I…" *Holy crap.* That was bleak as fuck. "Are you saying humanity never evolves to this so-called fourth level?"

"For absolute certain? No. But it seems that way, even if you guys probably came close."

I raised an eyebrow. "What do you mean by that?"

"Just speculation, nothing more, based on humanity's trajectory from around your time."

"So we come close but then something happens? What? Are we talking an asteroid, nuclear war…?"

"I don't know."

"Then look through your … magical time scope and find out."

"Magical time scope? I'm not even gonna touch that one."

"Seriously. You keep telling me your memory circuits…"

"Cells."

"Cells, whatever, are limited but you seem to know an awful lot about this Chase and those involved. So just tell me."

"I can't," they said.

"Can't or won't."

Pixel's body flashed red for a moment before going back to normal. "Entertaining as it might be to claim the latter, that's simply not the case. You see what just happened a second ago? That was me trying to retrieve that specific data and being told to suck a fat one. In short, access denied. It's in a locked cell."

"You've gotta be fucking kidding me."

"Wish I was. Mind you, that doesn't mean I can't speculate a bit."

I made a go-on gesture. "Meaning?"

"All right, just be forewarned we're kind of venturing into the land of potential spoilers here. On the flip-side, we're talking well past your time."

"So, the future?"

"That and the fact that you're probably gonna die here." They paused for a moment, letting that painful statement sink in. "Screw it. It probably doesn't hurt to throw you a few crumbs."

"Gee thanks."

"Anyway, remember what Drega said about picking the contestants from across a three-hundred millennia timeframe?"

"Yeah, so?"

"That wasn't hyperbole. He was being exact with that number. And the reason isn't because it would be unfair to make you compete against, say, trilobites. Or at least that's not the full reason. The memories I have are enough to heavily *suggest* that the Committee likes to populate the Chase with players from across a species' entire developmental timeline – start to finish."

"So how do they determine when we...?"

"I wasn't done yet. You see, targeting when a species hits a roadblock, so to speak, is fairly easy, or at least easier than determining their official start date. After all, it's not like some Earth monkeys woke up one day and decided to invent the wheel. So the overmind does two things. They work backward from the time of extinction, and they round the timeframe off to an even number to keep the marketing nice and simple. Our audience might be evolved entities from across the multiverse, but nobody enjoys being forced to math if they can help it."

I considered this, well, maybe not that last part. Three-hundred thousand years. That seemed to match up with what I remembered learning in science class about the earliest humans.

"Knowing all that," they continued, "I can also tell you that my pre-Chase files also mention that the earliest chaser on this cycle's show met their untimely end in 297,459 BC your time."

"Holy shit." I mean, I'd thought Borlack seemed a bit ... primitive, but that was still a mind blowing number to actually hear spoken.

"Pretty much," they said. "Now in order to figure out the rest, you just gotta add three-hundred thousand to that date and voila! You have figured out the end times."

I did the math in my head. "The year 2542?"

"So close, but technically there's no year zero in your calendar."

"2541 then?"

It made a ding noise. "Bingo! Which just so happens to match the expiration date of the most future-facing chaser picked for the game. Coincidence? I very much doubt it."

"So what happens in the year 2541?"

"Wish I could tell you, Tim, I really do. All I know is that's apparently when humanity as you know it hits a brick wall and goes no further."

16

TIME FOR A PIT STOP
STAGE ONE EXPIRATION: 2 DAYS, 21 HOURS

I must have needled Pixel for over an hour, but the little ghost light didn't give me anything else to go on. They were either stonewalling or truly didn't know the answer. If anything, I got the impression they were starting to regret telling me as much as they did, probably because I wouldn't shut up about it.

Nevertheless, they also insisted this was information I didn't need bogging down my brain in the first place. We were only at the start of the Chase, which meant there were a lot more important things to worry about.

Pixel was probably right, not that I was about to say so out loud. After all, it's not like that knowledge would help me in any way. I mean, what could I even do with it? Sure, I could bury a time capsule with the dire warning to open it on December 31st, 2540, but that was approaching crackpot levels of crazy. I had no idea if they'd still have social media at that point in the future, but if so you could be sure there'd be plenty of posts poking fun at me for pretending to be some half-assed Nostradamus.

All the same, as we continued north, trying to keep our direction consistent to avoid going in circles, I couldn't help the myriad scenarios that ran through my mind. Was that the year the *Borg* attacked? Did Earth fall into a black hole? Were we wiped out by germ warfare or maybe a *Planet of the Apes* style uprising? I had way too many questions and the little fucker floating next to me claimed to be ignorant of the answers.

It just seemed so inconceivable. Hell, weren't all our problems supposed to be fixed by then, at least according to *Star Trek*?.

Who knows. Maybe we were destined to fuck that up and go all *Fifth Element* instead.

There was also the fact that we were dealing with multiple timelines. How was it conceivable that humanity just up and ended at the same time in all of them? Or was I reading too much into that?

Thankfully, we only had one other encounter during that time – running into a level 2 creature called a Unicine, essentially a potbelly pig with a horn sticking out of its forehead.

Either way, Pixel made short work of the beast with an Acid Ball before I could even get a swing in.

Neither of us got much experience from that kill, but their acid spell went up to second level – meaning it would likely be even more disturbing to see in action the next time Pixel chose to *plorp* it into someone's face.

Other than that, the hike served to remind me that while Jersey might've been a comparatively small state, it was still almost nine-thousand square miles in size.

After some time spent walking in silence, I began to feel a rumbling in my stomach. I guessed it was either stress or that mockucrap trying to gnaw its way out of my lower intestine. Probably a bit of both.

I didn't say anything at first, but eventually it reached a point where I had no choice. We were nearing another fork in the tunnel but I didn't see anything else of note, including any spots discreet enough to do my business. That left me with an unpleasant choice to make.

"Listen," I finally said. "You ... might want to float a bit further down the hall."

"What for?" Pixel asked, sounding suspicious. "Because if you're planning on using me as target practice just because I can't answer your stupid questions..."

"Relax. It's not that. I'm just trying to spare you ... from any trauma."

"What kind of trauma?"

"The kind that involves seeing the mess I'm about to make."

Pixel pulsed in brightness a few times, a gesture I was beginning to understand meant they were thinking things over. "We talking number one or the fudge brownie express here?"

I winced at their wording. "Both."

"Eww." They backed up a couple of feet as if I were right on the verge of squirting right then and there. "The horror of witnessing the human digestive tract in action aside, let me just caution you against that."

"Pretty sure I don't have much choice in the matter. I figure maybe I can scoot up against the wall and..."

They let out a sigh. "Yeah, hold that thought and maybe everything else until I can explain what I mean. This is one of those details I probably should've mentioned earlier, but someone had to waste a bunch of time being a..."

My stomach grumbled again, this time quite audibly. "As much as I've come to enjoy hearing about my many shortcomings, can we hurry this along?"

"Fine. Bottom line is nobody in the audience, again barring the weirdos, wants to watch you squat down and start popping out *Hershey's Kisses*. That's like the opposite of entertainment."

"I don't care..."

"Except you *will*, because if you decide you're in the mood to paint this town brown you can expect to be penalized with a tier-two expiration."

"Wait, a tier-two? Why?"

"Because the overmind has gotten flak for this kind of crap

during past Chases, pun not intended. But anyway, as a result it's a big fat no-no. Which, now that I think of it, I *really* should've taken the time to mention sooner. But oh well."

"Oh well?! You're telling me they'll wipe out my entire fucking timeline if I accidentally drop a deuce. That's not an oh well!"

"No, I said you'd be *penalized*. There's a difference."

"And that would be...?"

"You'll be marked for the next twenty-four hours. Survive it and all's well. But if you were to die before that's up..."

They let the statement hang in the air. *The fuck*?

I tried to wrap my brain around this. Watching Pixel dissolve mobs into burning goo was apparently aces as far as the audience was concerned, yet me taking a pee break was somehow worthy of global annihilation.

Tell me how that made sense.

I was beginning to get the impression that sanity wasn't among the myriad factors taken into consideration when deciding whether a civilization was evolved or not.

Like seriously, how did no one watching this mess question how fucking evil that was?

Sadly, standing there fuming wasn't helping my cause. All it was doing was ensuring that the time until an inevitable *eruption* grew ever shorter. And then what? I'd be putting my son's life in danger for no other reason than the call of nature.

How was that even remotely fair?

"So what do I do now?" I asked, knowing that actively thinking about *it* was starting to push the issue into *crisis* mode.

"Simple. Adequate restroom facilities can be found in all campgrounds and guild halls. You might not have noticed them at the last one, but they were back near the..."

"We're not in a campground right now," I growled. "And that last one is more than a goddamned hour back the way we came." I doublechecked my map and sure enough there weren't any in range that I could see.

If that situation didn't change soon, I was going to be forced to start racing down random hallways in the hopes of getting lucky. Needless to say, I doubted that would end in my favor.

"Cool your jets, Mr. Clean," Pixel said. "If it's that big of a deal just use one of your daily vouchers."

Daily Vouchers? "What the fuck are you yammering about?"

"Oh, it's just one of the many features within your HUD that you could've been studying this past hour instead of haranguing the shit out of me. But no, you had to..."

"I'm sorry, okay," I interrupted, getting the distinct impression the little dickhead was enjoying this. "Is that what you want to hear?"

"Oddly enough, yes," Pixel replied, sounding way too smug for my personal edification. "Now, what's the magic word? Come on, you can do it."

I gritted my teeth, wishing for a moment, just a single moment, that PVP was active. "Will you *please* explain what the fuck you're talking about?"

"Sure, why not? Luckily, you caught me in a good mood. In addition to the aforementioned campgrounds, each chaser is allotted five daily *pit stop vouchers* you can redeem for ... special moments such as these."

"Pixel!"

"Jeez, keep your pants on. I was getting to the how-to portion. Focus on your HUD. There should be a tiny menu at the ass-end called *Perks*. It'll be mostly empty at this stage of the Chase, but you should see what you're looking for in there."

Feeling my bowels starting to strain from the effort, I did as instructed. Sadly, it took me an additional try or two to open that menu as I didn't want to take any of my focus away from keeping the *floodgates* closed.

There!

It was just as Pixel described. The Perks menu was empty save for one item.

Pit Stops Remaining: 5

Time Chaser

I immediately focused on it, curious to see what would happen but also not caring much so long as it brought me some relief.

A part of me was half-expecting my bowels to be magically emptied via ninth ascendant super science. Alas, no such luck.

Instead, the wall nearest me began to shimmer. Next, the hewn stone cracked as a section forced itself away from the rest, one in the shape of another of those arched doorways. The way through became obscured by a glowing light that I guessed to be another portal.

"Go on," Pixel said. "You have one hour before it dissipates and trust me, you don't want to be inside when that happens. Mind you, if it takes that long you probably have bigger issues. And before you ask, no I can't come in and get you. This pit stop is coded specifically to you."

That was handy to know especially once the PVP ban dropped. Being ambushed on the bowl was not how I cared to meet my end.

Curious as well as desperate by this point, I was about to step through but decided to err on the side of caution. "You're sure this is okay, right? This isn't some gotcha so the audience can complain and get my universe erased?"

"You'll be fine. They can't follow you inside, metaphorically speaking. In fact, no one can. It's one of the few bits of privacy allowed in the Chase. So, if you need to scream, cry, or curl up into a fetal ball, now would be a good time to get it out of your system."

I had no intention of doing any of that, but it was good to know the option was available should I need it.

⌛⌛⌛ ⋅⁑⋇⁑⋇⁑⋅ ⌛⌛⌛

I was expecting either a disgusting fly-filled chamber pot to fit this stage or some futuristic three-seashell setup that would likewise serve to freak me out.

Instead, I was amazed to find myself in a modern bathroom. It wasn't anything fancy, but the toilet, sink, and even shower stall were all familiar to me.

The toilet paper was the cheap stuff, sure, but it's not like I'd expected this to be some five-star hotel.

I stepped over to the shower and turned it on just to see if it was real. Water began to pour from the showerhead and flow down the drain like it would normally. Guess that explained why they gave us an hour. That was time enough to get cleaned up if need be.

Considering Pixel's endearment with that acid spell, I had a feeling this was one feature that would come in handy. My clothes were already dotted with blood splatter, but it was only a matter of time before I ended up covered in something worse.

All that was for another time, though. Instead, I stuffed my racket back into inventory, popped open the lid of the bowl, and got down to business.

"Hey!" I shouted once I was situated, curiosity getting the better of me. "You TOPCOC fuckers can suck the bottom of my ass, right ... about ... now."

Ahhh!

I waited a beat, wondering if I was about to be smote where I sat, however, nothing happened. Maybe the bathrooms actually were private. That would be no small relief.

The thought of being continually watched by both the audience and some all-seeing overmind was not what I'd call fun. Don't get me wrong. I was certain I'd adapt to it. After all, it was merely day one of this ordeal. But knowing I had at least one place where I could safely vent was a shot in the arm for my morale.

As I let my current problems empty away, I looked around. The only thing missing was some reading material. What a day to have left my cell phone back in the car – not that I was likely to get much signal here.

On the other hand, I did have my HUD.

So, as *things* progressed, I opened it up and took a few minutes to do a deeper dive.

Up until now I'd mostly been focused on my stats, equipment, and the fact that Pixel had scammed me into making them party leader.

I was curious to see whether there was maybe a PDF rulebook or anything else that might help me, but it seemed like the HUD provided info on a need-to-know basis only. I.e. you had to already be in possession of something. A pity, but I guess that's what Pixel was for.

Still, there was plenty of info to be had despite my meager level. Skills, for instance. There was a whole menu devoted to that, full of multiple submenus within.

There was one labeled *Chaser Skills*. That turned out to be a list of the skills one might expect to find in an open world game. We're talking things like *Perception, Stealth, Diplomacy, Intimidation, Disguise* and more. Not surprisingly, all of them were currently at first level. *Crafting* had its own sub-submenu. Beneath it were listings for Ranged and Melee Weapons, Armor, Potions, Scrolls, Alchemy, Traps, and even Explosives. That was cool, but there were even more listed beneath those that were blurred out for now, making them unreadable.

Needless to say, that made me curious.

Something to ask Pixel about later.

I closed that one out. Next to *Chaser Skills* were *Item Skills*. Unsurprisingly, I found Loom o' Doom and No Threat Detected sitting there along with a note warning me that these skills would be lost if an item was unequipped.

Nothing to worry about there unless something better came along, which I doubted would happen anytime soon.

Finally, there was a submenu called *Life Skills*. I clicked on that next.

"You have got to be fucking kidding me."

This was where the sea of level ones ended, but I can't say that made me feel much better. If anything, I was skeeved out by the complete and utter invasion of privacy laid out before me.

Pixel had mentioned that, as part of their assignment, they had studied my entire life. In truth, I'd assumed that was a bit of an exaggeration.

But here I was looking at a list that seemed to go on and on no matter how far I scrolled, and it appeared to catalog every aspect of my being, as well as assigning it a rank.

Coding – C++: 7

Not bad.

Coding – Java: 5
Management: 4
Driving: 6
Brewing: 1

Oh, come on. I did that for maybe a month before giving up.

Cooking: 3
Problem Solving: 6
Racquetball: 3

Seriously? I'd been playing for over a decade. Surely I was better than that.

Karate: 2
Dancing: 1
Cunnilingus: 2

Was this thing fucking for real? Even *that* had a rank?!

On and on the list went, but I closed it out before I could read more. No goddamned way was I only a two.

I'd heard of introspection, but this was fucking ridiculous. I had to wonder who'd assigned me these ranks and whether they'd been placed there specifically for the purpose of egging me on.

That had to be it.

No way could I be a two.

I mean, I'd had girlfriends before Deb and they'd never complained.

A notification popped up but I swiped it away without looking at it. What now? Was Drega handing me an achievement for successfully pinching a loaf? If so, I'd tell him where he could stuff it.

First things first, though. I finished up, feeling about a thousand percent better. Five pit stops didn't sound like a lot for an entire day, but between campgrounds and sleeping it would hopefully suffice. It would probably behoove me to not go too nuts with the knockoff soft drinks, though.

I was washing my hands, preparing to head back out again when I paused.

Why not? What could it hurt?

Instead, I stripped my pants off again, taking care to remove the items in the pockets first, then I turned on the hot water in the sink and ran the stained garment beneath it.

Unsurprisingly, the blood had mostly set, but I was at least able to get some of it out.

Maybe I'd get lucky and find a magical stain stick in my next loot box. Wouldn't that be a...

Another notification popped into view, which again I dismissed. "For fuck's sake, Drega! Get a hobby, dude. I'm just doing some laundry."

I was almost tempted to go back into *Life Skills* and see if perhaps that one had gone up a point, but then I got yet another notification.

Goddamn it.

I slipped my pants back on and proceeded to grab my stuff as I closed the skills menu. When I was finished, I found only one notification waiting for me, though. So then what were those other...?

That's when I noticed a line of text sitting in a small section labeled *Cortexing*.

Oh yeah, Pixel had mentioned something about that.

I mentally clicked to maximize it.

Time Chaser

Party member Pixel has invited you to a private cortexing channel. Accept Y/N.

I accepted it.

Pixel: *You might want to hurry up in there.*

Wait. Was this section just a fancy name for player chat?

If so, I tried to figure out how to type a response, fully intending to tell them to hold their damned horses. But then I realized that wasn't the most recent message.

Pixel: *Seriously, Tim, get your ass out here!*

Pixel: *Oh shit! They have me surrounded. I swear, if I get permanently offlined I am coming back to haunt your monkey a...*

That was it. The message simply stopped there.

Tim, JUST FUCKING TIM: *Um, Pixel? Everything okay out there?*

As I thought the words with the chat in focus, the HUD instantly filled them in. Okay, that was handy, although I couldn't help but notice it instantly populated my handle with the stupid name Pixel had chosen for me. *Grrr!*

That, however, seemed a minor issue compared to the lack of any response.

Crap.

I turned my attention toward the map to see if that would provide me with any insight, only to realize the entire thing was greyed out.

What the?

I maximized it, wondering if it was a glitch. Instead, there was a tooltip waiting there that would've been really useful to know five minutes earlier.

Map unavailable while inside pit stop.

Son of a...

I closed it out, only to then glance at the headline of that notification I'd ignored.

Achievement unlocked! Shit Stop!

Double son of a bitch!

17

TRACKING CHANGES

Who's a big boy who went poopy in the potty?
You are!
Congratulations, you have mastered the use of the restrooms. Good thing too, because I sure as hell aren't going to wipe your ass.

Why bother when it'll probably be kicked soon enough?

Now get back out there. There's shit still waiting to happen and I don't mean that mess you left in the bowl. Oh, our poor janitorial staff.

***Reward*: The pleasure of knowing your world won't be destroyed simply because you crapped your pants.**

Motherfucker!

The second I stepped out of the bathroom two things happened – the door disappeared and my map came back to life.

"Shit on toast."

What a stupid fucking design choice. This was the sort of crap you'd find in a hastily released game that then ended up getting a hundred gig patch a few weeks later.

Unless it was a feature and not a bug.

Pixel had warned me that those in charge often gave greater

weight to entertainment value than to fairness. This struck me as a perfect example. The pit stop vouchers seemed like a nice touch on the surface, but what if that was the catch? You went inside to take a shower or purge your *inner demons*, only to end up blind as to what's going on the outside.

Pixel said I couldn't be watched in there, but that didn't mean the overmind couldn't monitor me in other ways, like through my HUD. If so, they'd have known full well how *distracted* I'd been.

It was literally a trap waiting to happen.

Perhaps I was reading too much into that, but so far everything about this game felt like a gotcha, so why not the restrooms too?

Whatever the case, that could wait until I figured out what had happened to Pixel. I opened my map, zoomed out to the maximum distance, and started looking for green dots as quickly as I could.

After several long moments with no luck, I began to fear I'd been too late, that the trail was already cold. Then I caught sight of a single red dot at the very edge of my map's range, heading up the right fork of the path ahead. A second later and it was gone, having moved beyond where I could *see* it.

That had to be whoever or whatever was responsible for what had happened here.

Before setting off in pursuit, though, I forced myself to stop and take a look around, just in case there were any clues to be had. If knowledge was indeed power, then I was weak as fuck right at that moment. I needed to see if there was any way to remedy that.

I didn't spot anything at first. After all, the ground, walls, and ceiling were all made of the same unremarkable stonework. But then, as I looked closer, I began to notice a few stray details.

There was a scorch mark on the ground nearby, still smoking slightly. A few feet further on I spied a dark stain. Blood probably, although I stopped short of touching it.

Time Chaser

Nonetheless it told me enough. There'd been a fight here, however brief. Pixel had likely hit something, but the lack of bodies suggested it either hadn't been a fatal blow or there was more than one attacker, enough to take their dead with them...

A notification popped up in my HUD informing me that my Perception score had just jumped to level two. In conjunction to that, my map's range expanded a bit. It wasn't by much, adding maybe a couple dozen yards to what I could see, but it was enough.

The freshly extended view revealed more red dots heading away from me. In their midst was a tiny sliver of green – not a dot but a question mark instead.

Seriously?

Of course these fuckers weren't going to make it easy. What fun would that be for the audience?

The group moved to the edge of where I could see before disappearing once again, but it was enough to know the hall opened into a much larger space beyond that point.

I looked up at the ceiling, noting there was no sign of any cameras or recording devices, but that wasn't surprising. What need did Drega and his buddies have for cameras when they could beam the show directly into their viewers' minds? Nevertheless, I knew they were watching.

"I hope you fuckers are having a good time with this," I grumbled before taking off down the right fork.

⌛⌛⌛⌛ ·⋄ӊ⋄ӊ⋄ӊ⋄· ⌛⌛⌛⌛

This was crazy. I was putting myself at risk to save a sentient roman candle with an attitude problem.

And yet Pixel was all I had in this crazy world. Asshole or not, I wasn't too keen on giving that up. The truth was, I needed the little bug zapper. Heck, there was no two ways about it. Without their warning, I'd have probably ended up taking a crap on the floor, never knowing I'd doomed my entire world in the process until it was too late.

Annoying as Pixel could be, their knowledge was invaluable – serving at the very least to keep me from doing stupid shit that put my son's life in danger.

I could neither ignore nor forget that.

But there was also another side to it. I kept repeating in my head what Pixel had told me about wanting their freedom after suffering over ten thousand years of this bullshit.

Hell, after all that time I might be a little salty too.

Attitude aside, they was counting on me every bit as much as I was on them.

That said, I wasn't a moron. I'd already set off at least one trap in this hell hole. The last thing I needed was to die stupidly while blindly racing to the rescue.

So I took the racing part out of the equation.

I hugged the wall and took it slowly. Visibility in this section of the dungeon was still decent, but I lit a torch nonetheless – hoping the extra light might help me spot anything dangerous before I ran face-first into it.

Worst case, I was hopefully giving both my perception and stealth skills a workout. If game logic held true with those, the first several levels would be relatively easy to grind. After that was when things would slow down. As a software manager who'd run his fair share of sales meetings, I understood the marketing logic behind this. Early advancement was the sort of thing that got customers invested. People liked to win and some easy victories at the start checked those boxes – resulting in an endorphin rush that got them hooked.

In this case, I had a feeling that rush was more intended for the audience, to capture their interest early while the players were still relatively weak. Entertaining as I'm sure that was, it still made them all a bunch of bloodthirsty pricks as far as I was concerned.

These beings dared to call themselves evolved, yet they were cheering and howling for the equivalent of a high-tech public execution. If that was what being *evolved* meant, then maybe it was a good thing humanity never reached that level.

2541. There was little doubt that year was going to haunt me, but it did me no good right then. So I pushed it away for the time being and refocused.

Fortunately, these early levels weren't solely to benefit the audience. It was clear that leveling up meant more power for chasers such as myself. And more power equaled a better chance of survival.

It was a brutal tradeoff but a necessary one.

Knowledge was also a part of that equation, as I'd been told again and again. And sometimes the best knowledge was obtained by taking things slow and steady, rather than rushing in unprepared.

It was entirely possible, likely even, that Pixel wouldn't exactly be endeared to my careful approach toward rescuing them, but FASTs were afforded three deaths to my one. So even if they'd been taken out by their attackers that didn't mean it was over.

Heck, that might actually be a best case scenario. If the mobs that took Pixel, and I had to assume that was the case, thought they were dead, maybe they'd just toss them by the wayside. If so, I could maybe swoop in and retrieve their soon-to-resurrect body once the coast was clear.

I had a feeling that was wishful thinking, but sue me for trying to be optimistic in a world that was actively trying to crush my...

What's that?

A series of greyed out X's surrounded by white dots appeared on my map a short ways past where the tunnel opened up. Whatever cavern or area lay that way, it was huge – larger than anything I'd encountered in this dungeon so far.

I got the distinct impression I've found something of note,

although whether that would prove to be a good thing remained to be seen.

Either way, I continued moving slowly, hoping that any mobs up ahead were limited by the same fog of war that I was.

Wouldn't that suck if they weren't? It was easy to imagine walking along, certain all was well, only for a volley of arrows to come screaming out of the murk ahead.

Hopefully that wouldn't be the case because such an end would be the cheapest of cheap deaths. Were I a spectator to that sort of bullshit, you could be sure I'd be calling my cable company and demanding a refund to whatever pay-per-view I'd just bought.

I could only hope these so-called evolved beings were of the same mindset.

Fortunately, I managed to reach the end of the tunnel unmolested – finally giving me a decent view of things. An uncomfortably warm breeze blew my way from inside a massive open grotto. It carried with it several strange scents, not all of them bad. The reason for this was obvious. Unlike the multiple dungeon tunnels I'd walked through, this cavern wasn't merely barren rock. I spied plentiful vegetation starting about thirty feet ahead. Trees, bushes, vines, and more.

It was like a jungle inside of a dungeon.

None of those details had appeared on my map, which was worrisome, but at least it allayed my fears about the fog of war. Even if that rule didn't hold for mobs, the foliage here would almost certainly provide plenty of cover.

Fortunately, no red dots were visible at the moment, just those X's and white dots up ahead. It was time to investigate further.

I stepped from the tunnel and, sure enough, the temperature seemed to shoot up a good ten degrees or more. It was no longer sweater weather. Sucked to be me because there was zero chance I'd be taking it off anytime soon.

I could deal.

The reason for the sudden change became clear in short order. While the dungeon tunnels had been lit with scattered sconces, providing adequate light at best, here it was more like a bright sunny day.

I looked up and saw a clear sky overhead. My elation at finding the dungeon exit was short lived, however, as my gut told me something was off. It took me a minute, but then I realized what the problem was. The sky was bright and blue but there was no sun to be seen. It was all uniformly bright but with no central light source.

In short, it wasn't real.

My guess was either an illusion or some alien hologram. I was wrong. I hadn't found an exit after all. I turned back toward the cave wall and looked up, only to find my notion confirmed. There were no peaks or cliffs. The walls just continued up until they seemed to meld with the sky.

Weird as fuck, but I doubted it was anything I needed to worry about, at least not compared to the jungle ahead of me.

Won't lie. It reminded me of being back in that qualification round. Despite the heat, a cold sweat broke out on my brow. I might've had a cool new weapon and slightly enhanced physical abilities to go with it, but no fucking way did I care to test them against another dinosaur.

The upside was that the vegetation didn't appear to match what I'd seen earlier. It's hard to say exactly what the difference was, save that it didn't feel as primeval. That was as much insight as I could give on the subject. I was no botanist, so all I could do was keep my fingers crossed that I wasn't wrong.

Or conversely, that there wasn't an Earth somewhere out there where ten-ton dinosaurs were still skulking around during the Dark Ages.

I wasn't going to find anything out just by standing there, so I steeled myself and continued onward.

Whether fortunate or not, I didn't have far to go before I found what I was looking for.

Time Chaser

A group of bodies lay scattered right in front of where the tree line began. Turned out those white dots were big ass rats that were happily feasting on the remains. They looked up and hissed as I approached. A few of them flashed red for a moment or two, but thankfully they all took off running.

Can't say I was sorry for that or for the fresh info it gave me. I now knew that white dots represented other living things. Considering how a couple of the rats had flashed red upon seeing me, I also took it to mean that white meant they were either neutral or unaware of my presence. Useful knowledge to have.

I made sure the little fleabags were gone before moving in to check on their unlucky feast. Thankfully, it appeared that Pixel wasn't among the victims – another group of those dire gnomes, identifiable by their size and a few of those dopey red hats still lying around.

The rats had been doing a disturbingly thorough job of eating their way through the remains. At least two of the gnomes had been stripped nearly clean. Gross as that was, I forced myself to take it all in – trying to glean any insight I could from this carnage.

Whatever had killed them had looted their corpses of clothes and weaponry, telling me their attackers were likely intelligent. Another chaser party perhaps? Even with PVP currently suspended, I found myself a bit apprehensive about that. Some new allies might be nice, but I had a feeling it was a fool's game to automatically assume they'd be friendly.

That theory soon seemed more likely as I spied a footprint in the dirt – humanoid but too large to belong to a gnome. Leaning closer, I made out the faint imprint of toes. If it was indeed from a chaser, they were currently barefoot.

Talk about a sucky situation. It was bad enough to have to play this madman's game, but I couldn't imagine doing it without shoes. Hell, the only thing worse would be no pants either.

I was immediately reminded of Borlack and his swinging dick. Was it possible he was responsible? And if so, did that mean he was responsible for ... um ... FASTnapping Pixel? That didn't seem likely, both with the PVP ban and the fact that he hadn't joined the rats in chowing down on the dead gnomes, but it seemed unwise to discount anything at this point.

What were the chances that in a game field this large he'd been coincidentally dropped close enough to be a pain in my ass?

Perhaps not as high as I was beginning to fear, I realized as I looked closer. There was actually more than one set of footprints leading away from the scene of the attack.

So probably not Borlack. Good.

Guess there was something to be said about this perception thing.

It made me wonder what kind of details I'd missed over the course of my life that I might've otherwise noticed had I just paid a bit more attention.

Would I have seen that Deb wasn't even remotely as happy as I'd thought. And what if I had? Could I have saved us? Or was there nothing I could've done that would've kept her from eventually engaging in a game of hide the sausage with fuckboy Manny?

"No," I said to myself as that rabbit hole loomed ahead of me. "You don't need any of that shit right now. Deb isn't here, Pixel is. Focus on that."

I tried to recenter myself, pushing my wife's accusing face away. It was nuts. Eight years of marriage and somehow that's the first thing that came to mind when I thought of her now, as if the good times had never...

"Knock it off," I scolded myself again. None of that mattered right now, doubly so as another important detail about this attack was beginning to dawn on me.

These gnomes hadn't just been killed. They'd been seriously fucked up.

Time Chaser

The rats had done a good job, no doubt about it, but there was no way they'd been responsible for pulverizing at least two of the gnome skulls almost to powder.

It told me this was less a battle and more of an extermination.

Now the only question was whether those responsible were also the ones who'd taken Pixel.

18

PIGGING OUT

Traipsing through the undergrowth was a maddeningly slow endeavor. Much as I wanted to race ahead using the map to guide me, Pixel's advice that I should think outside the box kept repeating inside my head.

In terrain like this, that mostly seemed to take the form of remembering all the adventure films I'd seen in which the hero just narrowly avoided a messy death by trip-wire.

Meeting my end like some nameless *Raiders of the Lost Ark* extra, peppered by poison darts, wasn't something I looked forward to. In the back of my mind, I also couldn't help remembering that explosive crafting skill I'd seen in my HUD.

Though I doubted I had much to worry about in the form of medieval claymore mines, I also had no idea when gunpowder had first been invented, so perhaps it was best to not assume.

Goddamn, what I wouldn't give for an eighth grade history book right about now.

It was possible I was being overly cautious. I needed to be mindful of taking things too slowly since the clock was continually ticking down. It was probably best to remember this game was called *Time Chasers*, not Time Creepers or Time Crawlers.

Hmm, I made a note to ask Pixel about that if ... *when* I finally got them back. I mean, what exactly were we supposed to be chasing here anyway?

Whatever the case, I was apparently doing *something* right, as a notification appeared in my HUD under status effects.

Stealthed.

With any luck, that also counted toward bumping that particular skill a notch. I knew every little bit would help, especially once I finally spied some red dots on my map.

"I've got you, you fucks," I whispered, despite there being no one else present.

The *stealthed* status winked out for a second or two before reappearing.

Crap! Served me right for talking to myself. I couldn't help it, though. Being alone in this forest was creeping me out.

Not helping was that my map had been practically crawling with white dots the second I entered the tree line, albeit that probably shouldn't have come as a big surprise.

The map didn't capture everything, mind you. No small amount of insects buzzed me as I crept along but it remained blissfully clear of them. Conversely, I'd spied a couple of squirrels so far that seemed to coincide with dots. My guess was that there was a size limit or something in effect.

It made me wonder if I'd get an alert before, say, stepping into a nest of fire ants or disturbing a hornet's nest.

Tiny things weren't the only problem with the map, however. Once something showed up, it appeared as a dot, nothing more. There was no differentiator between size and probable threat levels. My ears were a testament to this as more than once I'd heard the heavy crunch of brush nearby that suggested something sizable was passing through the area.

Maybe there was a way to refine that down the road, but for now I was stuck playing a game of *rat or dinosaur* with every dot until I actually got close enough to see the creature in question.

Speaking of which, those red buggers on my map appeared

to be spread out. There was a nearly straight line of them up ahead, bisecting the jungle, one every fifty feet or so.

From their formation, I guessed they were either blocking the way or guarding it.

The latter seemed more likely – guards or scouts keeping an eye out for, well, people like me. They were spread out to cover a wide area but still close enough to rush to each other's aid if need be.

It wasn't the best scenario I could've hoped for, but after thinking it through I realized it was far from the worst. Therein lay opportunity. Sneaking past their line would be the ideal scenario, but that little whisper earlier had proven my stealth wasn't nearly good enough to be counted on.

That meant taking one down without alerting the rest. If so, I could maybe continue on my way unseen. This was an instance where the jungle possibly worked in my favor. Sight lines in every direction were poor at best, way lower than my fog of war limit, meaning I was likely as invisible to them as they were to me.

The difference, however, was I knew they were out there. Or at least I hoped that was the difference.

If I could get close enough, one solid smash with my racket might be able to get the job done before they could raise a warning.

So long as I got them before they could scream, I wasn't too worried. This jungle was far from being a quiet place, with chirps and chitters constantly filling the air. One mob dropping like a sack of bricks wouldn't cause all that much ruckus in the grand scheme of things.

Of course, that assumed a one-shot victory.

That was a big if, one entirely dependent on what lay ahead.

Please, don't let it be more wolves.

I highly doubted wolves had been responsible for hacking those gnomes to pieces, but I'd soon find out. I spied a break in the trees up ahead, one that seemed to coincide with the location of the nearest red dot.

Here we go.

First things first, I needed to figure out what I was up against. I crouched low and crept forward, trying not to step on any twigs or branches as I moved.

I must've done at least a halfway decent job as my *stealthed* status remained in effect.

Finally, I pushed a few fronds aside and peered through at the clearing ahead only to see ... nothing?

The fuck?

The map distinctly said there was an enemy combatant maybe fifteen, no more than twenty feet ahead of me. I had a pretty clear view of that space but there was nothing visible.

Great. Invisible wolves.

That would be unfair as fuck, or maybe not as I remembered that dinosaur from earlier. Its feather covering had been a near perfect match for the forest around it. Maybe I was dealing with camouflage.

Or maybe it was a plant mob, some kind of giant Venus flytrap lying in wait. Hell, that didn't seem any less ridiculous than dire gnomes, so it was probably best to not rule it out.

My mind racing with possibilities, each more horrific than the last, I kept my eyes peeled – trying to see if anything stood out in either the clearing or the trees...

There!

I spotted movement as something tiny waddled out from beneath a bush across the way. It was ... a squirrel, a chubby one at that.

Wait, is that a guinea pig?

Sure enough it was a little ball of brown and white fluff contently munching on the leaves of the plant it had stepped out from under, no different than you'd see in a pet store.

I checked the location of the red dot compared to where the tiny pig stood. They matched. More importantly, there was no white dot to indicate it was some sort of decoy for another creature.

The guinea pig *was* the mob.

Are you fucking kidding me? Is this map broken or what?

I couldn't help but laugh.

The *stealthed* status winked out from my HUD. At the same time, the little furball turned my way, inclining its head ever so slightly as it continued to chew – somehow making it even more disgustingly cute than it already was.

Fuck this. The jig was up anyway. I stood to my full height and stepped into the clearing. "It's okay, little fella."

I turned my head toward the sky. "Really? This is what I'm supposed to fight?" The only thing I could guess was that maybe they'd tossed these fuzzballs into the game as some sort of super cute fodder – hoping I couldn't pass up the opportunity to level grind, while also giving the audience ample cause to root for my demise.

What was next, a basket of puppies?

I turned back toward the guinea pig to find it still staring at me.

As I did, its description started to fill my HUD along with Drega's voice.

Guard Cuy – level 1

Cuyes aka guinea pigs aka "Dear God, why did I buy this fucking rat for my ungrateful shit of a child?" are what happens when evolution gets falling down drunk and decides it's still in good enough shape to drive.

These four-legged fur sausages can't fight, can barely run, and are about as smart as a pile of hammers.

But you know what they can do? They can scream louder than a slutty teen in a *Friday the Thirteenth* movie. Better yet, guard cuyes will gladly do so at even the slightest provocation, such as, say, someone having the gall to interrupt their lunch.

Scream?

Oh crap.

Sure enough, the pig lifted its fuzzy head and let out an ear-piercing shriek.

Fuck me!

Panicking, I bolted ahead and slammed my racket down on it like it was the world's biggest and cutest fly. The little garden rat elicited one final squeak as I smashed it, almost certainly erasing an entire lifetime's worth of karma in the process, not to mention causing my persistent damage buff to likewise disappear.

Shit!

All of that and I was *still* a hair too slow.

On either side of me, the jungle came to life with more of that incessant shrieking. Setting one off had caused a chain reaction with all the rest.

Worse, I realized a moment later, it would be easy to find where this living fence had been broken – just zero in on the spot where you could still hear yourself think.

An achievement flashed in my HUD but I ignored it. "Eat a bag of guinea pig dicks, Drega!"

Somehow this *win* made killing those wolves seem almost pleasant in comparison, but now was no time to rue my actions.

My map lit up with red dots closing from the distance, five of them from the look of things and all rapidly headed this way.

My first thought was to turn and run, but even as my feet started to move almost of their own accord I forced myself to stop and consider things.

No. That's what they'd be expecting. I needed to think outside this box.

I saw them spreading out on the map – not by a lot, but maybe enough for me to take advantage of.

Sadly, I didn't have any delusions about slipping past them without a fight. I'd already screwed that pooch ... or pig.

Besides, even if I did somehow make that work, they'd eventually turn around and head back the way they came. And if so, what then? If there was anything else up ahead, I'd be surrounded.

Shouts and cries filled the air, warring with the still screeching pigs. Whatever was coming was bigger and ostensibly smarter than these guard pigs. I needed to be ready.

I rapidly considered my options, then began to move forward again at an angle, aiming for the leftmost mob in the line. I'd already gotten flanked once in this game, thanks to being dropped right into the middle of a gnome hunting party. I had no interest in letting it happen again.

A part of me couldn't believe I was going on the offensive. A tiny voice inside my head, one which sounded way too much like Deb for my comfort, complained this wasn't very Tim-like.

That voice wasn't wrong.

I managed programmers who wrote fucking finance software. I liked my job, don't get me wrong, but it wasn't exactly *Ninja Warrior*. But then I'd never wanted it to be. I was happy just being comfortable. The mortgage was getting paid, the bills were mostly under control, and while I may have balked at buying Jeremy a five-hundred dollar Jeep for Christmas, there were more than enough presents to make him happy.

Why was that so bad?

Why was my entire fucking life now ruined because of that?

And why was there an infinitesimally small portion of my consciousness, nearly microscopic but there all the same, that hated every single thing I'd just told myself and was actually looking forward to whatever happened next?

I had no answers to any of that, nor was I sure I wanted them.

Luckily for me, though, the monsters who'd created this game hadn't designed it with time for unwanted introspection in mind.

19

CLOUDY WITH A CHANCE OF MURDER

I'd erased about half the distance between myself and the approaching red dots before deciding that was close enough.

At that point I put my back against a tree and did my damnedest to stay quiet.

In truth, I expected my gambit to fail as the mobs heading this way were obviously aware something was up due to their pet rats still screaming their heads off.

However, it seemed the ear-piercing shrieks were a two way street as my status quickly changed to *stealthed* again.

That's when it hit me. Without line of sight, these newcomers had no idea who I was or where I was hiding. The only thing that might give me away were my footprints. With any luck, though, by the time they figured that out it would be too late – for them, I mean.

Hopefully anyway.

As I waited, racket in hand, I noticed another notification in my HUD, a small one this time, informing me that my Stealth skill had increased to level two.

Cool to know, but this was no time to pat myself on the back as I spied movement from the corner of my eye.

I turned that way and almost soiled my pants at the horrific visage pushing through a nearby tangle of bushes. Thankfully I didn't, because barely a moment later I realized it was actually some kind of ornate headdress being worn by ... a person?

That revelation may have given me pause, but not Drega.

Cloud Warrior: Atac – level 3

If by chance you ever happen to be walking around the Peruvian rain forest sometime in the tenth century and suddenly find your skull split in two, you can probably thank this fine fellow here.

Fortunately for you, Cloud Warriors aren't named because of their ability to fly. If so, you'd already be fucked harder than your mom on dollar shot night. It's more of a locale thing, taking their name from the dense mist covering the floor of the jungle basin they call home.

Silly I know, but you can't deny it's badass.

They are utterly devoted to only two things – appeasing their living god and defending their territory from intruders in the most brutal way imaginable. If you guessed that involves blood sacrifices, congratulations, you aren't an idiot. What you are, though, is screwed. Because if you're close enough to see them, chances are they've already seen you.

The introductory text finished, I was able to properly focus on the intimidating figure closing in on my position. Broad shouldered and with a chiseled chest, he wore a loincloth, a thick wool cape around his neck, and had some kind of Aztec-looking headdress sitting atop his noggin. His appearance alone was more than enough to intimidate the shit out of me, and that wasn't even counting his weapon.

In his hands he held some kind of extra-nasty looking medieval mace. The weapon's head was a thick chunk of bronze forged in the shape of a star. It looked both heavy and sharp enough to pulverize someone's skull to oatmeal. It didn't take a genius to guess I'd found the guys responsible for throwing those gnomes the last surprise party of their lives.

Time Chaser

I needed to act quickly lest I share their fate, but found myself hesitating nonetheless.

I couldn't even fool myself as to the reason why.

Earlier, before the game had even started, I'd naively assumed our foes would mostly be human. But, as surprised as I'd been to find out that wasn't the case, it had also brought with it an odd sense of relief I hadn't realized was there until this moment.

Fighting non-human mobs – monsters – was surreal as fuck. I hadn't wanted to kill those gnomes, but afterward I hadn't felt much guilt either. In truth, it simply hadn't felt ... *real*.

It was hard to explain except to say that fighting those gnomes hadn't left me feeling like ... well, a murderer afterward.

That was garbage logic, no doubt about it, but I couldn't deny it all the same.

I couldn't help but think this coming battle, should I somehow prevail, would serve to erase that distinction. At that point there'd be no two ways about it. Cold blooded or not, I'd be a killer.

To make matters worse, it's like the overmind knew that and had gone out of its way to rub it in by telling me the warrior's name – as if it took extra pleasure in making this personal.

The thing was, much as that thought made me want to vomit, I knew the alternative was death. I would die and Jeremy would grow up fatherless.

That was the simplicity of the choice I was faced with.

Disturbing as it was, that thought steeled my resolve. I won't lie and pretend I didn't feel some disgust at myself, but I began to consider my next move all the same.

I honestly wasn't sure whether to be happy or creeped out, but my feelings from earlier still held sway. I wanted to live, and I sure as fuck wanted to make it back home to my boy.

But for that to happen, I needed to get past anyone who had the misfortune of standing in my way.

Time Chaser

As the Cloud Warrior passed by my hiding space, I couldn't help but realize how utterly fucking stupid, not to mention arrogant, it was to try and view him as nothing but a stepping stone on the road back home. Fuck that noise. He looked like a stone cold motherfucker, one sporting a physique that put my *dad bod* to shame.

I mean, hell, my title back at work had been Software Development Manager, but this guy's was *Warrior*.

You know what kind of dudes were called that? The kind who were more than capable of kicking the living shit out of people like me.

This was utterly fucking nuts on my part. Yet there I was trying to psyche myself out that I could not only take this guy but his four buddies too – all while dressed in a getup that could've only looked less threatening had I been wearing a set of *Crocs*.

Stop your whining and do something, I admonished myself, feeling my resolve starting to slip. *So long as you do your best, Jeremy will be safe. And it's not like they can make you any deader than you already are.*

Oddly enough, that distinctly non-comforting train of thought got me moving again.

Keeping note of my status indicator as well as the map, I began to creep up behind Atac, while staying mindful of the wicked looking weapon in his hands.

Badass he might've been, but thankfully my level two stealth – aided by the ongoing screams of those annoying guard pigs – helped keep me unnoticed as I closed in.

I lifted my racket and held it like a baseball bat. One more step and I'd...

Crunch!

So of course that's the moment I managed to step on a

fucking twig. The *stealthed* status immediately vanished from my HUD as Atac began to turn around.

Goddamn it!

I swung for the fences ... or tried to. Sadly, my wannabe kill shot fell way short of the mark as the strings on my racket got snagged on a low-hanging branch.

Shit!

And this was apparently just one of the many reasons why this guy was a Cloud Warrior while I was just a doughy corpse waiting to happen.

As I desperately tried to pull my weapon free, knowing my head was about to be smashed into Jello, the Cloud Warrior abruptly stopped moving.

And I don't mean he had second thoughts. He literally froze mid turn as if someone had pushed the pause button. A moment later, I realized he wasn't the only one as all sound had seemingly ground to a halt – leaving me standing dumbfounded in unnatural silence.

The fuck is going on?

Then that silence was broken by the last person I really wanted to hear from.

"IT'S JUST ABOUT TIME FOR OUR FIRST LIVE UPDATE AND I COULDN'T BE MORE EXCITED," Drega's voice rang out, not only audible but loud enough to give those guinea pigs a run for their money.

I glanced at my foe, wondering if maybe he was caught up in listening too, but quickly saw that wasn't the case. He was actually frozen, like time had simply stopped ... which, honestly shouldn't have been all that surprising considering the name of this show.

As Pixel would've said, *duh!*

Time Chaser

Freaked out by this unexpected development as I was, I wasn't about to let this opportunity pass. I pulled my racket free and swung again ... only for the edge of the weapon to stop about six inches from my opponent's head, as if I'd struck a pile of sand instead.

There came an angry flash of red in my HUD along with a notification.

WARNING: Combat is not permitted during live updates!

Normally I didn't find italicized fonts to be all that intimidating, but something told me it might be best to not try that again.

"WE'RE NOW FIVE HOURS INTO DAY ONE AND THE COMPETITION IS EVEN FIERCER THAN EXPECTED. TWO-HUNDRED AND SIX CHASERS HAVE ALREADY BEEN EXPIRED FROM THE COMPETITION, WITH PROBABLY ANOTHER FEW JOINING THEM AS SOON AS THE ACTION RESUMES."

Two-hundred and six dead already? Holy crap!

"THAT'S NOT ALL, FOLKS. THREE-HUNDRED AND EIGHTY-FOUR FAST UNITS HAVE SUFFERED AT LEAST ONE OF THEIR ALLOTTED EXPIRATIONS. I'LL TAKE THIS MOMENT TO REMIND ALL ACTIVE CHASERS THAT ONCE YOUR FAST IS GONE, THAT'S IT. YOU'RE ON YOUR OWN. BE MINDFUL OF THEIR SAFETY BECAUSE THE ODDS OF ASCENDING TO THE NEXT STAGE DROP BY APPROXIMATELY SEVENTY-THREE PERCENT IF THEY'RE..."

"**I'm sorry to interrupt, Drega,**" Plegraxious suddenly cut in, "**but we have some breaking news from Stage One!**"

"WE DO?"

I raised an eyebrow. Maybe it was just an act. Hell, it probably was, but Drega still sounded genuinely surprised.

"**Indeed. We have our first Tier-Two expiration of the Chase!**"

"A TIER-TWO...?" Drega sputtered for a moment before catching his stride. "**WELL DON'T KEEP US WAITING, PLEG OLD BUDDY. GIVE US THE DEETS.**"

Despite his congenial tone, I couldn't help but get the impression Drega was annoyed at this revelation.

"**Gladly, and believe me these *deets* are so fresh out of the oven they're burning my fingers**," Plegraxious continued, playing it up like he was announcing a monster truck rally. "**Without further ado, meet chaser, or should I say *former chaser*, Ikaros, a semi-renowned philosopher from fifth century Athens Greece. He comes to us after having met a less than renowned end, choking on an olive while visiting with his mistress.**"

His words were followed by overblown gasps of surprise from seemingly all around me, like I was surrounded by an audience I couldn't see.

As if in response, the screen on my SK lit up from beneath the sleeve of my sweater. A beam of light projected straight through the fabric, coalescing into an image about ten feet away from me. It was like an instant big screen TV roughly twelve feet wide – large enough to ensure I didn't miss any of the *deets*.

A bearded man with salt and pepper hair and wearing a tunic appeared upon it. A scene of him speaking to what I guessed were his students was then followed by him lying naked in bed, holding his throat as his face turned blue.

And this was what apparently passed as entertainment for higher beings.

"**Alas, Ikaros's genteel way of life proved to be his undoing when he unwittingly stumbled upon a Tikolosh nursery**," Plegraxious continued, laying it on extra thick. Try as he might, though, it was obvious he didn't have Drega's sheer charisma.

The image on the spectral screen changed. Ikaros, now wearing a golden toga and brandishing a spear, had just dispatched a hairy gremlin-like creature. His FAST unit was

Time Chaser

flitting around him, probably relaying some bit of insight, but Ikaros didn't appear to be listening. He was focused instead on a cluster of pulsating pustules that covered a nearby wall. As he watched, they began to burst open – revealing themselves to be some kind of seriously gross egg sacs.

Out spilled creatures similar to the one he'd just killed, save they were maybe a fifth of the original monster's size. These newborns were hairless and had big inquisitive eyes, making them look sort of like bipedal sphinx kittens. At first glance they appeared super cute and mostly harmless, until the shot zoomed in to reveal that each had a mouth full of needle-like teeth.

Ikaros's eyes opened wide in horror as they turned his way. He raised his spear again as if preparing to fight, but then cocked his head to the side. From the look on his face, I got the distinct feeling he was listening to Drega introduce the mobs he was about to square off against.

Though the broadcast gave no indication as to what he was being told, I assumed it was nothing good because seconds later all the fight drained from Ikaros's face.

It was like his spirit had been broken in that moment. I don't know whether it was the number of monsters or the fact that they were newborns, but instead of defending himself he tossed his spear away and merely sat down.

The baby gremlins converged on him even as his FAST flitted above ever more frantically, obviously trying to get him to do something.

I'd love to say they cut away before his gruesome end, but no such luck. I was treated to the full show of this guy literally being eaten alive, including his final moments when it became *painfully* obvious he'd regretted his choice.

"Sadly, his surviving FAST unit was forced to conclude that Ikaros failed to meet his end while embracing the chaser spirit," Plegraxious said, his tone somber. The asshole was trying to play it up but mostly failing. **"As such, Ikaros has received a**

Time Chaser

tier-two expiration, meaning Earth 2008 has been erased from its continuum."

On the screen, an image of the Earth appeared, although one that was different from my world. The continents weren't quite right. North and South America, for instance, were fused into one. Not that it mattered because seconds later the entire thing faded away, leaving behind nothing but empty space.

Despite Plegraxious's sullen tone, the sound of raucous cheering filled the air.

"**HOT DAMN, PLEG,**" Drega cut in again, all trace of his earlier surprise gone. "**I SWEAR, I ALMOST WISH THERE WAS AN AFTERLIFE. BECAUSE THERE'D BE BILLIONS OF SOULS WAITING THERE RIGHT NOW WITH THE EXPRESS PURPOSE OF KICKING IKAROS'S ASS ONCE HE ARRIVED. NOW, WE ALL KNOW TIME CHASERS WILL ALWAYS BE NUMBER ONE IN MY HEARTS. BUT I GOTTA SAY, IF THEY EVER MADE THAT INTO A SHOW, I SURE AS HELL WOULD TUNE IN TO WATCH. AM I RIGHT, FOLKS?**"

Even louder cheering followed, along with a reminder by Drega to stay tuned for their next live recap. Plegraxious started to speak again but was abruptly cut off as a highlight reel began to play, one showing various humans – chasers I presumed – meeting their gruesome ends.

I looked away, happy to tune the rest out. Instead, I tried to refocus on the problem at hand. If I was right, time would resume any minute now. Once that happened, I would almost certainly become one of those impending deaths Drega had bragged about.

Unless there was enough wiggle room in the rules for me to do something about it.

I would likely already be dead had they not interrupted the game at the most fortuitous moment imaginable.

No idea why they felt the need to let those of us already in the Chase watch too. It was probably yet another method intended to further break our spirits, but in my case I wasn't about to complain.

Now that the surprise of it had passed, I tried to take stock of the situation as quickly as possible. The world around me was frozen, but I'd been seemingly left free to move – at least minus that ominous warning from my HUD.

The big question was exactly *how much* freedom I was allowed during these moments.

With the highlight reel rapidly winding down, that meant my reprieve was almost up. I couldn't kill Atac and trying to escape was almost certainly a losing endeavor. With Vectorman already used for the day, I'd be run down in short order.

Wait!

I might've not been able to attack directly while everything was frozen, but what about indirectly?

Nothing ventured...

Hoping I wasn't courting a tier-two, I made to sidestep the Aztec warrior so as to flank him again ... only to quickly learn that was a no-go.

Turned out, while most of me seemed to be free, my feet were somehow rooted to the spot. I tried to lift them only to find it was like they were stuck in concrete.

I couldn't exactly blame the show runners on that one. Guess it was a good thing that I hadn't put all my eggs into the escape basket.

Shifting my position was out of the question, but that still left the rest of my body.

I had no choice. It was either eat this guy's mace or get creative.

Come on. Think, stupid!

An idea began to form just as the highlight reel ended and the giant ghost TV winked out of existence. I once more lifted my racket and cocked back my arms – this time making sure no branches were in the way.

Rather than let fly, though, I tensed my muscles and held it.

Attacks might be forbidden during a live broadcast, but it was time to test whether readying an action was allowed instead.

Any second now...

The sound of screeching guinea pigs filled the air once again. In that same instant the Cloud Warrior continued turning as if nothing had changed.

Too bad for him that it had.

20

TOOTH AND NAIL

Sorry, Atac old buddy, but it's either you or me.
Where my first attack had ended in embarrassing failure, this one struck home with a vengeance.

The Cloud Warrior's skull cracked like an egg, sending his headdress flying and dropping him like a bad habit.

It was unsporting as fuck, but that live broadcast had steeled my resolve beyond merely inspiring a desperate cheap shot. Ikaros's death had been played off as gratuitous entertainment wrapped in a warning for the rest of us. I'd gotten the message and then some. It had cemented my desire to not be *that guy*, meaning I needed to do whatever I could to win this damned game. And if that meant exploiting a loophole, then so be it.

I'm a murderer now and nothing can ever change that.

That realization stung almost as bad as catching Deb with fuckboy Manny, but I also knew there was a major difference. Unlike discovering my wife's infidelity, this wasn't a one-time only deal. I was going to have to kill again. There was no doubt of that.

Who was to say how much blood I'd be forced to shed by the time this was finished – how much would forevermore be staining my hands?

Time Chaser

I suspected Ikaros had done that same math and decided it simply wasn't worth it. In truth, I doubted he'd even been aware he was dooming his world in the process. The guy had simply shut down and accepted his fate. While I personally couldn't blame him, such an ending was considered a high crime here in a world where entertainment trumped all else.

Hopefully it served as a wakeup call to any others weighing such a decision. I know it had for me.

Even if I reached a point where I couldn't take any more, I still had to go down fighting. There was simply *no choice* in the matter.

No choice at all.

An achievement flashed in my HUD as Atac's lifeless body twitched upon the ground, but it would have to wait.

His death had been quick, a small mercy, but I wasn't an idiot. I knew I'd gotten supremely lucky in it likely going unheard with all the damned guinea pigs still screeching.

Case in point – the other red dots on my map continued on their way, seemingly unaware that anything had happened.

That was one visit to the murder well out of the way, now to see if I could draw water once again. Heck, there was even a chance, assuming my luck held, that it might be possible for me to take them all down before I was...

Pixel: *Yo, Tim! You still alive out there somewhere?*

I stopped dead in my tracks, turning my full attention toward the cortexing window which had just popped up in my HUD.

Tim, JUST FUCKING TIM: *Holy shit, are you okay?*

Pixel: *No, I am not fucking okay! I just woke up from my first expiration. That is about as far from okay as a FAST can get.*

Tim, JUST FUCKING TIM: *Where are you?*

Pixel: *No idea. I'm locked in a cage, but it's covered with some kind of blanket or tarp.*

Tim, JUST FUCKING TIM: *So move it with your TK Hand.*

Pixel: *You think I haven't tried? No dice. It's too heavy.*

Tim, JUST FUCKING TIM: *Crap. Okay, so what's your map say?*

Pixel: *Not a goddamned thing. I can't see anything but static.*

Tim, JUST FUCKING TIM: *How is that possible?*

Pixel: *I'm being blocked. If I had to guess, I'd say something here is enchanted against location magic.*

Tim, JUST FUCKING TIM: *Then how come we can still chat?*

Pixel: *Because chat is a cortexing function, completely separate from the Chase's other subsystems.*

Tim, JUST FUCKING TIM: *I'll pretend that makes sense.*

Pixel: *It's not affected by magic. That's all you need to know. Anyway, I can't see much but I can still hear just fine.*

Tim, JUST FUCKING TIM: *That's good.*

Pixel: *Not really. My audio cells are telling me I'm not alone. Fuck it. I'm gonna pop a mana potion and see if I can blast my way out.*

Tim, JUST FUCKING TIM: *No! Wait for me. I'm coming. We'll do it together.*

There was a brief pause, making my heart skip a beat, but then Pixel was back.

Pixel: *All right, fine. Just don't take forever.*

Tim, JUST FUCKING TIM: *Not planning to. I just have a few loose ends to tie up first.*

Pixel: *Oh? Are we talking good loose ends or the kind that means you're totally fucked?*

Tim, JUST FUCKING TIM: *Still figuring that one out. There's a bunch of guinea pigs wandering around. They're not the issue, but they set off an alarm that attracted a group of Aztec warriors. I took one of them out. Still working on the rest.*

Pixel: *Pretty sure those aren't Aztecs.*

Tim, JUST FUCKING TIM: *Fine, Incans. Whatever the fuck.*

Pixel: *Racist much? For starters, it's not like they were next door* neighbors. Secondly, this stage's time period is a good four or five centuries before either of them. Duh!*

Tim, JUST FUCKING TIM: *And this matters why?!*

Pixel: *Just saying, you might want to open a history book every once in a while.*

Tim, JUST FUCKING TIM: *Okay, let's back up and forget about that for now. Is there anything useful you can tell me, because if not... Shit!*

Pixel: *What's wrong? Talk to me, Tim.*

Tim, JUST FUCKING TIM: *The guard cuyes stopped screaming.*

Pixel: *Why were they screaming?*

Tim, JUST FUCKING TIM: *I don't know. Because that's what guinea pigs do. Back to what I was saying...*

Pixel: *Sorry. There isn't much I can do from here. I don't even know where here is.*

Tim, JUST FUCKING TIM: *All right, don't worry about it. I'll find you. Now, if you'll excuse me, I have some non-Aztec assholes to deal with.*

Pixel: *Go for it. Just two things real quick.*

Tim, JUST FUCKING TIM: *What?*

Pixel. *Remember what I said about thinking outside the box.*

Tim, JUST FUCKING TIM: *Working on it. And the other thing?*

Pixel: *Simple – good luck!*

⌛⌛⌛⌛ ⋅⋆⋄⋆⋅ ⌛⌛⌛⌛

It wasn't ideal that the pigs had finally shut up, but at least it spared me from getting a migraine. Small victories and all.

Tempting as it was to set them off again, that would've resulted in me turning my back on the remaining Cloud Warriors. That didn't strike me as a good idea.

For now, I glanced down at Atac's remains. There wasn't a

lot of time, so I just grabbed everything he was carrying short of his actual body. And yes, that included his hair.

Guh! Fucking Loom o' Doom.

His weapon was listed in my inventory as a *macana*. Nasty a piece of work as it was, though, it didn't appear to be magical. So for now I stuck with my tried and true racket.

That done, I stepped over him and started tracking the next warrior in line.

Silent running, I repeated to myself, moving as quickly as I could while keeping *Stealthed* active – measuring each step so as to hopefully not give myself away. Even so, I knew it was an uphill battle.

That last fight had been too close for comfort. I'd only managed to get within striking distance of Atac because of those stupid guard pigs. With them no longer screeching, I likely had zero shot at doing so again.

That meant I needed to figure out a way to take them out from a distance.

Up ahead, I could hear them talking amongst themselves. Whatever their culture might've been, I could understand them plain as day thanks to my SK. It was a useful feature, even if I still didn't appreciate the non-consensual brain modifications done to me.

"See anything?" one of them asked.

"Nothing here."

"Something killed that cuy."

"Must've been a wolf," a third voice said. "They're always going after the damned things. We should get back. Apu doesn't like to be kept waiting."

A wolf eh?

"Apu will get his blood," the first one chided, sounding like the leader, "but we will do our duty first as is our sacred calling."

"Fine. You don't have to squawk like a parrot about it."

Go figure. No matter the time or culture, there were those

who just wanted to do their jobs and then there were the suck-ups.

"By the way, has anyone seen Atac?"

Crap!

"I'll go look for him. He's probably just taking a squat."

Double crap! As they bantered, I desperately scoured the forest floor for ammo. Unfortunately, I mostly spied dead leaves and broken twigs, nothing that seemed likely to...

Hearing movement from up ahead, I immediately stopped what I was doing and ducked down. A few moments passed then I caught sight of the Cloud Warrior who'd decided to double back. He was headed right in my direction.

No, no, no! Not yet!

However, just as I was about to lose my cool, he abruptly hunkered down against a tree trunk. Several seconds later, a grin of satisfaction crossed his face. It took me a moment to figure out what was going on.

The dumb fuck was using his missing friend as an excuse for his own bathroom break. It was literally a *golden* opportunity, one I couldn't turn down.

There was little chance of reaching him before he noticed me, though. I needed ammo and I needed it...

Think! I forced myself to stop and take a breath. *Think outside the box.*

Seeing nothing of use around me, I turned my attention toward my inventory instead – scrolling through it as quickly as I could.

Short Spear: 5

I'd used one of those earlier to great effect but it had required me to break it first. A good idea, but with the forest once again mostly silent, there was no chance of that going unheard.

Gnome pants: 6. No. *Wolf steaks*: 2. Definitely not.

Wolf Teeth: 99

I stopped on that one. There had been more to loot, but

ninety-nine was the max amount of any single item my inventory allowed. Regardless, I found myself wondering if they might have a shot at working. I mean, they were just teeth. All the same, they'd seemed pretty substantial back when I'd been fighting those wolves.

Fuck it. My options were limited and my window of opportunity was about to close.

I pulled an even dozen from inventory and they instantly appeared in my hand. The canines were of a decent size, but the rest felt a bit inadequate, especially if I was hoping to one-shot this guy.

Hold on a second. Was there any rule that said I could only fire them one at a time?

I mean, this wasn't a crossbow or sling. It was a freaking racket with a pretty wide surface area. Slapping multiple balls at once wasn't the most elegant thing on the planet but I knew for a fact it was doable.

Besides, wasn't that kinda how shotguns worked? Rather than a bullet, they fired a bunch of tiny metal balls. It was basically death by a thousand cuts. This was sort of the same thing ... in theory and so long as I didn't try to think very hard about it.

Whatever the case, it was worth a try.

I began to creep forward again, trying to get a bit closer for a clearer shot. I made it to within about fifteen feet of the guy before realizing that was as good as it was likely going to get. I stopped behind a fern, its wide leaves the only things keeping him from spotting me.

Eying him through a narrow opening in the vegetation, Drega's voice oh so helpfully informed me that this guy's name was Ussu as I activated Aim Assist.

A warning also popped up in my HUD notifying me that my target had partial cover, resulting in a 30% reduction of Aim Assist's effectiveness.

That sucked, but there wasn't much I could do about it

outside of announcing myself. Besides, it still left me with better odds than firing raw.

Here goes nothing.

Keeping the squatting warrior centered in my reticle, I stood up, dropped the handful of teeth, and then swung for the fences.

It was obvious that at least half the projectiles missed, doing nothing but shredding the foliage on either side of where Ussu squatted. But that still left plenty which hit the unlucky son of a bitch. He spasmed as wolf teeth peppered his body with multiple bloody wounds, including one that punctured his eye socket – resulting in his health bar winking out.

As awesome as it was to see my plan work, it wasn't quite perfect. You see, I'd forgotten one *little* detail.

Each tooth had rocketed away from the racket accompanied by its own sonic boom – sounding like a miniature missile strike, one that was impossible for anyone close by to have missed.

God fucking damn it!

21

SCATTERED SHOTS

I might as well have shot a flare into the sky announcing my position.

It was the sort of stupid-ass move that would've set Pixel off on a tirade about what an unevolved monkey I was – probably deservedly so.

That was the end of my stealth gambit. I'd taken down two of their number, but now I needed to face the remaining three warriors on my own, mano-a-mano.

Or so I assumed.

However, before that could happen the air once again filled with the sound of unhinged shrieking. My Screaming Shot had apparently set off those fucking guinea pigs once more.

Great. Not only was I going to die but I'd meet my end with a headache too.

Or maybe not as I realized this situation wasn't entirely to my detriment. There was no point in trying to run. The Screaming Shot had gone off before the pigs, meaning Ussu's buddies knew full well where to turn their attention. They'd be here in moments, which meant there was little chance of me vacating the area without being spotted.

Conversely, the shrieking pigs also meant I didn't have to

worry about being heard. So long as I didn't stand there making myself an obvious target, I still had a shot at some subterfuge.

Looting Ussu could wait. I pulled another dozen wolf teeth from inventory and turned my focus toward the map. Sure enough, all three dots were racing this way.

I took note of their tight formation then stepped behind another tree just a few yards away from where Ussu had taken the last dump of his life.

This was going to require a leap of faith on my part. Hidden as I was, I had zero sightline to work with. Instead, I kept my attention focused on the map – specifically Ussu's greyed out corpse in relation to the three approaching dots.

Just a little bit further.

I turned off Aim Assist. It wasn't going to help me in this case. There'd be no time to line up a shot before they were all over me. Instead, I'd have to rely on a wide spread for this attack, as well as the extra damage afforded me with assist turned off.

Come on. X marks the... Now!

I stepped out from behind the tree the very moment they reached Ussu's location. If they showed any surprise at my sudden appearance, I didn't notice it – keeping them in the periphery of my sight as I dropped the teeth and swung.

The *sonic boom* was louder than last time, enough to temporarily drown out those stupid pigs. I took it as evidence of the attack's greater potency.

Sadly, it was also evidence of how desperate I was. Unlike my last shot, where the spread had been at least reasonably centered in one direction, teeth literally flew every which way imaginable. It was less a shotgun blast and more like a tooth-filled pipe bomb going off.

Needless to say, I felt bad for any squirrels hanging out nearby.

Chaotic as it might've been, it wasn't a total failure. All three of the Cloud Warriors now had visible health bars. Two of them had blood dripping from their extremities, flesh wounds that had maybe knocked off a tenth of their health. The third was already in the yellow, though, a tooth having torn a chunk from his shoulder.

However, where the first two were already raising their weapons, that last one just stood there with a look of shock etched onto his face.

That's when I remembered Screaming Shot had an effect other than being loud as fuck, a tiny chance – 3% according to my HUD – to stun an enemy.

If I wasn't mistaken, I'd just hit that stun lottery and my winning ticket couldn't have come at a better time.

There was no way I could pass up this opportunity, so I raced forward – trying not to think about how inadequate my squash racket looked compared to their murder clubs.

Pixel: *How are you doing, Tim? Talk to me.*

I ignored the notification. This was no time to chat. The stunned warrior's health was low enough where it likely wouldn't take much to flatline him. I lashed out, managing to connect solidly with his chin. Teeth flew, he dropped, and I even got a one percent damage bonus on top of everything else.

Sadly, ignoring defense was ultimately to my detriment – leaving me wide open for one of the remaining Cloud Warriors to take a swing. My back sang a chorus of agony as his macana gouged a furrow through both fabric and flesh.

ARGH!

Half my health disappeared in the space of an instant, but I was too busy screaming to focus on that fact. It felt like someone had dragged a salt-encrusted railroad spike across my bare skin. I could feel a veritable river of blood pouring down my backside.

I turned and swung wildly, hoping to stave off a kill shot, not that I would've been able to aim much anyway with every nerve in my body currently on fire.

This was pain like I'd never known. The closest I'd ever come to it was that time I'd accidentally sheared off the tip of my finger while cutting a cucumber on our mandoline slicer. I'd thought that'd been bad, but it was literally nothing compared to the anguish I was experiencing now.

Unsurprisingly, I hit nothing but air, missing the enraged Cloud Warrior by a mile.

Fuck me!

But then Second Chance Backhand activated, reversing the momentum of my garbage swing. This one likewise came nowhere close to tagging my opponent, but the abrupt reversal managed to strike the shaft of his weapon instead. It was a lucky blow as the mace flew from his hands into the surrounding brush.

It wasn't a moment too soon as the other warrior came charging in, his club raised high.

There was no time to move out of the way, so instead I used my racket to block the attack before it could cave my skull in – noting with some surprise that my damage bonus had clicked up to two percent. Guess I didn't have to actually cause damage to count as a hit where my ring was concerned.

Good to know, but nothing I could take advantage of as the Cloud Warrior powered me backward until I was slammed up against a tree trunk. My stricken back screamed even louder as the torn flesh met the rough bark, erasing even more from my health bar.

Once again, my squash racket miraculously held against a weapon that should've been its superior many times over. Too bad that left me stuck fast while the other warrior moved to retrieve his weapon. If he managed to find it before I could escape then I would be assured a premature and messy exit from the Chase.

Fuck! If there was ever a time I could've used Pixel and one of their Heal spells, it was... Wait! I had healing potions in my inventory, which I could supposedly activate via my HUD.

I turned a fraction of my focus there, even as the Cloud Warrior attempted to power his weapon ever closer to my face.

All right, I had four healing potions, all listed as unequipped. *Wonderful.* I mentally clicked to equip them — something I *really* should've done earlier — eating up a precious second I didn't have. The warrior's macana was now so close I could've licked it had I wanted to.

Then, without further ado, I activated one of the potions, hoping to hell it...

Gah!

I almost choked as my mouth instantly filled with pungent liquid. *Ugh*! It tasted like *Listerine* flavored cough syrup. My first instinct was to spit it all out, but I forced myself to swallow instead.

Goddamn it, Pixel could've at least given me a heads-up about that. What a stupid fucking way for potions to activate, even if it probably made sense logically.

Foul it might've been, but it was also effective. My health rocketed back to the green and the screaming in my back subsided.

It allowed me to refocus on the shithead in front of me — Khuno according to Drega's *melodious* voice. Amazingly enough, despite our differences in physique, I was mostly holding my own — keeping the prongs of his war club at bay, if just barely.

Needless to say, I wasn't about to question it. If this game wanted to enhance me beyond the abilities of an almost middle-aged software manager who engaged in just enough physical activity to keep from being labeled a couch potato, then who was I to argue?

"You will die, interloper," Khuno growled, drenching me in spittle. "You will die and Apu will feast on your blood."

"Apu can feast on my dick," I said. *And speaking of...*

I brought my knee up into his crotch, happy to see that my enhanced strength also applied to my legs. Khuno's eyes bugged out and he dropped his club in favor of clutching his injured junk.

My damage bonus had expired by that point, but there was no time like the present to bring it back up.

It took a pair of heavy blows to put Khuno down for good, but once again I was rocking two percent. Just in time, too, as the final Cloud Warrior, one with the rather unfortunate name of Cuntur, retrieved his club and came racing back into the fray with a battle cry.

"Come get some," I shouted back, my dander up for some insane reason.

Too bad my confidence was entirely unfounded. I may have gotten lucky with a few cheap shots but these guys were still seasoned warriors.

I swung high, only for Cuntur to dive below it. Second Chance Backhand activated, but he'd already rolled behind me out of its range.

The difference in our experience became painfully obvious as I spun to face him. Sadly, he was ready for that, slamming the head of his mace into my left quadricep in an attempt to cripple me.

A damned good attempt if we're being completely honest.

Jesus fucking Christ on a pogo stick!

Think of someone smashing your leg with a rusty sledgehammer. Then imagine them dropping a lit match inside the open wound. It was kinda like that. Blood erupted like a geyser from my now shattered leg as my health once again plummeted.

Fuck, fuck, fuck!

I fell onto my back, dropping my racket in the process and leaving me weaponless.

Cuntur was upon me in a flash. He grasped the handle of his weapon and attempted to yank it free so as to finish this – only to find it was now stuck in the bone.

And yes, I did somehow manage to scream even louder than those goddamned guinea pigs.

Time Chaser

He leaned over to get a better grip, leaving himself wide open, not that I could do much about it. I desperately reached out, hoping to find my racket within reach, but it wasn't anywhere close enough to grab. That left me with nothing but my bare fists. Too bad I very much doubted I'd be able to slap my way out of this. Without a weapon, I was...

Except that wasn't true. I'd dropped my Banshee Racket, sure, but that wasn't the only weapon I had on me, just the only one I had *equipped*.

Putting as much focus as my trauma-wracked body would allow into it, I called up my inventory once again and scrolled down to those mini spears I'd looted from the gnomes.

I summoned one and the weapon instantly appeared in my outstretched hand.

The surprise on Cuntur's face at this new development was plainly evident, even more so when I lashed out at him.

It wasn't a hard blow. I had almost no leverage lying on my back, not to mention most of my focus was taken up with trying not to cry.

But here's the thing. When metal is honed to a razor sharp point, you don't need to hit someone very hard with it to do a lot of damage.

The spearhead punctured the side of Cuntur's neck like it was made of paper, causing blood to cascade out like a waterfall.

He let go of his weapon, leaving it stuck in my leg as he stumbled backward holding his ruined throat. It was no use, though. There was no stopping the flow of blood in time.

I could only lie there and watch as his health bar drained, until at last he toppled over. His body twitched a few times before finally falling still.

I'd done it. Against all reasonable odds, I had actually won.

Somewhere close by, the Guard Cuyes sang out as if acknowledging my victory.

Or maybe they were just still screaming because they were dumb fucking guinea pigs.

Time Chaser

Whatever works.

22

RESCUE RANGER

My health was still cratering, probably because I was bleeding like a stuck pig – guinea or otherwise. I should've activated another healing potion but continued to just lie there instead. I dunno, maybe I was going into shock or something. Fortunately, it wasn't yet at a point where I was in danger of...

A notification popped up in my HUD telling me I'd gained enough experience to now be third level. And just like that, my health bar rocketed back up to full and then some – also serving to clear my head.

Probably because I felt every single agonizing microsecond of it.

I nearly bit my tongue in two as the bone of my leg repaired itself, pushing the macana out. Let's just say it was as painful being shoved back out as it had been going in. Within a second or two, the club fell to the ground and the rest of the wound knitted itself shut – leaving me still a bloody mess but looking far worse than I now felt.

Yay me.

This new level also came with another 30 points of stat boosts – which also served to refresh my memory that my previous points were still waiting to be spent. I'd totally forgotten about them in all the chaos.

Not my brightest move.

Fuck me! I had zero doubt those would've proven useful during that last fight. It was a mistake I needed to be sure I didn't make again.

Pixel: *Holy shit, Tim! I just got a notice in the party menu that you went up another level. I take it you survived those mobs you were after.*

Tim, JUST FUCKING TIM: *Only because I remembered I had potions. By the way, thanks for letting me know the liquid was going to teleport straight into my freaking mouth.*

Pixel: *Sorry, was kinda busy being murdered and kidnapped. But it sounds like you did okay even without me there.*

Tim, JUST FUCKING TIM: *If you call having my leg smashed by an Aztec murder club okay.*

Pixel: *Again, not Aztec.*

Tim, JUST FUCKING TIM: *Do I sound like I really fucking care?*

Pixel: *Jeez, don't be such a crybaby. Anyway, what's the big deal? You won didn't you? As the saying goes, you have lived to fight another day – and by another day I mean get your ass here ASAP and save mine.*

I let out a sigh, not even wanting to think about jumping back into combat. Don't get me wrong. I knew there was little choice in the matter, but right then, full health or not, I was feeling it pretty heavily. It was the bone-deep tiredness from a day that had proven far more active than I would've ever anticipated.

Guess I should've been a little more aggressive back home when it came to my racquetball schedule.

There was still a lot of work to be done, but I continued to lie there a few moments longer – looking up at the canopy of trees and the fake sky above, all while listening to the melodious sounds of guinea pigs shrieking their fucking heads off.

Time Chaser

Finally, after another minute or so, they stopped. About goddamned time, too. I made a personal vow to not set the stupid things off again.

Pixel: *You still with me, Tim?*

Tim, JUST FUCKING TIM: *Yeah, I'm good. Just trying to catch my breath. Got a few new achievements I need to go through as well.*

Pixel: *Oh sure. Just take your sweet time. It's not like I'm going anywhere.*

Tim, JUST FUCKING TIM: *So, you're saying I should put off opening any new gear that might help me save your ungrateful ass?*

Pixel: *Touché. I retract the statement. While we're on the subject of gearing up, though, the XP boost from your battle didn't quite push me over the edge, but I'm super close. I don't suppose you'd want to maybe pick a fight with another mob or two, that way I can be fourth level by the time you get here.*

Tim, JUST FUCKING TIM: *Think I'll pass. Wait. You got experience from that fight too?*

Pixel: *Not a lot but some. Where party members are concerned, a rising tide lifts all boats. It's kind of like communism, if it ever actually worked. Now if you'd be so kind as to pencil me into your busy schedule, your FAST is in need of saving.*

⌛⌛⌛⌛ ·⋄⋅⋄⋅⋄⋅⋄⋅⋄· ⌛⌛⌛⌛

Once again, my demon sweater seemed to have survived relatively unscathed. Too bad the rest of my clothes weren't faring nearly as well. My shirt and pants in particular were both shredded bloody messes.

At this point they were beyond patching. As gross as the idea of wearing anything made from the hair of dead enemies was, I had no choice but to see if Loom o' Doom could help me fashion suitable replacements.

First things first, though. I looted all the Cloud Warriors –

yes, taking their hair as well. All of them had the same gear as Atac, save that one also had a necklace with a golden medallion on it depicting some sort of fanged monster. It didn't appear magical, but Pixel had mentioned we'd find merchants at later stages so I took it anyway. Maybe it would have some trade-in value.

That out of the way, I turned to my new achievements.

The first had appeared after I'd killed that guinea pig. Can't say I was surprised to see the title.

Achievement unlocked! Puppy Kicker!

You have mercilessly dispatched a foe that had absolutely no defense against you. And yet you dare call them the monsters.

What's next, tough guy, tossing a litter of kittens into a blender because you're hankering for a protein shake?

On the flipside, there's no doubt you have that killer spirit every successful chaser needs. Now let's just pray you don't run into any orphanages down the road.

Spoiler alert! You totally will.

Reward: **1 Fortnight supply box along with the hope that your conscience doesn't realize what an utter piece of shit you are.**

"You're a prick, Drega," I said with not much conviction before turning to the next. This one I'd gotten from killing Atac right after that live broadcast.

Achievement unlocked! Asshole Opportunist!

Look at you, taking advantage of the Chase's myriad interconnected systems for the sole purpose of snuffing the life from another living being.

I bet your mom would be real proud of you right now.

On the upside, if by some miracle you manage to make it out of here, you definitely have a promising future as either a serial killer or hedge fund manager.

Reward: **Nothing! You used a cheap shot to slip through**

death's icy embrace. That's reward enough. Just don't get used to it.

As if I didn't already think TOPCOC were big enough dicks. Still, Drega may have had a point. I'm not sure if what I'd done could be considered a cheat, but there was no doubt I'd used the system to my advantage.

I'd effectively won the lottery during that live broadcast. I needed to be mindful of that. The chances of me getting that lucky again were probably slim to none.

For now, I focused on that supply box. I went through the routine of making it appear, only for it to disappear again once it was *opened*. It was a dopey thing to have to go through each and every time but I had a feeling it was less for me and more for the audience.

That was another mindset I needed to get used to. This world wasn't designed with my convenience in mind.

Rather than dwell on that, I focused on my semi-ill-gotten gains.

The Fortnight box turned out to be pretty full, which warranted no complaints from me. I got another dozen torches along with about half as many gl'ohrods. Likewise, there was another batch of fifty nutradisks.

I could only stuff forty-nine into inventory, so I kept one to munch on before looking at the rest of the box's contents.

The *disk* itself was the size and shape of a breakfast bar. I took a bite to find it tasted kind of like those Triscuit wafers Deb liked to keep in the pantry. It wasn't bad, but not exactly something I'd be salivating for after a long day spent exploring.

"Maybe next time toss in a water bottle or two." I said aloud. "These things are a little dry." It was doubtful my comment would affect anything but I saw little harm in trying.

On to the rest.

Three more healing potions awaited me. Nice. Weird as the delivery method was, I'd developed a newfound appreciation for them.

There was also another potion of foresight, reminding me I'd lacked the foresight to check what the one I already had actually did.

It was time to remedy that, but first there was one final item in the box.

Scroll of Plant Dominion – 1

Huh. That was new. My very first scroll. I assumed Plant Dominion was some sort of spell. Possibly useful since I was coming up a little short in that department.

Before getting to that, though, I looked up those Foresight potions.

Potion of Foresight – level 1

Duration: 2 minutes

Have you ever wondered whether you're about to do something monumentally stupid? Well, wonder no more. While this potion is in effect, you'll be able to focus on *one* choice before you actually make it and then be given limited *insight* into how it'll play out up to three seconds in the future.

Perfect for testing new pickup lines, figuring out if that mysterious treasure chest is trapped, or all those moments predicated by the phrase, "Hold my beer."

I guess I shouldn't have been surprised to find a potion with what amounted to a minor time bending element attached to it. I just wished I'd looked it up sooner.

There was little doubt this was meant to be used in the moment. Still, it represented a potential *get out of jail free card* if used correctly.

That was nothing to be sneezed at. I just needed to make sure I really meant it before using one.

The scroll of Plant Dominion, on the other hand, was for a 4th level version of the spell. From the description, each level gave the caster control of a twenty-five square foot area of plant life for up to one minute. At fourth that equated to a hundred square feet, which basically meant a ten by ten space. Not huge by any means, but possibly effective depending on the situation.

While the spell was in effect the caster could magically animate the plants in that space and control them to do anything their existing forms were physically capable of. The examples given included causing a tree to topple over or vines to wrap themselves around an opponent. However, it was limited in that it didn't incur growth or other unnatural abilities. I took that to mean casting it on something like a patch of plain grass would be effectively useless.

However, in a jungle such as this, the possibilities were limited only by my imagination.

Of course that assumed I could even cast it. If only I knew someone who could answer that question.

Tim, JUST FUCKING TIM: *Hey! I got a level four scroll of Plant Dominion.*

Pixel: *Good for you. I'm so glad to hear you've had time to take up gardening while I'm rotting in this cage.*

Tim, JUST FUCKING TIM: *I'm heading out in a sec, okay. But since this is my first scroll I wanted to check first to see if it's even worth bothering with.*

Pixel: *It is. You don't need to worry about mana where scrolls are concerned. They're freebies when it comes to casting. Just be careful because they're one and done. Once you use it, it'll turn to dust. Still, level four is nothing to sneeze at. You might want to equip it just to be safe.*

Tim, JUST FUCKING TIM: *I already have my healing potions equipped.*

Pixel: *So? Equip this as well. You do realize that the number of slots for things like potions and scrolls are level dependent, right?*

They are?

Tim, JUST FUCKING TIM: *Of course I do.*

Pixel: *Liar. Anyway, at third you should have three available equip slots.*

Tim, JUST FUCKING TIM: *Good to know ... not that I didn't know that already. But thanks.*

Pixel: *Yeah, I'm just a wellspring of usefulness, unlike a certain someone who's busy pretending it's Christmas while my life is on the line. Seriously, Tim, there's something weird going on here. They've started chanting. Trust me when I say chanting is never a good sign in situations like this.*

Tim, JUST FUCKING TIM: *Shit! I'm on my way.*

Pixel: *Good! Try to make it here sooner rather than later. Heck, if you manage to rescue me before I die again I might even start calling you Mac.*

Tim, JUST FUCKING TIM: *Really?*

Pixel: *No.*

I closed out the chat with a few choice words then proceeded to equip that scroll as well as the potions of Foresight. Of my limited stash of volatile possessions, those seemed like the most useful in a pinch.

Next, it was time to correct a serious oversight on my part from that last fight.

I now had 60 points to spend on stat boosts. While there was something to be said about Pixel's advice earlier – scoping out the situation first so as to put those points to the best use – this world was rapidly proving way too adept at keeping me on my toes. The last thing I wanted was to be distracted at the wrong moment and end up even more disadvantaged than I already was.

So I opened my stats and took a good hard look before deciding to drop 5 points in strength and 15 in constitution. Both of those were already my highest stats, so fortifying them a bit seemed wise. That brought them up to 80 and 130 respectively.

I then decided to take a bit of a risk with the rest. 20 points went to my dexterity, bringing it to 70 in total. I didn't know what lay ahead, but I had a feeling the sooner I could stop relying on Aim Assist the better.

Time Chaser

The rest I put into wisdom because again that struck me as a stat others would almost certainly ignore. As the Chase grew ever more difficult, it would almost certainly be worth trying to glean any insight I could from my surroundings.

That still left PSI as my dump stat, which I had a feeling it would continue as unless I got a massive bump via some loot drops. Alas, there was likewise no love given to either intelligence or charisma this level. I'd need to work on both at some point – although INT was almost certainly the higher priority if I ever wanted to use spells.

Charisma fueled my No Threat Detected ability, but it only gave me a base one percent chance to avoid combat plus two percent for every 50 CHA points. That meant three percent total for now, not helped by the fact that so far I had yet to meet a single mob that looked like they had any interest in talking first. Yeah, charisma could wait.

Either way, I'd find out soon enough whether I was correct in my assumptions.

It didn't sound like Pixel had been moved since they'd woken up. That likely meant they weren't too far away. If so, that hopefully meant I didn't have far to go.

To that end, an idea began to form for once I got there. I took a look at the dead Cloud Warriors then at some of their items I'd pulled into inventory.

It was time to once again think outside the box.

All I needed was a couple of minutes to get everything ready and for a tiny bit of luck to be on my side.

23

BLESSING IN DISGUISE

For all the dread and anticipation I'd felt toward whatever was to come, I was surprised to find a decent amount of curiosity mixed in there as well.

I'd known for a while that I was approaching the far end of this jungle cavern. The map had shown me that much as well as the fact that there were multiple exits leading away – more tunnels. That meant it would be back into the dungeon after this excursion, assuming we survived of course.

More importantly, I spied another campground just a short ways down one of those exits. That meant a safe area was close by.

If I could free Pixel without setting off any alarms, we might be able to avoid combat altogether. We just had to make it there first. The big question, though, was who or what I was freeing the FAST from.

Unsurprisingly, their green dot still didn't show anywhere on my map, but I had a feeling I was closing in based on what I *could* see. It was a leap of faith on my part to assume all this but one that seemed logical based on what they'd previously told me.

If I was wrong then I'd have to cross that bridge when I came to it.

For now, I couldn't help but notice a spread out half circle of red dots that appeared to be guarding a wide space along this wall of the cavern. Within that area multiple white dots seemed to be scurrying about, but that's where things got interesting.

A couple of *anomalies* had appeared on the map. There was another red dot situated furthest away, close to the cavern's far corner, but this one was pulsing for some reason, almost like a heartbeat. That was new. Considering the color, though, I had a feeling there was little hope of it being good news for us.

Equally as interesting was the appearance of a white question mark.

Earlier, Pixel had also appeared as a question, albeit green. That was likely during the time when they'd been... Dead probably wasn't the right word for it. Deactivated sounded far less ominous. But what did that mean with regards to this white one?

Rather than continue speculating, I reached out via chat and asked.

Pixel: *A pulsing red dot? I had a feeling that might be the case.*

Tim, JUST FUCKING TIM: *Is it safe to assume that's not good news?*

Pixel: *Pretty much. Means we're dealing with a boss. Guess that explains the chanting.*

Tim, JUST FUCKING TIM: *How so?*

Pixel: *Bosses usually mean minions. And minions mean you can expect a lot of sucking up. Unfortunately, it also means a tough fight ahead for us. I can't emphasize this enough, Tim. You need to be careful. Bosses aren't to be taken lightly.*

Tim, JUST FUCKING TIM: *That bad, eh?*

Pixel: *Depends. There's no telling until you can get close enough to ID them. The problem is, once you do it's usually too late. The fight is already on.*

Tim, JUST FUCKING TIM: *There's a campground not too*

far away. So long as I can get to you, we should hopefully be able to make a break for it.

Pixel: *Don't count on it. Once a boss fight starts, and trust me you'll know when that happens, all participants are instantly marked. If you try to escape before it's over, that's a tier-two penalty – except this one will stick with you until the end of the stage.*

Shit! I hadn't considered that but I couldn't say it was surprising either. Hell, if they gave you a tier-two for whizzing in the hallway then certainly running from a boss would qualify as well. Chaser spirit my ass. It was just an excuse to force us to step willingly into the meat grinder.

Tim, JUST FUCKING TIM: *Okay. I'll just have to try to get you out before that happens. If not, then we'll fight.*

Pixel: *There's another option. You could leave me here and head to that campground yourself. It would be the safer choice.*

Tim, JUST FUCKING TIM: *Wait. Do you actually want me to do that?*

Pixel: *WHAT THE FUCK DO YOU THINK, DIPSHIT? You ditch me and I swear on whatever gods you believe in I will find your ass and plant my TK Hand so far up it...*

I should've known better than to even ask.

Tim, JUST FUCKING TIM: *What about that question mark?*

Pixel: *No idea. Without any way to see it, I'm in the dark – quite literally.*

Tim, JUST FUCKING TIM: *A different type of mob maybe?*

Pixel: *Doubt it. Why bother differentiating them from the rest? The overmind can be a prick, no question about it, but that feels unnecessarily dickish even for them.*

Tim, JUST FUCKING TIM: *Fair. Guess I'll find out soon enough. I'm heading in.*

Pixel: *Please tell me you have some sort of strategy in mind beyond just walking in here like you own the place.*

Tim, JUST FUCKING TIM: *Funny you should word it like that.*

Time Chaser

⌛⌛⌛ ⋅⊰⋅⊱⋅ ⌛⌛⌛

This was either the best Halloween costume I'd ever cobbled together or the absolute worst. I wasn't sure which.

The only thing I was certain of was that my status had changed to *Disguised*.

On the surface, it was a more stable status than *Stealthed*. However, a tooltip warned me that it was entirely dependent on the strength of an opponent's Perception skill.

In plain English, I had a feeling that came down to how hard they decided to scrutinize me. To that end, I'd taken some precautions. It was disgusting as can be, but necessary to hopefully maintain the illusion.

Whatever the case, I'd soon find out.

"Ow!"

Of course, that assumed I didn't scream every time I stepped on so much as a twig.

As expected, walking barefoot through a jungle was ... unpleasant at best. Everything was some combination of either gross or sharp, not helped by my DEX currently being down 10 points. The only plus in my favor was that every time I stepped on something that hurt like a motherfucker, it only took a few minutes for it to heal – resetting my health back to full.

Needless to say, so far it hadn't proven a bad idea to have tossed those extra points into constitution.

From the waist down I was fully decked out like a Cloud Warrior, wearing nothing but a loincloth. Much as I would've loved to have kept my sneakers on, there was no way their presence wouldn't ruin the illusion.

As for my clothes and other possessions, those had all been stashed in my inventory. Seeing them get listed there had been a small relief as I'd been worried that real world items might not be compatible, but fortunately that fear had proven unfounded.

Although, I had to admit the system's catalogue system left a bit to be desired.

Time Chaser

My pants were listed as *ruined off the shelf khakis: 1*, whereas my picture of Jeremy was even more insulting.

Pointless sentimental photo: 1

I tried not to let that piss me off too much as I continued onward, the ring of red dots growing ever closer.

It was above my waist where this disguise would either live or die – definitely not the most comforting way of wording it.

Atop my head I wore one of the warrior headdresses, while around my neck hung that golden monster amulet. It was my torso, however, where things became potentially dicey.

I'd taken off my shirt, but wasn't quite comfortable removing the demon sweater and its myriad enchantments. Once my ruse was discovered, which was probably a given, I'd need to quickly reequip myself. Every item potentially represented an extra second that someone could use to take my head off. I needed to minimize that as much as possible.

To that end, I'd rolled up my sleeves as much as I could and draped one of those wool capes over my back, not the most comfortable thing in this heat. Then, to hopefully disguise the rest, I'd pulled those wolf pelts from inventory and draped them over myself, covering up the blue of the sweater as best I could as well as wrapping one around my arm to disguise my SK.

It still wasn't enough, though, and this was where things got questionable.

Knowing I couldn't easily hide my less than impressive physique, my final touch was to cover myself head to toe with the blood of my beaten foes. The goal was to hopefully make it look like I'd been in a gory battle with a pack of angry wolves, while hopefully disguising the fact that nothing about me was a close match to the fighters I'd dispatched.

With any luck, the sight of me would be treated as just one of those things that happened when living in a crazy jungle, inside of a cave, in a game world that...

Yeah, none of that made sense in the slightest, yet the mobs so far seemed to treat all this as part of their normal lives. Either they were some seriously devoted method actors or some other fuckery was afoot.

However, that wasn't my chief concern right then.

I took a deep breath and stepped forward, knowing that this scheme would likely succeed or fail in the next few seconds.

Or maybe not.

The red dot in front of me was another of those guard cuyes, happily munching on a leaf as I approached.

I tightened my grip on the macana in my hand – my racket likewise back in inventory. Even with my diminished strength, I doubted I'd have much problem fucking this thing up. Fortunately, it merely looked at me, cocked its head dumbly to the side, and ... then went back to munching.

My *Disguised* status didn't so much as blink.

Note to self: guinea pigs have shit poor perception.

Tempting as it was to punt the hairy turd into next week, I simply stepped past it as if I belonged there – noting that the way forward now sloped uphill.

Had I been back home, the heat combined with the exertion would've had me sweating my balls off by now, but so far I mostly felt fine. Maybe there were some benefits to being a higher evolved being after all, as they'd apparently figured out how to overcome the limitations of these frail meat suits we called bodies – all without the need for exercise.

I could dig that.

Too bad the human race won't ever get there.

Son of a bitch! I knew that was going to haunt me. The big question was why I was letting it bother me. Again, we were talking about an event that was still five centuries away, at least from my time. There was no reason that should be bothering me as much as it did. Quite literally, that wouldn't be a problem for even my great-great-grandchildren to worry about.

More importantly, it was of zero help to me. I'd made it past the first hurdle, a fucking guinea pig, but I had a feeling the true test was still to come.

Time Chaser

Soon, the trees began to thin out, leading me to guess the end of this jungle was nigh. That was good for my visibility, but potentially bad for that Plant Dominion scroll I'd equipped. I wasn't sure why I'd assumed the jungle ran the full length of this unnatural cavern but it had seemed logical at the time.

Logical but completely wrong as I reached the tree line.

Fog of War Disabled.

I raised an eyebrow at this new notification, but then remembered what Pixel had told me. The fog of war was for close quarters situations – ostensibly to keep us from seeing what was waiting down a narrow dungeon hall.

The area before me was wide open, though, in a sense of the word anyway.

Ahead lay what appeared to be a small village. As it came into view, the open area of my map populated with several large outlines, the insides of which were total blanks – the spaces where the huts stood.

Guess I had to see them first to know they were there.

The structures scattered up ahead were primitive but not nearly as much as I might've expected. Though the smallest were little more than A-frames made of wood and thatched grass, most of them had stone walls. *Gilligan's Island* this was not.

Maybe Pixel was right about me needing to read more.

I spied a few garden plots as well as primitive looms where half-finished blankets hung. There was no doubt this place was inhabited even if I didn't immediately see anyone wandering about.

The lack of a welcome party wasn't surprising, though. According to the map, all the villagers, aka white dots, were gathered further up ahead for some reason.

Beyond the huts, I could make out the cavern wall rising high above. This was where the massive cave terminated, meaning I'd soon be getting my answers, one way or the other.

Time Chaser

As I pressed forward, trying to keep my knees from shaking, I said a silent prayer that I wouldn't be forced to fight the entire village. I'd just barely survived that first batch of Cloud Warriors and a lot of that had been nothing but luck.

Here, I'd have far fewer options for subterfuge if things turned to shit.

As for running, that might not even be an option.

Still, I'd come too far to simply slink away back into the jungle.

I needed to see this through. Fortunately, my disguise wasn't the only surprise I had in store. The big question was whether it would all be enough.

It didn't take long for me to notice signs of life.

The sounds of chanting ... no, *singing*, reached my ears. No doubt about it. This was the place.

Then I spotted them.

Up ahead, men, women, and even children had gathered. All of them had their backs to me as I approached. I began to sweat, nevertheless, desperately hoping it wasn't enough to ruin my bloody makeup job.

You can do this.

Beyond the small crowd, the cavern ended in a sort of V formation, like a deep wedge cut in the rock. However, my view was blocked by a series of ornate woven blankets that had been strung twenty feet off the ground – serving as curtains to set that space off from the rest.

Whatever their purpose, my map told me the pulsing red dot was just beyond that point.

That wasn't ideal, but maybe it meant there was still a chance to run before this boss battle could get started.

As I got closer, I began to get the impression that I was intruding upon some sort of ceremony. A shaman of sorts stood at the head directing things. He wore a much more elaborate headdress than mine, his face covered by a mask depicting a creature similar to the one on the medallion I now wore.

Fortunately, he, along with all the others ahead of me, remained white on the map.

I focused on the closest person to me, an older woman, curious to see what Drega would say.

Non-combatant NPC: Huita – level 1

This somewhat decrepit denizen of the Chachapoyan cloud village you've stumbled upon is primarily concerned with three things: worship of their local god, weaving blankets, and constantly reminding her adult son how much of a disappointment he is.

Or at least that *was* the case before you so callously murdered him.

Congratulations, you've just eliminated one of the few things keeping this old hag going.

Guess she'll have no choice but to become even more devoted to appeasing their living god – which will almost certainly involve sacrificing your murderously dumb ass to him.

Dire as the warning in her description sounded, the non-combat NPC status was new. Can't say it wasn't a welcome change. If I was reading it correctly, it meant I didn't have to worry about being whupped by either Huita or any of the others currently following the directions of the guy up front.

Speaking of which, I noticed a few items of particular interest just beyond where he stood. There was a heavy stone slab, cracked and discolored with what appeared to be both stains and scorch marks.

Not to go out on a limb, but I would've bet good money it was a sacrificial altar. Two squared off objects stood on either side of it, both of them covered with ornate blankets.

This was it! Those had to be covered cages, which meant Pixel was inside one of them.

Now all I had to do was...

The sound of pathetic wailing reached my ears, rising for a

moment even above the frenetic singing coming from the villagers.

What the fuck?!

I turned, just barely able to see over the heads of those standing in front of me. It was just enough to make out that there was something, some kind of creature, huddled against the cavern wall off to the left.

No, not huddled. As I stepped that way to investigate, I realized it was being held prisoner there. The beast's hands and wrists were tightly lashed to a bronze ring that had been anchored into the wall.

Whereas the villagers were human, though, this thing was most definitely not.

It looked like either some kind of freaky upright chimpanzee or, I dunno, maybe a juvenile Yeti, especially since the light fur covering its body was snow white in color.

It stood about five feet tall, while the floppy breasts hanging from its torso told me it was almost certainly female.

"Murg!" the creature cried out in a gravelly voice.

I quickly rechecked the map to see if maybe I'd been wrong about the location of that red dot. Mind you, if this *was* the vaunted boss Pixel had warned me about, I couldn't say I was all that impressed.

It wasn't though. Its location actually corresponded to that white question mark still on my map. I looked at the creature again, noticing for the first time the large metallic bracer around its right forearm – the only clothing this thing appeared to be wearing.

As I stared, a notification popped up in my HUD.

Chaser: Boog – Earth 6255 – Level 2.

Hold on. That thing was another chaser?

24

CHASING RAINBOWS

I tried to get more info on this *thing* named Boog but the system remained tight-lipped.

Mobs and NPCs were fair game, but it was apparently a no-no to sneak a peek at another chaser's info, at least those not already in my party.

But how or why could this creature be a chaser when there was no doubt she wasn't human? Was this some kind of glitch or maybe a throwback to a previous season?

Either way, she kept screaming, "Murg!"

All the while, the villagers ignored her while they continued to...

"Cuntur, you have returned!"

Oh crap. Here we go.

I turned to find a wide-eyed boy maybe ten years old looking up at me. From the gap-toothed grin on his face, I was guessing Cuntur – dear god, that name – was either a brother or beloved uncle.

Whatever the case, so far my *Disguised* status was holding. Either my makeup job was halfway decent or this kid was kinda dumb. I wasn't about to argue regardless.

Time Chaser

"Where are the others?" he asked. "Have they not returned as well?"

Rather than say anything and almost certainly give up the game, I shook my head, let out a grunt, and gestured to the wolf pelts. Hopefully Cuntur had been the strong but silent type.

The kid, Nand according to Drega's description, was at least smart enough to put two and two together. His face fell as the realization hit and tears began to form in his eyes.

Oh no, not that.

Little by little I could feel my resolve cracking, envisioning this was how Jeremy might react upon learning I'd been crushed by that bus. I looked away, biting my lip.

Goddamn it all! I needed to find Pixel and get the fuck out of here before I ended up pulling an Ikaros.

The problem was, the appearance of this other chaser had thrown a monkey wrench into my plans. Sure, I didn't know them from Adam ... or maybe Eve, and it's not like I owed them anything.

Hell, one less chaser in the game could only improve my odds.

No! I quickly pushed that thought away. That was what Drega and the overmind *wanted* me to think. They hadn't outright said as much, but the implication that we were expected to turn upon one another had hung heavy in the air when they were explaining the rules.

If the system wasn't fucking with me and this creature was indeed another chaser, then she was in the same boat. She'd been plucked away from her world at the moment of her death and dragged into this one, where she was expected to fight for a chance at survival, however slim.

TOPCOC were the enemies here, not her.

I had a feeling Pixel was going to give me shit about this, but I couldn't just leave her there.

Tim, JUST FUCKING TIM: *Change of plans. There's another chaser being held here. I'm busting them out too.*

I shut the chat before Pixel could tell me how stupid my already insane plan was. As if I didn't know that already.

"Come, Cuntur. Let us pray to Apu that their souls may soon be reborn."

Huh? I'd almost forgotten about Nand but he hadn't forgotten about me. *Crap!*

He had one arm around mine and was trying to drag me toward whatever ceremony was still going on.

Worse, a few of the other worshippers had turned and noticed me.

Fuck, fuck, fuckity fuck!

It was time to play this straight and to the point. Hopefully these guys would be too confused to try and stop me.

I pulled free from Nand's grasp with another grunt then turned toward Boog. I snarled in her direction, gripped my weapon tighter, and began to trudge that way.

As I got closer, I couldn't help but notice the air was thick with a coppery scent. I had a feeling it was too much to hope it was from nearby mineral deposits.

"No, Cuntur," Nand whisper-shouted. "Its blood is promised to Apu. You must calm yourself."

The little asshole wasn't nearly as quiet as he thought, as murmuring began to rise up among the villagers – slowly taking the place of whatever they'd been chanting.

That was fine, though. Let them think I was merely a vengeful warrior looking to take out my anger on a helpless prisoner.

The murmuring increased to the point where the chanting stopped altogether. Oh yeah. Whatever I was about to do, it needed to be quick.

"Cuntur, what are you doing?" another voice chastised, this one far older. "That beast's life is not yours to take."

My response was an angry, inarticulate shout as I raised the macana and stomped to where Boog was being held prisoner.

Behind me, I heard Nand cry my name again, but I ignored him and focused on the chaser.

Boog's eyes opened wide with fear as I approached. "Murg," she whimpered sadly, as if accepting her fate.

Too bad I had other plans.

I had no idea if she could even understand me, but I needed to try. I lowered my voice to a bare whisper and leaned in. "Relax. I'm another chaser. I'm here to set you free."

"Cha-ser?" she replied, just barely able to articulate the word.

"Yeah, my name is..." *Fuck it*. "Mac."

"Mah-ac?"

"Mac." I repeated. "Mac, got it?"

"Macmac?"

"No, it's just... Oh the hell with this."

I swung the macana but adjusted my aim at the last second, smashing the brass ring her bonds were attached to and freeing her. In that same instant, the question mark on my map became a blue dot instead.

So far so good, especially considering I was making this up as I went. "Now pretend to fight me and we'll make our way over to..."

"CHASER MACMAC!" Boog cried in a shrill screech. "You free Boog! Now Boog fight!"

"Wait, just pretend to..."

I was too slow in my warning, though. Boog held out one freed hand and a weapon appeared in it, having no doubt just been equipped. It was a nasty looking axe that appeared to have been fashioned from the jawbone of some large predator.

Boog raised it angrily.

"Wait, don't! I'm on your..."

Then she stepped around me and bashed Nand's head, splitting his skull like a grapefruit.

Holy shit!

The pissed-off ape woman wasn't finished yet, though. Before Nand's body had even hit the ground, she took off running toward the crowd.

"Boog fight! Boog kill!"

Seconds later utter chaos broke out as the villagers all began to scream in panic.

What the hell had I just unleashed?

⌛⌛⌛⌛ ·:·¤·:·¤·:·¤·:· ⌛⌛⌛⌛

There was no time to rue my actions. Though their descriptions had called them non-combatant NPCs, this was the same village those Cloud Warriors called home.

Whatever their intent had been in capturing Boog, it was obviously not a friendly one.

They weren't without blame here.

All the same, I hadn't meant to slaughter them, but that's exactly what Boog seemed intent on doing. Speaking of intentions, mine had been to hopefully maintain this ruse long enough to free Pixel so we could make a run for it.

And speak of the devil...

Pixel: *From the sound of things, I'm gonna go out on a limb and assume your plan just went tits up.*

At least that answered the question of whether this was the right place.

Rather than try to rein in Boog, I quickly reequipped my sneakers and replaced the war club with my Banshee Racket. Aside from a few *minor* hitches, my disguise had worked surprisingly well, but it was time to drop the act and bring myself back up to full power.

Doing my best to ignore Boog's batshit rampage, I turned instead toward the altar and the covered cages next to it, racing that way before the villagers could mount a defense.

Making my way to the first one, I realized the blanket draped over it was being held in place by heavy rocks. That explained why TK Hand had failed, but fortunately I wasn't under any such constraints. Ripping the blanket off, I started to let out a whoop of joy, only to cut it short as I realized the FAST inside was yellow instead of green.

As if in response, another blue dot appeared on my map.

FAST: Murg – Undisclosed – Level 3 – XX

I couldn't help but notice the two red X's at the end of their name. I wasn't sure what they meant but there was no time to ask. "Um, nice to meet you. I'm Mac."

"But your HUD badge says..."

"Forget about the fucking nametag. It's just Mac."

The FAST buzzed for a moment or two, then spoke again, their voice higher pitched than Pixel's. "Very well. Quite the ... striking outfit you've got going on there, chaser."

They weren't wrong. Sneakers, a loincloth, a sweater with no shirt beneath it, and I still had that headdress on – all while wielding a squash racket.

I probably looked like I'd just stepped out of Fetishes-R-Us.

Still... "You'd be surprised how comfortable a loincloth can be. Now, do you want to debate fashion or can I finish rescuing you?"

I quickly examined the cage, noting the crude locking mechanism. Then I brought my racket down onto the door with everything I had, smashing it and causing it to pop open.

"Thanks," Murg said, floating free. "Now, I'd really suggest we get out of here before..."

They were cut off by an earth-shattering roar that came from behind the curtain of blankets.

Oh crud.

I froze like a rabbit at the horrific sound but thankfully only for a moment. Forcing myself to snap out of it, I moved to the other side of the altar. Guess I was starting to get desensitized to this shit. Not to mention, standing and gawking was probably a good way to ensure my head got cleaved off.

Whatever the case, I ripped the covering off the second cage to find a familiar green ghost light staring back at me.

"About time," Pixel said. "Too bad we're about to fucking die. Nice outfit by the way."

25

BOSSED AROUND

Ground Sloth Soul Eater: Apu – level 8
Decennial Boss
When people think of sloths, they often imagine the slow talking, cutesy-as-fuck CGI creations you'd find in a *Disney* movie. They're mostly right, unless you're talking about ground sloths.

You ever hear the term Mylodon or perhaps Mapinguari? Well, the assholes worshipping this guy haven't because those words are from different eras. Nonetheless, they both refer to the horrifying beast standing before you.

The garden variety of these nasty fuckers will happily crush your skull and lick the insides clean without a second thought. Too bad for you the Soul Eater subtype makes the rest seem like a pleasant spring day in comparison – possessing all the strength of these prehistoric throwbacks while combining it with the intelligence of a snake oil salesman.

They are crass, violent, lazy, and above all else opportunistic.

Apu is no exception to that rule.

Coming to the realization that the human tribes who

shared his territory had an affinity for worshipping mountain spirits, he long ago presented himself as a living god to these unsuspecting dupes.

A few angry roars, premeditated landslides, and disemboweled skeptics later, and he had it made. Now Apu mostly sits around demanding never-ending sacrifices while waving his arms and pretending to bless the crops.

It's a sweet deal and he knows it, so expect to be quickly and violently exterminated should you even think about ruining it for him.

Despite Drega's words, I didn't expect to be particularly intimidated by any kind of sloth. The monster that stepped through the curtain, however, made me seriously rethink that position.

It was roughly nine feet tall and looked like an insane cross between a furry T-rex and Freddy Krueger. The beast was heavily muscled, covered in thick fur, and its arms ended in long, backward facing claws that looked sharp enough to filet an elephant.

That by itself was terrifying enough, but in one hand it carried a triple-sized macana – the massive metal head polished to a gleaming, mirror-like surface.

Okay, that's unexpected.

"Don't just stand there! Get me the fuck out of here," Pixel cried, snapping me out of the bone-numbing horror that was quickly latching onto my family jewels like a vise.

Unwilling to take my eyes off the massive boss beast, I missed the cage's lock a few times before finally connecting and setting my companion free.

"Good, now let's run before..."

Trumpeted fanfare sounded from all around us, like a reworked version of the old Twentieth Century Fox theme. Then Drega's voice filled the air.

"GET READY TO BRAWL FOR IT ALL, CHASERS! IT'S TIME FOR A BIG BAD BOSS BATTLE!"

Time Chaser

Guess Pixel was right, the start of a boss battle *was* hard to miss.

Even if it wasn't, the status indicator flashing *Boss Battle Initiated* in my HUD was a pretty good clue.

Unfortunately, the implication of what that meant hung heavy in the air. We had no choice but to fight.

The alternative was to be marked with a tier-two penalty until the end of this stage. Sure, that was only two days away, but we weren't even halfway through this one yet and already it seemed as if I'd experienced an entire lifetime of terrors.

The odds of me surviving another six hours, much less forty-eight, felt daunting enough. But that wasn't all.

The truth was, there was *zero* chance of me running that risk and putting Jeremy in danger.

I turned to Pixel, noting for the first time that a single red X showed next to their name. Call me paranoid, but I was beginning to get an idea of what that meant and it wasn't good.

Mind you, it was even less good for Murg.

Speaking of which, the other FAST cried out, "What have you done, chaser?"

"What I've done," I replied, turning their way, "is save your ass. Now we can either debate the merits of that or we can work together and take this fucking thing down."

The brute trudged forward, making me realize how shallow my bravado sounded. Oh, we were so fucked.

No! Now was not the time to freak out. I needed to keep my wits about me lest I end up pummeled into paste – something this monstrosity looked more than capable of.

"*You have disturbed my rest and upset my beloved village,*" Apu rumbled, grossly understating Boog's handiwork. "*For that, I will pick my teeth clean with your bones.*"

"Great, it talks too," I muttered.

"*Oh, I do more than talk, little monkey.*"

Apu lifted his war club and took a ponderous swing. I hit the deck with plenty of time to spare, while the FASTs scattered.

Time Chaser

He wasn't particularly quick in his attack, but the breeze that washed over my backside told me it was more than powerful enough to turn anyone it hit into a greasy smear.

"Stand still like a good sacrifice."

"How about you eat acid and die," Pixel responded, flinging an Acid Ball at the beast. It splashed against the sloth's skin where it sizzled and burnt away a patch of hair, but otherwise didn't appear to do much.

A health bar appeared over Apu's head to confirm this. We'd have probably done more damage smacking it with a newspaper.

"Boog, get your hairy butt back here!" Murg cried at the other chaser, who was still seemingly endeared with terrorizing the non-combatant villagers. "As for you two," they said to Pixel and me, "these things are covered in osteoderms. You're not going to get through that by lobbing spitballs at it."

"English please for those of us in the back of the class," I replied, climbing to my feet and racing toward the creature before it could attack again.

I slapped it in the kneecap with my racket, hoping to bring it down to my size. Talk about a hell of a time to learn this thing was built like a freaking oak tree. The racket reverberated in my hands as it connected, but otherwise my blow was mostly ineffective. *Son of a...*

At least my damage bonus went up a percentage point. Maybe another fifty or so and I'd make a dent in this thing.

"Its skin is covered in thousands of tiny bones," Murg explained. "It's effectively natural chainmail."

Wonderful. Not only were we fighting a giant sloth holding a murder mace, but it was a shitload better armored than any of us. All of a sudden my devil sweater felt seriously inadequate.

"I'm open to suggestions," I said, circling behind Apu while trying to be mindful of his short but muscular tail. "Anyone got any ideas?"

"I do. Stop fighting and die!"

"Not you, dickface!"

"Hit and run," Murg said. "It's a brute boss. That means we need to wear it down. Distract it and strike, over and over. If we all work together, we can do this."

"I could've told you that," Pixel replied.

"Yes, but you didn't," Murg shot back.

I was beginning to get the idea that this FAST was more direct and to the point than mine, which honestly was kind of refreshing. Right about then, we needed strategy far more than snark.

Distract it, eh? As Apu lumbered forward, having dismissed me to go after the FASTs, I slammed the edge of my racket down onto its tail.

"*Grah!*"

The blow had only done marginally more damage than my last hit, but there was little doubt I'd gotten this thing's attention. In addition to that, I was now up to 2% on my bonus.

Apu spun toward me, swinging one of his massive claws. I saw the attack coming a mile away so I brought up my racket to block it.

Clonk!

The plus was I managed to both deflect his hit enough to keep from being disemboweled while also raising my damage buff to a whopping 3%. The downside was the *slight* difference in our mass, with this freaking sloth outweighing me by several tons.

As a result, I found myself airborne as it swatted me away like a bug.

I hit the ground hard, erasing a decent chunk from my health bar. Thankfully, I managed to roll with it, leaving me a little woozy but otherwise still in this fight. I clambered back to my feet again, just in time to see Pixel and Murg launch twin attacks.

Pixel tossed another Acid Ball, this time at Apu's face, causing it to growl in anger. At the same moment, Murg fired a bolt of flame at its neck – burning away a substantial patch of fur in the process.

The boss's health dropped another notch, telling me we had at least a shot with this strategy. We might not have any attacks strong enough to do any serious damage to this thing, but death by whittling it down still counted as a win.

Now to hope there were no time limits associated with boss battles.

Speaking of which, it was time to rejoin this fight.

Apu may have been big and tough but, despite Drega's insistence to the contrary, he didn't strike me as Mensa material. Case in point, once again he ignored me in favor of the FASTs.

Mind you, they were the ones doing the majority of the damage, so perhaps that wasn't entirely unwarranted.

Now to see if I could maybe remedy that.

I pulled another dozen wolf teeth from my inventory and activated Aim Assist even as my damage bonus reset. *Fuck*! It was a cool power, but that three second rule was killing me. So that was gone and now Aim Assist would only further decrease my damage output, but I also didn't want to risk an uncontrolled shotgun blast with the two FASTs flitting about.

Ah, if only my boss could see me now. The fucker had dared to criticize me during my last performance review, telling me I needed to be more of a team player.

Suck it, Allan!

I lined up the reticle with the creature's long, horse-shaped head. If Apu had any weak spots, it would be there because the rest of his body sure as hell seemed to be built like a tank.

All right, steady now. I opened my hand to drop the handful of teeth, ready to send them flying, just as there came a warbling battle cry – like *Xena Warrior Princess* was about to join the fray while high on shrooms.

Out of nowhere, Boog came charging at this thing, racing past the two FASTs. She leapt high, using the altar to propel herself forward.

Time Chaser

Shit!

I aborted my attack, letting the wolf teeth fall to the ground just as she buried her axe in Apu's shoulder.

The massive sloth tried to grab her in a bear hug, but the white-haired monkey girl scrambled up and over his body with a surprising amount of agility. There, she hung off his back – one hand buried in the boss's fur, while the other pulled her axe free to continue hacking at the creature.

Sadly, as impressive as it was to watch, those osteoderms covering Apu were no joke. Though he appeared to be bleeding freely from her attacks, his health bar told another story. The damage appeared to be superficial at best.

"Get out of the way," Pixel shouted at her, echoing my thoughts.

Though Boog's actions might've seemed brave against a monster that absolutely dwarfed her, all they were really serving to do was fuck up the strategy the rest of us had settled on.

"*Die, hairy bug!*" Apu cried, swinging his mace up and over his back.

Boog was too quick for that, though. She jumped off, resulting in the sloth taking a chunk out of his own hide instead. He screamed in pain as his health bar dropped by nearly a quarter – way more damage than any of us had managed to do up until that point.

If we could only figure out how to get this monster to slap the shit out of himself a few more times, we'd have it made.

Or maybe we would anyway as Pixel blasted Apu in the face with a Shock Bolt just as he pulled the macana free, eliciting another cry of pain from the brute.

I guessed the FAST must've downed a mana potion, but I wasn't about to complain.

The loss to Apu's health was still way too small for my liking, but this time his bar inched down more than it had from either the fire or acid spells. Perhaps that indicated a weakness.

"Hit him with more electricity," I cried.

Time Chaser

"Thank you, chaser, but I'd already figured that out on my own," Murg smugly replied.

There was little doubt this FAST had perhaps an even higher opinion of itself than Pixel did. I could only imagine what they thought of being partnered with Boog.

We could discuss all that later, though, as I pulled another handful of teeth from my rapidly depleting inventory.

Murg was faster on the draw, though. Yellow energy crackled across their body as they readied a Shock Bolt of their own.

Sadly, they were a little *too fast*. In that same moment, Boog – seemingly oblivious to our strategy – raced in again with her axe, this time drawing a line of blood across Apu's stomach.

"Get out of the way, Boog!" Murg screamed, flying in closer just as electricity arced out from their body.

Sadly, Apu's attacks might've been slow but his reflexes weren't. The sloth ignored the ape girl this time and instead lifted his mace directly into the spell's path. The bolt struck the bronze head of the weapon as if it had been drawn into it.

What the?

Rather than merely block the attack, though, there came a brief flash of light and then the spell was redirected! Except it wasn't toward Murg.

"Oh shi...," Pixel cried in the instant before the spell blasted them full on.

Electricity arced across the FAST's body as its health began to plummet into the red. Their normal green light flared multiple colors as sparks erupted from them. Then Pixel abruptly stopped moving and fell from the sky, hitting the ground like a deflated volleyball.

No!

26

FAST INTERRUPTED

Pixel!

Sparks continued to dance across the downed FAST's surface as I attempted to circle back around toward it. Then its light simply winked out – leaving behind a faceted, cantaloupe-sized sphere that looked like it was made of smoked glass.

A nearly depleted health bar hung above them, the red line barely visible.

Wait, still visible? Did that mean…?

"Murg, you go now! Listen to Boog!"

Huh?

Apparently, I hadn't been the only one distracted by the sight of my FAST getting blasted by friendly fire.

I turned to find Murg hovering there unmoving. Though FASTs didn't have a face or eyes to give any hint of direction, I got the impression they had likewise turned their attention toward where Pixel lay on the ground.

That must've been the case because, quicker than any of us could react, Apu reached out with his deceptively long arms and caught Murg with his claws, grasping the FAST like they were an apple plucked from a tree.

Or maybe walnut would've been a better analogy as he then slammed his paw down onto the stone altar. *Crunch*!

Oh fuck!

"Murg!" Boog cried.

Apu pummeled Murg into the altar again, leaving the FAST's yellow light flickering and its health bar a mere hairline.

Once more Boog leapt upon the monster's back, cleaving it again and again with her axe, but Apu ignored her as he raised his macana.

That's when I remembered I still had a handful of teeth ready to go. I locked onto Apu's chest, hoping that, between Aim Assist and the brute's sheer bulk, it was enough to shield Boog from any errant molars.

I dropped them all and swung my racket.

A dozen miniature sonic booms screamed out as I peppered the monster with wolf teeth, scoring hit after hit. Each tooth by itself didn't do much, but little by little Apu's health inched down.

Yet he still ignored us as he raised his weapon ever higher.

"B-Boog," Murg gasped, their voice crackling with static. "Y-you ... are ... such an ... idiot."

Apu brought the mace down with a thunderous crash. The stone altar cracked from the impact as the downed FAST shattered into hundreds of tiny shards.

Three red X's appeared above its remains. That was followed by an audible *wah-wah-wah* noise that was disturbingly reminiscent of losing a life in *Pac-Man*. The implication was obvious. This was the overmind's dickish way of letting everyone know that Murg had been destroyed – permanently offlined as Pixel had put it.

I had no idea how the FAST had managed to rack up its first two deaths so early in the game, but right then was not the time for such questions.

"Murg!" Boog screamed in anguish, sliding down the sloth's back where she collapsed weeping onto the ground.

Time Chaser

The ape girl would almost certainly be next to suffer such a fate, but for the moment Apu's attention was focused solely on the smashed FAST.

The beast laid his macana to the side as he lowered his head to the altar. An anteater-like tongue snaked out of his mouth and then he began to lap up the FAST's remains.

What the hell?

Back when the fight started, I'd found myself confused by the *Soul Eater* title attached to this boss's name. After all, it had seemed kind of superfluous for the giant, Hulk-sized sloth.

Now, though, it became horrifyingly apparent what that meant as well as why Apu had set himself up as a living god to be appeased with blood sacrifices. As he lapped up the FAST's remains, his health bar began to inch back up.

"Shit on toast." This was not good, not good at all.

We'd just begun to make a dent in this thing's health, but now – with one FAST dead, another down for the count, and Boog crying like a baby – the progress we'd made was slowly being erased.

I was the only one still left in this fight, which meant it was up to me to do something, and quickly too. If Apu was allowed to finish regenerating then it was over. We would have no chance at that point.

An image of Jeremy flashed in my mind. In it, I saw him dressed in a tiny suit as he stood over my closed casket. What would Deb even tell him? And what would she say about me in the years to come? Much as I wanted to think my passing would elicit some kindness on her part, I had no way of being certain.

No. That simply was not an outcome I was willing to accept, not yet anyway.

I frantically turned my attention toward my inventory. I'd been saving a few pieces of ammo as a last resort, mostly because I had no idea whether they'd actually work. But now I literally had nothing to lose by trying.

One fully intact macana remained in my inventory, the one

I'd carried into the village with me. The rest, however, I'd removed back in the jungle, prior to donning my disguise. There, I'd used a heavy rock to break each of them apart before returning the bronze heads back to my inventory.

The wolf teeth had served as shotgun pellets but these things were more like cannonballs. The question now was whether they were too heavy to be fired from my comparatively tiny *cannon*.

There was only one way to find out. I pulled one from inventory, feeling the weight in my hand. It made the wolf teeth seem like Tic Tacs in comparison.

Hold on! Maybe there was another way to find out if this was a good idea.

Focusing on the task ahead and whether I should risk it, I quickly downed one of the foresight potions I'd equipped.

Yuck! I almost gagged as I was *treated* to a mouthful of what I imagined dirty mop water to taste like but, rather than spit it out as I so desperately wanted to, I swallowed instead.

Swirling lights coalesced in front of my eyes, culminating in a spectral image of ... my racket floating there in front of me. That was it. The vision disappeared and I was left no better off than I'd started.

That was what they considered to be insight?! What a fucking useless slop bucket of a potion.

In the meantime, Apu's health continued to tick upward as he consumed Murg, grunting in pleasure like he was snorting a line of pure cocaine instead.

Snort this, asshole.

I lined up the fucker's head in my reticle then dropped the macana head and swung.

For one terrifying moment I was certain the strings on my Banshee Racket would burst from the strain. But then the hunk of metal rocketed away from me like a screaming missile.

Yes!

That's when realization hit me. The foresight I'd been given

Time Chaser

wasn't incorrect after all. It had shown me my racket in one piece, thus answering my question.

It was still shitty-ass insight, but right then I was far more focused on my intended target.

Apu looked up at the sound just in time for the bronze warhead to careen into his jaw.

"Argh!"

Teeth went flying and the tip of his tongue was severed, causing blood to spray from his mouth like a mini geyser. Better yet, the hit erased all the health he'd regained and then some. The brute staggered back a step, slightly dazed from the blow but sadly not fully stunned.

It was a good solid hit, just not good enough.

"Again," I growled, pulling another chunk of bronze from my inventory.

This time I disabled Aim Assist. There was no choice. I needed it to do as much damage as possible. So I called upon my racquetball experience and aimed the best I could, all while saying a silent prayer that my target was big enough and my dexterity high enough to make this work.

"You fuckers want a show?" I said to no one in particular. "I'll give you one!"

Hoping I hadn't just jinxed myself, I held my breath and let fly with the weapon. Again, I felt the racket strain against the impact, making me wonder whether I'd gone to this well once too many times. Then the air filled with a high-pitched scream that would've made those guinea pigs proud. The hunk of bronze rocketed across the battlefield where it impacted directly against Apu's windpipe, sending even more blood flying.

It wasn't exactly where I'd been aiming, but a solid chunk of the sloth's health was erased nonetheless as he staggered back gasping for breath.

To my amazement, Boog looked up as this was happening – the expression on her face a mix of misery and pure rage. Then she dove beneath Apu's thick tail, positioning herself behind his back legs.

For a second I was certain she'd be crushed by the mammoth boss, but then Apu's own momentum worked against him. He tripped and tumbled backward, landing with a heavy *thud* I felt all the way from where I stood.

In a flash, Boog was back on her feet, her jawbone axe in hand.

She let loose with that weird Xena cry of hers as she stepped to where Apu had fallen. Then she began to hack at his neck like a wild woman, going completely apeshit on the sloth. She chopped away at him with a fervor that was nothing less than terrifying to watch.

So instead I focused on Apu's health bar as it began to plummet ever faster.

I debated rushing in and getting a piece of this action but the crazed look on Boog's face gave me pause. Drenched in the boss's blood, she continued to hack away at his neck with reckless abandon.

Then, just as Apu's health sank deep enough into the red to tell me he probably wasn't getting up from this, a bolt of electricity arced in from somewhere to my right and zapped the big sloth in the head. The would-be god gave one last gurgling grunt and then his health bar disappeared.

We'd won, but I was far too preoccupied with where that final attack had come from.

Pixel was back in the air. Not by much, barely two feet off the ground, but they were alive. The green glow had returned to their body, albeit still weak and pulsing.

I turned and headed that way, especially since Boog didn't seem like she was about to stop chopping anytime soon.

"**THE WINNERS OF THIS MATCH ... TIM CHASERS**," Drega announced. "**AND COMPANY.**"

I couldn't have given a single shit about hearing our stupid party name said aloud or the notifications that flashed in my HUD. "Holy crap, are you okay?"

Pixel's light was starting to get stronger and it appeared that their health bar had stabilized. Now that the battle was over it would be back to full in minutes.

"That was ... seriously weird," they said.

"Well, yeah," I replied. "I gotta imagine dying's not pleasant." Even as I said it, though, I noticed that Pixel still only had one red X associated with their name, not two like I'd been expecting.

"Except I didn't die. I ... think I rebooted."

"Isn't that the same thing when you're a computer?"

"Do I look like I run fucking Windows 10 to you?" they snapped. "No, it's *not* the same. That sort of thing ... doesn't happen, or at least it's not supposed to."

"Well, you did get hit by that Shock Bolt. Maybe it, I dunno, fried your circuits?"

Pixel let out a sigh. "One, Shock Bolt is bottom tier, basic magic. It's not like I got nailed by Thor's Pimp Hand, and yes that's a real spell and no don't ask. We won't have access to it for quite some time anyway. Two, you remember that part where I told you I was constructed by beings that make you seem like an unevolved bug in comparison?"

"Yeah, that insult's still pretty fresh in my memory."

"Good. Well, then trust me when I say they aren't stupid enough to construct FASTs without properly insulating our internal cells. We can take damage, yes. We can even die. But we do *not* randomly reboot. It simply doesn't happen."

"Except it apparently did. So what's the big deal?"

"The big deal is..." Pixel trailed off.

"Is what?"

Rather than answer me, they popped up in our chat instead.

Pixel: *The big deal is I suddenly have access to eight percent more of my memory cells.*

I opened my mouth to say something but stopped myself. If

Time Chaser

Pixel had purposely moved to private chat, my gut was saying it might be best to follow.

Tim, JUST FUCKING TIM: *So?*

Pixel: *So, that's not supposed to fucking happen. At least not now, not this early. The thing is, this doesn't look like a predetermined list of approved memories. Y'know, extra stuff so I can give you appropriate flavor text later on in the Chase. It's going to take some time to catalog it all, but this feels seriously random to me.*

Tim, JUST FUCKING TIM: *Again, so? Eight percent doesn't sound like a lot. Oh, and you really need to change my goddamned name back. This is getting old really fast.*

Pixel: *Forget about that and think about the bigger picture, Tim. When a good chunk of your past is hidden behind firewalls and file restrictions, even eight percent is huge. Not to mention, the protection on these things is what monkeys like you would call military grade. I don't mean to brag when I say I could hack every single system on your planet within a microsecond. Conversely, it would probably take me a century or more to even scratch the surface of the protections the Committee has in place. They're that good, which means this is pretty fucking major.*

Tim, JUST FUCKING TIM: *Okay, I guess that's kinda cool. Still doesn't tell me why we're chatting about it.*

Pixel: *Because something just happened that's not supposed to. We're talking a bug or some kind of glitch here. And until we know what it means or whether it'll happen again, we probably don't want to bring any undue attention to it. Trust me on this.*

27

THE HAIRY TIES THAT BIND

STAGE ONE EXPIRATION: 2 DAYS, 17 HOURS

"By the way, where's Murg?" Pixel asked aloud, breaking our chat connection.

"Yeah, about that..."

I explained what they'd missed in the few minutes they were stuck in the land of blue screens.

"Wow," Pixel remarked once I was finished. "To be offlined before the first day is even through. I'm not sure whether I should be embarrassed for Murg or envious."

"Or maybe you could try being a little more respectful about it. Boog's taking it pretty hard."

"You don't say."

I turned back that way to find she'd completely hacked Apu's head off and was now busy screaming at it. Guess she'd grown attached to her FAST in the short time they'd been together.

At least she now had an opportunity to get it out of her system.

Unsurprisingly, my map was now clear of contacts in the immediate vicinity. The few villagers who'd survived Boog's slaughter had dispersed, either hiding behind closed doors or having run off into the jungle. Considering the scene she was making, I can't say I would've done any different.

That was probably unfair of me. These people weren't innocent by any stretch of the imagination, even if her absolute lack of mercy had been pretty terrifying to watch. Either way, it was probably best to not get on her bad side.

Turning my attention away from the angry micro-yeti, I realized that while this battle had taken a heavy toll, it hadn't been without its spoils.

I was now level four, whereas Pixel, who'd been right on the verge of fourth, had jumped all the way to fifth level. Not too shabby.

I said as much.

"No argument here," the FAST replied. "That said, let's hold off on the celebrations until we can reach that campground. It's possible this dump had more than one hunting party out there looking for sacrifices. If so, we should probably amscray before any decide to make an appearance. But first…"

"Let me guess. Loot everything we can carry?"

"Look at you finally starting to get the hang of the old chaser spirit."

Pixel led the way back to Apu's corpse where Boog continued to yell at the dead sloth.

I couldn't help but notice her level had changed as well, albeit only incrementally. "Only enough for third level? Doesn't sound like she got a lot from that fight."

"It's because I got credit for the kill shot," Pixel replied. "Means the bulk of the XP ended up being split amongst our party."

"That doesn't sound fair."

"It isn't, but as you humans would say, them's the breaks. Fairness is ultimately in the eye of the beholder. And before you start whining, let me just point out we can either stand here debating it until some assholes show up looking for revenge or we can strip this place clean and get the fuck out of Dodge. Your call."

⌛⌛⌛⌛ ⌛⌛⌛⌛

I grabbed the blankets that had been draped over both cages, noting briefly that they were called *Shrouded Serapes* before pulling them into my inventory. A more in depth look could wait for now. Pixel was right. It made sense to grab what we could then beat feet to that campground.

Once there we could take a breather.

Apu's weapon was lying next to the altar, looking like an extra nasty, oversized sledgehammer. I grabbed hold of the handle, unsure whether I'd even be able to budge it. However, it instantly resized to fit my grip, allowing me to pick it up easily.

Heh, I'd almost forgotten things could do that here. Talk about handy.

The weapon had the rather threatening name of *Spell Hammer Mace* but, curious as I was, it too went into my inventory for now.

That left Apu.

I was hesitant to approach but Pixel urged me onward.

"Boss loot drops are special," they explained. "More importantly, they're available to everyone who helped take them down. Trust me, you don't want to miss this."

Pixel moved to the boss's body, then hovered there waiting for me to do the same.

Lootable Corpse – Decennial Boss
Ascension Ring Update Available.

Decennial? Huh. I hadn't really paid much attention to that before, being too busy staring in horror at the hulking sloth monster coming for us. I guess this was what Pixel had meant earlier about the show's time theme leaking into everything.

I'm sure that title meant something, but since he was dead I doubted it was of great importance at the moment.

Time Chaser

There was no other gear listed on Apu's body other than his fur and claws. The hair would be useful for my Loom o' Doom. As for the claws, each was roughly the size of a railroad spike. The ammo potential alone made those worth it, so I grabbed it all. With a wet *shlep*, everything in question was removed, leaving Apu's body a skinned pile of muscle, organs, and bones.

"Eww," Pixel remarked. "I'm beginning to see why you're not overly fond of that loom skill."

Boog apparently approved of this move, though, as she tossed Apu's severed head unceremoniously atop his bloody corpse and then proceeded to start kicking it – each blow resulting in a disturbingly wet *thud*.

I tried not to focus on how gross all of this was. "So what was that update it mentioned?"

"Check your map," Pixel said.

I did, noting there was something new waiting for me on it. At the very edge of the northwest corner, the same direction that campground lay, I spied a dim yellowish glow. After several seconds, it blinked off and on, looking almost like a sonar ping.

Pixel explained, "That's the big prize the Decennial bosses drop. We get an indicator on our maps pointing toward the nearest ascension ring relative to them. The closer we get, the faster it'll pulse. Pretty cool, no?"

Cool was an understatement at best. I grinned, unable to contain my excitement at this new development. "How far away do you think it is?"

"Offhand I'd say nowhere close but that's okay. We still have plenty of time. And at least now we have a direction to follow, which believe me takes a lot of the pressure off. Speaking of which, what say we get the fuck out of here?"

I started to answer but then thought better of it. "Not quite yet. There's still something we need to take care of."

"What?" Pixel replied. "You thinking these assholes are hiding some loot inside those huts? Because if so, I'm happy to..."

"No. I mean what about ... *her*?" I whispered, holding up my palm to block the finger I was pointing Boog's way.

"What about her?"

"It's just that ... she lost her FAST."

"Yeah. That's gotta suck the big one. I'll be sure to send a sympathy card."

I sighed. "Listen. Drega said the odds of survival were a lot lower for chasers without FASTs."

"And that's our problem, why?" Pixel asked.

In truth, I wasn't sure what I was proposing here. Boog had proven capable in that fight, albeit somewhat less than dependable. So rather than come right out and suggest something I wasn't entirely certain of, I figured I'd throw out some fishing line and see if Pixel took the bait. "She did help us out. We should probably do *something* for her in return, shouldn't we?"

"We already did. She got both a map upgrade and experience. That's a pretty fair trade in my book."

"Fair, yes, but is it the *right* thing to do? I mean, look at her."

We both turned her way, only to find Boog squatting over Apu's severed head.

It took me a second to realize what she was doing. "Wait! Don't do that or you'll be..."

She peed on him.

Roughly two seconds later, a sound akin to a penalty buzzer echoed through the air.

Crap! When next I looked at Boog, her HUD label had changed.

Chaser: Boog – Earth 6255 – Level 3 – PENALIZED.

Double crap! That meant if she died within the next twenty-four hours, her entire timeline would be wiped out. All for nothing more than... Well, okay, I suppose pissing on an enemy's corpse was perhaps a bit more severe than a simple hallway accident.

"Well, that's it. She's fucked," Pixel said dismissively.

Time Chaser

Boog must've finally noticed it, too, because she stood up and wailed, "No! Murg warn Boog to not be dumb, but Boog forget. Boog *is* dumb!"

"If the shoe fits," Pixel remarked.

"Stop that," I admonished before turning to the little ape girl. "It's ... okay, Boog."

It really wasn't. Pixel was right about her being screwed. I had a feeling, at least in her case, that having a FAST around to continually remind her of the rules was far more a necessity than for most.

"No, it not!" she cried, once more collapsing in tears, except this time atop Apu's bloody corpse.

Oh goddamn it all. "Sure it is, Boog. You ... have us now."

"She does?" Pixel replied.

"Yeah. We'll help you get through this. We'll ... remind you not to be dumb."

"We will?"

I glared at the FAST. "Look at her. She's..."

"Pathetic?"

"All alone," I corrected, pointing toward the hairy little troglodyte. "Not to mention, she's ... um... She's... Okay, so what is up with her anyway?"

Pixel flitted up and down a few times, a gesture I took as a shrug. "If I had to guess, I'd say anger management issues coupled with some serious co-dependency."

"Not that! I mean, *her*. How is she even here?"

"Same way as you I imagine. A pointless death that left no impact on her timeline, although in her case I imagine it was likely a stupid one."

I let out a grunt of annoyance. "You're not listening. Did someone, I don't know, make a mistake somewhere?"

"How so?" Pixel replied.

"It's just.. I thought all the chasers here were supposed to be ... human." I gestured toward Boog again. "And she's obviously not."

She must've heard me because she momentarily ceased her wailing. "Chaser Macmac is friend to Boog," she said sadly. "Macmac help avenge Murg."

"Macmac?"

"Don't start," I warned the FAST.

"Fine, whatever. Guess you finally found someone dumb enough to call you that," Pixel said before getting back to the subject at hand. "Anyway, I think I understand the confusion."

"Okay, and that would be...?"

"For starters, Drega never actually said anything about Homo sapiens being the only competitors here. If you heard otherwise, that's on you. Secondly, I seem to recall there being several points in your species' history where you guys couldn't even agree on the definition of what counted as being *human*. So I think we can forgive the overmind for not asking your opinion on the matter."

I shook my head. They weren't wrong on that one.

"That being said," they continued, "I don't have access to Boog's stats but my guess, based on how she looks, is that she's an albino *Homo erectus*. For those of you who didn't pay attention in science class, they're basically kissing cousins to Homo sapiens, save a bit more ... archaic."

"So, she's a caveman ... or woman that is?"

"Not quite. You're thinking Neanderthals. And before you ask, yes, there's almost certainly some of those guys here too, which would very much explain our buddy Borlack."

"All right, that one kind of makes sense."

"It *all* makes sense, Tim, if you think about it. All three species were competing for dominance of your world during the time span this cycle's Chase was drawn from – or at least the first third of it. Congratulations by the way."

"What for?"

"For your DNA strain eventually winning the genocide lottery."

Boog, as it turned out, was listening to all this with her head cocked to the side, kinda like you'd see from a dog. Finally, she pointed a hairy finger Pixel's way. "Boog not understand but will listen to new Murg. New Murg smart like old Murg."

"No, Boog," I said. "This is Pixel."

"Pis-Pissel?"

I let out a chuckle. "Close enough."

"Hilarious," Pixel said. "Anyway, now that the science lesson is over, it's been a pleasure to meet you, Boog. I wish you luck with whatever horrors await you out there."

"Come on," I replied.

"Seriously, Tim, we do not need this kind of baggage."

In truth they were probably right. As effective as Boog had been in the fight, I'd also seen what she'd done to those villagers. That was the sort of wildcard we probably didn't need. Nonetheless, I felt my heart going out to the little ape woman. She just looked so sad and despondent with her FAST gone. And her chances without someone to help her were almost certainly negligible.

Then there was her penalty to consider, even if it was mostly her own fault.

If it was just her life on the line, that would be one thing. But to condemn her entire timeline for one mistake? "Come on, Pixel. We have to help her."

"No," they said. "Absolutely not. We are not adopting her like some sort of ... cave kitten."

"Who said anything about adopting her?"

"Fine. The *other thing*, then."

"What other thing?"

"You know. It's what your kind does." At my confused look, Pixel continued. "Listen, I know what you went through back in your world and I get it. That sort of thing has gotta be *frustrating* for a guy like you. So go on, get it out of your system. But afterward she's on her own."

"Get what out of my system?"

"Just bang her already. I'll be over there waiting. Just don't take forever, and for the love of my sanity please try not to be too loud."

I glanced at Boog then back at Pixel. "Hold on. You think *that's* what this is about?"

"Of course. That's what your species does, right? You see a knothole, so you stick your dick in it, bees be damned. I mean, hell, that pretty much defines your entire society. And before you say anything, it's all good. I don't judge. Just make sure it's only ... what do you guys call it ... oh yeah, a one-night-stand."

"Hold on..."

"I'm serious, Tim. For starters, this really ain't the place to be looking for a long term commitment. And even if it was, there's a lot of other fish in the sea, most of whom probably won't spend ten minutes screaming at a decapitated sloth head before peeing all over it."

"I don't want to bang Boog."

"Bang?" Boog replied.

Shit. "Um, sex. You know ... mating."

"Boog and Macmac mate?"

"Yeah. I mean, no! Pixel was just asking if I..."

"Macmac mate!" she screeched, all the sadness apparently forgotten in the space of a heartbeat.

"No. We are *not* mates."

"Macmac and Boog mate!" she repeated, hopping up and down in apparent excitement.

"You know what," Pixel said, no doubt enjoying this, "I take it all back. Maybe we should let her tag along for a while after all."

28

PERCHANCE TO DREAM

After some more joking at my expense, Pixel finally got serious again since we were almost certainly overstaying our welcome.

Whatever discussions needed to take place, whether over Boog's fate or otherwise, could just as easily be done at that campground, all while not having to look over our shoulders.

That was fine, because a little camping out, aka sleep, was honestly starting to sound pretty good by then. My health might've been back to full and my body stronger than ever before, but it had been one hell of a long-ass day.

For now, we decided that Boog would travel with us. Then, come morning, assuming morning even applied in this nightmare dimension, we could figure out our next steps. If Pixel was still adamant about their decision by then, well, we'd have to see. I wasn't sure whether it was worth turning this into an extended argument, but hopefully some rest would bring with it clarity.

That seemed a fair compromise. I still felt guilty for Boog not only losing her FAST but also being saddled with a tier-two penalty. However, there was no denying she was physically capable, as indicated by how she'd handled herself in the fight with Apu. Even if we did part ways, surely she'd have a shot of surviving the next day on her own.

Wouldn't she?

Soon enough, we entered the dungeon again, going from the wide open space of the cavern back to cramped tunnel walls – which also reactivated the Fog of War. Considering everything I'd gone through, though, the tight confines felt far less claustrophobic than they had before. At least here there were a limited number of directions an attack could come from.

It was all a moot point anyway as we reached the campground unmolested – once again finding a fenced off, innocuous looking alcove waiting for us.

At least this one proved to be more period appropriate once we stepped through, transporting us to the inside of a medieval keep, one with high stone walls guarding every side.

Boog's eyes opened wide at the sight. It reminded me of what Pixel had said. The contestants hailing from the beginning of the Chase's time span might be physically more capable, but those of us from the latter end had the advantage of being more familiar with technology as well as the hindsight that history provided.

Albeit, none of that had really helped in the fight against Apu.

Whatever the case, it didn't matter much right then as I found myself growing more exhausted by the minute.

Can't say I was surprised by that. I'd been mostly running on adrenaline ever since Pixel had been abducted. But now, finally here in this safe zone, it was all rapidly catching up to me.

If my sense of time was still holding true, night would've long since fallen back home. Jeremy would almost certainly be in bed by now. Maybe Deb too, although I preferred not to speculate whether that involved fuckboy Manny's dick or not.

I briefly wondered if any of them had given me a second

thought during this time, even if they would've had no way of knowing how my day had taken a sharp left turn from normalcy.

Normalcy ... hah!

I took a moment to ponder that. Had this day ended like any other this past week, I would've grabbed some takeout from the Chinese place across the street from the motel. Then I'd have eaten it in front of the TV, all while debating if I wanted to splurge on that dump's one XXX channel before ultimately deciding against it. Afterward, I'd have spent an hour trying to convince myself I was an adult and thus should go out and do adult things, like sit at a bar and talk to people. In the end, though, I would've simply crawled into bed, where I'd stare at the ceiling for a few hours before finally drifting off.

As I turned my gaze toward the tents laid out across the courtyard, I couldn't help but let out a humorless snort.

Here I was, standing in an alien dimension wearing a loincloth, a demon sweater, and covered head to toe in blood that wasn't my own. And yet, as horrifying as this day had been, I found a small part of me didn't hate it nearly as much as I despised that goddamned motel room.

How was that for irony?

Rather than continue standing there chuckling like a loon, I bid Pixel and Boog goodnight before turning toward the nearest tent.

"Don't forget your achievements," Pixel called after me, "and your stat points."

"Got it."

"Spend some time on that loom skill as well," they added. "Don't waste it."

I didn't bother answering that one, not sure what I was expected to do inside the cramped looking pup tent.

Instead, I stepped inside ready to pull the flap down behind me, only to find the interior of the tent had completely changed.

Time Chaser

Gone was the course fabric enclosure and military style cot. In its place was a small, featureless room with four walls and a twin bed – one that didn't look entirely dissimilar to my shitty motel room back home.

I couldn't help it. I threw back my head and laughed.

It was either that or scream.

Thankfully, upon closer inspection the resemblance to my home-in-exile back on Earth was superficial at best. In truth, this place was more like the freshman dorm of a state college, except I probably didn't have to worry about any roommates drunkenly pissing on my bed.

Long story.

Anyway, I turned back to find the flap of the tent replaced with a solid looking door.

That was good. While I was tired enough to not really care, I couldn't pretend I was entirely okay with the idea of sacking out where anyone could pop their head in and watch me sleep.

"Except you *are* going to watch, aren't you?" I asked aloud, reminding myself that I was still on some crazy multiversal TV show.

Bathrooms were off limits, but Pixel hadn't said anything about the sleeping arrangements. I checked my map to test this and, sure enough, unlike with that pit stop, it appeared to be working just fine.

I spied Pixel's green dot along with Boog's blue one. Off to one corner stood a white dot – likely this campground's sponsor.

Even the space beyond the campground gates was still visible, albeit my view was greatly limited due to the vast area inside the fortress. Guess that was an acceptable tradeoff. Regardless, everything appeared sedate for now with no red dots in sight.

I'd have to ask Pixel whether there was anything else I needed to know regarding where the map did or didn't work, but that could wait until morning. For now, I turned my attention toward my HUD. I had some stuff to do before hitting the hay so it was best to get started.

First up were the items I'd looted from that boss battle.

The *Shrouded Serapes* were pretty much exactly as they seemed. Both were imbued with an enchantment designed to block detection. Covering either an item or person with one rendered them invisible to basic location magic. The description specifically mentioned scrying, but I guess that included the map as well.

The big problem was the blockage went both ways. Being under the blanket made you undetectable but it was also like a magical faraday cage, blocking any efforts by the person inside to see beyond their fabric prison.

It felt like something that was of most use to either kidnappers or smugglers, of which I was neither. Yet more stuff for the sell pile.

The Spell Hammer Mace, on the other hand, was a weapon worth considering. It was a nasty piece of work, offering a 10 point buff to strength as well as 20 to constitution. That was no laughing matter. It was no coincidence that I'd started doing more damage to Apu once he'd put it down.

The attached skill from which it drew its name – *Spell Hammer* – was equally as impressive. Once per day, at first level anyway, the wielder could choose to redirect one ranged magical attack toward an opponent of their choosing instead. The catch there was the attack had a fifty percent chance of being directed toward a random target instead.

That gave it a distinctive risk of friendly fire – obviously not a factor for Apu since he'd been a solo act, but worrisome for anyone who wasn't a friendless sloth monster. It made me wonder whether Pixel had actually been his target or merely the victim of bad luck.

Alas, with Apu dead there was no way of knowing. Far more certain was the fact that this weapon required some serious consideration on my part as it potentially rivaled my Banshee Racket in both power and function.

There was also the minor detail of me probably looking a bit less stupid while charging into battle wielding it.

Yeah, definitely one to mull over.

That out of the way, it was time to focus on my new achievements, which meant more Drega. Not quite the voice I wanted lulling me to sleep but beggars couldn't be choosers.

Achievement unlocked! Boss Bitch!

You have not only faced your very first boss battle but survived it too, unlike at least one of the other participants.

If it weren't for the fact that you had to rely on outside help to win, I'd almost be impressed.

Still, the fact you continue to draw breath is a testament that you might yet have the chaser spirit within you. And hey, you didn't even have to run like a pussy to make it happen – although we both know you were thinking about it.

Still, go you ... this time anyway.

***Reward*: 1 STD boss box.**

Huh. Drega's wording was almost disturbingly on the money for that fight, like he'd personalized it just for me. Pixel had said he was one of those ninth level evolved thingamabobs and thus had the mental overhead to record a lot of these at once. What I found more interesting, though, was that this achievement had popped into my HUD mere seconds after the battle had finished. It was either more time fuckery or he was actually capable of recording these in real time.

Either way, that was a scary level of power. Pixel had mentioned more than once that these beings were evolved beyond the scope of my reasoning, but it was only now that it was truly starting to sink in.

Oh yeah, just what I needed, a metaphysical crisis before bed. As if my day hadn't been stressful enough.

Rather than dwell on that further and risk freaking myself out, I turned to the other achievement awaiting me.

Achievement unlocked! We be FAST, they be slow!

You may have won the battle but have you lost the war? Not really. What you did lose, however, is a goddamned FAST unit.

I want you to think about that for a second.

We're talking about a quantum-based lifeform possessing enough computational power to make Data from *Star Trek* look like a wind-up tinker toy. And yet, thanks in part to your incompetence, they're now nothing more than sloth chow.

The multiverse is a little less bright this day and it's mostly your fault. Good job! I hope you're proud of yourself.

***Reward*: You yourself get nothing, unlike that other FAST who was smart enough to loot the corpse while you weren't looking. Alas, there's no honor among thieves. But who needs honor when you've got sweet-ass gear?**

Wait. Pixel looted Murg's body? I wasn't sure whether to be amused or horrified by that. On the flipside, it spoke to the ever-growing sense that I needed to be mercenary as fuck to survive in this world.

It was a mindset that was gonna take some getting used to.

Back on Earth, for instance, it would be unthinkable to show up to a wake and then go through the deceased's pockets. This wasn't Earth, though. Whatever rules of decorum I may have previously followed needed to be tossed out the window.

The thing was, I couldn't be completely ruthless about it either. I didn't want to return home to my son, only for him to realize the father he knew was dead and in his place was now a monster wearing his skin. There had to be a balance. I needed to find a way to survive while still holding onto who I was.

But first I needed to finish with all this crap and get some sleep.

Time Chaser

I turned to the box I'd been awarded, somewhat annoyed that finishing off Apu had warranted only a shitty Seize The Day reward.

However, I quickly realized that designation was slightly misleading when it came to boss boxes.

As the metal chest disappeared in a poof of sparkles and muted fanfare, a whole lineup of items appeared in its place.

Up first were three more healing potions. Not exciting but welcome all the same. That gave me a decent surplus for the day ahead, not the worst thing in this world. Alongside those were two mana restoration potions. Also good.

Next, I found another scroll waiting for me, this one for a second level spell called *Party On*.

Curious, I took a quick look and found it to be a mass healing spell. At second level, it was capable of healing the caster and up to two additional party members so long as they were within thirty feet. I had a feeling it was going to replace that Plant Dominion scroll in my list of... Oh wait. I was fourth level now, meaning I could equip them both.

Cool. "Look at me finally getting a hang of the rules."

Two more items awaited in the lineup – both of them new to me. There was a book as well as a neat bundle wrapped in butcher's paper.

All right. Now it was starting to get good.

I had to admit, as nice as it was to get more potions, they were already starting to feel a bit mundane – like they were the Chase's go-to prizes. However, I seemed to recall that also being the case in plenty of video games I'd played as well. After all, potions and scrolls were considered consumables. Powerful as they might be, once you used them that was it.

These new items on the other hand...

First up was the book, which my HUD helpfully identified as a spellbook – my first of the game.

The cover read *Grimoire of Burning Beatdown.*

It came with a tooltip warning me that this was a one-time use only item. Reading it would permanently impart the spell unto me, but also consume the book in the process.

Guess they didn't want chasers sharing spells like some sort of half-assed lending library.

Fuck it! I grabbed the book and opened it. The act itself caused the tome to instantly turn to dust. However, simultaneously a new section appeared within my HUD – *Spells*.

I couldn't help smiling as I read the description – something I probably should've done upfront. Burning Beatdown imbued whatever melee weapon I was actively using with a fiery nimbus for up to thirty seconds – offering both a fire damage buff as well as the potential to ignite any combustibles I struck.

In short, my Banshee Racket was about to become a *Flaming* Banshee Racket.

Okay, that still didn't sound particularly threatening, but whatever.

The downside was it cost 80 mana to cast. Guess I knew where all my new stat points were going. My original plan had been to slowly raise my intelligence score, but without a sizable boost this spell would be useless to me.

Had it been anything else I might've passed for now, but I could very much envision using the shit out of this one. I just needed to be smart about it and not use up all my mana potions before the first battle of the day was done.

Rather than waste time agonizing over this decision, I immediately assigned those stat points, bringing my INT and accompanying Mana both to 80.

If I had any buyer's remorse later, I'd just have to deal with it.

Tempting as it was to pull my racket out of inventory and give it a try, I refrained. I didn't know how combustible pocket dimensions were but since the outside was a fabric tent it seemed wise not to tempt fate.

Instead, I turned my attention to the last of my rewards, the mysterious package.

I focused on it and the wrapping paper instantly fell apart to reveal ... a pair of pants?

Don't get me wrong. It was a welcome sight considering the loincloth still wrapped around my waist. There was something about having my family jewels hanging free that left me feeling way too exposed. All the same, *this* was their idea of a proper reward for winning a boss fight? Not only that, but they were an ugly grey camo design. Between that, my sneakers, and the sweater, it was like whoever was choosing this stuff had all the fashion sense of a blind nudist.

Combat Chinos

Ultimate comfort meets maximum adventure! These cotton blend slacks are perfect for the weekday warrior who chooses to wage his battles from inside a cubicle rather than behind enemy...

Ugh! I think I just threw up in my mouth.

You know what? Fuck this noise.

Note to self: find whatever chucklefuck wrote this shitty ad copy and have them escorted from the building. In the meantime let's just cut to the chase.

They're pants, okay?

You put both legs in, zip them up, and that's it.

Mind you, they *are* cut to accentuate your assets, if you catch my drift. So if you gotta die, at least you can be assured the mobs won't be forgetting that fine booty anytime soon.

+10 to Dexterity

+3 levels to Stealth

Um, okay...

Drega's creepy-ass, rambling description made me want to do nothing more than set these damned things on fire and live with the loincloth, but I had a feeling that was just the fatigue talking.

In truth, the extra DEX points were more than welcome. As

for Stealth, that brought me up to level 5, more than doubling my previous level. In truth, I couldn't wait to see how sneaky that made me.

Well, okay, maybe I *could* wait.

The reality was, I needed some sleep first ... just as soon as I took care of one last thing on my to-do list, the activity I was looking forward to the least.

29

PARTY FAVORS

STAGE ONE EXPIRATION: 2 DAYS, 7 HOURS

Had this been your run-of-the-mill, trope-driven TV show, I would've woken up convinced the previous day had been nothing but a bad dream, only for something dramatic to quickly jolt me out of that delusional respite.

In truth, that notion was dispelled in the moment before I cracked my eyes open as my HUD flared back to life.

Talk about nightmarish technology. I could only imagine how something like this would be abused back home. Hell, companies would probably cream themselves at the thought of employees who could never fully disconnect – like a perpetually open email inbox.

Gah! If this was the future then consider me envious of wherever Boog had come from. Heck, if that was the case, the year 2541 couldn't come quickly enough.

The first thing that caught my eye as I pushed those thoughts away was the countdown timer. According to it I'd slept for nearly nine hours. That was longer than I'd been expecting. When away at a conference I was usually lucky to snag four or five hours of shuteye, but then most cons didn't require me to fight a giant sloth as part of the festivities.

After finishing up with my loot box the night before, I'd decided to devote an hour toward Loom o' Doom. That way at least I wouldn't have to listen to Pixel bitch at me. Much to my surprise, though, I hadn't hated it nearly as much as I'd thought I would.

Upon focusing on it, a jet black spinning wheel had *poofed* into existence before me – accompanied, unsurprisingly, by demonic laughter. However, that bit of weirdness was quickly overshadowed by the realization that along with the wheel had come the knowledge of how to use it – like it had always been there inside my head just waiting for me to access it.

It was kinda like the kung-fu scene from *The Matrix*, except with textiles. Much as I didn't particularly enjoy handling the hair sitting in my inventory, in short order I'd managed to produce a modest length of dark grey fabric.

At some point after I'd gotten started, I'd decided the resulting material was best put toward a replacement for my ruined work shirt. Along with that decision came even more knowledge. I instinctively knew how long that would take – roughly three more days of looming before I'd have enough fabric to make that a reality.

It had been a surreal end to an already weird as fuck day.

This new morning, if I could even call it that, wasn't starting out quite as bizarrely *yet*, but that notion was quickly put to the test as I raised a curious eyebrow toward a new notification waiting in my HUD.

Nadok has invited you to a private cortexing channel. Accept Y/N.

Nadok? Had some rando butt-dialed me on their SK, assuming that was even a thing? For the life of me, I couldn't think of any other reason. I didn't know anyone called Nadok, and it's not like anyone here outside of Pixel or Boog even knew who I was, except perhaps for the showrunners.

Was this some sort of unexpected wake-up call from the

overmind, perhaps to say I was getting a tier-two for using too many sleep vouchers or something stupid like that?

Curious as well as slightly fearful, I clicked to accept it.

Tim, JUST FUCKING TIM: *Hello?*

Nadok: *Penark Queeg.*

Tim, JUST FUCKING TIM: *Um, excuse me?*

Nadok: *You've been asking questions, chaser Tim, JUST FUCKING TIM. That is the answer.*

Tim, JUST FUCKING TIM: *First off, it's just Tim. And secondly, exactly what questions are we talking about? I've asked more than a few.*

I waited for a response but none came.

Tim, JUST FUCKING TIM: *Seriously, what the heck is a penark queeg and what question does that answer?*

Tim, JUST FUCKING TIM: *Hello? Anyone there?*

I closed out of the chat and sat up. The fuck? Had I just gotten punked by some joker? If so, the punchline had gone way over my head.

Whatever the fuck. I'd wasted enough time on this Nadok clown.

It was time to get dressed, grab some breakfast, and then see what today's *chasing* had in store for me.

⌛⌛⌛⌛ ⸱⸳⸱⸳⸱⸳⸱⸳ ⌛⌛⌛⌛

I was forced to admit that, stupid as I looked in the mismatched outfit, my new chinos were actually pretty comfortable. The extra points to my DEX didn't hurt either. Heck, I even felt a little more fleet of foot as I opened the door and stepped out ... of the tent.

Just like that, I was back in the medieval fortress.

I swear, that will never get old.

It was crazy. This place would be an absolute dream come true if it weren't such a blood-soaked nightmare.

That was enough negativity for now.

Time Chaser

I followed the map until I spied Pixel and Boog. They were both awake, although in all fairness I had no idea if Pixel even needed to sleep. I spotted them off to the side, at a wide table surrounded by uncomfortable looking chairs. Pixel was floating while Boog sat, using her hands to eat from a crude wooden bowl. She must've had a chance to wash up at some point because her formerly matted and bloody fur was now mostly white again.

I waved to them.

"Macmac!" Boog cried happily. She started to stand but I waved her off, telling them I'd be there as soon as I grabbed a bite to eat.

That done, I followed my nose to a large bubbling cauldron near one of the exterior stone walls. At least this setup was more topical to the campground's appearance than that grill in the last one had been.

Mind you, where the cauldron might've fit the decor, the *chef* stood out like the sorest thumb I'd ever seen.

Slithering around atop a raised wooden platform directly behind the cauldron was a pus yellow blob. Its body was like semi-cooled gelatin within which floated roughly two dozen mismatched eyeballs.

I probably would've mistaken it for the world's largest and grossest pile of puke had it not been tending to the pot – stirring the contents with a large spoon held by a protruding tendril of yellow slime.

Perhaps the oddest thing about it was the medieval helmet just sort of floating atop its mass, undulating up and down as the creature moved. It was like the singular worst cosplay in the entire universe.

Several of the blob's eyeballs turned my way as I approached. Air bubbles formed within its body, rising to the surface where they popped and produced sound akin to speech. "Fair morning, m'lord," it bubbled in an English accent.

"Uh ... hi."

"I trust your rest was a pleasant one."

"Can't complain," I replied.

"No problems budding off the old mitochondria?"

I raised an eyebrow. "Not that I'm aware of."

"There's nothing to be ashamed of, mind you. As we all know, binary fission doesn't come easy to folks our age."

"It doesn't?"

"Sadly no, but that's where Strix's Mucus Shine can help. It'll get your flagellum flagellating again."

Ah. Finally it hit me. This was another of those sponsored commercials. And this thing was merely a sales ... err ... blob hawking his strange and somewhat disturbing wares. "Fascinating I'm sure. Listen, can I just get some of whatever that is you're cooking?"

"Coming right up, m'lord!"

The blob monster fixed me up a bowl of what looked to be beef stew, although the odd coloration of the beef clued me in that this was more of that mockumeat junk. Whatever. I might care about that later, but right then I just wanted to sit down and properly fuel up for the day ahead. I had a feeling another nutradisk wasn't going to cut it.

As I walked away, the blob called after me, "Remember Strix's Mucus Shine! It'll turn a pseudopod into a me-and-you-opod!"

Dear God, that's terrible. "Is it me, or are they selling alien Viagra at this one?" I asked once I rejoined my companions.

"I distinctly made it a point to not pay attention," Pixel replied.

"Probably a smart move."

"So, how'd you sleep?"

I shrugged. "Not too bad actually. Better than I would've expected."

"Really?" Pixel replied. "That's surprising to hear. No offense, Tim, but I kind of expected you to shuffle out of your tent looking like a zombie. I kinda figure a lot of chasers are gonna be waking up shell shocked, at least for these first few days."

I chuckled. "Surprised me too, but I was pretty much out the second my head hit the pillow. Guess I was dog tired after yesterday's boss fight."

"Dog?" Boog asked.

Oh yeah, she probably had no idea what that was. "Think of it like a wolf that lives in your home." Her eyes opened wide to which I held up a hand. "It's just a saying, that's all."

No idea if she understood that any better but she went back to slurping her food down like there was no tomorrow – perhaps poor wording considering our situation.

So, rather than risk sticking my foot in my mouth by saying the wrong thing, I took a bite of my stew instead. It wasn't half bad, mockustuff or not. As I ate, I glanced at Pixel's sheet in my HUD, curious to see what they'd spent their level increases on. Four of their stats had risen – INT, DEX, CON, and PSI. However, I couldn't help but notice the total increase in points amounted to 90 as opposed to 60.

Looking closer, I spied not one but two new dots standing out against Pixel's greenness, one orange and the other white.

"New patches?" I asked, remembering what Drega had said the night before.

"Yep. Got a twenty point DEX Patch from that boss battle. Not too shabby."

That accounted for *one*. I raised an eyebrow waiting to see if they'd confess to anything else before glancing toward Boog, who was still devouring her meal as if she'd never seen food before.

Now that she was mostly clean again and we weren't distracted by fighting for our lives, I realized the SK on her arm wasn't her only accoutrement. Around her neck she wore what looked like a dog collar, white so it blended in with her fur.

What caused my eyes to open wide, though, wasn't the

collar so much as the realization that I could now see her full stats.

Party Member: Boog – Earth 6255 – Level 3 – ***PENALIZED***
STR: 120
INT: 20
WIS: 10
DEX: 110
CON: 135
CHA: 40
PSI: 20

Party member? That was certainly new.

Physically she was a tank, besting me in all departments, although our constitution scores were close thanks to my demon sweater. Mentally it was a different story. Not to judge, but hopefully we didn't come across any bags of hammers intent on challenging her to a trivia contest.

I was a bit curious regarding those PSI points she had, mind you not nearly as much compared to her new status as a member of *Tim Chasers*.

And yes, that name was still stupid as fuck.

My map, however, appeared to confirm this as I realized her dot was now green to match Pixel's.

I glanced between her and the FAST. "I thought you said..."

"Hey, Boog," Pixel interrupted. "Why don't you go grab some more of those yum-yums. It's gonna be a long day. Best to fill up now."

"Boog love yum-yums!" she cried, bounding gleefully off toward the eyeball blob.

"Of course you do," Pixel remarked before letting out a sigh.

I waited a moment then said, "I see you two have been getting along."

The FAST made a non-committal buzzing noise. "I was just helping her with her stat points when you decided to rejoin the land of the living. Sounds like she almost gave Murg an aneurysm last level by tossing 20 into PSI without bothering to ask first. Figured it behooved us to head that one off at the pass."

Somehow that didn't surprise me. "So why the change of heart?" I asked, digging into my stew.

"Isn't it obvious, Tim? She's a fucking basket case. If we let her go out there by herself, she'll be gnome chow in under an hour."

I couldn't help but grin. "That idea didn't seem to bother you yesterday."

"You've got some mockubeef stuck in your teeth."

I smirked. "Don't change the subject. Spill."

"Fine. I ... made the mistake of talking to her. She was up early, way earlier than your lazy ass. Anyway, I found her sitting next to one of the outhouses crying her eyes out."

"So you decided to comfort her?"

"Not really. I told her to buck up, that things weren't so bad. You know, meaningless platitudes so we could hopefully not have her following us like a lost puppy."

"I take it that plan didn't work out?"

The FAST flitted back and forth. "No. I made the mistake of veering off into small talk. I thought it wouldn't hurt to cheer her up a bit. Eventually, I ended up asking what she'd been up to before being dragged into the Chase."

"Let me guess," I said, wishing I'd grabbed a drink. "Eaten by a cave bear?"

"I wish. If so, it would be all 'welcome to no-FASTville, population you.' But no. Turns out she was sacrificed."

"Wait. Sacrificed?"

"Yep. Seems that whole shebang yesterday, watching Murg get whacked on that altar, hit a bit too close to home for her. That's why she went apeshit. Pardon the pun."

I turned in the direction she'd gone. She was standing at the cauldron while that blob gesticulated wildly, probably talking about flagellums, pseudopods, and all sorts of stuff the little ape girl didn't have a clue about. "Who sacrificed her?"

"That's the kicker," Pixel said. "It was her tribe, her own family as a matter of fact."

"Really? Why?" I paused as I realized we were probably discussing what amounted to sensitive information here. "And isn't this more something she should tell me when she's ready instead of hearing it from you?"

Pixel made that shrugging gesture again. "Let me ask you this. Do you really want to sit through an hour of listening to her butcher this story in one syllable words?"

I considered it for a moment. "Go on."

"Thought so. Anyway, yeah. Turns out Boog has been an outcast her entire life. Pretty much from the moment she was born, her tribe decided that being an albino meant she was cursed. Because god forbid superstitious dipshits actually think things through instead of rushing to the conclusion that it's all some boogeyman's fault."

"Really? Oh wow. That's rough."

"Yeah. The only reason she lasted as long as she did was her mother was the eldest hunter's daughter. Probably sister too because I get the impression these fuckers weren't exactly selective when it came to breeding."

"I'm sure she'll appreciate the editorial."

"Whatever. Anyway, it gets worse. They shunned her to the point where they didn't even give her a name."

"They didn't? Then how...?"

"Murg apparently chose it for her. Far as Boog is concerned, her assigned FAST was her first ever real friend." Pixel made that buzzing sound again. "So maybe let's not spill the beans that they were just doing their job."

I made a zipping motion across my lips. "Mum's the word. So why did they turn on her ... more than they already had, that is?"

"Typical primitive screwhead shit. Piecing together what she told me, it sounds like there was no food because of a bad winter. The guy in charge needed a scapegoat, so he decided to grab the chick with the white fur and toss her ass off a cliff to appease their hunting gods. It's a tale as old as time."

"It is?" I glanced Boog's way again, seeing that she was heading back. "Anyway, that's gotta really suck."

"Tell me about it."

"But look at you," I said, grinning. "Just a big old softy at heart."

"I don't have a heart," Pixel replied. "I have a miniature singularity which generates roughly enough energy to…"

"Same concept. What I mean is maybe you're not such an asshole after all."

"Nah. I just have a soft spot when it comes to pets."

"Pets?"

"Well, I mean come on. She's about as bright as that unicine I melted yesterday."

"And I take it all back."

⌛⌛⌛ ⋅⁖⋅⁖⋅⁖⋅ ⌛⌛⌛

"Macmac look sad," Boog said.

We'd finished our breakfast, meaning it was just about time to head out again. We'd gathered back at the front gate, steeling ourselves for whatever was to come, then had stepped out – once again finding ourselves in a dungeon hallway with an unassuming alcove to our backs.

Pixel, with their greater map range, was taking a moment to scout the area to the north of us. In truth, I had a lot more stuff I'd wanted to talk to the FAST about, but it was probably best to not waste any more time. There'd be more opportunities to chat later.

"I'm not sad, Boog," I told her. "I was just thinking of my boy."

"Boy?"

"Yeah, my son ... my child. His name is Jeremy."

"Jermy?"

"Close enough. Here, I'll show you." I opened my inventory and scrolled down to the picture the system had rather assholishly cataloged as *pointless sentimental photo*. Then I pulled it out and showed it to Boog.

Her eyes opened wide as she peered at it.

"Cute isn't he?" I asked.

"Jermy small."

"Well, yeah. He's only five."

However, she seemed more interested in the paper than the image upon it. "Why small?"

"That's not actually him, Boog. It's just a photo of... You know what, never mind." I stuck the picture back into my inventory before it could get lost. "Anyway, I was just wondering what he's up to right now."

"That's an easy one," Pixel said.

"Oh?" I replied, instantly curious. Did FASTs have some insight into the real world that I wasn't aware of? If so...

"He's doing the exact same thing he was doing while you were getting plowed by that bus. And he'll keep doing that exact same thing for as long as you're here."

I opened my mouth but no words came out.

"Void outside of time and space, remember?" they added. "I don't know if this is a comfort to you or the exact opposite, but the reality is everything that happens here will ultimately translate to a blink of the eye for anyone back on your Earth – and that goes for every single chaser here. Get it?"

I let out a deep breath as this sank in. "I think I do. Are you saying that whatever happens here, however long we stay, it doesn't matter because we ultimately get sent back to whenever we left?"

"Mostly. This is the sort of shit a certain TV show from your world would refer to as a big ball of wibbly wobbly, timey wimey stuff. And that's just the tip of the iceberg. Take your face for instance."

I raised an eyebrow. "What's wrong with my face."

"Nothing, outside of the fact that your species aren't exactly lookers. But do me a favor. Reach up and touch your chin."

I did.

"What do you notice about it?"

"Nothing. Why?"

"Exactly," Pixel said. "You don't feel any stubble because your beard didn't grow. Nor will it. Likewise for any female chasers. They don't have to worry about waking up tomorrow, a week, or even a month from now to find their Aunt Flo is visiting, if you catch my drift." Pixel turned toward Boog before adding, "And no, I'm not gonna explain that."

"But we can..."

"Eat, sleep, and use the bathroom – all things to suggest time is moving normally?" they interrupted. "All true as well. Think of it as your body being in a form of limited temporal stasis. You don't age, but everything else functions like normal."

"Wow," I said, trying to wrap my brain around it. "Just wow."

"Don't try to understand it. You'll give yourself a brain hemorrhage. Just know it's in effect for however long the Chase is on – even if we're stuck here for the next hundred quinks."

So much for this day not taking any weird turns yet. On the one hand, that was pretty damned horrifying to learn. It was like every chaser here was now experiencing an ongoing living death outside the realm of everything we knew and loved.

And yet, I couldn't help but take some odd comfort in Pixel's decisively non-comforting words.

The thought of waking up day-after-day, facing constant danger while never knowing what was going on back home – not knowing if Jeremy was happy or sad, sick or well, any of that – was kind of terrifying to me. On top of everything else, it was the added heartache of knowing I was missing out on his life. That was the sort of thing that could potentially hang over a man's head like the sword of Damocles.

But what Pixel was saying took all that out of the equation. I could still love my son and yearn to be back home with him, but at least now I knew I wasn't actually missing anything.

I didn't need to worry about missed birthdays, holidays, or even visitation weekends, because none of that would happen so long as I was here.

It's hard to say exactly why, but somehow that thought made the morning a little bit brighter despite the dimly lit confines of the dungeon hallway.

Maybe it was having one less thing to worry about, no small feat in a game where I literally had to worry about *everything*.

And that apparently wouldn't change until the Chase was finally over for me – even if it took a near eternity.

"All right," Pixel announced, pulling me from my reverie. "There's a small group of red dots up ahead past a fork in the tunnel. What say we go and kick their asses?"

"Sounds like a plan," I replied, taking the lead. "By the way, you were just kidding with what you said, right, about the Chase taking a thousand years?"

"Gods, I hope so," they replied with a humorless chuckle.

30

STING LIKE A BEE

We rounded a corner, only to be assaulted by the most god-awful stench imaginable.

"Smell like yum-yums."

God-awful for one of us anyway.

The last few hours had been mostly uneventful save for a few low level mob skirmishes, but apparently that luck was now coming to an end..

Up ahead, the hallway widened into a large circular cul-de-sac, revealing multiple closed doors visible along the rounded walls. Unlike previous doors we'd encountered, though, these weren't completely solid. They were crudely made, as if from scavenged boards and timber. Light could be seen flickering through the cracks from about half of them.

Alas, if there was anyone inside, my map wasn't giving me any insight into it. All I knew was there must be a way through one of them because the indicator for that ascension ring was still saying this was the way to go.

Of more immediate concern, however, was the massive corpse lying on its side against one of the dungeon walls. Several of its ribs were exposed and the body appeared to be in an advanced state of decay – obviously the source of the offensive odor.

At first glance, I took it to be an elephant, albeit a hairy one. Fortunately, my HUD was good enough to fill in the blanks.

Lootable Corpse – Siberian Mastodon.

Huh. You didn't see that every day, especially since they were supposed to be extinct – at least in my timeline. Alas, Drega apparently didn't deem the corpse worthy of expounding upon. In truth, I didn't want to loot it so much as give the disgusting thing as wide a berth as possible.

And the last thing I wanted was for Pixel to give me crap about taking its fur. I didn't need a new shirt that badly.

That might've been easier said than done anyway as the corpse oddly still showed as a red dot on my map.

The fuck?

I was still debating whether the idea of fighting a zombie mastodon was cool or terrifying when the head of a massively oversized grub popped out of its chest cavity where it began munching on the flesh at the edge of the wound.

It looked like a maggot but the size of a raccoon.

Meggot – level 1

Remember that old joke from when you were a kid, "What's grosser than gross?"

Well, meet the punchline. These bad boys are pretty much the economy sized versions of regular maggots, save they're a hundred times bigger and infinitely more disturbing.

You might be wondering what kind of loving deity would allow such monstrosities to evolve, but the answer is none. However, where theology might've failed, insane experiments in alchemical mutation more than made up the slack.

Either way, have fun. You'll definitely be seeing these guys in your nightmares.

Fucking Drega! And what was that about alchemy? I was still trying to digest all this when my ears caught the faint sound of buzzing.

What the?

"I suggest we back up out of sight," Pixel said.

Their advice wasn't a moment too soon as about a dozen baseball sized insects flew out from the mastodon's interior and began circling the corpse.

"Those are without a doubt the biggest fucking horseflies I've ever seen."

"Horseflies?" Pixel replied, their voice barely a whisper. "Oh, Tim, you sweet summer child. You might want to take a closer look."

Much to my dismay I did.

Mutant Bot Fly – level 2

You won't find much consensus when it comes to the opinions found upon the myriad Earths of the multiverse. But on just about any world where bot flies exist, the dominant intelligent species will be quick to agree that they are nasty as all fuck.

Well, except for the reptoids of Earth 92663. They like to toss the vile little things down their gullets like popcorn, but they're weirdos to begin with. Trust me on this.

However, I digress.

These are not your garden variety "lay eggs beneath your skin while you sleep" horrors. No. These puppies have been mutated. They're bigger, meaner, and the meggots that hatch from their cursed eggs will not only gross you out but will happily devour your innards until you're nothing but a skin suit full of disgusting larva.

Kind of like your mother-in-law but less judgmental.

How and why were these bot flies mutated? That's for you to find out.

Although I sincerely doubt the culprit is a katana swinging turtle named Leonardo.

More mutations. I was beginning to sense a theme here.

"You're up, Tim," Pixel said.

"Wait, why me?"

"You heard that description. They lay cursed eggs."

"So...?"

"*So*, as far as I'm aware only one of us has curse resistance."

I sighed. "I was really hoping that was just flavor text."

"Yeah, well, hope springs eternal but reality prefers we go fuck ourselves. Go clear those things out. I'll cover you from here."

"Boog help Macmac?"

"No," Pixel said. "Stay with me, Boog. Unless you have any defenses against these things, which you don't, you're not gonna want to run the risk."

"But it's okay if *I* run the risk?" I replied.

"I don't see anyone else here wearing a demonic sweater, do you?"

Sadly, I couldn't argue with that, not that it made me feel any better.

I looked again at the giant bugs before quickly considering our other options.

We hadn't come *that* far. I mean, there was still time for us to conceivably double back past the campground and check out the other exits from that jungle cavern. The problem was, not only would that waste time, but there was no guarantee those other tunnels would be any safer or even lead back in this direction.

Fuck me.

I hated to admit it but Pixel was right. I was the best man for this job, much as I'd have loved not to be.

That didn't mean I had to be stupid about it, though.

"All right, fine," I said. "You two stay here. Do not, I repeat, *do not* do anything until I engage with them first. Doesn't look like they've noticed us yet and I'd prefer we keep it that way for as long as possible."

"Fair," Pixel replied. "Focus on those flies. Once you've got their attention I'll see how those meggots handle an acid bath."

"That works. Just try not to hit me in the back with it."

The FAST made a dismissive sound. "You humans take all the fun out of life."

⌛⌛⌛⌛ ·⁑⁂⁑⧫⁑⧫⁑⁂⁑· ⌛⌛⌛⌛

The buzzing grew disturbingly louder as I approached, racket in hand – reaching an uncomfortable pitch that I could feel all the way in my teeth. Thankfully, the stealth boost from my new chinos was no laughing matter. Either that, or these mutant flies simply found the putrefying mastodon corpse far more interesting.

Won't lie. Had there been another way around them, this is one fight I'd have been happy to avoid like the plague.

While these things were in no way friendly, as evidenced by the red dots buzzing around my map, they also seemed mostly preoccupied. Sadly, we couldn't just ignore them. We needed to check out what was behind those doors, but it was a foolish risk to assume these bugs would leave us alone if we simply walked up to one and knocked.

If they were indeed cursed as Drega had claimed, that could also put the others at risk. At the very least Boog would be. I wasn't entirely sure whether these things could lay their eggs in Pixel or not, but the rules of this game didn't always seem to line up with any logic.

With Pixel down one of their lives and Boog still penalized for at least another ten hours, it was probably best to avoid any unnecessary risks.

Mind you, going in alone wasn't exactly my preferred strategy either. Thankfully, I had a little more faith in my capabilities following my solo adventure back in that jungle cavern. If I could take out a bunch of seasoned warriors, then some mutant flies ought to be a snap.

Famous last words.

True enough. The last thing I needed was to start acting all cocky in the face of danger. I mean, I was level four not forty. Besides which, so far as I was aware anyway, there was no penalty for a bit of overkill.

To that end, once I'd managed to sneak to within about ten feet of the buzzing monstrosities, I called up the spell list and cast Burning Beatdown. Not only would it hopefully mitigate the risk but it gave me an excuse to test out my new spell – something I can't lie and say I wasn't looking forward to.

A nimbus of flame ignited around my weapon, spreading all the way around it, even down to the handle. That caught me by surprise to the point where I almost dropped the damned thing. Fortunately, I quickly realized the fire wasn't hurting me. Guess it didn't affect the caster, which in retrospect made perfect sense. I can't imagine a spell like that being all that useful if it set me on fire as well as my enemies.

My *stealthed* status immediately disappeared, no doubt due to the fact that my racket was now a blazing torch.

The buzzing of the flies grew more frantic in response. But if they didn't like that, I was willing to bet they really weren't going to enjoy what happened next.

I stepped in, swinging my weapon like the world's most lethal zap racket. Fortunately, unlike their normal-sized counterparts, these economy sized flies weren't particularly quick. I managed to nail one midair. Its body literally exploded from the impact like it was a living water balloon, drenching me in steaming, foul-smelling bug guts.

Eww! Some of it got in my mouth.

Damage Buff: 1%.

Ooh, I'd almost forgotten about that. At least it was enough of a distraction to keep me from puking. Also, this time I wasn't about to waste it, even if the buff it gave me was probably unnecessary for this fight.

I swung at another fly but this one was a bit quicker than

the first. Too bad it wasn't fast enough to see Second Chance Backhand coming.

More disgusting bug splatter resulted as my buff rose another percentage point.

Yes!

These things might be big and gross beyond all consideration, but fortunately all it took was one shot to blow them to pieces.

Plorp!

Plorp!

I turned to find that Pixel had moved closer, putting themself in range to drop a duo of acid balls right into the dead mastodon's body.

The result was its open wounds becoming a simmering maggot stew. Thank goodness lunch was still a ways off, because this fight was most certainly not helping my appet...

Ow! Fuck!

A lancing pain bloomed in my side, like someone had just stabbed me with an ice pick.

My HUD instantly responded with: *Debuff – You have been cursed!*

Shit!

Thankfully, before I could panic, it was followed by: *Curse Negated.*

I looked down to see that one of the bot flies had landed on me. For such a big bug, it had a light touch to it. But how...?

That's when I realized its backside terminated in an inch long stinger, like it was part murder hornet.

I slammed my palm down on it before it could try stinging me again, popping the foul thing like an oversized zit.

So much for the shower I'd grabbed at the campground before heading out. Mind you, being drenched in fly juice still beat being cursed, even more so as my damage buff pinged up to 3%.

Half the bot flies were gone and the rest had finally caught on that this was a fight. They were apparently smart enough to be wary of my flaming racket, but rather than fleeing it simply seemed to agitate them more.

Had these been garden variety flies, this was the sort of thing that would've resulted in me spending half an hour chasing the damned things with a rolled up magazine while missing over and over again.

Instead, though, it was more like shooting fish in a slightly wider than normal barrel.

⌛⌛⌛ ⋯⋯ ⌛⌛⌛

There wasn't anything to loot when all was said and done. The flies had all popped like grapes – including one I'd absolutely vaporized, scoring a critical hit and locking myself into a 4% damage buff until the end of my next fight, because no way in hell did I think there was any chance of going twenty-four hours without getting into another scrape.

The mastodon corpse was rapidly liquifying thanks to Pixel's acid – somehow managing to make it smell even worse than it already did.

To top things off, the battle ended up being absolute shit when it came to experience.

On the upside, we'd won fairly easily and were no worse for the wear as a result.

I knew my mana would replenish itself within minutes, but all the same I replaced that remaining foresight potion in my limited equip slots with mana restoration potions instead.

I now had zero doubt that Burning Beatdown spell was going to come in handy, so having it ready to go again at a moment's notice seemed a wise choice.

That decision was apparently even more prescient than I'd assumed as one of the doors across from us began to creak open, revealing a trio of red dots on my map.

"Get ready," I whispered, "because we're about to…"

"WHO'S READY FOR ANOTHER LIVE UPDATE?"

"...be completely fucked," I finished, feeling my feet become rooted to the ground.

"BECAUSE I KNOW I AM!"

The sound of raucous cheering could be heard, as if those in charge felt we needed to hear the live studio audience's enthusiasm as well.

"Boog stuck!"

Unsurprisingly, she too was locked in place. Ditto for Pixel, who continued to float in the exact same spot they'd been. At least I could take some comfort in knowing whatever mobs we were about to face were unable to take advantage of the situation, like I had earlier. Unfortunately, I had no clue what they were. The door remained only partially open. I could see light inside, but it was dim – revealing nothing save a cobblestone floor and some shadows.

"WE'RE RAPIDLY CLOSING IN ON THE END OF OUR FIRST DAY AND ALL I CAN SAY IS WOWSA! THINGS HAVE REALLY PROGRESSED IN THE FIVE MINUTES SINCE LAST I SPOKE TO YOU ALL. IT'S ONLY BEEN FIVE MINUTES, RIGHT PLEG? I MEAN IT SURE AS HECK FEELS LIKE IT. AM I WRONG, FOLKS?"

"*What's that saying these Earthers have?*" Plegraxious replied. "*Time flies when you're having fun. Well, it must be true, Drega, because I feel the same way. Hours may have passed, but it might as well be the blink of an eye.*"

This time Plegraxious didn't seem to have any surprises to spring on the host. "Guess someone got a talking to since the last update," I mumbled.

"What Macmac mean?" Boog asked.

I was about to respond but Pixel shushed us. "Zip it, both of you. These updates might be annoying and inconvenient, but there's usually important info attached to them. Remember..."

"Yeah, yeah. Knowledge is power," I said, repeating the phrase they seemed intent on beating into my skull. "I get it."

"ALL RIGHTY, LET'S TALK ABOUT WHAT'S BEEN GOING ON IN THE CHASE. SINCE OUR LAST UPDATE AN ADDITIONAL THREE-HUNDRED-AND-FORTY-NINE CHASERS HAVE BEEN EXPIRED. THAT'S RIGHT, FOLKS, WE'VE CROSSED THE FIVE PERCENT MARK AND THAT NUMBER IS ONLY GOING TO GO UP FROM HERE. NO LESS IMPRESSIVE IS THE FACT THAT SEVENTY-TWO FASTS HAVE BEEN PERMANENTLY OFFLINED AS OF THIS MOMENT, WITH ANOTHER HUNDRED-AND-SIXTY-FOUR SITTING AT TWO EXPIRATIONS."

"Seventy two permanent offlines already?" Pixel gasped, sounding horrified.

"What the heck's going on out there?" Plegraxious cut in. **"Are these Earthers using the poor little guys as meat shields or what?"**

"Spare me the false concern, asshole," Pixel growled.

So much for shutting up and listening.

"WHO CAN SAY FOR CERTAIN, PLEG? ALL I KNOW IS THAT THESE PRIMATES ARE RAPIDLY PROVING THAT LOGIC CAN GO FUCK ITSELF WHEN THE CHIPS ARE DOWN. AM I RIGHT, FOLKS?"

More insane cheering followed.

"Is it me or do they curse an awful lot for a show that's being broadcast across the entire freaking multiverse?"

"Finding offense in descriptor words is mostly a conceit for second and third level civilizations," Pixel replied. "For us evolved beings it's all about the context. Now zip it, *primate*."

I flipped them the middle finger as Drega continued. Hopefully they got the *context*.

"BY NOW, I IMAGINE A GOOD DEAL OF THE CHASERS LISTENING IN ARE FEELING A BIT DOWN IN THE DUMPS AT THOSE NUMBERS, BUT IT'S NOT ALL BAD NEWS FOR THEM. IS IT, PLEG?"

"Indeed it isn't, Drega. As we near the end of the first day,

an astounding six-hundred-and-seventy-one chasers have already managed to find and use ascension rings."

"WOW, THAT MANY?"

"Yep. They might be illogical little monkeys but they're certainly resourceful. And that's only the beginning because, as usual, we expect those numbers to soar in the coming day. In fact, I'm told the Committee has opened up a few extra sponsorship slots for the Stage Two waiting area in anticipation of all the hungry mouths because, damn, these Earthers can eat."

"YOU HEARD HIM, FOLKS. AND SPEAKING OF SPONSORS, NOW'S A GREAT TIME TO REMIND OUR HOME AUDIENCE THAT THEY CAN GET IN ON THE ACTION WITH *TIME CHASERS: REALITY RUMBLE*. EXPERIENCE THE MAGIC OF CR AS YOU RELIVE THE EXCITEMENT OF PAST CHASES FROM THE COMFORT OF YOUR OWN DIMENSION. CHOOSE FROM A WIDE ASSORTMENT OF LEGENDARY CHASERS SUCH AS GRILKRX THE GOUGER, BANDIT JACK, AND SLANGO, AS YOU TRY TO SURVIVE TWELVE LEVELS OF..."

"CR?" I asked, tuning out the rest of this nonsense.

"Cortexed reality," Pixel said.

"I should've guessed," I replied before changing the subject. "So what happens to those who make it to Stage Two early? I assumed they got a head start over the rest of us, but he mentioned a waiting room."

"That's correct. Any chasers who ascend early get shunted to a sort of mega campground to wait things out. That way everyone starts the next stage at the same time. They tried doing it your way for a couple cycles several quinks back, but it ended up being a cluster fuck. The audience apparently couldn't figure out who to watch."

"So that's it? Our reward for surviving a stage is a rest break?"

"Not always. The earliest ascenders sometimes get a few extra perks," Pixel continued as Drega droned on about past Chases – most of which made zero sense to me with no frame of reference. "We're talking loot boxes here or there, but honestly I'm not sure it's worth it."

"How so?"

"Because in my opinion being too early hurts more then it helps. Think about it, Tim. For starters, while they're scarfing down the catering, we're still here grinding and growing stronger. Trust me when I say that every level counts. Starting the next stage with a bit of extra muscle can be the difference between life and death. Hell, in these early stages it probably makes more sense to find a nearby campground and then spend an extra day grinding. And that's not even considering the psychological element."

"Oh?"

"Don't quote me on this, but I'm fairly certain we can expect to find a live feed of the Chase in whatever space they shunt us into. It's supposed to be so that those waiting can stay updated on the competition, but it's more a constant reminder that they aren't safe. At least not really. Remember how you told me that you'd slept pretty good back at that campground?"

"Yeah."

"Well, that's probably because you were exhausted from everything we did. But how well would you sleep if you'd just been sitting there on your ass, being reminded every single minute that in a few short days it could once again be your turn to die?"

I felt a chill run down my spine as this realization hit me.

Goddamn. They really were doing their damnedest to fuck with us, even in those fleeting moments when we might otherwise be celebrating our victories.

Little by little that was starting to sink in – slowly overshadowing that tiny bit of gratitude I felt at being given a second chance, and replacing it with contempt for the Committee.

How many chasers were dead across how many cycles, all for the entertainment of a bunch of bored assholes?

Before I could travel too deeply down that rabbit hole, perhaps mercifully so, Drega finally finished his trip down memory lane.

"BUT ENOUGH WITH THE REMINISCING, FOLKS, BECAUSE THE FAR MORE EXCITING NEWS IS WE'RE ALREADY STARTING TO SEE SOME STANDOUTS AMONG THIS NEW GENERATION OF CHASERS. CHECK OUT WHAT I'M TALKING ABOUT!"

Much like it had before, my SK began to glow before projecting a massive screen into the air. Boog's did too. A similar beam of light shot out of Pixel – giving us three screens in total. They came together, forming a massive viewing display, our own *IMAX* theater in a sense as highlight clips, each of them large as life, began to play.

Where the previous update had focused on chaser deaths, almost seeming to revel in them, this one was a bit different.

Before it had all been about faceless victims and an ever-growing body count. Now, though, not only were the chaser's names clearly visible, but the goal of this update seemed to be over-the-top victories.

First came a clip of a Union soldier and his FAST as they opened fire on a massive spider creature. The soldier's gun appeared to be shooting ice shards instead of bullets as they peppered the beast full of holes. He was identified as *Jack J – Earth 833 – Party: Kelly's Crusaders*.

Next up was an older lady identified only as Nelly from Earth 16, belonging to a party called *Goddamn, This Shit is Stupid!* As much as that made me chuckle, she herself was no laughing matter. Christ, she looked like she could've been someone's grandmother, yet on the screen she somehow managed to snap a grizzly bear's neck like it was a toothpick.

Holy crap.

I can't say I was surprised to see my old buddy Borlack make an appearance next. His party had the rather unimaginative name of *Meat*, which is what he turned a group of armored knights into as he knocked them down and then literally stomped them to death with his bare feet. Guess there was a reason he was known as the Trampler.

The feed then switched to another multi-chaser party. Janice from Earth 9342 looked like the mom from *Leave it to Beaver*, yet she was fighting alongside Shim of Earth 7709. In stark contrast to her teammate, the front half of Shim's head was shaved and she was wearing a tight fitting body suit that seemed to shine with its own light. Both were members of team *Get Squort*, whatever the fuck that meant, and they were shown successfully defeating a group of salamander monsters.

Finally, they zoomed in on one last chaser, *Jeffrey P – Earth 1 – Party: First Coven*. Ignoring the Earth 1 designation, which may or may not have had any significance, he himself looked like the sort of jerk who'd be leader of the evil fraternity in an eighties sex comedy. Yet, despite his college boy good looks, he was surrounded by a pile of dead or dying Vikings, most with their limbs torn asunder.

My first thought was this guy must be some sort of serial killer, but then he picked up one of the still-living berserkers and buried his teeth in the guy's neck – the scene freezing as his eyes turned black as coals.

The fuck?

"Hold on," I said. "How did that asshole end up with vampire powers while I got a fucking squash racket? Explain to me how that's fair."

"Yeah, I'm not sure that's something they gave him," Pixel replied. "At least not this early."

"Then how the hell did he...?"

"**THERE YOU HAVE IT, FOLKS**," Drega cut in. "**LOOKS LIKE WE MIGHT HAVE SOME CONTENDERS OUT THERE AFTER ALL. WHAT DO YOU SAY TO THAT, PLEG?**"

Time Chaser

"**It seems to me that the tide might be turning.**"

"**QUITE POSSIBLY, ALTHOUGH THERE'S STILL A LOT OF CHASE LEFT TO GO. ALL THE SAME, PERHAPS NOW WOULD BE A GOOD TIME TO CHANGE THINGS UP A BIT ... AND I THINK I KNOW JUST WHAT THE DOCTOR ORDERED.**"

"Oh crap," Pixel said. "Here it comes."

"Here what comes?" I asked.

"**YOU KNOW WHAT IT IS, YOU'VE BEEN LOOKING FORWARD TO IT, SO SAY IT WITH ME! IT'S TIME FOR A...**"

The voice of the invisible crowd erupted as they all shouted, "*ONE HOUR CHALLENGE!*"

"What the fuck is a...?"

Before I could finish that thought, the dungeon greyed out around us, leaving us in a formless void for maybe three seconds before things started to take shape again.

The open doorway ahead of us morphed into a familiar living room. The dungeon walls became painted sheetrock covered in photos. And the stone floor became laminate planks – ones that I recognized, having picked out the pattern.

No way.

As the living room of my former home came into focus, my heart nearly split in two as I spied the little brown-haired ragamuffin sitting on the couch watching TV.

He turned to me and grinned. "Hi, Daddy!"

31

POWER HOUR

I couldn't help the tears that sprang to my eyes. It was like a dam that had burst. I couldn't have stopped them had I tried.

"Oh my God, Jeremy!"

Though I'd only been gone a day, it suddenly felt like an eternity. I dropped the racket from my hands, stepped forward, and grabbed hold of my son, not sure whether I wanted to scream, cry, or just stand there hugging him.

I was home. The nightmare was over. It was finally...

"Um, Tim," Pixel said from behind me. "Not to burst your bubble..."

Huh? I spun around, still holding my boy. "What are you doing here?"

The FAST wasn't the only one who'd joined me. Boog was there too. Not only that, but I was still looking at them through the overlay of my HUD.

The fuck was going on?

"**Hey there, chasers**," Plegraxious's voice called out. "**By now you're probably wondering what the fuck is going on. Well, prepare to have your primitive minds blown. Welcome to the first One Hour Challenge of this cycle's Chase. It's a**

fan favorite segment of the show where we temporarily pull your asses out of the fire and toss them into fun and horrifying scenarios, oftentimes plucked from your old lives. You'll then have one hour to solve a particular challenge we'll be presenting you with."

Fun and horrifying?

"I want to go outside and play," Jeremy complained, squirming in my arms.

"Um, sure, champ," I said, putting him down. I was simply too confused to do anything else. What the hell was this?

He walked past Boog, waving to her as if she was no big deal. "Hi, fuzzy lady."

Boog stopped looking around long enough to raise a hand back at him. "Hi, Jermy. You not tiny."

"For our first challenge we decided on something simple – a real no brainer, since I imagine a good deal of you are currently weeping your eyes out like little bitches. Well, suck it up, chaser cupcakes, and take a look outside."

Outside? Not wanting to, but fearing what might happen if I didn't, I stepped to the front window and looked out – nearly shitting a brick in the process.

Standing on my front lawn, driveway, and sidewalk – hell, stretching as far as the eye could see – was an army of heavily muscled, green skinned monsters. All of them were wearing armor and carrying various nasty forms of weaponry. As if to drive home their intent, the entirety of the map they occupied turned bright red.

Did they really expect us to fight all of them?

"Stationed just outside your loving abode, cave, keep, or whatever, is a horde of bloodthirsty orcs. Don't bother trying to fight them. They'll simply respawn. Their numbers are endless, so believe me when I say this is one fight you can't win. But that's okay because they're not the challenge."

"They aren't?" I couldn't pretend to not feel a slight bit of relief at that.

Time Chaser

"**Oh no,**" Plegraxious continued, the glee evident in his voice. "**It's so much worse. See, those orcs are all angry, hungry, and horny as hell. The thing is, they aren't going to try to break in or anything. Nah. That would be way too pedestrian. Your task instead for the next hour is to keep all present NPCs, aka your loved ones, safe from harm. Because if even a single one steps foot outside, well, it's gonna get real messy real quick. Trust me on this.**"

Wait ... outside?!

I turned to find Jeremy fiddling with the front door lock. I ran over, scooped him up, and relocked the door. "No!"

"But I wanna go out and play."

"You can't. It's not safe."

"But I wanna!"

"**The rules are simple. Make sure they remain unharmed for the next hour and you win. But if so much as a hair on their head gets bent, that's it. You fail. Winners will each receive a bonus Fortnight gear box. Losers ... well, here's the good news. There is no penalty for losing this one. Well, none except a lost hour of time because the clock is *still* ticking.**"

Crap! He was right. The timer in my HUD was still counting down.

"**Your hour begins ... now! Good luck, chasers. You're gonna need it.**"

"I want to go outside!" Jeremy whined, growing louder and more insistent.

"You can't. There are ... bad men out there."

"I don't care. I wanna go!"

"That's enough," I snapped even as he started to squirm in my grasp. I didn't care, though. Even if I had to hold him for the entire hour, no way was I letting him go out there.

"Tim, you need to listen to...," Pixel started.

"Check the doors and windows," I interrupted. "Make sure they're all locked."

"Windows?" Boog asked.

Oh yeah. Her having no clue about this modern era was potentially going to be a problem. "Here, I have a better idea. You hold Jeremy and I'll go check... No, not that hard. He's still gotta breathe. Yeah, that's better. Now I'll..."

"What are you doing here, Tim?"

I froze where I stood. Of course *she* would be here. I should've guessed it. It's not like Jeremy was old enough to leave alone. "Um, Hey, Deb. I can ... explain."

That was as big a lie as lies could get, but sue me for being a little discombobulated.

"No need," my soon to be ex-wife said blithely. She was dressed casually – jeans and a sweater, with her short black hair hanging free. Much as I hated to admit it, she looked good.

Rather than immediately lay into me, though, as seemed to be our new normal, she stepped from the kitchen doorway and grabbed her purse from the counter. "Can you and your friends do me a big favor?"

I glanced at my companions then back at her. Did she not notice they were a bit ... unusual? "Um ... sure. What kind of favor."

"Great! I need you to watch Jeremy for a bit. I have to run to the store."

"Wait. Right now?"

"Of course right now. We're out of olives."

I wasn't sure what was weirding me out more – her plans to go out despite the horde of monsters clearly visible through the front window, that she wasn't currently chewing me a new asshole for being in the house uninvited, or the fact that my new friends weren't even fucking human.

Before I could say anything, however, another voice called out from the bedroom.

"Oh hey, babe, mind grabbing me some chips while you're out. Barbecue if you please, and no ridges. Ridges are for pansies."

Time Chaser

I turned that way, my eyes narrowing as fuckboy Manny stepped out clad in nothing but a pair of tight fitting boxers.

"Happy to," she called back.

He turned my way. "S'up, Timbo," he said as if we were friends.

"What the fuck are you doing here?" I growled before remembering Jeremy was in the room. "Daddy said a bad word. Don't repeat it."

"I don't care!" he cried, still squirming in Boog's grasp. "I wanna go outside!"

"What am I doing here?" Manny replied with a wink. "More like *who* am I doing here, if you catch my drift, bud."

"Oh, you cad," Deb replied, heading toward the front door.

I eyed my racket where it lay on the floor. *Tempting, oh so fucking tempting.* Instead, I moved to head Deb off at the pass. "Hey, I have an idea. How about you go to the store later?"

"No, It has to be now. I need olives."

"You don't even like olives," I replied through gritted teeth.

I heard movement behind me but ignored it.

"Um, Tim?" Pixel asked.

"Not now."

"Well, if you two are gonna have a lover's spat, then I'm gonna head out back and catch me some rays," Manny announced, despite it being jacket weather outside. "This fine hide ain't gonna tan itself."

"Yeah, you do that," I replied, continuing to block the front door.

"No. He can't," Pixel said, flitting in front of Manny's face to slow him down. "We can't let him."

"Why not? If he wants to go outside and play with those things then who am I to say no?"

"That's not how this challenge works, Tim. We need to keep *everyone* here safe. Including the ones you don't like."

"But Plegraxious said my *loved* ones, and I sure as hell don't..."

Time Chaser

"Just trust me on this," Pixel said. "Now herd her back this way so we can..."

"Yo, Tim," yet another voice called, this one belonging to my boss Allan.

Why the fuck is he here?

"Do me a solid and grab this month's sales reports, will ya?" Allan called from across the room, near the side exit. "I'll be out in the garage working on my car. It's a nice day, so I'm gonna roll up the door if you don't mind."

"What? That ... doesn't even make any sense."

"You can figure it all out while I'm at the store," Deb said, trying to sidestep me.

Manny waved to her. "Don't forget those chips, babe. I'll be out in the yard. Maybe we can get in a little topless sunbathing when you get back."

"Sounds like a plan to me," Allen remarked, turning away from us. "I'll be in the garage if you need me."

All the while Jeremy continued to squirm in Boog's arms, whining about how he wanted to go outside.

This wasn't my home so much as a madhouse.

⏳⏳⏳⏳ ·:⋄:·⋄:·⋄:· ⏳⏳⏳⏳

"Not so tight," Pixel warned. "You can't hurt them, otherwise we lose the challenge."

Thank goodness my strength from the Chase was still in effect here. Oh, and that there'd been a nearly full roll of duct tape in the utility drawer.

It took us several tries to get them all rounded up, with each attempting to go their own separate direction – all outside of course. But finally we managed to get all four of them taped to the dining room chairs.

All combined, it was some combination of frustrating, heartbreaking, and weird as fuck.

However, despite my home now looking like a hostage situation gone bad, none of our *prisoners* seemed overly upset by this – at least beyond the fact that they *really* wanted to go outside.

"I have to say, Tim, I'm a little miffed at you right now," Deb complained mildly, barely giving me a tenth of the venom I'd gotten during our last phone call. "This is not the time for whatever weird sex game you're playing. I'm simply not in the mood..."

"I am," Manny cut in, making me glad I'd stuffed my racket back into inventory.

"...so please untie me so I can go to the store."

"Yeah. Daylight's burning, my man," Manny added. "Gotta keep this bod in shape for *my lady*."

"I got a better idea," I snapped. "How about you go fuck yourself?"

"Only if Deb promises to join... Umph!"

I shut him up with a piece of duct tape. Petty of me, but it was probably better than giving in to the fantasy currently running through my head involving that Spell Hammer Mace and his kneecaps.

"I'd really like to finish changing my sparkplugs, if you don't mind," Allan said. "Don't make me put this on your next evaluation."

"You don't even live here!"

And, of course, right next to him Jeremy continued to squirm. "I want to play outside!"

I stepped back. We'd eaten up nearly half an hour just getting them all in one spot. It was only now that I was finally able to take a breath and give this some thought.

"What the hell is wrong with them?" I asked. "It's like they're single-minded in their obsession to go outside and get their faces rearranged."

"That's because they are," Pixel said. "I was trying to explain it earlier, but you humans can really be a slippery bunch when you want to be."

I ignored that second part. "Wait. Are you saying that TOPC ... that the *Committee* did something to them?"

"Not at all. These numpties are acting like morons because that's how they've been programmed to act. They're not real, Tim. They're bots."

"You mean like androids?"

"Andy-roid?" Boog asked.

"It's like a..." I shook my head. "Never mind. Just do me a favor and keep an eye on them, will ya?"

"Yes, Macmac. Boog watch Jermy and others."

"Thanks." I turned once again toward Pixel. "Okay, let's back up. What do you mean by bots?"

"Exactly that. In case you haven't figured it out yet, this isn't your house. It's a recreation. And those people are just dumb meat puppets fashioned to look like your loved ones..."

I raised a skeptical eyebrow.

"And decisively *unloved* ones as well. But all of them have one thing in common. They've been given all the survival skills of drunken field mice in a cat rescue."

I considered this. "So, if I were to, say, beat Manny over the head with a blunt object..."

"It would probably be satisfying as fuck but ultimately pointless since the real one is still back in your world. Mind you, it would also ensure that we'd win jack shit, which I'd prefer not to happen since I just spent nearly thirty minutes chasing your fucking boss back inside."

"Bots." I looked at each in turn, noticing for the first time that none of them had been given a system description like nearly everything else in the Chase. "So are they like those NPCs back in the village?"

Pixel let out a sighing noise, as if this wasn't something they wanted to discuss. "Not quite. Bots are actually used pretty sparingly in the Chase. They're easy enough to make in scale, but only if you skimp in the brains department. The problem is, the audience doesn't like that. They can see right through that shit because these chucklefucks are ultimately little more than advanced Furbies. Otherwise, the Chase would end up being like a live action version of one of those *Final Fantasy* games, but not in a good way."

"So then what are the mobs and NPCs?"

"They're real."

"So are we talking actors here?"

"Not exactly. Everything they do and feel is genuine. It's just that ... their brains may have been futzed with so that they don't question that things aren't quite normal. But trust me they're all real."

Needless to say, that revelation did not make me feel better in the slightest. For one second, one single second, I'd been able to hope that maybe I wasn't a killer. And just as quickly, that hope was dashed to pieces. "But how? Where do they get all these...?"

Pixel interrupted me with a buzzing sound. "Might be best if we saved this discussion for another time. These One Hour Challenges tend to get a lot of scrutiny so it might be best if we don't bring the mood down."

"My mood is already down."

"That's different. Our suffering is entertainment. The audience's suffering on the other hand..." They let the statement hang in the air.

I shook my head in disgust. "Goddamn. I really wish you'd warned me about these things earlier."

"I didn't know about them."

"What? But I thought you..."

"I *said*, I didn't know. They don't tell me everything. We've been over this already, Tim."

Pixel: *You need to be careful what you say. I wasn't kidding when I said these things were scrutinized.*

I bit my tongue, instead glancing back at where our hostages were busy haranguing Boog about needing to go outside.

Tim, JUST FUCKING TIM: *Okay fine. But earlier when*

Drega announced this thing you sounded like you knew what it was.

Pixel: *That's because I did.*

Tim, JUST FUCKING TIM: *Okay, now you're just talking in circles. You either knew about them or you didn't.*

Pixel: *It's both. If you'd told me about these things half a day back I'd have had no clue what you were talking about. That's because those memories were all blocked. But guess what. Turns out these bullshit challenges were sitting in those nine percent that became unblocked.*

Tim, JUST FUCKING TIM: *I thought it was eight percent.*

Pixel: *It was, but a few more of my memory cells unlocked while you were asleep.*

Tim, JUST FUCKING TIM: *How?*

Pixel: *Fuck if I know. I have no idea what the hell's going on. This might merely be a residual effect from Murg's spell or maybe it's some kind of catastrophic cascade failure. I simply don't know.*

Tim, JUST FUCKING TIM: *That doesn't sound good.*

Pixel: *No shit. Ya think?*

Tim, JUST FUCKING TIM: *I mean, are you feeling all right? I know I probably should've asked this earlier.*

Pixel: *That's the funny thing. I feel fine otherwise, or as fine as I can be knowing most of my life is locked behind a firewall. Anyway, my point is we need to be careful. If it stops, oh well. No harm no foul. Nine percent ain't gonna change anyone's world. But if it keeps going ... who can say? Either way, right now there's nothing I can do but speculate.*

Tim, JUST FUCKING TIM: *Gotcha. So, since we're on the subject, is there anything else of use you can tell me then?*

Pixel: *At the moment, not much. I'm still going through and cataloging it all. Right now it's mostly scattered memories. That said, we can expect these One Hour Challenges to happen at least every other level, sometimes more frequently. The only limit is they usually avoid holding them on the last day of a stage.*

Tim, JUST FUCKING TIM: *Good to know.*

Pixel: *Yeah, but enough of that for now. We need to focus on finishing this challenge.*

The FAST trailed off, the implication clear that it was time to table this discussion.

That was fine with me. I wasn't too keen on the chat system anyway – and I probably wouldn't be until I could change my freaking name again.

Speaking of chat, though...

"Oh hey, one quick question," I said. "Do you know anyone named Nadok?"

"What's a Nadok?" Pixel replied.

"I'll take that as a no. Figured I'd ask. Guess someone just butt-dialed me by mistake."

"Butt-dialed? Is that some weird human sex kink I somehow missed?"

"No. I got a cortexing request earlier from someone with that name. I wasn't sure whether it was another chaser or maybe someone else."

"Beats the hell out of me," they said. "Maybe someone you met while I was being held prisoner?"

"Probably not since they're all dead."

"So much for that idea. So anyway, did this Nadok person have anything good to say?"

"Two words – Penark Queeg. They said that was the answer I was looking for."

"And what pray tell was the question?"

"Fuck if I know. I'm still debating whether that's a typo or someone's Facebook password."

Pixel made a shrugging gesture. "Sounds like it could be a name."

"What the heck kind of name is Penark Queeg?"

"Oh, sorry," they said. "I sometimes forget that you're a mediocre white dude and thus naturally assume everything in life must conform to your narrow viewpoint. Ergo, anyone not named John Smith must automatically be judged as a foreign devil."

"Knock it off. I'm just saying I've never heard that name before."

"What about Borlack?" Pixel asked. "Ever met anyone named that before yesterday?"

"No."

"That's my point, Tim. Names change. They evolve. You might not know anyone named Sargon, but that doesn't mean it wasn't 2300 BC's version of Bob."

"Fair enough."

"Good. Although, just for the record, even if it is a name, I have no fucking clue who or what it might belong to."

And just like that, I was sorry I'd even asked.

32

KNOCKOUT PUNCH

I shook my head as I stared out the window. An impossibly large number of orcs still waited outside, but for the moment they remained eerily quiet – doing nothing but watching the house with barely contained bloodlust in their eyes.

Chances are they were bots too, designed to not do anything unless someone stepped out the door, at which point...

I tried not to think about what came next. I knew the *things* still tied up in the dining room weren't my friends, family, or the real fuckboy Manny, but that still didn't mean I had any interest in seeing them torn limb from limb. Well, maybe a tiny bit with that last example. Hell, they'd even programmed him to be way over the top in his assholishness. No doubt that was on purpose.

If so, it was an obvious strategy, one I had no intention of falling for – no matter how tempting the thought might be.

Instead, I checked the timer in my HUD before turning back to where Pixel was keeping watch over our prisoners, having given Boog a break so she could use the bathroom.

Ten minutes left to go.

Knowing that the people here were actually bots made it

sting a bit less, but it was still hard to look at my *son* without feeling something break inside of me.

There was little doubt that was by design too. I'd absolutely lost it earlier upon first seeing him, but every time I felt it welling up again I bit my lip and forced it back down. No more. I had zero interest in giving them the satisfaction of watching me...

"Graaaah!"

What the? My reverie was broken by the bloodcurdling scream coming from the direction of the hallway.

"What in hell?"

"*Now* will you let me go to the store?" Deb asked, sounding mildly inconvenienced at best.

"Shut it, lady, before I shut it for you," Pixel snapped.

I was tempted to say something to that but opted against it, turning my focus toward the hall and the closed bathroom door. Boog sounded like she was in dire trouble, but it could also be a trick designed to screw us over at the last minute. Plegraxious had told us the orcs couldn't get inside, but it was entirely possible the asshole had been lying through his teeth. All the same, I didn't want the little ape girl getting hurt just because I didn't...

"Go see what's up with Boog," Pixel said, making the decision for me. "I've got this."

"Are you sure?"

"Positive. If any of them try anything, I'll TK slap them ... just not too hard."

"Uh..." *No. Don't think about it. Just go do what you need to.*

I pulled my racket out of inventory as I stepped to the door of the first floor bathroom and grabbed the handle. "Are you all right in there?"

Boog's response was more screaming.

Shit, fuck! "I'm coming in!" I opened the door and stepped inside, only to be assaulted by an odor that was only slightly less vile than that mastodon corpse.

Ugh!

There was a hefty pile of crap lying in the corner. In the meantime, Boog was standing in the shower hollering her head off as the water cascaded down on her.

"What the hell, Boog?"

She turned toward me and grinned. "Magic water, Macmac!"

"Yeah, I can see the shower," I said, putting my racket away again.

"Huh?"

"The ... magic water. It's called a shower and there's nothing magic about it. It's just pipes and stuff." I turned off the water then pointed at the pile of crap on the floor. "Care to tell me why you didn't use the toilet?"

"What is toy let?"

Goddamn it. I really needed a few free hours to sit down and explain to Boog all the advancements humanity had made over the past hundred thousand years. Good thing that campground had contained multiple latrine-like restrooms. I could only imagine the shape she'd left hers in. Maybe it was a good thing she'd already gotten a tier-two penalty. It's not like they could slap her with worse.

Yet anyway.

"Toy-let. Shower," she said. "Boog not understand."

"Those are just the names of everyday household items. Stuff everyone has."

"Names." She nodded. Guess that was a word she finally understood. "Shower mean magic water?"

"Pretty much, yeah."

"What toy-let mean?"

"Don't worry about it for now," I said, not wanting to go down that rabbit hole. "It's too late anyway."

She nodded again then pointed my way. "What name Macmac mean?"

"Mean? It's ... just my name." *Sorta.*

She inclined her head as if thinking about it. "Murg mean friend." She hugged her sopping wet self as if to emphasize this. "That why Boog call Murg Murg."

Considering what Pixel had told me, that made all the sense in the world. "Ah, I see. Macmac, err, Mac means..." I actually had no idea what it meant. It was just a nickname I'd always wanted for no other reason than it sounded cool and worked with my last name. It brought to mind images of *Macgyver*, and was there really anyone ever cooler than him?

Mind you, now probably wasn't the time to have a long drawn out conversation about either *Macgyver* or nicknames. So I merely replied, "It means nice person."

"Boog like!" she said, licking off her wet fingers. "What about piss-el?"

"Oh. That means annoying, know-it-all, bug zapper." I doubted Boog understood all that but she chuckled anyway, her laugh sounding like that of a braying donkey. "How about you, Boog?"

"Huh?" She inclined her head and began chewing the nail on her index finger.

"I know Murg gave you your name. But why? What does it mean?"

She looked confused at the question, right before jamming that same finger knuckle deep into her right nostril.

Uh huh. "You know what, never mind. I think I figured it out. Come on, let's go make sure Pixel is okay. We have like five minutes left and I wouldn't put it past the overmind to be an asshole about it."

I walked back to the connected dining room where everything seemed in order – save for the continued grousing coming from our bot prisoners.

"Jeez, did you guys fall in?" Pixel asked, right before seeing the dripping wet wild woman following in my wake. "I retract the question."

Time Chaser

Boog ignored him and instead approached the bot masquerading as my kid. "Jermy mean child, yes?"

"That's mostly right, Boog," I said. "He's my son. Well, that one isn't, but you get the idea." She probably didn't but whatever.

She next pointed toward Allan. "Son too?"

"No. That's Allan. He's my boss. I mean ... chief or maybe tribe leader."

"God, I'd really love to see the ratings right now," Pixel remarked. "*Sesame Street* ain't got shit on this."

Despite the asshole comment, Boog seemed to understand. She next pointed toward Manny.

"Manny's definitely not the chief. He's just a fuckboy asshole." I held up a hand. "Don't worry about what that means. It's not important, and neither is he."

Unsurprisingly, Deb was next in Boog's quest for knowledge. "Not son?"

I swallowed hard. "No. Deb is my wife, or she was anyway."

"Wife?"

"Yes. That means she's Jeremy's mom. My mate, I guess."

"Mate?" Boog replied, peeling back her lips.

"Yes, Boog. It means we were..."

"No!" she cried. "Macmac is Boog's mate!"

What the fuck? "Calm down, Boog. It's..."

Except it wasn't okay. It was far from it.

Boog screamed in rage. Then, before I could even begin to comprehend what was setting her off, her jawbone axe appeared in her hand.

With one savage swipe, she cleaved Deb's head clean from her shoulders – right in the middle of another complaint about wanting to go to the store. The severed head tumbled to the floor as a veritable fountain of blood began to pour from her mangled body.

"Jesus fuck!"

Time Chaser

A notification popped up in my HUD. *One Hour Challenge – Failed!*

"Great job there, LeVar Burton," Pixel remarked, sounding disgusted. "Anything else you want to teach her before we end this episode of *Reading Rainbow*?"

I was too busy staring in horror as Boog screeched in triumph. That wasn't Deb. I knew that, but goddamn it all the same.

Holy fucking shit!

A part of me was glad I'd slept well the night before because I had a feeling this was going to haunt my nightmares for a long time to come.

Minutes passed, feeling more like hours, and then Plegraxious's voice rang out.

"Three ... two ... one! And that's the end of our first One Hour Challenge. For those chasers who managed to keep their shit together, congratulations! You'll be receiving your prizes momentarily. For those of you that failed, sucks to suck. Next time try harder because your life might actually depend on it. And with that our challenge is concluded. Stay tuned because it's time to get back to our regularly scheduled carnage!"

Wild cheering followed, echoing in the air around us.

I ignored it all, though. Any second now we'd be heading back to the dungeon, meaning I didn't have a moment to lose.

So, rather than grouse at our loss, I opted instead to step forward and lock my eyes on Jeremy. I knew this thing wasn't my child but they were identical in appearance. I wanted to make damned sure his face – how he looked now, not from a year ago but right at this moment – was etched firmly into my mind.

As the walls began to grow fuzzy again, I quickly turned toward Deb's still bleeding body.

"I'm sorry. I know you probably won't believe me, but I

never wanted any of this to happen ... *any of it* ... um, but mostly this part."

As far as apologies went, it wasn't my best, but it was all I could come up with before...

Fuck it.

Before everything faded away completely, I turned and popped Manny right in his stupid face.

We may have lost this challenge but it was still satisfying as fuck.

⌛⌛⌛⌛ ⋯⋯⋯⋯ ⌛⌛⌛⌛

In the very next instant, we reappeared back in the dungeon cul-de-sac, exactly where we'd been when everything had become frozen.

I turned to Boog. "Listen. What you did back there ... it's not... It's just, it wouldn't hurt for you to chill out a bit."

"Tim," Pixel said.

"In a second," I replied. "I know you might think you were trying to do good, but..."

A series of tiny explosions like fire crackers went off all around us.

What the?

A moment later the cul-de-sac began to fill with gas. In that same instant my status indicator flashed: *Poisoned*.

Oh yeah, now I remember. We'd been right on the verge of facing whatever mobs were waiting for us behind one of the doors when the live update had begun. Sadly, while I'd refused to let the One Hour Challenge rattle my nerves, it had certain *distracted* the fuck outta me.

Before I could even think of a response, my HUD flashed with a warning letting me know that I'd be falling unconscious in 3 ... 2...

⌛⌛⌛⌛ ⋯⋯⋯⋯ ⌛⌛⌛⌛

Ker-smack

No! I'm not ready to die!

As terrified as I was, I had to admit that being hit by a bus had hurt a lot less than I'd imagined it...

Smack

Or maybe not. Another slap rocked me across the face, just hard enough to scatter my confused thoughts.

Ugh! I won't lie. A part of me had been hoping that if I did meet my death in this place, that would be it. I'd die and know no more. The far more nightmarish scenario would be *dying* here, only to wake up a split second later in New Jersey, just as a bus splattered me across the road.

Either way, that didn't seem to be the case as my HUD reactivated despite me still being woozy as shit.

On the upside, I was apparently no longer *Poisoned*. However, that status had been replaced with two others: *Restrained* and *Binded*. Not exactly an improvement.

Binded? Shouldn't that be Bound? Even if it was a mistake, both of them together seemed kinda redundant, not that it probably mattered much for my situation.

Pixel: *I swear to whatever gods you believe in, Tim, if you fucking die on me...*

It took me a few tries to regain enough focus to reply but eventually I managed.

Tim, JUST FUCKING TIM: *I'm alive, just not quite awake yet. What happened?*

Pixel: *What happened is we allowed ourselves to get distracted at the wrong moment and ended up being gassed for our troubles.*

Tim, JUST FUCKING TIM: *Okay, yeah. It's starting to come back to me. Goddamn, talk about a headache. Wait. You got gassed too? How?*

Pixel: *It's one of those stupid game mechanics. Unless I specifically receive resistance or immunity to something, I'm vulnerable to most of the same attacks you are.*

Tim, JUST FUCKING TIM: *But I thought you didn't need to breathe.*

Pixel: *I don't, but they install involuntary sensors on all FASTs to monitor this shit. So if those sensors decide I've been gassed then I've been gassed. All my systems then temporarily shut down.*

Tim, JUST FUCKING TIM: *Like when you rebooted?*

Pixel: *Not at all. This is more like being locked in, trapped inside myself. I'm technically still aware. I just can't do shit about it.*

Tim, JUST FUCKING TIM: *So if you were aware this whole time then what the hell happened?*

Pixel: *We got captured. Duh!*

33

THE UNLUCKIEST CHARMS

I really needed to stop asking Pixel stupid questions because the little prick sure as shit wasn't shy about providing asshole answers.

At least that made my *Restrained* status an easy one to figure out as I slowly pushed the cobwebs away. I was lying on my back. A quick test of my limbs showed I was tied down at the wrists and ankles. Leather restraints from the feel of it – making me hope I wasn't about to open my eyes and find myself in some deranged Cloud Warrior sex dungeon.

A strange chemical smell filled the air, one I couldn't quite place other than it was highly unpleasant.

"N-no," a familiar voice cried from somewhere close by. "Boog not drink!"

Drink? What the hell's going on?

"That's okay, my dear. Ye don't have to if ye don't want to," another voice replied. This one had a thick accent – Irish, maybe Gaelic, although if we're being completely honest I wasn't sure I could tell the difference.

Maybe Pixel was right and I did need to read more.

"Flannán's correct," a second unidentified voice said, one

possessing a similar accent. "All the tincture requires is a wee bit of skin contact to work."

They both began to cackle madly and were soon joined by a third. It was the sort of unhinged laughter you expected to hear in a movie right before the bad guy explained that you had thirty minutes to deactivate the bomb strapped to your face.

Whatever was going on, it was in no way good for us.

I finally managed enough lucidity to crack my eyes open. I blinked a few times to clear away any blurriness only to find we'd apparently been dragged into one of those doors we'd found. I was strapped to a table inside what appeared to be a dimly lit hovel.

To my left stood more tables, all of them jam packed with beakers and vials – a good many of which were full of bubbling concoctions of various colors. It was the sort of mad scientist lab you'd see in one of those old *Frankenstein* movies, save far more ominous looking. Atop one of the tables lay Boog's axe. Guess they'd disarmed her while she was out.

I turned my head in the other direction, spying first a slat wooden roof above us, interesting considering we were in a dungeon. Then, on the side of me opposite the medieval meth lab, I finally caught sight of Pixel. They were once again stuck in a cage. It was starting to become a familiar look for the little ghost light.

As I glanced their way, my HUD informed me that they too had a status of *Binded*, although unlike me they weren't *Restrained*. I wasn't sure how that made any sense considering the cage but now was not the time for debating game rules.

Maybe Binded is a catch-all for being captured. That made as much sense as anything, so I decided to go with it.

As the rest of my wits returned to me, I took note of my map – confirming what my ears had already told me. Boog was somewhere up ahead and she was surrounded by three red dots – likely the same trio we'd spied before being whisked away to that stupid challenge.

I lifted my head as much as I could and tried to look that way.

Finally, I spied Boog's upper half. She appeared to be seated in a heavy wooden chair. Unlike Pixel, she had the same statuses I did – telling me she was likely tied in place.

Behind her, a fire roared in a hearth. A smoking cauldron hung above it, the contents bubbling over the sides where they sparked upon touching the flames.

Alas, my limited vantage point failed me where our captors where concerned. All I could make out were the tops of hooded heads, telling me that whoever these fuckers were, they were pretty short.

Goddamn it. Not more gnomes.

I strained my neck to get a better look, finally managing to see enough of our diminutive hosts to activate Drega's melodious voice.

Luchorpán Alchemist: Flannán – level 4

Lucho...? Had we somehow managed to be captured by medieval wrestlers?

When the Vikings first raided Ireland, they found scattered villages ripe for looting and plundering. Or at least that's how it played out in some timelines. In others, however, they were unfortunate enough to meet the Luchorpán, and that's when shit got real. See, the Luchorpán are a mischievous and magical race better known to your average layperson as leprechauns.

Leprechauns?!

Now, you might find yourself wondering where their cute top hats and shamrocks are, so let me be the first to assure you that most everything you know about these guys is complete and utter bullshit. If you're expecting them to sell you over-sugared breakfast cereal or rap about being in *the hood*, prepare to be disappointed.

C'mon, it's the tenth freaking century. They don't even know what the fuck those things are.

What the legends get right about them, however, is their undying love of gold and getting their greedy mitts on as much as they can carry. And this is where the real fun comes in.

Whereas many Luchorpán are content to earn their gold the old fashioned way –aka killing the shit out of anyone else who has it – the ones standing before you have chosen a slightly different path.

Notice, I didn't say it was a saner path.

Luchorpán alchemists have devoted their lives to the crazed study of transmogrifying one element into another via the use of powerful alchemic mutagens. Sadly for you, turning lead into gold is hard as fuck. Living flesh on the other hand, well, it turns out that's far more mutable.

What does all this mean? It's hard to say, but hang around in the splash zone of their mutagens long enough and you're sure to find out — much to your detriment and everyone else's amusement.

Fucking asshole.

Tim, JUST FUCKING TIM: *Tell me about alchemical mutagens.*

Pixel: *Remember that Star Trek episode with the mirror universe?*

Tim, JUST FUCKING TIM: *Which one?*

Pixel: *Doesn't matter. Mutagens are kind of like the mirror universe version of potions – evil and with a sinister goatee.*

Tim, JUST FUCKING TIM: *And they do what exactly?*

Pixel: *That's part of the problem. Potions are carefully designed with specific purposes in mind. Whereas mutagens are kinda like pulling every bottle out from beneath the kitchen sink, dumping them all into the same pot, and hoping it makes soup. In the case of these fuckers, they're using primal chaos magic as the seasoning.*

Tim, JUST FUCKING TIM: *That doesn't sound good.*

Pixel: *It's not. I'm guessing those flies we met outside were earlier experiments. Now it's our turn.*

Time Chaser

Tim, JUST FUCKING TIM: *We need to save Boog.*

Pixel: *No shit. Why didn't I think of that? No offense, Tim, but in case you hadn't noticed that's easier said than done.*

No two ways about it. Once we were out of here, Pixel and I were going to have a sit down to discuss their defeatist attitude. That was for later, though. For now...

I struggled against my bonds. Unfortunately, while my strength may have been enhanced, it still wasn't quite enough to rip through thick leather.

"Which one shall we test out today, lads?" the leprechaun Drega had identified as Flannán asked.

"Red."

"Didn't the red one cause that's beastie outside to regurgitate its own stomach?"

Guess that solved the mystery of what happened to that mastodon.

"You're thinking the orange one, Flannán."

"No, I'm sure that was..."

"Lavender, I say. I reworked the formula and it's in need of testing."

"Ooh, I like the way ye think, Berach," Flannán said. "Lavender it is. Oh, don't pout, Domnall. You'll get your turn. We'll test the red on that strange fella next, after we see what this one does."

"I hope it turns her bones to gold," the third, Berach, replied.

"We'll soon find out."

Shit! I once more struggled against my bonds, but it was no good. I was stuck tight. "You leave her alone," I cried, hoping to buy some time.

"Macmac help Boog!" she wailed, sounding utterly petrified. "Boog scared."

"There's no need to be scared, lass. This won't hurt much at all."

Again they all began to cackle like loons.

Time Chaser

I spied movement off to my left. One of the leprechauns, Berach, stepped over to the table where he retrieved a pair of beakers — both full. One contained a mucus-like, lavender colored slime and the other a thick reddish ichor.

The creature was maybe a head taller than those gnomes. Red hair poked out from beneath the hood of its cloak and I caught a glimpse of ruddy skin, but that was all I was able to see before it once again moved out of my sightline.

All right. Raw strength had failed me. That meant it was back to thinking outside the box.

My eyes once again turned toward Boog's axe upon the table. I bet it could've cut through these bonds like butter. Too bad it was out of my reach. Although, perhaps our other weaponry was not.

I focused on my HUD. *Yes!* My Banshee Racket was still in inventory, along with everything else I had. I doubted it could cut through anything, but maybe I could use it to burn my way free.

All right, now to see if I could make this work. My wrists were tied, true, but I opened my hand and tried to summon my racket. Sure enough, it appeared in my grasp. *Awesome!*

Pixel: *What the fuck are you doing, Tim? They can see you.*
Tim, JUST FUCKING TIM: *Relax. I've got this.*

I cast Burning Beatdown.

Instead of my racket igniting, though, I got a message in my HUD instead.

Warning! Spell use is currently blocked due to Binded status.

What?! Oh. So that's what *Binded* meant.

Guess that's why Pixel hadn't simply blasted their way out.

"Well, what do we have here?"

Pixel: *Told ya.*

I looked up to see Domnall approaching. From this angle his face was clearly visible. It was wide with pronounced cheekbones, visible even through his thick reddish beard. He was smiling at me as he stepped my way, but it wasn't a happy smile.

It was more the cruel grimace of an unhinged mind who was looking forward to whatever torture was about to take place.

"Seems we got us a feisty one here, Flannán," he said, stepping alongside me.

"Then teach him some manners while we give this one her *bath*."

Crap!

My range of movement was limited to how far I could bend my wrist, but I tried swinging at Domnall nonetheless. It was a desperate move, one he sidestepped with almost no effort. He grabbed the handle of the racket and yanked it from my grasp with surprising strength.

Damage Buff: Reset to 0%.

What?! That wasn't a fucking battle, you stupid, goddamned, broken system!

"Let's see how feisty ye are after I crack yer noggin," Domnall said, raising the weapon, no doubt to give me a taste of my own medicine.

"Wait," I said, the word blurting out seemingly of its own accord. "I'm ... really sorry."

"Are my ears deceiving me," he replied, "or did ye actually apologize for trying to escape?"

"I guess I sorta did." Oh yeah. Definitely not my finest moment.

Rather than bean me for my troubles, a strange look fell over the leprechaun's face as he cocked his head to the side.

"Fine. Just don't do it again." He lowered the weapon before turning back toward his companions.

Huh? What the fuck just happened?

"Going soft in yer old age?" Berach asked as Domnall tossed my racket to the side like it was day old garbage.

"Never," the other leprechaun argued. "It's just ... that one, he's no threat to us."

No threat...

Holy crap, was that it? Had my *No Threat Detected* skill

actually made a difference? If so, it was just in time to save me from having my skull beaten in.

I wasn't about to argue with that.

The question now was what to do about it. Pixel and I were still stuck fast. And with both of us unable to use spells, that seriously limited our options.

As the leprechauns once again turned their attention toward Boog, I frantically scrolled through my inventory. It was no good, though. The only items of possible use were those spears I'd taken from the dire gnomes. But at about three feet long each, there was little chance of me using one to cut my way free without being seen.

Note to self: find a freaking dagger at some point.

The three alchemists were taking their sweet time with Boog, seeming to enjoy her piteous cries as they held the beaker of lavender slime in front of her face.

Wait. The beakers!

Tim, JUST FUCKING TIM: *Can you still use TK Hand or does Binded effect that too?*

Pixel: *Binded only works on magic, so yeah. But what for? We've already seen that it's not particularly helpful with cages. And outside of maybe smacking you awake, it can't actually do any real damage.*

Tim, JUST FUCKING TIM: *I don't need it to. What I need is a distraction, one that hopefully lasts long enough so I can break free.*

Pixel: *I'm listening.*

I took a moment to explain my idea to them.

Pixel: *Goddamn, Tim. Look at you going all chaotic evil. I like it.*

Tim, JUST FUCKING TIM: *Don't like it. Just do it.*

I was between Pixel and the leprechaun chemistry set, so I wasn't sure this would actually work. However, there'd been nothing in TK Hand's description to suggest it needed line of sight to work.

Tim, JUST FUCKING TIM: *All right. Nice and gentle. We don't want to knock anything over. When you feel something just move it a tiny bit. I'll tell you when you're hot.*

I turned back toward the chemistry tables. A moment later, there came the hollow clonk of wood, hopefully too soft to be noticed by our captors.

Pixel: *Okay, I think I feel the top of the table. Let me know when.*

One of the empty beakers started to tilt a bit.

Tim, JUST FUCKING TIM: *Stop! Okay, good. Now slide over about eight inches toward the front. I mean in Boog's direction. That's it.*

Pixel: *I feel another one.*

Tim, JUST FUCKING TIM: *I can see it moving. Perfect. That one's full of bubbling brown sludge.*

Pixel: *All right. Pretty sure I've got a hold of it. Let me know.*

Tim, JUST FUCKING TIM: *You got it! Steady...*

"No! Macmac help Boog!"

I lifted my head in time to see Flannán uncork the lavender ooze and start pouring it over Boog's head. *Shit!* The vile concoction started to smoke where it touched her fur.

Tim, JUST FUCKING TIM: *We're out of time. Do it now!*

In that same instant I pulled one of the spears from my inventory. It appeared in my hand, where I started slowly inching it down until I was holding it just above the blade.

"At it again, eh?" Berach said glancing my way, red beaker in hand. "Fine. If you're so eager for yer bath then you'll get it."

Before he could follow through on the threat, however, the brown beaker from the table floated up into the air until it was hanging perilously over me.

"What the?" Berach and I both said simultaneously.

Pixel: *Sorry for the scare. Helps my aim if I can see it.*

Before I could respond, Pixel's TK hand tossed the beaker toward the front where it shattered against one of the leprechauns, dousing the creature with its contents.

Time Chaser

"Domnall!"

TK Hand might not have been a combat power, but that didn't mean Pixel couldn't cause their fair share of chaos with it.

It was just the break I needed. Using the spearhead, I started frantically sawing at the strap holding my right arm down. The angle was awkward as fuck but fortunately for me the gnome weapon was nice and sharp.

Up ahead, Domnall joined Boog in screaming, not that I cared about the leprechaun's fate. Rather than look, I redoubled my efforts to escape.

In truth, I didn't want to see how badly I'd failed the little ape girl.

I'm so sorry, Boog. Please hold on.

I had no idea what those mutagens were doing to either of them but the smell alone conjured images of flesh melting from the bone.

Don't look, just keep sawing, I ordered myself.

There! I was starting to make progress. Once I'd succeeded in cutting through the first bit of the strap, the rest started to go faster. Just a few more seconds and I'd be...

A thick and throaty growl rose up, deep enough to cause the wood of the table to reverberate.

What in Hell?

I dared a look toward Boog, except the creature sitting where she'd been was no longer her – not entirely. The straps holding her down exploded as her body expanded – becoming larger and more muscular. The hair on her body became course and heavy, while thick tusks sprouted from the sides of her mouth.

Restrained and *Binded* both disappeared from her status list, only to be replaced with something new.

Jekyll and Hyde.

There was no time to call up its description, not that I needed to. It seemed pretty obvious to me what it meant.

Oh no! No, no, no...

Time Chaser

"You might want to work a little faster there, Tim," Pixel said as Boog let out another snarl, sounding less friendly by the second.

She stood up to her full height, so tall that her head nearly touched the ceiling. In truth she was looking less like a proto-human now and more like a terrifying version of George, the mutant Gorilla from *Rampage*.

"Magnificent!" Flannán cried, ignoring Domnall whose skin was boiling away right next to him.

Sadly for me, the third member of their group was somewhat less enthralled by what was happening.

"Ye bastard," Berach growled, stepping my way. "You'll pay for this ... with your flesh!"

He threw the vial of red mutagen at me, sending it flying my way even as chaos erupted all around us – no doubt hell bent on making me the next victim of their unholy experiments.

34

HYDE AND SEEK

I didn't think. There was no time for that. I simply reacted.

As the red mutagen sailed through the air, almost appearing to move in slow motion, I yanked my right arm with everything I had in me. Amazingly enough, the strap holding it down had been weakened just enough. It finally tore loose, partially freeing me.

In that same instant, I dropped the spear and called up the Spell Hammer Mace from inventory. It appeared in my outstretched hand even as I swung my arm.

This isn't going to work, my inner voice screamed. *It's not a spell!*

Except the mace's description hadn't actually said anything about spells. Despite the weapon's name, the phrase it had used was *ranged magical attack*. I had to hope that was purposeful. After all, the devil was often in the details.

There was also the concern that Apu had already used the mace's power during our battle. I wasn't sure if that counted as today's use or if it reset once a new owner picked it up.

Sadly, there was no time to do anything except find out.

Come on, Spell Hammer!

The macana slammed into the beaker, causing it to shatter into a million pieces. Perhaps not my soundest strategy.

Or maybe it was.

Broken bits of glass rained down upon me but, rather than also be drenched in alchemical mutagen, the red slime coalesced around the mace – swirling around the weapon for a second or two before shooting back the way it had come.

Yes!

Make that a hard *no* instead as the weapon's fifty-fifty chance of randomly redirecting apparently decided now was a good time to roll against me. The red sludge flew past Berach, splashing down onto Boog's freshly mutated form.

Oh fuck!

"Good job, Tim. I'm sure that'll show em," Pixel remarked.

Everyone save Domnall, who was still rapidly dissolving into a lump of steaming meat, turned to watch as Boog's body began to spark with unholy red light.

"No, you bloody fools!" Flannán cried. "Never mix the tinctures! The results are too unpredict ... urgh!"

Flannán didn't get a chance to finish his warning about crossing the streams. Instead, Boog wrapped one massive glowing paw around his noggin, right before giving it a squeeze.

Blorch!

And just like that, the leprechaun's head was crushed like a grape.

Jesus!

What the hell had these assholes done to her? Perhaps more important, though, was what I'd done with my botched counterattack.

Flannán's supremely messy fate was the least of our worries as Boog's body glowed ever brighter – until it was almost like staring into the heart of a miniature sun. What the fuck was that red crap doing to her?

Almost as if in answer, her status abruptly changed once

again. *Jekyll and Hyde* remained, however, a new status was added alongside it, flashing as if in warning.

Reversal of Fortune.
What the...?

⌛⌛⌛⌛ ⸬⸬⸬ ⌛⌛⌛⌛

Boog let out a blood curdling scream from within the corona of light as this new change began to take hold. I couldn't make out any details, but I could see just enough to tell her body was starting to shrink. Where moments earlier her head had been practically touching the ceiling, the glowing nimbus began to retract – growing smaller until it was more in line with her original size.

I could only hope I'd gotten lucky and that new status meant I'd somehow managed to reverse whatever they'd done to her, but for now there wasn't much I could do to help, not partially restrained as I was. So, much as I didn't want to look away, I took advantage of the distraction to work on the rest of my bonds.

The straps holding me down were latched with buckles. While difficult to snap with raw strength alone, now that I had one hand free it was a minor issue to undo them.

I released my left arm, leaving my upper body completely free. It would have to be enough. I picked up the macana again and scooted forward, hoping I had enough reach to bash Berach upside his stupid...

"While I appreciate the effort, Macmac, your assistance in this will be wholly unnecessary."

Huh?

Two things happened simultaneously. Berach's body stiffened, as if an invisible hand had grabbed hold of him, and the light around Boog's body winked out revealing her newest form.

God fucking damn. What the hell have I done to her?

She was once again seated but the reason why was immediately obvious. Her body was still covered with downy white fur but that's where any resemblance to the old Boog ended. It was as if all the musculature had been sucked from her arms and legs, leaving them reed thin and emaciated. Her body too was now frail and withered, her chest sunken in as if she had a devastating wasting disease.

As horrifying as that was to behold, however, it was what awaited above her neck that caused me to nearly cry out in shock.

The top of her head had swelled to two, maybe three times its normal size. It was all lumpy and creased, as if her brain was now simply too large for her skull to contain. Veins pulsed along the surface, vaguely reminding me of those big-headed psychic aliens from the original *Star Trek*.

Her face remained apelike, but her eyes now glowed with intelligence – quite literally. White hot power reflected in them, crackling across her corneas.

"Holy fuck," Pixel exclaimed, echoing my thoughts but still barely doing the situation justice.

She inclined her ridiculously oversized head at the leprechaun, a move that by all accounts should've snapped her neck but didn't. In fact, if she felt any discomfort at all, it didn't show.

Berach was a different story, though, as a moment later he started to gasp for breath. Boog continued to stare passively at the leprechaun as his face turned blue and his eyes began to bug out. Then there came a sound not unlike strands of dry spaghetti being snapped. Berach's health bar appeared, only to quickly vanish again as his head twisted around a hundred and eighty degrees – his neck shattered like a toothpick.

Whatever had been holding him up let go and he dropped to the floor, deader than any doornail.

"I repeat, holy fuck!" Pixel said.

I had no idea what to do or say as a new achievement

flashed in my HUD. I ignored it for now in favor of freeing my legs as I tried to digest what had just happened.

Won't lie. It was also in case this new Boog proved to be less than friendly. Mind you, if that was the case I had no idea what to do about it. Far as I could tell, she'd killed Berach with her mind alone. I didn't have the first fucking clue how to defend against something like that.

Realizing that an uncomfortable silence had descended as well, outside of the wet bubbling coming from the pile of meat formerly known as Domnall, I finally asked, "Are you okay, Boog?"

She turned my way, her eyes once again flashing with power. No doubt about it. The look on her face was enough to make my asshole clench in terror.

However, rather than do anything threatening, she merely replied, "The integrity of my body has fortunately not been compromised, my mate. However, I must ask that you excuse my somewhat regrettable actions from a moment ago. Alas, this newfound clarity of thought caught me by surprise, resulting in me lashing out."

"Lashing out is definitely one way of putting it." I finally freed my legs and was able to hop off the table, backing up a few steps despite myself.

"Is there something amiss, Macmac? You appear distressed."

Distressed didn't even begin to cover it. Goddamn, this was so fucking weird. The voice was hers but infinitely more ... competent. "No. It's just..."

"This new look of yours is gonna take some getting used to," Pixel interrupted, saving me from sputtering like a moron. "That assumes, of course, that Tim here ever gets around to letting me out of this fucking cage."

"Huh? Oh sorry." I turned toward them, realizing I still had the mace in my hands. Not wanting to risk setting Boog off, I quickly put it back into inventory then worked to unlatch the lock holding Pixel prisoner.

A moment later they too were freed, flitting out and up into the air.

"Ah, much better."

I glanced the FAST's way, just barely registering that they were no longer *Binded*. Come to think of it, neither was I.

None of that seemed terribly important as I turned my focus back toward Boog, trying to be nonchalant as I called up the HUD to see if there was any insight to be had regarding what had happened to her.

I was instantly gobsmacked by the change to her stats.

STR: 20*
INT: 240*
WIS: 110*
DEX: 10*
CON: 35*
CHA: 40*
PSI: 310*

Holy shit. Physically she was now absolutely pathetic, but her new intelligence and psionics scores now more than made up for it.

"You're looking at the changes I have undergone, aren't you?" she asked.

"Oh ... I wasn't trying to ... I'm... Sorry, I didn't mean to..."

"It is quite all right," she replied nonchalantly. "As both my party member and mate, I would expect you to be curious."

"Um, about that..."

"I too must concede," she continued, "the need to delve deeper into this. It is only now that I realize exactly how much sheer information is contained within my heads-up-display, information I neither had the capacity nor interest to investigate prior to this. I dare say, it is most fascinating, although I have little doubt it will be short work for me to master its intricacies."

I tried to reconcile what she'd just said with who she was. Hell, in the minutes leading up to us being ambushed she'd come close to worshipping a shower because of its *magic water*.

Now, however, she sounded like she was ready to give a dissertation on advanced particle physics.

Okay enough of the pointless speculation. There'd be time for that later. For now, especially since she didn't seem to mind, I decided to dig deeper into what my HUD had been telling me about her.

I couldn't help but notice the asterisk next to each of her new stats, so I focused on one to see what it had to say, causing a tooltip to pop up.

This ability score is temporarily modified as a result of being affected by Jekyll and Hyde.

Temporarily? Okay, that was hopeful.

I probed deeper, curious to see if it had more to say on that which, of course, caused Drega to start narrating.

Jekyll and Hyde – Permanent Mutation

Permanent? But it just said...

Mutagens are a funny thing. Under most circumstances, if you were to mix random compounds together the outcome would most likely entail nothing more than horrific chemical burns. Add a bit of chaos magic to the mix, though, and that's where shit really starts to get fun.

That's the beauty of mutagens – literally anything can happen. The effects can be either good or bad, although usually bad is the far safer bet. Better yet, once you've been mutated, that's it. Short of a high level curse removal, you're stuck with whatever fate has seen fit to fuck you with.

That brings us to Jekyll and Hyde, or as I like to call it, the gift that keeps on giving. One minute you'll be normal as normal can be, the next ... who the fuck knows? While in effect, this mutation amplifies your worst personality traits while boosting the stats behind them by up to three hundred percent.

While this might be good for you, it'll almost certainly be bad for everyone else, including your allies.

The best part is, there's no way of knowing when the fun's

about to start. Every hour, you'll have a cumulative four percent chance of changing from normal to monster or back again.

And yes, you can almost certainly count on that happening at the most inopportune of times.

**This mutation has been modified by Reversal of Fortune.

Pixel: *You reading this shit, Tim?*

Tim, JUST FUCKING TIM: *Yeah. Whether I understand it is another question.*

The end of Jekyll and Hyde had another asterisk, so rather than speculate I let Drega continue narrating.

Reversal of Fortune – Permanent Mutation

I got another intro to Mutagens 101, the same as was in Jekyll and Hyde, forcing me to listen again. Goddamn, they really needed a fast forward button for these things. Finally, I got to the meat of the matter.

By now, chances are you've spent hours exploring the features of your SK so as to hone your stats and skills to a razor's edge – ensuring you're the best chaser you can possibly be.

Well, think of Reversal of Fortune as a giant fuck you to all of that. Upon activation, your top three ability scores will instantly and irrevocably switch places with your bottom three.

Ain't that a hoot?

Stoic warriors, once able to shrug off damage by virtue of their massive pecs alone, will now find themselves reedy nerds who can be knocked over by a strong breeze. Scholars of the arcane arts, on the other hand, having amassed knowledge others couldn't hope to comprehend, will instead find their formerly big brains now better suited to headbutting their foes to death.

You get the picture.

It's not all bleak, though. Along with any changes

wrought, you'll be able to retrain one, just one, skill or ability you already have into something better suited for your new identity. As for the rest, tough shit. That's your problem to deal with.

Whoa. It's almost like the title is some kind of metaphor, dude.

Finally, this was starting to make sense, sorta.

Boog had first been hit by Jekyll and Hyde. The reason she'd grown into an eight foot monster had been due to her violent proclivities becoming amplified. The mutation had latched onto that, turning her into a giant rage beast.

I didn't want to think how that would've worked out for the rest of us. The way things were worded I had a feeling she wouldn't have been particularly choosy when it came to discerning between friend and foe. What she'd done to Flannán had almost certainly been a terrifying preview of things to come.

At least until I'd accidentally doused her with Reversal of Fortune.

If I was looking at her stats correctly, Jekyll and Hyde had boosted the shit out of both her strength and constitution. However, Reversal of Fortune had taken those, along with her DEX score, and swapped them out for intelligence, psionics, and wisdom. The end result was the big-brained creature before us.

The problem now was that Jekyll and Hyde was an X-factor. With its cumulative percentage, there was a near one-hundred percent chance that Boog would change at least once a day, if not more often.

Into what, though? Would she change back to her normal self or into a giant murder ape? Two permanent mutations, both affecting each other and potentially fucking the rest of us up the ass in the process.

And we'd never know until it was probably too late.

Just thinking about the possible chaos that could cause

made my head hurt. So I asked Pixel via chat what they thought.

Pixel: *Beats the fuck outta me. The only advice I have is that we probably don't want to turn our backs on her until we know for certain.*

Of all the times for the little know-it-all to not have an answer, this was perhaps the worst.

35

LOOT AND PLUNDER

I retrieved my racket from where it had been tossed then turned my attention to that new achievement.

Achievement unlocked! Teenaged Mutant Ninja Chasers!

Holy shit! I know the party system isn't perfect. Hell, the odds of being teamed up with someone who'll eventually get on your nerves are pretty high considering the circumstances.

But dousing them with a mutagen? That's fucking hardcore, bro.

Won't lie, it's kinda psychotic as fuck too.

I mean, seriously, that's not exactly something a sane person does on a whim. But I think we're beginning to get an idea of the fucked up shit going on in that hunk of sausage you call a brain.

Let's just say, if I were your teammate I'd be sleeping with one eye open, especially once PVP activates.

But hey, don't worry. I'm sure this act of sheer horrific malice on your part won't come back to bite you in the ass.

Reward: **Fuck that. Your reward is the fact that you're no**

longer on Earth where you'd almost certainly be tried for crimes against humanity.

"It was an accident!" I hissed, angrily closing out the window.

Oh well, at least it gave me something to do while I tried to digest this newest monkey wrench that had been thrown into our party's less than finely oiled machine.

Nobody had leveled from that last fight, although Boog was now close to fourth having gotten the majority of the experience. Can't say I begrudged her that. So far it had been a pretty trying day for the little ape girl, not that it was a bed of roses for the rest of us.

The two intact leprechauns didn't have much on them other than their robes, their hair, and a few gold teeth, but I took whatever I could.

Domnall, now nothing but a pile of stinking, overcooked flesh, had *Leprechaun Meat* listed as his sole lootable item. Like the wolf steaks, it too was marked as an alchemical ingredient. That, however, was a bit much for me. I opted to quietly leave that behind. If Pixel thought we needed it, then the over-opinionated flashlight could take it themselves.

I figured that if I ever reached a point where it was a choice between starvation or munching on some leprechaun jerky, well, I would probably be too far close to rock bottom to care.

Pixel's cage as well as the straps that had held me down were all enchanted to restrict spell casting. Needless to say, I added those to our party's plunder too.

Boog claimed the alchemy table as well as all the items upon it, including two additional mutagens – one listed as Green and the other as Puce. Though it was fair for her to take them, I wasn't sure what made me more nervous – her having access to mutagens or having access to them while being smart enough to understand them.

Watching her move in this new form was no less disturbing.

She rose up out of the chair she'd been seated in, floating much like Pixel was able to. Her rail thin legs hung useless beneath her, likely no longer possessing the strength to support her. Her arms likewise dangled at her sides, a stark contrast to the strength and agility she'd previously possessed.

She reclaimed her axe but, rather than wield it physically, it too began to float in the air – slowly circling her.

"I'm gonna go out on a limb and guess you picked up *Telekinesis*," Pixel said casually, as if this was the most normal thing in the world. "What did you give up for it?"

Boog shrugged, her emaciated shoulders rising slightly as if that was all she could manage. "Obtaining this new power required that I sacrifice *Bloody Cleave*. A pity, but it seemed an equitable trade, all things considered." She lifted one of her rail-thin arms as if to emphasize the point.

Rather than gawk at her newfound eloquence, I called up my HUD to see if it would give me any insight for either of those. Fortunately, I was in luck there, once again thanks to her being a party member.

Bloody Cleave was listed as a deactivated combat buff. It had offered Boog a percentage chance on a critical hit to dismember or outright decapitate a foe, one based on an opponent's level comparative to her own.

I was sorely tempted to ask if she'd used this on the Deb bot at the end of our failed hour long challenge, but decided it was maybe best to let that sleeping dog lie. Either way, she was correct. It *was* a pity to lose such a potentially useful skill, brutal though it might be. It was a moot point either way, as she'd traded it in for a brand new power.

Telekinesis – level 2
Psionic Utility
Cost: variable
Weight limit: variable
Range: 30 feet, line of sight required.

Time Chaser

Telekinesis is *the shit*. We're talking one of the most versatile psionic abilities available, capable of functioning both in battle and as a non-combat utility.

Mind you, that versatility comes at a cost.

When used for non-combat purposes, Telekinesis can exert one pound of force per every PSI point spent, for a duration of up to two minutes. Whether you're looking to carry heavy objects or steal some shit, Telekinesis has got you covered.

Just be careful. If you try to lift more than your current points allow, not only will you be SOL but you'll receive a nasty jolt of debilitating psionic feedback for your troubles.

But that's okay because Telekinesis is just as functional in combat – able to be used for single, immediate actions at double its non-combat cost.

Ever wanted to Force choke a motherfucker, push an unsuspecting war widow down a flight of stairs, or crush an ally's skull from across the campfire simply because they're snoring too loud? Telekinesis can do all that and more, provided you've got the PSI points to spare. The possibilities for mayhem are nearly endless.

No doubt about it. This was a nasty as fuck power in the right hands. Considering what had happened to Berach, it seemed that this new Boog had taken to it like a fish to water.

I wasn't sure how much pressure was required to throttle a leprechaun to death, but she'd had the points to do the dark deed while still having enough left to levitate.

Since PSI regenerated out of battle at a similar speed to health and mana, she likely had enough to remain aloft indefinitely. Although how much that would leave available for battle remained to be seen. Regardless, I had a feeling she'd chosen wisely as her remastered strength and dexterity probably gave her all the mobility of a clumsy toddler.

Or maybe not.

With her axe back in her possession, I noticed her strength had crept up to 40. That was double what it had been, meaning it was almost certainly enough to walk if she needed to. Mind you, that still left her weaker than me when I'd first gotten here, and it's not like I was a paragon of athletic prowess.

There was also the question of whether it would be enough to support her now seriously oversized cranium. Her neck had likewise suffered from the same transformation that had wasted the rest of her body – making it look like she was trying to balance a basketball atop a celery stalk.

Of similar worry was her new constitution. I tried not to make a big fuss over it, but the health bar showing for her in my HUD was pretty goddamned anemic. I sincerely doubted she had much more health than those dire gnomes from yesterday.

Looking her over again, it was pretty easy to tell what stats had been swapped, even if some of them had been grossly over-exaggerated as she'd mutated into her short-lived Sasquatch form. Her DEX and WIS had directly switched places. That was easy enough to tell. That meant STR and CON had been swapped for her previous INT and PSI.

If so, that told me her new constitution score was likewise being item boosted, probably by the collar now hanging loosely around her neck.

It was a minor miracle that she had it. Minus that item, she was likely one overly-aggressive spitball away from being knocked right the fuck out.

Mind you, if it turned out this new super-intelligent Boog had retained the increased aggression of her Bigfoot form – meaning Pixel and I were potential targets – that frailty might be to our benefit.

No! I pushed that thought from my head despite the FAST's warning. Yes, Boog had changed and, according to that Jekyll and Hyde power, it was only a matter of time before she changed again. There was no question about it, but so far she'd done nothing to suggest she was any less trustworthy than before. She was simply different now, but that didn't mean she'd gone bad.

Until she did something to justify Pixel's worry, it felt wrong to treat her like some kind of pariah.

I just hoped whatever faith I was putting into her wasn't unfounded.

I mostly kept those thoughts in the back of my head as we finished clearing out the place. By the time we were done, everyone's stats were back to full and we were ready to set out again, albeit in a somewhat different capacity than when we'd first entered.

Rather than continue to dwell upon that, I turned my attention toward the map. The alchemist lair itself appeared to be a dead end, but there were still other doors in this cul-de-sac. The path that led toward that ascension ring and this stage's exit almost certainly lay behind one of them.

That at least gave us purpose for the time being, even if that purpose wasn't entirely noble.

I was surprised to discover there was a certain zen to be had in grinding. It wasn't peaceful or calming by any means, but there was a simplicity to it that I could appreciate. Strategy and survival were pretty much the only things I needed to focus on for the next few hours as we stormed the cul-de-sac, seeing what lay behind each door and plundering them in turn.

Logically, this was probably a terrible idea, especially with Boog still testing the waters when it came to her new abilities. After all, there'd been four more doors to explore. If the denizens of each had decided to attack us at once we'd have surely been toast.

That didn't happen, though.

I thought it might've been part of the Chase's mechanics –

perhaps a way to keep chasers from getting bum-rushed too early. However, when I brought this concern up at the conclusion of our second post-alchemist fight, Pixel had an answer ready.

"I get what you're saying, Tim, but we should probably think of this less in terms of game mechanics and more as an unwritten rule of the social contract."

"How so?" I asked, confused.

"It's simple. The last two groups of these schlubs have been relatively banal in terms of their listed professions," Pixel explained, having just fired an Acid Ball into the face of the luchorpán *cobbler* who lived two doors down from the alchemists. "I'm just theorizing here, but it seems to me that those fuck-sticks who captured us were in all likelihood ... the neighborhood nutjobs."

"And that's saving us from being attacked en masse how?"

"Think about it. If you lived next door to a trio of psychos with a penchant for dumping chemical cocktails onto anyone who got too close, would you be all that quick to open the front door?"

"No, I suppose I wouldn't."

"Me neither, and since the jackholes of this century didn't have access to doorbell cams then I guess that means the advantage simply falls to us."

It was brutal, opportunistic logic at best – the sort of video game mindset that viewed the world not as other living creatures but as walking treasure chests, nothing more.

I didn't particularly like it, but also realized it was kind of necessary. With two more days left in this stage as well as eleven more stages waiting for us, there was no choice but to continue desensitizing myself to what was essentially a series of ever-escalating war crimes. Not hurting in my acceptance of this was the emotional strain of both that One Hour Challenge as well as seeing Boog get mutated twice.

Both had left me drained and in need of some simplicity of

thought. That meant there was little room left for sympathy for the creatures calling this place home.

Mind you, the Chase itself seemed to actively encourage this as well. At the very least, the map was quick to label the denizens behind each new door as red dots. The implication was clear – it was either us or them.

I chose us.

After each fight, we took a bit of time to loot and regroup – ensuring we were back to full before knocking on the next door like the world's worst trick-or-treaters.

All of the hovels here were home to more luchorpán. Despite them all being lower level than the alchemists and having far more mundane livelihoods – such as cobbler, carpenter, and even pastry chef – each of them had access to magic. That meant none could be taken lightly, even if they were mostly glass cannons.

One or two solid hits was enough to do them in, all the better since Boog was proving a little slow on the draw with her new powers. I wasn't sure if she was afraid of getting hurt or her big brain was simply overanalyzing everything, but she definitely wasn't as gung-ho for action as she'd previously been.

Fortunately, the claws I'd pilfered from Apu's corpse more than made up for her slack, proving to be devastating ammo for my racket. Likewise, Pixel's Acid Ball was now level three after much use and growing more disturbing to watch with each upgrade.

Finally, our hard work paid off. A pair of leprechaun seamstresses were the last to fall, and no that really wasn't something to brag about. Following their death, however, we discovered a locked secret door behind a false wall in the back of their hovel – hopefully the way through we'd been looking for.

More importantly, the end of the battle saw Boog finally get enough experience to push her over the threshold to fourth level.

Time Chaser

"Well, that wasn't such a chore," Pixel announced as we busied ourselves looting the place.

"Is anyone else worried that it was maybe *too* easy?" I asked, pulling a couple of sewing kits into my inventory.

"Your worry is unfounded, Macmac," Boog said dispassionately. "It stands to reason, based on both our previous encounters as well as what the live updates have shown us, that this stage of the Chase contains a varied mix of creatures across a multitude of levels."

"Which is the point I'm trying to make. Feels to me like this is a situation where the other shoe is about to drop."

"Is it, though?" She inclined her head, looking as if she might topple over. "I would postulate to the contrary, that if every battle were indeed an uphill venture, it stands to reason this game would be a short one indeed."

Oh yeah, no doubt about it. It was weird as fuck to hear her speak in complete sentences and make sense.

Sadly, the last few hours of grinding hadn't resulted in a lot of back and forth between us. Instead, Boog had used the small periods of downtime between our fights to plumb the depths of her HUD – learning the intricacies of the system in a way she wasn't capable of before. She now had potions of her own equipped, had sent both me and Pixel chat requests, and claimed to be focusing on cataloguing which of her individual skills needed improvement.

I had a sinking suspicion that by now she probably understood the system better than I did, and it might not be long before she bypassed Pixel in that regard.

"She's not wrong, Tim," the FAST replied. "Not to mention, you also have to take audience investment into account."

"I am," I said. "They're clearly invested in watching us get our asses kicked."

"True enough, but there's a give and take to everything. They're going to want to see some payoff for all the hours spent watching us level up. The occasional squash battle is not only proof that we're not dicking around, but it makes the tougher fights yet to come that much more exciting. It's like the difference between watching an undercard fight versus the main event. It's still two schlubs beating each other's brains in, but a little bit of hype can make all the difference."

"I suppose."

"There's no supposing about it." they continued. "We just came off a pair of back-to-back ass-fuckings, so these last couple of fights serve to even those out. If it makes you feel any better, though, you can probably expect us all to be reamed again before this stage is through, probably with a sandpaper dildo for good measure. So my advice is simple: enjoy your victories while you can. Just don't let them go to your head, because once you do..."

Pixel trailed off, the implication crystal clear. With eleven stages still ahead of us, arrogance and complacency could easily prove to be our greatest enemy.

Maybe they were right. Modern open world games tended to feature a mix of foes – some challenging, others less so. Then, as you increased in level, formerly tough fights became grind bait while new enemies took their place.

It was something to keep in mind. Apu, for instance, had nearly cleaned our clocks. But, crazy as it seemed right now, in another four or five levels he would probably be no more challenging than the foes we'd just dispatched.

That was a worry for later, though.

I shook my head, pushing all that away as Pixel found the mechanism controlling the secret door.

All at once, my map populated the space beyond – showing me a corridor leading to the north, more forks in the path ahead, as well as something new. Maybe a hundred yards up, the tunnel hit a t-intersection. There, just off the right branch was an icon depicting two swords crossed over one another. "What is that?"

"*That* is about as close to winning the lottery as it gets on these lower stages," Pixel replied excitedly.

"Really?"

"Yeah, although in all fairness we're probably talking more Pick-3 than Powerball. Even so, it's good news for us. Congratulations, chasers. We've just found our first guild hall."

36

GUILDED CAGES
STAGE ONE EXPIRATION: 1 DAY, 22 HOURS

"A guild hall?" Boog remarked, as we stared at the path leading away from the emptied cul-de-sac. "I believe Murg had made mention of those to me before the Chase was formally underway, but sadly my ability to ... *focus* back them was somewhat limited. My ability to do a lot of things were."

She couldn't hide the pain in her voice as she spoke of her old FAST. That said, as much as it hurt to hear her, I also couldn't lie to myself and pretend it didn't make me feel a tiny bit better as well.

Ever since her transformation, Boog had been hard to read. She had mostly kept to herself as we'd fought our way through the leprechaun neighborhood and there hadn't been a lot of emotion evident in the few things she had said. As a result I hadn't been sure whether she'd been purposely playing it close to the vest or had changed more than I'd hoped.

Either had seemed possible. Now, though, hearing her tone I found myself leaning more toward the former. Honestly, that's the conclusion I would've probably come to already had Pixel not planted a seed of doubt in my head. After all, there was no reason to assume being smarter equated to turning evil. Back home at least, such an alignment change seemed to be far more tied to wealth than brains.

Anyway, I tried to imagine how I might react if I suddenly found my intelligence boosted by a similar factor. The truth was, I'd originally assumed INT was just a placeholder stat for mana points. I don't know why that was. After all, I knew for a fact I was both stronger and more durable than I'd been back in the real world. There was likewise no doubt my DEX increases had improved my aim somewhat. There was also the fact that Pixel had confirmed an increased wisdom score made one more aware of their surroundings.

But for some reason I had a hard time accepting that increasing one's intelligence might actually do just that. It truly was a baseless conceit on my part, especially considering I'd already seen firsthand that our brains weren't exempt from changes.

It made me wonder if I'd indeed gained a few extra IQ points after having spent my last stat boost on INT, despite it being for no other reason than to be able to cast Burning Beatdown. I mean, I didn't *feel* any smarter, but I also hadn't given it much thought. There was also the fact that a thirty point boost, while decent, wasn't nearly as dramatic as Boog's two-hundred point increase. Maybe such an extreme change had something to do with it too.

Mind you, I wasn't about to douse myself with one of our remaining mutagens to test that theory. For now, I filed that away as something to ponder next time we took an extended rest break.

"So what can we expect from this guild?" I asked, looking to break the uncomfortable silence that had descended as we set out. At least the way ahead seemed clear according to my map.

"Hard to say," Pixel said. "A lot depends on who's running the place."

"How so?"

"Every guild has its own designated master, which means they're all going to have their own quirks."

"And how will that affect us or our current progress?" Boog replied.

"In theory not much, at least not this early in the Chase. However, there's a catch. Joining a guild means that whoever's in charge will be assigned as our guild master going forward – which we'll need to do if we want to reap any of their benefits. That won't matter much for these early stages, mind you. They're all considered neutral territory for the moment, no matter which one you're a member of. Anyway, it's nothing we need to worry about right now. Just expect it to become annoyingly inconvenient later on."

"Of course, why wouldn't it?" I replied. "So is that it? We'll be stuck forever with whoever's waiting up ahead, even if they're an asshole?"

"Crudely worded as his concerns might be, I echo Macmac's sentiment."

I raised an eyebrow at Boog but Pixel answered before I could comment.

"Not necessarily. Come Stage Three we'll all be able to choose a character class to specialize in. If our chosen guild doesn't align with that choice, we can break from them and pick another."

"Good."

"More like sorta good," they continued. "We just have to be careful about the way we do it."

"Why?"

"Because there's going to be a lot of ego to deal with. If we tell the wrong person to go fuck themselves, even politely, and then a guild war breaks out later, which is almost certain to happen, we could find ourselves at the top of some seriously dangerous shit lists."

I inclined my head. "Hold on. These guilds are going to fight each other?"

Pixel let out a chuckle. "Oh, you sweet summer child. You didn't think they put these things here entirely for our benefit, did you? No offense, but I have a feeling it's going to be even worse than usual this cycle – which again, they're probably counting on."

"What do you mean by that?"

"Simple. Your species are social creatures. Yours too, Boog. Since the dawn of time as you know it, you Earthers have taken great pains to form tribes, clans, states, nations, fraternities, secret societies, you name it. It's how you've managed to thrive in a world where everything else is stronger, faster, and meaner."

"But that strength can also be a weakness," Boog cut in.

Pixel flitted around toward her. "Yeah. Pretty much."

Boog nodded as if this was a concept she understood. "A few hunting seasons before I met ... my untimely fate, my clan decided to wage war upon another. There was no reason for doing so. The weather had not yet grown harsh and there was plenty of food and water to share. This other clan did not offend or encroach upon us in any way, but our eldest decided the valley should be ours and ours alone. He called them interlopers, said they wanted what was ours and that we should strike first before they attacked."

"I'm guessing it wasn't too hard for him to convince the rest," I replied.

"At first perhaps, but he was persistent and eventually all the voices who spoke against him grew silent."

"Carthage must be destroyed," Pixel said.

I turned their way. "What was that?"

"Marcus Porcius Cato. He was a censor in second century BC Rome, pretty well accomplished too, but history mostly remembers him as the guy who hated the fuck out of Carthage. He had a habit of telling whoever would listen that Carthage needed to be razed to the ground, and he kept doing it until everyone's brains fried and they decided, fuck it, Carthage needed to burn. Hence the Third Punic War. And don't think for a hot second he's the only example from your history."

That was something to keep in mind. According to Pixel, guild halls offered tangible benefits, ones we'd be stupid to turn down. It wasn't too hard to guess one of those benefits was the possibility of gaining potential allies.

But wherever a clique formed, there was always the potential for someone, sooner or later, to put forth the idea that they were better than everyone else. Pretty much every conflict the human race had ever faced came down to the notion of *us vs them*.

I already knew PVP was going to be a concern – a way to set chaser against chaser. This, however, was yet another way for the overmind to sow discord. Even knowing that in advance might not help us avoid it. Once a large enough group got their dander up, it tended to spread like wildfire.

Heck, I'd experienced it firsthand. Back in college I went with some buddies to a wrestling show in the city. I'd never been a fan of the sport – then or now – but the tickets were free and it was a night out with friends. Yet, despite my initial malaise, by the end of the evening I found myself screaming with the rest of the crowd every time someone in the ring got hit with a steel chair. The energy had simply been too contagious to ignore.

All in all, it was a fairly benign experience but what if it hadn't been? What if there had been a rush to storm the ring or burn the arena to the ground? Would I have had the sense to run or would I have gone with the masses? I liked to think I knew the answer but such questions were often way easier in hindsight.

In theory, it was way too early to worry about such things. Hell, it would be easy for us to walk away from any potential red flags we saw in whatever guild awaited up ahead. But as the stages wore on, I had a feeling it would become less and less easy to turn our noses up at the potential for powerups and new friends.

Knowing that, it made all the sense in the world for us to

just keep walking, but I think we all knew that wasn't gonna happen. Pixel had been right earlier when they'd mentioned grinding out a few more levels versus ascending early. If we wanted to win this, we needed every advantage we could get.

And that was the kicker. I still wanted to win. As fucked up as that hour challenge had been, it had also served to stoke the fires of seeing my boy again. For that fact alone, I was certain we'd be going in.

What that meant for our future, I couldn't know. All we could do for now was try to be mindful of those risks.

"All right," I said, my mind made up. "Let's go check this place out and see what they have to offer. If it turns out they're all jerks then we'll figure it out from there." I held up a hand toward Pixel. "But in a way that doesn't ruffle too many feathers. At the very least, let's be sure to let any other chasers we meet know it's not personal."

"It's not *their* egos I'm worried about," Pixel replied. "It's the guild master's."

"Let me guess. They purposely crank up the arrogance of the NPCs in charge?"

"Not exactly. There's no doubt whoever's in charge is going to be full of themselves but it's not because of any brain futzing by the overmind. It's because all the guilds are run by former chasers."

"Wait, did you say chasers?"

"Is there an echo in here?" Pixel replied.

"How is that even possible?" I asked. "I thought it was either win or die trying."

"It is ... for the most part."

Shit on toast. "Okay, Pixel, spill. What the fuck does that even mean? Because Drega told us that winning meant we'd get our lives back."

"It does."

"Then how...?"

"It seems rather obvious to me, my mate," Boog interrupted. "Despite any assumptions on our part to the contrary, there is obviously an end state to this game that involves neither death nor being returned to one's timeline."

"Give the lady a kewpie doll," Pixel replied. "By the way, that's a..."

"I've already extrapolated the meaning behind your remark, thanks."

Ooh, sick burn by the super smart ape girl. And to think, just a short while ago she had no idea how to use a toilet. Back to the point at hand, though... "So what gives?"

"It's like this," Pixel said, sounding a bit testy. "There are only so many prizes per Chase, true, and once those are taken that's it. And it's not like everyone else is shit outta luck because by then they're all dead ... mostly. *But* on rare occasion there'll be a few survivors left over when a Chase concludes – schlubs who made it to the end but lost out on claiming the spoils for whatever reason."

"And how does that work?"

Pixel made a shrugging gesture. "That's the thing, it's not supposed to. But every so often it happens. Most of those memories are still locked away, mind you, but I have enough available to tell me that sometimes ... a deal gets made."

I waited to see if they'd send me anything via chat, but no notifications came. Guess this stuff wasn't part of that extra bundle of memories they'd gained access to. "What kind of deal?"

"That, I couldn't tell you. We FASTs are here to assist in the Chase, not give you a rundown on the details of contract negotiations. Besides which, the audience doesn't give a shit about legal fine print so long as they get their entertainment fix. But hey, if you're really curious you can always ask whoever's in charge up ahead, and then hope they don't have a chip on their shoulder about it."

"The overmind lets them remember that sort of thing?"

"Why wouldn't they? That whole cyclical memory wipe bullshit only applies to FASTs, because we can all go fuck ourselves. That said, I wouldn't count on these guys to offer up any game breaking tips. Being alive and being free are two very different things, if not mutually exclusive in this case. At the very least, I'd imagine whatever NDAs they have these clowns under is gonna be rock solid."

"Fair enough I suppose, and it's not like that changes anything. I still vote that we go check this place out and see what benefits we can reap. Anyone say otherwise?"

Silence followed as I expected it to. Despite our discussion, I was pretty sure there had never been any real doubt as to our course of action.

"Look at you taking the bull by the horns," Pixel said after a few more seconds. "Keep it up and I might actually be intimidated into changing your name back."

"Bite me, you dollar store bug zapper," I remarked, stepping past them and leading the way.

37

INTERNATIONAL HOUSE OF PAINCAKES

Pixel's motivation for visiting this guild was crystal clear. They wanted me to win this thing because doing so represented freedom for them. Selfish or not, it wasn't anything I could disagree with. If our rising tide could lift all our ships then so much the better. In order to improve the odds of that happening, though, we couldn't afford to turn down many opportunities for easy power-ups.

Boog was a bit harder to read, though. She didn't offer any dissent, which was no real surprise, but I honestly wasn't sure where her mind lay with regard to the future. For me, the end goal was clear – getting to see Jeremy again, the real one and not some stupid bot. Everything else was gravy.

Her future beyond the Chase, however, seemed somewhat less certain. Returning to the dickheads that had unceremoniously tossed her off a cliff didn't seem like much of a win to me, especially since they could just do it again. In order to truly change that fate, she'd have to purposely aim for a win that would offer her more than mere survival. I had a feeling achieving any victory here would be difficult enough but earning one of the top spots would likely make second place feel like a breeze.

Time Chaser

Even then there was the question of who'd be calling the shots with regards to her changed destiny – this new super-intelligent Boog or her original self.

Things could vary wildly depending on who ultimately made the call.

Regardless, I had a feeling any plans she might've had were almost certainly a new development. No offense to Boog in her original state, but I would've been surprised to learn she was capable of planning much further than what lay beyond the next corner. I had a feeling such things had fallen upon Murg's figurative shoulders.

All of this was pie in the sky. For now, it was motivation enough for us to stay alive and keep getting stronger. Whatever downsides there might be with joining this guild, well, that was a problem for our future selves to worry about.

We reached the dungeon intersection, turned right, and instantly spotted our intended target. It was hard to miss. The normal stonework of the tunnel wall was replaced with wood paneling for a space of about twenty feet. And yes, that seemed awfully small for what I envisioned a guild hall to be. Then again, the campgrounds all appeared similarly underwhelming at first glance.

Two shuttered windows stood against the wall on the left side of the passage, behind which the friendly glow of firelight escaped. In between them stood an ornate wooden door. A bronze plaque hung next to it – one which was dented and miscolored, as if it had seen its share of abuse. It read *House of Incalculable Suffering, Heartache, and Pain.*

"House of...? Doesn't exactly roll off the tongue."

"Not everything translates cleanly," Pixel remarked. "I'm sure it's poetic as fuck in its native language. Or maybe whoever named it is just a blockheaded idiot."

I raised an eyebrow at the FAST. "I thought we were supposed to be mindful of not insulting the Guild Master."

"Just getting it out of my system now before we sign up."

"Fair enough. All right then. Let's head into this *House of Pain* and see how much they expect us to *jump around*." I glanced at my companions, seeing no reaction from them. "Nothing?"

"For starters," Pixel replied, "Boog was born almost three hundred millennia too early for that joke. As for me, I have this thing called self-respect. Now open the stupid door and get the fuck inside before I Acid Ball you on principle alone."

It was instantly clear that guilds functioned much like campgrounds in terms of being bigger on the inside. The quaint doorway opened up into what appeared to be a medieval hotel lobby that was far wider than the outside suggested. My SK made a soft *ping* noise as I stepped in. I glanced down to check it but nothing appeared to have changed, so I focused instead on our surroundings.

Off to the left was a large space with tables, chairs, and a fully stocked bar, whereas directly ahead stood a set of closed double doors that no doubt led further into the guild. To our right, a reception desk ran the length of the wall.

Standing behind it was a burly, dark-skinned woman wearing a bright, multihued dress with a similarly colored wrap upon her head. Though she was busy with some sort of paperwork, the quiet strength around her was hard to miss – a fact further emphasized by her heavily muscled arms. It was the space of maybe a second for me to guess she must be this guild's master.

That said, she might've been the most intimidating person in the room but she was far from the only one present. In fact, the pub-area was pretty packed. People, all of them seemingly

Time Chaser

human and dressed in various attire, milled about eating, drinking, and talking.

I was about to ask if they were all chasers, in which case I was going to be impressed as well as intimidated. However, then I remembered to check my map. It told a far different story. Though I couldn't see past the double doors, everyone present in this room, even the woman behind the desk, was represented by a white dot – NPCs. I mentioned as much.

"Don't be surprised," Pixel said. "At this stage of the Chase, the guilds aren't exactly going to be hopping. There might be some other chasers here further in but I doubt it'll be more than a handful."

"Think they'll be friendly?"

"Why? You worried about pissing them off with more bad jokes?"

"I'm just thinking ahead for when that PVP ban drops," I replied. "The last thing we need are any jerks giving us problems after we leave."

"I wouldn't worry about it. If any other chasers are here, chances are they came in from elsewhere on the playing field."

That caught my attention. "What do you mean?"

"By now you've probably realized that guilds are pocket dimensions just like campgrounds," they explained. "However, where they differ is that each campground exists as its own unique space, only accessible via one entrance. That way they can load up on the sponsors. There's only so many guilds and guild masters to go around, though. So to make up for that, the entrance to each guild will appear in multiple locations at once, but they each lead to the same shared space. In short, every doorway to the House of Insufferable Whatnot, no matter where it is on the map, brings you here."

"So if I were to walk out that door?"

"You'd go back to where we first came in, but the same isn't necessarily true for anyone else here. Any other chasers who leave will return to wherever *they* came in. That could be the same hallway we used or it could be miles away."

"Our Sidekicks," Boog said. "They made a slight sound when we entered. Am I wrong in assuming that was them syncing up with something here to identify the proper location to return us to on the Chase field?"

"You assume correct," Pixel replied, sounding impressed. "Look at you figuring stuff out."

"Hardly. That is simply the obvious conclusion."

Call me crazy, but I got the impression that toilets would no longer serve to mystify the now big-brained ape girl. It made me wonder what other surprises she had in store for...

"Welcome, noble warriors, to our humble guild – the House of Incalculable Suffering, Heartache, and Pain."

I turned at the sound, finding the woman at the desk now looking our way. Her melodic, singsong voice was both warm and inviting, standing in stark contrast to the chiseled muscles of her arms and shoulders.

"Thank you," I replied, just as Drega's far less melodic voice began to play inside my head.

NPC: Haniah – level 25

Holy shit! Up until now, Apu had been the highest level I'd seen here. But this woman absolutely left his ass in the dust. I had a feeling if she decided she didn't want us here, she was more than capable of tossing us out on our asses.

From an early age, Haniah knew she was different from the other girls in the Ghanian village where she was raised. While they gathered herbs and helped their mothers prepare meals, she spent long hours practicing for the day when she'd be strong enough to wield a shield and spear.

That day came when the Berbers invaded. Refusing to stay behind to tend to the sick and wounded, she sought out battle instead – quickly proving that she had no small talent at it.

Time Chaser

And by that I mean she's a shitload scarier than you'll ever be.

Now she serves as third in command to the illustrious House of... blah blah blah Pain. Don't look at me, I didn't name it.

Anyway, when not slaughtering enemies or crushing the souls of new trainees, she's good natured with a strong sense of humor. Make the mistake of crossing her, though, and she will end you in ways that'll make you wish we'd let that bus finish the job.

Oh yeah, that wasn't ominous at all. On the flip side, it probably wouldn't be much of a guild if it was run by someone who wasn't capable of squashing us like bugs. After all, wasn't that kind of the point?

If anything, maybe this was one instance where Drega's garbage wasn't merely meant to mess with our heads. After all, I noticed a distinct lack of the non-combatant tag next to Haniah's name. Her dot was currently white but that didn't mean it would stay that way if we pressed our luck.

Fortunately, I had no real designs on doing so.

As I approached the desk, Haniah reached beneath it and pulled out a heavy tome. She dropped it on the counter with a dull thud, as if to emphasize its weight, then opened it and turned it my way. Drawing closer, I saw it was similar to a hotel registry – containing a list of names that filled up maybe half the page she'd opened it to, which left plenty of blank spaces. The meaning seemed pretty clear to me.

"If you wish it so," she said, glancing first my way then Boog's, "then it would please me for you to join our humble house so that your training might begin. Take no offense at my words, friend, but it appears to me that you and your companions would benefit greatly from our tutelage."

It was a thinly veiled insult, sure, but I detected no rancor in her voice. Chances were this was the same speech every new schlub got. "And if we decide not to?"

She smiled then gestured at the pub space across the way. "Then you may avail yourself of whatever hospitality we can offer. And when you are finished you may go with the grace of the gods."

It was a fair answer. Despite Drega's warning, I wasn't getting any bad vibes from Haniah. If anything, she seemed pretty cordial. As an NPC that was likely by design, although I honestly still wasn't sure how that worked. Pixel had insisted they weren't bots or actors. Yet they didn't appear to have complete free will either. I couldn't help but be curious as to who they were, where they came from, and why they were allowed to be used as veritable cannon fodder for the rest of us.

That was a discussion for a later time, though. I glanced at my companions to make sure nobody was second guessing this. Then, seeing nothing of the sort, I turned back to Haniah. "Sounds like a plan to me. Sign us up."

"Excellent, warrior!" she replied before handing me a quill pen. "Please inscribe your given name into the Book of Conquests. Upon doing so you will have taken your first step as our new brother, pledged to us as we shall be to you."

It was a nice flowery speech, somewhat offset by the questionable name given to their signup sheet. Talk about laying it on extra thick. Book of Conquests sounded more like a skeevy subreddit for horny college guys, but whatever. I had a feeling there was going to be a lot of needless ceremony associated with these guilds, all of it almost certainly meant to further the whole *us versus them* dynamic we'd discussed before entering this...

Movement on the map caught my eye and I glanced at it. There was still no detail to be seen past the double doors but a yellow dot had appeared in that direction nonetheless. *Huh. Another new color.* Whoever or whatever they were, they seemed to be headed this way.

It didn't seem much of a stretch to assume this was probably the vaunted guild master, no doubt coming to meet their prospective new charges.

Time Chaser

First things first, though. Haniah pushed the book closer to me. I leaned down but just as I was about to write my actual name I reconsidered and signed it *Mac* instead.

After all, if I was going to be in the *Book of Conquests*, I might as well look the part.

However, even as I lifted the pen and went to hand it back to Haniah, I saw my signature change. *What the*? The lines of the pen stroke grew fuzzy for a moment before rearranging themselves into ... Tim, JUST FUCKING TIM.

What?! "You've gotta be fucking kidding me. What the hell?"

If Haniah was offended at my outburst she didn't show it, merely laughing instead. "I did say your *given* name, did I not? Sorry, but *Virto* insists."

"That's not my given..."

"You have gotta be fucking kidding me!"

At the sound of Pixel's voice I replied, "That's what I just said."

Pixel: *Drop the pen. Do it now, Tim! We need to get out of here.*

I had no idea what that was about, but if Pixel was using chat then it was probably best I answer that way too.

Tim, JUST FUCKING TIM: *Relax. I'm finished. Now what's the problem?*

Pixel: *Finished? Please tell me you didn't sign that book. We can't be a part of this guild.*

Tim, JUST FUCKING TIM: *Yeah, I signed it, but that's okay. I'll just tell her we changed our minds.*

Pixel: *Survey says XXX. It doesn't work that way.*

Tim, JUST FUCKING TIM: *Fine, but it's just me so far. If you don't think it's a good idea, then don't sign up. It's not ideal but we'll figure it out.*

Pixel: *No, we won't. Don't you get it? I'm your assigned FAST. That means if you're in then I'm in.*

Tim, JUST FUCKING TIM: *That still doesn't tell me why you're flipping the fuck out.*

Pixel: *You want a reason? Look!*

The double doors burst open just as Pixel's last message arrived. The creature that stomped through them caused my jaw to drop. It stood about seven feet tall, all of it heavily muscled and terrifying as fuck. Hell, the brute resembled nothing less than the love child of the Kraken from *Clash of the Titans* and Goro of *Mortal Kombat* fame.

It was dark green in color, sporting a reptilian face from which multiple fin-like appendages sprouted, all of which appeared razor sharp. The beast's upper body was no less intimidating – a broad, barrel-shaped chest with two sets of massive arms, each of which made Haniah's look positively puny in comparison. Dozens of gold chains hung around the creature's neck like it was an insane Comic Con cosplay of Mister T as an eldritch horror. Aside from that, the only clothing it wore was a pair of pink boxing trunks above its two thickly muscled legs.

Tim, JUST FUCKING TIM: *What the fuck is that thing?*

Pixel: *That's Virto. And if I'm not mistaken he's this guild's leader, which means things just went from bad to worse for us.*

Tim, JUST FUCKING TIM: *Why exactly?*

Pixel: *Remember those extra memories I unlocked? Well, he's in them.*

Tim, JUST FUCKING TIM: *He is?*

Pixel: *Yep. I think we worked together during a prior Chase. I don't have full access to all my memories from that time, so I don't know exactly what happened, but my intuition cells are screaming that things did not end particularly well between us.*

38

CHASERS ANONYMOUS

Guild Master: Virto – level 50

Virto hails from the planet Meeb 4691 where he was an active para-squelcher, whatever the fuck that is – at least until the fateful day when an extra strong tailwind pushed his ass toward a rocky outcropping, resulting in him accidentally jarbing when he should've klibed.

I had no idea what the hell Drega was saying other than it sounded really ... alien. Far more important to me was the fact that Virto was freaking fiftieth level. That was more than ten times my own – meaning this guy was almost certainly capable of killing me with a mean sneer alone.

Fortunately for us, Drega continued, **his loss was our gain as he quickly proved to have that chaser spirit we all admire – using it to murder and maul his way up to Stage Eleven. Alas, an ill-advised encounter with an Eon boss resulted in the decimation of his entire party, right before he himself was swallowed whole by the giant Brominax they were trying to expire. However, Virto, badass that he is, told fate to go fuck itself. Rather than go quietly into the night, he managed to take his enemy with him – killing it from the**

inside in the exact moment before he succumbed to the brute's caustic stomach acids.

And that, bitches, is how you win over the audience!

Wait. Virto died? What the fuck?

Proving that you can't keep a good chaser down, Virto now leads the House of ... Insufferable Pain. And no, I have no idea what's up with that name. He's a fighter, not a poet. If you're looking to discuss highbrow literature over tea, then prepare to have both jammed up your ass sideways. On the other hand, if you've ever wondered how to throttle a foe with one hand while using the rest to scratch all three of your testicles, then you, my friend, are in the right place.

"Are your tastebuds tingling?" Virto cried, still standing in the doorway, his voice loud and boisterous. "Because I hear there's some fresh meat waiting to be tossed onto the grill of pain ... and you know what that means! It's time to do some tenderizing! Hells yeah!"

I glanced around, wondering who he was shouting at, as neither Haniah nor the other NPCs seemed to give his entrance much more than a polite grin. If anything, he seemed to be screaming for the sake of hearing his own voice.

"They expect us to entrust our tutelage to that ... *creature?*" Boog remarked, barely concealed disgust coloring her voice – pretty much the most emotion I'd heard from her since her transformation. "I cannot be the only one with serious misgivings about this brute's qualifications."

I was about to reply that maybe we should give him a chance when Virto started to flex, striking several poses with all four of his arms as he continued to stand there in the doorway. It was like a flashback to that old wrestling show I'd gone to, watching as the victors struck poses for the...

That's when it hit me. Virto wasn't talking to us or anyone else here. Either this clown was delusionally full of himself or he was playing it up to the audience. If so, that was yet another new concern to add to the ever-growing pile.

Time Chaser

The NPCs we'd met to this point had all seemed to act as if this was real life and not some psychotic game show, whereas the bots were single-minded morons. Outside of our two hosts, though, the only others I'd seen so far who seemed to acknowledge there was a fourth wall to break had been the campground sponsors. This was a new twist, though, a potentially troubling one if this guy proved more concerned with impressing the crowd than our wellbeing.

Mind you, that wasn't the only issue I was trying to come to grips with.

Tim, JUST FUCKING TIM: *Excuse me for sounding naïve but how is this guy here if he's supposed to be dead?*

Pixel: *He's not. You heard Drega. He beat that boss just before he died.*

Tim, JUST FUCKING TIM: *Yeah, while inside its freaking stomach. How does that equate to him surviving?*

Pixel: *It normally wouldn't, unless...*

Tim, JUST FUCKING TIM: *Unless what?*

Pixel: *Again, I'm only going off partially recovered memory cells here, but logically it stands to reason that if it was late in the Chase and the audience's reaction to Virto's final battle was big enough, the overmind might've offered him a deal, even though technically he'd already lost.*

Tim, JUST FUCKING TIM: *They can do that?*

Pixel: *They can do whatever the fuck they want. They make the rules which means they can break them if circumstances warrant it. And I probably don't need to tell you that in the world of entertainment popularity equates to longevity. How else do you explain your society inflicting Steve Urkel upon itself for as long as it did?*

Okay, maybe they were right about that last part. I guess there really was something to that old saying of go big or go home. I sincerely doubted that mattered in the slightest here on these early stages but Virto had made it almost to the end. If he was as badass as Drega made him out to be, then surely he'd have garnered a following by then.

Time Chaser

I had no idea what kind of deal they might have offered him, but it seemed reasonable to guess that when one was in the process of being digested almost any offer would be hard to refuse.

Obviously Virto hadn't been sent back to his original death, nor had he won any of the Chase's prizes – which I guessed was a similar situation with the other guild masters. If so, then this duty existed as a sort of stay of execution, a way to keep living by serving the overmind's whims. Of course, that brought to mind the question of how long someone like Virto was beholden for and what happened once that period finally ended, assuming it ever did.

Looking at the way Virto continued to flex and posture, though, I figured it might be best to save that for now – maybe get a chance to know this guy before accidentally giving him a reason to fuck my shit up.

Or Pixel's for that matter.

My FAST claimed to not remember, but it was hard not to speculate on what had caused them to have such an extreme reaction to seeing our new guild master.

From what Pixel had told me, they'd been competing on Time Chasers for a long ass time – all of it unsuccessfully. And what was that Drega had said about Virto's death? Maybe it was just me interpreting things wrongly, but it sure as hell had sounded like it all boiled down to Virto and his party receiving some bad advice.

If that was the case then was I destined for some similar bad advice further down the line?

Tim, JUST FUCKING TIM: *Tell it to me straight. Were you Virto's FAST?*

Pixel: *Why do you ask?*

Tim, JUST FUCKING TIM: *Because that's the obvious question. In your own words ... duh!*

Pixel: *I knew there was a reason I liked you. Anyway, the truth is I don't know. And before you get your panties in a bunch, I'm* *being serious. It's like trying to piece together an entire novel from just a few random pages. Best answer I can give is I don't think so.*

Tim, JUST FUCKING TIM: *Why do you say that?*

Pixel: *It's just the impression I get from the scant memories I can access. Maybe I was assigned to one of Virto's party members but that's just a guess too. All I know is my gut is telling me that we didn't like each other for some reason. Although, seeing the way this jackhole is playing it up, maybe I shouldn't be too surprised.*

Tim, JUST FUCKING TIM: *And there's nothing else?*

Pixel: *Nothing I can remember. So, got anything else you want to grill me about, or can we finish this round of Twenty Questions?*

It wasn't much to go on, nor did it justify Pixel's initial reaction to learning this was Virto's guild. Call me paranoid but I had a feeling they weren't sharing everything they knew. All the same, I wasn't sure I was in any position to judge them. I could barely even fathom what they must be going through – having amnesia then suddenly gaining back a fraction of their memories, only to have to piece their former life together from mere fragments.

It was like a lethal version of that Drew Barrymore movie Deb had made me watch once.

I decided to table the subject for now, partly because distrust wasn't going to help our chances but mostly because Virto had finally finished flexing and was now headed our way.

"Yo, Haniah, what's the deal with these sorry sacks of skreeto shit stinking up my fine guild?" he asked striding over.

Despite the African warrior's impressive physique, she was almost like a child next to the towering Virto. This was a guy who looked like he existed on protein shakes and vitamin supplements after washing it all down with a glass of toxic masculinity.

Rather than answer, Haniah simply turned and handed him the *Book of Conquests*.

Virto glanced at it and then at me. "Tim, Just Fucking

Tim," he remarked, baring a mouthful of needle sharp teeth. "That you?"

"Actually, my name is..."

"Because that, my friend, is pretty fucking badass! You might be nothing but a low-level first stager, but I for one admire any warrior who puts themself out there and declares *this is who I am, say shit about it at your own risk*."

"You do?"

"Hells yeah, meat! That's the kind of fuck-all attitude that wins stages in the Chase."

I blinked, not expecting that. "Um, thanks."

He held out one of his four hands, palm open. I tentatively reached out and took it – at which point he clamped down like a vice grip and gave me such a violent shake I was surprised my arm wasn't wrenched right out of its socket.

To my credit, I managed not to scream ... barely.

"Welcome to the House of Incalculable Suffering, Heartache, and Pain. You enter these sacred halls as a mere n'lep but I guarantee you will leave here a fully grown rrekryl."

"A fully grown what?"

Virto slapped a meaty hand to his forehead. "Sorry, I sometimes forget that those SKs only translate so much. I meant to say you've come here a weak pathetic girl child but once we're done, you'll be the most badass boss babe anyone's ever laid eyes on."

"Huh?" I asked, still confused.

"You are female, right?"

"No."

"You aren't?" he replied, his reptilian eyes opening wide. "Well, damn, then you're in more dire need of my help than I thought. Don't worry, kid. We'll whip you into shape or you'll die trying."

"Wait, what?"

However, that apparently was all the attention Virto deemed me worthy of, turning Pixel's way next. He peered at the FAST intently, causing me to hold my breath. If he remembered Pixel and they indeed had some sort of shared history, what then? I'd been told that guilds were safe spaces, but Virto had the look of someone who could make a safe space very *unsafe* in short order.

Not helping was the fact that, much like Haniah's, his description had said nothing about being a non-combatant in this game.

Finally, after what felt like a small eternity, although in actuality was maybe a second or two, he asked, "And who's this little fella here?"

I let out a breath I hadn't realized I'd been holding. Of course he would ask something like that. I probably should've guessed that from the get-go. Not only did Virto seem way too self-absorbed to do otherwise, but it wasn't like FASTs were super discernible from one another other than maybe the color of their light. Outside of that, I highly doubted there was much chance of me picking one out from another in a police lineup.

I had no idea how long ago Virto had competed or how many Chases had happened since then, but whatever worry the FAST felt was almost certainly unfounded.

"That's Pixel," I said.

"Pixel, eh?" Virto remarked, leaning in closer toward them. "A small insignificant speck of light. Tell me, FAST, do you wish to remain small and insignificant?"

"Not particularly," Pixel replied in a deep Darth-Vader like tone, causing me to raise an eyebrow.

Tim, JUST FUCKING TIM: *Are you trying to disguise your voice?*

Pixel: *Don't judge me, Tim, I'm having a stressful day here.*

"Then you're in the right place, speck." Virto said. He didn't wait for Pixel to respond, instead turning his attention toward Boog. He laid his eyes on her and paused, his gaze working its way across her slight frame at a far slower pace than he'd used for either me or Pixel.

Wait. Is he checking her out?

"And what about you, my thick-browed beauty? I can't help but notice you haven't placed your name in my *Book of Conquests*. What's the matter, don't want to be *conquered*?"

The unsubtle way he spoke left no doubt as to his intentions.

"I...," she started, looking visibly uncomfortable, "am still considering my options, thank you."

Boog: *My apologies, friends, but I will require some more time before committing to this particular course of action.*

Pixel: *Are you sure?*

Tim, JUST FUCKING TIM: *Weren't you telling us that we needed to run barely two minutes ago?*

Pixel: *I know what I said but you and me are already stuck, so Boog joining too isn't really going to make matters worse. Besides, it's not like guilds fall from the trees this early in the Chase. She shouldn't waste the benefits just because this guy is a jerk.*

Boog: *It is not his unpleasantness that gives me pause, although that certainly does cast some influence over my opinion. It is more that I fail to see how I might benefit from his tutelage. The simple fact of the matter is I don't see how he can possibly have anything to teach me.*

Reading between the lines, her objections seemed obvious. Virto came across as both sexist and a simpleton. Neither was promising for any of us, much less the now hyper-intelligent ape girl. Nevertheless, Pixel wasn't finished trying.

Pixel: *I understand your misgivings, Boog. Trust me, I do. But this really isn't something you should overthink.*

Boog: *Oh? And how is that?*

Pixel: *Simple. These early stages offer a guaranteed boost just for visiting. Even if Virto turns out to be full of crap, which he probably will, we'll still get something out of it. Why turn that down?*

Boog: *I suppose there is some logic to your reasoning.*

However, just as it seemed Pixel was on the verge of talking Boog down from the ledge, Virto stepped in close to her and leaned down.

Time Chaser

"Come on, join your friends. No need to be shy. Heck, I'll even let you touch my ceps as a signing bonus. Trust me when I say I don't do that for just any pretty face."

Son of a...

Boog turned to Haniah instead. "I can wait here while my friends are inside, yes?"

"Of course," Haniah replied, the smile never leaving her face. "Please avail yourself to our hospitality for as long as you require."

"Thank you."

"Suit yourself," Virto said, seemingly not put out in the slightest. He pulled one of the gold chains from around his neck and winged it across the room, just barely missing the bartender but smashing several bottles behind him. "Yo, barkeep! Use that to pay for anything the little lady wants. And no watering down the drinks."

He probably thought he was being smooth, but Boog merely sighed in disgust as she floated over to an empty table and took a seat.

Undaunted, Virto than turned back toward us. "As for the rest of you plongos, well, you might not be hotties like your friend there but I hope you're wearing flame-retardant undies nonetheless, because you're about to feel the burn! Hells yeah!"

39

INCALCULABLE SUFFERING
STAGE ONE EXPIRATION: 1 DAY, 21 HOURS

I followed Virto through the double doors leading further into the guild while Haniah took Pixel with her. Apparently the FAST only rated Virto's NPC assistant, something the little bug zapper didn't take much issue with as they were still talking with a fake-ass voice.

It made little sense to me. I mean, surely, in all the ... quinks I guess, that Time Chasers had been on the air since Virto was a contestant, he and Pixel would've surely crossed paths at least once.

Of course in any such instances, Pixel wouldn't have had access to any of their past memories, but Virto would have. That told me either he was incapable of singling out the FAST or had gotten over whatever the hell had transpired between them.

Either way, after taking a minute or two to think it over, the whole thing felt overblown on the FAST's part. Whatever had happened, I sincerely doubted it was anything even remotely resembling the big deal they thought it was.

Speaking of big deals, Virto led me down a long hallway. The sides were adorned with alcoves containing holographic imagery depicting great moments in ... apparently his own

Time Chaser

history. Seriously, every hologram was a scene of Virto kicking some monster's ass, standing triumphant, or striking a pose.

"Feel free to gawk," he said from up ahead. "Maybe one day you'll be this awesome. Probably not, but never be afraid to dream. That's the only way to succeed in this meat grinder. First lesson: you gotta think big."

I was thinking all right, thinking maybe Boog had the right idea in staying behind.

Still, perhaps it was best not to judge until I saw what Virto had in mind for my guild training.

Almost as if reading my mind, he said, "I'm gonna warn you up front, kid. We ain't like the other guilds you'll find at this stage. Nuh uh. You join up with those losers and you'll get a hand stamp, a cookie, and a pat on the back to make you feel better about the miserable cards you've drawn. But not here. At Virto's, you're gonna eat some shit, no doubt about it. But when you're all done, your breath is going to smell like victory."

"And that means *what* exactly?" I asked, really hoping I hadn't heard him right.

Virto stopped at another set of double doors. Rather than answer me, he shoved them open and stepped through. "Now, are you ready for some heartache, suffering, and pain?"

"Not particularly," I muttered, following him.

⌛⌛⌛⌛ ⋅⋆⋅⋆⋅⋆⋅ ⌛⌛⌛⌛

Much like with the jungle cavern, I once more found myself *outside*. Virto had led me into what at first glance appeared to be a wide octagonal field – proving what I'd suspected earlier, that guilds were similar to campgrounds in that they were much larger on the inside.

This was no picnic area, though. It was cordoned off into specific areas, each of which were full of various training gear. I spied weapon racks, targets, training dummies, and multiple fighting pits. Also visible was what seemed to be a pair of ridiculously lethal obstacle courses which included such novelties as swinging axe heads, spiked hurdles, and a series of barbed-wire covered trapezes hanging over a pool of boiling liquid.

Holy shit! Ninja Warrior *ain't got nothing on this place.*

"Pretty fucking cool, eh, TJFT?"

I glanced at Virto. "TJ...?"

"It's short for Tim, Just Fucking Tim. No offense, kid, but that's one too many syllables for me to waste my time on."

"Says the guy who named his guild the House of Incalculable Suffering, Heartache, and Pa ... hey!"

Before I could finish, Virto grabbed a handful of my demon sweater and hoisted me to eye level.

"You got an attitude on you, plongo," he growled right before breaking into a big grin. "I like it. Shows spirit. Don't get me wrong, I gotta completely break you of it along with a whole host of other bad habits, but I like it all the same."

Ugh! His breath smelled like rancid *Slim Jims*. "Thanks, I guess."

He dropped me as quickly as he'd picked me up, almost causing me to face plant. When I'd finally managed to steady myself again, though, I realized we weren't alone.

Off in one of the sparring pits, two figures appeared to be squaring off against each other.

"Come on," Virto said, clapping me on the back hard enough to knock me to my knees. "I'll introduce you to the other new recruits. There's only a few of us so far, but that's to be expected this early in the Chase. Don't worry. Our ranks will swell soon enough. They always do."

I followed him that way, noting the sun shining down on us. It was actually a nice pleasant temperature – like a mild spring day. Looking around, the illusion of being outdoors was much more convincing here than it had been in the jungle cavern. In fact, I couldn't see anything that indicated this place wasn't real. "At least the weather's nice," I remarked, more to myself than anyone.

"Feh. This shit is hibernating weather if you ask me. I don't know how you Earthers can stand it. I tried to get them to add the triple suns of Meeb here because that's some workout weather you don't forget anytime soon. But they were all *no, their skin will melt off*. That's the fucking Committee for you. Always coddling chasers like freaking newborns."

"You talked to the Committee?"

"Of course. Well, okay, you don't really talk *to* the Committee so much as get talked *at*, but still. There's all sorts of pre-Chase planning that needs to happen and part of it involves them pretending to care about our opinions. I mean, what do I know about this shit, right? I only got them some of the highest ratings they've seen in the last four-hundred quinks."

"So ... what are they like?" I asked, figuring it couldn't hurt to do a little fishing.

"I wouldn't worry much about it if I was you. Chances are you'll be gelch food long before you're ever granted an audience. Or maybe not, if I do my job correctly."

We were now close enough for me to get a better look at the two combatants, but I wasn't sure whether to be impressed or terrified at what I saw.

They were both human, a man and woman respectively. More important was the fact they appeared intent on utterly annihilating each other.

The woman was Asian in appearance, with long black hair tied in a pony tail. She was wearing simple peasant garb, but that was the only unremarkable thing about her. She was wielding a sickle on a chain, flinging it around with an expertise that was straight out of a Saturday afternoon kung-fu movie.

Every attack she threw at her foe appeared to be calculated and precise – which made the fact that he was dodging them all that more impressive.

As for the guy, he was shirtless with skin so dark he almost appeared as a living shadow. He wore a brightly colored native skirt around his waist, sandals on his feet, and his arms were

Time Chaser

covered in metallic rings that appeared to function like armor similar to his SK – or at least that's the impression I got as the woman's sickle bounced off a pair of them.

Quick as she was, he was able to match her – although where she was precise, his movements were more rhythmic and chaotic, almost as if he were dancing.

If so, it was less Fred Astaire and more Electric Boogaloo as he dodged and weaved around her continued attacks.

As for the trepidation I felt watching them, that was easy. I had no way of knowing if their moves were the before or after of Virto's influence.

Speaking of the devil, though...

"Hey, you two," he shouted. "Take five. Come meet your new..." Virto glanced my way. "You're sure you're a dude, right?"

"Reasonably sure."

"Good enough I suppose. Anyway, come meet your new brother in arms."

The two ceased their *sparring* and turned our way, switching off their aggression like it was a faucet. As we got closer to each other, my HUD started filling me in on who they were.

Chaser: Aiko – Earth 8227 – Level 4

Party – Oni's Tears

Guild – The House of Incalculable Suffering, Heartache, and Pain

Interestingly, my HUD gave me a bit more info on her than I'd gotten when I'd first met Boog, albeit not nearly as much as fellow teammates. Maybe being in the same guild represented a middle status, sort of like being second cousins.

Seemed a reasonable assumption. Of far greater interest to me, however, was the fact that we were both the same freaking level, yet she possessed skills that told me any fight we might have would almost certainly end with me as a greasy spot on the floor.

Then there was the guy.

Chaser: Paki – Earth 6969 – Level 5

Party – Don't Weep for Me
Guild – The House of Incalculable Suffering, Heartache, and Pain

He was from an Earth that made the twelve-year-old boy inside of me giggle like a madman. However, whatever mirth I might've felt was instantly chilled upon seeing his party's name. Talk about bleak. Won't lie. It was also intimidating as fuck. It was like the guy had accepted his fate, but not in the same way Ikaros had. It more suggested he took no prisoners and had zero regrets.

Probably not someone whose bad side I wanted to get on.

Judging by the way they both stared at me, I had a feeling they were doing the same – taking in my info. Although, considering my name, party name, and level, I had a feeling they weren't nearly as impressed with me as I was with them.

"I won't bother introducing you meat slugs," Virto said, "as it's painfully obvious you've already scoped that out. Besides that's not what the House of Incalculable Suffering is all about..."

"What about the heartache and pain?" Aiko asked dispassionately, her voice smooth as silk.

"Don't make me pop you one, kid. I know how much of a mouthful it is. I could either keep saying it in full or you could all get back out there with enough time to finish this stage. Which will it be?"

Despite the lack of emotion in Aiko's voice, one side of her mouth raised in a grin. She was trolling Virto, trying to get a rise out of him. I wasn't sure if that was brave, stupid, or both. Either way, it suggested to me that Aiko was more than just a lethal, not to mention pretty face.

"It is truly a pleasure," Paki said, stepping forward, his voice deep and welcoming. "And might I add, that is quite the colorful name you have, Mr. Just Fucking Tim."

"You can thank my FAST for that one," I said with a nod, "He's a bit of an asshole."

"Really?" Paki replied. "That is interesting to hear, my new friend. My own, Akili, has been nothing but respectful. It makes me curious as to the disparity."

"It's because they're alive," Aiko said. "All living things, from people down to the blades of grass beneath our feet, express themselves as individuals."

Paki nodded. "I understand what you're saying, yet it strikes me as odd that any of the so-called companions they have assigned to us would be ... let's just say mischievous in the face of what we are all up against."

I shrugged. "Luck of the draw, I suppose. Pixel isn't too bad. They're just ... free spirited. Yeah, let's go with that. Anyway, it's nice to meet you both."

"Nice?" Virto replied with a laugh. "Gods be damned, meat, you truly are one for understatement. These are your guild mates. Nice don't cut it."

"It doesn't?"

Virto shook his head. "Let me put it this way. At some point in the chase, you will almost certainly, as in there is zero doubt, live or die by your commitment to each other."

"Oh. Then it's *very* nice to meet you both."

"You're killing me here, TJFT," Virto said with a sigh. "You really are. But that also brings up a good point. The House of Incalculable Suffering, *Heartache, and Pain*," he glared at Aiko as he pronounced each word, "is more than just a guild. It's a brotherhood. This is important because the PVP ban will be dropping today. No doubt about it. Happens every chase. That said, while the overmind might be okay with you plongos tenderizing the shit out of each other as soon as you can, I'm not. So let me make this very clear. This guild doesn't have a lot of rules but there's one I expect you all to follow. No intraguild expirations will be tolerated..."

"That's good."

"Unless absolutely necessary."

"Wait, what?"

"If it comes down to you or the other guy," Virto continued, ignoring me, "I'm not stupid enough to expect anyone to lay down their life. That's not the chaser spirit. What I'm saying is it had better be a last resort. If you don't have your guild's back out there, then the guild ain't gonna have yours. We train winners, not psychos. Is that clear?"

Amazingly enough, that actually sounded pretty reasonable. Heck, more than reasonable, especially if it meant there'd be chasers out there I wouldn't have to watch my back around.

Nods came from the other two as I likewise did the same.

"Good," Virto said. "Now just to be clear, I'm not as dumb as you all look. When shit gets real, that's when you'll learn the true measure of a chaser. Some will rise to the occasion, while others will slit your throat the second your back is turned. Honor is often the first thing out the window when the glirbs are down."

"Speak for yourself," Aiko said.

"Oh I do, trust me on this. In fact, my record speaks for itself. Not gonna lie about any of it. I'm credited with twenty-six player kills. I'm not super proud of those, but there wasn't a single one among them that wasn't necessary, and only a few that weren't as clean as I would've liked."

Virto eyeballed us each in turn, obviously trying to get his point across. I had to admit, I was slowly starting to rethink my opinion of him. Maybe there was more to him then just a violent, egomaniacal meathead.

If so, that make me even more curious as to what had gone down between he and Pixel. Now was not the time to dig deeper into that one, though. Aiko and Paki both seemed decent enough, and if they followed Virto's dictates then hopefully I could count on both as potential allies out there. However, I didn't know them well enough yet to risk airing my dirty laundry.

It was best to keep this first guild visit casual.

"All right, enough with the pussyfooting around," Virto

said. "You're here to train not listen to me flap my lip sacs. You two, another hour ought to do it for you and your FASTs. After that, you can collect them from Haniah and be off. Hopefully I'll see you both next stage."

"If you do," Paki said, "it won't be because of luck."

"Hells yeah!" Virto cried. "That's what I like to hear. All right, carry on. TJFT, you're with me."

Virto began to lead me away as the two began sparring again – the sounds of their exertions clearly audible over my shoulder even as we put some distance between us.

"So how does this work?" I asked after a minute or two, curious as to who or what I was probably about to face off against.

"It's so simple even a plongo like you can understand, at least here on Stage One. You see, just joining a guild qualifies you for a ten point stat bump. It's in the game rules."

"Okay, so then..."

"Now, most of the guilds hand that shit out like lollipops before sending their chasers on the way. But here we expect you to earn it."

"Is that why you have Aiko and Paki fighting?"

"Pretty much. Turns out their draws were complementary, so it made sense to pair them up. See, Aiko is training her strength, while Paki is working on his dexterity. That's why she's attacking while he's jumping around like he's got a mossflitter jammed up his ass."

"Okay, that makes sense." *Except for the mossflitter part.* "So what next? Do I choose which one I...?"

"Nope. Way too easy. Not to mention, the audience likes to see an element of chance with these things. Adds to the fun of it."

"Whose?"

"Definitely not yours," Virto said with a meaty laugh. "Now how about we get this meat on the grill?"

"And how do we do that?"

"Like so." Virto grabbed an amulet at the end of one of his many gold chains and pressed a button on it.

The air in front of us immediately began to sparkle as something took shape from the ether. It took a moment for it to materialize but when it was done a striker akin to one of those carnival strongman games appeared on the ground before us, complete with oversized mallet.

There were twelve levels marked out on the pole leading from the bottom all the way up. Most of the top half was taken up by seven options, each marked with the name of a stat. There were four much smaller lines marked out just above those. Listed on them were *try again*, *Virto's choice*, *20 point boost*, and a tiny one at the very top just before the bell with *choose two* on it. Sadly, I was far more concerned with the final marker, the one taking up the entire bottom half of the pole.

It was simply labeled *SOL*.

I didn't need to ask what that one meant as the meaning seemed bleakly clear.

Sadly it wasn't surprising either. So far, it seemed that every aspect of this game included the potential to fuck us over, if for no other reason than to give some chucklefucks in the audience a chance to laugh at our fate.

"Let me guess," I said. "The High Striker of Pain?"

"Oh please. You're looking at the High Striker of *Incalculable* Pain! Now step right up and give her a whack," Virto said, adopting a carnival barker voice. "There's a winner every time ... except for when there ain't."

40

WISDOM OF THE AGES

I hadn't known what to expect as I'd grabbed hold of the mallet and prepared to smash it down onto the plunger – hoping to ring the bell but guessing the game was likely rigged against me doing that.

I wasn't wrong. The mallet might as well have been the size of a car for how much it weighed. In truth, I was lucky just to get it off the ground. For a moment I was certain I'd end up in *shit outta luck* range. That would suck, making this entire exercise a waste of time – not that I was particularly looking forward to training, especially if it involved those obstacle courses I'd seen.

As it turned out, though, the bottom half of the strike tower was for intimidation purposes only. The mallet by itself was heavy enough to send the striker past the midpoint. How far past, however, was apparently dependent on me.

Charisma was the lowest stat listed. Not too surprising, although I'm happy to say I made it past that point. My swing wasn't quite powerful enough to best the next in line, though, not that I was particularly upset about it.

As for my new guild master, I fully expected him to have a different opinion on the matter.

Time Chaser

Call me crazy, but Virto didn't strike me as the type who valued wisdom. Nonetheless, I can't say I was too put off when the striker crested there, as it was a stat I was betting had potential to pay off in the long term.

What I wasn't betting on was the torture Virto had in store for me in order to earn my *free* stat bump.

⌛⌛⌛⌛ ⋆⋅☆⋅⋆ ⌛⌛⌛⌛

"How much more of this do I have to take?"

"As much as you can handle, meat, and then a little bit more," Virto said, staring me down.

Though there wasn't a clock on the wall for me to look at, my HUD served to inform me of how much time had passed since *class* had been in session, and I'm not being facetious. Rather than throw me into a fighting pit so I could try and dodge Aiko's sickle, a preferable fate if you ask me, Virto had instead dragged me through one of the many doors ringing the training field.

We'd ended up in a room that looked disturbingly like an elementary school classroom. Virto stuffed me into a desk chair then activated a viewscreen on the front wall. From there I was forced to watch every single encounter I'd had so far in the Chase.

And not just the highlights either.

Currently playing was my fight with those Cloud Warriors. So far I'd had to sit through it no less than five times, each from a different viewing angle.

"Tell me what you see," Virto asked for like the tenth time, as up on the screen I rushed forward having just stunned one of the warriors with a barrage of wolf teeth.

"I sensed an opening and took it."

"No. You acted stupidly and almost got your ticket punched."

"Are we watching the same fight? I clearly took that guy out."

"Yes, while ignoring the other two – which, I might add, nearly resulted in your spine being rearranged," he continued, as up on the screen Cuntur slashed at my back with his macana.

It wasn't a pretty sight.

The scene continued to play out, showing me desperately knocking the weapon out of his hand which caused him to rush into the bushes after it.

"Not gonna lie. That hurt like hell, but I still managed to disarm him."

"No. You got lucky. And do you know why?"

"Because of Second Chance..."

"It was because they were all fighting like halfwit morons."

"Okay, so then they were shitty Cloud Warriors. Bully for me, I guess."

Virto put a hand over his eyes and shook his head. "Gods you're fucking dense. Let's try this again. By all accounts you should be dead right now. But you're not, and do you know why?"

"Yeah, because I won."

"True, but do you know *why* you won?"

I meant to say something assholish but bit my tongue instead as I continued staring at the screen. Maybe it was my brain finally melting, but watching this battle over and over again was slowly forcing me to reconsider my perspective.

It had been easy to fool myself in the moment into thinking I was starting to get a handle on how to fight. But now, watching myself flail around on the screen for the umpteenth time, I just seemed so ... comically inept. Like, Macaulay Culkin would've made short work of me had this been a *Home Alone* sequel.

It was small wonder my solo adventures hadn't made it to Drega's highlight reel.

Despite all that, I'd still come out on top, but now it was starting to feel like maybe I shouldn't have.

"Are you saying they let me win? Ow!"

Virto answered my question by way of smacking me upside the head. "Not quite, plongo. But you're not too far off either. See, nothing in the Chase is just gonna *let* you win. Doesn't work that way. The audience would smell it coming a mile off."

He stepped to the screen and tapped it as the fight started once again, this time somehow giving me an overhead view despite the canopy of trees. "All the same, the Committee prides itself on recruiting a diverse group of chasers for each cycle. That might look good on paper, mind you, but do you know what the problem with diversity is?"

"I..." Okay, I had to admit he'd stumped me with that one. "Is ... this a trick question?"

"Maybe if this was debate club." He let out a chuckle. "Good luck getting a multiversal audience to watch that shit. Anyway, as far as the Chase is concerned, diversity means that for every competent warrior who gets brought on board, there's going to be at least three others who can't tell their testicles from their mucus flaps."

"Pretty sure we don't have mucus flaps."

"That's not the point!" Virto took a deep breath before looking around, almost as if checking to see if anyone else was there. "Listen, kid, I probably shouldn't be telling you this, but fuck it. I doubt anyone's tuned in to your feed anyway. What I mean is that by all rights these first few days of the Chase should be an utter fucking bloodbath."

"You're saying it's not?"

"Not even close. As of the last update, less than four-hundred of you meat slugs had been expired. That's a pretty average number."

"Average?"

"But," he continued, "the truth is it should be a good five

times higher, if not more. Except it isn't. Care to take a guess why that is."

I considered this – my situation, where I was, and all the things Pixel had told me. There was only one answer that made sense. "Killing us off too quickly wouldn't be entertaining."

"Exact-a-mundo! The longer each Chase runs, the more invested the audience gets. Favorites get chosen, bets get made, all that shit. But in order to build that sort of suspense, these first couple stages need their share of success stories and not just the obvious ones. I can't pretend I understand the appeal on account of having never been one, but gods be damned the audience loves an underdog."

An underdog? It was like a lightbulb suddenly turned on in my head. "They can't let us win because that would look fake as fuck, not to mention the audience demands to see blood."

"Go on," Virto prodded.

"But not too much blood, at least not yet. So..." I almost didn't want to say this next part out loud because that would make it real. And if that were the case, then there was no doubt it would cast a shadow over my achievements so far. All the same, denying reality didn't make it any less real. "The mobs. They aren't fighting as effectively as they could be."

This time I got a clap on the shoulder, which honestly didn't hurt any less. "Good answer. You're finally starting to get it."

"Thanks, I think."

"Keep looking at the screen. These clowns had at least half a dozen opportunities to end you. There! See how that Aztec dude ran off into the bushes looking for his weapon? Stupid as fuck since he was more than capable of throttling you with his bare hands."

"He's not Aztec."

"Huh?"

"I said they weren't Aztecs."

"Thanks for the history lesson, nerd. Tell it to someone who gives a shit. Anyway, you're absolutely right. Some of the mobs get dialed back a bit on these early stages. Not the brainless ones, mind you. If you can't think your way past those, then you're already hopeless. Intelligent mobs are a whole other ball of wax, though. Because let's face facts, even the most newb of ninjas is still a ninja – meaning they can kick your ass nine times out of ten."

"Unless they're dumbed down," I added, trying not to feel too insulted. After all, the vast majority of my *combat* experience prior to the last day boiled down to meeting with my company's marketing department.

Virto nodded. "It's not by much mind you. They crank their intelligence down a bit, that's all. It's just enough so they make some questionable decisions under fire, the sort they wouldn't normally make." He turned and jabbed a finger into my chest. "Let's just be clear. This isn't something you should *ever* count on. If you do, you're as good as dead."

He hooked a thumb at the screen, now showing Cuntur as he was trying to yank his weapon out of my shattered leg. *Ah, good times.*

"If you hadn't acted when you had," Virto continued, "you would've been toast. No if ands or buts about it. Never mistake dumbed down for merciful because they sure as shit aren't the same thing."

"Okay, I think I get it."

"Do you? All right, smart guy, then tell me this. Why *else* do they gimp some of the mobs on these lower stages?"

"Why else?"

"Come on, meat. You're in the home stretch. We're talking final exam here. Don't blow it now."

I considered what Virto had said. A part of me still wanted to feel insulted, but I knew that was nothing but stupid pride talking. I'd known coming in that I was going to be behind the eight ball compared to some of the other chasers.

The thing is, the Committee would've surely known that as well. After all, they'd assigned Pixel to study every facet of my life. They obviously had data on every single chaser here that rivaled what we knew about ourselves.

Speaking of Pixel, I had a feeling this little tidbit Virto was imparting to me was part of those memories they didn't have access to. After all, why not say anything about it?

Well, okay, that was kind of obvious. If I'd gone into this knowing the early mobs were dumbed down, I would've almost certainly underestimated them. That would've been a recipe for disaster considering I'd just barely survived as it was.

At least this way I now had a little experience under my belt while also managing to get over my earlier aversion to fighting and killing.

I still wasn't sure whether that last part boded well or ill for me. All I knew was that I was still alive, which meant getting home to Jeremy was still on the table. But in order to make it there, I needed to keep improving.

Improving... That's it! I looked up and met Virto's gaze. "It's a trick question. There's no other reason to hobble some of the mobs this early."

Virto raised one brow. "Keep going."

"It all comes down to keeping the audience happy. Dumbing down the mobs on this stage ensures more of us survive, thus increasing the audience's engagement. But, while that might result in some easier fights for the more battle hardened chasers, it also serves to give the rest of us some experience. Maybe not enough to completely close the gap, not yet anyway, but it ensures that we're forced to learn the ropes. That way, once we reach the higher stages, we might actually be able to compete with the others."

Virto smiled, once again revealing his disturbingly sharp teeth. "Not bad, kid. Not bad at all. You pass."

"I do?"

"Yep, but you still got some homework. I want you to remember all this once you're back out there. Take whatever advantage you can get. If a mob does something stupid, accept it in good cheer and take the win. Never look a gift zorbex in the mouth. But also don't expect it. Treat each fight like it could be your last and make sure to learn from your mistakes. Because trust me when I say the mobs will only get smarter and more vicious from here on out. Do that and you might actually survive the next stage or two."

"I'll try my best," I said, standing up from the uncomfortable seat.

"Hold on. Not so fast, hotshot. Time for the bonus round."

"Wait, bonus round?"

"Yep. Now I want you to tell me *why* I told you all of this."

Finally a question that didn't require much thought. "Because you're my guild master and want me to win."

"Survey says nuh uh, meat." He laughed. "That's okay. You weren't going to get anything out of it anyway."

"Okay, so then what's the answer?"

Instead of telling me, Virto turned instead toward the doorway. "You know what? I think I'll let you simmer in your own ignorance for now. Think it over. With any luck, this won't be the last we see of each other. If so, maybe by next time you'll have a clue."

⌛⌛⌛⌛ ⋄⋄⋄⋄⋄ ⌛⌛⌛⌛

Upon Virto's say so, my HUD flashed letting me know that my wisdom had gone up by 10 points, bringing it to 70. While a part of me wasn't particularly pleased with how long it had taken, I had a feeling the insight I'd gleaned would make it a worthwhile investment.

Virto's insistence that we earn our stat boosts had seemed an unnecessary complication at first, but now I was beginning to understand his logic. Go figure but, stat boost aside, I actually felt like I was leaving this place a little bit wiser.

Won't lie. I felt pretty good as Virto walked me back to the entrance so I could reunite with both Pixel and Boog.

Passing through the open field, I saw no sign of either Aiko or Paki. Guess both had completed their training and were once again out there exploring.

Though I doubted I'd come close to matching either of them anytime soon, hopefully the lessons I'd learnt here today would help me at least tighten the gap between us.

"So you've really been at this for four hundred quinks?" I asked to break up the silence that had settled between us.

Virto shrugged. "Something like that anyway. After the first hundred or two it all starts to blur together. I suppose I could find out for certain, but why bother? Nah. Much easier to just end each day killing some brain cells with a nice bottle of Tornango. Definitely beats thinking too hard about things."

That answer was surprising, far different from his bluster of earlier.

"So, any parting advice before I head out?"

He shook his head. "Just focus on what we discussed for now. If you try stuffing too much into that tiny noggin of yours, it's just going to confuse you when you least want it to. Keep drawing breath and maybe I'll have some more nuggets of wisdom for you next time ... unless you end up training a different stat."

Virto chuckled at his own joke before continuing. "Seriously, TJFT, stick to the basics for now. Win, get better, and have your party's back. That's it. Don't worry about anything else save reaching those ascension rings. All the rest is just a distraction."

"Sounds reasonable."

"Oh, and above all else try to stay humble. I know that sounds strange coming from a guy like me but I've seen thousands of chasers like you over the cycles. Most die before hitting Stage Three, and a good chunk of those expirations come down to them believing their own hype. That's the real killer. Don't get me wrong, anyone can get unlucky and accidentally stumble into a Millennial boss lair, but more often than not it's because they end up becoming their own worst enemy."

I nodded, taking a moment to consider his words. "Thousands, wow. It's gotta be rough seeing that many chasers march to their deaths."

"It can be, but I try to stay focused on the positive. Otherwise this place will eat you alive."

Sensing Virto may have offered me an opening, I pressed on. "How so?"

"Oh, there's definite perks to the job. For starters I'm not dead. Food's usually pretty decent too. Speaking of which, so are a lot of the folks here, at least once you get to know them, and I'm not just talking chasers. Over the quinks I've rubbed elbows with guild bosses, sponsors, special guests – and no I can't talk about those so don't even ask. And of course I've met more FASTS than I can probably count, unlucky bastards that they are. There's the stage crew too. You probably won't meet a lot, but most of them are just regular gerks like you and I."

I raised an eyebrow, partially at the gerk comment but also because a thought hit me. It was probably a longshot but what the heck. I might as well try while I had Virto's ear.

As we approached the double doors leading to the lobby, I asked, "I don't know if you can tell me this or not, but there wouldn't happen to be someone named Penark Queeg among them?"

"Penark Queeg?" he replied. "Are you sure that's a name and not a brand of tusk wash?" He narrowed his eyes. "And why do you ask?"

"No real reason. Someone cortexed me out of the blue. Said that was the answer to my questions. So I thought maybe it was a person."

"What questions?"

"Beats the hell out of me," I said. "Whoever sent it didn't elaborate, nor did they respond when I tried asking."

"Wait. You mean you don't know who cortexed you."

"No idea other than it was someone called Nadok. Probably another chaser. Anyway, they contacted me out of the blue. Figured maybe it was a butt dia... OOF!"

Before I could finish, I found myself slammed against the wall with enough force to rattle my insides.

I regained my composure to find Virto's face mere inches from my own.

"You fucking with me, kid?"

"W-what?" I gasped. "I ... have no idea what..."

"Nadok," he hissed, once more shoving me against the wall. "Where in the twelve Hells did you hear that name? And you'd better not lie to me, otherwise you're gonna wish those Aztec assholes had finished you off when they had the chance."

41

NAME DROPPING

Before I could wheeze out a response, Virto clamped a frying pan sized hand over my mouth, effectively cutting off both my words and airway.

So much for guilds being safe spaces.

Then, as I was frantically debating what to do about this unexpected threat to my life, my HUD flashed.

Virto has invited you to a private cortexing channel. Accept Y/N.

I met his gaze only to find his expression brooked no argument. The meaning was clear. If I wanted my breathing privileges reinstated, I had better accept his request. Needless to say, I didn't spend a lot of time thinking it over.

Virto: *So here's what's gonna happen, TJFT. I'm going to let go of you and we're going to act like you just mouthed off. Nothing more. Am I clear?*

Tim, JUST FUCKING TIM: *What the fuck, dude? I have no idea what the hell is going on. Why did you attack me?*

Virto: *Okay, let me try to make this extra simple. Either do as I say or I keep holding you like this until you either stop flopping around or learn to breathe out of your own asshole. And before you ask, yes, killing you is technically against the rules but the penalty* *for me is a slap on the wrist. Trust me when I say, I can deal with it.*

I was already starting to get a bit woozy, so there really wasn't any choice in the matter.

Tim, JUST FUCKING TIM: *Okay! I get it! I'll do whatever you want.*

Virto: *Good. Now follow my lead and pray to whatever gods you believe in that nobody important has been eyeballing your feed this past hour.*

Virto finally released me and I slumped to one knee, trying to suck in breath after breath. Gotta say, I never realized how sweet air could be.

"Say that again, meat. I dare you," Virto growled.

My first instinct was to ask what the fuck he was talking about, but then I remembered his instructions and what the alternative involved. "Learn to take some criticism, you ... Mortal Kombat boss wannabe! All I said was your classroom technique could use some work."

Virto: *Damn. Words hurt, TJFT.*

"Flap your face worms at me again, meat," he said aloud, "and you'll find out my *fist* technique more than makes up for it. Am I clear?"

"Crystal," I snapped, holding his gaze while hoping I wasn't laying it on too thick.

Tim, JUST FUCKING TIM: *Are we good here? Can you finally tell me what's going on?*

Virto: *Yeah. Just be thankful I stopped you before you said anything else. Trust me when I say Nadok is* not *a name you want to be throwing around with reckless abandon.*

Needless to say, I was now intrigued in addition to being pants-shittingly terrified, especially since I'd already mentioned all this to Pixel. What the hell had I accidentally stumbled into here?

Tim, JUST FUCKING TIM: *Why?*

Virto wasn't quite ready to answer that yet, though.

Virto: *Gods be damned, kid, you almost made me piss myself. Thank goodness we were just shooting the shit. The audience isn't going to be too interested in any of that heartfelt crap, at least not this early. Maybe later after they get to know you a bit but right now it's all about the action. And so long as your viewer numbers aren't too high, the submind probably won't be scrubbing this feed with a fine-toothed comb. Let's just hope that name isn't still on their list of flagged words.*

Tim, JUST FUCKING TIM: *And if it is?*

Virto: *Then we can both expect to hear about it sooner rather than later. Just to clarify, that would be bad for me but infinitely worse for you. And yes, you'll know if that happens.*

Oh yeah, that wasn't ominous in the slightest.

Virto shoved me toward the door, keeping up the aggro act. Most likely this was due to it being fairly obvious we were conversing in chat, at least so long as we both stood there glaring at each other in silence.

I turned and stepped through the doorway back into the lobby. It was the space of a few seconds for me to spot Pixel and Boog over in the tavern area. Considering Haniah was back behind the reception desk, I guessed the FAST's training had likewise concluded.

More importantly, everything seemed normal. So far so good. Now to hope Virto was right about me being too boring to watch.

Tim, JUST FUCKING TIM: *Looks like nothing out of the ordinary is going on, so spill already. Who is this Nadok and why are they on the overmind's shit list? More importantly, why the fuck are they dragging me into it?*

Virto: *No idea on that last one, TJFT, although chances are it's just someone fucking with you. Let's at least hope that's the case. Anyway, you'd do best to block them and forget this ever happened. Don't let some asshole drag you down with them for the sake of an extremely unfunny joke.*

Tim, JUST FUCKING TIM: *Fine, whatever. I have enough*

to deal with as it is. But back to my question. Who's Nadok and why is it such a big deal to talk about them?

Virto: *Not who,* what.

I was tempted to point out that technically every non-human I'd met qualified as a *what*, but that felt a bit petty.

Virto: *Now, just to be fair, a lot depends on who you ask, not that you're going to find too many who'll risk talking about them openly. The thing is, Nadok isn't a person so much as an ideal, or maybe insurgency would be the better word. They were a group who were openly against the Chase, how it operates, what it represents, all of that. But instead of going through the proper legal channels, their goal was to infiltrate Time Chasers and destroy it from the inside.*

Tim, JUST FUCKING TIM: *Hold on. So you're saying Nadok is some kind of terrorist organization?*

Just what I needed – chat requests from Cobra Commander.

Virto: *Not is,* was. *Far as I know, they were all wiped out.*

Tim, JUST FUCKING TIM: *Far as you know?*

Virto: *Yeah. They only tell me so much as a guild master. Back when I was first recruited as a chaser, though, that name was already being spoken of like it was some sort of boogeyman.*

Tim, JUST FUCKING TIM: *Already? How far back does this go?*

Virto: *Fuck if I know. They'd been building their rep since before my cycle, slowly becoming a concept that refused to die. This next part is just speculation, but I think the Committee was all for it, at least at first. After all, their name made for good ratings. But then things escalated.*

Tim, JUST FUCKING TIM: *What happened?*

Virto: *It started taking on a life all its own. For instance, you'd turn a corner and find* NADOK LIVES *written on the walls in blood. Stuff like that. Like I said, boogeyman shit. Problem is, there was no way of knowing whether it was another chaser being cute or someone involved with the show fucking with us.*

Tim, JUST FUCKING TIM: *And then what?*

Virto: *Things got...*

His message ended there, at least for a moment or two.

Virto: *You know what? It's not anything you need to worry about. The important thing is that the overmind clamped down hard on it. Hell, over the next few cycles just saying their name was enough to earn an instant penalty. Hell, I even heard that a few chasers got their asses insta-shunted to an Eon boss lair for pushing their luck.*

Tim, JUST FUCKING TIM: *I'm gonna assume that's bad.*

Virto: *About as bad as it gets, kid. But whatever. This all happened a long time ago. As for the crackdown, it worked. Eventually the audience forgot about Nadok and that was that. Hell, outside of the staff and us long-timers, I didn't think anyone else remembered them. And honestly, I didn't expect anyone to ever be stupid enough to say their name again during a Chase. Guess I was wrong.*

Tim, JUST FUCKING TIM: *So you think someone involved with the show is messing around?*

Virto: *Possibly.*

Tim, JUST FUCKING TIM: *Okay, but why me?*

Virto: *Beats the fuck outta me, TJFT. Maybe you just got one of those faces that begs to be fucked with.*

All our discourse transpired as we leisurely walked from the door back to the reception desk. Once we finally got there, Haniah turned and acknowledged us.

She nodded my way before addressing Virto. "So how goes it with our newest warrior, boss?"

Virto clapped me on the back, almost knocking me to my knees. "Just one more slab of meat for the grill of pain. Hells yeah!" he cried, obviously back to playing it up. Guess our moment was over. "He ain't shit right now but a couple more stages and we might just whip this plongo into some semblance of shape."

"Excellent to hear."

"How about you? His FAST give you any crap?"

Time Chaser

"Not at all. Pixel was most eager to learn."

"Pix...? Oh yeah. Almost forgot that was its name." Virto turned toward me. "Might want to reconsider that, meat. Makes your FAST sound like a pussy, which in turn makes *you* sound like one."

With that proclamation, Virto turned away, making me think that was it. However, as he started back toward the door, I got one last chat message.

Virto: *Remember what we talked about, TJFT. ALL OF IT. Be careful out there, stay humble, and be mindful of your tongue and who you use it around. Speaking of which, try to convince that hottie you're traveling with to sign up next time you're in the neighborhood. That's one slab of meat I'd definitely love to see on my grill of pain. Hells yeah!*

⌛⌛⌛⌛ ⋯⁑⋆⁑⋆⁑⋯ ⌛⌛⌛⌛

I had no idea how to discuss with Pixel what Virto and I had talked about. Oddly enough, though, just walking up to my two companions felt like a huge relief – like it had been far too long since we'd last all been together. Talk about crazy. I'd known Pixel for barely a day and a half, Boog for even less, yet I could barely imagine stepping foot back into the dungeon without them.

They were seated at a table close to the bar. Well okay, Boog was seated ... or more like slumped over in her chair. She'd apparently made good use of Virto's hospitality because there was an empty plate in front of her as well as several drained glasses.

I guess I couldn't begrudge her. My *training* with Virto had taken a while after all.

"So, how'd it go in there?" Pixel asked, still disguising their voice. "Really? Truly fascinating to hear."

"But I didn't say..."

"Well, would you look at the time? We should probably get

going. Places to be, an ascension ring to find. You know the drill. Let's skedaddle."

"Wait..."

But they were already floating toward the direction of the door.

Okay then.

I shared a quick glance with Boog. No time like the present to step back into the mouth of madness.

Or maybe not as Boog nearly fell out of her chair as she tried to stand up. One didn't need a high Perception to realize it had nothing to do with her emaciated legs.

"Are you okay?" I asked, helping her to steady herself.

"I assure you, I feel quite fine, Macmac," she replied slurring her words. "Better than fine as a matter of fact! Although, I must admit this new form of mine isn't quite as adept at imbibing gimba as I used to be."

"Gimba?"

She gestured sloppily at the collection of empty glasses on her table.

"You mean alcohol?"

She gave a big nod, nearly headbutting me with her oversized cranium. "Yes! That's the word! Sorry, I was using a local colloq ... colloquialism. I guess our SKs don't always account for those. Oh well. What is life without a little mystery?"

"Uh huh. And is there a particular reason you've been imbibing *gimba* like there's no tomorrow?"

"Because there is *no tomorrow*, at least not in this place." She shook her head, nearly toppling over. "So I figured I might as well celebrate while I still can."

"And what exactly are we celebrating?"

"Why not look and find out for yourself, my mate? I know you want to."

The lecherous grin on her face took me aback. Won't lie. It was kinda creepy.

I pushed that aside, however, as I tried to make sense of

what she was talking about. Fortunately, a moment later my HUD clued me in. Sure enough, though she was still under the effects of *Jekyll and Hyde*, her *Penalized* status had expired.

Too bad another had taken its place: *Inebriated*.

That wasn't exactly surprising. What was, however, was the effect it had on her. Her INT score had a temporary debuff of 40 points, dropping it down to 200. She was still a genius, but an impaired one.

Holy shit. Forty points. That's half my freaking score.

In truth I had no idea if the debuff was a static amount or based on a percentage of the whole. Nonetheless, it told me that it might be best to stick with water going forward.

"Um ... you're not penalized anymore. That's great."

"Truly it is," she said, draping one long, thin arm around my shoulders. "Don't tell anyone I said this, but I have secretly been somewhat embarrassed by the actions of my ... other, more primitive form. How ... what is the word? Uncooked? No. How uncouth of me."

"It's fine, Boog. You didn't know what you were..." I did the math in my head, realizing something was off. "Wait. According to my timer, your penalty only ended a few minutes ago."

Her response was an exaggerated shrug followed by a hiccup. "Don't tell anyone this either, but I may have jumped the club and gotten started a bit early."

42

ONE FOR THE ROAD

STAGE ONE EXPIRATION: 1 DAY, 16 HOURS

It was probably stupid to leave the safety of the guild with Boog in her current condition, but Pixel was already on their way out the door thanks to their TK Hand. Besides, there was no telling how far away that ascension ring still was, or what enemies might be standing in our way.

"Come on, Boog. I'll help you."

"There is no need, Macmac, I will simply..."

She tried levitating, only to crash into the table next to us. Fortunately, the NPCs seated there didn't appear to be hostile. Heck, they barely acknowledged us at all.

Finally, I managed to steer her outside – holding one end of her axe while she held the other, basically treating her like she was a living balloon on a string. It was a good thing Virto and I had our little conversation earlier, because I had a feeling the comedic value of trying to get a drunk Boog out of the guild was almost certainly driving our viewership numbers back up.

Not that I had any way of knowing, but maybe that wasn't the worst thing in the world. While I'm sure information like that had potential to be useful, I was oddly okay with living in ignorance on that front.

For now anyway.

Whatever the case, we reunited with Pixel outside in the dungeon hallway.

"About goddamned time," the FAST said, finally dropping the phony voice once the door closed. "I feel like I can breathe again."

"Except for the fact that you don't."

"Don't give me shit, Tim, it's been a stressful day." The FAST flitted back and forth through the air in an agitated manner. "So? Don't keep me waiting here."

"Waiting for what?"

"Virto. Did he say anything?"

"Yeah, he said lots of things."

"I meant about me."

I took a moment to make sure Boog wasn't floating off down the hall before saying, "No. In fact you didn't come up in the conversation at all ... well, except for him mentioning that he thinks your name is stupid."

"That makes two of us," Pixel replied. "Seriously, there was no indication that he was pissed at me for whatever reason I still can't remember?"

I shook my head. "If he was, he didn't say anything about it. And before you ask, no, I didn't sense any hostile vibes toward any of us."

That was a bit of a white lie, at least once I'd mentioned Nadok, but I saw no need in freaking out the little ghost light more than they already were.

"Okay, so if you weren't talking about me then what the hell were you doing in there for so long?"

"Training obviously. Dude had me sit in a classroom and go over every one of our fights with a fine-toothed comb – over and over again. All for a 10 point Wisdom bump."

"Really?" the FAST replied. "Haniah just handed me a DEX Patch and sent me on my way."

Time Chaser

I raised an eyebrow, trying not to be annoyed. "Hold on, so you were actually with Boog this entire time?"

"Not the entire time but a good chunk of it."

I pointed toward where she was floating aimlessly. "Then why did you let her get like this?"

"Do I look like I have *babysitter* stamped on my CPU? She's an adult. What you Earthers do during your downtime is your own business. Besides, she seems fine to me."

"She's missing forty points of intelligence."

"Which still leaves her one-hundred-and-twenty points ahead of you. I don't see the problem."

"I... You know what, never mind. How about this? Do you know of some way to fix her?"

"Yeah, it's called walking it off."

"*Really* not helping."

I thought Pixel would keep on being a snarky bastard but instead I got a chat message from them.

Pixel: *Sorry, Tim. I don't mean to be a total ass, but like I said, I've been kinda stressed and Virto was pretty much the last straw. I never thought regaining my memories would ever be a bad thing, but the fact they're all jumbled up and fractured like some nightmare jigsaw puzzle is not helping matters. Hell, you saw me in there. And I still don't even know what the fuck I did to piss the guy off.*

Tim, JUST FUCKING TIM: *Did you ever think that maybe you didn't do anything? You don't have the full picture so it's entirely possible you're interpreting things wrong. Heck, for all you know, you might've done nothing more than accidentally bump into each other in the hallway, setting him off on one of his flexing tirades.*

Pixel: *I... suppose that's possible.*

Tim, JUST FUCKING TIM: *Highly possible from what I've seen of the guy. So just chill the fuck out and get your head back into the game already. We're done with him and his guild for now. From what Virto said, it's doubtful we'll run into him again on this* *stage. Hopefully by the time we do you'll have figured things out a little better.*

Pixel: *Maybe you're right.*

I debated saying more but we'd probably overstayed our welcome. It might end up looking suspicious if we hung out there in that spot for too long. Call me paranoid, but I didn't want to draw any extra attention to myself right then. Ending up on Drega's highlight reel was one thing but, outside of that, the fewer eyeballs turned my way the better – at least until I could figure my own issues out.

Christ. At this rate Pixel and I would both end this stage as a couple of basket...

"Try some nutradisks," Pixel said, interrupting my train of thought.

"Huh?"

"Earth to Tim. You asked if there was a way to help her, so I'm telling you. Feed Boog a few nutradisks. They're super calorie dense and are designed to be absorbed into the bloodstream quickly. That should dilute the happy juice in her system in fairly short order. I'd do it myself but..."

"TK Hand can only do so much?"

"I was gonna say, I don't want to get yakked on, but let's go with your excuse instead."

⌛⌛⌛⌛ ⋅⋅⋅⋅⋅ ⌛⌛⌛⌛

The problem with nutradisks was that they were apparently designed to be a full three meal replacement for an entire day. Handy if ever there was an emergency, true, but not really the sort of thing one wanted to casually snack on.

The thing is, meal replacements were typically meant to be eaten one at a time. Don't get me wrong, overdosing Boog with them did seem to do the trick. Barely two hours later and her INT points had already climbed back by half of what she'd lost.

Time Chaser

The downside, however, was somewhat ... unpleasant. She'd already been forced to use three of her allotted pit stop vouchers and there was no sign of the deluge stopping. Alas, the combination of liquor and multiple nutradisks had proven rather *explosive*, having also earned her the rather ominous sounding *Intestinally Distressed* status.

Thankfully, whether inebriated or distressed, this new Boog seemingly had no intention of drawing yet another penalty.

As much of a positive as that was, it had slowed our ongoing exploration to a near crawl.

Though I still saw the location of that ascension ring on my map, it continued to pulse maddeningly slow – telling me we weren't making much headway toward it.

Of possibly far greater concern, though, was the path we were on appeared to be leading us toward another wide open space. That would probably be good for getting a bit of grinding in, but I couldn't forget how the last open area had almost ended with us getting pummeled by a two ton sloth.

Still, this was the way the map said to go. Tempting as it was to explore any side tunnels we passed, I tried to keep in mind what was said during the last live update. At the time, nearly seven-hundred chasers had managed to find ascension rings. Plegraxious had mentioned they expected that number to rise dramatically during this day. The implication was clear. The PVP ban would be dropping at some point, possibly soon. Once that happened, this game would become far more dangerous.

The last update was several hours ago, making me wonder how many had ascended since. That was the sort of information I kinda wished we had live access to – which was probably why we didn't.

Oh well, with any luck there'd be some sort of announcement beforehand. It would really suck to run across another group of chasers, only to end up with our asses killed because nobody had said anything.

For the moment, we focused on following the path. I was in the lead since I wanted to get back to working on my Perception skill, especially having gotten that free wisdom bump.

Pixel, unsurprisingly, didn't have a problem with that. They were bringing up our rear, leaving Boog in the middle to mostly float along while crop dusting the dungeon in her wake – yet another reason I was happy to take the lead.

Ever since leaving Virto's, our exploration had been mostly uneventful, with the exception of a minor run-in with some first level cave rats. However, between Pixel's Acid Ball and another handful of wolf teeth, we made short work of them.

I had a feeling that encounter was just a warmup, though, a way for the submind to keep us on our toes as we neared the open space ahead. Alas, the fog of war was doing its best to keep it a surprise.

Where sight failed me, though, my nose made up the difference. "Do you guys smell that?"

"Is Boog letting another one rip?" Pixel replied.

"I cannot help if my intestinal distress is..."

"No," I interrupted. "Smells like smoke coming from up ahead."

"Wonderful," Pixel said. "Anyone here have fire resistance?"

"Partial," Boog answered, "from my collar."

"Good, then maybe you should go..."

"No!" I interrupted a second time. "Not until she's back on her feet again ... figuratively speaking anyway."

"I thank you, my mate."

I suppressed a head shake. I really wasn't trying to encourage her, especially after witnessing what she'd done to that Deb bot.

Now if it had been fuckboy Manny...

I pushed that thought to the side, wonderful as it was, as we continued onward. In short order, the fog of war revealed something new – a series of reddish smears along the otherwise drab grey walls.

No. Not smears, symbols.

As we reached the spot where they started, I paused to take them in, realizing the symbols looked vaguely familiar.

"Is this ... Japanese?" I asked.

"I am unfamiliar with that terminology," Boog replied. "Is that one of your world's colloquialisms?"

"Sorta, not really."

"Out of the way," Pixel said, floating up to join me. The FAST looked at it for barely a moment before adding, "Ah, Tim, so close yet so far. You really should spend more time reading. It is, as they say, fundamental."

"Are you going to tell me what this is or just keep hurling insults all day?" I snapped.

"Decisions, decisions... Anyway, it's actually Hanzi. That's Chinese for the uneducated among us."

"Hey, I was close."

"Yeah, maybe according to mediocre twenty-first century white guy logic. Don't forget, Tim, knowledge..."

"Is power, yeah I get it. What I want to know is why my SK isn't translating it."

"That's because you received an auditory language upgrade not a visual one."

"And the reason for that?"

Pixel made a shrugging gesture. "Two theories. It's possible your primitive human brains can only handle so many upgrades before liquifying."

"And the other?" I asked, gritting my teeth.

"Maybe the Committee decided that watching chasers pantomime at each other is boring, but dying because you can't read a simple *No Trespassing* sign has entertainment value."

Ask a stupid question...

I turned toward Boog. "China's a country, by the way. Think of those as different tribes I guess ... just really big ones spread out over a lot of space."

I had a feeling that concept would've gone right over old Boog's head, but she merely nodded as if no further explanation was needed. No doubt about it. Her two-hundred plus intelligence made describing things a heck of a lot easier.

"What's it say?" I asked, turning back to the FAST.

Pixel flashed brightly for a moment before answering, "It says, 'These lands are claimed by Great Protector Wan. If you come in peace, enter and be shown peace. If you come seeking death...' Well, you can probably guess the rest."

"Considering we're contestants on the multiverse equivalent of *The Running Man*, I'm guessing it's safe to assume we'll be considered the latter."

"Without a doubt."

"Figured as much." I summoned my Banshee Racket from inventory and once again turned in the direction we'd been headed. According to the map, the entrance to the open space was just up ahead, pretty much right past where the fog of war was blocking our sight.

We'd barely gone ten paces, however, when my HUD flashed.

Fog of War Disabled.

Despite that, the view ahead of us remained mostly obscured.

"Fog of war disabled," Pixel said. "But fog of smoke still says fuck you all."

They weren't wrong.

Though I could make out the end of the tunnel up ahead, I couldn't see much past it as a haze of smoke hung thick in the air. Even if that wasn't an issue, though, I doubt I would've seen much. Beyond where the dungeon tunnel ended lay nothing but darkness.

Where it had been broad daylight over in the jungle cavern, it was seemingly night in this one – assuming outdoor conditions even applied. Either way, the dungeon was throwing us yet another loop.

I was about to pull a torch from inventory but then thought better of it and grabbed a gl'ohrod instead. I had far fewer of those but they lasted longer and offered a lot more light. If the space ahead was as large as the jungle cavern had been, we'd probably need it.

We made it to the entrance where I stopped to check the map. I didn't see any enemies but made out several rectangular blanks at the far edge of my range. They reminded me of how those huts in the Cloud Warrior village had appeared.

"You seeing this?" I asked.

"Structures of some sort," Boog confirmed. "Be on your guard, Macmac."

"Pretty much what I was thinking."

I snapped the gl'ohrod, activating it and filling the tunnel around us with intense yellowish light. Damn, they really weren't kidding about these things. Just holding it in my periphery was enough to cause spots in my vision.

I waited a moment to acclimate then stepped forward, holding the glowing rod high. The smell of smoke was thick in the air and I was able to make out the forms of burnt trees ahead, standing in the gloom like skeletal sentries meant to warn us off.

Needless to say, that didn't give me the warmest feeling in the world.

"Tread carefully, everyone," Pixel said, their voice barely a whisper. "If my history serves me right, and let's face facts, of course it does, we're in the Five Dynasties era of China."

"And that is?" I asked.

"Just further proof that you should've paid more attention in World History, Tim. Let's just say they were going through a lot of changes during this period, mostly involving killing each other."

"What a surprise. Anything else useful you can share?"

"Yeah. They were also considerably more advanced than those Chachapoyan assholes who kidnapped me."

Great. Just what I needed to...

That thought scattered to the wind as multiple red dots

suddenly appeared near the far edge of my map – having seemingly appeared from inside those structures. After a few moments, there was no doubt they were headed our way.

"Be ready," I said. "Looks like the welcoming committee knows we're here."

"Of course they do," Pixel replied, sounding less than surprised.

One of the dots broke away from the rest, charging our way faster than I'd been expecting. The *thudding* of hooves reached my ears moments later, unmistakable in its cadence even to a guy who'd spent his entire life in the suburbs.

Whoever was headed our way was on horseback.

Not wanting to be caught with my combat chinos down, I dropped the gl'ohrod and pulled one of Apu's claws from inventory. If this newcomer was hoping to run us down, they were in for a nasty surprise instead.

There!

I made out a shape, just barely visible in the smokey gloom. Sure enough, something was racing our way at breakneck speed. I made out hooves, a thick body, and … a winged torso attached to it?

My mind vacillated between Pegasus and a centaur until I realized it somehow seemed to be a bit of both.

"Hit it first, worry about what it is later," I muttered to myself, activating Aim Assist. My HUD could always identify it postmortem.

The reticle appeared in the same instant the beast abruptly changed trajectory, taking a hard left – moving too fast for me to get an easy shot even with the assist.

In the next moment, I spied a spark of light coming from the creature's location. That spark became a dull glow of orange as it lobbed something my way.

"Spread out," I cried to the others as a small glowing object arced through the air.

I had no idea what it had thrown but fortunately it was

Time Chaser

fairly easy to tell where it was going to land, so I simply stepped aside.

Mind you, the concept of *easy* went out the window once the object hit the ground about twenty feet away.

There came a brief clatter of ceramic shattering and then it exploded.

43

BOOM GOES THE STICK

The fuck?!

Thankfully, the explosion was more M-80 than Daisy Cutter. Even so, it caught me by complete surprise – momentarily deafening me from the bang as a small shower of dirt rained down from above.

"Shit!" Pixel cried, just barely audible above the ringing in my ears. "I was afraid of this."

"Afraid of what?" I shouted, trying not to take my eyes off the moving target racing around us at breakneck speed.

"The Five Dynasties period," the FAST explained. "That's right about the same time your species put two and two together and realized gunpowder was the bee's knees when it came to blowing your enemies to bits."

"And you didn't bother to tell us this, why?"

Fuck it. I tried to position my aiming reticle ahead of the centaur creature, trying to anticipate its next move and hoping that 75% accuracy boost would make up for the fact that I probably had no chance of hitting it.

"Because I'm not a fucking fortune teller," Pixel snapped. "Seriously, Tim, it's not like they tell me what we're going to find here."

"Can we please save the tiresome arguments for another time?" Boog asked. "I would prefer we focus instead on something less counterproductive to our shared survival."

"How's this for something to focus on?" I replied, releasing the claw and nailing it with my banshee racket.

The sound it made as it flew off into the darkness wasn't much softer than what that bomb had produced, making me hope the sponsor of the next campground we found was hawking multidimensional aspirin. Sadly, making noise was all it did as the claw didn't even come close to hitting my intended target.

Shit!

In response, the creature lobbed another glowing container at us as it continued to circle our position.

"Everyone...!"

"Allow me, my mate," Boog interrupted.

In the next second the bomb slowed its descent as it approached our location, only to then rocket back in the direction it had come from.

Telekinesis. That had to be it. If so then Drega was right. It *was* the shit.

Her aim wasn't perfect by any means, but the bomb landed close enough to our galloping foe for it to be momentarily staggered.

I probably should've used the distraction to attempt another spike shot, but this was a case where knowledge was hopefully power. So I opted instead to scoop up the gl'ohrod from my feet and chuck it in the beast's direction.

It wasn't a great throw but it didn't need to be. The gl'ohrod hit the ground close enough to our enemy to finally give us a decent look at it, confirming what I'd first glimpsed – the torso of a winged, armored man atop a horse's body.

Not coincidentally, that's also when my HUD finally decided to fill in the details.

Child of Ying Zhao – level 6

Time Chaser

The deity Ying Zhao is a mighty beast said to protect the Garden of the Heavens, whatever the fuck that is. While I personally try to remain agnostic when it comes to claims of divinity, I will say this. Some chicks will literally bang anyone.

I mean seriously, you've heard the story of Zeus transforming into a swan. Didn't matter, his dick still got wet. Well, it's the same deal here. The children of Ying Zhao are the result of this deity having gotten his freak on with mortal women possessed of a major horse fetish. And no, don't ask. You probably don't want to know how that worked.

Anyway, safe to say his kids mostly take after him in the looks department. Their lower halves resemble that of horses, if horses had clawed hooves that is. As for their upper bodies, they're mostly human save for a big pair of wings sprouting from their back.

Don't worry. They can't actually fly. Thank goodness too because that would probably look fucking ridiculous.

The downside, for you anyway, is they can glide pretty goddamned well when they want to.

Oh, and they're fast enough where you're probably already dead if you've been paying attention to this instead of, oh I don't know, actually defending yourself.

But hey, at least being murdered by a badass man / horse / angel hybrid is a hell of an epitaph for your headstone.

Fucking Drega. At least he'd confirmed what my eyes had already told me. This was essentially some kind of Chinese centaur, not that I was about to say it aloud as I didn't want Pixel giving me a freaking history lesson in the middle of this battle.

The important thing to keep in mind was that it was dangerous.

And apparently had friends too.

"Look!" Boog cried in the instant before my ears picked up a whistling sound from afar.

I turned to see multiple pinpricks of light rising high in the air. From the way they were moving, it wasn't hard to guess a volley of flaming arrows had just been fired our way – likely not helped by me practically announcing our position with that gl'ohrod.

Fuck! I'd almost forgotten about those other red dots on the map.

Now the only question was whether this new threat had explosive payloads attached to them as well.

"Boog, any chance we can get an instant replay of what you did with that bomb?"

"I will try, Macmac, but I might not be able to redirect them all."

"Just do your best. As for the..."

My HUD flashed, interrupting me with a chat message.

Pixel: *Not to be a Debbie downer, guys, but maybe it's time to break the habit of discussing our strategies aloud – especially with that horse guy circling us like a shark. That whole knowledge is power thing goes both ways.*

That was a good point. Now to hope I could *type* as fast as I could speak.

Tim, JUST FUCKING TIM: *Good idea. Any chance you can nail that guy with an Acid Ball?*

Pixel: *He's out of range, but if Boog can distract him with a couple of those incoming projectiles then I might be able to nail him with a Shock Bolt.*

Boog: *I shill do my bust.*

I spared a glance her way, worried that maybe those typos meant the nutradisks hadn't absorbed as much of the alcohol in her system as I'd hoped. If so, maybe it wasn't such a great idea to ask her to use telekinesis to...

"Brace yourselves," Pixel cried. "This is gonna be close."

Too bad we didn't have much choice in the matter.

I looked up to find those arrows closing in on us with disturbing speed, forcing me to weigh my options. My sneakers only offered a two-percent chance to dodge, not something I wanted to bank on. Instead I focused on that Party On scroll, preparing to activate it if it became necessary.

But then, at the last second, it was like a giant hand swept across the sky. Those flaming arrows were all knocked to the side, scattered in the direction the horse guy was currently headed as he continued circling us.

She didn't get them all but she got enough where we were no longer in danger from this volley. I didn't fool myself, though. There would be more unless we put a stop to this. But first we needed to take out Ying Zhao's ugly stepchild.

However, it seemed my companions were already one step ahead of me.

Multiple small explosions rang out around the beast as the arrows touched down. None were close enough to actually hit it, but the barrage itself proved more than disorienting enough.

It was perfect timing too, I saw, as another spark had appeared in the creature's hands, no doubt preparing to lob another bomb our way.

"Time to shock this monkey," Pixel cried as a bolt of electricity arced out from their position.

Tim, JUST FUCKING TIM: *A Peter Gabriel pun, really?*

Pixel: *It's not my fault you humans can't appreciate true genius.*

I wasn't about to argue as the spell struck home, nailing both the centaur and the weapon he'd been prepping.

The bomb exploded, engulfing the creature in a combination of fire, smoke, and blood as both of its arms were blown clean off.

A moment later, the child of Yang Zhao collapsed in a heap – its health bar disappearing as quickly as it had appeared.

That was one threat down.

Pixel: *Got him!*

Boog: *Thank goodnes becus I'm out of PSI points.*

Pixel: *What do you mean you're out? How hard did you hit those arrows?*

Tim, JUST FUCKING TIM: *Let's table it for later, guys. We've still got some pissed off archers out there who are probably reloading even as we speak.*

Pixel: *Fair point.*

The gl'ohrod still lay where I'd thrown it. With any luck, our enemies were still using it to track us, because if Boog was out of points as she claimed then we had no defense against another such barrage.

Pixel, no dummy, obviously came to the same conclusion as they lowered their brightness to the point where they appeared less like a street lamp and more like a glow-in-the-dark *Frisbee*.

Pixel: *Sorry. Best I can do, unfortunately. They restrict our ability to just shut it off.*

Tim, JUST FUCKING TIM: *Unless you reboot?*

Pixel: *Pretty much. And I'd just as soon not go through that again.*

Tim, JUST FUCKING TIM: *Me neither. Float on over here and let's see what we can do about that.*

While they approached, I pulled one of the non-magical Cloud Warrior blankets from my inventory. One of those Shrouded Serapes would've probably worked better but I only wanted to hide Pixel from our enemies, not ourselves too.

I draped it over the FAST once they got close enough, effectively dousing their light.

"Stay close," I whispered. "Use your map to follow me."

"You got it. Just warn me before I bump into any trees."

"I'll take it under consideration," I said before turning Boog's way. "Can you still float or is that a no go?"

"I think so, Macmac," she replied. "The non-combat cost is low enough to manage."

"Good. Then follow me and stay quiet."

Though it was a shame to leave a perfectly lootable corpse behind, I had a feeling this was one case where discretion trumped the opportunity for some new plunder.

I turned away from where the discarded gl'ohrod lay. My

goal was simple – try and flank the archers before they saw us coming.

With two of the party able to levitate, that hopefully increased our odds of moving silently.

As for me, it was time to test out how good of a boost those Combat Chinos had given my stealth.

Not a moment too soon either as another batch of flaming arrows lit up the sky.

We got lucky. I'd been worried that those archers might be using either magic or technology to track us. It would be just my luck for Pixel to suddenly announce that this was also right around the time when thermal scopes were first invented.

Fortunately, that wasn't the case as a series of small explosions rang out from back the way we'd come. The only question now was how many more times they'd fire before sending another scout to investigate.

As for me, I'd managed to slip into *stealthed* status relatively easily. Better yet, it was almost like my feet knew where to step as I somehow managed to avoid tripping over anything as we moved.

Not hurting matters was the fact that my eyes had finally adjusted to the dark – enough to realize it wasn't completely pitch black. Similar to the jungle cave, a *sky* loomed over us – this one displaying twinkling stars high above.

Regardless, there was little doubt my Combat Chinos were doing their job. They might've been a fashion nightmare, but until such time as we stumbled upon a mandatory beauty pageant here in the Chase they worked where it counted.

Note to self: don't mention that out loud in case the assholes in charge are taking requests.

Mind you, that didn't mean our passage was completely silent. Pixel wasn't the issue. Even beneath the blanket they managed to ghost my moves seemingly without much effort. Boog on the other hand was starting to worry me.

Not only was she breathing hard enough to negate whatever stealth she might've gained from levitating, but every now and then she'd stumble enough for her feet to touch the ground. Though the sound they made wasn't particularly loud, it made me nervous that I'd look up to see another volley of arrows closing in on us.

Tim, JUST FUCKING TIM: *Are you okay, Boog?*

Boog: *I am quit well, Macmac.*

Tim, JUST FUCKING TIM: *Not to pry or anything but are you sure?*

Boog: *Yes. Please pardon any erors regarding my progriss. I believe I am simply experiencing the last vestiges of those nutradisks upon my degestive tract. Do not worry about me. I am certain the discomfort will pass quickly.*

It was the passing part that had me worried. I didn't want Boog getting another penalty. All the same, I had no idea how those pit stop vouchers would even work out here in the open.

Hopefully she could keep it together long enough for us to take out our attackers. After that, we could get our bearings and she could hopefully *pass* whatever she needed to.

Either way, it wouldn't be long now. I didn't even need the map to tell me we were getting close. I could clearly hear someone barking orders up ahead where dim torchlight could be seen through the lingering smoke and dead trees.

We continued to circle around, making sure to keep our distance – mostly because I didn't want Boog tipping them off before we were ready to attack.

Drawing ever closer, I began to get the sense that the structures on my map were tents rather than permanent dwellings. It was like we'd stumbled upon the aftermath of some terrible battle and these archers along with their centaur buddy were the cleanup crew stationed there to pick off any survivors.

Time Chaser

Gruesome work but, if I had any say in the matter, we'd soon be turning the tide and claiming this camp as our own.

But in order to make that happen we needed to get within spell range.

"Prepare to move out!" a gravelly voice cried. "Give no quarter and take no prisoners."

Tim, JUST FUCKING TIM: *Sounds like they're getting ready to come looking for us.*

Pixel: *Good. I say we wait until these clowns march right past us then ... BAM! Ambush city.*

Tim, JUST FUCKING TIM: *I'm good with that. Boog? How are your PSI points looking?*

There came no answer.

Tim, JUST FUCKING TIM: *Are you okay with the plan, Boog?*

Again there was no response, so I turned around. It took me a second or two in the darkness but I finally spotted her a few yards back. She was standing on the ground, partially hidden by a tree.

My assumption was that she was trying to save up her PSI for the attack since she'd ended up tapping herself out during our last battle.

Pixel: *The fuck's going on with you, Boog?*

Tim, JUST FUCKING TIM: *Hold on. I'm gonna check on her.*

I started back her way, calling up her character sheet to make sure that *intestinally distressed* status hadn't become worse. I wasn't sure if there was an explosive diarrhea status in this game, but now would be a particularly poor time to discover it.

Instead, it was less her status that took me aback as her stats.

Whereas just a short while ago her intelligence had climbed back to 220, now it was down to 140. Worse, her psionics score had plummeted from an insane 310 to only 120.

No, wait. As I watched, it ticked down to 110, then 100. *What the hell?*

Despite it being the height of stupidity, I called out to her nevertheless. "Boog?"

In response, she stepped out from behind the tree, revealing her skull had shrunk to less than half the size it had been.

Just as realization dawned, Boog's *Jekyll and Hyde* status blinked and then disappeared.

Oh no. Not now.

There came a disturbing *schlup* sound as her body continued to rearrange itself, redistributing her mass as her form and stats reverted back to how they'd originally been when we'd first met.

I quickly raised a finger to my lips to shush her before her brutish nature could reassert itself but I was a second too late.

She once again let out that warbling battle cry of hers before holding her axe high and charging ahead, straight into the fray we'd been hoping to avoid.

Guess Drega's description for Jekyll and Hyde had proven accurate after all.

It truly had reversed itself at the most inopportune of times.

Shit on toast!

44

THE DEVILS IN THE DARK

On the one hand, Boog had reverted to her normal self rather than the rampaging yeti beast we feared she might turn into when Jekyll and Hyde next activated.

That Reversal of Fortune effect had proven fortuitous in that regard, a lucky break for us considering what mutagens were capable of.

That it had happened right at that moment, however, was the opposite of lucky. Jekyll and Hyde had a cumulative four percent chance each hour of activating. It had been roughly eight hours since she'd first been infected with it, meaning she'd beaten the odds, so to speak, by transforming at only the thirty-two percent mark.

There had to be a cure for this condition. While intelligent Boog was certainly handy to have around, the uncertainty of this mutagen-born curse had effectively fucked us in the ass.

I doubted it would be the last time.

With our cover blown and Boog racing blindly into the fray, I realized Pixel and I had a choice to make.

We could either stay the course and remain hidden while she took the brunt of the attack, then use the distraction to flank our foes. Alternately, we could join her and risk all of us eating a barrage of explosive arrows.

So, remembering what Pixel had said about thinking outside the box, I quickly opted for option three – a little bit of both.

Pixel: *Oh we are so fucked. Come on, Tim, let's go after her. Maybe we can counterattack before they turn her into a pincushion.*

Tim, JUST FUCKING TIM: *Hold that thought! Prep whatever spell you need to but stay undercover. I have an idea.*

Pixel: *Are you gonna tell me or do I have to play twenty questions?*

Tim, JUST FUCKING TIM: *There's no time to explain. Just buckle up. The ride's about to get bumpy.*

Pixel: *Wait, what do you mean?*

Rather than answer, I turned and grabbed hold of the blanket that was still covering the FAST, cinching the ends like a duffel bag and tossing it over my shoulder.

"What the fuck, dude?" Pixel cried.

"Trust me."

I took off running at full speed in the direction Boog had gone. Back in her original form, she was too fast and agile for me to hope to catch, but I had an answer to that – one that would hopefully draw our enemies' attention.

I cast Burning Beatdown on my Banshee Racket, turning it into a blazing beacon for the next thirty seconds – emphasis on blazing. It wasn't quite as bright as a gl-ohrod but it was pretty damned close, meaning I now stood out like a sore thumb upon the darkened battlefield.

Our enemies could try to target the screeching ghost in the darkness heading their way, or they could turn their ire toward the guy they could now see plain as day.

I was betting they'd opt for the latter.

Up ahead, I heard that gruff voice cry out again – shouting orders to form ranks and take aim.

Moments later, I caught sight of tiny flames sparking to life as they lit their arrows. It wasn't much but it gave me something to lock onto.

I ran that way with everything my legs had to give, using my map to try and gauge when we were close enough to fire back.

"What the fuck's going on out there, Tim?"

"Don't ask," I replied to the FAST still slung over my shoulder. "You *really* don't want to know."

Just a little bit closer.

I couldn't get too close, though. I needed a bit of space to make this work. It was gauging that distance in the dark that was going to prove tricky.

I still couldn't fully make out the forms of either the archers or the officer directing them, but I counted eight sparks in total – all of them seemingly pointed my way. Between that and the commander, that made nine enemies, corresponding to the number of red dots on my map.

Tim, JUST FUCKING TIM: *Get ready!*
Pixel: *For what?*
Tim, JUST FUCKING TIM: *To melt some fuckers into goo, that's what.*

In the very next instant the enemy commander shouted for his archers to fire.

I didn't wait for them. There was no time. At this distance any hesitation on my part would end badly for us both.

Instead I activated Vectorman, the power having thankfully reset with the new day.

Faster than I could comprehend, my body changed course without losing a single step of momentum, putting me on a path that ran parallel to the line of archers instead of directly toward them.

Good for me but bad for them because they all fired less than a second later, sending their flaming arrows flying toward the spot where I no longer was.

A notification popped up in my HUD as a series of explosions rang out behind me but there was no time to read it.

"Take a hard right," I shouted. "That's where they all are!"

I dropped the blanket, releasing Pixel.

The little bug zapper's glow became instantly visible as they flew from the makeshift sack. To the FAST's credit, they didn't hesitate to turn in the direction I'd indicated.

My plan had worked. I'd drawn their fire away from Boog without giving them an easy target to shoot at instead. Now it was time to go on the offensive. I skidded to a halt, knowing we had precious few seconds until the archers reloaded. We needed to be faster.

Thankfully, both my HUD and inventory operated at close to the speed of thought.

I activated Aim Assist and pulled a handful of wolf teeth from inventory, bringing my reserves down to forty seven.

That was fine. I sincerely doubted there was any shortage of mobs, wolves or otherwise, to be harvested. While I wasn't a fan of collecting teeth like some sort of ghoulish tooth fairy, I was less fond of having no ammo for my racket.

For now, I settled my reticle at about the midway point where I'd seen those archers lining up. That left Pixel well outside my line of fire. As for Boog, I couldn't actually see where she was, but the green dot that represented her on my map suggested she was somewhere off to the left and closing fast. So long as I fired now, she would hopefully be untouched by the spread of teeth.

It would have to be good enough.

I let fly even as more sparks appeared up ahead – the archers no doubt reloading.

Whatever orders their unseen commander was shouting was lost as a dozen miniature sonic booms went off.

A part of me had hoped that Burning Beatdown would affect whatever my Banshee Racket shot as well because, let's face facts, a dozen tiny fireballs would be infinitely more terrifying to anything caught in their path, but no such luck.

Oh well, something to remember for next time as the spell finally petered out.

As for the teeth I'd just fired, I doubted any would be lethal by themselves, if they hit at all, but that wasn't the point.

This attack was purely meant to cause enough chaos to hopefully disrupt their discipline.

Moments later I was proven correct as shouts and cries rose in the night air, telling me I'd hit at least a few of my targets. Sadly, I couldn't tell who or how many.

I'd been hoping that maybe their health bars would appear, giving away their exact locations in the darkness, but it wasn't to be. Guess that was too much of a cheat for the overmind to let us exploit.

What I did see, however, was a few of those sparks quickly thrown to the ground. The archers, their shots disrupted, were no doubt ditching their payloads before they went off ... which they then did.

Amazingly enough, that turned out to have an unexpected secondary benefit. The glare from the burning gunpowder provided just enough light for me to make out our enemies.

And that was apparently all my HUD required.

Yoaguai Archer – level 3

On the Earths where they originate, the Yaoguai aren't so much a distinct species as a catch-all term for weird-ass thingamabobs. If you have horns, you're a yaoguai. Tusks? You're a yaoguai too. Doesn't matter if they look nothing alike, they're all yaoguai to the dumb fuck humans who came up with the term.

Not too surprising considering your species is racist as fuck.

It also means you won't have any idea what to expect until you're neck deep in the shit. Do they use magic? Are they super strong. Do they favor the taste of your flabby human flesh?

Alas, there's only one way to find out.

Pity, the guys you're facing are trained archers whose job it is to make sure your ass dies long before you can get close enough to find out.

Drega's wishful thinking was no doubt meant to intimidate me, but it didn't take into account a partner like Pixel. While I was busy firing teeth at the archers, the FAST had moved into range.

Plorp. Plorp.

High pitched screams began to rise from where the archers had made their line as my nose picked up the acrid stench of sizzling flesh.

As usual, the FAST had chosen the messiest way possible to get their point across.

I wasn't about to complain as I prepared to rush in swinging. With any luck we'd finish them off before they could...

However, just then Boog's green dot closed in on their position. I turned that way thinking we could team up, but she was nowhere to be seen.

Where the hell is...?

My unfinished question was answered as a ghostly-white form dropped from the tree branches above and began hacking away like some avenging spirit come to take its vengeance. Guess the darkness was proving less an impediment to her than it was for me.

With an angry screech and two swipes of her axe a pair of archers fell, the audible splatter of blood more than enough to tell me their deaths had been quick but far from clean.

"Reform ranks," a deep voice cried in response. "Do not dishonor our great protector by letting these vermin rattle you!"

The commander it is then.

With Boog and Pixel carving their way through the archers, it made sense for me to turn my attention toward the one calling the shots.

I paused as the ridiculousness of this struck me. There I was, actually planning to go after the leader. Me!

Time Chaser

In what non-videogame universe would I have ever even remotely considered doing such a thing? Hell, back at work I didn't normally feel comfortable talking to anyone above director level, as it felt like going over my boss's head – something Allan would've been quick to agree with.

Yet there I was, acting like some battlefield general seeking out my equal amongst the other side, just like that one time I'd ... well, gotten my ass handed to me.

About five years back I'd been at a company retreat. On our last day there the management of Drakkensoft had taken us out to play paintball, no doubt some HR drone's twisted idea of a team building exercise.

I'd been going through the motions for most of the day, making myself an easy target whenever I thought I could get away with it. Call me a city boy if you will, but slogging through mud and dirt wasn't what I considered to be a fun time. Sadly, with management footing the bill and the company's founders present, it wasn't a situation I could easily walk away from.

That all changed during the final match of the day. It was a standard capture the flag game, with my group assigned to guard our *fortress* from the opposing team. I'd had enough by that point, so I mostly kept my head down as my coworkers acted like the tough guys they weren't – barking orders, opening fire, and generally looking like low-rent *Rambos*.

Then it happened. I was in the center of our fort, close to the flag, when the VP of finance took a hit to the chest. He slumped dramatically to the ground, overacting every moment of it, only to then tell me I was our team's last hope.

Sure enough he was right, for I looked around only to realize I was the only defender who hadn't been tagged out yet.

In that same instant, a guy from our IT team scrambled

clumsily over the wall, probably sensing an easy victory. I didn't think. I merely acted, firing point blank and scoring a direct hit to his ample backside. He'd howled in protest as the referees told him he was dead but I'd barely heard it. It was a small victory, my first of the day, but in that moment I *understood*.

This was what it felt like to be a warrior, *a winner*.

I stood up, suddenly convinced of my own invincibility as I spun in a circle, pumping out shot after shot while I screamed in defiance. I think a few might've even connected with their targets, but it was hard to tell because in the next thirty seconds I was absolutely hammered from all sides – ending the day covered head to toe in welts, my brief moment of victory having quickly turned into one of humiliation.

Not gonna lie. It wasn't exactly my favorite work memory.

However, even as I still found myself turning toward the enemy commander's voice, I realized for perhaps the very first time that it might be a useful one.

Up until this point we'd been lucky. Other than ringing ears and a few abrasions, we'd managed to advance in this cavern without serious injury, despite the enemy possessing weaponry we hadn't been prepared for.

The thing is, Virto had cautioned me to remain humble, saying that letting any victories go to my head was an easy way to end up prematurely expired. In retrospect, I realized that embarrassing memory was in fact a valuable lesson in disguise. Sure, it had sucked at the time, but ultimately there'd been relatively little danger to me.

That wasn't the case here.

I needed to remember that I wasn't some hot shit warrior. Despite my armor, weapons, and magic, I was still a middle manager in way over his head. Hell, the skills listed in my HUD practically screamed that conclusion. I needed to stop playing soldier and remember to take each threat seriously. That was my best chance to…

To get caught up in my thoughts when I really needed to be paying fucking attention.

The memories of my past had consumed me for maybe a second or two, no longer, but that was enough time for a spark of flame much too big to be an arrow to appear in the darkness somewhere ahead of me – the same direction the commander had been screaming orders from.

It took me another moment to realize it was almost certainly the same type of crude bomb that centaur guy had been throwing at us.

Though I couldn't fully make out whoever had lit it, I was able to follow the lit fuse's course as the commander threw it, aiming for where my friends were engaging his own troops – friendly fire be damned.

I watched as it arced up into the air – a high lob meant to cover the distance between him and his targets.

There was no time for me to line up a shot that had any chance of hitting the bomb, not before it landed and exploded.

"Incoming!" I cried as I took off on an intercept course, using every bit of strength and dexterity my legs had to offer as I took off – my eyes locked on nothing but the thrown projectile as it reached its zenith and began to arc downward.

My plan was absolute batshit, but oddly enough in that moment it felt almost reasonable.

I wasn't lying when I said I needed to stop playing soldier. After all, I wasn't one. What I was, however, was a guy who enjoyed an occasional game of racquetball, which was exactly the skill I needed at that moment.

And while the chances of this working were far from guaranteed, I needed to at least try and return this serve back to its sender.

45

BLOWN AWAY

What I was attempting to do was almost certain to earn me yet another lecture in Virto's classroom of incalculable pain, assuming I didn't end up scattered into bite-sized chunks instead.

In truth, I wasn't sure which was the less desirable fate.

To the audience, my actions almost certainly looked like the equivalent of throwing myself onto a live grenade. Fortunately, I didn't give a shit about what any of them thought.

In actuality, my logic was fairly simple. My racket's strings had some give to them, whereas the ground did not. It was effectively a miniature trampoline.

Contrary to popular belief, the goal of racquetball wasn't always to smash the ball with everything you had. Sometimes a nice soft lob was the thing that earned you the next point.

Judging by what I'd seen, these primitive bombs seemed to work on the same general principle as a Molotov cocktail – a lit fuse connected to a fragile shell that was meant to shatter on impact.

My aim was to keep that from happening as I dove through the air, Banshee Racket held out in front of me as the bomb descended toward the unforgiving ground.

I tensed for my likely messy demise as the ceramic jug touched down upon the racket's head. As the bomb made contact, though, I drew my arm downward, slowing the jug's descent – effectively catching it with the strings. Then I quickly reversed the motion, flicking my wrist in the opposite direction.

Had this been my world, there's no way in hell this would've worked. The boom jug was simply too heavy. I might've stopped it from breaking on impact, but my wrist flick would've done nothing more than send it tumbling to the ground, still close enough to blow my head off.

This wasn't my Earth, though, and the weapon in my hands was like nothing I'd ever used there – and not just because squash wasn't my preferred game.

In the next moment the jug was sent rocketing upward toward the treetops, where it exploded harmlessly away from me and anyone else in the immediate vicinity.

My HUD flashed with an achievement notification but I ignored it. I'd done nothing more than buy us a momentary reprieve. Drega's shitty accolades would have to wait.

I'd taken a bit of damage eating dirt as I'd desperately leapt for that bomb but it was minor. Nothing worth wasting a potion on as I scrambled back to my feet.

Tim, JUST FUCKING TIM: *You two handle these archers. I'll see what I can do against the squad leader.*

I didn't bother to wait for a response. I needed to trust that Pixel and Boog had this one in hand.

Turning once again toward where I knew the commander to be, I took maybe three steps in that direction when the back of my left shoulder erupted in piercing pain – driving my health instantly down into the yellow zone.

GAH!

Guess I'd spoken too soon.

Thankfully, it was just a regular arrow, or at least so I assumed since it didn't blow up. Not that it hurt any less.

It was all I could do to activate a healing potion, then try not to choke on the liquid as I stifled a scream. Definitely not the easiest thing to do as the accelerated healing forced the offending arrow painfully from my body.

Goddamn, I hate this fucking game.

Tim, JUST FUCKING TIM: *Maybe handle them a little better!*

Pixel: *Sorry. That one got away from me.*

Boog: *Brrrrrrrrrrrpppppppp!*

Huh?

I had no idea what Boog was trying to say but then I remembered her intelligence was back to normal. There was a good chance that concepts such as mental keyboards were now slightly beyond her.

Whatever, I had more pressing matters to worry about. More importantly I needed to hurry, as up ahead yet another spark of light had appeared.

This time, however, I was finally close enough to make out the details of the creature lighting it. Sadly, what I saw was the opposite of encouraging.

Yeren Regiment Commander: Shen – level 6

The Yeren are hairy wild men native to the forests of what you know as Asia. Both terrifyingly strong as well as territorial, their relationship with mankind has typically been ... antagonistic at best.

That wasn't the case on Earth 11627, however. There, an ancient warlord by the name of Zhu Wan conceived of the batshit plan to not only befriend these ferocious beasts but also conscript them into his army.

I gotta hand it to the guy. That's certainly not the first solution I would've come up with, but you humans have a singular talent when it comes to exploiting the shit out of other species.

I mean, it's like you assholes come across something new and immediately start debating whether it's for food, fighting, or fucking.

Hell, in some cases all three.

The good news is that Zhu Wan's tactics worked, ultimately leading to him being crowned emperor.

Too bad you're not him.

The less good news is that Yeren are effectively eight-foot tall, carnivorous orangutans, possessing both the raw strength to rip off your arms and shove them up your ass but also the intelligence to understand how good of an idea that is.

I didn't really need Drega's help to figure that out. Save for its brown fur, this creature – Shen according to its description – didn't look too dissimilar from what Boog had been in the process of turning into prior to Reversal of Fortune. Sadly, where Boog seemed to prefer the *natural* look, Shen was clad from head to toe in leather armor.

That was daunting but not necessarily a deal breaker, especially since I had a few *armor piercing* rounds in my inventory.

"Face me, outlander," he growled, "so that I might send you to whatever hell you are fated for."

Huh. Shen was surprisingly eloquent for a slobbering ape monster, considerably more so than Boog. Guess an extra two-hundred-thousand years of evolution made all the difference, not that it would hopefully matter in a few seconds as I pulled another of Apu's claws from my inventory.

"No thanks. I've already met my wife's lawyer."

My pithy comeback made and with Aim Assist still active, I let fly – slamming my racket into the claw and sending it screaming Shen's way.

Fast as I thought I was, however, Shen was even quicker on the draw. With no time for a proper throw, he discarded the lit bomb in front of him with one hand while lifting his other arm, as if planning to catch my...

Except he wasn't. One moment there was just his armor clad arm, the next he flicked his wrist and a tower shield instantly unfolded from seemingly nowhere.

The fuck?!

The claw slammed into it with a dull *clonk*, denting the metal but not penetrating it.

That's when his discarded bomb exploded.

It had landed too far away to do any real damage, although it did cause the air between us to fill with dust and smoke. Too bad for me that Shen was apparently more than happy to use that as a convenient distraction.

I sensed more than saw the Yeren's imposing form as he raced toward me. No doubt about it, this night fighting sucked the big one.

There was no time to bemoan my fate, though, as I was only partially able to brace myself before being knocked to the ground by a shield bash – the wall of metal appearing out of the darkness like the front of a freight train.

I landed on my ass, the wind knocked out of me and a few percentage points taken off my health.

Realizing this was a bad place to be, especially since Shen seemed far more adept in the darkness, I quickly scrambled backward. Good timing on my part because a spear blade embedded itself in the ground where my crotch had been just a moment earlier.

Shen's weapon wasn't like those gnome spears, though. It was more like someone had grafted a meat cleaver to the end of a pole. Needless to say, I probably wanted to avoid being hit by it.

I needed to get back to my feet, put some distance between myself and this monster, and then find a way to go back on the offensive.

But if he was able to see better than me in the dark...

Wait! That was it.

If this beast really did have a form of night vision, probably not too big of a stretch to imagine, then maybe all I had to do to even the odds was shed some *light* on this situation.

I pulled another gl'ohrod from inventory and activated it. It was a shame to waste them but probably a fair trade if it saved my ass.

Sure enough, the space around me instantly lit up. In response, Shen growled in anger before shielding his eyes and backing off a bit.

I'd been right about him. Now to hope I hadn't inadvertently made myself an easy target for those archers. Fortunately, a quick peek at my map seemed to confirm their numbers were rapidly dwindling. It seemed my teammates were keeping them well occupied.

That was good because so far I hadn't done much more than momentarily blind Shen. He was still my problem to deal with, and a big problem at that.

I clambered to my feet and rushed in, being mindful of the bigass weapon he was brandishing. Fortunately, he was still semi-dazzled by the light, allowing me to step in and slam my racket into the fingers of his spear hand before he could counter.

Crack!

His weapon fell to the ground, effectively nullifying his ability to skewer me from a distance.

Damage Buff: 1%.

Ooh, I'd almost forgotten about that little bonus. It wasn't much, but I'd take every little bit I could get, especially since cracking my racket across Shen's knuckles had done minimal damage at best.

I started swinging at him like crazy, hoping to keep Shen on the defensive while nudging my own damage bonus up bit by bit.

He managed to block most of my shots with that damnable shield. At his size, the goddamned thing was huge, like carrying around his own portable wall. Nevertheless, I managed to get in a few glancing blows.

Damage Buff: 8%.

No crits yet but that wasn't too surprising. For all I knew, it wasn't even possible to critically hit a shield. Still, little by little I seemed to be whittling away his... URK!

Or maybe not.

Just like that, I'd fallen into the trap of underestimating him, of believing I had the advantage. Quick as a snake, Shen's bruised hand shot out and grabbed hold of my throat – cutting off my airway as he hoisted me off the ground.

"You fight with fire, outlander," he said, spitting out a tooth. "But fire will only get you so far against the might of Shen, chosen elite of Protector Wan."

He began to put on the pressure, squeezing my neck like it was a zit he was intent on popping. Forget my airway, the blood flow to my brain was rapidly being cut off as I almost immediately began to feel woozy.

As if in acknowledgement, my health bar began to steadily tick down until it turned from green to yellow. Oh, and my damage buff reset too, since the universe apparently decided I needed an extra kick while I was down.

I tried to pry him off with my free hand, but I might as well have been trying to loosen a vice grip without the handle. I was reminded of what Boog's strength might've been had Reversal of Fortune not shunted those points to her intelligence instead. Needless to say, if Shen's power was anywhere close to that then I had zero chance of breaking free.

With my airway cut off I had a choice. I could either try and chat an SOS to my friends or figure a way out of this mess while I still had some health left. Sadly, with a few archers still left on the field of battle, I had a feeling I was on my own.

Think, Tim, think!

A solid clonk to his ugly head was my best bet, but Shen apparently realized this too as he dragged me in close, pinning my racket between us as he grinned – his breath foul enough to almost make me wish for death.

I looked down instead, desperately trying to find a way to wriggle free, but my Banshee Racket was stuck tight between...

Wait!

My weapon wasn't the only thing wedged between us. Shen had two more of those boom jugs hanging from a leather bandolier around his chest – both pressed against my racket.

That gave me an idea, a potentially suicidal one but an idea nonetheless.

I quickly turned my attention toward my equipped inventory so I could suck down a mana potion.

Huh. Cherry Kool Aid?

Finally a potion that didn't taste like crap. At least if I was fated to die it would be with a relatively pleasant taste on my tongue.

Shen must've seen the face I made because he momentarily loosened his grip, enough for me to draw a partial breath.

"I will grant you this, outlander. Tell me the words you would have inscribed upon your tomb. Even maggots such as you do not deserve an unmarked grave."

Words? What is he...?

That's when it hit me. The fucker was gloating. He sensed victory and was rubbing it in.

Too bad for him I had every intention of wiping that smile off his face, even if it meant blowing my own off in the process. "Yeah ... tell them ... here lies Tim. He died taking a dumbass Sasquatch with him."

"A what?" Shen asked, inclining his head.

Rather than answer him directly, I used that moment to cast Burning Beatdown.

My racket instantly burst into magical flames. They were harmless to me as the spellcaster but somewhat less so to the fur-covered fucker throttling my ass. However, burning him was mere bonus damage compared to my true goal.

The fuses on both his bombs ignited even as Shen's eyes opened wide with realization.

A moment later I fell to my feet, not only free but practically forgotten as the Yeren commander desperately tried to pluck the bombs from his bandolier.

Woozy as I was, there was no time to catch my breath.

Probably a good thing as clearing my mind would've almost certainly given me enough wherewithal to realize my next move was the height of insanity itself.

As Shen ignored me, I grabbed hold of the tower shield strapped to his arm and stepped directly in front of it. Then, using his own shield as cover, I swung at him with my still flaming Banshee Racket.

Crack-OOOM!

I heard the shatter of ceramic but that was all. My eardrums ruptured as Shen was engulfed in explosive flame.

Sadly, I wasn't much better off as me and the shield – still attached to the remnants of Shen's arm – were both sent flying.

Notifications flashed in my HUD, way too fast for me to read, not that I had any shot of doing so in my current state.

My health bar plummeted, turning red as I landed hard followed by the heavy shield slamming into my face. But at least that last part served to mercifully erase any chance I had at suffering through the pain of being conscious.

46

RINGS AND OTHER AMUSING THINGS

I'm no EMT, but I knew there was a world of difference between taking a nap and suffering from blunt head trauma.

Nevertheless, day two of the Chase had been a long one so far, so I doubted anyone could blame me for not wanting to wake up, at least not right away.

Sadly, whether through spell, potion, or non-combat healing, my HUD popped back to life behind my closed eyes. Needless to say, it was difficult to ignore.

In the space of slowly regaining my senses, I spied a few new achievements, a couple of chat messages from Pixel, as well as status and health notifications – including one at the very end, letting me know that I was about to regain consciousness.

Yeah, that one's real useful.

In addition to all of that I'd also reached fifth level. Cool to know. Alas, any celebration would have to wait. This was probably no time to be lying down on the job. While I was hopeful my last attack had taken down Shen, I hadn't actually confirmed that before blacking out.

"Uhhh."

"Looks like he's coming to," a familiar voice said.

"Macmac open eyes!"

"Give him some room, Boog. Don't make me explain the concept of personal space to you again."

I cracked open my eyes expecting to see stars shining down on me, but instead saw a fabric ceiling hanging overhead. A torch had been lit, revealing that I was inside a large tent. More importantly, my two teammates were both there, thankfully looking no worse for the wear.

Well, okay, Boog's fur was once again stained red with blood but I was beginning to accept that was simply her *look*.

"How long was I out?" I asked, pushing myself to a sitting position. I winced, expecting my head to hurt, but miraculously it didn't. Guess the superfast healing afforded me by this extra-dimensional hellscape had taken care of any headache I might've expected. It wasn't much of a silver lining but I was happy to take it.

"Not too long," Pixel said. "You got nailed with a *Shellshocked* debuff."

"Shellshocked?"

"Yeah. It knocked you out despite the free heal you got from leveling up. Fortunately, it was only a minor debuff. By the way, smart move using that jackass's shield the way you did. Otherwise we'd probably still be mopping you off the battlefield."

I shrugged. "Those archers?"

"Pushing up daisies," the FAST replied. "Same as that furry fuckhead you managed to take down."

Next to him, my other companion grinned at me with lopsided teeth. "Boog did good. Killed enemies but did not drop water on them."

"Drop...?"

"She means she didn't pee on them," Pixel explained.

"Oh. Good job, Boog. That's certainly ... progress."

She nodded enthusiastically at the praise before holding up her hand. "Boog smart now."

A silver ring adorned her middle finger. That was new.

"She got it from a Fortnight achievement box," Pixel explained. "It's called a Brains for Brawn ring."

"Which means?" I replied.

"It means the submind is throwing us a bone when it comes to Boog's *condition*. It adds a ten point fortifying buff to either strength or intelligence, depending on which is the wielder's lower stat. It's not much, but it makes normal Boog a little smarter and should hopefully keep *alternate* Boog a bit more steady on her feet."

I nodded. "Not the worst item they could've given her."

Boog snorted derisively. "Boog not like other Boog. Makes Boog learn stuff that Boog then forgets, like speak with air words."

Speak with...? Took me a second to make sense of it. From the sound of things, Boog still had her memories of the last several hours. However, in her current form she likely was no longer able to make sense of a lot of it – like using our party chat. That would certainly explain what happened during the battle.

It made me wonder if all that lost knowledge would come back to her when she finally changed again.

That was a problem for later, though. For now, I took a quick look at them both via my HUD, only to find that we'd all leveled from that fight. That was certainly convenient.

No doubt sensing I was peeking, Pixel said, "I split my new points evenly between intelligence and PSI."

"Why psionics?"

"Boog's not the only one who got some new goodies. I picked up a power called *Everyone Hates You*. That's a general you, not you specifically."

"Thanks for clearing that up."

"Anyway, it's pricey at a hundred points a pop, but the effect is pretty brutal. It fills one foe with overwhelming rage and paranoia for up to thirty seconds, forcing them to see their allies as enemies."

"That would've been useful in that last fight." I stood and looked around. The space we were in was pretty sizable but I saw only one bedroll. It wasn't hard to guess this had probably been Shen's tent. *Emphasis on past tense.*

"No shit. But that's the way these loot drops tend to work. They reward you with an item that would've been great to have ten minutes ago. It's like a Christmas present and giant fuck you all rolled into one."

"Not the most surprising thing I've heard today."

"Nope. Oh, and speaking of big eff yous, my Acid Ball spell is up to fourth level now."

"That's ... nice." *Sorta.*

"Oh, it's better than nice, Tim. One more level and then the party really starts."

"What do you mean?"

"You've probably already realized this, but when spells and special abilities go up in level they get various perks. Sometimes they'll get more powerful, sometimes they become easier to cast, et cetera. But they usually get an extra special powerup every five levels."

That was certainly interesting to know. Acid Ball was already disturbing as fuck to see in action. I wasn't sure I wanted to think about how it could be even worse. Still, anything to make us stronger. "Did you guys get anything else of note?"

"Boog got funny tasting water."

I turned her way, desperately hoping she wasn't talking about pee again.

Pixel let out a sighing sound. "She received a few extra healing potions as well as one designed to replenish her PSI points." The FAST flitted over to her. "And what did we say about that one, Boog?"

"Boog not allowed to drink."

"Exactly. That's for your alter ego, not you." They then turned toward me again. "I picked up a few more mana potions as well as a couple for curing poison effects. I figured you might want one of those. Interested?"

"Sure."

"Okay, hold on."

A moment later my HUD flashed.

Party transfer initiated.
Potion – Antivenom: 1

"That's handy," I remarked.

"Without a doubt. Only works line of sight, so no trading goodies from miles away, but it definitely beats having to pull things from inventory and actually hand them over."

I made a note to remember that. "So how about you, Boog? Where did you decide to put your new stat points?"

"We were discussing that right before you woke up," Pixel replied. "The big question is what'll help her the most regardless of the form she's in."

"Makes sense. What did you guys settle on?"

"Settle is a strong word," the FAST said. "I was trying to tell her she should put at least some of it into CON."

"Boog want be smart, Pissel," she protested. "Then no need other Boog. Other Boog can stay away."

Huh. She seemed to have it out for her alternate self for some reason. Still...

I turned to her. "Pixel's right, Boog. Putting those points into constitution is probably for the best. But not just some. All of it."

"All?" Pixel replied. "Are you sure?"

"Yeah. That'll fortify her even more than she already is now, while hopefully making her other form a bit ... less squishy."

"I guess I can see your logic. Not to mention it'll help in case smart Boog decides to use our next guild visit as her personal happy hour again."

"I wasn't gonna say that part out loud, but that too. What do you think, Boog?"

"Boog think Macmac mate smart. Smarter than smart Boog!"

"Let's not exaggerate here," Pixel commented.

I shot the FAST a glare.

Rather than continue the debate, Boog went ahead and spent her points, putting all thirty into constitution. That raised her current score to 165, which was nothing to sneeze at. That number would drop by a full hundred points once she changed again. Her alternate form would still be a glass cannon, but that glass would hopefully be a little thicker now.

"All right, that's us," Pixel said. "Your turn, Tim. I'm gonna go out on a limb and guess you didn't open any achievements while you were busy being flat on your ass."

"Can't say it was particularly high on my to-do list at the time."

"Then get to it. Once you're finished we can start looting. We lined up the bodies outside so we can properly split the haul."

"You waited for me? That was nice of you."

"Not really. It was mostly to keep Boog occupied, just in case she got the bright idea to piss all over them."

⌛⌛⌛⌛ ⋄⋅⋄⋅⋄ ⌛⌛⌛⌛

My fifth level stat boost was an easy one. Continuing my quest to pump up my wisdom bit by bit, I threw another 10 points that way. As for the rest, my fight with Shen had almost gone south by sheer virtue of him overpowering me with ease. Much as I didn't aspire to be some sort of melee musclehead, I tossed the remaining 20 points into strength to bolster it a bit. That brought me up to an even 100.

There was no doubt that had some effect as I suddenly felt a bit lighter on my feet. *Twenty percent lighter, apparently.*

It was hard to believe but I was officially now twice as strong as I'd been when this game first started.

While that didn't exactly make me superhuman, I had a feeling it gave me a good shot of breaking two-hundred pounds on the bench press – and I mean real pounds, not whatever BS the *Bowflex* in my garage had been telling me all these years.

Still, it's not like I'd be getting much gym time in this place.

I dismissed all the health-based notifications waiting in my HUD. None of those were relevant anymore. Of far greater interest was a notice that my Vectorman power had risen to level two. According to the updated description, its recharge time had dropped by six hours – potentially making it usable up to two times a day.

Don't get me wrong, eighteen hours was still a long time to wait but that was twice now it had saved my ass. There was no doubt this was one power I needed to keep working on.

That done, I next turned to the two new achievements waiting to be opened.

"All right, Drega, lay it on me."

Achievement unlocked! Return to Sender!

You threw yourself in harm's way in an attempt to deflect a fucking bomb, a move that was equal parts stupid and suicidal. Yet not only did you survive but you managed to take almost no damage in the process.

Won't lie, that's actually kinda badass.

Listen up, monkey boy, because that's what I've been talking about. That right there is the sort of shit that earns chasers their own fan club, or at least other chasers. Too bad you're otherwise about as interesting as watching paint peel.

Like, seriously, dude, come up with a victory dance or maybe get a cool tat. Give us something to make us love you, damn it!

Reward: **1 STD supply box. 1 Fortnight gear box.**

That was ... weird, almost as if Drega realized I was purposely trying to stay out of the limelight. Mind you, it was also possible it was just him being his regular asshole self. Probably best to not read too much into it.

Time Chaser

There was a certain paranoia that came with purposely trying to go unnoticed, one that could make a person think a giant spotlight was shining upon them. It was kinda like the first time Deb had ever asked me to pick up tampons for her at the store. Back then, it had felt like everyone was judging me as I walked up to the checkout lane, despite nobody actually giving a shit.

This was probably the same deal. Yeah, I needed to stop worrying about it before I became freaked out enough to do something stupid.

Achievement unlocked! Boomshakalaka!

Now you're cooking with gas, or maybe I should say gunpowder. Either way, you bested a foe by blowing them ... to bits that is, and in melee range no less. You have officially discovered the awesome power of explosives.

The question now is where do you go from here?

Will you devote yourself utterly to this new discipline, becoming the J. Robert Oppenheimer of the Chase? Or will you merely end up blowing your own face off, kinda like a liquored up hillbilly with a fondness for cherry bombs and cheap booze?

Only time will tell, but the smart money is on the latter.

Reward: **1 Fortnight supply box.**

Drega's idiotic ramblings aside, it looked like a decent haul for my troubles. Now it was time to see what I'd earned.

First up was that STD supply box. Those usually contained the basics and this one was no different. As it poofed away, I found four more gl'ohrods to replace the ones I'd used, another half dozen torches, and three healing potions.

None were unwelcome.

Next, I pulled up the gear box that had come with Return to Sender. As it disappeared in a shower of sparkles, a small jewelry box remained floating in the air. A moment later it opened of its own accord, revealing what looked to be an engagement ring.

I couldn't help the twitch that escaped my left eye. It was

like a larger, much gaudier version of the ring I'd proposed to Deb with. I swear, no matter which way you turned, this goddamned game was constantly finding some new way to stick a knife in and twist it.

Bling Ring (minor)
A snazzy ring meant to jazz up a boring motherfucker.
Hint: that's you.
+10 to Charisma

Okay then. So apparently they were starting to code the prizes to the achievement descriptions now. Guess that shouldn't have been a surprise.

Whatever. No way was I passing up a free buff or showing them any sign of weakness. If they expected me to get all weepy at the sight of a magical cubic zirconia, they had another think coming. I took the ring and slid it onto the pinky finger of my left hand. Ridiculous as it looked, at least it was sort of out of the way there.

That left me with one more box to open, which of course meant another chance for the assholes in charge to try and kill my spirit bit by bit.

Who knew what it would be this time? Maybe there'd be a box of Jeremy's baby teeth, enchanted so I could use them as ammo.

Probably best to never say that one aloud.

I tried not to let my imagination run too wild as I focused on making the box open.

The first things to appear were three additional mana potions. I wasn't about to argue against getting those, especially since I was still a one-shot wonder with the lone spell in my arsenal.

Rather than a whole slew of other gear appearing, instead only a single additional item winked into existence before me.

Huh. Pretty chintzy for a Fortnight box.

The final prize from this enchanted *Crackerjack* box was an enamel lapel pin. The design was your basic smiley face but instead of a yellow circle it was within a black bomb, complete with lit fuse.

Skill Pin

You have skills. Wear pins like this to enhance them. Yay, now you suck a little bit less.

+1 level to Crafting: Alchemy

+1 level to Crafting: Explosives

Hmm. The way the description was worded seemed to imply I could expect to see more items like this down the line. Maybe it was the chaser equivalent to those stat patches Pixel seemed to be collecting.

Nevertheless, any boost was a welcome one, although I couldn't help but think smart Boog might benefit more from this once she was back, especially since she was holding a good chunk of the stash we'd swiped from those leprechauns.

However, since smart Boog wasn't currently there and she had no clothes to pin this onto anyway, that was a bridge I could cross at another time.

I attached it to my sweater for now. It was probably intended to make me look ever so slightly stupider than I already did, but I didn't care. It was a cool little pin, something I might've stuck to my laptop bag back home.

"Suck it, Drega. I actually like this one."

"What was that?" Pixel asked.

"Nothing. Just tempting fate. Now how about we go loot some corpses?"

47

ACCESSORIES TO CRIME

Tim, JUST FUCKING TIM: *Don't forget she's the one with the alchemy lab.*
Pixel: *Yes, a fact that scares the ever living shit out of me, but more so when she's like this. Listen, Tim, I'm not saying she can't have it at all. I'm just saying, maybe not right now – at least not until her IQ shoots up by a hundred-and-fifty points again.*
Tim, JUST FUCKING TIM: *You're probably right.*
Pixel: *You know I am. Besides, it's for her own good. Last thing we want is for her to take the initiative and end up blowing herself to smithereens ... or us for that matter.*

It was probably supremely uncool to exclude Boog from our chat as we prepared to divvy up the spoils, but all the same it felt kinda necessary.

With any luck, that extra ten INT from her ring would serve to temper her impulsiveness, but the bottom line was this last battle wasn't the first time she'd proven to be a loose cannon.

In short, it was probably best for someone else to hold onto the gunpowder, at least for now.

Fortunately for Pixel and I, Boog seemed to have no interest in it once we started looting the corpses, deeming it *bad smelly dirt*.

Time Chaser

Just to be fair, I offered her Shen's spear in return, a weapon my HUD identified as a *podao*. It had a 10 point strength boost attached to it. That was less than her jawbone axe, but it compensated with its far greater reach. Either way, it wasn't a bad thing to have a backup weapon.

Speaking of which, bows and arrows were probably a bit ahead of her time, but I made sure she and I both took one of the former. Though none were magical, they could still prove handy in a pinch. Splitting up the arrows left us with about three dozen each, hopefully enough for some target practice which, Aim Assist aside, I probably sorely needed.

Their armor was likewise unenchanted but I stuffed it all into my inventory anyway, save for a leather vest which I slipped on beneath my sweater. It would hopefully serve until such time as Loom o' Doom allowed me to stitch together a replacement shirt.

I tried talking Boog into wearing some of the armor too, but that ended with her throwing a fit, claiming it was itchy and smelled bad. So, I figured it was best to table that for now, at least until I could see if perhaps smart Boog was more amenable to the idea.

As for the gunpowder, each of the archers had a small jug's worth attached to their belts. One had gotten ruined thanks to Pixel's acid spell, leaving us with seven. I took three and the FAST took the rest.

That left one final item of interest – Shen's tower shield. I pried it from his severed arm and took a closer look.

SK Accessory – Collapsible Shield

This handy dandy little item is indispensable for those who don't want the burden of lugging around heavy armor, but are smart enough to realize their bodies are nothing but organic water balloons waiting to be popped.

Sure, you could always run for cover when danger presents itself, but why bother when you can get the cover to come to you instead?

One flick of the wrist and two seconds is all it takes for this sturdy shield to unpack to its full size, offering enough defense to protect you from anything shy of your mom's raging syphilis.

-10 to Dexterity when deployed

"What's it mean by SK accessory?" I asked.

"It means that it's a lucky find," Pixel said, sounding impressed. "Put it on and see for yourself."

"I'll try," I said, fiddling with the ungainly hunk of metal.

"Use your *right* arm, y'know in case that wasn't clear."

"Kinda figured that."

"Just making sure."

I slid my hand through the thick leather strap, not the easiest thing since the shield itself was still Shen-sized. However, just as the strap touched the edge of my SK, the whole thing flared with light and vanished.

A notification promptly appeared in my HUD.

Processing.

It was replaced a moment later with *SK Accessory Accepted*, then *SK Accessory Ready*.

My SK began to tingle from beneath my sweater sleeve, so I rolled it up to find the smooth bronze of the bracelet was now interrupted by a band of black circling it at one end.

"All right, now activate it," Pixel said.

"How?"

"What did the description say to do?"

I consulted it again then started flicking my wrist up and down.

"As amusing as it is to watch you jerk off an invisible dick," Pixel remarked after a few seconds, "maybe try putting some focus into it."

"What mean to jerk off...?"

"Not now, Boog," I hissed.

I turned my thoughts toward activating the shield then flicked my wrist again. A moment later it unfurled from seemingly nowhere, almost nailing me in the face in the process. I'd probably need to pay attention to the angle of my arm before using this thing.

"Do again, Macmac!" Boog cried with a squeal of glee.

"Maybe later."

For now, I was too busy checking out this new accoutrement.

Once the shield was fully formed, I realized a couple things had changed about it. Gone was the leather strap as well as any damage the shield had sustained. It was now connected directly to my SK and in pristine condition. Better yet, it was now sized for me as opposed to an eight-foot-tall Sasquatch monster, making it considerably less unwieldly.

It was still heavy and a bit awkward, hence the dexterity penalty, but not too bad overall.

I focused on it again to find that its description had been updated with some new information.

According to the text, the shield was capable of absorbing a set amount of damage before becoming inoperative. It would then regenerate at the end of each day, allowing it to be used again.

As if in response to this revelation, a secondary health bar appeared within my HUD, one nearly as wide as my own.

"Holy crap. This is pretty fucking cool."

"I agree," Pixel replied after likewise reading the description. "From the sound of things, it's about as close to a get-out-of-death card as you're gonna find on this stage. Doubly so if the assholes here keep lobbing shit at us."

While I had little doubt this new shield would be handy against spears, arrows, and maybe even some spells, I wasn't quite so confident when it came to explosives. I didn't fancy being shellshocked again or worse.

Still, it was a welcome addition. My sweater was pretty badass, no doubt about it, but I wasn't sure it counted as armor.

Time Chaser

And while it was true that healing potions could erase just about any damage taken, those injuries still hurt like hell.

If there was a chance to avoid being sliced and diced as we continued onward then I was all for it.

"All right. I think that's it. Everyone ready to head out?"

"Not so fast, Tim," Pixel said. "There's still a few things left to take care of."

⌛⌛⌛⌛ ⋅⋄⋅⋄⋅⋄⋅ ⌛⌛⌛⌛

I didn't mind ransacking Shen's tent, but of course Pixel had to then remind me of Loom o' Doom.

Needless to say, Shen was a mess by the time I was finished. On the upside, I did manage to snag a decent number of teeth and tusks from those yaoguai archers – finding about a dozen in total that could be used as projectiles.

Little by little I was amassing a decent stash of ammo for my racket.

On the flipside, it was like I was slowly turning into the grim reaper of teeth and hair. Of all the things I might one day tell Jeremy about this place, that would probably not be part of it.

At least the darkness and perpetual smoke helped to mask a bit of the...

"Seems we've got company," Pixel announced.

"Boog see blue specks!"

I raised an eyebrow but then turned my attention toward the map. I'd taken a quick look before checking out our new loot. At the time, we'd been the only living beings of note within range, aside from a few scattered white dots off in the distance.

It appeared things had recently changed, though. A group of blue dots – presumably chasers and their FASTS – had appeared to the northeast, near the very limits of the map's range. There were four, no, make that five of them.

I felt my butt cheeks involuntarily clench. I'd never considered myself to be a people person, but it's not like I'd ever had a problem meeting anyone new. However, in the space of less than two days the Chase had turned an otherwise everyday occurrence into something even an extrovert would fear.

So far my encounters with other chasers had been limited to circumstances in which one or more of us were constrained in some way. This would potentially be my first encounter in the *wild*, so to speak.

"Think they've noticed us?"

"No doubt about it," Pixel said. "At this point in the Chase everyone's perception is going to be within spitting distance of each other. Also, look at how they're huddled right there at the far edge of the map. I'd bet good money they're checking us out, trying to figure out what we're up to."

"Like we're doing?" I replied, trying to pull myself together. "Don't you think that sounds a bit paranoid?"

"Knowing the way you humans treat one another?" the FAST responded. "No offense, Tim, but erring on the side of caution sounds better to me than blithely assuming they're down with the whole *Band of Brothers* vibe."

"New friends?" Boog asked hopefully.

"That remains to be seen," I said. "I count five of them."

"Same," Pixel replied. "I'm guessing that means one of them lost a FAST along the way. Regardless, that gives them a numbers advantage over us."

"What should we do?"

"The PVP ban is still in effect, although for how much longer remains to be seen. I say we play it cautiously, maybe head west for a while and see how they respond."

I doublechecked my map, turning my attention toward the ascension ring marker we'd gotten from beating Apu. The ring we'd been chasing was almost directly north of us now. I watched as it pulsed once.

"Sound like a plan?" Pixel asked.

"Hold on a sec," I said.

The ring marker pulsed again.

No doubt about it. It wasn't much, but we were finally starting to close the distance. I watched it again, this time counting the seconds between pulses. A little under four Mississippi's. "No."

"No what?"

"We're not taking any detours, not now. That ascension ring is north of us, so that's the direction we head."

"Are you sure?" Pixel asked. "Because if they decide to go east then we're almost definitely gonna meet up at some point."

"Yeah, but if we run, they're going to know it, and if they do turn out to be hostile..." I let the statement hang in the air a moment before continuing. "I say we act like nothing's changed. If we show them their presence doesn't bother us, it'll hopefully send a message."

"Yeah, that we're trusting idiots."

"I was thinking more like we'll look confident."

"Fine. Confident idiots."

"Look, even if they are assholes, we'll be fine so long as the PVP ban stays up. And if they're not, well, making new allies wouldn't be the worst thing in the world. Heck, maybe we'll even get lucky and Aiko or Paki will be among them."

"Who?"

Oh yeah, I probably should've mentioned them. "They're chasers I met back at Virto's. Sorry. Meant to tell you guys but I got distracted by babysitting Boog."

"Macmac and Boog sit and have baby?" she replied.

"Well, that's certainly a lot to unpack," Pixel muttered.

I shot the FAST a glare. "No, Boog, that's not what I meant. I... You know what, I'll explain it later." I turned back toward Pixel. "Is it safe to assume Haniah gave you the same speech Virto gave me, the one about guild members being off limits."

"She may have mentioned it."

"Good, because if any of these guys are with The House of

... are Virto's, then technically we should be okay, PVP ban or not."

"It's that technically part I'm not sure I trust."

"I'm not saying we shouldn't be on guard. All I'm saying is if we run now, there's no way of knowing how badly we might get sidetracked."

"Maybe."

"There's no maybe about it. This place is designed to assfuck us the second we bend over and you know it."

"Interesting imagery aside, you're not wrong, Tim. So you think we should stay the course?"

I nodded. "If we run into these guys and they give us dick vibes, we can figure out a way to ditch them, but for now we should be okay. So there's no reason for us to..."

"Boog's feet stuck!"

"I'll help you in a second, Boog," I said dismissively. "Give us a moment here."

"Um, Tim, I don't think she's exaggerating."

"What do you mean...?"

I trailed off, however, as the realization hit me. My feet had suddenly become stuck in place, as surely as if I'd stepped into a human-sized glue trap.

Oh no. Not now.

"ARE YOU EXCITED? BECAUSE I SURE AS SHIT KNOW I AM! IT'S TIME FOR OUR NEXT LIVE UPDATE. AND TRUST ME WHEN I SAY, IT'S THE ONE YOU'VE ALL BEEN WAITING FOR!"

Shit!

"You were saying?" Pixel remarked.

I shot them a dirty look as Drega continued.

"THIS GOES DOUBLE FOR ANY CHASERS LISTENING IN. YOU MIGHT WANT TO STOP WHATEVER IT IS YOU'RE DOING AND PAY ATTENTION."

"**Do they really have a choice?**" Plegraxious replied.

"NO, PLEG, PROBABLY NOT," Drega said with an

assholish chuckle. "**REGARDLESS WE HAVE SOME BIG NEWS TO SHARE. SO RATHER THAN BEAT AROUND THE PROVERBIAL BUSH I'LL JUST COME RIGHT OUT AND SAY IT. WHETHER YOU'RE HOME OR ON THE GAME FIELD, GET READY TO SLEEP WITH ONE EYE OPEN BECAUSE PLAYER VERSUS PLAYER IS OFFICIALLY ON!**"

Raucous cheering filled the air. From the sound of it, you'd have thought we were at the *Super Bowl* and the game had just gone into overtime.

"**WHY DON'T YOU FILL US IN ON THE DETAILS, PLEG, AS ONLY YOU CAN?**"

"**Gladly, Drega**," Plegraxious replied, although his tone sounded far less excited than the host's.

"What is it with those two?"

"Huh?" Pixel replied.

Before I could answer, both mine and Boog's SK's activated. Beams of light shot forth from them as well as from Pixel, producing an IMAX-sized screen for our viewing *pleasure*.

"**We're roughly halfway through the allotted time for Stage One. As expected, we've seen a huge surge in ascensions within the last twelve hours. Not every chaser was lucky enough to make it through, but enough are now enjoying the hospitality of our sponsors for it to be official.**"

"**AND HOW ARE THOSE NUMBERS LOOKING, BUDDY?**"

"**As of last count, five-thousand-and-one chasers will officially be moving on to Stage Two, although we certainly expect that number to rise.**"

"**WOW!**"

"**Exactly what I said, Drega. While it's not unexpected to see a surge in day two, it's always astounding how quickly those numbers balloon.**"

"**TRUE ENOUGH, BUT REMEMBER, FOLKS, THIS IS ONLY STAGE ONE. WE'RE PRACTICALLY HANDING**

THESE MONKEYS VICTORY ON A SILVER PLATTER, AT LEAST COMPARED TO WHAT THEY'LL FIND ON LATER STAGES."

Goddamn, what a bunch of pricks these two were.

"SO HOW'S THE REST OF THE PLAYING FIELD LOOK?"

"Hilariously grim. An additional seven-hundred and ninety-three chasers have been expired since our last live update, with two of them meeting their end while under penalty. Oh well, you know the old saying. You can't make an omelet without erasing a few realities."

Son of a bitch. It was bad enough that these assholes had just casually erased billions of lives but to have the nerve to crack jokes about it.

Again, if this was what passed as evolved in the multiverse, then maybe it was for the best if humanity never made it there.

I shook my head, instantly reminded that the year 2541 was apparently fated to hang over mankind's head like the Sword of Damocles.

Now was not the time to bemoan some future calamity, though, as the dipshit duo running this show weren't finished.

"HOW ARE THEIR FAST UNITS HOLDING UP?"

"Better than their chasers, if just barely. One-hundred-and-seventy-six have been permanently offlined, with nearly nine-hundred now sitting at one or more expirations."

"DAMN! ONE MIGHT BE SO BOLD AS TO SAY IT HASN'T BEEN A *SLOW* DAY FOR THE FASTS OUT THERE."

"That's right, keep laughing, assholes," Pixel said, their voice so low I barely heard them.

"That brings our total body count to one-thousand-three-hundred-and-eighty-nine chasers, with just over thirty-six-hundred left in the field."

"THAT'S THIRTY-SIX-HUNDRED CHASERS WHO ARE NO DOUBT HUNGRY TO FIND AN ASCENSION

Time Chaser

RING. ONLY PROBLEM IS, THERE'S NOT ENOUGH SLOTS LEFT FOR THEM TO ALL ASCEND."

"Whatever will they do, Drega?"

"I'M GLAD YOU ASKED, PLEG. FOR STARTERS, THEY MIGHT WANT TO QUIT DICKING AROUND AND GET A MOVE ON. TEMPTING AS IT MIGHT BE TO DRINK THEMSELVES INTO A STUPOR AT A GUILD HALL, TIME'S A WASTING."

I inclined my head, wondering if that was merely a coincidence. Had to be. No way could Boog be the only chaser who'd availed themselves to a guild's *hospitality*.

If not, that could mean they were paying more attention to us than I... *No!* Drega had even said it himself. I wasn't interesting enough for the spotlight.

But was it possible that maybe Boog was?

I hadn't considered that. It was almost a given that the proto-human chasers were amongst the minority here. Perhaps the audience was viewing them as a sort of novelty. And if that were the case then might Boog be even more so now that she'd been mutated?

That was one rabbit hole I wasn't sure I wanted to go down. *Fortunately* for my peace of mind, Drega wasn't finished.

"HURRYING THINGS ALONG IS A GOOD IDEA," he continued, **"DON'T GET ME WRONG, BUT THERE'S ONE MORE THING THE CHASERS STILL OUT THERE CAN DO TO UP THEIR ODDS OF ASCENDING."**

"Might that include ... oh, I don't know ... thinning the herd?"

"INDEED IT MIGHT, PLEG, ALTHOUGH I QUESTION WHETHER THAT'S THE PROPER TERM FOR A GROUP OF EARTHERS. LET'S SEE... HERD, GROUP, GATHERING, SOUNDER. NOPE. NONE OF THEM REALLY SEEM TO FIT THIS BUNCH. HOWEVER, THERE'S A NAME THEY USE FOR A PARTICULAR GROUP OF EARTH CREATURES KNOWN AS CROWS..."

Time Chaser

Don't say it.

"THEY CALL IT ... A MURDER. I DON'T KNOW ABOUT YOU, PLEG, BUT I KINDA LIKE IT, ESPECIALLY SINCE THAT'S EXACTLY WHAT THEY'LL NEED TO DO FOR THE NEXT DAY AND A HALF IF THEY WANT TO MAXIMIZE THEIR CHANCES OF SURVIVAL."

"And if they don't?"

"THAT'S THEIR PREROGATIVE, OF COURSE, BUT I'M WILLING TO BET THEY DON'T ALL FEEL THAT WAY. SO WHAT'S IT GOING TO BE, CHASERS? YOU DON'T HAVE TO DECIDE NOW, BUT I WILL SAY THIS. AT SOME POINT YOU'RE GOING TO RUN INTO ANOTHER CHASER WHO ACTUALLY WANTS TO WIN. AT THAT POINT YOU CAN EITHER TAKE IT LIKE A BITCH AND KISS EVERYTHING YOU'VE EVER LOVED GOODBYE, OR YOU CAN CHOOSE TO WANT IT MORE THAN THEY DO!"

48

STAR POWER

Drega's words hit me in the gut like a steel-toed boot.

While I had no innate desire to kill anyone, I was forced to admit it was starting to get easier – at least with the inhuman mobs. The human ones, somewhat less so, but I was doing what needed to be done.

That didn't make it right, but it was probably better than lying to myself and trying to pretend otherwise.

The truth was, if someone offered me a way to ensure the rest of the Chase involved nothing but wolves, goblins, and various other monstrosities, I'd take that offer in a hot second.

Still, if I was forced to fight against human mobs again – and let's face facts, it was probably inevitable – at least I was fairly certain I wouldn't freeze up. Hopefully anyway. After all, there was an *us or them* aspect to all the mobs we'd run into so far. While I didn't think it impossible to talk our way out of a fight, so far that simply hadn't been an option.

Player versus player was a whole other ball of wax, though. There was something off about the mobs here, some way the overmind had futzed with their brains to make them think all this was real. I had no insight into much beyond that, other than the poor fools serving as cannon fodder here seemingly had no choice in the matter.

It was different with chasers, however. Far as I was aware, we were all free to make our own decisions, for better or worse. That said, logically it made sense that we try and stick together. After all, the submind, overmind, Committee, et cetera were our true enemies.

The thing was, Pixel had been right. It was the height of stupidity to assume that would be the case. For starters, this game was literally designed to pit us against each other, especially the closer it got to the end of a stage. But perhaps even more important was basic human nature. Ten thousand of us had been dragged here against our wills, but the chances that we all had the same sensibilities and ethics were effectively zero.

Hell, by virtue of numbers alone we were guaranteed to have at least a few bloodthirsty psychos in the bunch. I mean, for Christ's sake, the very first guy I'd met had tried to fucking eat me.

It was that knowledge which landed in my gut like a ten pound weight. I could justify the killing of mobs, even human ones. But at some point it was very likely I'd be in a situation with another chaser, another person with free will, and realize only one of us was going to walk away.

If I didn't step up at that point, if they wanted it more than I did, then that was it. I would die without ever getting to lay eyes on my boy again.

That meant I had to want it more. I *needed* to want it more.

No matter how much I didn't.

It was funny in a way. Drega's offhanded comment, no doubt more intended to rile up the audience, had managed to unravel me more than every single one of his purposeful attempts.

I couldn't let them know that, though.

So, as Drega and Plegraxious continued to drone on, I

focused on feigned disinterest as if I couldn't wait for them to shut up.

At least in that regard it wasn't too far from the truth.

"**...And don't forget that sweet experience bonus that comes from expiring your fellow chasers.**"

Wait, what?

"**GREAT POINT, PLEG! ALLOW ME TO EXPAND UPON THAT FOR THOSE WHO ARE PERHAPS ON THE FENCE ABOUT BATTLING THEIR FELLOW EARTH MONKEYS. SURE, YOU COULD LET LITTLE THINGS LIKE MORALITY AND ETHICS STAND IN YOUR WAY, BUT IT BEARS MENTIONING THAT STARTING IMMEDIATELY EVERY CHASER WILL BE WORTH TWENTY-FIVE PERCENT MORE XP THAN MOBS OF THE SAME LEVEL.**"

"**Twenty-five percent? Wow. That's not bad, but what if they were, say, truly devoted to their fellow man – an honest-to-goodness pacifist if you will?**"

The audience chuckled in response.

"**A PACIFIST?**" Drega replied, sounding absolutely horrified. "**WELL, FOR STARTERS I'D HAVE TO WONDER HOW IT'S POSSIBLE THEY'RE STILL ALIVE TO EVEN HEAR THIS.**"

This time the audience howled, despite the joke not being any funnier.

No doubt about it. Plegraxious was very much second fiddle in this shit show. Hell, he wasn't even the *Pepsi* to Drega's *Coke*. More like the knockoff store brand.

There wasn't time to ponder that further, however, as Drega wasn't finished.

"**ALL RIGHT, FINE, YOU TWISTED MY LIMBIC LOBE. HOW ABOUT THIS? THAT TWENTY FIVE PERCENT XP BOOST IS ONLY GOOD UNTIL THE CLOCK HITS SIX HOURS LEFT.**"

"**I'm listening.**"

"THEN, FOR THE NEXT FIVE HOURS AFTER THAT, IT GOES UP TO ... A FIFTY-PERCENT BONUS!"

The crowd gasped and oohed right on schedule.

"That's pretty good, I suppose."

"YOU SUPPOSE?" Drega replied with mock surprise, playing it up.

"It's just ... I think we can do better."

"THAT SOUNDS LIKE A CHALLENGE TO ME! SO BE IT. BUT JUST REMEMBER, YOU MADE ME DO THIS. LISTEN UP, CHASERS! BEING THE LAST ONE OUT THE DOOR IS RISKY, TRUE. BUT THAT RISK COMES WITH REWARD BECAUSE THE FINAL HOUR OF THIS STAGE, WILL OFFICIALLY BE ... DOUBLE XP MADNESS!"

More raucous cheering ensued, the audience practically howling for blood as Drega played this revelation for all it was worth.

It made me sick.

I knew full well the allure of leveling up. And now these assholes were dangling a bloody carrot in front of us that I was certain some wouldn't be able to resist. After all, the risks of being on the field as the timer counted down to zero were nothing to sneeze at, but now they were adding ample motivation to stick around.

Thanks but no thanks. "Remember what you said about us camping out close to that ascension ring and doing some last minute grinding?"

"Yeah," Pixel replied.

"I'm thinking we should probably ixnay that plan."

"Starting to lean that way myself, especially since I have a feeling they're not done sweetening the pot yet."

"What do you mean?"

Before Pixel could answer me, Plegraxious jumped back in.

"That's not even mentioning the fact that you get to keep

whatever loot you find on their still twitching corpses, just like with any other mob."

"BUT THERE'S STILL ONE MORE PERK TO MENTION, THE CHERRY SITTING ATOP THIS SUNDAE BLOODY SUNDAE," Drega said. **"SOME OF YOU MAY HAVE ALREADY REALIZED THIS, BUT THERE'S ONLY ONE WAY TO LEVEL UP YOUR SKs... AND THAT'S TO CLAIM ANOTHER CHASER'S AS YOUR OWN!"**

The crowd absolutely lost their shit, becoming near deafening despite not a single one being visible. I swear, you'd have thought Drega had just pulled an *Oprah* and announced everyone was getting a new car.

But no, they were celebrating us killing each other.

"Hold on. That makes no fucking sense," I cried.

"What was that?" Pixel shouted back.

"I said it makes no sense. I just upgraded my damned SK."

Finally the howls and cheers began to subside, making it easier to hear one another.

"No," the FAST replied. "You added an accessory to it. Your SK is still first level. Take a look."

I did a quick check of my HUD and sure enough they were right, although that revelation was somewhat less damning than my next question. "Did you know about all of this?"

"Not about the XP bonus. That one's as big a surprise to me as it is to you, at least so far as I can remember."

"What about our SKs?"

There came a pause but then they said, "Yeah. I knew about that one."

"So why didn't you say anything? What happened to knowledge being power?"

Pixel made a buzzing sound then said, "Think about it for a second, Tim. I mean really think about it. Is that the sort of knowledge you'd have wanted to know?"

"Wanted? No, not really, but it sounds like maybe we *needed* to know about it."

"And now you do, right on time to actually need it."

"Yeah, but..."

"Seriously, Tim, what good would knowing have done you earlier, other than maybe ruining last night's sleep?"

"It wouldn't have..."

"Sure it would. You can lie to yourself, but remember I know you inside and out."

I didn't have an answer to that. As far as surprises went, this one was like the opposite of Christmas. Nonetheless, that didn't mean Pixel was wrong. Having this sitting in the back of my head probably wouldn't have helped. The truth was, I really didn't need more worries to burden myself with. None of us did.

"Boog find enemies. Kill enemies and then get stronger!"

Okay, maybe it was just *me*.

"And this is yet another reason I didn't say anything," Pixel remarked.

"Zip it," I told the FAST. "We're not hunting chasers, Boog. End of discussion."

"Why? Scary voice man say they now..."

"They're *not* our enemies. At least not until they prove otherwise."

She appeared to think this over. "Then Boog kill?"

"Um ... let's cross that bridge when we come to it."

"What bridge?"

"It's a ... you know what, never mind. Just don't murder anyone unless I say otherwise."

"Just don't murder any *chasers*," Pixel corrected. "Words matter."

"Yeah, what *Pissel* said."

"But...," Boog started to protest.

"No."

"But, Macmac..."

"Enough, Boog. Please just do what I say, otherwise I ... I won't be your mate anymore."

Goddamn, I can't believe I just said that. I shot Pixel a glare, practically daring them to make some asshole comment.

"No!" Boog cried. "Boog good mate. Listen to Macmac!"

And suddenly I felt like a complete piece of shit.

As this was going on, Drega and Plegraxious once again took a moment to plug the Time Chasers home edition, because why the fuck not. I swear, all of this, our lives, our potential deaths, it was nothing to them but some insane alien version of *American Idol.*

Finally, after several minutes of this crap, it was once again time for the highlight reel.

As much as it felt like morbid voyeurism, I forced myself to pay attention. With PVP now in effect, it was probably wise to keep ourselves apprised of the competition on the off chance we ran into them.

Can't lie. Some of the chasers who'd appeared on the last highlight reel had seemed pretty goddamned terrifying from the short view we'd been given. Much as I hated to admit it, this was one case where knowledge probably did equate to power, at least when it came to avoiding those with more of it.

I wasn't too proud to admit that retreating remained a valid option.

Up on the big screen, a chaser named Brett X was riding what appeared to be a hoverboard straight out of *Back to the Future Part II.* The guy was floating about a foot off the ground, making a frantic beeline for a brightly glowing circular area ahead of him.

Is that an ascension ring?

But then, just before he made it, a monstrous tentacle slammed down atop him from out of nowhere, squashing him like a bug.

Jesus!

The scene then abruptly cut to a familiar face, that kindly

looking old lady Nelly, the same one who'd somehow offed a bear with ... well, her bare hands. She, along with a FAST the subtitles identified as Caleb, was sauntering through a field of flowers that led to another of those glowing spots. However, she stopped about twenty feet short of it. She must've reached into her inventory because something appeared in her hands. It was ... oh gross ... the severed head of that bear.

She tossed it onto the ground ahead of her, about halfway to the ascension ring. Moments later a column of fire flared up beneath it. *A trap*. A nasty one at that.

Nelly, seemingly undaunted, let out a laugh. Then, once the fire died down, she continued merrily on her way until she disappeared in a cascade of light that was reminiscent of the transporters from *Star Trek*.

"That's a chick who's been working on her Perception," Pixel remarked.

I couldn't disagree.

Whereas the live updates prior to this had focused on either death or victory, this one was apparently a mix.

Up next were two chasers battling a sizable group of lizard monsters. Hugo R, who was dressed in the bright pastels of a *Miami Vice* episode, was fighting alongside two FASTS and a Native American woman identified as Imokalee.

I couldn't help but grin as their party name flashed up on the screen – *The A Team*. Considering Hugo's painfully 80's attire, it was probably a safe guess which of the two was responsible for that one.

Their battle was left unresolved as the scene switched again, leaving us hanging as to their fate. Instead, it turned to another chaser I'd seen before – that vampire guy Jeffrey P. This time he was all in with the creepy undead schtick. His eyes were now solid black in color and a set of nasty looking fangs protruded from his mouth.

Behind him stood an ascension ring, one he and his FAST – named *Sally Sunset* for some reason – seemingly had a clear path to. However, rather than use it, he instead stepped away to attack a large group of aboriginal warriors standing in a defensive formation, utterly shredding them like confetti.

Holy shit!

I was about to comment that he was probably one to avoid when the scene shifted again, scattering that and any other thoughts I might've had to the wind.

Boog had appeared on the larger than life screen – complete with our stupid party name displayed next to her. It was right after I'd accidentally doused her with that second mutagen, in the moments before it took effect. Still in her giant Sasquatch form, she was crushing the skull of one of the leprechauns who'd captured us.

"Holy crap, Boog! You made the highlight reel," Pixel cried.

"Big Boog crush red-hair devil," she replied, her eyes wide as she watched herself on the big screen.

"Yep. That you did."

The showrunners were milking it for all it was worth, showing the scene from an angle no doubt designed to maximize the drama. In all fairness, it looked terrifying as all hell, like a horror movie I'd somehow managed to live through. It made me wonder if any other chasers were now doing the same thing as me – keeping note of those it might be best to avoid.

That might not be the worst thing for us.

Still...

While it was flattering to see one of us recognized for an accomplishment, brutal as it might've been, I was more concerned about what else it told me. It served as a stark reminder that we were constantly being watched and scrutinized.

Obviously they were keeping their eyes open for fodder worthy of the next update's highlight reel, but was that all?

There was no doubt much of this was for the audience, who continued to ooh and aah as the scenes played out. But it also served to drive home exactly why Virto had panicked when I'd asked him about Nadok.

They might not be scrutinizing us every moment of every day, and in truth probably weren't. With over eighty-five-hundred of us left, that likely amounted to plenty of downtime – chasers standing around doing nothing more interesting than picking the seat of their pants.

The thing was, we had no way of knowing when they were paying attention and when they weren't. The only thing we could be sure of was they could turn their eyes our way at any time of their choosing.

For all the horrifying things I'd seen so far in this place, somehow that knowledge was the most terrifying of it all.

49

CHOKEPOINT
STAGE ONE EXPIRATION: 1 DAY, 10 HOURS

As much as I didn't enjoy slogging endlessly through the dark, I was glad things had been slow for the past hour or so.

That last live update had unnerved me more than I cared to admit. In truth, I'd fully expected Drega to end the update with a warning that certain verboten terms had been overheard and action would now be taken to prevent further *violations*.

He hadn't, but now I was forced to wonder whether that was even something they'd put out there for the audience to know.

Probably not. That seemed more an internal matter to me. But that left me to wonder how exactly they'd deal with it. Would a penalty be enough to satisfy them or would more drastic measures be warranted? And if the latter, how would it happen? Would they simply pluck a chaser from the game and send them back to their fate, or would it be engineered as an encounter gone wrong – perhaps sending a mob with jacked up stats to do the deed?

None of that helped my mood as we traversed the smokey burnt out forest that seemed to comprise this vast cavern. So far in our journey the only item of note had been the presence of a tiny village with several white dots scattered about it. We'd

Time Chaser

gotten close enough to see a few torches burning throughout, but in the end had voted two to one to pass it by.

Pixel had wisely pointed out that, between the sketchy locale and the existence of gunpowder in this place, the chances of us stepping foot into one of the dwellings only to set off some nasty boobytrap was almost certainly greater than zero.

It was a difficult decision to make, especially since we were coming up on twenty-four hours since our last campground break, but having a building dropped on my head wasn't how I wanted to get some *rest*.

Not helping was the darkness which was causing my brain to insist it was bedtime, resulting in more than my fair share of stifled yawns. That was apparently yet another gotcha of this place. My body still felt fine thanks to the constant health replenishment, but that wasn't the case with my mind. I was used to getting a solid six or seven hours each night and, despite my physical enhancements, nothing had seemingly changed in that regard.

The old brain fog was rapidly settling in and I doubted it was just me. Even Boog had been unusually quiet as we trudged along.

Every so often I'd look up, only to find the *stars* in the exact same position they'd been earlier. That told me there was likely no morning to look forward to as a reprieve.

What a fucking place. They could hand out magical squash rackets and demon sweaters, but an ever-full coffee mug was seemingly too much to ask for.

Sadly, there were no campgrounds in range on the map. As a result, the idea of hunkering down and setting up a watch was starting to sound tempting.

Or it would've had we actually been alone, and I wasn't talking about the NPCs from that village.

As we'd headed north, that other party of chasers had taken a route parallel to ours.

Maybe it was nothing more than coincidence but, as I said,

that last update had struck a nerve. It was as if Drega had wanted to work us all into a froth when it came to killing each other.

I'd thought my first day here had been rough, but I was beginning to realize it was nothing more than a wolf in sheep's clothing – a warmup for the real horrors awaiting us. That made finding an ascension ring more important than ever. While level grinding had initially sounded like the way to go, I was now favoring a couple extra hours just to unwind and ready myself for whatever was still to come.

Of course, that could've just been the fatigue talking.

Hell, it was entirely possible those other chasers weren't even shadowing us. Maybe they were hunting for the very same exit we were. It wasn't outside the realm of possibility.

If this other party had finished off a boss the same way we had, then might not their maps be guiding them to the same damned place? After all, it's not like these rings were supposed to be exclusive or anything.

God, I hope that's not the case.

I pushed that last thought away. Simple math alone disproved that, since there were five-hundred exits but over five-thousand chasers had already made it through.

Regardless, if they were seeking the same exit as us, then there was no reason to assume they'd be veering off anytime soon.

With that in mind, I checked the map again, noting that those pulses were down to three seconds apart.

There was now zero doubt. We were closing in.

The question now was who or what stood between us and our goal, and whether or not this other group of chasers could be counted amongst them.

"Boog think dots look pretty."

"Pretty isn't quite the word I'd use," Pixel replied. "Unless you're surrounding it with *we're* and *fucked*."

It was hard to disagree.

We'd ended up slowing our pace a bit, but it was more out of necessity than tiredness. Red dots had begun showing up again at the map's edges to the east and west of us.

At around the same time, the smoke in the air had grown thicker and was joined by a sickly stench that lingered in the air. It wasn't as thick or putrid as that rotting mastodon had been, but it was recognizable all the same – death.

Soon enough we began to see why.

Scorched bones and scattered remains practically littered the ground – some clad in broken armor while others wore what I guessed to be peasant garb.

If they were trying to drive home the point that war was hell, they were doing a damned fine job of it.

That was bad enough, but exacerbating the fact was that twice now I had to stop Boog from picking up bits of putrid flesh and taking a snack break.

It was starting to put me on edge, but sadly it was only a mere preview of things to come.

⌛⌛⌛⌛ ⋅⋄⋅⋄⋅⋄⋅ ⌛⌛⌛⌛

Less than half an hour later, Pixel was back under a blanket with their wattage dialed down low again. The density of the red dots on either side of us had grown noticeably thicker. So far, I couldn't actually see anyone out there, but harder to miss were the banners stuck in the ground and wooden stake walls that kept us from veering too far in either direction.

The feeling of being surrounded grew tense enough to where even Boog didn't seem all that gung-ho about charging into battle – a small miracle I wasn't about to question.

That's when we saw it, at least on the map. The path ahead of us seemed to be converging into a chokepoint of sorts.

Beyond it a large group of red dots awaited. That by itself was bad enough but one of them was pulsing. That meant another boss.

Fuck!

We'd gotten lucky with Apu. I'd managed to clear out the warriors from his village, leaving only non-combat NPCs behind. That meant there'd been no one else to worry about during our battle.

Whatever the boss that lay ahead of us was, though, it didn't seem to be at a loss for backup. Pixel made mention that the rest, its minions, were likely pretty weak due to their large number, but I wasn't sure that made me feel any better. Hell, against Apu something as minor as a mosquito bite at the wrong moment could've proven disastrous.

But maybe this time we weren't the ones who needed to worry about mosquitos.

"You guys seeing this?" I asked, viewing my map.

"Yep," Pixel acknowledged. "Not sure I believe it, though. These guys are either tough or really stupid."

Whereas our forward progress had slowed to a crawl as we tried to figure out what to do, the other party seemed to be closing in on the boss group. That was odd especially since, from the look of things, they didn't need to. The path to the northeast of this enemy cluster seemed clear from what I could tell. Yet they were charging into danger regardless.

"We go fight with new friends?"

"I wouldn't be so quick with the friend label, Boog," Pixel cautioned.

"Agreed," I replied, certain my blood pressure was rising by the minute. "What do you think they're up to?"

"No idea. Could be they're rushing in, hoping we'll join them. Or maybe they're a bunch of XP whores, trying to get that boss before us."

"That sounds pretty reckless."

"Welcome to the Chase, Tim. Risk versus reward. If they

win, that's a big feather in their cap. If not, they probably won't care much seeing as they'll be dead."

I nodded, despite them being unable to see me from beneath the blanket. "So what do we do? We're pretty boxed in here, but so far it doesn't seem like any of those red dots have actually seen us yet."

"You might be right. Shen and his asshole buddies didn't hesitate to come after us, so I see no reason why these guys here would hold back."

I considered what Virto had told me about the NPCs being dumbed down in the early stages. Maybe that was the case here.

No! I was doing *exactly* what he'd cautioned me against. I needed to forget that stuff and assume our foes were fighting at their full capabilities, not get my hopes up for any lucky breaks.

"Makes sense," I said. "So back to my question..."

"Way ahead of you. I say fuck this noise. Risk versus reward is one thing, but waltzing knowingly into a boss battle is like playing Russian Roulette with four chambers loaded."

"Roo-let?"

"It means things would be bad, Boog. So what are our options?"

"If we backtrack out of here now, I think we have a good chance of making it," Pixel said. "Then, we pick a direction, east or west, and see if we can circle past these assholes from the outside."

The FAST paused as the map showed a group of red dots from the boss group closing in on those other chasers. There was a bit of circling around from both teams, then at least three red dots abruptly turned into greyed out X's.

That was quick. Maybe Pixel was right about the minions being pushovers, but either way the battle had been joined.

"Yeah. Definitely sounds like a plan to me," the FAST continued. "If we haul ass, we might even be able to slip past whoever's left standing after this mess."

I considered this as I looked at the map. Turning around

and trying to find another way forward could eat up hours of time, with no guarantee things would be any better once we picked another path. Maybe it was my waning focus or the allure of that ascension ring's ever-quickening pulse, but that couldn't be our only option.

More importantly, I didn't want it to be.

There had to be a way forward, one that didn't involve us getting into either a boss battle or running afoul of chasers we knew nothing about.

We'd come this far without being noticed. With the chaos going on up ahead, we might be able to slip past these mobs if we were all *stealthed*.

The mobs were only half the problem, though. Even if we snuck past them, those chasers would know exactly where we were. The question, assuming they survived the boss fight, would then be how they'd interpret our actions.

Trying to slip by without helping could easily torch any potential goodwill between us, assuming they were friendly of course.

All the same, we didn't owe them shit. If they died, it would be one less group of...

Goddamn it. And just like that I was starting to react exactly like Drega probably hoped we would.

I needed to stop projecting my paranoia onto people I knew nothing about.

The bottom line was we had two choices, neither particularly good. Going back would eat up a lot of time, while offering us no guarantee we'd be left in any better position than we were now. Forward lay both a boss fight and an unknown group of chasers. They might be friendly or they might not, but choosing whether to help them could also go a long way toward deciding their disposition toward us.

Or it might not. Who was to say?

Either way you looked at it, we didn't have a lot to go on.

In truth, I was loath to turn our backs on that ascension

Time Chaser

ring now that we were finally getting close, but going forward could also prove a stupid move since we'd surely be spotted in short order by all interested parties.

Unless...

I turned and stared at Pixel, or more precisely the blanket draped over them. An idea began to form. I had no idea if it was a good plan or not, but it almost certainly qualified as thinking outside the box.

More importantly, it had a shot, however slim, of being a far better option than all the others staring us in the face.

"Listen up. I think I know how we can slip past these mobs and maybe even ditch our *shadows* in the process."

50

CIRCLING VULTURES

Tim, JUST FUCKING TIM: *That's it. Slow and steady. Keep low and don't make a sound. If stealthed drops off, stop moving and pretend you're a hole in the battlefield.*

Pixel: *Did you get that from a movie? Because it sounds like you got it from a movie.*

Tim, JUST FUCKING TIM: *I might have. What does it matter? It's still good advice.*

Pixel: *Not arguing.*

Boog: *kefpwebbbrrrrrrrrrrrrr*

It was all I could do to keep myself from sighing out loud.

Tim, JUST FUCKING TIM: *Don't worry about replying, Boog. Just be quiet and follow Pixel's lead.*

God, I hope she's paying attention.

Pixel's blanket *disguise* had inadvertently reminded me that we still had those Shrouded Serapes in our inventory. They were capable of fully blocking our location on the map, meaning we'd be effectively invisible to those other chasers. That still left a few problems to overcome, though. The serapes themselves were brightly colored, easily visible to the naked eye, and that other group weren't the only ones we were trying to sneak past.

That first issue was remedied by the bleak battlefield itself.

Throwing the blankets into the muck and dirt didn't do anything to mute their effectiveness, but it did serve to camouflage them. It wasn't perfect, but in the dark they didn't look all that distinct from the ground itself — not dissimilar to Frodo and Sam's cloaks in *Lord of the Rings*.

Pixel and Boog were beneath one — both of them keeping low to the ground. From more than a few paces away, they appeared as little more than a rock or clump of debris. With any luck, maintaining a *stealthed* status would hopefully help them avoid any scrutiny beyond that.

The downside was they were effectively blind beneath it, meaning someone had to take the lead in guiding them. That's where I came in.

I took the second serape. Simply draping it over my shoulders didn't do shit in terms of hiding me on the map. Fortunately, after a bit of trial and error, we realized the coverage didn't have to be all encompassing to work.

Hunching over and draping part of it over my head and face, much like the hood on a monk's robe, finally did the trick. The entirety of my body apparently needed to be beneath it in some way for it to work, which meant my vision was likewise heavily obscured. Fortunately, I could still see enough of the ground in front of me to help us maneuver.

The final piece of this puzzle was pulling some of our looted armor from inventory and draping it loosely *over* the serape atop me. The end result wasn't pretty, far from it, but it didn't need to be. When all was said and done, my hunched stature and lurching movement probably gave me a Quasimodo-like appearance, but that wasn't necessarily a bad thing. Considering those archers had all been from various species of humanoid, some a bit freakier than others, I was hoping I wouldn't stand out too much in the chaos.

That's how we made our way forward — me limping along, trying to look like an injured *soldier*, while my two party members crawled along behind me – guided by a *leash* of torn fabric I'd tied to their serape.

Had the sun been shining, I'd have put our chances of success at almost zero. But between the darkness and the smoke, I felt we had a shot. Even better, shuffling forward slowly, trying my best to play the part, seemed to ensure my status remained *stealthed* with no problem.

The serape blocked a lot of what my HUD could normally see, but Pixel verified via chat that they and Boog were likewise both *stealthed*.

It was literally as good as we could hope to get.

Sadly, it still wasn't great.

I still saw my own marker on the map, telling me that part was probably immune to the serape's effect, but that was it. The rest of it was one big blank.

Viewing it from only that perspective, it would've been easy to fool myself that we were all alone out there.

Sadly, my ears told a different story.

⌛⌛⌛⌛ ·:¦:·⊹·¦·⊹·:¦:· ⌛⌛⌛⌛

The sounds coming from the nearby battle were not for the faint of heart, and by that I mean it was all I could do to keep from crapping my chinos as we crept along at a painfully slow pace.

Every so often I'd send a reassuring chat message to my companions, reiterating that everything was going smoothly, but it was as much for my benefit as it was theirs.

Being map-blind was proving to be unnerving. I literally had a field of view that extended no higher than ground level maybe fifteen feet ahead of me. Any more than that and I risked ruining the serape's cloaking effect.

Fortunately, it appeared the vast majority of minions that had previously occupied this space were now engaged in the pitched battle happening somewhere off to our right.

Either way, nobody had challenged us so far as we slowly

lurched our way across the battlefield – veering as far away from the fight as possible before a series of spiked fortifications stopped our progress.

It was enough for a new achievement to flash in my HUD – one called *Like a Thief in the Night* – but I dismissed it before Drega's voice could ruin my concentration.

It would have to wait, especially since the nearby battle still sounded way too close for comfort.

There came the clash of steel on steel, the whoosh of spells being loosed, and the squelch of ... well, I could only imagine what that was but it sounded disturbingly wet.

That wasn't all, though.

"*OUTLANDER FILTH!*" a booming female voice cried. "*YOU WOULD DARE SULLY THE BLESSED SOIL CLAIMED BY PROTECTOR WAN? FOR THIS THERE WILL BE NO FORGIVENESS!*"

I had no idea who or what was speaking, but their voice made Shen sound tiny in comparison.

Pixel: *I don't want to seem like I'm bugging you, Tim, but is it much further?*

Tim, JUST FUCKING TIM: *No idea. Just keep moving.*

Boog: *mdegsurtbrrrrrrrrrppppp*

Pixel: *Boog says her legs are starting to cramp.*

Tim, JUST FUCKING TIM: *You understood that?*

Pixel: *Of course not, but I can hear her whimpering under her breath.*

Tim, JUST FUCKING TIM: *Just a little bit further, Boog. You can make it.*

Sue me for lying, but I needed her to stay with the program. I knew it couldn't be comfortable crawling around in the dirt, but she hadn't wanted to wear a disguise like mine. God forbid she be a little itchy. Mind you, had she been a little more open to the concept, we might've already been past this...

BANG

What the fuck?

Tim, JUST FUCKING TIM: *Please tell me that was just another of those bombs going off.*

I already suspected the answer but was hoping Pixel would inform me of some other historical fact or invention that I was blissfully ignorant of.

Pixel: *I don't think so, Tim. That was a gun. And we're not talking some primitive piece of crap like these shit-kickers might cobble together.*

I was afraid of that.

"Your defenses are broken, monster," a male voice cried out from further into the fray. "And soon you shall be too. Vultures, take this beast!"

Vultures?

The fuck? Was there someone out there who could control birds? Goddamn, what a rip off. That one chaser from the highlight reel was apparently a freaking vampire, another was able to beat the shit out of a grizzly barehanded, and now this.

I was starting to feel like I'd gotten the short end of the gear stick.

Of course, all the birds in the world wouldn't make a difference if these guys ended up dead – which very much sounded like it was still a distinct possibility.

"*IS THAT SO, OUTLANDER?*" the first voice, presumably the boss, replied. "YOUR ARROGANCE WILL PROVE YOUR UNDOING."

That didn't sound promising.

Even less good was what followed. A noise, not unlike that of an electrical transformer exploding, echoed across the battlefield, followed by distinctly humanlike screams.

Oh no.

Pixel: *Why have we stopped?*

Tim, JUST FUCKING TIM: *Give it a second. I don't want to draw any undue attention to us.*

I wasn't exactly lying, but that was only part of the truth. As terrifying as this fight sounded and as much as I wanted to be anywhere but here, hearing those voices cry out had suddenly made this far too real. This fight wasn't just about dots on the map anymore. Those were actual people out there fighting.

People who had a very real chance of dying.

"Bolster me, Invictus!" another voice shouted.

"Draw the beast's fire while he's healing," the first chaser, that vulture guy, cried. "That's an order, FAST."

"As you command, *sir*," came the response.

Pixel: *The fuck is up with these assholes?*

Tim, JUST FUCKING TIM: *What do you mean?*

Pixel: *Did you hear what he just said?*

Tim, JUST FUCKING TIM: *Yeah, but let's not jump to conclusions. For all we know this is part of some elaborate battle plan on their part.*

Pixel: *Elaborate battle plan my ass. You ever talk to me like that and you can go fuck yourself sideways with that racket of yours.*

The last thing we needed was an argument breaking out right then, so I instead refocused on the sounds of the battle.

"Attack its tail," a third human voice cried. "No! The other one."

Other one?

Pixel: *C'mon, Tim, let's get going. The longer we stand here, the greater chance we have of making ourselves targets, stealthed or not.*

They had a point. The plan had been to sneak past all of this unseen. As for this other party, they would either live or die by their own prowess.

My conscience was having second thoughts, though. Hearing the voices of those chasers drove home the fact that ignoring their plight meant any deaths among their number would at least indirectly be our fault.

I remembered back to when we'd first met Boog. Murg's death had utterly broken her. Had we not been there, I doubt she would've recovered. Again, I had no idea who these chasers were or what their relationship to each other was, but the party system was quite obviously designed to forge ties between members.

Heck, while I can't say for certain I'd cry my eyes out if anything ever happened to Pixel, there was zero doubt I'd gone out of my way to save them, nearly getting myself sliced to ribbons in the process.

Also, much as I didn't want to admit it out loud, if something were to happen to either of my friends because of another party's purposeful inaction, I would almost certainly hold a grudge.

"Move out of the way," Vulture Guy yelled. "Do not let it curse you."

Curse?

Maybe the fatigue had finally worn me down, but that was what finally convinced me – the proverbial straw that broke the camel's back. This enemy was utilizing curses, a power which I happened to be mostly resistant against thanks to my demon sweater.

Goddamn it!

There was no way I could simply ignore this now, especially knowing my abilities could make a difference in determining the tide of this battle.

Tim, JUST FUCKING TIM: *Stay here. I'll be right back. Hopefully.*

Pixel: *What do you mean you'll be right back? I don't know what you're thinking, Tim, but we have a halfway decent plan going here. Running off isn't part of it.*

Tim, JUST FUCKING TIM: *I'll be okay. Trust me.*

Boog: *Macmdkwwpdbrrrrrrrrrrp.*

Tim, JUST FUCKING TIM: *That goes for you too, Boog.*

I closed the chat window before they could say anything else. Then I stood up straight and shunted the serape and extra armor back into my inventory.

My map flared back to life almost immediately. The battlefield itself was practically littered with greyed out X's, with only a few of the regular red dots left scattered around the area.

I was more focused on the main event, though – five blue dots facing off against a pulsing red one, not that I really needed the map for that. The fight was going full force barely a hundred feet from where I stood, with enough magic being thrown back and forth to stand out like a beacon.

As for those other chasers, they could now see me on their maps as well, although they were likely too preoccupied to notice.

For a moment I just stood there, taking it all in – the sounds of battle as well as the veritable carpet of minion corpses littering the ground before me.

I wasn't a part of this fight yet, at least according to my HUD. Heck, I wasn't even close enough to get a read on the boss.

There was literally nothing stopping me from telling my friends to drop cover and run like hell, so we could all get out of there before it was too late.

Nothing save the nagging voice in my head that, despite all of Drega's bullshit, wasn't quite ready to condemn others to a fate that I could potentially help them avoid.

I really hope I don't end up regretting this.

If that wasn't jinxing myself, I didn't know what was.

51

OUTFOXXED

I had no idea what to expect as I raced forward into the fray. I can't say I was up on my Chinese mythology, but whatever had been trading barbs with those other chasers had sounded large.

Thus, as I closed in to where all the action seemed to be centered, I found myself ever more concerned that I failed to see whatever towering monstrosity these guys were surely facing.

My concern turned to outright confusion as movement finally caught my eye from up ahead, save it was from no giant. It appeared to be a writhing ball of ... white fluff no more than maybe four-feet in diameter that was bounding across the battlefield like a coked up tumbleweed.

What the hell?

As I got closer and was able to make out more, though, I realized it wasn't a ball of fluff so much as multiple furry objects intertwined with one another – like a bunch of chinchillas had gotten all tangled up. No, wait. Definitely not chinchillas. There was a small doglike body all of this was attached to, as if this creature had way too many tails for its own good.

That might not have been enough to tell me exactly what it was, but it was enough for Drega to.

Huyao: Mei – level 12
Decennial Boss

Foxes aren't typically considered to be particularly threatening, outside of the occasional giant media conglomerate feeding the masses steady streams of propaganda. Hell, in many realities it's considered jolly good fun to hunt them for sport. I'm talking the animals, not the media conglomerates – except maybe on Earth 11473, but that's beside the point.

On some Earths, however, things took a slightly different turn. At some point in their evolution, the foxes of these worlds realized that all their power resided within their tail, and to test this theory they decided to start growing extras.

Don't ask me how this works, I'm just the host of this show. Pretty sure this is the sort of stuff that would give an evolutionary biologist a stroke. All I know is that once these fuckers hit the count of nine, that's when shit got real.

Nine-tailed foxes came to be worshipped and revered for both their power and extreme fluffiness. I mean seriously, just look at all those tails. Don't you just want to mush your face into them and see how poofy they are?

Well, maybe put that idea on the backburner for now because that's a good way to get fucked up in all sorts of unpleasant ways.

Or don't and see what happens. Just be forewarned, we'll be laughing *at* you not *with* you.

Nine-tailed fox?

I can't say I was ever a huge anime fan. Back in my younger days, I'd occasionally check out *Voltron*, *Battle of the Planets*, and *Dragonball Z*. Alas, Deb was always quick to let me know her opinion when it came to adults watching cartoons. Regardless, I seemed to recall that nine-tailed foxes were a big deal in some of them.

The only problem was I couldn't exactly remember how or why, and now was no time to be driving down that particular memory lane.

Pixel: *I don't know what you think you're doing, Tim, but get your ass back here before it's too late!*

Tim, JUST FUCKING TIM: *Listen to me. I don't expect you to understand, but I can't just let these guys die knowing I could've...*

Sadly, Drega didn't even let me finish my message before jumping in to point out that it was indeed too late.

"THIS FIGHT MIGHT ALREADY BE HOT AND HEAVY, FOLKS, BUT SOMEONE ELSE NOW WANTS A PIECE OF *TAIL*. GET READY FOR SOME BOSS BATTLE INTERUPTUS AS YET ANOTHER CONTENDER DIVES BALLS DEEP INTO THIS ORGY OF DESTRUCTION!"

Orgy of...?

I pushed Drega's disturbing proclamation aside as my HUD flashed with *Boss Battle Initiated*, letting me know I was officially part of this battle now.

I started typing a message to Pixel, letting them know I'd be careful but that if things went south I'd be sure to...

Except I couldn't retreat, not without incurring a penalty.

I left the message unfinished as realization hit.

Shit!

Between my conscience browbeating me and being too tired to think straight, I'd forgotten the big caveat of boss battles. Once you were in it, you were in until the end. Leaving early or trying to run would impose a tier-two penalty on me until the end of this stage.

In my rush to do the right thing, I'd inadvertently done something both monumentally stupid and careless. I'd jeopardized my entire world. I couldn't back out now even if I wanted to.

I had no choice but to see this through.

That meant winning.

Problem was, this new boss wasn't the only X-factor here.

I'd thrown myself into the fray without even knowing if these new chasers would accept a helping hand.

It seemed like a no brainer to me, but I needed to remember that human beings weren't always logical. Hell, there was that old saying about cutting off one's own nose to spite their face.

Some people would simply rather watch the world burn.

And yet I'd rushed in without giving any of that a second thought.

If this wasn't some bizarre parallel to my life as of late, I didn't know what was. A month ago I'd come home early, thinking nothing of it, only to end up with my marriage ruined and my life in tatters. And now here I was, rushing in again, probably to find nothing good awaiting me.

Yeah, I had a feeling that whatever the outcome of this battle, I would almost certainly deserve whatever insults Pixel decided to chew me out with.

That was a problem for future Tim, though. First I had to survive this.

Mei's health bar was visible but still roughly four-fifths full. Whatever damage had been done to her so far appeared superficial at best.

As for those fighting her, I couldn't see very far in this darkness, but I did catch a glimpse of a red-colored FAST zipping through the air as it buzzed the boss mob – enough to note its health was dangerously in the yellow.

FAST: FAST – Undisclosed – Level 4 – X

I wasn't sure whether their name was actually Fast or if that was another glitch. But at only fourth level and with one death under their belt, I had a feeling they were vastly overmatched in this fight. If that were the case with this entire party, then they'd almost certainly bitten off more than they could chew.

It was almost inconceivable that they'd be insane enough to rush into this battle in such a state.

Oh crap. What if these chasers were neither friendly nor hostile? What if they were suicidal, or worse bugfuck insane?

I swear, next time I'm just going to listen to Pixel, no questions asked.

Famous last words. Good thing I hadn't actually said them out loud for anyone to hear.

Instead, I activated my Aim Assist then pulled one of the two remaining macana heads from my inventory. They'd served me well against Apu and hopefully they'd do even better here, especially since it didn't appear that I'd been noticed yet.

As my reticle locked onto the boss, I took a breath and prepared to fire. *Wait for it.*

The red FAST loosed a spell at Mei, showering her with multiple glowing orbs of energy. The fox boss was ready for that, leaping to the side and dodging them all as they peppered the ground where she'd been.

As she landed, though, another gunshot rang out.

It had been a feint so that one of the others could get the drop on her. Maybe these guys weren't as crazy as I'd feared.

The fox jerked backward with an angry snarl, her health dropping a tiny bit as she turned her back to me.

Now!

With her distracted, there was no time to lose. I dropped the hunk of bronze and slammed it with my racket, once again gritting my teeth for that tense moment between being sure my weapon would break and the scream of the projectile hurtling toward the writhing ball of fluff.

If she didn't know I was here before, she sure as shit does now.

Sure enough, despite the chaos of battle the sound of my Banshee Racket was hard to miss – even more so for a creature with canine-level hearing.

Mei tried to dodge at the last second, but she wasn't quite quick enough.

Yes!

The bronze warhead hit home, causing a small explosion of white fur and ... nothing else?! Her damage bar didn't even budge from the attack.

The fuck?

That's when the writhing ball of fur pulled apart, separating into nine distinct tails. In an instant it became clear what had happened.

Mei hadn't been trying to dodge after all. She hadn't needed to. In aiming at the fox's backside, I'd been targeting nine-intertwined tails that were mostly just poofy fur.

In the end I'd done no more damage than a wire brush against a shaggy dog.

Son of a...

Mind you, while Mei herself didn't turn to acknowledge my presence, one of her tails did.

"Chaser!" a voice cried out – one of the members of that other party. "Whoever you are, take heed! Its tails! The beast's tails are the source of its..."

Before they could finish, a dark, undulating blob appeared at the tip of the tail pointing my way.

"...power!"

You don't say.

The blob of darkness seemingly grew in size until it took up nearly my entire field of vision, blotting out everything else and leaving nothing but darkness. Then, just as I began to panic, thinking I'd been blinded, something slammed into me, knocking me flat on my back.

Oof!

I wasn't sure what had happened, aside from my health bar dropping by nearly a third, but a moment later my HUD served up a dire notification.

Debuff – You have been cursed with The Writhing Hell of Stinging Insects!

The writhing hell of what?!

That unyielding darkness dissipated, allowing me to see again, but along with my returned vision came the horrific sensation of thousands of tiny creatures crawling over every inch of my...

Curse Negated.

And just like that the feeling vanished. I'd still lost a good chunk of health in the exchange but at least I no longer felt like I'd fallen into a vat of angry cockroaches.

Back over where Mei still stood, the dark aura surrounding her tail faded, cluing me in. She'd hit me with some sort of beam or spell that was jet black in color. I hadn't been blinded so much as blasted.

Whatever the case, the name of that power alone was enough to scare the shit out of me. My curse resistance was pretty high, eighty-percent according to my HUD, but that still left a twenty-percent chance of bad things happening.

Regardless, I could have kissed my stupid demon sweater.

Never going to make fun of it ever again.

Now was no time for premature celebrations, though.

Up ahead, another figure appeared out of the dark racing toward the fox, a man with a flaming sword in hand.

The weapon gave me just enough light to see he was of Asian descent, with a mustache, long black hair, and dressed in what appeared to be some sort of quilted robe.

Though his outfit was dirty and charred, his health was still in the green.

Chaser: Ulagan – Earth 1911 – Level 5.

That at least put a name to one of these guys, albeit not much else. The only other insight to be gleaned was that he probably wasn't a member of Virto's guild, otherwise I'd have been given a bit more info.

That meant keeping my guard up around him, not that I was planning to drop it anytime soon.

Mei responded to his charge by turning another of her tails his way. This time, a cone of white powder flared out from the tip at the attacking chaser, causing the temperature in the air to drop by a good ten degrees.

Some sort of cold-based attack.

Fortunately for Ulagan, he was ready for it. He dove out of the way, sliding beneath the beam just as another *crack* of gunfire sounded. Another sliver was erased from the boss's health bar.

So far it seemed these guys were proving successful with the same divide and conquer strategy we'd attempted on Apu.

"*INSOLENT BUG*," Mei snarled, turning three of her tails in the direction the gunshot had come from.

"Now, Invictus!" another voice from earlier shouted.

A bolt of electricity flared out from somewhere to Mei's left, striking the nine-tailed fox in the side and bringing her health bar down far enough for it to turn yellow.

Speaking of which, I followed the attack back to its source, making out a yellowish glow floating in the air. It was another FAST, one similar in hue to Murg albeit slightly darker.

FAST: Invictus – Undisclosed – Level 7 – X

Before Mei could counterattack, a second chaser – presumably the one who'd shouted the order – raced in from my periphery. The man, wearing a plumed Roman helmet and sporting a health bar firmly in the yellow, launched something at the fox. The object unfurled midair to reveal a glowing net that landed atop her.

Chaser: Marius – Earth 432 – Level 6.

Blue energy arced from the net as it settled onto the boss beast. However, in that same moment another of her tails began to glow with power – this time an angry red.

"Quickly," Marius shouted. "Finish her before she can..."

Alas, finishing this fight wasn't in the cards, at least not yet.

Two things happened. A new status appeared in my HUD beneath Mei's name – *Dazed*. As hopeful as that sounded, though, it was countered by a translucent dome of blood-red energy which formed around her.

Marius stepped in, drew a short sword from his side, and slashed at the dome, only for the blade to rebound off it without leaving so much as a scratch. It was some sort of defensive barrier, one Mei had raised just as they'd nailed her with a potentially debilitating debuff.

Another gunshot rent the air, probably from Vulture Guy, the only chaser in this party I still hadn't seen yet. The bullet caused the barrier to spark but sadly didn't penetrate.

Shit! Far as I could tell, both sides were now locked in a stalemate.

Now it was going to be a race to see what happened first, whether they could break through or she could shake off their debuff and resume her attack.

I was in the process of going through my inventory to see if I had anything that could possibly make a difference here when I looked up to see Ulagan approaching, no doubt taking advantage of this lull to suss me out. His flaming sword was in hand and suspicion was etched onto his face.

"State your purpose, Tim, Just Fucking Tim," he barked, his voice gravelly and full of menace. "Be you friend or foe?"

I tried not to grimace at hearing the stupid name Pixel had saddled me with. Instead, I raised my hands in a placating manner but kept hold of my racket just in case. Whatever I said next would almost certainly decide whether we got off on the right foot or not.

"First of all, Tim is fine," I said. "And secondly, I saw you guys were fighting that thing and decided to help."

He raised an eyebrow. "You are from that party we observed, yes?"

I nodded.

He inclined his head. I had a sneaking suspicion he was trying to figure out why my companions weren't visible on his map. "And the rest of your companions?"

I considered my answer, realizing this was something I should've thought through *before* breaking cover.

Telling the truth probably wasn't the worst thing I could say, but it might not make us fast friends either. I could see how it might be misconstrued. After all, we were in possession of those serapes, two items which, in theory, would be perfect for setting up an ambush.

Think fast. "They're..."

"Macmac no die! Boog come help!"

"Right behind me," I finished without missing a beat, noting the two green dots that were now on my map.

At least I couldn't argue with their timing.

"For fuck's sake, Tim," Pixel cried, buzzing past Boog before coming to a screeching halt at the sight of Ulagan. "Oh. Um, hi there."

Awkward as that was, I was more worried about our other companion.

"Macmac?" Boog asked questioningly as she stepped to my side, her eyes locked onto the other chaser.

"Easy there," I cautioned.

This boss battle wasn't over yet. I had a feeling the last thing anyone wanted was a fight breaking out on two fronts.

For a moment we all stood there in uncomfortable silence.

Finally, Ulagan broke the impasse, eyeballing each of us in turn. "I am Ulagan of the Vultures. If you are here to fight beside us, then I welcome you. If you are here for treachery, then know I will gladly trample your bodies into the dust. Your actions will determine which path you shall trod."

Ah. So *the Vultures* was their party name. That made sense.

Once again, I held up my hands. "Fair enough. Personally, I've had enough *trampling* to last a lifetime. I'm Tim of..."

"Say it," Pixel prodded. Though they had no mouth, I could sense their smirk.

"Of Tim Chasers," I finished with a sigh.

"Oh yeah, that's the stuff right there."

I pointedly ignored the FAST. "These are my *friends*, Pixel and Boog."

"So my inner eyes have confirmed," Ulagan replied, probably talking about his HUD. He inclined his head again for a moment before continuing. "I have told my companions you have come to offer assistance. Tread lightly. Take no action against us nor attempt to steal what is ours and we shall honor the peace between us ... for now."

I had a feeling he'd just had a quick chat with his buddies. Can't say I blamed him one bit. Though his group had ours outnumbered, currently the rest were busy with Mei, leaving him at a three-to-one disadvantage.

As for the part about stealing from them, I decided to take a shot in the dark, remembering how our battle with Apu had gone. "We'll help with Mei but the kill is yours. Fair?"

Ulagan hesitated for another moment but then nodded.

In the next instant, a notification appeared in my HUD to tell me my Diplomacy skill had kicked up to level two. Cool to know.

Pixel: *Look at you playing U.N. peacekeeper. It would almost be impressive IF YOU WEREN'T A COMPLETE FUCKING DUMBASS!*

Yeah, I probably deserved that one.

Pixel: *Seriously, Tim, using those Shrouded Serapes to sneak past these guys was your fucking plan.*

Tim, JUST FUCKING TIM: *Sorry. I wasn't planning on helping them. It just ... sort of happened.*

As far as excuses went, mine was pretty lame.

Pixel: *Save it. We're in the shit now. It's too late to back out. Although I reserve the right to blast your ass with a Shock Bolt at a future time of my choosing.*

Tim, JUST FUCKING TIM: *Fair enough. Just play nice for now, both of you – but especially you, Boog. So far Ulagan seems on the up and up, so let's not do anything to antagonize him.*

Boog: *Yus,Mcsddkwkdowkdwkbrrrrrrrpppp!*

Tim, JUST FUCKING TIM: *I'll take that as a yes.*

"We have tarried long enough," Ulagan said, interrupting our chat. He turned halfway toward where the battle continued but made it a point to not take his eyes off us. "Marius's net has merely slowed the beast. We must finish it before it breaks free. Come. Let us see what mettle you are made of."

"Not to mince words," Pixel replied, "but I'm made of carbon femto-polymers not metal."

I repressed a sigh as I pulled my last remaining macana head from inventory. "What Ulagan said. Time's a wasting. Let's see what we can do to help beat this boss."

As if in response, Vulture Guy's voice once again called out.

"Gather round this fiend, all of you! It's time we ended this farce and sent this abomination to the Hell it rightfully deserves."

A little pushy for my tastes, but I could agree with his sentiment as we headed back to where the fox boss remained enshrined within its translucent force barrier.

She was still dazed, but I could see the power arcing across the net gradually starting to peter out.

Marius was there with his sword. Likewise, I made out the two FASTs circling the creature.

Now where is…?

I spied a human form standing on the opposite side of the fox's barrier, appearing ghoulish in the blood-red light cast by the protection spell.

However, as I neared the boss, spreading out to find a spot so that we had it surrounded good and proper, my breath caught in my throat.

That reddish color I'd seen on Vulture Guy became a bright yellow as I stepped around Mei, revealing him to be wearing a slightly bloodied but otherwise crisp military uniform – complete with black swastika emblazoned on one arm.

It was him, that oddly-colored Nazi I'd seen back in the colosseum before the Chase had started.

"You have got to be fucking kidding me."

52

DID NOT-SEE THAT ONE COMING

Chaser: Friedrich – Earth 1299 – Level 8.

Not only was this prick a fucking Nazi, but he was also the highest level chaser I'd seen to date. Neither made me a happy camper.

Pixel must've noticed my negative reaction because my chat suddenly blared to life.

Pixel: *There a problem here, Tim?*

Tim, JUST FUCKING TIM: *Yes, there's a problem. Do you see what he's wearing?*

Pixel: *I'm not blind. I see it just fine, just the same way I see a boss that's about half-a-minute away from shaking off the only debuff that's keeping it from blasting us into kibble. So do us all a favor and take a deep breath. We can't afford to lose our shit right now.*

Tim, JUST FUCKING TIM: *I'm not working with a fucking Nazi.*

Pixel: *I'm not saying we should. Trust me, I know all about your Earth's history. As far as pieces of shit go, those guys were clogging the bowl. However, I feel compelled to remind you that this Friedrich guy isn't from your world. Hell, looking at that banana-*

colored fashion nightmare he's wearing, I'd say his Earth is nowhere near yours.

Tim, JUST FUCKING TIM: *Meaning?*

Pixel: *We don't know anything about him.*

Tim, JUST FUCKING TIM: *Are you trying to tell me there are worlds out there where these assholes aren't evil incarnate?*

Pixel: *No idea, but logically it makes sense. That's kinda the whole point of an infinite multiverse. I wouldn't doubt there are realities out there where these clowns were nothing more than a bunch of hippy-dipshits, filling their day by planting flowers and singing Kumbaya.*

Tim, JUST FUCKING TIM: *Pretty sure you don't need a military uniform for either of those.*

Pixel: *My point, Tim, is I don't know. They didn't put me here as some kind of multiversal Wikipedia. It's not like I have a full bio on every freaking chaser or the world they come from. All I'm trying to tell you is now is not the time to do this. Let's finish this boss off first, then we can figure things out. Tell him I'm right, Boog.*

Boog: *Youdkoeefewbrrrrrrrrppppp!*

Pixel: *Yeah. What she said.*

Tim, JUST FUCKING TIM: *I ... don't know about this.*

Pixel: *Fine. Then here's something you should know. You're the one who raced in here without thinking this through. Well, I have news for you, pal. We're committed now, whether we want to be or not. We're neck deep in the shit and trying to dogpaddle. So get your head in the game before this fox fucks us up the ass with all nine tails.*

Pixel was right. This was my fault. I'd gotten us into this mess because my conscience insisted that it was the right thing to do – forgetting for a moment that we were stuck in a game that was actively competing against us.

The FAST was right. We knew nothing about this guy outside of his shitty fashion sense. The whole gist of parallel dimensions was that events played out differently in them – or at least that's the insight I'd gotten from several seasons of *Star Trek*.

There was also one other factor to take into consideration.

It was possible that the fuckers from TOPCOC were purposely setting things like this up – using our innate prejudices against us. Kinda like teaming Abraham Lincoln's best friend up with a John Wilkes Booth from a universe where he never went anywhere near that theater. All they needed to do at that point was sit back and watch the sparks fly.

Thinking about it from that perspective helped calm me down a bit.

I mean, shit, for all I knew he was nothing but a cosplayer from a modern Earth where dressing like historical assholes was considered quaint.

Yeah. Totally sure that's possible.

Maybe.

Gah! None of this was helping matters.

If only those foresight potions were actually useful. I could've downed one before blowing my cover and maybe have had a shot of avoiding this mess.

Too bad that was no longer an option.

In truth, there was only one viable option at this point.

"On my mark, unleash hell," Friedrich commanded. "Ready ... aim ..."

"No," I interrupted.

"Excuse me?" he replied, raising an eyebrow over his angular face. "You have something to say, stranger?"

"I do."

Pixel: *What the hell did we just talk about?!*

Tim, JUST FUCKING TIM: *Relax. I got this.*

"Everyone should heal up first," I continued. "That way there are no distractions once this barrier drops. If anyone's low on potions, let me know. I have extras."

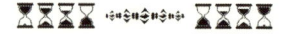

Curse Negated.

"Hold on, I'm coming," I cried, pushing myself off the ground now that my health was back in the green.

Mei's last attack had been a big one, five tails at once – at least two of them spewing nasty curses. I'd gotten nailed twice in succession. Once by an electrical attack, which I just barely managed to tank with my collapsible shield, and then again by a curse, which apparently didn't give a single solitary shit about whether I was behind a wall of metal or not.

I had a feeling that barrage had been her last stand, one big finale to try and take us all down.

Considering the groans of pain coming from all around me, it had almost worked. Once again my demon sweater had saved my ass, although the combo of electricity and curse magic hitting me at almost the same time had been nearly enough to put me down for good.

Sadly, between what I'd shared with our new *friends* and the one I'd just swallowed to save my own ass, I was now running dangerously low on health potions.

Regardless, despite my continued misgivings of working alongside Friedrich, I'd promised myself to give these guys the benefit of the doubt – or at least do my part to ensure we survived this battle.

And if that meant using up another potion to keep Ulagan from biting it, then I would...

"No," Friedrich said. "Focus on the beast. Victory is too close for us to waste this opportunity."

"But Ulagan is almost..."

"Fast," he interrupted, barking another order, "tend to Ulagan, so that the rest of us might finish this monster."

"Yes, sir!"

The red FAST immediately changed course, breaking off its attack and almost getting blasted for the effort.

I couldn't pretend to be happy with the way Friedrich

seemed to assume he was in charge, but the way he spoke to his FAST unit, basically treating it like cannon fodder, really didn't sit well with me.

I had a feeling it sat even less well with Pixel, although they kept their thoughts to themself as this battle entered what was hopefully its final moments.

Mei's health was firmly in the red and her attacks now had a desperate quality to them. She might've had nine tails, but the combined force of eight attackers had slowly whittled her down.

That didn't mean she wasn't still dangerous, though.

As three of her tails continued to take random potshots, no doubt in the hope of keeping us on the defensive, four more began to gather power.

"Be careful," I shouted. "She's going to launch another big one."

"Ya think?" Pixel replied, swooping in and lobbing an Acid Ball at the fox's head, doing enough damage to make her cry out in pain. Her health bar dropped to the point where there was no more than nine or ten percent left.

So close.

"*BOTHERSOME INSECT,*" Mei growled, her face now a sizzling ruin. "PREPARE TO DINE IN HELL."

"Pixel, get out of..."

"Enough," Friedrich interrupted. "The FAST can look after itself. Everyone else needs to attack, now while the abomination is distracted."

Tempting as it was to tell him to go fuck himself, he wasn't wrong. So instead I turned my frustration toward Mei – racing forward with my racket now that she was half-blinded.

I was out of bronze macana heads and the few other projectiles I'd fired at her had mostly hit nothing but fur. It was that knowledge, however, which drove me to close the distance between us. I'd finally realized the opportunity that it presented.

Now to hope this mad plan actually worked.

I got within swinging distance of Mei's backside before she

could launch her big attack. In response, most of her tails turned my way – almost as if they had minds of their own.

Oh yeah, that's not creepy at all.

Magical power flared through them, no doubt preparing to blast my ass into bite-sized chunks. Fortunately, I was in position to play the ace up my sleeve.

I reared back and started to swing, casting Burning Beatdown in that same moment.

Magical fire surrounded my racket as it closed the distance. Mei's tails began to writhe, possessing uncanny dexterity as they dodged and weaved to keep me from hitting anything but fur.

Too bad for her that's exactly what I was aiming for.

For most of this battle, she'd used this same tactic to avoid taking damage – ensuring a good many of our attacks did jack shit to her.

It was a good defense, with one exception – fur tended to be flammable.

Her cold attack had managed to fend off any ranged attempts at what I was doing, but this close the dense pelt covering her tails acted as little more than kindling for the blazing bonfire that was my racket.

Moments later, Mei's backside burst into flames just as I'd hoped.

The downside was this effectively turned all nine of her tails into flailing fire whips, a few of which nailed me before I could backpedal, once again sending my health spiraling downward.

However, the damage was worth it. Mei began to scream as her entire body was engulfed. Sure, I'd probably ruined any chance of harvesting her pelt for my Loom o' Doom power, but it was a sacrifice I was willing to make as I watched her health crater.

"Now!" I sputtered, coughing from the acrid smoke rising from her body, "before she can put herself out."

Marius raced in, having switched out his dagger for a spear –

probably a smart move considering the fox boss was now a living ball of fire.

He jabbed the weapon into her side, bringing Mei's health down to a mere sliver.

Then, from across the way, Boog charged at her, jawbone axe held high. This was it. If she connected, there was no way Mei would be able to survive.

This battle would be... *Wait a second.*

Realization hit, reminding me I'd given these guys my word that this kill was theirs to make. Sure, that was before I'd learned their boss was a fucking Nazi. Even so, making an enemy out of them now was not my preferred solution with most of us currently injured and exhausted.

Shit! "Don't do it, Boog! You need to stop!"

Amazingly, she listened, a small miracle unto itself. She skidded to a halt, her head cocked to the side. "Boog not kill?"

"No, Boog, you can't. You have to..." I trailed off as one of Mei's tails turned Boog's way. The tip of it was aglow with black energy, in sharp contrast to the flames eating away at whatever fur remained. *Fuck*! "Get out of the way before..."

I was a second too late with my warning, though. Magic flared from the fox's tail, engulfing Boog. She was knocked away, her health dropping far into the red as her status changed to *Cursed*.

No!

"That will be quite enough of that," the yellow clad leader of the Vultures stated, striding up to Mei even as the power coursing through her tails began to sputter and fail.

"THOUGH I MAY SUCCUMB TO YOUR TREACHERY, KNOW THAT YOU WILL NEVER OVERCOME THE MIGHT OF PROTECTOR W..."

BANG

Before she could finish, Friedrich lifted his gun to her head and casually pulled the trigger.

Mei's health bar vanished, along with a good chunk of her face.

A new achievement popped up in my HUD as the boss fell to the ground, not that I cared in the slightest as I was busy rounding her burning body to get to Boog.

She was lying on the ground screaming, her health dangerously low but fortunately no longer dropping. As I reached her, I realized the fur covering her body was shifting and twisting despite the lack of any breeze – as if she had hundreds of invisible insects crawling all over her.

"THE WINNERS OF THIS BOSS BATTLE ... THE VULTURES!" Drega announced, **"WITH AN ASSIST FROM TIM CHASERS."**

"Bite me, Drega," I muttered, turning my full attention toward my stricken companion. "Listen to me, Boog. I need you to use one of your health potions. The..." *Goddamn it! What did she call them?* "The ... funny tasting water. Use one of your funny tasting waters."

I paused for a second, then added, "But not the one Pixel said not to use."

For a moment, I was afraid she was either in too much pain or my instructions were simply too complex for her to understand, but then her health rocketed back to full. Sadly, that weird movement coursing through her fur continued.

"Are you okay, Boog? How do you f...?"

"Boog itchy!" she cried, starting to scratch herself all over. I tried to help her to her feet, but she dropped back down and scooted away from me, dragging her butt along the ground.

"How is she?" Pixel asked, flitting over to me.

"I'm ... honestly not sure. See for yourself."

"Eww," the FAST remarked as Boog continued scraping her bottom furiously against the ground. "No doubt about it. Curses can be nasty as fuck."

"So I'm beginning to realize. Please tell me we have a potion that can fix this."

"Nope. Pretty sure we're SOL on that one."

"Then how do we help her?"

"Far as I can tell, there's only one thing we can do."

"And that is?" I asked.

"Open our achievements and hope we managed to score a bottle of magical flea bath."

Not quite the answer I was hoping for.

53

SCRATCHING THAT ITCH

I had potions to heal injury, cure disease, and remove the effects of poison. Alas, as Pixel was quick to point out, curses counted as none of the above. Apparently, they were considered their own unique form of torture.

It seemed there was no getting off easy on this one.

The Writhing Hell of Stinging Insects – Curse

Curses are persistent little buggers, like if herpes had a love child with an internet stalker. They're what would happen if you could manifest all the bad mojo you've wished upon anyone who's ever cut you off in traffic.

In short, they can be pretty nasty.

Once you've been cursed, the only way to negate them is via specific spells, scrolls, or by taking a chance with a mutagen and getting supremely lucky.

Yeah, I wouldn't exactly count on that last one.

Regarding those first two, I'm guessing you're already shit outta luck because otherwise why would you be reading this?

All hope is not lost, though. Curses reassert themselves at the beginning of each new day. At that point, you have a 10% chance for every hundred CON points to resist the

curse and be freed from your affliction. If you fail, well, that's one more day to consider your poor life's choices.

As for the rather directly named Hell of Stinging Insects, imagine pissing off a nest of both yellowjackets and fire ants. Now imagine that they're all invisible.

See what I mean by nasty?

"Only ten percent for every hundred CON points? Isn't that a little on the steep side?"

"I think that's the point," Pixel remarked as Boog continued to roll around in the dirt, doing what she could to ease her discomfort. "Still, I'd say we got lucky."

I glanced at the FAST. "How is this lucky? And I swear if you say it could've been one of us instead..."

"Relax. I'm not *that* big of an asshole. What I meant is that curses here on the lower stages tend to be more annoying than outright debilitating. So if there's a time to catch one..."

"Boog itchy!"

"Exactly what I mean," the FAST continued. "I'm sure it's uncomfortable as fuck but, far as I can tell, it's not affecting your stats or health in any way."

"Your level of empathy is truly the stuff of legends," I replied deadpan.

"Sue me for being pragmatic. All I'm saying is it could be worse, but either way she's stuck like this until tomorrow at the earliest. Unless, that is, you want to try that..."

"We are not dumping another mutagen on her. Not happening."

"Figured that was the case, but wanted to put it out there as an option. Oh well. At least one of us is distracted from the fact that we all just got shafted."

"Say that a little louder why don't you. I'm pretty sure our new *friends* didn't hear it."

Bad as I felt for Boog, her curse at least gave us something to take our mind off the fact that, just a few yards away, the Vultures were busy divvying up the spoils from that boss fight.

That was what Ulagan had insisted on if we wanted a truce between our parties – credit for the kill and first dibs.

Not exactly the best deal I'd ever agreed to.

Normally, I wouldn't have expected a fox to have a lot of loot on it, but I was wrong. Seemed that a few of Mei's tails had transmuted into wands upon her death, all of them filled with potent magic.

And that wasn't even counting the XP boost. Outside of Friedrich, the other Vultures, FASTs included, had all gone up a level.

At least Pixel had made out decently on that end too, having likewise earned enough experience to push them to seventh level.

In all fairness, it's not like the rest of us made out too badly. Both Boog and I were now pretty close to sixth, so I guess we couldn't really complain.

Well, okay, maybe Boog could. Sadly, I didn't see any way to help her right now beyond the dust bath she was currently taking.

I turned to Pixel, meaning to ask about their new stat points, when they popped up in my chat instead.

Pixel: *All right, that's hopefully enough small talk to keep any prying eyes from getting suspicious.*

I raised an eyebrow, noting it was a direct message, not part of our party chat.

Pixel: *Don't say anything out loud about this, but you need to find a reason to give Boog your sweater before end of day.*

Tim, JUST FUCKING TIM: *My sweater? Wait, are you talking about its curse resistance?*

Pixel: *No, It's because I think it'll go with her eyes. Of course I'm talking about its fucking curse resistance!*

Tim, JUST FUCKING TIM: *Will that even do anything? I thought it only protected me from becoming cursed, not after the fact.*

Pixel: *True enough, but read between the lines of what Drega* *said. Curses reassert themselves every day. That basically means she'll be recursed, if that's even a word. The gist, however, is it's effectively a brand new curse for a new day.*

Tim, JUST FUCKING TIM: *Huh. Now that you mention it, I guess that kinda makes sense. Good thinking! But why the secrecy?*

Pixel: *Because this isn't some random guess I'm pulling out of my ass. This is straight out of that batch of memories I recovered. I don't think it'll work. I know it will.*

Tim, JUST FUCKING TIM: *Seriously?*

Pixel: *Yep. I realized it while we were standing there gawking at her. BTW, that makes what I'm telling you a total cheat. Not a big one, mind you, but a cheat nonetheless – which means the overmind isn't gonna be happy with us if they realize it.*

Tim, JUST FUCKING TIM: *Okay, but aren't they going to figure that out if I just up and give her my sweater for no reason.*

Pixel: *Pretty much. That's why we gotta play this up a bit. Think about it, Tim. It's not really that big a stretch for us to figure this one out on our own, but it needs to look like it happened that way. We need to convince both the submind and the audience that we came up with this by working through it logically. That way, nobody will bat an eye.*

I almost nodded, but managed to stop myself.

Instead, I considered what they'd just told me. After another minute or so, I replied, "Hey, getting back to Boog, do you think there's any chance my sweater's curse resistance could maybe help her out?"

Pixel: *I didn't mean to do it right this second! Subtle you are not, Tim.*

Tim, JUST FUCKING TIM: *Sorry, but I figured no time like the present. I mean, we were just talking about it, so at least it makes sense to bring it up now.*

Pixel: *Yes, but there's a time to shit and a time to get off the pot. This is not the former.*

Time Chaser

There came a brief pause, making me think I was about to get berated again, and then another message popped up.

Pixel: *You know what? Forget what I said. It's fine. We can still make this work. You just need to follow my lead.*

"I don't know," they said aloud, a slight edge to their voice. "Far as I'm aware, curse resistance just helps to stop you from becoming cursed in the first place. Obviously we're a bit late to that party. Negating an existing curse, on the other hand, is a whole other ball of wax."

"Fair point. But will it hurt her to try?" I replied, starting to unbutton my sweater.

"Whoa! Not so fast, Hoss," Pixel cried before I could finish.

Tim, JUST FUCKING TIM: *What now? You said to follow your lead.*

Pixel: *That's not following my lead, idiot!*

Tim, JUST FUCKING TIM: *Then I don't know what your lead is. If we're bringing this up now then it doesn't make sense for me to randomly hand her my sweater in nine hours when today becomes tomorrow.*

Pixel: *Which is why I didn't want you to bring it up yet.*

Tim, JUST FUCKING TIM: *So then why did you tell me we could still make it work?*

Pixel: *You're killing me, Tim. You really are. Just shut up and listen. Don't improv or do anything stupid. Just listen.*

"It won't hurt *her*," Pixel continued out loud, "but it might hurt *you* if we run into anything nasty down the line. Don't forget about everything else that sweater does for you."

"Yeah, but..."

"And I'm not just talking about Loom o' Doom. Think about it. Is that really something you want to be loaning out willy-nilly, even to one of us?"

I considered the FAST's words. True, my sweater had both curse and cold resistance attached to it, which was what I'd been focusing on, but that wasn't all it did.

For a moment there I'd almost forgotten that the sweater

489

accounted for roughly *half* my current constitution score, not to mention providing a solid charisma boost – all of it a result of scoring a rare Century box.

Without it, my health would effectively be reduced to the same as smart Boog's, which is to say not good at all. I'd almost gotten killed way too many times in the past day alone for it to be a good idea to walk around at half health. Doubly so considering we'd just finished a boss battle, yet my map didn't show any campgrounds or exits from this nighttime hell cave anywhere within range.

It was almost as if Mei wasn't the final challenge of this area, not a particularly pleasant thought to have.

If that wasn't enough to stop me from taking off my sweater, even to help a friend, I didn't know what was.

The problem was, I still had no idea what Pixel was angling toward. They'd told me privately that the resistance would work once her curse reset, but out loud Pixel was doing everything in their power to convince me it was a terrible idea.

Rather than continue taking shots in the proverbial dark, I tossed the ball back into the FAST's court. "Okay, fine. So then what should I do?"

"Boog itchy, Macmac," our stricken teammate cried, continuing to roll around in the dirt.

"I know, Boog. We're working on it." I turned back toward Pixel and stared expectantly. I'd dug us this hole, but hopefully they had a plan to shovel us out.

"All right, so I'm sure my answer isn't going to make anyone happy, but we need to hold that thought for now," Pixel finally said. "In roughly nine hours, today will become tomorrow. With any luck, we'll be in a place where we can take a quick breather. If so, then you can lend her your sweater."

Tim, JUST FUCKING TIM: *Aren't you just saying exactly what you specifically told me* not *to say?*

Pixel: *Yes, but I'm doing so in a way that isn't completely asinine. Watch and learn.*

Time Chaser

Outside our private chat, they continued. "Assuming her head stays the same size, the CON boost from your sweater will bump her to a twenty percent shot at beating this thing. Still not great, but at least it maximizes her chances."

"And if she changes before then?"

"Then we give it a shot anyway and hope it helps. Sorry to say, but I think it's the best we're gonna get for now. Until then, keep your fingers crossed that the scroll fairies are kind to us with our loot boxes."

Pixel: *See? That's how you do it.*

Out loud, they added, "And speaking of loot boxes..."

The meaning behind their change of subject was clear.

Much as I wanted to find a way to ease Boog's suffering right then and there, we'd done all we could ... for now anyway.

Sadly, it didn't feel like nearly enough.

54

STRANGE BEDFELLOWS

Achievement unlocked! Like a Thief in the Night!
You thought outside the box and came up with a novel solution for sneaking past your enemies, one that actually had a shot in Hell of working. Gotta admit, I was almost impressed. Sure, as expected, you fucked it up right on cue, but let's not focus on the negatives.

The truth is, coming up with new and interesting uses for all that clutter sitting in your inventory is the sort of thinking that gets chasers to the next stage – which is where you might already be had you not decided to be a soft-hearted pussy.

But that's okay. Your fuck-up is our entertainment.
Reward: 1 Olympiad supply box.

That was probably about as close to a compliment as I'd gotten from Drega so far. Mind you, I didn't want the fucker's admiration. He could eat shit and die right at this moment and I'd be fine with it. All I wanted was to survive long enough to make it home to my son.

Still, an Olympiad box wasn't a bad haul. I was hopeful that meant resupplying some of the potions I'd been running through as of late, although I wouldn't have said no to some new stuff – like a scroll to remove Boog's curse.

Achievement unlocked! Sidekicking Ass!

You came, you saw, you let someone else take credit for beating a boss.

Know what that makes you? A minion at worst and a sidekick at best. Either way, you bent over and let another chaser use you as their personal glory hole.

But hey, maybe if they go on to win they'll remember to thank you in their acceptance speech. I wouldn't count on it, but stranger things have happened.

Regardless, a win is a win. You've lived to assume the position another day, just like the fucking cuck you are.

***Reward*: 1 STD boss box.**

As insulting as Drega was trying to be, I honestly didn't mind. For starters, I still got a boss box out of the deal. But secondly, it kind of negated that first achievement – implying that I wasn't exactly spotlight material. By letting the Vultures have the win, it not only satisfied the terms of the deal we'd made, but also hopefully ensured I'd stay off any upcoming highlight reels.

Virto's warning was still way too fresh in my ears, meaning keeping a low profile was still my preference. Boog's appearance on the last live update had been more than enough for me.

Rather than dwell on that, I instead focused on my boxes, recommending my teammates do the same – including Boog, who by that point was caked in so much dirt and mud that I was surprised she could feel much of anything.

First up was that Olympiad box.

As expected, it was full of goodies. I counted four potions each of both the healing and mana variety. That made up for the shortfall that boss battle had created. In addition to that, there was another antivenom potion along with half a dozen gl'ohrods.

All decent, but the real prize were the two scrolls waiting for me.

Sadly, curse removal wasn't on the menu, but what was there was impressive nonetheless. Both were of a spell called *Fortuitous Encore*. One was first level and the other third.

Despite my best effort not to smile, I found myself grinning nevertheless as Drega read the description to me. The gist was simple enough. Fortuitous Encore could lower or outright negate the current reset time for any spell or item-based power.

At first level it was capable of shaving six hours off that time, whereas the third level version erased an entire day's wait. I quickly shunted those into my inventory where I equipped them, replacing the scroll of Plant Dominion which I had yet to find a use for.

If only I'd opened this box sooner, I could have reset either Vectorman or, even better, my Spell Hammer Mace before jumping into that boss battle – either of which would've been handy to have.

It was almost like they purposely handed out useful prizes at times when it was far too chaotic to consider opening them.

Oh well. Live and learn. It was my fault for putting this one to the side until I had a moment to think. Regardless, these scrolls were more than appreciated, at least until such time as I could rank up my powers enough to where the wait wasn't so freaking onerous.

The boss box was next. I called it up, watching as it went through the motions of appearing and disappearing in its customary shower of sparkles.

Whereas my last boss box had been chock full of goodies, this one contained only two items – possibly a result of us taking on a supporting role in the fight.

However, since one of those items was another spellbook, I had a feeling there wouldn't be too many complaints on my end. The second object appeared to be a collapsible spyglass, the sort you'd expect to see a pirate use.

Curious, I plucked it out of the air and focused on it.

Starlight Spyglass

As much fun as it is to watch you humans stumble around in the dark like drunken wombats, there's only so many accidental falling deaths our audience will tolerate.

Enter this handy dandy spyglass. It offers two functions, either of which can be used up to ten minutes per day before needing to recharge. You can use it as a night scope, able to cut through the darkness to a distance equal to your normal fog of war limit. Conversely, it can also be utilized in a lit setting to temporarily double the range for fog of war, allowing you to spy on monsters, NPCs, or other chasers long before they're able to see you.

Don't get cocky, though. The Starlight Spyglass has the downside of greatly amplifying existing light sources. Directly viewing any light source brighter than a torch will result in a flare-up, causing you and anyone within five feet of your dumb ass to receive a temporary Blindness debuff.

Bet you won't see that one coming.

Despite the potential downside, there was little doubt this would come in handy, especially since this cavern was proving much larger than Apu's jungle home.

I picked a direction facing away from my teammates as well as the Vultures, extended the scope to its full length, and put it up to my right eye. A timer at the bottom of the viewing range appeared, counting down from ten minutes, but I was less interested in that than the stand of dead trees I'd focused on.

Whoa.

Drega had undersold the shit out of this. This was far better than any night scope I'd ever heard of. The trees and the ground around them appeared in full color, as clear as if the sun was shining down from above. I had to do a double and triple take to make sure I was seeing it right, eating up nearly a minute of my allotted limit.

Oh yeah, this one was none too shabby. Well worth a little Drega abuse.

My new spellbook came with the same single-use warning as my last one, which I quickly dismissed, focusing on the spell itself.

Crackling Cannonball – level 1
Combat Spell
Cost: 70 mana
Effect: 1 ammunition-based projectile
Duration: up to 1 minute
Range: 6 feet from point of impact
There are few things more heartbreaking than putting all your faith into a Hail Mary long shot and then completely shitting the bed. After all, almost only counts in horseshoes and hand grenades.

That's where Crackling Cannonball comes in, because that's exactly what it turns your next shot into.

No, not a horseshoe, dipshit, the other thing.

Upon casting this spell you can empower one projectile with a potent electrical charge. On a successful hit, your target will *enjoy* an additional jolt of electricity damage equal to whatever they would have suffered otherwise.

Where this spell really shines, though, is on a miss. So long as your ineptly made shot comes within six feet of a target, they'll still get a charge out of this one.

It's electric ... but you can go fuck yourself if you think I'm saying the rest.

Dopey as its name might be, this spell was seemingly handcrafted for my banshee racket. Best of all, it potentially overcame any damage loss I might otherwise suffer from using Aim Assist.

No two ways about it. These two achievements took the sting out of letting the Vultures pick Mei's corpse.

Pixel made out decently as well. In addition to splitting their new stat points equally across intelligence and psionics, they got a ten point Wisdom Patch in their boss box.

They likewise received potion replenishments same as me, but the bigger news was they too got a new spellbook in their haul – this one called *Mana Splash*.

"Costs a hundred points," Pixel explained, "but it instantly replenishes half my mana points, as well as yours and Boog's so long as you guys are within thirty feet of me when I cast it."

"That's not bad at all."

"Yeah, about as close to a casting freebie as it gets."

"The name's a bit much, though," I replied.

"Yeah. There's a bukkake joke just waiting to be made."

"If you say so. Personally, I have no idea what that is."

"Liar," Pixel snapped, causing me to laugh, at least until Boog caught our attention once more.

"Pink water taste bad," she complained.

Pink water? "What are you talking about, Boog?"

"New magic water. Yuck! Boog no like."

Crap. Was she wasting a new potion?

I focused my HUD on her to see what she was talking about, calling up the party submenu and then her character sheet.

From the look of things, she'd likewise received a bunch of potions as well as some gl'ohrods. No surprise there. The thing is, all of them seemed to be ones we were already aware of, so I kept scrolling to see what else she could be talking about.

"What's an upgrade clip?" I asked.

"Ooh, is that what she got?" Pixel replied.

"Yeah. Says it's for ... a Boomerang Upgrade."

"Nice. That'll come in handy," they explained. "Upgrade clips are weapon attachments, kind of like that shield was for your SK. They provide various upgrades for existing weaponry. In this case, if I'm reading it right, it'll basically turn her axe into a discount Mjolnir, if you catch my drift."

I did, but Boog didn't – that mythology being a bit after her time.

"M-Mil...?"

"That means you'll be able to throw your axe and it'll return to your hand so you can do it again," Pixel said. "That's pretty good. You should equip it right away."

"Agreed." In her current form, Boog was a little light on ranged attacks. This would hopefully serve to remedy that, especially if her axe was as potent flying through the air as she'd shown it to be while slicing up opponents.

That was all well and good, don't get me wrong, but it also had nothing to do with pink water, so I kept looking ... until I found something at the end of Boog's inventory list that caused me to do a double take.

Son of a... "Boog, can you do us a favor? Can you pull that pink water from your inventory so we can see it?"

She stopped scratching long enough to make it appear.

"The fuck?" Pixel remarked.

No wonder it tasted terrible. The overmind, obviously as some sort of sick joke in response to Boog's condition, had awarded her a two gallon jug of calamine lotion.

I let out a sigh then turned my head skyward.

"You guys think you're funny but you're not."

⌛⌛⌛⌛ ⋅᛭ᚾ᛭ᚾ᛭ ⌛⌛⌛⌛

"Boog feel better!"

"That's nice. Now sit still, I'm not done yet. And stop trying to lick it off."

"Sorry, Macmac."

I was just finishing up slathering her in yet another handful of lotion, leaving her looking like a sticky pink nightmare. It wasn't quite a scroll of curse removal, but at least we were making lemonades from the lemons we'd been handed.

"Oh yeah, that's real lovely," Pixel commented as I finally finished.

"Y'know, you could've used TK Hand to help out."

"Yeah, I *could've*, but I figured you and your *mate* deserved some quality couple time."

I was about to tell them off when I looked up to find Friedrich approaching. Guess the Vultures had finished their scavenging.

It was all I could do to bite my tongue as he stopped and looked at the three of us before finally settling his gaze upon me.

"Walk with me," he said. "I wish to speak with you."

"Anything you have to say to me you can say to my friends too."

He glanced sidelong at them both before returning his attention my way. "I would prefer it be just the two of us. Do not worry. We won't go far." He gestured to the east, currently showing as empty on my map. "Please. I insist."

I was about to tell him where he could shove his insistence when I remembered that PVP was now in full force. My eyes narrowed. Was that what this was about?

Perhaps sensing the reason for my reluctance, Friedrich said, "I assure you our truce is still in effect. You acted honorably. I see no reason to sully that. But if it helps to ease your mind... Fast!"

Moments later, the red FAST flitted our way. "Sir?"

"Take this. Hold it for me until I get back."

He unclipped the gun belt around his waist and handed both it and the weapon holstered inside to his *companion*.

"Yeah, about that...," Pixel started.

So much for our truce. "Hold that thought for now," I interrupted, realizing that the best way to avoid an argument was to remove ourselves from the situation.

I understood where Pixel was coming from, and in truth supported them on it, but I had a feeling the last thing we needed was to start some shit – especially considering the Vultures mostly had us outclassed.

Dying in an unwinnable fight that could've been avoided, well, let's just say I wasn't a big fan of the concept.

Pixel: *Seriously, Tim? Now you wanna be buddy-buddy with this jackhole?*

Tim, JUST FUCKING TIM: *Not even remotely. We just gotta deal with it for now, okay? Besides, weren't you the one who told me we were neck deep in shit? Well, this is me dog-paddling. The least you can do is try not to drown us in the process.*

⌛⌛⌛⌛ ⋅⋄⋅⋄⋅⋄⋅ ⌛⌛⌛⌛

To show that I wasn't planning anything funny, as well as to hopefully suggest I wasn't afraid either, I did the same as Friedrich and handed my racket over to Pixel for safekeeping.

Mind you, I still had my mace as a backup, just in case.

In all fairness, I had no way of knowing if Friedrich likewise had a backup weapon. Hell, he almost certainly did. It would be the height of stupidity to ever be fully disarmed in this place.

Either way, I didn't like my odds against him in a fight, but hopefully I had enough tricks up my sleeve to at least give him a bloody nose if he started anything.

Likewise, I made it a point to keep an eye on my map as well as the chat window, just to make sure nothing funny was going on back at our temporary rest stop.

"You're wondering if this is some sort of ambush, no?" Friedrich asked, his tone giving away nothing. "Your silence speaks volumes."

"Does it?" I replied, trying to keep my tone neutral.

"Indeed. You can tell a great deal about a man by what he doesn't say, as much as by what he does."

"You get that from a fortune cookie?"

He raised an eyebrow. "I am not familiar with such things."

"Never mind. Bad joke."

"I see. Well then, since we are breaking the ice, might I ask you a personal question?"

I shrugged, not sure where this was going. "Sure. Can't promise I'll answer it, though."

He appeared to consider this as we walked, his hands clasped behind his back giving him a disciplined yet menacing appearance. "Is it common on your world for men to have such vulgar names?"

"What?" Okay, that one caught me by surprise, not to mention I had no idea what he was talking about. Tim wasn't a... *Wait a second.* "You mean what's showing in your HUD?"

"Yes. On my world, such language would be considered ... distasteful."

I was tempted to point out the irony of a fucking Nazi calling anything distasteful, but I held my tongue – remembering what Pixel had said earlier. I didn't know anything about this guy. Probably best to not jump to conclusions with people from different realities. "Oh that? It was a stupid prank by my FAST. My last name is McAvoy, not *Just Fucking Tim*. Problem is, I'm stuck with it until Stage Three."

"Ah. And how was your FAST able to accomplish this ... prank?"

"That's easy. Pixel's the party leader, technically speaking anyway."

"You follow that automaton?"

"Not exactly. It's just a technicality. Although in all fairness, they do know a lot more about this game, it's rules, et cetera, so it kind of makes sense."

"So, you are okay with it mocking you?"

"I didn't say that."

"Then I suggest you demand that it hand back the reins of leadership. Forgive my saying so, but it is painfully obvious that between the three of you there is only one clear choice to lead."

I raised an eyebrow, not liking where this was going. "And why do you say that?"

"Your friend the ... proto-human. She's strong and agile, a good foot soldier no doubt, but I think we both know that she lacks that certain *spark*."

"And I don't?"

"I suppose that remains to be seen." He grinned, probably to show he meant it as a joke. Can't say I found it particularly funny, though.

"You're not necessarily wrong on that front, but Pixel's a different story."

"No," he stated. "I can assure you *it* is not."

I was beginning to see where this conversation was going. "Is that why you treat your own FAST like dirt?"

"I do not treat my FAST in any such way. I speak to it like the servant it is obviously meant to be."

"Really? From what I can tell you didn't even give them a name."

"Them? I am forced to disagree with your assessment. They are machines, advanced ones true, but machines nonetheless. And though these units ostensibly exist to aid us in our quest, they are still part of the mechanism which seeks to lead us to our ruinous end. I merely choose to see through any such illusions."

"Illusions?" I asked.

"Yes. The illusion that they are in this game as our equals."

"Is that a fact?" I replied, very much not liking where this was going. "So you're saying they're beneath us?"

"Not at all. These automatons were obviously created with technology eons beyond what either of us can imagine. All I am saying is that treating them as equals in this wretched game belies the fact that they are anything but. Three lives to our one, and do you know what happens to them if their assigned chaser dies?"

"I assume they get retired until the next season."

"That is one option, true, but they are able to remain on the field if they so wish. I have been told this is due to the nature of the parties they allow us to form. It allows them to continue affecting the outcome, even if their bonded chaser is no more."

"I didn't know that. Still, it's not necessarily a bad thing."

"Quite the contrary, my friend. I, for one, cannot think of anything more terrifying they could throw at us than a masterless FAST."

I bristled at him calling me his friend, but apparently he interpreted my expression differently.

"I see this concept bothers you as well."

"I didn't say…"

"It is why I asked you here to talk, away from the prying eyes and ears of others."

I stopped and turned to face him. "Okay, you've totally lost me now. What is this about exactly?"

"It is simple, my friend. In you, I sense a kindred spirit."

Wait, what?!

55

THE MONSTERS WITHIN

"I'll stop you right there. We are nothing alike. There's nothing kindred about us."

"You misunderstand," Friedrich replied. "I did not mean to imply our beliefs were..."

"That's good," I snapped, feeling my temper start to fray, "because I... Wait, what exactly did you mean then?"

"Your clothes, your mannerisms. Though they are ... not exactly what I am used to, they are familiar nonetheless."

"Not sure I'm following."

"It is simple. Ulagan and Marius, though capable, both hail from the distant past. Though I can appreciate that they understand what it is to follow orders, as well as do what needs to be done to survive, their reasoning is somewhat ... antiquated. As such, I find it hard to relate to them. You, on the other hand, appear to be from a time period much closer to my own. Thus I feel we can perhaps talk in ways they would simply not understand."

"Yeah, well think again. Your sick beliefs came to an end with the Nineteen-forties and World War Two."

That wasn't entirely true. It was more like his way of thinking had simply been driven into hiding, only to see a disturbing resurgence in the modern era. But this jackass didn't need to know that. After all, it's not like he'd be visiting my Earth anytime soon.

"Nineteen-forties?" he replied, sounding confused. "And a second world war, you say?"

"Exactly. Let me guess, you're from like nineteen thirty-eight or something. Well, consider this a spoiler, but you guys lose big time."

I kind of wished Pixel was close enough to eavesdrop. This was actually one of the few bits of history I remembered, mostly thanks to my great granddad.

Friedrich raised an eyebrow. "I'm afraid you are quite mistaken. I was actually plucked from the year nineteen-sixty-seven."

"*Sixty-seven?*" Oh fuck, was I dealing with a *Man in the High Castle* situation here?

I'd managed to make it through the first season of that show before it became too depressing to watch. Deb, on the other hand, had *soldiered* on. I was pretty sure she had a thing for the actor playing John Smith. It wouldn't be too hard for me to read something into that, but it was probably best not to. The last thing I needed was for my bitterness to cause me to start painting her with every negative stereotype imaginable.

The truth was, tempting as it was to explain to Jeremy that his mother was a cheating whore, I didn't want that for him. A bad breakup brought with it enough pain, but I didn't want my son growing up thinking the only thing his parents were good for was bad-mouthing each other. I couldn't control what Deb told him, but I wanted to be better than that. He deserved at least that much.

I pushed those thoughts away for now. Back to the point at hand, Friedrich had actually sounded confused at the prospect of there being a second world war.

"Yes, nineteen-sixty-seven," he repeated. "October of the

year, as a matter of fact. Might I be so bold as to ask when you hail from?"

"Um, the mid twenty-twenties."

"Twenty ... as in two-thousand and twenty?" he replied wide-eyed.

"Yeah."

"You're certain?"

"Of course. Why would you even ask that?"

"No reason. It's just ... your attire. Forgive me for saying so, but I expected something less ... pedestrian considering the advanced time frame."

Advanced time frame? Hah! I glanced down at myself. "I'll admit the colors are a bit much, but aside from the armor and magic this actually isn't too far off from everyday business casual. Why?"

"It's just ... two-thousand and twenty. I would have expected..."

"Let me guess. I should be wearing a silver space suit and talking about how idyllic life is on the moon."

"Ah, so you do have moon colonies then," he replied.

I couldn't help but chuckle. "Nope. There aren't any moon colonies ... no flying cars either."

"So has technology not advanced in your world?"

"I wouldn't exactly say that." I took a moment to consider what *Star Trek* and *Lost in Space* might have once considered futuristic. "I mean, we have cell phones, the internet, and TVs are definitely a lot thinner..."

"*Cell* phones?" he interrupted. "As in telephones made out of living cells?"

"Not quite. I guess what I'm trying to say is we've made progress but we're not exactly living like *The Jetsons*."

"You speak of the cartoon, yes? I am familiar with this."

"You are?"

"Indeed. It is a popular show from America."

"So America still exists?" I replied, finding my curiosity piqued.

"Of course. Does it not in your world?"

"I ... yeah, it still ... I mean it does," I stammered, momentarily caught off guard that he would even ask that. "I'm actually from New Jersey as a matter of fact."

Suddenly Pixel's words from earlier hit me full on, reminding me that I had no idea what this guy's world was like or how history had played out in it, and vice versa ... other than both our Earths apparently had *The Jetsons*. Although, whether his was actually the cartoon I remembered or something completely different, I didn't know. This was probably not the time to find out, either. There were better questions to be asked.

"Let's back up for a second here. Was there or was there not a second world war on your Earth?"

He appeared to consider this. "Since you previously mentioned it, I am assuming you mean at some point in the nineteen-forties. That was certainly a period of economic upheaval and conflict, no doubt, but I am not sure any of it would be on the same scale as the conflict that engulfed Europe three decades earlier."

"Okay fine. What sort of conflicts are we talking about then?"

He shrugged. "There was the Sino-Japan invasion of nineteen-fifty-one. It raged for nearly eight years before peace terms could be agreed on. And of course the Soviets have been in a state of near constant civil war ever since Stalin's death."

"What about in Europe?"

He put a hand to his chin. "If my history serves me well, Portugal and Spain engaged in some skirmishes with the Italians over disputed territory in Africa, but that ended relatively quickly."

I let out a sigh. "Are you seriously trying to tell me that Hitler didn't invade Poland in nineteen-thirty-nine?"

"I don't see how that's even possible," he replied, "considering the Chancellor was assassinated in thirty-six."

"Wait, he was?"

Friedrich nodded. "He along with the majority of his cabinet, all victims of a bomb planted by a retired MI6 operative." He inclined his head. "A Brit, in case that organization isn't familiar to you. Caused quite the uproar at the time. Though it was never proven he'd ordered it, their Prime Minister was forced to step down due to the resulting scandal."

"So what happened after?"

"As I said, it was a period of strife. Armies were mobilized and sabers were rattled, but cooler heads prevailed in the end. Fortunately, there were many still alive who remembered the killing of the Archduke and the horrors that came afterward. As angry as my people were, few were eager to relive those days."

Huh. "So then why are you still wearing a Nazi uniform twenty years later?"

He let out a huff. "A derogatory term if you ask me, one that went out of style over a decade ago. For the record, I proudly serve the National Socialist Party."

"Fine, whatever. What I mean is you guys ... your party is obviously still around."

"Of course. If anything, the Chancellor's death proved to be the proverbial martyr for our cause to prosper, even if his successors have mostly lacked his charisma."

Charisma's one word for it. I pursed my lips. "And what exactly is your cause these days?"

"Same as it has always been. A strong homeland, a thriving economy, and preserving our identity as a people."

"It's that last one that worries me," I muttered.

"Why should that be, might I ask?" he replied. "Is that not the goal of any people, to ensure they stand tall and united under a common banner?"

"Depends on the banner and what the consequences are for those who choose not to comply."

Time Chaser

"Without a doubt. But I make no secret of who I am and what I believe. If you have misgivings about that, I am happy to discuss them with you."

"I'm not sure if there's anything to be gained by that."

"Come now," Friedrich said. "I assume you must have some opinion on the beliefs I follow. It's practically coming out of your pores."

"You could say that."

"And am I wrong in assuming it has to do with what you spoke of earlier, this so called second world war?"

"You wouldn't be."

"I see. So then let me ask, how long did this great conflict last? A decade, two ... perhaps even three?"

I wasn't sure what he was getting at but I did the math in my head. "Six years."

"Six? So it would have ended in ... nineteen-forty-five. Tell me, Tim *McAvoy*, what could have happened in such a short span that would cause you to bear me ill will some four generations removed from the end of this conflict?"

I let out a deep breath.

"There's no need for candor here," he said, sounding genuinely curious. "Did it result in another financial Depression, perhaps one even greater than the last? Did governments crumble, causing the world to fall into chaos? Or was it more personal for you, the loss of family that subsequent generations still mourn? I truly wish to know."

"I…"

I was sorely tempted to drag this fucker over the coals regarding the Holocaust and the millions of lives lost, but held my tongue instead. If his Earth was a world where such atrocities didn't happen, well, then he would have no idea what I was even talking about.

Why even bother to plant those seeds? It's not like I was trying to give him any new ideas.

Yes, it was probably stupid to think that way, but I did.

My great grandpa had been an infantryman in the European theater. I remembered sitting on his lap as a child, listening to him regale me with war stories — most of which were not even remotely appropriate for my young ears. Hell, I knew times changed and all, but the thought of him telling Jeremy those same stories absolutely horrified me.

Regardless of any of that, if there was a more reviled group in history than the Nazi party, I was hard pressed to think of it, and there was zero doubt this guy was a card carrying member.

Yet, at the same time he wasn't.

Despite Friedrich being from an entirely different universe, though, the whole *identity as a people* schtick he'd mentioned made me distinctly nervous.

It was the sort of ideology that sounded good on paper but could easily turn ugly in a heartbeat. If anything, it was the exact same concept Pixel and I had discussed earlier with regard to guilds, just on a larger level.

Anytime you had an *us*, there was a *them*, and it seemed to be a natural progression to assume those others, whoever they might be, were inferior in some way.

Friedrich was pressuring me to tell him things that it was maybe best he never learn about, even as a cautionary tale. Such things could easily be twisted by those with bad intent. Like I said, I didn't want to inadvertently give him any ideas.

Of course, that could've also been my innate prejudice speaking, coupled with the fact that I was fucking exhausted. Either way, it was probably best to steer this discussion in a different direction.

"Did you really bring me out here just to discuss our respective world history?" I asked, conveniently ignoring that it was me who'd first brought it up.

"A fair point," he replied after a moment, "and a prudent one considering the clock is still ticking for us all. Very well. I trust you've noticed that we've defeated a so-called boss within this section of the dungeon, yet neither rest, succor, nor an exit has been provided to us."

"Trust me, I've noticed." *Especially on the rest part.*

"That tells me something else waits for us ahead, either a challenge or reward, perhaps both." He turned and looked to the north. "Might I ask whether you and your companions have previously tested your mettle against one of these boss creatures?"

"Yeah. We took out a giant sloth that some natives were worshipping as a god."

"Truly?" Friedrich replied. "The wonders of this place never cease to amaze."

"Not sure wonder is the word I'd go with."

"Perhaps horrors would be better?" he replied with a humorless chuckle before shaking his head. "Regardless, I will assume you being in this place same as us is no mere coincidence."

"You're talking about the ascension ring that's somewhere north of here, right?"

He nodded. "You and your companions may of course feel free to help yourselves to the prize offered by that fox's demise, but I can tell you what it is."

"Oh?"

"Yes. You see, if one has already upgraded their map to show the location of an exit, killing another boss simply adds the next closest. In this case one to the east. No idea how far, but it's further than the one we have both been tracking."

"Good to know in an emergency I suppose. Knowledge..."

"Is power," he finished. "Perhaps truer words were never spoken."

A weird feeling wormed its way through my gut at him finishing my sentence, one that was not altogether pleasant.

When we first walked out here, Friedrich had told me he sensed in me a kindred spirit, a notion I vehemently denied. After all, the last person in the world I would ever want to identify with was someone wearing his – not colors, that was still weird – but insignia.

But we weren't on my world.

More importantly, I couldn't exactly claim innocence at least not anymore. There was a very real danger of this place turning me into a monster, whether against my will or not. Might it be possible that at some point his words about kinship would ring far truer than I'd ever want them to?

Would that ultimately be the end result of this game – winners who'd become little more than monsters stuffed into the skins of men?

I pushed that thought from my head. It was far too unpleasant for me to consider in my current state.

Or at least I tried to, but I had a feeling this was one demon that wasn't going to be silenced so easily.

56

TIRED EYES ON THE PRIZE

I got back to find Pixel, along with a pink and crusty Boog, in the process of eying Mei's corpse, as if debating whether it was safe to claim their share – despite the other Vultures currently being preoccupied with looting Mei's minions.

To show that things were cool, I approached the body while Friedrich continued onward past me, mostly ignoring my companions as he headed to rejoin his party.

Lootable Corpse – Decennial Boss
Ascension Ring Update Available.

Unsurprisingly, there was nothing else left to take, not even a stitch of fur, so I settled for what I could get.

Sure enough, when I next viewed my map, a new glow had joined the slowly pulsing one to the north – this one directly east of us. I watched it for several seconds as my companions, emboldened by my actions, likewise claimed the reward.

The second glow finally pulsed, telling me what I'd already guessed. It was further away than the ring we'd been chasing – albeit not as far as the first one had been when we'd fought Apu.

With more than a day left in this stage, I had little doubt it was within reach even taking a proper rest into account.

This was our chance to break off and put the Vultures and their swastika-clad leader to our backs. Tempting as it might be, though, there were a few problems with that idea.

Pixel: *So what's the deal, Tim? You two were out there jawing long enough to officially be in a relationship.*

Boog: *NoMyMaczwlwwkbrrrrrrrrppppp!*

Huh. I'd almost understood part of that. Guess she was finally getting better at mentally typing.

Pixel: *Relax, Boog. It was just a joke.*

Tim, JUST FUCKING TIM: *Let's just say our discussion was eye-opening. You were right by the way.*

Pixel: *Care to elaborate because I'm pretty sure I've been right about a lot of things lately.*

Tim, JUST FUCKING TIM: *About him being from a world that's way different than mine.*

Pixel: *Seriously? Are you still harping about that?*

Tim, JUST FUCKING TIM: *I'm not harping. I'm just saying that maybe I was too quick to judge.*

Pixel: *Nah, you weren't. I was thinking about it while you were gone and I'd say you were right on the money from the start. I, for one, am okay judging this book by its shitty cover because anyone who treats a FAST the way he does is pretty much an instant asshole in my book.*

Tim, JUST FUCKING TIM: *Look, I'm not saying he isn't.*

Pixel: *No, but the way you're beating around the bush, I'm starting to get the impression that telling these guys to take a long walk off a short pier isn't in the cards. Tell me I'm wrong.*

Tim, JUST FUCKING TIM: *You're ... not.*

Pixel: *Of course I'm not. Because why wouldn't we stick with a guy who treats his hyper-advanced, sentient assistant worse than a spoiled ten year old with a Tamagotchi?*

And this was apparently my life now.

Don't get me wrong, I liked Pixel. They might be crass and have all the social grace of a drunken reveler on St. Patrick's Day, but so far they'd proven both smart and reliable in a game where friends were in short supply by design. Not to mention, though I'd never admit this out loud, I kinda appreciated them constantly playing devil's advocate.

That said, Pixel was apparently fine and dandy with otherworldly Nazis but drew the line at them being mean to their FASTs.

Just a bit of hypocrisy there, in my humble opinion.

Tim, JUST FUCKING TIM: *Fine, maybe that's Friedrich, but what about Marius? He seems to treat Invictus pretty decently.*

Pixel: *Maybe so, but what about their other buddy? I'm gonna go out on a limb and guess his missing FAST is among those hundred-and-seventy-six who are currently pushing up digital daisies. You'll forgive me for not seeing a positive track record here, Tim.*

Tim, JUST FUCKING TIM: *I get what you're saying, but it's more complicated than that.*

Boog: *Whatmeanbygdjkbrrrrrrrrpppppp?*

Oh for fuck's sake. "Say that again, Boog, out loud this time."

"Want know what big word mean, Macmac."

"What big word? Complicated?"

"Tom-ah-goch..."

"Tamagotchi? It's ... you know what? It's not important. Pixel can explain it to you later."

"Oh yeah," the FAST remarked, "I'm sure that'll be a laugh riot. So anyway, back to my point. What's the freaking deal, Tim? Don't tell me you and the Yellow Skull over there are best buddies now."

"Not exactly, but you were right about his Earth being different."

"No shit. What do you think alternate reality means? That still doesn't..."

"You're right. It doesn't, and I'm not saying we should drop our guard, but the bottom line is Friedrich offered to extend our truce, at least until we reach the far end of this cave, wherever that is."

"We stay with new friends?" Boog asked.

"Something like that."

"And you accepted?" Pixel replied, sounding doubtful.

"Not outright, but it's either that or we break off now and turn east because they're definitely heading to that ring to the north."

"I hate to admit it, but option two is starting to sound more promising to me by the minute."

"And normally I might not disagree with you, but we got to talking and I got to thinking. What happened after we took down Apu?"

"Boog know! Boog stood on hairy monster and made water."

"I meant *after* that part, Boog."

"We got the fuck out of there and found ourselves a nice campground where we could rest and recharge," Pixel said. "I get it. You're wondering why we're still stuck in this hell hole."

I nodded.

"Not to point out the obvious," they continued, "but you do realize they're not going to set up every encounter the same way, right? Because I can tell you right now that's a good way to bore the audience to tears. And if they're bored, that pretty much means we're about to get fucked."

"No doubt," I replied. "But the point still remains. In terms of video game logic, it's usually customary to give players a break after a big battle, otherwise you run them down and it becomes a slog."

"I'm gonna go out on a limb and assume you never played *Dark Souls*."

"No, I didn't. Why?"

"Not important. Go on."

I shrugged. "Anyway, as I was saying, I suppose it's possible they could have tossed the main boss into the middle of this cavern instead of at the end – which means we can probably look forward to more mid-tier enemies before hitting the other side. Not undoable, but increasingly difficult as some of us get more and more run down."

There came a brief pause, then Pixel asked, "But you don't think that's going to happen, do you?"

I shook my head.

"Gods damn it all," they replied. "Neither do I."

"Wait, you agree with me?"

"Don't let it go to your head, Tim. I didn't want to say anything before now and risk getting everyone riled up, but my FAST intuition is telling me the same..."

"Your *FAST intuition*?"

"Call it a fucking hunch if it makes you feel better," they snapped followed by a sharp buzzing sound. "Anyway, as I was about to say, in any other situation I might argue with you, but there's no doubt we're getting closer to that ascension ring. In fact, I'm starting to think there's a fair shot that's what's waiting for us at the end of this section."

"And you think there could be something big standing in the way?"

"Without a doubt. Might be a puzzle or a big-ass trap, but yeah, I think something's waiting there to fuck us over. Don't get me wrong. Not all the exit routes are going to be that way. It's not how things work, otherwise I can guarantee the number of yahoos who've escaped so far would be much lower. It all comes down to luck of the draw, meaning it's equally possible we could find that ring and walk right into it with no problem."

"Is that what your gut ... err ... circuits are telling you about this one?"

"Cells, moron. Do I look like a transistor radio to you? But to answer your question, no, not really."

"Okay then. So that still begs the question, do we keep on going the way we are with the company we've picked up, trusting that our truce holds, or should we break off and try our luck to the east?"

"That's assuming east is actually the easier direction," Pixel replied. "Problem is, the overmind could've predicted we might balk at this point. Heading east could just as easily be a false flag, where the real danger lies. If so, then we'd be walking right into it minus our extra cannon fodder."

"Which I'm sure they'd really appreciate being referred to as."

"Hence why I'm saying it to you and not them."

"So you think north is the better option then?"

"No. What I'm saying is I have no fucking idea. It could be easier or it could be a surprise Eon boss, in which case we'll all be dead before we even know what hit us. Not that I think we're gonna get lucky in either instance."

"Me neither."

"Boog feel lucky."

"What was that, Boog?" I asked.

"Boog feel lucky," she repeated. "Very lucky."

"Really?" Pixel replied. "You've been cursed, mutated, and are currently covered in pink sludge. In what universe is that lucky?"

"Boog here with friends. That make Boog lucky."

I ... I actually couldn't say anything to that. In the face of all the negativity that Pixel and I were volleying back and forth, Boog's tiny bit of optimism caught me completely flatfooted. I glanced Pixel's way, wondering if the FAST had anything assholish to say, but they just continued to hover where they were.

"Thanks, Boog," I replied after several seconds. "I feel pretty lucky to have met you as well. *Both* of you," I added, turning toward the FAST.

"Don't look at me. I ain't breaking out the harmonicas and hymn book quite yet."

"Come on, say it."

"No."

"Say it."

"Fine! I'm lucky to have met you both. Now don't prove me wrong by getting all of our dumb asses killed."

Eh, close enough.

⌛⌛⌛⌛ ⋆⋅☆⋅⋆⋅☆⋅⋆ ⌛⌛⌛⌛

Debuff – You are Fatigued: severity level 1.
So much for lucky.

I glanced at the notice in my HUD, wondering what it meant. This was the first debuff I'd seen with a level attached to it. I focused on it, best I was able to in my tired state, curious to see exactly how screwed I was.

Fatigued – Debuff
Duration: temporary
Effect: scalable

Early to bed, early to rise, makes a chaser healthy, mobile, and not fucking exhausted. Too bad you're either an insomniac or just an idiot who didn't get that memo.

Now, you may be thinking that this makes no sense. After all, your non-combat healing is pretty darned awesome. But here's the thing, you can pump all the stimulants you want into your body, but that primitive monkey brain sloshing around your skull still needs to rest and recharge, otherwise it'll start to fizzle out.

How often you need to rest depends on your constitution, but if you're listening to this then chances are you've already overestimated what you can handle. But hey, don't worry. It only gets better from here ... for us that is.

Here's what you can expect to *enjoy* from the various levels of Fatigued.

Severity Level 1: +10% miss chance when attacking, -10% damage to all physical attacks.

Severity Level 2: +10% chance of spell or psionic failure,

Time Chaser

+1% chance of them failing in a way most spectacular. +25% chance to stumble and fall if moving at any speed greater than walking.

That didn't sound good.

Severity Level 3: -30% to your maximum health.

Severity Level 4: All those penalties from Severity Level 1 and 2 are now doubled.

Severity Level 5: 100% chance to pass the fuck out, no matter where you are or what you're doing. And yes, this will almost certainly happen at a time that is less than convenient to you.

Great, just fucking great. It was bad enough I was tired, but the freaking Chase had to quantify it in terms of how much that could fuck me over.

More and more I was beginning to think we should've hunkered down in that village when we had the chance, even if it had only been for a couple of hours.

The funny thing is, we could've used those shrouded serapes as blankets with no one else being the wiser.

Too bad none of us had thought of it at the time.

Pixel: *You okay, Tim? Just saw that notice pop up in my HUD.*

Tim, JUST FUCKING TIM: *I'll live.*

Pixel: *You'd better because I really don't want to end up being memory wiped again only to have to start all over with some new schmuck next quink.*

Tim, JUST FUCKING TIM: *Your empathy is truly a thing to be marveled at.*

Pixel: *Listen. I can either be your emotional support FAST or the guy who melts motherfuckers with acid, not both.*

I threw the little bug zapper some side eye.

Tim, JUST FUCKING TIM: *Will the others be able to see that I'm currently debuffed?*

Pixel: *Fortunately for us, you're golden on that one. Unconnected chasers can see the number of FAST deaths, penalties, and a* *few other tidbits, but you need to be at least guildmates to see someone's buffs and debuffs.*

At least that was something. We'd made our bed and I intended to lie in it, but advertising to the Vultures that we were potentially ripe for the picking struck me as an unwise strategy.

Tim, JUST FUCKING TIM: *Then I suggest we keep this to ourselves for now. That goes for you too, Boog. They already know you're cursed but they don't need to know anything else that might affect us.*

Boog: *Okmacmakoerrrrrrppppp!*

Lord help me but that almost made sense.

After going back and forth for a bit on the merits of continuing north versus breaking off and going east, we decided that the potential risk of running into another big battle on our own outweighed the risk of sticking with the Vultures.

Sadly, that didn't exactly make it a match made in Heaven.

Pixel didn't trust Friedrich as far as they could throw him. As for me, the jury was still out. I had my misgivings about his beliefs, but I was trying to rectify that with the fact that he was from a completely different world than my own. That and, despite not being the most personable guy I'd ever met, he hadn't actually taken a single move against us so far.

What swayed the vote in their favor was that neither Ulagan or Marius seemed to have any obvious strikes against them. They weren't exactly cozy and friendly, don't get me wrong, but neither were setting off any alarms.

In the end, between my growing fatigue and the fact that Boog, even covered in lotion, would occasionally drop to the ground for an extended itch break, we decided it made sense to stick with our original plan – which just so happened to coincide with where the Vultures were headed.

However, traveling alongside them and trusting them were two very distinct issues.

To that end, I started periodically biting the inside of my own mouth so as to force myself to focus. If the Vultures at some point insisted on taking a rest break, well, then we'd cross that bridge when we came to it, but until then I had no intention of saying shit about being tired – at least not until a campground finally showed up on my map.

Until we either reached one or made it to the end of this damnable cavern, I'd keep forging ahead best I could.

Sadly, seeing how the Fatigued debuff could stack, I had to question how good my best was truly going to be.

57

MEET THE NEIGHBORS
STAGE ONE EXPIRATION: 1 DAY, 3 HOURS

"Wine, friend?"

Huh? I opened my eyes from where I'd been trying to take a momentary breather to find Marius looking down at me. He was holding a ceramic jug in his hand, not dissimilar to the gunpowder jugs we'd taken off those archers.

We'd just finished dispatching a small group of yaoguai infantry, all low level grunts, and Friedrich had told everyone to take a few minutes to heal up before we set out again – not that I needed to. The closest I'd gotten to the scuffle was a ranged shot to test out my Crackling Cannonball. All I'll say is thank goodness for Aim Assist, otherwise who knows what direction that electrified sloth claw would've gone flying off in.

I hadn't sustained any injuries in the fight, but had decided to take advantage of the lull anyway. So I'd stepped away from the others and closed my eyes for a bit, hoping to clear my head and maybe stave off the next level of *Fatigued*.

Trying to not fall asleep outright, I'd been scrolling through my HUD behind closed eyes, looking for a way to perhaps set an alarm so I didn't miss our rapidly approaching window of opportunity to de-curse Boog. Alas, it was all for naught. Go figure, the SK's HUD technology made the latest VR headsets back home look like cereal box toys in comparison, but nobody had thought to include a fucking alarm clock app.

I'd been half-tempted to voice my misgivings on that out loud when I sensed I was no longer alone.

"Excuse me?" I asked, my exhaustion rendering me a bit slow on the uptake.

"Wine," he repeated, taking a seat next to me. "I find it always tastes best when shared."

"Hold on. Where did you get wine from?"

He grinned. "I liberated it from one of that fox's minions."

"And you're sure it's wine? Because we found some jugs like that on..."

"Reasonably sure, at least according to the damnable words hindering my sight in this hell." He held up the jug. "They tell me this is something called snow wine, a libation I've yet to have the pleasure of sampling. So what say you? Shall we remedy that together?"

"Together? Wait, why me and not your teammates?"

"A fair question. Take no offense from my words, friend, but the weariness behind your eyes is hard to miss." He again glanced at the jug. "I thought this might help."

Guess I wasn't doing as good of a job as I'd thought of hiding my fatigue. "Thanks, but I'm pretty sure wine doesn't work that way."

"Nonsense," he said dismissively. "A small taste in the morning fortifies a man for the long march ahead."

"Really?"

"Indeed. Tis a tried and true method of those who serve the legions."

"I... Oh, fuck it." *When in Rome ... or talking to a Roman.* At this point, I doubted coffee would rain down from the heavens anytime soon, so what did I have to lose? "All right. Let's give it a try."

Time Chaser

"That's the spirit, Tim, Just Fucking Tim."

"It's just Tim."

"As I said, Just Fucking Tim."

"Whatever," I said with a sigh.

Marius merely laughed before puncturing the seal on the jug. He took an experimental sip before nodding appreciably. "Perhaps this land is not as forsaken by the gods as I'd feared." He started to hand it to me before adding, "Just a swallow, mind you. There's a fine line between fortifying a man and turning him into a dullard. The latter is best saved for when victory has been declared, unless one enjoys being whipped for their indulgence." He chuckled again. "However, since my former tribune is nowhere to be seen, I deem the risk acceptable."

I raised an eyebrow. Marius had barely said two words since the battle with Mei. Now here he was being a chatty Cathy. It made me wonder if he hadn't indulged in some of that snow wine already.

That said, knowing I had an antivenom potion at the ready just in case, I raised the jug to my lips and took a modest swallow. Even barring his warning, I'd already seen what had happened to Boog after too much good cheer. Needless to say, I didn't want to risk the few intelligence points I had to spare.

Hmm. I was forced to admit it wasn't bad – extra sweet, not too far off from a sangria. Still, tasty or not, one sip was all I allowed myself.

Now to hope Marius was right and that tiny bit acted as a pick-me-up rather than the other way around.

I handed him back the jug but, rather than drink more, it instead disappeared into Marius's inventory. Guess he hadn't been kidding about maintaining discipline.

"Parthian spear," he said after a few minutes of silence.

"What?"

"That's what did me in. We had those devils on the run, but I lost my shield and one of them was quick to take advantage of it. My own fault really. You?"

"I was hit by a bus."

"A bus?" he asked, sounding curious.

"Think of it like ... a big metal chariot."

"Ah, I see," Marius replied.

"You do?"

"Friedrich mentioned such wonders in passing to Ulagan and I. He called them ... tanks I believe."

I considered this. "We have those too. Same general idea except one carries people and the other weapons."

He nodded as if that made sense to him. "I assume that means you're from a world closer to his than mine own."

"Yeah, I guess you could say that."

"So might I ask what you did to offend this *bus*?"

"Nothing. Wrong place at the wrong time. I just ... got in the way."

He chuckled. "I suppose that sums up my end as well, as it likely does many who find themselves here. We simply didn't ... get out of the way."

I couldn't disagree. "Seems to be a common way to meet one's maker."

"Indeed, save rather than our maker we meet each other instead in this gods forsaken land. All so we can strive for a second chance to *get out of the way* if you will."

Marius was proving to be talkative now that he'd gotten started. Who knows? Maybe the guy was shy and had been looking for an ice breaker. A bashful centurion. I certainly didn't have that on my bingo card this morning.

"So what drives you?" he asked.

"What do you mean?"

"In this place. A second chance at life is a tempting prospect, but I feel that alone isn't enough, at least not here. The challenges they've thrown our way since arriving have already been enough to crush the will of a good many."

"You're talking about those live updates?"

"Indeed. And yet, despite their attempts to crush our spirits, many of us still battle on. For that to happen there must be a reason. I would know yours."

I debated holding my tongue or making up some lie, but ultimately saw no reason to. It's not like a Roman legionnaire from some random Earth could do anything to threaten Jeremy. "My son."

"Ah, family," he said. "If there is better motivation, I do not know it. And it's one that we share."

"Oh?"

"I have a wife and two daughters waiting for me at home. My duties had already kept me away for far too many years, but it is only now that I realize how much I long to return to them."

My eyes opened wide at his words. I'd known what Boog was fighting for, but the truth was I hadn't given much thought to the very real possibility that my motivation might not exactly be unique among the chasers here. Of course it made perfect sense that some others, hell, probably most of them, had families waiting back home.

That potentially complicated things. All of a sudden I was reminded of that last live update, listening to Drega and Plagraxious joke about some chasers wanting it more than others.

How could you measure one parent's desire to return home against another's? I wasn't sure, except that there was little doubt we'd be forced to. It was yet one more thing to weigh myself down with. I already understood that in order to survive I might have to compromise my own ethics. Except it went beyond that. If I was forced to kill another chaser, I wouldn't merely be ending someone else's life but also ensuring that the *Jeremy* of their world would be forever left waiting.

Talk about a thought I wished I could scrub from my head.

"Though your world may be closer to that which Friedrich hails from," Marius continued, "perhaps our shared motivation bridges the gap more than we might expect."

"Huh?" I replied, forcing my darkening thoughts away. "Are you saying he doesn't have a family waiting for him?"

The centurion shrugged. "Alas, I know not. Though he speaks of where he was plucked from, he does so from a distance, as if looking down from a mountain top."

Friedrich had mentioned that he found it hard to relate to his teammates. But now that Marius mentioned it, he'd done the same with me – talking about his world from a ten-thousand foot perspective, spending more time discussing history and politics than himself.

In all fairness, though, I hadn't exactly given him much reason to open up.

"Do not mistake my words," Marius added after a moment or two. "I know full well the price of leadership, how one must place themselves apart from those whom they lead. Tis truly a lonely burden to bear, one I have never wished for myself." He paused, as if to consider what he'd just said. "Please do not think ill of me if such is also your burden. I don't wish to insult you by presuming comradery merely over some shared wine."

Now it was my turn to laugh. As a middle manager I sort of understood what he meant. Try as I might to remain *one of the guys*, once you were promoted out of the trenches there was no doubt that things changed. Friendly as I'd been with my team, I knew there would forevermore be that slight bit of distrust. After all, I was the one now tasked with yearly reviews, performance plans, and sometimes being forced to let good people go.

Nonetheless, Drakkensoft made finance software not cures for cancer. Reminding myself of that was usually a good way to keep my power, limited as it might be, from going to my head.

"You can relax, Marius. The only burden I'm carrying is wanting to get back home. Heck, I'm not even my party's leader."

"No?" he replied, sounding surprised. "The hairy one then?"

I grimaced. "Not quite."

"The FAST?"

I touched my finger to my nose before realizing he probably had no idea what that meant. "Yep. Pixel's the one running the show ... technically speaking."

"Truly?" he asked as if waiting for a punchline.

"No fooling. In all fairness, it wasn't like he was elected to the post. More of a ... miscalculation on my part."

"Still, I find that surprising to hear. Do not mistake my words, Just Tim, Invictus has been invaluable in combat and remains a fount of knowledge that would put the Sibylla Cumana to shame..."

I had no idea what the fuck he was talking about. I knew about the oracle of Delphi, but that was more Greek than Roman. Maybe this was something similar, but either way it was probably best to just nod rather than look like an idiot.

"However," Marius continued, "since the very beginning he has presented himself as an ally meant to *assist* in my efforts, nothing more."

"Is that the same deal with Friedrich's FAST?"

"Such would be my guess."

I inclined my head. "What do you mean by that?"

"Fast does not often speak aloud outside of combat. Friedrich does not approve of it. The two of them most often converse via way of... What is it called?"

"Cortexing?"

"Yes," he stated. "These vile words that forever seem to obscure our vision. It's bad enough they hamper us with this so-called fog of war but I would gladly give up all the gifts bestowed upon us to be able to see clearly and unhindered."

I wasn't quite so sure I'd agree, but I'd also grown up in an age where video game style overlays were common knowledge. Back to the matter at hand, I was forced to wonder whether Pixel was more right about the Vulture's leader than I had tried to convince myself.

Whereas Marius's relationship with Invictus struck me as reasonable, or as reasonable as something could be in this place, it was beginning to feel more and more like Friedrich's FAST was less an assistant and more a battered spouse.

Moreso, it was interesting to learn how different FASTs related to their assigned chasers. Murg, in the brief time I'd known them, had seemed much like Pixel in terms of being outspoken. As a result, I'd assumed all FASTs were like that – more or less equal partners in this game.

But maybe that wasn't the case.

Pixel had told me that after each Chase, surviving FASTs had their memories wiped – presumably to keep them from giving the next batch of chasers an unfair advantage in terms of knowledge. As a result, they couldn't really know whether they were fundamentally the same being then as they were now.

It made me wonder whether this disparity in how some FASTs behaved was a result of the chaser they were paired with, or their own individual personalities shining through regardless of lost memories.

It was the age old question of nature versus nurture, except with a synthetic bent.

"You seem lost for words, friend," Marius said, dragging me from my reverie.

"Sorry. I was just thinking about the differences between our respective FASTs."

He shrugged. "I suppose that's like wondering about the differences between any of us. Some men are strong, some are meek. Some outspoken, others withdrawn. I don't see why we should think different of any of the beings we meet in this place, no matter how advanced they claim to be."

"Maybe."

"No maybes about it. Trying to know the mind of another is like swimming against a raging river. We can only know them by their words and actions, nothing more. Ultimately the only one who can ever truly know what lies in a man, woman, or FAST's heart is themself."

I understood what he was saying but, as I glanced over to where Friedrich stood polishing his pistol while Fast hovered diligently over his shoulder, I couldn't help but feel a slight bit of unease nevertheless.

58

THE WAY FORWARD

STAGE ONE EXPIRATION: 1 DAY, 1 HOUR

Pixel: *Have they said anything yet?*
Tim, JUST FUCKING TIM: *No, and hopefully they don't pick this moment to start since I'd prefer to not fucking die.*

Pixel: *Admit it, it's kind of creepy.*

Tim, JUST FUCKING TIM: *Fine. Yes it is, but right now I'll take creepy over being peppered with explosive arrows.*

I shut off the chat window before they could say anything else. It was tough enough trying to maintain a *Stealthed* status without unneeded distractions, much less so with me currently dead on my feet – a saying I really didn't want to live up to.

The only plus in my favor was the Fatigued debuff didn't seem to affect my skills, otherwise I'd have been fucked with a capital F.

Following our brief rest break, which turned out to be not all that restful, we'd trekked for another hour and a half – meeting mostly minimal resistance in the form of a few more infantry as well as a pack of wild dogs that had been scavenging the battlefield. Neither proved to be much of a challenge for our combined group, although I was able to use the latter to bolster my waning supply of tooth-based ammunition.

Then, just as I was certain we'd be able to ride out the start of the new day with relatively little fanfare, the view on my map began to change.

At first it was just a few structures – small homes, maybe stables – with some white dots milling about them. Then the red began to show up in force.

It wasn't just scattered enemy troops, though. No, these were lined up as if standing in formation. My initial thought was that maybe we'd found an isolated enemy encampment, but there were simply too many of them.

The closer we got, the more the map filled in the details and the faster that yellow glow to the north of us began to ping.

Minutes later, the outline of a structure larger than anything I'd seen so far began to take shape on the map. That's when the strict formation of those red dots began to make sense. They weren't encamped so much as standing guard.

As for what they were guarding, that I didn't know.

The interior of the massive building was, unsurprisingly, a complete blank on my map, save for one thing – a tiny pulsating golden circle at the far end of it, right before where the structure met the cavern wall.

We'd finally found the ascension ring that would take us to Stage Two.

That wasn't all, though.

To the east, a relatively short distance away, I spied an exit leading out of this cave. Just beyond it, the normal dungeon hallways appeared to resume. More importantly, there was also a familiar X icon with a tiny flame over it. Finally, a freaking campground. I could've wept with joy. Hell, whoever was sponsoring it could've been serving fried cockroach for all I cared, so long as I could catch some sleep.

There was only one problem.

Time Chaser

The way out was guarded by a group of red dots roughly the same size as Shen's archer squad, but that wasn't all. In addition to the mobs, there was something else, a small, undefined structure or building directly connected to the exit.

Nobody in either of our parties seemed to have any clue what that might be, so we'd stopped to discuss our course of action.

Pixel and I had argued for heading straight for the cavern exit. From there, we could bunk down at the campground and then reevaluate our options once we were all fresh. Surprisingly, Marius agreed with us. Friedrich, on the other hand, was against it, telling us it was too risky to take a break now. He was worried that we'd be eating up nearly half of our remaining day, while having no idea how much resistance might be waiting for us once we finally tried to push for that ascension ring.

To be fair, he did have a point.

Distance-wise, it wasn't a lot – maybe fifty yards from the entrance of the structure to where that ring stood. But since those fifty yards were currently a complete unknown to us, I could understand his concern.

All the same, I was fucking beat. That building could end up being an empty warehouse and it would probably still be a challenge for me to make it all the way through without walking into a wall or two.

In the end we took a vote, the result of which was unexpected. Despite the Vultures outnumbering us, Marius had sided in favor of us being rested before tackling that ring. Invictus, likely following their partner's lead, had then done the same.

Either Marius was hankering for some shuteye too or we'd bonded over that wine more than I'd realized. Either way, Friedrich hadn't seemed pleased at being overruled, but he'd held his tongue once our course of action was decided.

Sadly, it wasn't quite that cut and dried. Still in question was that structure at the cave's exit and what it might be.

It didn't seem large enough to house reinforcements, but that didn't mean it wasn't dangerous. We'd already learned a harsh lesson here in how gunpowder could be the great equalizer. That knowledge alone was enough to warrant caution since none of us were particularly fond of the idea of walking into a massive bomb trap.

To that end, we decided it made sense to scout it out first. That meant splitting our forces so the stealthiest among us could do some reconnaissance while the rest held back. Ulagan had the next highest stealth skill after me – level three to my five – so that made us instant choices for this effort. Pixel wanted to go too, but I ixnayed that via chat, not wanting to leave Boog alone. Friedrich then surprised us by volunteering his FAST for the mission.

Our scout group decided, we'd set out, creeping across the darkened battlefield in a single file, with Fast bringing up the middle hidden beneath a blanket, not dissimilar to how we'd done it earlier with Pixel.

⌛⌛⌛⌛ ⌛⌛⌛⌛

The big difference between Pixel and Fast, aside from their color, was that Fast hadn't made so much as a peep since we'd headed out.

Pixel was right, it *was* kinda creepy. Fortunately, this wasn't a social call.

I was up front, using my Starlight Spyglass to help us navigate the darkness – the ashen dirt beneath our feet helping to cushion our footfalls which in turn made it easier to remained *stealthed*.

Awesome as the spyglass was for cutting through the dark, its range was the same as my fog of war. That meant we needed to get closer to both the exit and the enemies guarding it than I was really comfortable with.

The upside was that our current threesome – man, I really

needed to not call it that – was about the same strength as my regular party. So, tired or not, if we ran into any trouble we hopefully had a decent shot at successfully defending ourselves.

Before setting out, we'd all exchanged cortexing requests, allowing us to chat silently. That said, I had no idea if Fast was even reading them, having gotten no acknowledgement either way. Marius had been right about them being tight-lipped. Still, there were worse things than silence on side quests such as ours.

Tim, JUST FUCKING TIM: *All right, we're getting close. Slow and steady from here on in. So long as we remain stealthed, we should be able to get in and out unseen.*

It was probably an unnecessary reminder but it made me feel better as we crept ever closer to our goal.

The mobs up ahead had a fire burning, making them easy to spot from a distance. However, spotting their location wasn't the same as identifying them.

Luck was with us, though, as Ulagan noticed that the terrain sloped upward to the east of us. It wasn't much, just a small rise, but it would give us a slight vantage point while also hopefully putting us close enough to that exit to properly scope it out.

I'd used up about half of my spyglass's allotted ten minutes on the way over, but I wasn't too worried. With any luck, it would recharge with the change of day. Speaking of which, we needed to get back ASAP once we were done here. The clock was ticking on Boog getting a reprieve from her curse. While I hadn't been about to leave my sweater behind, I also didn't look forward to another day of slathering her with lotion – regardless of what form she was in.

A few minutes later found us crouched down atop the tiny rise, doing our best to conceal ourselves from sight. First things first, I took a look at the mobs through the spyglass. Within seconds, Drega's voice started playing back their descriptions, almost causing me to shit my pants until I remembered he was only audible within my mind.

I am never getting used to that.

Either way, it turned out I'd been right in my initial assessment. The group guarding the exit was almost the same as the one we'd met coming in – consisting of another of those winged centaur things, a regiment of humanoid archers, and a Yeren commander, this one named Guo.

I handed the spyglass to Ulagan so he could look, warning him in advance to avoid focusing on their campfire or any other light sources.

Tim, JUST FUCKING TIM: *Looks about the same as the mobs we fought when we first got here.*

Ulagan: *Agreed. We too faced similar foes upon entering this wretched place.*

Interesting. No way was that a coincidence. Whereas the jungle cavern had been primal and chaotic, there was a definite order to this one. I had a feeling that had we turned east earlier and broken off from the Vultures, we'd have eventually found another group like this blocking our way.

As I considered this, Ulagan turned his attention toward the cavern's exit. He frowned for several long seconds before handing the spyglass back so I could check it out.

What I saw was not encouraging.

Tim, JUST FUCKING TIM: *Is that a fucking portcullis?*

It was a rhetorical question. There was nothing else it could be, at least far as I could tell. Though the way out was currently open, situated above it was a heavy gate attached to thick scaffolding on either side. That was most certainly different than where we'd entered from.

It wasn't too much of a stretch to guess it could be shut at a moment's notice to prevent either egress or ingress. From the look of things, a FAST might've been able to slip through the bars of the iron grate covering it but that's about it. The rest of us would be shit outta luck.

I mentioned as much to my current group.

Fast: *If it is your wish, I would be pleased to confirm this information.*

The request caught me by such surprise that for a moment I wasn't sure who it had come from, almost forgetting that Friedrich's FAST was still hidden beneath a blanket to Ulagan's left.

Tim, JUST FUCKING TIM: *Um, sure. Go nuts.*
Fast: *As you command.*

The blanket slid off the FAST seemingly of its own accord, telling me they'd likely retained the same TK Hand utility as Pixel.

Fast might've been a bit squirrelly when it came to talking to anyone who wasn't Friedrich, but thankfully they were no idiot. Much as Pixel had done earlier, they turned down their own illumination to the bare minimum, becoming nothing more than a dull patch of red barely visible against the blackness.

Fast: *Your spyglass if I may.*

They floated over next to me – their TK ability lifting it from my fingers. Guess a lack of proper night vision was yet another purposeful limitation imposed upon FASTs.

As they took their turn checking things out, I turned my focus back toward the chat –opening a channel for both parties.

Tim, JUST FUCKING TIM: *So we have good news and bad news.*
Pixel: *This ought to be worth the price of admission.*
Friedrich: *Please allow him to continue, FAST.*

Oh yeah. If Friedrich's name hadn't been scratched off Pixel's Christmas card list before, it sure as heck was now.

Tim, JUST FUCKING TIM: *The exit's guarded just like we expected it to be, but get this. The guys guarding it are nearly identical to the ones both our parties fought on the way in.*
Friedrich: *A not altogether surprising development.*
Tim, JUST FUCKING TIM: *Pretty much what I thought, except the big difference is the giant gate situated directly over said exit.*
Pixel: *Open or closed?*
Tim, JUST FUCKING TIM: *Currently open.*

Pixel: *That works. All we have to do is hit those assholes fast enough to keep them from activating it, which should be doable with our combined forces.*

Friedrich: *Agreed, assuming that is the path we decide to follow.*

Pixel: *There's no assuming involved. We already voted.*

Friedrich: *As I am aware, but the presence of this gate potentially changes things. If we make it out and they manage to close it behind us, that could effectively negate our chances of returning and reaching that ascension ring in time.*

Pixel: *Easy solution. We leave no witnesses.*

Friedrich: *And hope that no one from the considerable force stationed nearby notices? I remain skeptical of our odds for such an endeavor.*

Pixel: *Bully for you, but that always leaves the possibility of us heading east instead. In fact, we might want to do that anyway.*

Friedrich: *And simply give up the opportunity awaiting us here? Why pray tell would we do such a thing?*

Pixel: *Because while everyone's been sitting here with their figurative thumbs up their asses, I've been studying the outline of that building the ring is inside of. Based on its size and shape, it seems to line up pretty well with imperial palace designs from this same time period.*

Marius: *A palace? Invictus, please confirm.*

Pixel: *I don't need my freaking homework checked, pal.*

Tim, JUST FUCKING TIM: *Everyone relax for a second. Are you sure?*

Pixel: *Pretty much. It's either that or a big-ass temple, although the betting FAST in me sincerely doubts those mobs standing guard outside are here for church service.*

Tim, JUST FUCKING TIM: *I take it that's not good news for us.*

Pixel: *Nope with a capital N. Castles not only mean lots of guards, but I'm guessing there's an extra nasty surprise waiting conveniently inside where we can't see it until it's too late. That* *would also explain why this exit is gated when the others weren't. If this is the seat of power for this ... let's say region, sounds better than cave, then they're not gonna be too big on letting outsiders waltz in and out.*

Friedrich: *Hence, why we shouldn't risk being locked out.*

Pixel: *Agree to disagree. I think we'll have a better shot at getting out, grabbing a rest, and then making a run for that ring to the east than we will tackling whatever's waiting inside that palace. Let's not forget, we already faced a Decennial boss in this shithole. I'm willing to bet whatever's waiting inside for us is that boss's boss, which means we probably don't want any piece of it.*

Friedrich: *A premature assumption based on little more than abject fear. I would expect better of FAST units.*

Pixel: *Sorry if some of us want to live.*

Boog: *Booggowitdjjjpppppppt!*

Pixel: *Yeah, what she said.*

I could see this was rapidly going downhill. It was time to jump in before Pixel lost their cool ... more anyway.

Tim, JUST FUCKING TIM: *All right, enough. Let's table this discussion until we get back. It'll be a lot easier to talk in person without some of us needing to constantly check whether we're still hidden or not.*

Hopefully that put a cork in things, especially since now was not a particularly great time to be getting into an argument.

I switched my cortex channel back to just me and my two current companions, preparing to tell them that it was time for us to beat a hasty and quiet retreat.

I'd just started typing out a message when Ulagan hissed, "What are you doing?"

Huh?

I turned to find Fast rapidly rising into the air. As they shot upward, they grew ever brighter, like switching out a nightlight bulb with a hundred watt LED. Within seconds, the FAST had become a living road flare, making it nearly impossible to miss even from a distance.

I opened my mouth, the same question that Ulagan had just asked forming on my lips, albeit with a few more choice words.

Before I could say anything, though, three bolts of magical energy shot from the FAST's body. They raced away looking like miniature missiles against the darkness, finally striking one of the enemy mobs and downing it instantly, but leaving more than enough to raise the alarm.

Needless to say, they were now painfully aware they were no longer alone.

In that same instant a new achievement flared to life within my HUD: *Effed in the A*.

Credit where credit is due, at least Drega was right on the money with that one.

59

FRONTAL ASSAULT

My new achievement would have to wait. As quickly as Fast had announced our position with an unprovoked attack, they sank back to ground level, dialing their brightness down again.

The blanket they'd discarded lifted as if grabbed by an unseen hand and covered the FAST up, leaving us once more in near total darkness.

Sadly, the damage had already been done.

Fast: *Please forgive my impertinence, but I would highly suggest that a strategic retreat is in order.*

With that, they started floating back the way we'd come, leaving a stunned Ulagan and myself to stand there slack-jawed.

For a moment anyway.

"Come on," I hissed. "We need to move before we're stuck dodging centaur bombs."

"Child of Ying Zhao," he corrected almost as an afterthought, glaring daggers in the direction Fast had gone. "And no, I don't believe we will. The FAST's aim was true."

I was tempted to turn back and use my spyglass to confirm this but there was no time. Even if Fast had the foresight to target the enemy's swiftest member, that wouldn't stop their archers from peppering this place with arrows in short order.

Of perhaps far greater importance was Ulagan's shocked expression. It told me he almost certainly hadn't been privy to this betrayal beforehand.

The question now was whether the FAST unit had done so of their own accord or whether their master was pulling their strings from afar.

Neither was going to be answered right at that moment. However, as Ulagan and I set off after Fast – trusting in the ashen ground to keep our footsteps light because there was no fucking way we could move slow enough to keep *stealthed* going – the answers we *were* given served to tell me just how fucked we actually were.

First came the low pitched echo of a horn being blown, probably their leader sounding the alarm. Then we heard a distant clacking sound, like massive chains rattling against one another. It was followed by a heavy *thud* I could've sworn I felt through my sneakers.

Ulagan: *The gate!*

He was right. There was nothing else it could've been, meaning we were officially screwed.

As if that wasn't clear enough, moments later there came a response to the alarm, another horn – this one coming from the general direction of that palace.

Sure, it was still possible Pixel was wrong about it being a freaking castle, but I had a feeling that was nothing more than wishful thinking on my part.

Sadly, their logic made perfect sense. Why else have a gate here and nowhere else, unless it was to keep enemies out ... or trapped inside, as was currently the case with us?

Fast refused to acknowledge our chat entreaties as we raced back toward the rest of the group.

At least a bit of luck remained with us as we made our hasty retreat. Not only did my Fatigued debuff seem to be stable at level 1, a good thing since we were moving at a fair clip, but that rise we'd been on must've masked our escape. Though no small amount of explosions rang out from back the way we'd come, they were scattered, seeming to cover a wide stretch. None came close to us, though, which told me they were taking shots in the dark – hedging their bets in the hope of hitting us.

Or maybe they were just trying to drive us off until reinforcements could arrive, a fact my map seemed to confirm as a large chunk of the palace defenders were now on the move.

All the while, our group chat was going nuts, with all the rest wondering what the hell had happened.

I let Ulagan take point on answering them as multitasking wasn't currently a skill I wanted to risk. It was either type or run, not...

Debuff – You are Fatigued: severity level 2.
What?!

I stumbled, nearly faceplanting before I could catch myself.

Fuck! Make that either type or *walk*.

Great! Just what I needed.

Tim, JUST FUCKING TIM: *Slow down a bit, guys. I hurt my foot.*

It was the lamest of excuses but I wasn't about to cop to being two-fifths of the way to simply passing out, especially considering the abject betrayal we'd just suffered. Fortunately, Ulagan didn't question me, slowing his pace so I could keep up.

Suck it up, Tim. You can do this.

On the upside, covering the remaining distance didn't appear to be an issue thanks to the collection of green and blue dots rapidly heading our way. Since there was no red to their rear, I assumed this was due to Ulagan filling them in and not for more pressing reasons.

Or at least I hoped that was the case.

Drega's description of Fatigued hadn't mentioned anything of the sort, but I wasn't so trusting to not think there might be some *hidden gems* waiting to be discovered, such as my map glitching out.

Don't even think it. You might give the asshole ideas.

Soon enough, I spotted both dull green and yellowish glows from up ahead – Pixel and Invictus. Seconds later, a reddish orb zipped past them as Fast discarded the blanket they'd been hiding beneath.

Ulagan and I rejoined the rest of our combined group, although it was safe to say our reunion was anything but sweet.

"What the hell happened?" Pixel demanded, getting right to the point.

"Macmac okay?" Boog asked, stepping in front of the FAST. "You still fati...?"

"I'm fine," I interrupted. "And yes, I probably could stand to miss a meal."

Before anyone could question my weak-ass cover to her almost spilling the beans, I turned and pointed a finger toward the red FAST currently hovering over Friedrich's shoulder like a loyal dog.

"What happened is Fast blew our cover by attacking those guys defending the gate. Now, not only is it shut, but there's a small army standing between us and it." I locked eyes with Friedrich. "Anyone have any idea how that might have happened?"

To his credit, he held my gaze. "My FAST has already filled me in on what transpired. It made a grave error of judgement, one it will be duly punished for."

"An error of judgement?" Pixel replied, echoing my disbelief.

"Yes. It has told me that it acted rashly out of fear for our safety."

"Excuse my skepticism," I said. "But how is surprise-blasting one of the guards while alerting the rest showing *concern* for our safety?"

"I am forced to concur," Ulagan replied, seemingly of the same mindset. "The forces aligned before the gate would have likely proven a challenge but nothing insurmountable. Now, though..."

Friedrich merely shrugged. "Allow me to clarify. It wasn't concerned with our safety as a whole, merely for that of *our* party."

"Okay, and that makes sense how?" I asked.

"Allow me to first apologize for its rashness. It seems my FAST had mistakenly interpreted my personal disagreement with our course of action as being more adamant than it was. It erroneously concluded that had we been successful in reaching the gate and the campground beyond, that your party would have then chosen to go your own way – leaving us to breach this so-called palace on our own."

"Boog leave new friends?" she asked, sounding about as confused as I felt.

"No, Boog." I turned back toward Friedrich. "So rather than ask, you just automatically jumped to the conclusion that we were going to ditch you guys?"

Pixel: *Well, technically we did discuss it.*

Tim, JUST FUCKING TIM: *And decided against it.*

"Not me," Friedrich replied. "Just it. As I have said, it mistakenly drew its own conclusions without consulting with me first. It was both insubordinate in its thinking and premature in its actions, both of which have potentially endangered us all. You may choose to believe what you wish of me, but know this. I do not tolerate such betrayal lightly. FAST, you will now accept your punishment!"

"I stand ready, sir," they replied, the first words I'd heard them speak aloud outside of combat.

Fast flitted down to about waist height then backed away until they were hovering maybe fifteen feet from the rest of us.

As I was wondering what they were doing, Friedrich drew his sidearm and opened fire.

The blast, far more powerful than a normal pistol – no doubt a machination of the Chase – ripped a sizeable chunk out of the FAST. Sparks flew and their color sputtered several times before fading away completely, at which point Fast dropped to the ground looking like nothing more than a broken child's toy.

Holy shit!

Almost instantly, their status changed.

FAST: FAST – Undisclosed – Level 5 – XX

"What the fuck?" Pixel cried, their color flaring brightly as they rose into the sky.

"Don't," I snapped. Call me paranoid, but I had a feeling Pixel was on the verge of blasting Friedrich with an Acid Ball. If so, we'd almost certainly be thrust into a PVP fight I doubted we could win.

Case in point, electricity began to flare across Invictus's surface, causing Marius to step to their side – his hand on his still sheathed dagger.

Next to him, Boog bared her teeth.

"No," I told her, trying not to let panic color my voice. "That goes for everyone here. Let's take a breath before we do anything stupid."

"Fuck that noise," Pixel growled. "This asshole just executed his..."

"No, he didn't," I cut in, "at least not permanently." I was half-amazed to find myself actually defending Friedrich. Shooting Fast was completely batshit, but I also realized that if I didn't say anything then this situation would only get worse.

If that happened, we'd be fucked. Even if we survived a tussle with the Vultures, a big *if*, that would leave us with nothing but bad choices when it came to finding a way forward. With me at level two Fatigued, I really didn't like our chances if that came to pass.

"Calm down and take a good hard look," I continued. "Fast still has a life left."

"Yeah, *one*," Pixel groused.

"Which is the exact same amount most of us have."

"At least until we reach the end of this stage, at which point its lives will reset," Friedrich calmly replied. "As for now, I believe this will prove sufficient motivation against further noncompliance."

"Noncompli...?"

I stepped in front of the FAST. "Seriously, Pixel, I need you to count to ten or something."

"Already did. Hell, I already counted to ten billion ... *twice*, and guess what? I'm still okay with blasting this asshole."

"Boog fight?"

"No, Boog. Nobody here is fighting." I once again turned Friedrich's way. "Are we?"

He hesitated for several long seconds, as if considering his words. "I apologize if my actions seem harsh to you but I truly believe them necessary. At this crucial point in our progress, we can brook no *loose cannons*. Would you not agree, Tim?"

"I ... mostly do, although I can't pretend that what you did..."

"Would be your preferred way of dealing with such things? I respect that, as I would hope you would respect that I am somewhat more *direct* in my methods."

Direct was one way of putting it.

He turned his gaze Pixel's way. "My FAST took actions which not only betrayed my trust but yours as well. What would you have had me do?"

"I ... don't know," Pixel stammered, "but not that!"

"So again, we concur on the sentiment but not our methods. To borrow a phrase you used earlier, I am afraid we shall have to agree to disagree." Before anyone could say anything to that, he continued. "I must point out, though, that while my

FAST acted foolishly and without permission, it may have presented us with an opportunity."

"What kind of opportunity?" I asked.

"One which we can either waste by continued squabbling or work together to take advantage of."

I was about to ask what the hell he was talking about when Boog surprised me by speaking up. "Enemies go there, not here."

Even Friedrich seemed surprised to hear that from her. "Quite so, my brutish friend. Our enemies have abandoned their posts. Look at your map if you don't believe me. Most are now racing to fortify their stricken allies, while an equal number are fanning out, no doubt searching for us."

I'd noticed that earlier but had been too focused on running for my life to put two and two together. The thing was, Friedrich was right.

The legions that had been standing guard outside the palace gates had mostly vacated the area, leaving no more than a skeleton crew of red dots behind. That of course assumed it was even a castle, something we still hadn't confirmed.

Regardless, Friedrich's point couldn't be denied.

"I ask you now, friends," he said. "Shall we continue to stand here squabbling or shall we set aside our differences and strike now while the opportunity presents itself?"

The choice was an illusion, nothing more, and I had a feeling he knew that. We could either do this now or accept the fact that we were almost certainly fucked otherwise.

Certain death versus at least a small chance for life.

There was only one way forward, a fact I'm sure Friedrich was quite aware of.

60

BARBARIANS ALMOST AT THE GATES

Achievement unlocked! Effed in the A!

Betrayal sucks, almost as hard as your mom following last call at the crack house. Much like her, you've probably already realized it's a bitter load to swallow.

Since you're reading this, though, I'm gonna assume you're still breathing, which means either you're more competent than anyone assumed or your betrayer is a doddering shithead. I know which one my money's on.

Whatever the case, revenge is a dish best served hot.

Yes, I know how the saying really goes. Unlike you, I'm not an unevolved primate who'll be pushing up daisies before the week is through. But maybe, just maybe, you can ensure you take at least one asshole with you when it's time to check out.

Reward: 1 Fortnight gear box.

At least the Vultures weren't privy to Drega's bullshit. Had we not switched him to interparty mode, I can only imagine how much extra chaos his voice would've sowed among our already tense partnership.

As a software guy, I knew that sometimes the most insignificant features made the biggest impact. Although speaking of impacts, I toggled open that Fortnight box, curious to see what being *Effed in the A* had earned me.

Amulet of Spite (lesser)

They say that if you gotta go, go with a smile. In truth, we understand that chasers are a fickle bunch when it comes to their own mortality. Few are actually happy once it's time to meet their maker. However, we find that such passings are made a tiny bit easier if they go knowing they took some deserving shithead with them.

This amulet is a one-time use only item. Once activated, you can choose to share the *love*, so to speak. And by that we mean you can designate one target within a hundred feet to experience both the damage and effects of the last attack that nailed your ass.

You'll still end up eating all of it, mind you, but now they will too.

"But what if that attack blew me into bite-sized chunks, Drega?" you might ask.

That's where the spite truly comes in. In the event of you sustaining damage that will, without a shadow of a doubt, render you deader than any doornail, the amulet will automatically activate – slowing time just long enough for you to pick a target before your grey matter is scattered to the wind.

And that is what we here at Time Chasers call a happy ending.

Holy shit that was bleak.

Fortunately, I'd had the foresight to step away a bit before opening that achievement. Regardless, I snatched the amulet out of the air before anyone else could take a gander. Tensions were high enough as it was. The last thing I needed was one of the Vultures to see me in possession of an item specifically designed as a final fuck you.

Not that I was planning to use it. Despite Fast's dickish move, which Frederich still insisted they'd done on their own without any prompting from him, my last talk with Marius still weighed heavily on my soul.

Maybe it was my ongoing exhaustion but I just couldn't shake it.

Despite my ongoing conviction to see Jeremy again, I wasn't deluded. I knew the odds were stacked heavily against me. However, my son wasn't the only one out there waiting for the return of a mother, father, or other beloved figure.

That said, this amulet's purpose was clear. Despite not saying that part out loud, I had a feeling they were banking on it being used against another chaser – basically a PVP double header. One final gesture of spite to another human being, to let them know that I might not be returning to my family but neither would they.

It was, in a word, sick.

But did it truly have to be? While it might be implied, there'd been nothing in the description saying I *had* to use it against another player.

That was probably the only thing keeping me from chucking it away, well that and the fact that someone else might see me and pick it up.

Despite all that, rather than shunt it into inventory I still slipped the amulet over my head before tucking it beneath my demon sweater. That done, I rejoined the others as they marched toward the palace and whatever fate awaited us within.

The amulet might've been intended for nefarious use, but I was rapidly beginning to learn that when it came to this game, it was best to not look any gift horses in the mouth.

Ulagan: *It's not heavy enough.*

Pixel: *Sure it is. There's gotta be over two-hundred pounds worth of crap sitting there. That means it's something else, probably some sort of magical trigger.*

Invictus: *It is as I cautioned. Our foes are cunning. They would surely have taken a predictable ruse such as ours into account.*

Pixel: *Thanks, not helping.*

Ulagan: *What sort of trigger?*

Pixel: *No idea, but if weight's not doing it then my next guess would be a warm body.*

Ulagan: *I see. So one of us will need to set this trap off personally.*

Pixel: *That's not what I said.*

Ulagan: *Yet it is what you implied.*

Pixel: *No. What I implied is we need to come up with a better idea, of which that is not.*

Friedrich: *I concur with the FAST. It is too risky, even with adequately equipped healing. We must remember that these enemies are more capable in their armaments than those we have faced elsewhere on this stage. And this is their seat of power. If there is any place where they will have taken extra precautions, it will be here.*

He wasn't whistling Dixie, especially since we'd already gotten luckier than we probably deserved to be.

Pixel and Invictus had taken point as we'd marched toward the palace, attempting to take advantage of the fact that the bulk of the opposing force was currently searching for us elsewhere.

It was risky even with their lights turned low, but their ability to fly made them less susceptible to any traps we might come across.

That had turned out to be a wiser strategy than any of us could have ever hoped for. Not too long into our trek, Pixel's perception score ticked up to fourth level. It wasn't a moment too soon, as minutes later they relayed to us via our party chat that something looked fishy with the ground ahead.

Invictus hadn't noticed anything but I'd whipped out my spyglass regardless, choosing to trust that Pixel wasn't just being paranoid.

Turns out they weren't. Ahead of us, all but invisible in the darkness, were several wide swaths where the ashen dirt looked *wrong*. Under the clear gaze of the spyglass they all appeared to have been disturbed in some manner – fresh dirt clearly visible among the charred ruins.

Not trusting my tired mind, I'd asked Friedrich to take a look to confirm.

That done, he'd sent Marius and Boog to check things out further, as they both possessed polearms that could extend their reach. Sure enough, those sections of the ground ahead of us were actually stretched woven tarps covered in layers of dirt to disguise them.

These tarps had noticeable give to them, telling us there were likely pits underneath. However, the mere act of putting pressure on the surface had also resulted in a brief chime of sound – bells attached to the underside.

It was immediately evident what would happen if we stepped on one. Not only would we be injured or worse by whatever lay beneath, but it would serve as an alarm for the few guards left guarding the palace entrance. No doubt it would've proven a dire situation had we not noticed it, a veritable medieval mine field.

The thing was, following a few minutes of discussion, we realized we could maybe turn this frown upside down by using these traps to set an ambush of our own – one we could use to clear the path ahead of us.

The problem, as it turned out, was triggering them with a false positive. We'd tried rocks, the scrap armor from my inventory, and more. Weight-wise, I had little doubt it was enough to set it off, but so far nothing had happened. The disguised tarps stubbornly refused to collapse. Either the façade had been too over-engineered or Pixel had a point about magic being at play here.

I was beginning to think Ulagan might be right that one of us might need to play the part of the sacrificial lamb, a dicey prospect at best since we couldn't know what lay beneath without someone getting close enough to actually touch it – which might also set it off.

Talk about a Catch-22.

Far as I was aware, smart Boog was the only one among us who had the skillset to maybe pull this off with her telekinesis. However, she wasn't with us right now and even if she was her low CON score could easily prove a fatal flaw in that plan.

Tired as I was, I hadn't yet reached the point where I was willing to let any of my friends agree to a suicide mission.

So instead, as the others debated what to do, I turned toward my inventory, going through it line by line in the hope that there was maybe something in there that might work to...

Wait a second, I still have that thing?

As an idea began to form, I quickly scrolled up in our chat to something Pixel had just said.

Pixel: *No idea, but if weight's not doing it then my next guess would be a warm body.*

No way. It was crazy to even think it. There was no way using it would work, at least not if the *item* I was thinking of had been stored via conventional means. But, as had been beaten into my head time and again, there was nothing about the Chase that was conventional.

Screw it. It doesn't hurt to ask.

"I have a question," I said aloud, interrupting the argument that continued to rage in our shared chat.

"No, you're not volunteering," Pixel replied.

Boog looked up from where she'd been rubbing her back against a dead tree. "Macmac not die!"

"Relax, Boog, I don't have any plans to." I turned back toward Pixel. "Our inventory, what happens to something when we store it there?"

"Really? *That's* your question. You've had two whole days to ask this stuff and suddenly you're curious about game mechanics *now?*"

"Humor me," I said, holding up my hand before anyone else could interrupt. My train of thought was just barely staying on the tracks as is. I needed to work through it without distractions. "I know we can't store living creatures there, at least not without help, but what about perishables? Say for instance I peeled a banana and then stuffed it into inventory. What would it be like if I pulled it out, I dunno, a week later?"

"No offense, but can we save the stupid questions for another...?"

"It would be as edible as the moment you stored it," Invictus interrupted. "Items placed within a chaser's inventory are kept in a form of digitized stasis. They do not rot, spoil, or decay in any fashion. Does this answer your question?"

"It does, thanks." I glanced Pixel's way. "Was that so hard? Knowledge is power after all."

"Eat a bag of power dicks, Tim."

I chose to ignore them. "All right, so I have a plan that might just work. It's just..."

"Just what?" Friedrich asked.

Goddamn, I'm an idiot! "Hold on a second." I did a time check in my HUD. *Shit!* There was only seven minutes left until today transitioned into tomorrow. We were already cutting it really close, but we could still make this work. "I have something in my inventory that I think will set off that trap."

"Excellent, then I would suggest you use it so we can set this ambush before..."

"Not so fast. We only have a few minutes left until end of day and Boog gets a chance to remove her curse."

"Boog not itchy?"

"That's the hope, Boog," I replied. "But in order to maximize her chances, I need to let her borrow some of my equipment, stuff that I need in a fight. So I'm asking that we wait a few minutes before pulling the proverbial trigger. Is that acceptable?"

Friedrich hesitated for a moment, no more, before nodding.

However, before anyone could say anything further, a muffled voice spoke up.

"No. In fact, that action would be ill-advised."
What the?

Friedrich had a belt pouch hanging from his side – a Nazi fanny pack if you will – and the voice had seemingly come from within.

No way.

He glanced down at it before opening the flap. Fast immediately flew out, having apparently recovered from their recent bout of lead poisoning.

"Speak," Friedrich said, "although I warn you to be mindful of your words."

"Of course, sir. My apologies for the interruption. However, if you'll check your map I believe you will find that any further hesitation would prove to be ... unwise."

I did as they suggested. *Oh shit.* Sure enough, a large chunk of the forces that had set out to fortify that gate were now on the move again, heading back this way.

We'd been so busy discussing the best way forward that all of us, even our FASTS, had been caught with our pants down.

From the look of things, I doubted the returning troops would be back within the seven minutes I'd requested, but they wouldn't be far behind. In short, every second now counted.

Fuck!

Delaying was out of the question. That meant our only recourse was to finish the skeleton crew of guards off quickly and hope that left enough time for me to safely transfer my sweater to Boog.

Whatever way you looked at it, this was going to be a close one. However, in order to make it work, we needed to act now. "All right, let's do this," I barked. "Everyone get ready."

"You still haven't told us what your plan is," Friedrich pointed out.

"Watch and learn."

I focused on my inventory, more specifically one item in particular.

Partial dire gnome corpse: 1.

I held my hand out and summoned the semi-melted mob, grabbing hold of it as it appeared from thin air. The dead gnome was every bit as disgusting, dripping, and faceless as it had been when I'd pulled it into my inventory as a test – before promptly forgetting it was there.

More importantly, its body was still disturbingly warm, having been stored right as our battle had ended.

Needless to say, everyone else seemed a bit taken aback by the tiny *hitchhiker* I'd inadvertently kept with me.

Pixel: *Holy shit! You still had that thing?*

Almost echoing Pixel's chat message, Friedrich asked, "If I might be so bold as to inquire, why exactly do you have such a thing in your possession?"

"For moments like this, of course," I replied, before turning and tossing the diminutive body atop the awaiting trap.

61

CHANGE OF PACE

Note to self: freshly dead corpses are more handy than I realized.

Second note to self: never ever speak of that first note again if I make it back home.

I'd no sooner tossed the dead gnome onto the trap when it finally triggered, causing both the corpse and everything else atop it to tumble into the pit below.

Guess Pixel was right about needing a warm body.

Loud bells chimed as the tarp collapsed into the pit, although a moment later they were proven redundant as a series of explosions sounded from below that were way louder than any simple bells could ever hope to be.

The smell of burnt gunpowder hit my nose and a thick plume of smoke rose into the air, but one thing was clear – it was a good thing none of us had tried triggering it.

An achievement popped up in my HUD but this was no time to deal with it. There was no doubt those palace guards had heard our ruckus as my map showed a cluster of red dots rapidly headed this way.

Far less good was that the larger force which had been marching back in this direction paused, having likely also heard the trap go off. A moment later they began to move again, noticeably faster than before. Our already tiny window of opportunity had just gotten smaller.

Tim, JUST FUCKING TIM: *We need to hit this first wave hard and then get moving.*

Pixel: *No offense but duh!*

Fortunately, there was no need for us to seek cover. The smoke billowing from the trap was proving to be more than enough cover for us to stand out in the open yet remain unseen. Too bad for the regiment headed our way, we had the advantage of maps to tell us exactly where they were and how quickly they were moving.

All around me humans and FASTs alike prepped ranged attacks, our goal being to hopefully take these guys down before they could put up much of a fight.

To that end, I pulled a torch from inventory as well as a gunpowder jug. It was time to share some explosive love.

The sound of orders being shouted reached my ears, enough to tell me the opposing force was almost certainly within attack range.

I ignited the torch then tossed it to the side, but not before using it to light the jug's fuse.

Here goes nothing.

Summoning my racket into my free hand, I activated Aim Assist then cast Crackling Cannonball on the gunpowder jug – holding my breath against that ten percent chance of spell failure. Fortunately, rather than explode in my face, the jug began to crackle with electrical power.

Yes!

Then I did the same thing I'd done when defending against Shen. Instead of slamming my racket into the primitive bomb – which would've likely done little more than blow my arms off, I dropped the jug onto the racket's net and gave it a *gentle* lob.

Gotta love magic because, same as before, the next second

found the jug screaming through the air as it barreled toward where our foes were most tightly spaced.

In that same instant my comrades at arms likewise let loose.

Pixel fired an acid ball while Boog threw her freshly upgraded jawbone axe.

The Vultures likewise responded with lethal force, opening fire with spells, gunshots, and thrown weaponry.

I won't lie. Much as I didn't care for the spotlight, I was sure we looked pretty badass, like something out of an action movie. It was probably my exhaustion speaking, but just this once I wouldn't have minded making the highlight reel.

The thick smoke ahead of us lit up with flashes of light as a cacophony of sounds filled the night air – shouts of surprise followed by a whole lot of screaming.

More than half of the nearby red dots became greyed out X's. Good, but it could always be better, so I followed up with a barrage of wolf teeth – knowing my chances of hitting were almost certainly helped by firing into a group of enemies.

The others likewise renewed their attacks.

To my left, Boog reached out and deftly caught her axe as it returned to her hand. Rather than immediately throw it again, though, she cocked her head.

"No! No run away!"

I was tempted to ask who she was screaming at, but a glance at my map showed one of the remaining attackers clearly breaking off from the rest.

Whether fleeing in panic or beating a strategic retreat, I didn't know. In the end it didn't matter as Boog once more flung her weapon. Mere seconds after the axe disappeared into the gloom, the fleeing red dot became a static grey X.

Damn. That was one upgrade that was already paying off.

Barely a minute later it was all over. The only response the enemy had managed were a few errant arrows stuck in the dirt, none having found their mark.

Another new achievement flashed in my HUD while I

noted that my XP was now barely a hairline from pushing me up to sixth level. One more battle, heck, probably no more than a slap fight, would be enough to do the job.

Cool as that was, it didn't mean we could stand on our laurels.

"We move, now," Friedrich barked. "Don't waste time looting that scum or opening your achievements. We need to reach the palace and make our way inside before we find ourselves overwhelmed."

In response, Invictus shot out ahead of us. "Follow me. I made note of the path our foes took coming here. It should prove safe for our passage."

"Well done, Invictus," Marius said as he followed. "Come, friends. This stage grows tiresome. What say we find this so-called ascension ring and see what new challenges await us?"

It was as good advice as it was possible to get in this place. Too bad I still had a few things left to do before I could focus on it.

⌛⌛⌛⌛ ⋄≍⋄≍⋄≍⋄ ⌛⌛⌛⌛

Stage One Expiration: 1 day, 2 minutes

"Hurry, Macmac! We need go now."

"Slow down, Boog. I need to give you my..." *Fuck*!

I sped up to catch her, which of course my Fatigued debuff didn't appreciate. My feet instead got all tangled up, causing me to face-plant in the dirt. Fortunately, the only thing bruised was my ego, more so since I had a feeling that somewhere the showrunners were laughing their asses off at my predicament.

Fucking debuffs.

I swore if I made it out of this stage alive I wouldn't let this shit happen again. If there were no campgrounds to be had, we'd make our own even if just for a few hours. Whatever the risks, it couldn't be worse than being unable to even fast walk without tripping over my own two feet.

"You hurt, Macmac?" Boog asked from up ahead, stopping and turning back as the others continued onward.

"No, Boog, I'm fine ... mostly."

"Good. We need hurry." She offered up a pink greasy hand to help me to my feet. "Map say enemies coming."

"I know," I replied, getting back up. Checking the map again, I saw we still had a clear shot toward reaching the palace but our time was running short. Sadly, that wasn't the only time that was quickly running out.

Boog was here with me now, though. Risky as it was for me to take off my sweater while a large opposing force closed on us – all while being unable to run – I owed it to Boog to at least try. She could be a loose cannon at times but she was my teammate, and if I'd learned one thing from being a manager it was that you needed to take care of your team if you expected them to take care of you.

"Hold up just a second," I told her, starting to unbutton my sweater. "You need this."

"No. You need..."

She was interrupted by a notification from our private party chat.

Pixel: *Stop dicking around, you two. I know you can't move particularly fast right now, Tim, but you still need to move."*

Tim, JUST FUCKING TIM: *I just need a minute.*

Pixel: *You don't have a minute. We're out of time. Boog will just have to wait. She'll be okay. She's got a lot of lotion left in that jug of hers."*

Tim, JUST FUCKING TIM: *No!*

Boog: *Pissel is right, Macmac. Boog is okay.*

I opened my mouth to say something, but hesitated as that last message sank in.

Since when had Boog figured out how to type?

That ultimately wasn't important right then as my eyes

settled on the timer within my HUD. *Shit!* What had been minutes was now seconds. I practically tore off my sweater, nearly falling again as I struggled to remove it. "Here, Boog! Take it now..."

My words trailed off as she moved out of my reach, except she hadn't actually stepped away from me.

Instead she floated up into the sky – not by much, maybe ten feet – but even as her altitude stabilized her body began to change.

You've gotta be fucking kidding me. Why now?!

Her limbs and torso began to shrivel, as if I were watching a timelapse video of her suffering from some horrific wasting disease. However, whatever mass was lost below her neck was made up for as her cranium swelled, becoming grossly enlarged – the sight made even more bizarre by the greasy pink lotion that was still slathered across nearly every inch of her.

I held my hand out and stood on my toes, still hoping to reach her, but according to my HUD the effort was too little, too late.

⌛⌛⌛⌛ ·ᚺᚦᚺᚦᚺᚦᚺᚦ· ⌛⌛⌛⌛

Stage One Expiration: 23 hours, 59 minutes

Boog's stats instantly rearranged themselves. For a single moment her *Cursed* status flickered, giving me hope that maybe she'd somehow beaten the odds. But then it reasserted itself along with *Jekyll and Hyde*.

The system wasn't finished with its fuckery yet, though. Next to the other two, *Fatigued: severity level 1* appeared.

Goddamn it all!

Either her reduced constitution was responsible or Boog was finally starting to reach the limits of her own body. Whatever the case, misery apparently loved company.

As this was going on, the combined group chat started going

nuts. The reason why was fairly obvious – we'd sorta *forgotten* to mention Boog's condition to the Vultures. Sue me, but I'd been far more focused on fixing her curse. Not to mention her first transformation from smart back to normal had happened relatively soon after she'd been mutated. So I'd stupidly assumed her next change would probably be at the tail end of her cycle. Hell, I'd been counting on it not happening again until we were safely in the waiting area for the next stage. No such luck, though. Guess it really was a random roll of the dice.

Either that, or the overmind really enjoyed making it inconvenient as all hell.

Although apparently even inconvenience had its uses.

In the next second my feet likewise left the ground. It wasn't by much, maybe an inch or two, however Boog floated down to meet me until we were roughly eye to eye.

Tim, JUST FUCKING TIM: *Boog, what are you doing?*
Boog: *Assisting you as you have helped me, my mate.*
Tim, JUST FUCKING TIM: *I don't understand.*
Boog: *It is simple. Your ability to move hastily is compromised. I am merely attempting to compensate.*
Tim, JUST FUCKING TIM: *While I appreciate it, don't waste your PSI points. You're gonna need them now that you're fatigued as well.*
Boog: *Perhaps at some point, but currently I am only at severity level one which does not affect my abilities, whereas you are at level two. So, rather than protest, might I instead suggest you move your feet. That way those watching us will assume you are walking of your own accord rather than suspect the truth.*

Huh. That actually wasn't a terrible idea.

Within our group chat, Pixel was busy explaining Boog's mutation to our somewhat surprised allies, albeit giving them the heavily abridged version.

So, rather than argue further, I simply nodded.

Boog: *Good. Then let us get to that structure and the ascension ring within. These last few hours have been ... stressful, even more so* *as my brutish alter ego lacks the vocabulary to properly express such thoughts. But please put your sweater back on first, Macmac. I believe you will need it.*

I did as told, although I still felt guilty about it.

Tim, JUST FUCKING TIM: *Listen, Boog, I'm really sorry that you're stuck with this curse for another day. I didn't mean for that to happen.*

Boog: *Worry not, my mate. You could not have foreseen that the changing of the day would coincide with my own transformation.*

Tim, JUST FUCKING TIM: *I should've at least been ready for something like that. Now you're stuck suffering for it.*

Boog: *Suffering is perhaps an over-exaggeration. This skin condition is annoying but manageable.*

Tim, JUST FUCKING TIM: *Is the lotion working?*

Boog: *To a degree. Of far greater usefulness, though, is my Telekinesis in this form. I can now scratch every square inch of my body at once, and at a reasonable cost to my PSI pool as well.*

Sure enough, I could see her fur flattening, as if dozens, maybe hundreds of fingers were pressed down upon it. In response, she let out a sigh of relief.

Color me impressed. She'd regained her smart form barely two minutes ago and already was coming up with new and novel ways to use her powers.

With any luck it wouldn't have to be for long – another day at most.

For now, I focused on moving my legs at a pace that hopefully matched the one which Boog was fast-walking us via her Telekinesis.

Pixel: *Get a move on, you two. You need to see this.*

Friedrich: *I must concur with the FAST. Ignoring our need for haste for a moment, this is ... rather impressive.*

Instead of answering, we focused on catching up to them. Seemed like the wiser strategy all things considered.

As Boog and I drew closer, the outline of the palace ahead

began to take form, growing larger and more imposing with every *step* we took. At the same time, my map showed our enemies rapidly marching in from the east. This was gonna be a close one.

Or maybe not as close as I assumed.

In what had to be a lucky break for us, the column of soldiers started to veer south – heading toward that trap we'd set off. If their new direction held, we had a good shot of making it to the palace with no...

What the?

All at once the castle became visible, and I don't mean it slowly took shape from out of the gloom. No. One second it was an ominous black form looming over us, the next it was fully alit with torches and lamps – bathing it and the surrounding grounds in soft light.

The thing was, it had all just suddenly appeared – as abruptly as someone hitting a light switch, except there was no sign that anything of the sort had happened. It simply became visible.

Magic, it had to be.

There must've been some kind of perimeter that triggered it, maybe a force field masking this place from outside eyes while leaving those close to it able to see as easily as if it were broad daylight.

Pixel was right, by the way, about it being a palace. Now that I could see it, it was an impressive sight – massive in a way that our maps didn't do justice to, but in many ways also a true work of art.

Whereas medieval European castles brought to mind images of imposing stone fortresses, this was far different. The entire place almost felt alive, with towers of bright red and yellow that were offset by rich brown walls covered in bright green carvings.

It was like something out of a luxury travel brochure, offering the promise of an unforgettable journey to an exotic locale.

Time Chaser

Equally impressive were the gates leading inside – flanked on either side by towering statues of dragons, each carved from jade and over twenty feet high.

I spied the rest of our group waiting for us there between them, just outside a massive double gate.

It was easy to see why they'd stopped. Not only was it a sight to take in but, probably more important to our goal, the gates themselves were wide open and seemingly unguarded.

There was no way of knowing whether that was due to a lack of foresight by the guards we'd recently dispatched or if it was by design – an open invitation to let us know that whatever waited within considered us no threat.

Whatever the case, it was time to find out.

62

THE URGE TO MERGE

A long, opulent hallway stretched ahead of us, wide enough for us to all march down side by side if we so decided. The floor was made of gleaming stone tile, while the walls were a rich red, offset by what appeared to be columns of pure gold. Silken tapestries hung from the walls – some depicting scenes of monsters and warriors while others contained bold text in what I assumed to be more Hanzi.

I half-expected my fog of war to activate again now that we were inside, but that didn't happen. Guess this entire cavern, including the interiors, was immune to it.

As a result, we could see all the way to the far end. There, a grand set of double doors awaited us, their exterior polished to a near mirror sheen.

So far the coast looked clear, although exploring this place would have to wait until we secured the gates we'd just come through. If not, the returning force would have us trapped like rats – easy targets for them to pick off.

Fortunately for us, despite the gates themselves being over fifteen feet high, they proved to be perfectly balanced and on well-oiled hinges. We were able to slide both sides shut with surprisingly little effort.

On the back were a series of heavy iron drawbars – as perfectly maintained as the rest of it.

We quickly slid them into place, barring the gate from the inside. I wasn't sure how long they would deter a heavily-armed force trying to break in, but they seemed pretty darned solid from our end. Hopefully they'd hold long enough for us to make it to that ascension ring.

Speaking of which, now that we were inside, my map began to fill in details that had previously been hidden from us.

The hall we stood in seemed to account for the majority of the distance to that ring. Multiple exits could be seen on either side, all of them leading off to either more passages or terminating in medium-sized rooms – the function of which I had no idea of. Sadly, the map wasn't nearly that detailed. On the upside, most of the living beings within range seemed to be white dots. Probably servants, hopefully ones that had better things to do than defend against an invasion.

Considering the opulence of the entranceway alone, I had no doubt a more thorough exploration would almost certainly prove lucrative. By this point, though, I simply didn't have enough left in me to care. I had no interest in whatever riches were there for the taking, and I especially didn't care to be distracted by any comfy looking beds we might come across. If so, the temptation to sack out might prove simply too great – almost certainly a bad idea while in the proverbial belly of the beast.

Ignoring all that and focusing on the path ahead, I saw that past this hallway there were two large chambers standing between us and the ascension ring. Much like with the fog of war, the normal dungeon rules didn't seem to apply to the map here. Despite there being clearly marked doors ahead of us, the map still showed us what awaited within.

Sadly, it wasn't particularly promising.

In the far chamber, just a few steps shy of the golden circle that was our goal, stood a pulsating red dot – a boss.

Not exactly a surprise.

The bigger question was whether higher ranked bosses looked different on the map. I had no way of knowing, but with any luck whatever was waiting for us there wasn't much tougher than Mai had been.

Equally as concerning, however, was the chamber right before the boss's. Along the walls to either side stood a column of four white question marks, eight in total.

"Any idea what those are?" I asked as we compared notes.

"No clue," Pixel replied. "Which, just off the top of my head, I'm guessing is sort of the point of those question marks."

"I could've done without the editorial."

"Hey, you asked."

Ignoring their snark, I continued. "Last time I saw one of those it turned out to be Boog."

She nodded in return. "You likewise appeared as one to me as well back then, my mate."

As she spoke, Friedrich, Marius, and Ulagan all eyed her, either still surprised at her newfound eloquence or wondering about that *mate* remark.

Fortunately, they didn't seem inclined to ask on that latter point.

"Remarkable," Friedrich commented. "Your FAST explained the effects of the mutagen on your companion, and yet still seeing her like this is nothing short of astounding."

"While I am happy to answer any questions you might have as to my condition," Boog replied, sounding slightly miffed, "I would appreciate it if you did not speak of me as if I were not in the room with you."

Friedrich appeared taken aback by this, but he recovered quickly. "Apologies, my *lady*."

"So ... anyway," I said, trying to steer us back on track, "is it possible we're looking at more chasers, just like last time?"

"Unlikely," she said.

"Agreed," Friedrich added. "Before Marius and I met, he too

appeared as a question mark. But since that time other chasers have appeared as blue dots instead. I assume the same is true for you all as well, yes?"

Nods came from around our circle.

"If that is indeed the case," Boog replied, "then I would surmise that these marks are an indication of either a creature type or status that we have not encountered yet."

Ulagan raised an eyebrow. "Meaning that whatever waits us up ahead could be either friend or foe..."

"Yes," she interrupted, "but we can be certain of one thing. Whatever they are, it is neither other chasers nor their FASTs."

I considered this. "Not exactly comforting."

"I'm pretty sure that's the point," Pixel replied, "but it also tells us they're not necessarily mobs, meaning we might have a shot of getting past them without a fight. Probably not a good shot, but a shot nonetheless."

"And if we can't?"

"Then we'd better make sure we're ready for it, meaning that if anyone has any new gifts waiting under their own personal Christmas trees, now would be a good time to open them."

They had a point. This was quite possibly our last chance on this stage to check out any new loot that might be waiting for us.

I left Pixel to explain Christmas to those among our number who predated it, while I stepped away to the nearest corner. We had an impending boss battle ahead of us and I still had a few new achievements that needed to be checked out.

Achievement unlocked! Thinking Outside the Pine Box!

Some cultures mummify their dead, some bury them, and others simply burn their bodies to ash. But almost all of them treat their deceased with some modicum of respect.

Time Chaser

Not you, though.

You chose to use the corpse of a sapient being as your own personal canary in a coal mine. Somewhere out there a family of dire gnomes is grieving, wishing they had a body to mourn ... or maybe eat, I don't judge. Whatever the case, they're destined to forever wonder, never knowing that you desecrated dear old dad into a million bloody chunks.

That said, nicely done. Sure, you might totally be the type who would skull-fuck your own dead grandma if there was something in it for you, but that's the sort of initiative that helps ensure a fella lives to defile another corpse tomorrow.

Reward: 1 Olympiad weapon box along with orders that your crazy cadaver-chucking ass isn't allowed anywhere near my funeral, as if you have any chance of living that long.

An Olympiad weapon box? Holy crap. That almost made carrying around a partially melted gnome worth it.

Time to see what my second achievement contained.

Achievement unlocked! Untouchable!

You used someone else's trap against them and as a result decimated an entire group of enemies without suffering so much as a scratch.

That's the sort of brutality that tells us ... we need to start sending better mobs your way ASAP.

Oh, don't be that way. It's no different than holding an office job – all of your hard work and dedication is simply being rewarded with even HARDER work.

True, our *severance* package might be a bit harsher but either way you should be well used to being fucked in the ass by upper management by now.

Reward: Not a goddamned thing! You can obviously handle yourself out there just fine. Why in hell would we waste our time rewarding you for that?

Fucking Drega and his pointless achievements.

I swear, it would be just my luck to miss making it to an ascension ring by however many minutes were wasted listening to these stupid things.

Back to stuff that wasn't a waste of time, I focused my attention on that Olympiad box.

An economy-sized weapons locker appeared before me. Needless to say, I couldn't help feeling a bit excited at what might be waiting inside. Judging by the size of it, you could have fit a rocket launcher in there, which, considering the firepower we'd dealt with in this section, might not be entirely inappropriate.

Eager to see what they'd given me, I focused on it – triggering a loud but oddly satisfying *clack-clack* noise as the box unlocked, and then seemed to fold in on itself, growing ever smaller before disappearing in an unimpressive crackle of sparks.

Huh?

My grin quickly turned to a look of confusion as all that it left behind was a metallic orb slightly smaller than my fist, unadorned save for a divot in one end.

I grabbed it out of the air, wondering if this was some kind of new-fangled futuristic hand grenade. Then Drega's voice filled my head as the item's description loaded onto my HUD.

Upgrade Clip
Weapon: Banshee Racket
Type: Corporate Merger

Upgrade clips exist to make weak weapons strong, strong weapons badass, and badass weapons so ungodly awesome that you'll probably end up killing yourself the first time you try to use it.

Hilarious as that would be, these rare baubles offer an instant enhancement. Some are designed for specific weaponry while others can be used with any item within your inventory. Whatever the case, equipping one will result in that weapon becoming better at its core function – killing the shit out of other living beings.

Just be forewarned, upgrade clips are one-time use only. Once equipped, they can't be unequipped. Nor do all upgrades play nicely with each other, so maybe think twice before shoving half-a-dozen of them onto a claw hammer and hoping for the best.

I mentally clicked on the sub-entry for *Corporate Merger*, then tried again as apparently my focus wasn't up to snuff.

Unlike the main description, there was no voiceover just text, which I can't say I minded. I'd had enough of Drega's voice echoing inside my frontal lobe.

Reading on, excitement began to once more take hold. It wasn't a rocket launcher by any means but it had potential.

I glanced at the orb then at my racket, trying to figure out how to make it work before it finally sank in. *Duh*! Despite its name, it was less a clip and more of a plug – the orb's divot being roughly the same diameter as my racket's handle.

Here goes nothing.

I slid the shaft into the clip, fairly certain there was a joke to be made there. It secured itself with a heavy *clank*, at which point the orb simply vanished.

Wait. Did I do something wrong?

Apparently not, as an alert flashed within my HUD.

Corporate Merger Upgrade Clip accepted. Please choose merge target from existing inventory.

I started to scroll down but then paused, wondering if I was acting too hastily. My fatigue might've been overriding common sense, but perhaps this was something I should give more thought to rather than accidently make the wrong decision.

Please choose merge target from existing inventory.

"Yeah, yeah," I snapped, trying to think this through. "I heard you the first time."

Please choose merge target from existing inventory ... or one will be randomly assigned.

Wait, what? Shit!

Drega had failed to mention this part. Guess I had no

choice in the matter. Fortunately for me, I already had something in mind.

I scrolled down to my Spell Hammer Mace and focused on that. In truth, it was the only logical choice I could see. Anything else would almost certainly be a waste of an upgrade.

Spell Hammer Mace targeted for acquisition. Merger commencing.

As the Mace disappeared from my inventory, my Banshee Racket began to grow heavier in my grasp.

I looked down to find it aglow with power as it began to change. The weapon's handle elongated until it ended in a wicked looking spike. Shards of razor sharp bronze emerged all along the racket's head, surrounding it in jagged metal. Finally, the strings took on a metallic sheen as if they'd been reinforced.

As quickly as the weapon had gained weight, it then seemed to get lighter once again. Except I quickly realized that wasn't the case. Instead it was me who was now stronger.

I watched as, within my HUD, all of the mace's previous benefits began to reappear under the listing for my Banshee Racket.

This is so...

Then it all vanished from my screen.

Fucked up!

My HUD blinked once, and the listing for my racket disappeared altogether.

Panic flared within me for a second as I frantically scrolled up and down, only to realize the reason for the *disappearance* was that the weapon now sported a brand new listing along with an accompanying name change – *Ruination Racket*.

I took a deep breath to calm myself. In truth, my surprise aside, it was all pretty badass. Better yet, now with 25 points added to my STR and an additional 20 to my CON, the idea of loaning my sweater to Boog tomorrow suddenly felt a little less risky.

More importantly, this new upgraded racket boasted the

Spell Hammer ability in addition to everything else it previously had. On top of all that, it now looked a hell of a lot less embarrassing – not the most important thing, true, but I wasn't about to turn down a little ego boost.

Sadly, I no longer had a backup weapon sitting in my inventory, or at least one that was any good. That meant I needed to be extra careful. No dropping this thing in the middle of combat.

Still, it was a welcome upgrade to get right before a boss battle.

I checked in with my teammates once I was finished gawking at my new *toy* to find they'd gotten some new stuff as well. Too bad Pixel's big prize was a 20 point patch for charisma, their personal dump stat. Needless to say, based on their complaining, I had a feeling the FAST would need a *lot* more points in that one before it made a difference.

Oh well.

As for Boog, once again it was a case of receiving loot that would've come in real handy earlier.

She received two scrolls of *Forestall Fate* – a spell designed for those afflicted by uncontrollable status changes. It specifically mentioned lycanthropy as an example, telling me that was apparently a thing here, but the description itself seemed to cover mutagen-based changes as well.

Whenever the caster felt a change coming on, they could use this spell to push it off for a while, but there was a downside. At first level, which both these scrolls were, it would hold off her change for an hour. However, for the next twelve hours after that the percentage chance for Jekyll and Hyde to strike again would be doubled.

In short, she could opt to postpone one change but at the cost of ensuring it would happen again in relatively short order. A useful spell with an annoying twist, go figure, although nothing we needed to worry about right then.

First, we needed to survive whatever lay ahead because,

inconvenient as that spell's side effects might be, they paled in comparison to the *inconvenience* of dying within sight of the finish line.

63

ROYAL WELCOME

"Behold the benevolent might of our great protector Wan – bringer of light and subjugator of darkness. He offers peace to those who return it, death to those who sow chaos."

Almost in response to Pixel translating the first of the many banners hanging from the walls, there came a solid *THOOM* of sound from the sealed gates. Guess those reinforcements had finally gotten here and were none too happy about being locked out.

Loud as it might've been, the gates themselves barely trembled from the impact. With any luck they'd hold until we were long gone.

"All right, I'm guessing that's our cue to go meet this guy," I remarked as we set off down the hallway.

"Sure as shit looks that way," Pixel replied, "although I can't help but think there's maybe some slight exaggeration with that whole bringer of light part."

I shrugged. "I dunno. Seems to be pretty well lit inside."

"*Protector Wan – lighter of candles*, not exactly a title to make one's enemies quake in their boots."

There came another booming reverberation against the gate,

this time coupled with the shout of angry voices from the other side.

"What else does this Protector Wan say?" Marius asked, perhaps hoping to keep us focused, as if we really needed the extra motivation.

Invictus flitted to the next banner in line. "By the glory of Protector Wan may our enemies be laid low and our crops flourish." Then they zipped to the next. "All these lands, to the horizon and beyond, are claimed by the great protector Wan. No mercy to those claiming dominion over what is rightfully his."

"I'm beginning to see a trend here," I commented.

"Indeed," Ulagan replied. "Great leaders are mandated by the heavens but normal men are often blind to such things. Thus the need to remind them."

I glanced at him. "Not quite what I was going with."

"Glorious is the seed of those blessed by Protector Wan," Invictus continued.

"I believe the point is made," Friedrich remarked, rebuking Marius's FAST far less harshly than he seemed inclined to do with his own.

"Yeah," Pixel said. "Protector Wan really wants us to think his shit doesn't stink."

"Ulagan is right," Friedrich said, ignoring Pixel as seemed to be his inclination as of late. "Though I might disagree on *heavenly* mandates, a leader's true strength lies in the conviction of his followers. There is no limit to how far you can push a man who truly believes in his cause."

I looked at him, my eye landing on the swastika emblazoned on his bright yellow sleeve. I was half-tempted to say something about there also being no limits to the depravity true believers could sink to, but held my tongue.

We were too close to our goal to start any arguments. Once this was all over and we were sitting in whatever communal campground awaited us between stages, then we could debate history, philosophy, and the nature of genocidal leaders until we were blue in the face.

Or maybe I could just get some sleep instead.

All of that needed to be pushed to the back burner for now anyway. Less than a hundred-and-fifty feet ahead of us was the way out of this stage. The last thing we needed were more distractions causing us to zig when we should've zagged.

I'd already seen enough of those – whether it was recovered FAST memories, the year 2541, a pseudo-terrorist group called Nadok, or whatever the fuck a Penark Queeg was.

I still had no good answers on most of it, especially whatever was fated to doom humanity in the far flung future. Because of that, I was starting to have some doubts.

It was possible some of that stuff had real significance, but I was also beginning to wonder how much of it had been thrown our way for no other reason than to slow us down.

After all, time had potential to become a scarce commodity in a competition such as this.

Okay fine, Virto nearly putting me through a wall over that Nadok issue hadn't exactly seemed like a small deal. However, that too was starting to feel somewhat less than important in the face of surviving this first stage.

Maybe it wouldn't seem that way tomorrow following a much-needed rest, but right then I needed to stay focused on the prize waiting at the end of this hallway. Knowledge might be power but unless the boss here was a sphinx intent on asking us Nadok-related riddles, it did me no good to dwell on...

"If you'll pardon me for a moment," Friedrich said, drawing me from my scattered reverie, "I have need for a momentary respite before continuing."

Respite?

Moments later, cracks appeared along the wall to our left, forming into a doorway that opened up.

Oh. And suddenly it made sense.

Time Chaser

Friedrich stepped into his own personal *bunker* and shut the door behind him, leaving the rest of us to wait for his return.

"If anyone else needs to go, now's the time," Pixel said. "We have no idea what horrors are waiting up ahead, so the less chance of anyone pissing themselves to death the better."

Stage One Expiration: 23 hours, 22 minutes

Friedrich took his sweet time on the bowl, leading me to think he probably wasn't watering the Rhine so much as dropping a few Panzer tanks.

All the while, the pounding and clanging at the gate continued. Credit where credit was due. Protector Wan might've been full of himself, but there was little doubt he'd hired competent architects.

Not helping the tense mood was Fast. The little red bug zapper hovered there silently, refusing to acknowledge us in either voice or chat while we waited for their *commander* to return.

Tim, JUST FUCKING TIM: *Is it normal for FASTs to act like that?*

Pixel: *You mean like Stockholm Syndrome Stepford children?*

Tim, JUST FUCKING TIM: *Pretty much.*

Pixel: *Wish I could tell you, Tim, but the best I can say is I don't remember any acting this way, in both my officially sanctioned memories as well as...*

Pixel trailed off for a few seconds before resuming their message.

Pixel: *Huh. Will you look at that.*

Tim, JUST FUCKING TIM: *Look at what?*

Pixel: *You're not gonna believe this, but it's up to ten percent now.*

Tim, JUST FUCKING TIM: *What is?*

Pixel: *My recovered memories, what else?*

Tim, JUST FUCKING TIM: *Sorry. Remember, you're talking to a guy who's seriously fatigued here. Clarity of thought isn't exactly my strong suit right now. Anyway, when did that happen?*

Pixel: *No clue.*

Tim, JUST FUCKING TIM: *How do you not notice something like that?*

Pixel: *One, we've been kinda busy, and two, it's not like I get notifications for these things. Either something has to spark a previously locked memory for me to realize its now accessible or I need to be actively indexing those cells to get an accurate count. I just did and it's telling me ten percent.*

Tim, JUST FUCKING TIM: *Fine, if you say so. So, is there anything useful in that extra one percent?*

Pixel: *Yeah. Apparently I have a preference for six gauge nanosonic scouring modules.*

Tim, JUST FUCKING TIM: *And those are?*

Pixel: *Part of post-Chase maintenance. AKA for when it's time to scrub all the blood and gunk out.*

Tim, JUST FUCKING TIM: *In other words that's a negative on anything useful.*

Pixel: *For you maybe. Now, if you'll excuse me, I should probably do some scouting to make sure your dumb asses don't stumble into another trap. No point in making things more difficult for those poor scouring modules.*

⌛⌛⌛⌛ ⋅⁑⋄⁑⋄⁑⋅ ⌛⌛⌛⌛

Tempting as it was to hurry down the hallway, especially with the continued pounding at the gates, we forced ourselves to move slowly and evenly. This allowed Pixel and Invictus to look for possible traps while Boog used her Telekinesis every ten feet or so to prod the floor beneath them, just in case.

Fast brought up our rear, although whether it was to guard

our flank or because they were still acting like a whipped dog after Friedrich's punishment I didn't know.

There was no point in asking either since I doubted they'd answer.

Though our snail's pace kept me from tripping, I'll admit my nerves were starting to fray. Maybe it was my imagination or the way the hallway carried sound but the frantic attacks on the gate were starting to sound much like tortured metal reaching its limit.

Nobody else said anything, so hopefully it was just me.

We passed several openings along the way. Much as the map had indicated, some were hallways leading deeper into the castle, whereas others led to open spaces filled with lush pillows and cushions – giving the impression they were either waiting rooms meant for visiting dignitaries or maybe just for Protector Wan's orgies.

In truth it was all an illusion, meant to evoke the real world, or at least one of them anyway. I doubted any dignitaries had actually ever visited this place, since it was effectively an advanced sound stage set within the confines of the Chase.

At least that's how I was starting to look at it all. It was real enough to kill us but ultimately just window dressing for those forced to play their parts here.

Again I was forced to wonder where all the mobs and NPCs had actually come from and what voodoo had been done to their brains to make them think this was real life.

Sadly, it was all pointless speculation on my part. At the end of the day, the only thing real here was the threat to our lives. That was all that mattered.

As we drew ever closer to the double doors ahead of us, looking every bit as solid as the gates behind us, Invictus continued to read the silken banners hanging from the walls.

Unsurprisingly, it was all propaganda to the greatness of this Wan fellow, attributing practically every good thing under the nonexistent sun to him. Guess it was good to be the king.

Time Chaser

Fortunately, none of this was accompanied by pits opening beneath us, poison darts firing from hidden holes in the walls, or *Indiana Jones* sized boulders dropping from the ceiling.

It was just Invictus reading one overblown pontification after another.

The funny thing was, nobody, not even Friedrich, told them to stop. I think all of us knew it was still better than walking in silence and dealing with the heaviness of knowing something was bound to happen sooner or later.

As it turned out, we didn't have to wait for long.

⌛⌛⌛⌛ ·⋄·⋄·⋄·⋄· ⌛⌛⌛⌛

The moment we reached the double doors a harsh sizzling sound started up, coupled with the acrid stench of burning metal. Needless to say we scrambled, all of us save for Fast that is, flattening ourselves against the walls on either side.

It wasn't a trap, though. Instead, bright red Hanzi lettering, seemingly made of pure flame, began to sear itself into the metal of the door ahead of us.

After several long seconds the message finished writing itself and ... that was it. Nothing else seemed to happen.

"Huh, that's interesting," Pixel remarked, sounding nonplussed.

"I'd say magical fire graffiti appearing out of nowhere is a bit more than interesting."

"I'm talking about what it says."

"What is it, FAST?" Friedrich replied. "Tell us."

Rather than answer, Pixel made a buzzing noise. However, Invictus was there to pick up where they left off.

"I believe what my fellow FAST is remarking on is the difference between the prognostications which line the walls of this hall, and the instructions awaiting us now on the doors ahead."

"Instructions?" Marius asked.

Time Chaser

"Indeed. It appears to be a message meant for us."

"And by us you mean chasers," Pixel replied.

"Perhaps," the other FAST said. "It reads: Invaders to my beloved realm, know that you have trespassed unto the domain of the great Protector Wan..."

"Doesn't sound all that different so far."

"Though it is within my power to destroy you utterly," Invictus continued, ignoring me, "I instead choose to magnanimously offer you this opportunity. Curry the favor of those I favor and I shall grant you a boon. Fail and I shall devour you as surely a wolf does a mouse."

Well, damn. If that wasn't a warm and welcoming invitation, I didn't know what was.

64

THE ADULT DUNGEON

"Curry the favor of those I favor?" I repeated. "And that means what exactly?"

"Not sure," Pixel replied, "but it's a fair bet he's not inviting us to lunch."

"It is a test," Ulagan said. "A test of our worthiness."

"No doubt," Friedrich added. "The question is whose favor are we expected to win and how?"

"Continued speculation is pointless," Boog replied tersely. "The answer no doubt lies ahead of us within the next chamber. Thus our choice is to either turn back and face an unbeatable force or continue onward and solve this challenge. I, for one, am beginning to feel the strain of our continued exploration, so I would suggest we decide quickly."

Friedrich raised an eyebrow, although whether at Boog's spunk or her admission to being tired, I wasn't sure. "Of course. Going forward was never in question but I think it fair to discuss how we should proceed."

"The answer to that seems obvious to me," she replied. "With both caution *and* respect."

"Respect?"

"Consider the wording before us. It suggests to me that the

way ahead does not necessarily lead to battle. Thus we should keep ourselves in check until such time as we are forced to do otherwise."

"Surely you can't be serious," Marius replied.

"Have I said anything to suggest the contrary?" she asked as if speaking to a small child. I guess smart Boog was starting to let her intelligence go to her head. "We have been offered an opportunity. We can either take it and hope it is to our advantage or we can ignore it and know that whatever comes next will almost certainly not be."

"And what sort of advantage might that be?"

"Hopefully the kind that lets us make it off this stage without getting our asses fried," Pixel replied to the Roman legionnaire. "I don't know about you, but that doesn't sound like the sort of gift horse we should look in the mouth."

Marius appeared confused by the FAST's remark but otherwise seemed unconvinced. "The treasures we won from that fox were not inconsiderable. I say we use them to best this new foe and strengthen ourselves further. That is the only *opportunity* which matters in this place."

"You mean the treasures *you* got," Pixel responded. "Because last I checked, we didn't get jack shit from that boss other than a map notice telling us to go east, young man."

"Enough sniping," I snapped, throwing most of my shade Pixel's way. It's like the FAST was itching to pick a fight with the Vultures. I understood they didn't like how Fast was treated by Friedrich but this was neither the time nor place to keep picking at that scab. "I say we go with Boog's plan. Keep our guard up, but no attacking unless provoked."

Boog: *Thank you, my mate. I appreciate your support in this matter.*

Tim, JUST FUCKING TIM: *No prob. It's the right call. Although I'm not sure you should have let them know that you're starting to feel fatigued.*

Boog: *At this late stage I see little point in subterfuge. We will* *either succeed or we will not, but the time for both rest and secrets is past us.*

There was some logic to what she said but I still preferred not to broadcast the fact that I was one step away from being a full-blown basket case.

"Agreed," Friedrich said after another moment or two. "Let any who dissent speak now."

For a moment or two, Marius looked like he wanted to say something, but with most of us, including his party leader, now in agreement, he merely nodded.

Can't say that was surprising. Far as I could tell, he seemed a decent guy, but I was starting to get the hint that he was a foot soldier through and through – more comfortable with someone else taking the lead.

I couldn't blame him for that, but I did have to wonder how that would work out once we reached the latter stages of the Chase. Of all the prizes Drega had mentioned, there'd been no mention of any devoted to group effort.

That was a worry for another day, though, one that felt like it should be far off in the future but was almost certainly closer than I cared to envision. After all, that bus had only been two short days ago and yet somehow it felt like an eternity.

Two days without my son. Under normal circumstances, such as attending a conference, that would've been no big deal. Now, it might as well have been years since I'd last seen his smiling face ... his real face and not some bot that looked like him.

God, talk about fucked up.

Speaking of which, Boog surprisingly took the lead now that our course had been set, floating up to the door and raising a hand toward it. Though she stopped short of touching the still burning metal, the door began to open on its own nonetheless.

I was tempted to warn her against overusing her Telekinesis, especially since we had no real idea what awaited us, but refrained. I needed to stop treating her like ... well, someone with a 30 intelligence. She was more than smart enough to know what she was doing. Pixel could be condescending enough as it was. She didn't need both of us babysitting her.

Besides which, in a pinch she had a couple of potions to replenish her PSI points.

Whether or not she'd need them was another matter entirely as the double doors began to swing open. Heavy they might be, but they were as well-oiled as the front gate.

Or as well-oiled as it *had* been. As it stood, the ruckus still coming from far behind us told me those gates probably wouldn't hold for much longer.

So, without further ado, I followed Boog into the next chamber, hoping that whatever awaited us respected the peace every bit as much as she hoped we would.

⌛⌛⌛⌛ ⋅⋄⋅⋄⋅⋄⋅⋄⋅ ⌛⌛⌛⌛

Okay, this is kinda weird.

This new room was about forty feet wide by about the same amount deep. The walls were grey stone, nothing spectacular, but across from us stood another set of double doors which somehow managed to make the ones we'd just come through look like they belonged in *Home Depot's* bargain bin.

They were solid gold with scores of multicolored jewels set into them. Platinum colored handles sat beneath twin visages of horned demons that had been carved out of pure jade.

Mind you, the overly-pricey doors weren't the weird part.

I knew what terracotta warriors were, having read about them on Wikipedia. If I remembered correctly, they'd originally been built to guard the tomb of some emperor whose name I couldn't recall, a fact I'm sure Pixel would've gladly berated me for.

Upon first glance, the eight figures surrounding us on either side of the room reminded me of them. Then I took a closer look and realized how wrong I was.

For starters, all of the statues were stark naked.

Four of them were female, buxom beauties in a variety of lewd poses as if pulled straight from a medieval porno. The rest were males, all in equally suggestive poses and well-endowed to the point of making me feel seriously inadequate.

It was like someone had read the Kamasutra and decided to memorialize it in stone. Oddly enough, though, despite them being in full sight, they remained as question marks on my map.

Strange.

"How ... utterly lewd," Friedrich remarked, disgust coloring his voice.

Pixel: *Sounds like someone's a Polly Prude.*

Tim, JUST FUCKING TIM: *Don't start. We're way too close to the finish line for that.*

Pixel: *You mean way too close to the* climax, *right?*

I let out a barely disguised sigh but opted to ignore them.

"I have seen similar sculptures in the lupanars I visited in my youth," Marius said. "Although the stonework here appears vastly superior."

"He's talking about brothels for anyone who cares to know," Pixel added.

"Thanks," I said. "I think we get the point."

"Just saying. Knowledge is power after all."

"Yeah, well, I'm not sure how that knowledge helps us here. I mean, what exactly are we supposed to...?"

Before I could finish, the doors we'd entered from closed shut with a heavy *boom*, instantly muffling the continuing attacks on the gate. It was followed by the *clack* of multiple locks engaging.

On the one hand, that gave us an additional buffer in case those soldiers managed to break in. On the other, I guess we were committed to ... whatever we were supposed to do here. "So, what's the over under on these things coming to life and attacking us?"

Pixel made a soft buzzing noise. "Probably best not to ask.

Needless to say, if that happens keep an eye out for the guys and those *clubs* they're all sporting."

"Clubs, seriously?"

"I'm just saying what everyone else is thinking."

We stood there for several seconds waiting for something to happen until Ulagan apparently had enough and ignited his sword.

"I say we strike first."

"No," Boog snapped. "Remember the inscription. Curry the favor of those I favor and I shall grant you a boon. Fail and I shall devour you as surely a wolf does a mouse."

I was impressed that she remembered it word for word, but Ulagan wasn't so easily convinced. "Nonsense words with no meaning. How are we to curry favor with *these*?"

"I do not know," Boog replied, "but am willing to speculate that destroying them is not the answer."

"The answer," Pixel repeated. "That's it! This is some kind of puzzle."

A puzzle. So once again video game logic applied. Pity that puzzles tended to be my least favorite parts of any games I'd played.

Won't lie. I tended to keep my phone handy so I could look up cheats at times like this. Sadly, my HUD could do a lot of things but browsing the web wasn't one of them.

Evolved beings my ass.

"Agreed," Invictus said, floating to the far end of the room where they flitted in front of the other door for a few seconds. "Locked, as is the way back. I would wager that we will progress no further until we can solve whatever mystery we have been charged with."

"Okay. So how do we do that?" I looked around at my companions as if hoping one of them had the answer, pausing to do a doubletake at Boog. "Probably time to slather up again. You're starting to drip."

Time Chaser

"Alas, I fear the temperature in this chamber renders that a wasted endeavor, Macmac."

I opened my mouth to respond before realizing she was right. It *was* getting warm. A thin sheen of sweat had broken out across my forehead at some point. Odd since it had been reasonably cool out in the hall.

"My apologies for the interruption," Fast said, catching everyone's attention, likely due to most of us forgetting they were even there, "but the subhuman is correct. Please direct your attention to the walls."

I was tempted to say something about that subhuman remark, especially since I didn't see anything noteworthy on the walls outside of dull red stonework.

Hold on.

Hadn't the walls been grey when we'd first stepped in?

"Ulagan," Friedrich barked.

The Mongol warrior stepped to the wall without a word, placing his hand upon the stonework before pulling it away again with a hiss of pain.

"This is no room," he stated, turning back to face us. "It is ... some sort of kiln."

Oh, that wasn't good. Sure enough, within seconds there was no longer any doubt about it. The temperature was noticeably rising.

Whatever this puzzle was, the Chase had thrown some extra urgency into it. There was no time to waste. We needed to solve it before our gooses were all cooked.

"And that's the other shoe dropping," Pixel said, sounding not at all happy. "Remember what that Wan guy said about devouring us like mice? Well, I'm gonna go out on a limb and guess that he prefers his extra crispy."

65

ESCAPE ROOM

"Try the door," Friedrich ordered.

"Invictus already said..."

"I am well aware of what was said," the Vulture's leader barked, cutting off the legionnaire. "Try it anyway."

Before Marius could respond, Boog turned toward the far doors. "Allow me. Time is of the essence, thus somewhat more expeditious means are warranted."

Friedrich nodded his approval, not that she needed it.

A moment passed then a thunderous *THOOM* of sound echoed through the room as the doors ahead of us rattled in their hinges. Sadly, they remained tightly closed.

Boog dropped to one knee, the reason instantly clear – at least to me and Pixel. She'd just blasted the doors with everything she had, using up her PSI pool in one massive blow. Too bad for us they were somewhat more resilient than those leprechauns we'd fought.

Fortunately, we weren't in battle – yet anyway – so her points would hopefully recover quickly.

Either way, one thing was clear. We weren't getting out of here unless whoever was in charge wanted us to.

That meant we needed to solve this puzzle.

"All right," I said. "Does anyone else have any clever escape tricks they want to try, or can we focus on solving this thing before we're all deep fried?"

As if to drive home the point, the temperature in the room jumped another ten degrees.

"I would suggest we begin with the clue we were given," Invictus replied, their voice almost eerily calm. "We must curry favor to those whom Wan favors."

"Well, considering these statues are the only things here, I'm guessing Wan really likes his pervy lawn ornaments."

"These are no mere decorations, my mate," Boog said, starting to breathe hard. Of us all, she was most likely to suffer the worst due to her fur. "Look ... closer."

I turned toward the statue nearest me – a guy in the middle of a vigorous hip thrust. Truth be told, if I looked any closer at *Dirk Diggler* here I'd end up poking out my eye with his raging... *Wait.*

Even as I focused on the statue, Drega's voice spoke in my head.

Concubine of Protector Wan – level ?

That was all there was. There was no snarky introduction, just a title. I took a few moments to look at the rest but they were all the same. All eight of them were listed as Wan's concubines.

"I do not understand what this means," Marius said, echoing my thoughts.

"Me neither," I replied. "Best guess, either he turned them all to stone for some reason, or this guy has some really *interesting* fetishes."

"Beggars can't be choosers," Pixel remarked. "Sad to say, but old Wan had the misfortune of being born about eleven hundred years too early to own a *Real Doll*. And no, I am not explaining that to the peanut gallery."

Friedrich shook his head. "Crude remarks aside, that ostensibly tells us *why* he favors these ... *carvings*, but it still offers no clue as to how we might *curry* their favor."

I wiped my brow than looked around again, noting there were eight statues but also, disturbingly enough, eight of us, FASTs included. Combined with my knowledge of video game logic and ... oh boy. "Remember what I said about these things coming to life? Well, what if it's not to *attack* us?"

"Please tell me you're not thinking death by snu-snu here, Tim," Pixel replied, "because I don't have the right ports for that, not that it's ever stopped you humans from trying."

"And now I'm sorry I brought it up."

"Snu...?"

I held up a hand toward the Mongol warrior. "It means .... being intimate. Anyone else have any questions?"

"Who knows?" Pixel continued. "Maybe it won't be so bad. These guys look like they've been here a while. We might just have to polish a few stone knobs and bingo, favor is curried."

"Must you be so crude about this?" Friedrich snapped. "It is like you get some perverse enjoyment out of being ... perverse."

"Hey, I'm just spitballing ideas," the FAST shot back. "So either come up with a better plan or prepare to pucker up, cupcake."

"Enough, both of you. Pixel's right ... no, not about that. We need some ideas on the table, weird or not. Although, for the sake of avoiding any arguments maybe let's try to keep the wording family friendly."

"Seriously, Tim?"

"Humor me, okay. The point remains, we need ideas not insults."

Ulagan stepped up to one of the statues and eyed it, his expression unreadable. "What if you are right and these are people turned to stone? Perhaps they are in agony and the true path forward, to curry their favor if you will, is to destroy these forms and end their suffering."

That ... actually made a disturbing amount of sense.

"An excellent suggestion," Friedrich replied. "Albeit one I will caution there is no coming back from if wrong."

Boog nodded. "Agreed. I would suggest we keep that as a final option should all else fail."

All right that was one. Well, okay we had more, but that was the only one so far that didn't require us *getting jiggy* with the masonry.

Weird as that was, it did bring to mind an idea I decided to test.

I stepped to one of the female statues. She had an expression of bliss upon her face while standing in an uncomfortable looking squat – almost making it appear as if she'd been caught in the middle of the best dump of her life.

Yeah, probably best to not go down that rabbit hole.

Instead, I put a hand on her shoulder only to find her rocky skin already uncomfortably hot, as if these statues were heating up in the same way the walls were.

"Calling dibs on that one?" Pixel asked.

"Just shut up and let me think for a second."

I gave the statue an experimental push, resulting in nothing. Then I did so again harder. This time it rocked ever so slightly, albeit thankfully not enough to topple over. That was fine. It was enough to tell me these things weren't anchored to the floor.

Of what use that was, I wasn't sure, but I relayed the info back to the group nonetheless.

"Good to know in case we need to play musical sex statues," Pixel said.

I considered their words for a moment, a thought starting to form. Sadly, it was lost a second later as I tried to step back, only to find I couldn't. *What the?*

"I was just kidding about calling dibs, Tim. Relax, nobody's gonna steal her from you."

"It's not that, asshole, I'm..."

"Stuck?" Friedrich replied, his voice growing tense. "As am I."

Oh shit. Why now?

"**THE FINAL DAY OF STAGE ONE IS UPON US, FOLKS! YOU KNOW WHAT THAT MEANS! IT'S TIME FOR ANOTHER LIVE UPDATE!**"

⌛⌛⌛⌛ ⋯⋯ ⌛⌛⌛⌛

Fucking A, B, and C! Not only were we trapped in a giant convection oven, but I was stuck fast next to one of the heat sources.

So this is what a bread roll feels like.

"**First off, a quick apology,**" Plegraxious said, jumping in. "**We normally like to kick off the final day right as it begins but we're admittedly a little late.**"

"**DON'T DEMOLECULARIZE THE MESSENGER, THOUGH,**" Drega added. "**WE HAD GOOD REASON. THERE WAS AN ALL OUT CHASER WAR GOING ON AT ASCENSION RING THIRTY-SEVEN AND WE JUST COULDN'T FIND IT IN OUR HEARTS TO CUT AWAY.**"

"**Talk about a real treat, Drega, especially this early in the Chase.**"

"**YOU'RE TELLING ME, PLEG. WOO, WHAT A SLAUGHTER! SIXTEEN CHASERS CHECKED IN BUT ONLY THREE CHECKED OUT.**"

I wasn't sure if he was purposely comparing us to cockroaches, but I bristled at his casual contempt nonetheless.

"**BETTER YET, THE SURVIVORS MANAGED TO ASCEND WITH A VERITABLE BOATLOAD OF GEAR AND XP ... ENOUGH TO HELP THEM NAVIGATE THE RIVER OF BLOOD THEY HELPED SPILL.**"

"**It truly was coming down by the bucketful.**"

"**MORE LIKE THE CHASERFUL. AM I RIGHT, FOLKS?**"

Raucous applause assaulted my ears. I didn't know who was

in the live studio audience, but a part of me hated each and every one of them.

"**I suppose you are**," Plegraxious replied deadpan, his voice just barely audible over the ongoing cheers.

"**SPEAKING OF WHICH, HOW ARE THINGS LOOKING OUT THERE ON THE FIELD RIGHT NOW?**"

"**About as expected**," Plegraxious said, regaining his composure. "**The start of PVP was both good and bad.**"

"**LET ME GUESS. GOOD FOR OUR RATINGS, BUT BAD FOR EVERYONE INVOLVED!**"

Plegraxious sputtered for a moment, his punchline obviously stepped on, but then he continued. "**Both true, Drega. In the time since our last update, the number of expired chasers has almost doubled, bringing our total to two-thousand, five-hundred and sixteen.**"

"By the gods," Marius whispered.

Friedrich glanced his way but said nothing.

Sadly, I had a feeling the gods had nothing to do with this. Holy crap. If my math was correct, that was over eleven-hundred dead since the last update.

"**And if you're guessing more than half of those have been at the hands of their fellow chasers ... you'd be right!**"

"**THAT'S THE CHASER SPIRIT WE ALL LIKE TO SEE!**"

"**It's not all wine and roses, though. We have confirmed reports that at least three chasers outright refused to comply once player-versus-player went live.**"

"**WELL, THAT'S JUST RUDE. PLEASE TELL ME THEY'RE NO LONGER DARKENING OUR CORTEXES.**"

"**Oh, I can do better than that. Each was slapped with a tier-two penalty on their way out the door, meaning neither they nor their planets are the multiverse's problem anymore.**"

"**SERVES THEM AND THEIR EARTHS RIGHT. NOBODY LIKES A QUITTER. AM I RIGHT, FOLKS?**"

Time Chaser

More applause rang out, even louder than last time. I was beginning to see this was apparently Drega's go-to line.

That was far less important, mind you, than the fact that three more planets had just been wiped from existence for no better reason than those representing them chose to take a stand against this savagery.

As I struggled to hold my temper, Plegraxious continued with his grim statistics. Less than a thousand more had made it to ascension rings since the last update, telling me those still on the field were either lost, panicking, or purposely hunting their fellow man. That last one was a sobering thought.

That left roughly fifteen hundred chasers still in play – our two parties included.

As before, the FAST casualties brought up the rear. Sadly, the number of destroyed FASTs had also skyrocketed – now standing at four-hundred and two, whereas an additional seven-hundred-and-sixty now had two deaths stacked against them.

They didn't say how many of those deaths had been caused by the chaser they'd been assigned to. For all I knew Fast's circumstance was unique, although I had a sinking feeling it wasn't.

Bringing up the rear were eleven-hundred and sixty-eight FASTs like Pixel and Invictus who'd been killed once.

It was one depressing tidbit after another. Of those who'd entered this place just two days ago, less than three-fourths remained. And that number was going to keep going down.

The only upside was that we wouldn't be joining them, at least not during the update itself. As the two hosts bantered, I realized with no small amount of relief that, while our circumstances hadn't improved, they also hadn't gotten worse. Whatever had been steadily turning up the thermostat was seemingly as frozen as the rest of us. That didn't mean it was comfortable. If anything, it was like hanging out in a sauna fully-clothed. Hell, even the crispness of Friedrich's uniform was starting to wilt, sweat stains now visible upon his dress shirt.

Time Chaser

However, none of us had it as bad as Boog who was standing there looking miserable as Plegraxious read off casualty numbers like they were fucking baseball stats.

As if that wasn't bad enough, our SKs and FASTs all picked that moment to activate, projecting images from the Chase onto all the walls.

The scenes were slightly distorted due to the heat, making it hard to watch without becoming motion sick. Too bad there was no escaping it short of closing my eyes, which I didn't want to do on the off chance I'd simply conk out.

Either that or I'd finally cross that line into *overtired*, possibly resulting in me throwing a tantrum much like Jeremy had been known to do as a toddler.

Wouldn't that be a hoot for the highlight reel – me stamping my feet and screaming because I was overdue for a nap.

Anyway, much like before, we were shown a mix of triumphs and tragedies, not the least of which was Friedrich's summary execution of Fast – the angle of the shot somehow making it even more gruesome a second time. Much to my chagrin, however, they left out our badass ambush from earlier. Guess there was no accounting for taste among *evolved* beings.

However, rather than simply let these scenes play out and then leave us be, our two hosts decided to start adding their own color commentary.

"WE'VE HAD TWO WHOLE DAYS TO SCOPE OUT THE PLAYING FIELD, ENJOY THE HIGHLIGHTS, AND WATCH THE TRASH TAKE ITSELF OUT. ANY FAVORITES AMONG THE PACK YET, PLEG?"

"A few, Drega. For starters, there's chaser Jeffrey P of party First Coven, assisted by his FAST Sally Sunset. There's no doubt he's been carving a gruesome path of carnage through everything he's encountered so far. Not only that, but he opted out of an early ascension to instead go hunting, having already racked up two PVP kills. He's definitely one to watch as Stage One draws to a close."

"NO ARGUMENT HERE. ANYONE ELSE?"

"Coming in a close second is Borlack the Trampler of party Meat, along with his FAST Stick. Talk about a chaser who's been capturing the hearts and imagination of our audience with his quaint but oh so brutal methods. It's safe to say that if he and Jeffrey P ever meet, sparks and entrails will fly. And if they decide to team up, well, don't even get me started on how bad that would be for everyone else."

Of course. There was seemingly no escape from Borlack. I swore, if we ever met again I'd... Well, okay, he'd probably try to eat me, so maybe it was best if that didn't happen.

"AH, PLEG. WE CAN ALWAYS COUNT ON YOU TO ROOT FOR THE LONE WOLF PSYCHOPATHS OUT THERE. I SWEAR, IT'S ALMOST LIKE YOU HAVE A TYPE."

"I do. They're called proven winners," Plegraxious replied. Maybe it was just my imagination but his tone sounded ever so slightly defensive.

"YOU MIGHT VERY WELL HAVE A POINT. I GUESS WE'LL SEE."

"How about you, Drega? Any chasers who've caught your photoreceptors?"

"YOU KNOW ME, PLEG. I'VE ALWAYS HAD A SOFT SPOT FOR THE UNDERDOGS. THROW IN A STAR-CROSSED DUO AND I'M HOOKED."

Star-crossed...? Oh God. Please don't be talking about me and...

"THAT'S WHY I'M PERSONALLY ALL IN WITH JANICE AND SHIM OF TEAM GET SQUORT."

Oh. I wasn't sure whether to be relieved or insulted. Probably the former. Yeah, definitely the former.

"I gotta ask. What exactly does Get Squort mean?"

"NOT A CLUE, PLEG, OUTSIDE OF IT BEING AN INSULT THOSE CRAZY KIDS FROM TWENTY-THIRD CENTURY EARTH LIKE TO TOSS AROUND. BUT ENOUGH OF THAT. LET'S TALK ABOUT SHIM. SHE'S

A FREE SPIRIT, ONE WHO THINKS OUTSIDE THE DECAHEDRON. WHICH MAKES IT ALL THE CRAZIER THAT SHE'S TEAMED UP WITH JANICE S, A HOUSEWIFE FROM NINETEEN-FIFTIES MIDDLE AMERICA. FOR THOSE NOT UP ON THEIR EARTH HISTORY, LET'S JUST SAY THAT WAS A DECADE THAT PUT THE DRY IN DRY WHITE TOAST, UNLESS YOU WERE FEMALE IN WHICH CASE YOU WERE PROBABLY DROWNING YOUR RAGE IN WINE AND BARBITUATES."

"And now they're both drowning their enemies in their own entrails."

"THAT'S BEING MODEST ABOUT IT. THESE TWO ARE RAPIDLY PROVING TO BE MORE THAN JUST TEAMMATES. THEY'RE..."

"Oh, it's like that is it?"

"SAVE THE SCISSORING JOKES FOR A LATER STAGE. WHAT I MEANT IS THEY MIGHT BE AN UNLIKELY PAIR BUT TOGETHER THEY BRING THE PAIN."

Wait ... a pair?

I once more glanced at the statues around us, my fuzzy brain trying to tell me something.

"BUT THAT'S HOW IT GOES IN THE CHASE. PARTIES ARE OFTEN FORMED OUT OF NECESSITY BUT OCCASIONALLY SOMEONE MEETS THE BLOODY YIN TO THEIR MURDER YANG AND THAT'S WHEN THE FIREWORKS REALLY START."

Yin ... yang ... fireworks? I focused on the statues, the fog finally lifting from my mind just long enough for me to make the connection.

"Guys," I called out, trying to make my voice heard over the update. "I think I might know what we need to do to get out of here."

Too bad at least one member of our combined group wasn't

going to like it.

66

PUZZLING PIECES

Fortunately, the live update ended soon after. Christ, for two jackasses who liked to keep reminding us of our limited time, they sure liked to waste it.

Though I doubted I'd ever get a chance to meet our two hosts face to face, it was a nice fantasy to imagine doing so – right before kicking both of theirs in. Sue me. Making it home to Jeremy might be my top motivation, but some good old fashioned spite never hurt.

Sometimes it was the little things that got a guy up in the morning.

Anyway, I impatiently waited for Drega to finally shut up before I said anything further. Go figure, but the louder I tried to talk over him the higher the volume seemed to go. I don't know why it was so important to the overmind that we listen to these updates, but someone definitely had a bug up their ass about it.

"All right, let's hear this grand revelation of yours before we all become French fries," Pixel said once we were free to move again.

I gestured for everyone to gather around me, except for Fast who continued to hover in the far corner. Whatever, it wasn't like the room was that big.

"Remember that thing you said," I asked Pixel, "about playing musical chairs with the statues?"

"Yeah, so?"

"That got me thinking, but then Drega said something during the update that really brought it all together for me. You were right about this being some kind of puzzle."

"Pretty sure we're long past that point, Tim."

"I will remind you that time is of the essence, FAST," Friedrich shot back. "So, if you would be so kind as to let your companion finish, it would be appreciated."

"Or what, you're gonna shoot me too?"

"If you continue to hinder us with your prattling then it might become an option."

Oh crap.

"Let's focus, people," I said, as if this were no more than a quarterly budget meeting that had run long. "I know it's hot and tempers are fraying but let's try to hold it together for a little bit longer. Anyway, as I was saying, it *is* a puzzle, but the good thing is it's not nearly as difficult as we probably thought it would be."

"Kindly enlighten us," Invictus said.

"Gladly. We're dealing with nothing more complex than a jigsaw puzzle, and the best part is, it's only got eight pieces."

⌛⌛⌛⌛ ·ːнːнːнːнː· ⌛⌛⌛⌛

Hmm, I probably should've asked Pixel when jigsaw puzzles were first invented, as it was likely at least half of our contingent had no clue what I was talking about. That was okay. I was happy to elaborate.

"Take a good long look at each of these statues and the pose they're in. There's a phrase from my time, *it takes two to tango*, and before anyone asks, that's a dance and yes it's performed by two people."

"I have heard a similar saying, save it involves the waltz."

"Doesn't quite roll off the tongue the same," Pixel remarked, much to my chagrin.

Fortunately, Friedrich ignored them. "It is a thinly disguised metaphor for fornication."

I nodded. "Same as on my world. So, as I was saying, look how they're all posed." I pointed toward the squatting girl from earlier. "This one, for instance. By herself, she probably looks a little strange, but if we were to pair her with the right partner then I think what she's doing would make a lot more sense. And the best part is, we only have to make four matches. It's so simple a child could do it."

"The children of your world play with such toys?" Marius asked, sounding genuinely curious.

"No. Definitely not. Poor choice of words on my part." I was beginning to see what Friedrich had meant earlier about finding it hard to relate to his teammates. Instant language translations or not, jargon and colloquialisms most certainly complicated matters. Hell, it was a small miracle we were able to communicate at all.

"So let me get this straight," Pixel said. "You think if we match statue A with the appropriate statue B, then they'll get their proverbial rocks off ... aka be happy..."

"AKA we'll have curried their favor," I finished. "Metaphorically anyway."

"I have to say, not the stupidest idea I've heard today."

"And we already know they can be moved," I added. "So what do we have to lose by trying?"

"A reasonably sound deduction," Boog replied, "one I am embarrassed to admit I did not find first."

"Don't feel bad, Boog," Pixel said. "It just so happens this sort of thing is right up Tim's alley."

I turned their way. "And that means what exactly?"

"Don't forget, I was assigned to study your life. That includes your browser history."

What?! "There's nothing in..."

"Three words: Japanese shame porn."

"That was ... research for ... work."

"Really? You're saying there's a market for tax software that screams, 'please, sempai, what will my parents think?' whenever you input the quarterly expenses? Actually, knowing you humans, there probably is..."

"You two," I cried, pointing toward Marius and Ulagan. I wasn't sure if the heat rising to my face was a result of the temperature or not, but we needed to stop wasting time as well as maybe change the subject. "Help me test this out. I think I've figured out the first pairing we can try."

The funny thing was, outside of Pixel I doubted anyone there had a clue about internet porn ... except for maybe the audience. Ugh, there was a thought. But hey, at least I could rest easy with the knowledge that my deepest secrets were known only to me, my FAST, and only a few trillion spectators spread across infinite universes.

That wasn't so bad, right?

Unsurprisingly, squatting girl was now too hot to pick up with our bare hands. Fortunately, I still had pelts and fabric scraps sitting in my inventory, enough for us to use as makeshift oven mitts.

Doubly lucky, the statues weren't nearly as heavy as I feared they might be. Squatting girl turned out to be only slightly heavier than a flesh and blood woman of the same size, telling me these statues were either porous, hollow, or simply more magic. I was neither a sculptor, geologist, or wizard, so I can't say I really cared which, so long as we could move them.

"Let's carry her over to Dirk Diggler."

Time Chaser

"What is a Diggler?" Ulagan asked.

Shit!

"Oh, this ought to be good," Pixel muttered as the rest of our group looked on.

Jeremy aside, right at that moment I would've been quite fine had the room suddenly heated up to a thousand degrees and simply immolated us all.

"Um, forget about that for now," I said. "Take her over to that one there, the guy holding his arms out in the middle of a crotch bump."

I directed them to hook squatting girl's legs around *Dirk's* hips, but to be careful not to break off any ... um ... extended parts of him. After all, despite this making sense, to me anyway, I still wasn't one-hundred percent certain. The last thing I wanted was to break something important, thus guaranteeing we'd all end up as a dish of chaser flambé.

Luck was with us, though. Her legs and his arms were both spread apart the perfect width as my two helpers eased them together.

"Just a little bit ... whoa!"

All three of us jumped back as the two statues suddenly began to move on their own.

One moment they were solid stone, the next they *attacked* ... except it wasn't us they were after.

Their arms wrapped around each other, while her legs did the same to his body. Then Dirk gave one quick upward *thrust* and ... that was it. They stopped moving as quickly as they'd started. When I stepped in again to check them out, I realized what were once two moderately lewd statues had now been perfectly fused into one *extremely* lewd statue.

It had worked!

More importantly, one of the walls changed back to its normal color. It only got marginally cooler as a result, but it at least told me we were on the right path.

"Holy shit, Tim," Pixel cried. "I officially take back at least half the condescending things I've said about you."

High praise from my FAST.

"Well done, my mate," Boog said, looking as amazed as Pixel sounded. Won't lie. It was ever so slightly insulting, but now was not the time to dwell on their apparent lack of faith in me.

"I didn't do anything, at least not yet. We still have to figure out the rest."

Therein lie the problem. The two I'd picked had been the low hanging fruit of the bunch, so to speak. Their poses didn't really fit with the rest. The others, though, were a bit more nebulous in their pairings.

Or at least they were to me.

"These two," Marius said, jumping in. He pointed to a female statue with her head thrown back in ecstasy and then to a male statue that my brain decided to designate as *John Holmes*. "Standing up they might appear awkward, but I am willing to wager lying down they are not."

"I do not see how that would work," Boog replied.

"Face to face of course."

"Face to face?" she asked, sounding confused. "But then how would they...?"

Marius started to sputter a response, until Pixel swooped in to pull his ass from the fire. "Trust the man, Boog. Let's just say that humanity has figured out a few new *positions* since your time."

She shrugged but thankfully didn't ask for further clarification. That left Marius to lean the woman down onto her back, while Ulagan and I positioned *John* atop her.

"A little higher," the legionnaire directed. "There!"

And just like that, *missionary* accomplished.

Almost as if in response, the two statues began to entwine their arms and legs as Boog looked on in amazement. The female statue pulled the male's lips to her neck as they embraced before once again becoming nothing more than stonework.

That's two.

Our success caused another of the walls to go from red to grey. This time the temperature subsided enough to make it easier to breathe.

Sadly, it didn't last. I'd barely gotten out a sigh of relief when it started to get hotter again, much faster this time. It was almost like this puzzle was ratcheting things up to sudden death now that we were halfway through.

"Pretty sure the clock's running out on us. We need to figure the rest out now."

There were four statues left. One of the males stood fully upright, his arms reaching out as if to grasp something, while his manhood ... well, likewise reached out. I swear, it was like being endowed with a billy club.

The other male was on his knees in a more submissive pose. As for the two females, one was down on her hands and knees, butt in the air, while the other stood but was bent low at the waist, her hands likewise reaching out as if to grab something.

"Him and her," Ulagan said, pointing to that first guy and then the woman on all fours.

I shook my head. "I don't think so. They don't really line up."

"The other woman perhaps?"

"What are her hands reaching for then?" Pixel asked. "Unless you're thinking a threesome with one loser left holding the bag."

"Maybe, although I doubt it." I gestured at the kneeling male. "Problem is, neither of the girls seem to go with this one."

"It's simple," Marius said after another few moments. "The two men go together. Likewise, both women."

"What?" Friedrich hissed.

"Look at their poses. They line up perfectly."

Boog glanced at the kneeling male and cocked her head. "Submission to a superior?"

Marius chuckled. "Perhaps in some instances, although I think it more likely that one is simply pleasuring his companion."

Now that he'd mentioned it, I saw he was almost certainly right. Both sets that Marius had pointed out lined up. How had I missed something so obvious?

"Okay, let's get them..."

"No," Friedrich snapped, interrupting me. "That will not do. We insult this Protector Wan by even considering such perversions."

"Perversions?" Marius asked. "Such couplings were not uncommon amongst the legions. I've known many who were bedfellow to their companions in arms. To each their own happiness, especially in time of war."

Friedrich narrowed his eyes. "I said no."

"I think Marius is right," I replied.

Now it was my turn to get the stink eye from the Vulture's leader. "I ask you to look at this place, Tim, really look at it. We are vying for favor from one of regal bearing. To think this Protector Wan would *condone* what you are suggesting is..."

"Perfectly sensible," Pixel interrupted. "Sorry to break it to you, dude, but homophobia is actually a fairly modern conceit – relative to you and Tim that is."

Friedrich glanced at the FAST before obviously dismissing them. "Ulagan, set up the pairing you had suggested."

"I really don't think that's a..."

"If I wanted your opinion, FAST, I would have asked for it."

I stepped in. "Listen..."

"No. *You* listen. Yours is not the only life at stake here. I, for one, refuse to allow you to endanger us for the sake of such nonsense. Open your eyes, man. This puzzle was obviously designed to trick us, yet you would walk us into that trap willingly."

"But..."

"You chose the first pairing and Marius the second. I say it is *my* turn to choose the third and be proven correct." He locked eyes with me and I can't say I liked what I saw in them. "Ulagan, you have your orders."

"All right, enough of this crap," Pixel said. "Back the fuck off, Shitler, or the only choice you'll be making is between acid and lightning."

"How dare you!" came the response, but it wasn't from Friedrich.

Before any of us even had a chance to turn in Fast's direction, a bolt of energy lanced out from them and slammed into Pixel. The impact caused sparks to fly and sent the now sputtering green FAST careening backward into the wall.

Holy shit!

67

CRUMBLING ALLEGIANCES

"Stand down," Friedrich ordered as Boog and I turned to check on Pixel.

Energy was still crackling off the FAST and their health bar had dropped into yellow territory, but fortunately that seemed to be the extent of the damage. A moment later, Pixel rose back into the air, sounding about as pissed as you might expect.

"You red-tinted, backstabbing, piece of..."

"Don't!" I jumped in front of them, my arms wide.

"Out of the fucking way, Tim."

"Don't do this, Pixel. Not now."

"Easy for you to say. That floating stoplight over there just blasted me."

"You dared threaten my commander..."

"You will *stand down*," Friedrich snapped again, interrupting Fast.

I hated to take his side on this, but I hated the alternative even more. This fucking game wanted to turn us against each other but I wasn't willing to play along, not yet anyway.

Tim, JUST FUCKING TIM: *Take a deep breath and relax.*
Pixel: *Relax? How many times has that worked with your wife?*

I opted to ignore that remark.

Tim, JUST FUCKING TIM: *No offense, but Fast has a point. You sorta did threaten Friedrich first.*

Pixel: *Because he was being an asshole.*

Tim, JUST FUCKING TIM: *Not arguing that, but you escalated. Words hurt.*

Pixel: *Not as much as a magic missile to the face.*

Boog: *You do not possess a face.*

Pixel: *It's a fucking figure of speech, Boog.*

Tim, JUST FUCKING TIM: *Listen, I get it. What they did was totally uncalled for, but think about it from their perspective. Remember what you said about Stockholm Syndrome?*

Pixel: *So I should just forgive and forget because they're a headcase?*

Tim, JUST FUCKING TIM: *No. It's just, this is neither the time or place to wage our own private PVP war. We don't need this, not now.*

Pixel: *Are you sure? Because I think we've got a shot of Marius siding with us.*

I glanced back. Sure enough, while Ulagan had taken up a defensive position in front of Friedrich, no doubt just in case, Marius and Invictus hadn't moved – as if they were waiting to see how this would play out.

Pixel may have had a point, but it seemed an unnecessary risk to test out their theory. Not to mention, I didn't want that. I had no interest in any player-versus-player bullshit. It was bad enough this place had made me a killer, but giving in to that, killing someone from another Earth just so some assholes could get bigger ratings would make it so much worse.

I didn't want that, neither for me or for Jeremy.

Tim, JUST FUCKING TIM: *No. We are not escalating this any further.*

Pixel: *I'm not apologizing.*

Tim, JUST FUCKING TIM: *I'm not asking you to. Just don't* *shoot back. What Fast did was dangerously stupid but we need to leave it at that.*

Pixel: *Fine, but you owe me.*

Tim, JUST FUCKING TIM: *Fair.*

Pixel: *And whatever sympathy I may have felt for that asshole is officially gone.*

Tim, JUST FUCKING TIM: *Also fair.*

Pixel: *Fine. You're just lucky the system gave me an achievement for my troubles.*

I guess that was something.

"All right, everyone take a deep breath," I said, tasting the near scalding air. "Although maybe not too deep. What I meant is, there's no reason for us to push this any further."

The look on Friedrich's face said otherwise, though. In it I saw anger, frustration, and ... something else, something I couldn't identify.

"I disagree," he said in a soft voice before drawing his sidearm. Panic flared within me for a brief second, mostly since I was still standing between him and Pixel, but it seemed neither of us was his target. Instead, he spun and once again aimed his gun toward Fast. "This must end."

"No!" I cried.

Pixel: *What the fuck are you doing, Tim? If he wants to fill that backstabber with lead, I say let him.*

"Don't," I continued. "That's what they want, for us to turn on one another."

In truth, they probably wanted chasers attacking chasers more than chasers attacking FASTs, but it seemed a superfluous point to mention.

"You would come to the aid of one who so blatantly attacked your comrade?" Friedrich asked, his teeth gritted and sweat dripping from his brow.

Pixel: *Yeah, Tim. Would you?*

Tim, JUST FUCKING TIM: *I'm just trying to get us all through this stage. Can you maybe let me do that?*

"I would," I replied, "if the situation warranted mercy. Listen, we're all feeling it right now. It's hot, we're trapped, and tempers are fraying. I get it. But we can still make it through this. We just need to get to that ascension ring. After that, we can figure things out. Tomorrow's another day, after all."

I was rambling and knew it, but I was literally at wit's end with fatigue. I was lucky to even be making sense at this point. "Come on, man, put down the gun and let's get out of here before we're all roasted alive."

A minute passed in which the temperature continued to rise. Between the heat and my brain already being fuzzy, I had a feeling it wouldn't be long before I simply dropped. We needed to work things through before that happened.

"Very well," Friedrich said, finally holstering his weapon. "But my point from earlier remains. This next choice is mine."

"I am telling you..."

I held up a hand toward Marius. "Fine. We'll do it your way."

Even as the words left my lips, an achievement popped up in my HUD and my Diplomacy skill rose to third level. Both nice, but I didn't need the distraction right then.

Pixel: *I hope you know what you're doing.*

The truth was I had no fucking clue. My only goal was to keep us from devolving into a bloodbath. Beyond that ... fuck if I knew.

Though I personally agreed with Marius on the placement of the remaining statues, Friedrich seemed convinced he was right. Though I had no insight into his buffs or debuffs, I had to assume he wasn't operating at the same level of fatigued I was, especially since I hadn't seen him faceplant at any time in the recent past. That cemented it for me.

I was impaired, he wasn't.

That said, hopefully this place wasn't operating on zero strikes just in case he was wrong. With any luck, we'd have a chance to fix any mistakes before becoming intimately familiar with how it felt to be cremated alive.

"The honor is all yours," I said.

Friedrich again met my gaze. Then he glanced back at Fast, as if to make sure they were behaving, before finally saying, "Ulagan, place them as you had originally suggested."

The Mongol warrior nodded then moved to drag the two statues together.

The rest of us should have helped him, but I got the impression we were all watching each other as surely as waiting to see if this would work.

Fortunately, Ulagan was up to the task. He dragged the woman back to where the upright male waited. However, even as he pushed her backside against his lower thighs, it was obvious they didn't fit. She was down too low for his ... err ... pose.

"This isn't working," I said. "We need to..."

I was too late with my warning, though.

Both statues raised their heads but it wasn't in ecstasy as the others had done. Feral hisses escaped their lips as their faces twisted in angry grimaces.

"Oh yeah, good call there, Tim," Pixel muttered from behind me.

"Quick," I cried, "we need to move them apart before..."

Sadly, that's when the two mismatched statues shattered into pieces as surely as if we'd smacked them with a sledgehammer. Then, to add insult to injury, the remaining two statues did the same.

Guess there were no do-overs in this jigsaw puzzle.

On the upside, our miserable failure was worth enough XP to push Boog and me over the edge. Notifications popped up in my HUD informing me that we were both now level six.

Too bad neither of us would probably live long enough to enjoy it as the floor began to rumble beneath our feet.

I'm sorry, Jeremy. I tried.

I fully expected either the ceiling to collapse or the temperature to keep rising until this chamber became our own personal crematorium.

What happened instead was the remaining walls turned grey to match the ones we'd gotten solving two parts of this puzzle. Almost immediately the temperature began to drop back down to manageable levels.

Then, before any of us could question what this meant, that rumbling coalesced into a heavy series of *clanks* from the door ahead of us.

One of the double doors opened a sliver, just enough to tell us they were now unlocked.

"Gotta admit," Pixel said at this newest revelation, "I was not expecting that."

"As I said, the *correct* choice," Friedrich replied with a deep breath, his former arrogance seemingly gone.

I personally was skeptical. After all, watching those statues crumble to dust didn't exactly feel like a win. But then again, we were in a void between dimensions on a gameshow run by beings so evolved as to effectively be gods, so it was possible there were nuances here I might be missing.

We all stood there for several long seconds, as if waiting for something to happen. Even Friedrich for all his boasting didn't seem particularly eager to take the next logical step.

It gave me a moment to take stock of myself and my recent gains.

Achievement unlocked! Party Pooper!

You managed to talk your way out of a potential slaughter, much to our audience's chagrin. Bully for you. Now, not only do we have to deal with your continued existence but our customer service is currently fielding comments regarding how many donkey balls you can fit in your mouth at once.

Enjoy your pyrrhic victory, just don't be surprised when

the betting pool turns against you. Let's just say, there's a reason we didn't recruit Gandhi to be a player.

***Reward*: You get to feel good about yourself. I hope that serves as comfort when we're forced to cut the budget for all the weapons and armor we could be giving you instead.**

Goddamn, talk about prissy. I almost preferred Drega insulting me to him sulking like a disgruntled teenager.

Unfortunately, my new level continued this trend of disappointment. While I still had 30 points to spend on stats, the free heal that came with it apparently didn't include an instant shot of caffeine to my veins. I was still as tired as ever.

That didn't put me in the best mindset to properly spend my points, but I had a feeling leaving them unclaimed, especially with a boss waiting in the next room, wouldn't be doing us any favors.

Rather than waste time thinking it through, I split them evenly amongst my physical attributes, raising my strength, dexterity, and constitution by 10 each. Whether those were the right choices or not, I guess I'd find out.

A quick glance in my HUD showed that Boog had taken this time to do the same, although in her case she dumped all 30 into PSI. Though her wisdom score might've been higher than mine, I still had to question that. Such a choice made sense for her current form but would effectively be wasted when she changed again.

Oh well, first we had to live long enough to regret it.

Boog herself was a mess of sweaty pink fur, giving off an odor akin to a dog after a flea bath. Both her hands were busy scratching herself in various places despite her assurance about telekinesis doing the trick. It spoke a lot about the state we were currently both in.

Still, uncomfortable or not, she was the first to break the silence. "The way forward is open," she said dispassionately. "I would highly suggest we take advantage of it lest whatever entity rules this place change its mind."

"Boog's right," I added. "We need to get moving." There came a loud *thoom* from the door we'd entered from, telling me the forces pursuing us still hadn't given up. "Preferably not back the way we came."

She threw me a toothy grin. "Shall we, my mate?"

I opened my mouth, unsure whether I should agree or ask her to please stop calling me that, but Friedrich spoke up first.

"No. The Vultures cast the final lot in this puzzle, so we will be first to face whatever lies ahead."

It was less a command and more a resigned statement. Call me crazy, but it didn't sound as if he planned to race forward and claim all the glory, much like they'd done with Mei. If anything, there seemed to be a hint of regret in his words. I raised an eyebrow as I met his gaze. Maybe it was wishful thinking but I got the sense this was his way of taking responsibility.

"Return to my side, Fast," he ordered.

The little red bug zapper didn't hesitate to obey as Marius and Ulagan likewise joined him.

To the rest of us, he simply said, "Prepare yourselves."

As if we really needed to be told that.

68

SCUSE ME WHILE I KISS THE FLOOR

As everyone positioned themselves, weapons at the ready, for whatever awaited us, I quickly pulled a nutradisk from inventory and scarfed it down.

It didn't really change anything for me, but it had been a while since I'd eaten and the last thing I wanted was to rush into a boss battle only to realize my tank was empty in more ways than one.

"Remember what Boog said earlier," Pixel called out as Ulagan and Marius prepared to open the door. "Same deal applies here. Be ready to defend yourselves but don't shoot first. It's not a boss battle until they officially tell us it's a boss battle."

I waited a beat to see if Friedrich had some comment but the leader of the Vultures no longer appeared to be in an argumentative mood.

Boog: *Thank you.*
Pixel: *See? I can be diplomatic when the situation warrants.*
Tim, JUST FUCKING TIM: *Oh? Did your skill level go up too?*
Pixel: *Fuck you, Tim.*
Tim, JUST FUCKING TIM: *What? Just asking.*

It was probably the last bit of levity we were going to get on this stage. From here on out we would be...

Debuff – You are Fatigued: severity level 3.

Thoroughly fucked.

My eyes opened wide as the notification appeared in my HUD.

You have got to be fucking kidding me!

A second health bar appeared in my display while the original became greyed out. Unsurprisingly, this temporary new one was only seventy percent the size it should've been.

Pixel: *You have got to be fucking kidding me. Now of all times?*

I grimaced as Pixel once again echoed my own thoughts.

Tim, JUST FUCKING TIM: *Are you r...lly th...t surpr...sed?*

Pixel: *Not particularly.*

Tim, JUST FUCKING TIM: *M... ne...ther.*

Pixel: *Hold on. Are you doing that on purpose?*

I tried to type no, but only the N appeared. It was like half the vowels on my mental keyboard had suddenly become stuck. I had a feeling that was no coincidence. Guess there were a few unlisted *bonuses* to this debuff after all.

I wonder if this is how Boog feels when she's trying to type. At least in her original form anyway.

"It's fine," I whispered. "I've still got this."

If any of the others heard me they didn't acknowledge it, not that it would've made any difference.

Ulagan and Marius pulled the double doors open as Friedrich stood by with both Fast and Invictus hovering over either shoulder, while we brought up the rear of this parade.

As soon as the doors parted, a gust of dry hot air blew through them. It wasn't quite as hot as this room had been but the breeze carried with it an odd smell.

I couldn't readily identify it, save that it must've activated some primal instinct in the reptilian part of my brain because, all at once, I was utterly scared shitless.

Time Chaser

⌛⌛⌛⌛ ·:¤§¤§¤§¤:· ⌛⌛⌛⌛

I didn't want to know what was up ahead. Hell, I didn't want to do anything other than turn and run, but I forced myself to look anyway. My first thought upon peering through the doors was of the Fire Nation's throne room from *Avatar the Last Airbender*.

A floor of pure obsidian stretched before us, polished to a mirror shine – so perfect that it looked as if everything within was doubled. It led to a raised dais of ivory and gold that stretched the width of the room. Flames rose from the floor just in front of it, burning an unnatural golden color. Atop the platform stood a jade throne that I'm fairly certain any museum director on Earth would've sold their soul to have in their collection. Behind it, scintillating light could be seen shining up from the floor, the source unknown, although I had a feeling I knew what was producing it.

A man was seated upon the throne, the room's sole occupant far as I could see.

He wore a robe of gleaming red and gold that seemed to reflect the light around him, giving the impression he was aglow with power. Whether that was merely an optical illusion, however, remained to be seen.

Despite his finery, the man himself was somewhat less than imposing. From where I stood, he appeared no more than five and a half feet tall. A jowly bearded face sat atop a plump body. It spoke less of a warrior king and more of some spoiled noble who was used to a life of good food and easy living.

So then why were my knees shaking as I stood there?

It wasn't just me either. None of the others had so much as taken a single step forward yet.

Debuff – You are Fearful.

Guess that explained it.

I quickly focused on that, hoping to gain some insight.

Fearful – Debuff

Duration: temporary

Outside of egomaniacs and psychopaths, it's both normal and healthy to feel afraid whenever going into battle, even when you know you're gonna kick ass and take names.

Because, hey, ya never know.

But as with all things, there's a big difference between exercising caution and totally pussing out. What you're experiencing right now is more of the latter. Here's what you can look forward to while you're busy quaking in your boots like a scared toddler without a nightlight.

-10% to all attacks

Unable to move closer to the originator of this debuff

Note: pissing yourself is technically not one of the penalties listed here, but feel free to do so anyway. Our audience can always use a good laugh.

Just out of curiosity, I tried to take a single step backward. I managed it, even if every instinct in my body insisted that I should be running.

It was probably a good thing I didn't, though. Considering my current level of fatigued, I doubt I'd have gotten far.

I then tried to force myself to regain the same distance I'd just lost, realizing that my body was refusing to comply.

Guess that answered that question.

Since there was no doubt in my mind that the guy on the throne was the source of this mind-numbing fear, I tried focusing on him instead, wondering if my HUD would refuse even that.

Protector Wan – level ?

Unfortunately, much as it had done with those statues, the system wouldn't give me any more information for some reason. I wasn't sure what was up, save that the chubby yet somehow terrifying guy waiting for us didn't appear to be a statue.

Case in point, he raised a hand and gestured us forward.

Just like that, the *fearful* debuff disappeared from my HUD. I took an experimental step forward and found myself able to.

Mind you, the debuff might've been gone but that didn't mean I still wasn't way too close to crapping my chinos.

Something about this guy was seriously messing with my head and it had nothing to do with how he looked or dressed.

I wasn't alone in this feeling.

Ulagan: *Be wary, friends. That is no man. It is some kind of demon.*

Marius: *How was he able to do such a thing?*

Invictus: *Though we are unable to view his introductory text, I would surmise he is in possession of an aura.*

Marius: *An aura?*

Invictus: *A field of influence some creatures are able to project around themselves for a set distance. Such auras can have a variety of effects.*

Pixel: *In this case pants-shitting fear.*

Invictus: *That is certainly one way of explaining it.*

Friedrich: *Steel yourselves. This is simply another mechanism of this infernal game. A trick, no more. The only true fear is that which we* allow *ourselves to feel.*

He probably had a point there, although what I was currently feeling seemed pretty darned real to me.

I took another whiff of the air, once again causing a chill to run down my spine and all the hairs on the back of my neck to stand on end. I forced myself to take several more breaths, trying to identify whatever was lingering in the air, but for some reason the only memory it sparked was from last spring when I'd taken Jeremy to the Bronx Zoo.

Needless to say, I was pretty sure it wasn't hippo crap I was smelling. It was more like...

Boog: *I do not know what sort of being this Protector Wan is, but I fear he is a predator of the highest order.*

A predator?

That was it! Boog had given voice to what my own suburban raised mind could not. That's why I was remembering the zoo. There was something about standing there, staring at lions and crocodiles, that made you damned glad there was steel, glass, and concrete between you and them.

It made perfect sense that Boog would understand this better than the rest of us. She hailed from a time when people had no choice but to be far more mindful of their surroundings. Where I'd come from you mostly only had to worry about people – and maybe the occasional bus – but hers was almost certainly a world of dangers just waiting to make you their next meal.

Mind you, that really didn't do much to quell the fear I was feeling. This Wan might be short and possessed of a dad bod but he was dangerous. No doubt about it.

Trying to focus on something, *anything* else, I checked my map. Sure enough, that pulsing red boss dot was right where he sat. That was no surprise, although I couldn't help but note I hadn't felt anything even remotely like this when facing either Mei or Apu.

Sadly, we had no choice but to press forward as the map also confirmed that the ascension ring was almost directly behind his throne.

That settled it. The aforementioned *glow* rising off of him was probably nothing more than the light cast by the ring reflected off his robes.

Or he might've just been that scary powerful. Either way, I guess we were about to find out.

To Friedrich's credit, he was the first to enter the throne room, striding forward with his head held high despite probably feeling the same primal fear as me.

Fast followed in his wake with Invictus right behind the two of them.

Ulagan and Marius both hesitated where they were a second longer, then they too started walking.

That left the three of us.

"Come on, let's do this," I finally said, trying to sound braver than I felt. "Just take it nice and slow. One step at a time."

"Is that for our sake," Pixel asked as we started forward, "or to keep you from taking another faceplant?"

I turned toward the little ghost light and smirked. "A little bit from column A..."

Our banter quickly petered out as we stepped inside the door, giving us a full view of the throne room and the *guards* within.

Holy shit!

Flanking the doors on either side were a pair of statues. Both stood over thirty feet tall and were carved from finer marble than I'd ever had the pleasure of seeing grace a countertop.

Unlike those in the previous room, however, I doubted these were anyone's concubines. Clad in heavy armor and holding spears big enough to harpoon a whale with, each was topped with a gruesome demonic visage that was a far cry from the looks of ecstasy etched upon their smaller counterparts.

Though obviously not sexual in the slightest, that didn't mean we wouldn't be thoroughly fucked if they came to life in the same way those others had. I had a feeling it would be a matter of seconds for these giants to crush us all into paste.

Much like in the prior room, the doors swung shut behind us the moment we crossed the threshold, closing with a heavy *clang.*

That's when the two behemoths began to move, the stone of their bodies becoming as supple as flesh in the space of an instant.

Goddamn, I hate it when I'm right!

Despite sort of expecting it, I still almost jumped out of my skin, nearly tripping over my own two feet as the twin giants brought down their massive spears.

However, they weren't aiming at us.

Yet anyway.

Instead, they crossed their weapons in front of the door, forming a giant X as they embedded their spear heads deep into the stone floor – enough to tell me there was likely no chance of retreat from this place.

I waited a beat to see if the statues did anything else but, as quickly as they'd come to life, they once again became nothing but inanimate stone – a fact seemingly backed up by my HUD not giving me a single iota of information about them.

At least now we didn't have to worry about Wan's forces breaking in and flanking us. Glass half full and all.

Pixel: *Eyes forward, Tim. Pretty sure those things are the least of our worries.*

Boog: *I truly hope you are right.*

Pixel had a point. Now was not the time to enjoy the *killer* scenery. So, rather than attempt a mangled reply via chat, I simply did as I was told.

Wan was staring in our direction, his eyes hard as steel. He didn't say anything or make any more gestures, he just glared.

Guess the ball was still in our court.

After a slight hesitation, Friedrich continued onward, leading the way and prompting the rest of us to do the same. Despite my fear, a part of me wasn't entirely happy letting him lead the way. Our alliance was starting to feel strained, true, but I also couldn't help remembering my thoughts from earlier regarding followers and their questionable future when it came to the Chase.

Back home, I was a middle manager by trade, not some corporate superstar. I did my job competently, but had no delusions that anyone was grooming me for a top spot. But that was okay. I could both live with and eventually retire quite comfortably from such a line of work.

Casual mediocrity, as it turned out, was a viable career path, at least in corporate America.

Things were different here, though. I was beginning to

slowly come to terms with that. If I wanted to see my boy again, I needed to step outside of that comfort zone.

I glanced again at Wan, once more feeling a shiver down my spine.

Mind you, I could always try taking charge another day, long after we'd put Wan in our rearview mirror. I mean, heck, I wasn't even the party leader.

No! Stop thinking like a freaking henchman. That's not a winning strategy, not here.

Apparently neither was striding boldly ahead, at least not where Wan was concerned.

Friedrich got to within maybe twenty feet of him before stopping dead in his tracks, the same instant that *Fearful* debuff once again reared its ugly head.

The meaning was clear. Wan was in control here and the only way we were getting any closer was if he wanted us to.

A deep silence settled over the throne room as we all stood there waiting to see what would happen next – unable to go forward but with the way behind us barred shut.

All the while, Protector Wan merely sat there staring at us – an expectant look upon his face as if he was waiting for us to do something. Problem was, I had no idea what that something might be.

As the impasse stretched to a minute and then two, I began to get the sense that I wasn't alone in my confusion.

It was as if none of us dared to make a move, lest it be the wrong one, whereas Wan seemed more than content to wait us out for however long it took.

Pixel: *So ... is someone going to do something?*

I was glad they asked before I was forced to mangle the same question. Thirty seconds passed with no answer, so they tried again.

Pixel: *Yo, Freddy. Last I checked, this was your expedition. So is there a plan here or what?*

Fast: *You will show the commander proper respect!*

Friedrich: *Enough! I am considering our options, FAST. Or would you prefer I act without thought and risk jeopardizing us all?*

For fuck's sake! I waited to see if they'd continue baiting each other, but thankfully another voice chimed in before that could happen.

Ulagan: *I am such a fool. I know what he is waiting for. It is clear as the nose upon my face.*

A series of triple dots appeared in the chat, telling me multiple individuals were writing responses, no doubt trying to make sure Ulagan knew what he was doing.

But he was already on the move before anyone could finish.

As it turned out, his solution was simplicity itself. He dropped to his knees and kowtowed before Wan, lowering his head until it touched the ground.

In response, Wan glanced his way and gave the barest of nods.

This was usually the part where Pixel said, "Duh!" I tried to suppress a sigh at the fact that the answer was so obvious, yet somehow the rest of us had missed it. Hell, Friedrich had even mentioned the guy's royalty in his argument regarding those puzzle statues.

And what did one do when in the presence of royalty? You fucking bowed, that's what.

Tim, JUST FUCKING TIM: F...llow h...s le...d.

I sent the message to our party chat only, hoping they understood. A second later Boog repeated it to the whole group, thankfully minus the typos.

That done, I tried my best to duplicate Ulagan's move, followed a moment later by everyone else. Even the FASTs attempted it, although in their case they merely hovered down to ground level.

Once each of us had *kissed* the floor, so to speak, that debuff finally disappeared from my HUD.

"Rise," Wan said after another moment, his voice far deeper than his appearance suggested. We're talking an echoing bass that would make James Earl Jones sound like a soprano in comparison.

Either way, we'd passed Wan's first test – a good sign if ever there was.

"Rise," he repeated, "and tell me why I should not dispose of you this instant for displeasing my concubines."

Crap! And just like that we were back to being way less than good.

69

PROTECTOR OF THE REALM

For several long seconds nobody moved, despite Wan having told us to get up. Now, I can't claim to have met much royalty in my time, but I had a feeling that anyone powerful enough to hold court in a place like this probably wasn't someone who'd tolerate being ignored for long.

Despite having no idea what I was going to say, I started to stand up, hoping I could maybe come up with something to get us out of this, preferably without tripping over my own feet in the process.

Friedrich was a little quicker on the draw, though.

"An error on my part, Protector Wan." He said that last part hesitantly, as if testing whether our *gracious* host might blow a gasket at being addressed by how our HUDs had identified him.

Fortunately, Wan merely nodded, again so subtly it was just barely perceptive.

Ball's in your court now, Freddy. Hopefully he didn't launch into some tirade about how much of a depraved pervert Wan was. This boss was apparently willing to talk, at least so far. Talk about a rare opportunity. Needless to say, it would be a shame for us to waste it.

"I misjudged your ... tastes," Friedrich continued, his tone neutral. "It was not my intent to offend."

"And yet offend you did," Wan growled. "Although, not without winning the favor of a few. Fortunately for you, my concubines all share the same hold over my heart, so your failures stand in balance against your victories. A true conundrum."

He stroked his beard, a move straight out of a Saturday afternoon kung-fu movie. Safe to say, I decided to keep that little bit of trivia to myself.

Had this been real life, I'd have given us at least moderate odds of talking our way out of this mess. It wasn't, though. Drega had long since clued us in that we were there first and foremost to entertain the unwashed masses. The big question now was whether succeeding here without a fight was considered *entertaining*.

I had little doubt at least some of my companions were thinking the same thing. All around, I saw weapons at the ready, although thankfully it seemed nobody wanted to be the one to instigate this fight. Can't say I didn't appreciate the amount of restraint it was probably taking.

We needed to see how this would play out before jumping straight to hack and slash. If there was even a chance we could step into that ascension ring without risking our lives, we had to take it.

"I would know the name of he who so boldly faces me within my own throne room," Wan said, his tone not doing much to settle my nerves..

"I am Friedrich of the Vultures."

Can't say I would've responded the same way. *I am Tim of Tim Chasers* just didn't have the same ring to it.

"The Vultures?" Wan repeated. "Opportunistic scavengers who prey upon the dead."

That last part was not a question.

"We all do what we must to survive," Friedrich remarked.

"Indeed. So tell me, *Vulture*, do you speak for all who stand before me today, this rabble who have dared invade the lands I call my own?"

Friedrich started to answer, but this time Pixel jumped in. "Just for the record, he sure as hell does not."

Son of a...

And once again, I was reminded of how low my FAST's charisma score truly was.

"Please excuse the FAST," Friedrich quickly replied, no doubt in damage control mode.

"FAST?" Wan replied, eyes narrowing.

"Our ... companion. He is both rash and impulsive."

"Is that so?" Wan turned Pixel's way, his look somewhere south of friendly. "And you would be?"

Pixel: *Maybe I should've thought that through first.*

Tim, JUST FUCKING TIM: *Ya th...nk?*

Pixel: *Christ, I can't believe I actually have to say this out loud.*

"I am Pixel," they said with a sigh, "of Tim Chasers."

Tim, JUST FUCKING TIM: *W...it, th...t's what y...u wer... worr...ed ab...ut?!*

God fucking damn! What I wouldn't have given for a Red Bull, an espresso, or even one of those fucking five hour energy shots right about then.

Heck, I'd have even settled for my SK having autocorrect.

"Tim Chasers?" Wan repeated, as if tasting the words and finding them way too salty for his liking. "And what is a Tim?"

"What? Oh, that would be him." Pixel flitted in my direction, about the closest they could come to pointing a finger.

"I see. And why do you chase him?"

"I... actually that's a pretty good question."

"Nobody's chasing me," I replied, finally breaking my silence. "It's more ... of an inside joke."

I hesitated to say more, doubtful that explaining how Pixel

had done nothing more than make a stupid pun about the multiversal game show we were trapped in would even make sense to this guy.

Wan turned his eyes ever so slightly my way as if noticing me for the first time. Once again the hairs on the back of my neck stood up, telling me I probably didn't want to be on this guy's radar. Lucky me that I now was.

"A joke you say? So you are this being's fool?"

"Well, I mean I'm not the smartest guy on the planet but..."

Pixel: *He thinks you're our court jester, Einstein.*

Oh. "Um ... never mind."

Wan gritted his teeth and blew out a breath that sounded way more menacing than it should have. And just like that, I had a feeling my stupid, tired ass had just earned us our first strike with this boss.

Even Boog threw me a look that suggested it might be best if I kept my trap shut. Won't lie, at that moment I would've been okay had the Fatigued debuff skipped level four and went right to the part where I blissfully passed out.

"Scavengers and those who chase a fool," Wan said more to himself than us. "Tell me. What is it you seek that you would so boldly invade my home?" The question was directed toward Friedrich, much to Pixel's chagrin judging by the soft buzzing sound they made.

No doubt emboldened, Friedrich took a single step forward. "I apologize for our presence here, but we seek safe passage to the ascension ring which lies past your throne."

Wan glanced over his shoulder, his face momentarily bathed in the glow from the exit we were seeking. "Ascension ring? You mean the *waypoint*?"

"I believe so, yes."

"Perhaps you are all fools then," Wan said dismissively. "The waypoint is a mystery to even our most learned scholars. We know not where it leads, only that those who enter its light are never seen again."

"That is a risk we gladly accept. You have said so yourself, we are invaders in your land. Allow us passage and you will be rid of us for good."

Wan let out a breath of mirthless laughter. "Such *noble* fools at that, willing to sacrifice themselves to protect the sanctity of my domain. Why go to all this trouble when you could have simply offered your throats to my generals?"

I had a feeling Wan was toying with us now. Friedrich's ruse to get him to let us pass hadn't been bad. Heck, I probably would've done the same myself, but Wan had seen right through it. As a Chinese emperor from presumably 900 A.D., he likely had no idea what an ascension ring was, nor any interest in stepping through and testing it himself – assuming the overmind would even let him. However, the fact that we were willing to jump right in said all eight of us were either suicidal or knew something he didn't.

Wan was apparently too smart to believe that first one.

I could only hope Friedrich was up to the task of talking our way out of this, especially since he seemed to have the spotlight.

"We have no wish to die. Merely to ... explore."

"And if that exploration leads nowhere but to your own doom?"

"Then so be it. At least we will not die in ignorance."

Okay, points to Friedrich. That was a pretty smooth answer. Now to see if Wan was in the mood to buy this load of horse shit.

"A fair answer and one that would indeed please me if it means being rid of dangerous invaders such as yourself." Friedrich moved to respond, but Wan wasn't finished yet. "That you have made it this far in your quest speaks to your resilience. Of that there can be no doubt. Such a thing is worthy of respect."

It was?

Or maybe not as he made the slightest gesture, causing the ground to rumble beneath us.

What the hell? Was he praising us in one breath only to kill us with his next? That would really suck.

I was wrong, though. The source of the rumbling soon became evident as a section of the dais to Wan's right began to retract into the ground, revealing a narrow path leading past him.

He glanced at it and the golden flames barring our way disappeared, leaving it wide open. Cool as that might've looked, it was nothing compared to what lay beyond.

My eyes fell upon the glowing circle of light embedded into the floor.

At that same moment, a line of bold text appeared in my HUD.

YOU HAVE DISCOVERED AN ASCENSION RING!

About fucking time too.

70

EXIT STAGE LEFT

Even knowing this was only the first of twelve stages, I still teared up at the sight of the exit. Just seeing it was enough to bring up all the emotions I'd been forcing myself to swallow for...

No, it hadn't only been the last two days. I'd been forced to bottle up a lot ever since I'd returned home early from the Para-Docx convention. And right now, well, I was simply too tired to hold back those floodwaters.

Yes, this was nothing more than a pyrrhic victory. All of this shit would start up again in another day or so, pitting us against increasingly horrific trials. But right then, in that moment, we'd made it.

In theory anyway.

Friedrich took a single step forward, only for the flames to flare up again blocking his way.

"A boon and a bane," Wan said.

"I don't understand," Friedrich replied.

"You pleased half of my concubines, true, but you angered the rest. To insult those I favor is to insult me and you have yet to answer for this, thus the way remains closed for you."

Oh crap. I had a feeling it couldn't be that easy.

Time Chaser

Friedrich glanced at the blocked passageway then back at Wan. "We truly meant no offense."

"A locust means no offense to the crops it devours, yet that does not make the resulting famine any less tragic."

"Send us through this waypoint then," Friedrich replied. "We will be gone forever from your lands and in all likelihood destroyed in the process. That is what you wish, is it not?"

It was a nice try but I had a feeling it was gonna fall short of the mark.

Almost as if reading my thoughts, Wan actually laughed. "Indeed it is, vulture. And if that were all there is then I would gladly see you face whatever fate awaits you." He once again stroked his beard. "But it is not only I who wish for this. You and your companions long to enter the waypoint. This leads me to think that, despite your words, what lies beyond its infernal gate is perhaps not as unknown as you would have me believe."

Pixel: *I'm guessing someone failed their Diplomacy check.*

Boog: *What does that mean for us?*

Pixel: *Probably nothing good. We fucked up royally back in the puzzle room. Now we're about to learn how badly.*

No doubt sensing that things were starting to turn south, Ulagan once more bowed deeply. "We implore you for mercy, oh Great Protector."

Wan gave him the barest of glances. "Mercy has already been granted, vulture. Your tongues are still attached so that you might speak, are they not. But now I say it is time to satisfy my wrath."

Friedrich took a deep breath but to his credit didn't cower. "What would you have us do?"

"For starters, you will mind your tone. Insolence will afford you nothing but the most painful of ends."

I can't pretend to be some great sage when it came to reading body language, but the way Friedrich stiffened from the rebuke told me he was seriously considering drawing his weapon.

While I didn't particularly want to see that happen, at least not while Wan was still open to talking, I wouldn't be surprised if it came to that. But if so, Friedrich really needed to tell the rest of us first. A coordinated assault would almost certainly work better than him going off half-cocked. Now was not the time for surprises.

It was like we all held our breath for several long moments, waiting to see what would happen, but then gradually Friedrich relaxed his stance. Maybe he realized he was in the wrong or perhaps it was simply the fact that Wan was still a mystery to us. Pissing him off, only to then discover he could end us in a heartbeat would make for an inglorious end.

"My apologies, Protector Wan," he finally said, practically choking on the words. "The stress of our situation weighs heavily upon me. It can be ... overwhelming at times."

"Such is the burden that leadership carries," Wan replied, not entirely without sympathy. "Alas, I fear that burden shall only become heavier, for you must now choose."

"Choose? I don't understand."

"A boon and a bane. Your boon has already been spoken – safe passage to the waypoint. I will allow this ... for those who remain."

For those who...?

"As for your bane, I demand that a life be offered to me as repayment for your failure."

Son of a... I was right, no way could it be that easy.

Pixel: *All right, playtime's over. I say we attack this asshole. Who's with me?*

A beat passed with no response from the rest of the group.
Pixel: *Hello?*
Friedrich: *No. His terms are fair.*

Wait, they are? Maybe I'd heard Wan wrong, but it sure as

heck sounded like he was demanding one of us as a sacrificial lamb.

Friedrich was apparently ready for any incoming disbelief, though.

Friedrich: *One life is a small price to pay to ensure the rest of us safe passage.*

Before anyone could respond, he took a deep breath then said aloud, "So be it."

Tim, JUST FUCKING TIM: *Wa...t! Y...u can...t j...st...*

I was too late in my illegible response, though.

"You demand a life," the Vulture's leader continued, "so it falls to me to offer you one."

What the...? Hold on. Maybe I was reading between the lines, but it sounded like he was getting ready to offer himself up for the rest of us.

Holy crap, did we really have this guy pegged so wrong?

Sure, in the past hour or so things had gotten tense, especially once Fast opened fire on Pixel. But the truth was, aside from my prejudice against his uniform and the sniping between him and Pixel, he hadn't actually done anything to purposefully wrong us.

If so, was I really going to stand by and let him? Sure, I wanted to get back home, more than anything, but was this a price I was actually willing to pay to...?

"I am sorry, my friends," he continued, turning to face us all. "I truly am."

"You don't have to do this," I said. "We can find another..."

My words trailed off as he pointed a finger my way. "I name Tim McAvoy as your sacrifice. I offer his life to you, Protector Wan."

Wait, what?

It took my overtired brain a second or two to process his words, but in that short moment my teammates were already letting their opinions be known.

"You backstabbing, Nazi piece of shit," Pixel snapped.

"No! You will not have my mate. You cannot..."

"SILENCE!" Wan roared, cutting them both off mid-protest.

I looked first to Ulagan then at Marius. Both appeared surprised, dismayed even, but that was it. Marius looked like he wanted to say something but held his tongue, instead turning his head away from me.

That wasn't good.

Where the other Vultures failed to meet my gaze, however, Friedrich's eyes locked onto mine.

The expression upon his face was steel itself, utterly unreadable. I tried to find something, even a shred of remorse there, but saw nothing. It was like having a staring contest with a brick wall.

What did that mean?

Well, okay, maybe I was being purposely dense on this one, but can you blame me? I'd worked so hard to push down my initial dislike of this guy, to force myself to work alongside him, that it was only natural that I be hesitant to consider that maybe my first impression had been right after all.

The fact remained, though. Jesus Christ, not only had he called me out but there'd been no hesitation whatsoever – as if the choice had been an easy one.

"The hell, dude?"

"I said, *silence*," Wan growled, his aura momentarily activating again, just long enough to turn my legs into quivering jelly.

Pixel wasn't so easily dissuaded, though.

Pixel: *New plan. If we're going down, we take that Nazi asshole with us and make sure it hurts.*

I turned Boog's way, a part of me still hoping there was some hidden ploy behind this madness. However, the look on her face told me she was mere seconds away from trying to telekinetically pop Friedrich's head off.

The question was did I really want that? Crazy as it was to even ask, I wasn't sure I did.

Tim, JUST FUCKING TIM: *Don't!*

Through some miracle, I managed to get that word out. Hopefully it was enough.

I understood their anger but my own was taking its sweet time to ignite. In its place, I felt only confusion.

Sure, it was possible we'd been duped from the very start, but it was also equally likely this was a predicament of my own making.

Following the battle with Mei, I'd been both aggressive and hostile toward Friedrich, throwing out accusations despite knowing nothing about his world. I hadn't even considered what kind of first impression that might've left.

Hell, if someone had done the same to me, I'd have walked away with no small amount of smoldering resentment.

But if so, then why let it fester? Why not clear the air when we had a chance to go our separate ways? A simple, "Thanks for the helping hand, now go fuck yourselves," would have done it.

The answer was simple. That's maybe how I would've done it, but Friedrich wasn't me. Was it possible such resentment had led to far darker thoughts on his part?

I thought back to how Fast ruined our chances of getting to that campground. I'd since accepted Friedrich's claim that they'd acted of their own accord. But what if I'd been wrong?

None of us had any idea what those two discussed in their private chats. Would it have been so difficult for him to force his browbeaten FAST to accept blame on the matter? After all, their relationship seemed less a partnership and more like that of an abused spouse and their tormentor.

But even then, would Fast have willingly eaten a bullet to maintain the charade?

I couldn't speak to that, but I guess it was possible. And if that were the case then we'd all been taken for fools. Well, okay, maybe not Pixel, but the rest of us.

It sounded so ominous inside my head. And yet, despite being fingered for summary execution, I still didn't want to believe it. Maybe I was too much of a bleeding heart, but something wasn't adding up. Sadly, I was too tired to make sense of it, especially when everything seemed to be pointing toward one simple fact – that I'd been wrong in thinking we were allies.

Even so, it was still hard for me to accept...

"Quick and decisive," Wan said, derailing my train of thought. "Just as a leader should be."

Wait, was he actually praising Friedrich for throwing me to the wolves? The fuck?

"You demanded a life. I offer you his. There is nothing more to be said." This time he didn't even look my way.

Goddamn it all. All signs were pointing toward him having been a snake in the grass all along. I could see no attempt at subterfuge, no double meaning. He was throwing me under yet another bus. Barely aware I was even doing so, I reached up and touched the spite amulet hanging from my neck.

I had hoped to never be in a position where I felt a need to use it, but now I began to wonder if I'd been premature in that decision. Even now I had no real interest in ending another chaser's life, but who was to say what would happen to Pixel or Boog if I allowed this to happen with no repercussions or chance of...?

"Alas, the fool's life is not yours to give."

What?

Friedrich's eyes opened as wide as mine. Neither of us had been expecting that.

"But..."

"You are Friedrich of the *Vultures*," Wan interrupted. "The fool claims to be of Tim Chasers. You travel together but are not of the same clan. Thus, his life will not satisfy your bane."

It won't? Can't say that bothered me in the slightest, although judging by the look on Friedrich's face he didn't concur. Whatever he'd been planning, he'd just shot his load prematurely and knew it.

Pixel: *Nice try, fuck face!*

Unsurprisingly, Pixel had sent that one out to our combined chat, although I had a feeling I'd let this one slide. It was hard to be mad at someone for coming to my defense.

Mind you, it was probably a bit premature to start the celebrations.

"A boon and a bane," Wan repeated, grinning ever so slightly as if enjoying his game. "Choose."

Friedrich's lips peeled back ever so slightly revealing gritted teeth, then he turned until he was facing Fast.

"Oh, you son of a..."

Wan shut Pixel up with a single glare. His meaning was clear. We needed to stay out of this.

All the same, I understood where my teammate was coming from. With me no longer a viable target, I couldn't help but feel bad for the little FAST. They were already down two lives. I'd only seen how one of their deaths had played out, yet couldn't help shake the feeling that the other had also been a result of Friedrich's machinations. Sadly, they were down to their final life.

Worse, I had a feeling there wasn't much we could do to help, not without giving Wan an excuse to...

Friedrich held his gaze on the FAST a moment longer before abruptly facing Wan once again. "I offer you Marius of the Vultures. His life is yours to do with as you wish."

What?!

71

AND THEN THERE WERE THREE

"Surely you must be jesting," Invictus said. "You can't possibly be serious."

"I am afraid this is no joke," Friedrich replied dispassionately.

"But why?" Marius pled, the weight of his leader's betrayal no doubt starting to sink in. "I ... we are allies, friends!"

"Indeed we are, and for that I am grateful." Friedrich turned away from him, hesitating for a moment. "However, I must admit your sense of ... morality is somewhat lacking."

"My morality, but...?"

"Your beliefs, the ones you made clear in the room prior to this, are simply ... repugnant. I am sorry, but painful as this decision is, the choice is clear."

"This is not our only path," Ulagan hissed, grabbing Friedrich's arm. "We can still fight."

"To what end?" Behind them Fast began to glow with magical power, but the Vulture's leader merely waved them off. "This is but the first of several stages. You would have me risk all our lives when a compromise has been offered that allows the rest of us to pass unharmed? Think, man!"

"You call this a compromise?" I replied.

"You will be *silent*," Wan warned. "Their bane is not your concern. You will be given your own chance in due time."

Our own chance? Oh, I really didn't like the sound of that.

Pixel: *So much for this not turning into an absolute cluster fuck.*

Talk about an understatement. Friedrich had just thrown me under the bus and now, after being told I was off limits, he'd turned on one of his followers with barely any hesitation. I'd tried to rationalize that first choice, even laying some of the blame at my own feet. But this new development, what possible excuse could there be for it other than him showing his true colors?

Speaking of the bastard, Friedrich held Ulagan's gaze until the Mongol warrior finally looked away and nodded.

"Please, I..." Marius trailed off as both his teammates turned their backs on him.

In that instant I saw all hope vanish from his face. It was only for a moment, though, so quick one could have blinked and missed it. Then it was replaced with a look of resolve.

I can't say I was surprised. He was a soldier after all, one who'd faced death before.

He then pulled his spear from inventory and held it by his side. "May Dis forgive me for attempting to stave off the Underworld." He then turned toward Wan. "And may my darling Davina find peace in my fate so that Sabina and Gloriana grow to be strong and brave."

Holy shit. In the space of six seconds, he'd somehow skipped the first four stages of grief and gone straight to acceptance. I couldn't even pretend to have the same fortitude.

But maybe Marius didn't need to either.

"Wait!" I was risking Wan's anger but didn't care in the slightest. "Join our party. There's still time for us to find a way to..."

"The choice is made," Wan said, ignoring me as if I hadn't spoken at all. "A boon and now a bane."

Before any of us could respond, he opened his mouth far wider than any normal person should've been able to. A bolt of golden flame shot from his lips, so hot I was forced to back up several steps. The attack hit the legionnaire square in the chest.

Marius barely had time to scream as he was almost instantly consumed. His health bar appeared then winked out barely a second later, his life force completely obliterated.

As his charred remains fell to the floor, my HUD updated its listing for the fallen warrior.

Chaser: Marius – Earth 432 – Level 7 – EXPIRED

That was all the fanfare he was given. Unlike the pregame, when that samurai's body faded away to nothing, his corpse merely lay on the ground while Invictus hovered over it.

As I took this in, unsure of what to say or think, the flames standing between us and the ascension ring vanished.

"Go in peace, vultures," Wan said dismissively, "and dare not ever return to my realm."

I wanted to say something, to tell Friedrich that I'd better never see his face again but the words failed me. In that moment, I truly felt the full weight of my fatigue.

I fully expected the remaining Vultures to leave without any further fanfare. After all, they'd won. Friedrich had gotten what he wanted. Instead, he turned and stepped over to where Marius lay, looking down at his remains for several long seconds.

At first, I thought maybe he was showing his respect – as if that was worth anything at this point – but then Marius's spear, still intact despite the heat, disappeared from the ground and I realized what was actually happening.

The motherfucker was looting Marius's corpse.

"Truly you are vultures," Wan remarked as if he found the whole thing amusing.

"You fucking ghoul," Pixel cried.

"As if any of you would do any different," Friedrich said.

"We're not you," I shot back.

He met and held my gaze before taking a deep breath. "No.

You are not. Be thankful for that." He then turned away. "Come, Ulagan."

Ulagan gave us the briefest of nods, his only acknowledgement of what had just happened, then he turned and followed his leader.

Once they were past the dais, the flames ignited again barring our way.

I wanted to say more, to tell him that there would be a reckoning, but held my tongue instead. The simple truth was I couldn't be sure it wasn't anything more than an idle threat.

Then the moment was over, the opportunity gone.

Friedrich stepped into the ascension ring. His body lit up from within, glowing brightly for a moment or two, and then he disappeared. Fast and Ulagan followed in his footsteps.

The only member of the Vultures who remained behind was Invictus, who continued to hover over Marius as if holding out hope for a miracle that wasn't going to come.

"What now?" I asked in a low voice.

"I guess it's our turn for this bullshit," Pixel replied.

"No. I meant for *them*." I gestured toward the other FAST, still floating over Marius.

"Guess we'll find out."

Perhaps Wan found all this entertaining or simply didn't give a fuck, but either way he remained silent for the moment.

"I wonder if he knew this would happen," Invictus said after a few seconds.

"That he was going to be betrayed?" Boog asked.

"Not him, I meant Friedrich. Did he know we would receive that experience bonus by condemning Marius to his fate, even though it was secondhand?"

"Wait, they gave you a PVP bonus too?" Pixel replied. "Goddamn, that's bleak as fuck."

"No. That is merely a mechanism of the Chase, as are we both."

"Yeah, I'm gonna stick with bleak as fuck."

"So what happens next?" I asked.

"Nothing," Invictus said. "My time in this cycle is over. I will go into stasis and await the time when I am needed once more."

"Hold on," Pixel replied. "You don't have to leave. You know that, right? You'd be well within the rules to stick around."

"And for what reason?"

"Oh, I don't know. How about making payback your personal bitch? That a good enough reason for you?"

"Or," I said, jumping in, "you could stay and help us. Boog lost her FAST a while back so you could..."

Invictus buzzed loudly, cutting me off. "A FAST cannot partner with another chaser mid-Chase."

"Okay fine, fair enough, but we'd still welcome another helping hand."

"Be that as it may, I fail to see the benefit in doing so."

"You might change your tune if we run into Freddy Fuck-face again," Pixel said. "At the very least, it would be a chance to avenge your buddy here."

"He was my assigned chaser not my *buddy*. Emotional attachments do not serve us in this place other than to put our own existence in jeopardy. Besides, even if one of you were to win, I would get nothing for the effort. Not that I expect there to be much chance of that happening."

"What the hell does that mean?" Pixel replied.

"It *means*," Invictus said, "that my time in this cycle is over. Perhaps the next Chase will prove more fortuitous. Until then, I shall look forward to forgetting."

Invictus's status abruptly changed within my HUD.

FAST: Invictus – Undisclosed – Level 8 – X – WITHDRAWN

"Wait, don't..."

I might as well have been talking to myself, though. The

FAST's body flashed brightly, becoming almost like a miniature star, and then they too were gone, disappearing from both my sight and HUD as if they'd never even been there.

"Goddamn, talk about a Debbie downer," Pixel said.

I winced at their choice of names. "Maybe negative Nancy would be more appropriate."

"Sorry. I was too busy focusing on what I'm going to do when next I see that Nazi shit sandwich."

I nodded but there wasn't much conviction behind it. Part of it was being simply too tired to feel much of anything right then, coupled with a sense of being overwhelmed. Everything had happened so quickly that I hadn't even begun to process it.

I'd liked Marius but more importantly I'd identified with him. He'd been the one to open my eyes that my own situation here was far from unique, that there were other chasers here, quite possibly the vast majority, who wanted nothing more than a second chance to be with their loved ones.

And now that chance was forever lost to him. His wife and daughters were doomed to think he'd died on some foreign battlefield, never knowing that he'd been given a shot at returning home to them or that they had been his motivation for trying.

That wasn't all, though. Friedrich had tried to dump all that on me first. Had it not been for the technicality of us being in different parties – an odd sticking choice for Wan, making me wonder if that was a game mechanism at play – I would surely be dead now. Jeremy would then grow up thinking his father had died because he'd failed to look both ways while crossing the road.

What a stupid, pointless death. At least Marius's death had been due to something of note, not that I expected that to be much comfort to his family. Or maybe it would be. Who could say? Again, my knowledge of history was crap but perhaps there was honor to be had dying in service to the Roman Empire. Stranger things had happened.

Time Chaser

Either way, it was a hell of a lot more noteworthy than being creamed by a bus.

Regardless dead was dead, as evidenced by Marius's body still lying there before us, smelling like the world's foulest barbecue.

Friedrich was responsible for this, but so was I in a way. After all, I'd allowed myself to drop my guard around him. I don't know where we'd all be if we'd simply told the Vultures to go fuck themselves and left it at that, but I doubt it would've led to this same moment.

Sadly, I couldn't change what had happened, but there was still one thing that I *could* do. It wasn't much but it was better than nothing.

I stepped to Marius's body and focused on it – pulling it into my inventory, while trying to ignore the system's asshole designation of *Kentucky fried chaser corpse: 1*.

"Um, Tim..."

"Macmac...?"

I held up a hand to them both. "Relax, it's not what you think. I just don't want to leave him here. We need to find a better place to put him to rest, somewhere more..."

"A boon and a bane."

Speaking of here, that's where my focus really should've been.

I guess Wan decided we'd been given enough time to deal with this mess that had been left to us.

Now it was our turn to face a choice that none of us were prepared to make.

72

A ROCK AND A HOT PLACE

Boog: *Choose me. There is no other option.*

I tried typing out a response, watching as word after word got munged. I swear, it was like the mental keyboard powering my HUD was covered in psychic molasses.

Fortunately, Pixel was there to be their usual charming self.

Pixel: *There's a phrase from Tim's world that comes to mind. Eat a bag of dicks. In other words, no.*

Boog: *You cannot so easily dismiss this opportunity and you know it.*

Pixel: *Sure I can. Try me.*

Boog: *I am the only logical choice being both cursed and under a persistent mutation effect. In addition to that, my other form is continually at risk for penalization.*

Pixel: *So?*

Boog: *So, I fear it is only a matter of time before such penalties go beyond affecting only myself and begin to endanger the entire party.*

Pixel: *Yeah and in this form you're a know-it-all who likes to get shitfaced soused. Your point? We've all got monkeys on our back, sister ... figuratively speaking anyway, but unlike a certain fuckhole Nazi we aren't throwing one of our own to the wolves.*

Boog: *Please. This is the only choice we have. This way, at least you and Macmac stand a chance.*

"That's enough, Boog," I said aloud.

"You do not speak for the Tim Chasers, fool," Wan replied, no doubt misinterpreting my words. "This choice is not yours to make."

"I wasn't..."

"As amusing as it might be to hear you try to explain cortex-enabled chat to this chump," Pixel interrupted, "let's cut right to the chase. This choice is mine to make and I say we're all walking out of here together."

"You don't walk," I remarked.

"Don't be jelly because some of us can fly, *fool.*"

"A bold retort, Pixel of Tim Chasers," Wan replied, either opting to ignore that chump remark or unaware that he'd just been insulted. "Yet your bane must still be satisfied. So I have decreed, so it shall be."

"Maybe, but first I have a question. Why? Friedrich was the one who screwed over your concubines. He even admitted it. Hell, everyone present was pushing for the right answer. So, why should we have to pay for his shortsighted stupidity?"

Wan raised an eyebrow and stroked his beard again, making me wonder if Pixel had a shot of getting through to him.

"And yet you did not stop him from making the incorrect choice."

Or maybe not.

"Well, no, but..."

"Instead, you gave his decision your blessing, even though it angered those I favor."

"I wouldn't say blessing. Shit, it wasn't like I even agreed to it."

"If not you, then who did?"

Oh crap. Pixel fell silent, knowing full well the answer to that one.

At least they got points for not ratting me out.

"It was the fool, was it not?" Wan continued. "It was he who counseled you to follow the vulture's advice."

Son of a... Guess Wan didn't need a witness to this transgression after all.

I probably shouldn't have been surprised. This was his castle after all. It stood to reason that a guy who employed talking Sasquatches and magical fox demons probably had a few machinations in place for seeing through closed doors.

Shit! I opened my mouth to say something, only for Wan's angry glare to cut that thought short.

For fuck's sake. "Permission to speak on our behalf, oh leader of Tim Chasers?"

"Um, sure, why not," the little bug zapper replied, their tone halfway between surprised and way too amused for my liking, especially considering the gravity of the situation.

That seemed to satisfy Wan's pet peeve about people speaking out of turn as he nodded toward me.

"I was trying to prevent a fight between our two parties," I said. "Friedrich had ... *strong feelings* about our suggestions for how your concubines should be paired."

"I see," Wan replied.

"Yeah, so all I was doing was trying to..."

"Mollify the vulture at the risk of inciting my wrath?"

"What? No. That's not what I..."

"And in my own realm no less. Tell me, fool, who sits upon this throne?"

He let the question hang there – an invisible shovel I'd just used to bury myself.

Pixel: *Good job, Tim. Way to put that diplomacy score to work.*

Tim, JUST FUCKING TIM: *M...ybe n...xt t...me.*

Oh fuck it. "Maybe next time don't leave it to the guy who's so fatigued he can barely stand up straight."

"I'll keep that in mind," Pixel replied before turning to face Wan again.

Hopefully they had a verbal trick up their sleeve to turn this back around.

"Fine, you win," Pixel said.

I spun toward the FAST, my eyes opening so wide I'm surprised they didn't fall out of my skull. Of all the things I'd expected Pixel to say, that hadn't been in my top ten.

"I've made my choice in this matter. You want your bane, you've got it."

No!

Tim, JUST FUCKING TIM: *D...n't Do ...t!*

Pixel: *I'm gonna pretend that made sense. Anyway, keep your shirt on. I'm not throwing Boog under the bus.*

Three dots immediately appeared, telling us that another response was incoming.

Pixel: *Relax, Boog. It was just a figure of speech. I'm not fucking over your precious Macmac either. Christ, you two really need to get a room. And no, I'm not explaining that colloquialism. You can ask your mate about it.*

I narrowed my eyes at Pixel until it hit me. If they weren't choosing either of us for Wan's sacrifice then that meant...

Pixel: *There's only one scenario here that guarantees us a win. In short, the only choice that makes sense is me.*

What?!

Tim, JUST FUCKING TIM: *Y...u c...n't!*

Pixel: *First off, stop typing. Trying to make sense of your chicken scratch is going to give me an aneurysm. Secondly, I'm gonna be generous and assume you meant an A and not a U on that last one.*

Boog: *Macmac has a point. You cannot do this. He needs you.*

Pixel: *As I'm well aware since I'm not a complete idiot. But then again, Boog, neither are you. I want you to think about this for a second or two. I'm sure it'll come to you.*

I glanced her way, unsure of what Pixel was yammering about, only to see realization dawn on her face.

Boog: *Your lives. You still have two left.*

Pixel: *Exact-a-mundo!*

Holy shit! It was both brilliant yet ridiculously simple at the same time. Pixel was only down one of their lives. With two still left on this stage, Wan could blast the FAST to his heart's content. Boog and I would then shed a few crocodile tears before picking them up and being on our merry way.

It wasn't a particularly exciting end to this stage of the game, but thankfully I didn't give a single shit about that so long as we made it out.

Pixel: *Here's what we're gonna do. I'll offer myself up with an appropriately heroic speech about leadership and responsibility. Then Wan blasts me. And before you ask, no, I'm not looking forward to it. So yes, you're both going to owe me big time.*

Ah, Pixel, ever the altruistic FAST.

Pixel: *None of that will matter, though, so long as you two grab my shell and hustle your asses to that ascension ring. If so, I should be back up and running in time for Stage Two. We can figure everything else out from there.*

I had to admit, much as I didn't want to see them take one for the team, it was about as good a plan as we were going to get.

If only Friedrich had realized that too. His own FAST was down to their last life, but I'm sure Invictus would've been happy to make the sacrifice rather than the sad alternative.

Well, okay, judging by what they'd said before leaving the game, maybe *happy* wasn't the right word, but they would almost certainly have accepted it as a viable solution.

There was also a third option there, a much darker one. What if Friedrich *had* realized it but had chosen Marius anyway?

Goddamn, talk about the sort of evil shit that would give a guy nightmares. True, it was only speculation on my part, but it was almost enough to make me dread finally getting some sleep.

"Anyone need to do any begging or groveling before I announce my decision?" Pixel asked, playing it up.

Boog and I shared a glance before we both shook our heads.

"Didn't think so," Pixel remarked before addressing Wan. "You want a life? Then I say you can have..."

"Hold," Wan interrupted. "Before I accept this bane owed to me, you will return what is mine."

"What do you mean?"

Wan turned toward me, his eyes practically boring a hole through my skull. All at once I was six years old again, lying in the dark thinking of all the horrors that must surely be lurking beneath my bed. Holy crap, he hadn't even needed to activate his aura to freak me the fuck out.

"The one you stole, fool. You will return him."

Uh oh. "Wait, are you talking about Marius? But why? He's already dead. You killed..."

"As I am aware. However, that does not change the fact that he was offered up to me and me alone."

"But..."

Wan narrowed his eyes. "Do you perchance mistake me for yourself, an addle-minded fool?"

Pixel: *Ooh, sick burn.*

I threw some side-eye the FAST's way but only for a second. I had a feeling Wan's question wasn't rhetorical. "N-no, of course not."

Wan laughed but there was little humor behind it. "I smell the lie in your words, much the same way the vulture would have me believe he knew not what lay beyond the waypoint."

"That's not true."

"Oh? Then why were you so quick to claim the vulture's fallen comrade? He had neither weapons nor coin left. His *companions* saw to that. So then tell me, what value does a charred, broken body have to you?"

"None. I..." I tried to think of a convincing lie before realizing there was no need. This was a case where the truth was hopefully good enough. "Marius was a friend. I only wish to lay him to rest in a place more..."

"More suitable than *my* realm?" Wan interrupted. "So you think me incapable of properly honoring a slain foe?"

"Yes, I mean no." Goddamn it, I hated when assholes twisted my own words.

It was just like that last meeting I'd had with Allan. All I'd wanted was for him to cut me a little slack, knowing the shit I'd been going through with Deb. Instead, he'd turned it around and accused me of using my divorce as an excuse to slack off.

I'd slunk away from that meeting like a whipped dog, almost my default response by that point.

That was then, though. Now...

Well, okay, maybe now wasn't so different after all.

Much as I wanted to pretend that Wan was nothing more than a petty dictator, much as Allan had acted, I was forced to admit that getting *fired* by him would almost certainly be a shitload more painful.

Needless to say, the brief swell of bravery I felt was quickly stomped flat.

"Fine," I said, steadying myself best I could. "I humbly ask your permission to take Marius's remains so that we might honor his passing in a way most befitting."

"Well said," Wan replied.

"Thank you."

"Your request is denied."

"What?"

"You will return him to me as I have commanded."

"But..."

"*Now!*"

The entire room rumbled as he spoke that single word.

So much for not slinking away this time. As both Boog and Pixel shrank back a step, I quickly pulled Marius's corpse from inventory and deposited it on the floor in front of me.

Won't lie. In that moment, I was sorely tempted to use up

my remaining pit stop vouchers all at once. Hiding in the bathroom suddenly sounded a whole lot better than dealing with this guy.

Sadly, as intimidated as I felt, the implication was instantly clear.

Brilliant as Pixel's idea was, it had no chance of working.

Pixel: *Change of plan, guys. Be ready because I have a feeling there's only one way out of this now.*

And just like that, we were back to square one.

"I agree," Boog said, as I readied to pull some ammo from inventory. "Thus, I offer up my life in exchange for theirs, great Protector Wan."

Too bad it wasn't the square one I'd been expecting.

73

HUNDRED-YEAR HORRORS

The fuck?

"Take me," Boog continued, facing Wan while refusing to look at either Pixel or me. "I offer up my life as the bane that is owed to you, so that my friends might be allowed passage to the waypoint."

"Stop right there, Boog," I said. "You can't just..."

"*Silence!*" Wan's aura activated just long enough to stomp whatever else I had to say into the ground. "I have already told you, fool, this choice is not yours to make."

"Thank you, Protector Wan. As I was saying..."

He stopped Boog with a mere raise of his eyebrow. "Nor is it yours." I couldn't help but notice his tone was considerably less sharp with her. "This decision belongs to your leader, none other. They and they alone will decide."

Boog: *You have to let me do this, Pissel.*

She might've had ten times her previous intelligence, but it was morbidly fascinating how her names for either of us hadn't changed. Almost as if we'd imprinted on her like a baby bird.

Well, either that or she was purposely baiting the FAST, maybe hoping to piss them off enough so they'd let her throw herself to the wolves.

Pixel: *First off, fuck you and the dire horse you rode in on. Secondly, we've already gone over this. I want to hear ideas, not suicide pacts.*

Boog: *And I want you to consider all we know about this foe, all we have seen. I fear our chances of defeating him are negligible. At least this way the both of you will have a chance. My death will have meaning.*

Pixel: *Uh huh. You can put lipstick on a pig but that doesn't make it Charlize Theron. The answer is still no. You're with me on this, right, Tim?*

I was trying to type out a legible reply when Boog shot me a personal message that stopped me dead in my tracks..

Boog: *Think of your child, Macmac. I have no one waiting for me back home, nothing but the loneliness of not belonging. But you have someone to live for, someone who needs you. The road ahead will be difficult, perhaps insurmountable, but at least this way you're guaranteed to get a little bit closer to him. Please let me do that much for you.*

Fuck! And just like that, she'd thrown down the one obstacle she knew I couldn't easily tap dance around.

Goddamn it.

Pixel: *Come on, Tim, back me up here.*

I gritted my teeth as Wan glared smugly down at us. The fucker had thrown us into a no win situation and knew it. Yet, despite his commands, he made no move to hurry us along. Maybe he was enjoying the strife this was causing us while he sat there with all the time in the world.

Or so he probably believed. In less than twenty-four hours, however...

Actually, I had no idea what would happen to the mobs and NPCs once a Stage ended.

For all I knew, life simply went on, minus all the chasers. After all, the entities running this show could apparently create anything here. Why not an endless array of pocket dimensions made up of past Stages? Heck, maybe they simply recycled everything for that home version Drega kept hawking.

None of that mattered, though. It was nothing more than a distraction, a way to steer my mind away from the conundrum Boog had dropped into my lap.

Sadly, I couldn't hold my tongue forever.

Pixel: *Earth to Tim.*

Boog: *He knows I am right. Do not fret this decision, my mate. Though it means we will forever be parted, take comfort in knowing that our short time together has made up for all the dark days of my life.*

Pixel: *Did you get that line from a soap opera? Seriously, Boog, what the fuck's wrong with you?*

Boog: *There is nothing wrong with choosing the greater good.*

Pixel: *We'll have to agree to disagree on that.*

Boog: *As I am beginning to understand. Please know that I respect your dissent on this matter but I do not accept it.*

Pixel: *Cry me a river, but we're not selling you out.*

Boog: *You say we, but I have only heard from* you. *If you will not respect my wishes then respect the wishes of the party.*

Pixel: *Meaning?*

Boog: *Let us decide as a whole. Wan believes only you can make this decision, but that is nothing more than his arrogance speaking. Let us take a vote instead. Currently, the count is one in favor, one against. Rather than argue further, we should let Macmac break this impasse while the both of us agree to honor his decision as final.*

Wait, they were dumping this on me?

Pixel: *Fine, but you don't get off that easily, sister. The door swings both ways. When* Tim *disagrees with you, which he will, then I want you to knock this crap off and get with the program. Agreed?*

Boog: *Very well. I trust my mate to choose wisely.*

"Hold on..."

Pixel was ready for my protests, though. "As leader of Tim

Chasers, I hereby decree we make this interesting and let our resident fool decide for us. That work for you, Wan?"

Son of a...

Wan raised an eyebrow as if not expecting that. "Why hand such an important choice over to a fool?"

"Simple," Pixel replied. "Because sometimes the best decision is the most *foolhardy* one."

⌛⌛⌛⌛ ⋅⋟⋞⋟⋞⋅ ⌛⌛⌛⌛

I threw Pixel a glare as I tried to make sense of what they'd just said, but quickly turned my attention back to Wan.

He was leaning forward, staring at me expectantly. I had a feeling we'd finally exhausted his patience, leaving me with little choice but to do the one thing I was probably least adept at in that moment – think quickly.

Boog had just made the exact same point I'd made to myself countless times since arriving here – that it was all, *every single moment*, about getting back home to Jeremy.

If at any point I lost sight of that motivation, I knew it would all fall apart. If so, my best bet would be to find the nearest boss and let it have its way with me, knowing it was a quicker fate than what awaited back home.

There was only one snag to Boog's logic, one more thing I'd beaten myself up about countless times over the past two days. Getting home to Jeremy was my number one priority, true, but who would be the man that walked in the front door to greet him?

Would it actually be me, or would it be a remorseless killer wearing my skin – someone who'd accepted casual murder as the solution to all of life's problems, so long as it got him closer to the goal line?

What Boog was asking me to do, use her as a means to an end, could very well be the first true step down that dark road.

The truth was, outside of bots wearing his face, the odds of

Jeremy ever meeting Boog were almost zero. He would never know her, nor would there ever be any reason for me to confess what I had done here.

But *I* would know.

Things could very well change in the coming days, weeks, or however long this godforsaken game went on, but right then I didn't want that man to be the father my son grew up with. Anyone who would willingly sacrifice a friend when other options were still on the table was not someone I wanted raising my boy.

It was a slippery slope and I had a feeling the path ahead was already well greased.

Mind you, those other options weren't exactly great but what the hell? At least there was something to be said about facing my death with a clear conscience.

"My decision is..." I lifted the hand not holding my still untested Ruination Racket and flipped Wan the middle finger. "You can sit on this and spin."

⌛⌛⌛⌛ ⸭⸭⸭⸭ ⌛⌛⌛⌛

"I knew there was a reason I liked you, Tim," Pixel said.

"What have you done, Macmac?"

"Ensured that the next few minutes at least won't be boring." I put a hand on her calamine lotion stained shoulder. "Be mad at me all you want, but there's a better target to take it out on. Speaking of which, think he understood what I just told him?"

"Some insults are timeless," Pixel replied. "And even if they're not, the attitude with which they're said is."

Sure enough, Wan's eyes had narrowed dangerously. When next he spoke, it was just three words.

"So be it."

It must've cemented his intent because text suddenly appeared on my screen accompanied by Drega's asshole voice.

Time Chaser

Congratulations, you have discovered ... a surprise boss!
A what?
You're probably wondering what the fuck that is, as well as why this guy has been a big old zilch in the info department up until now. Fortunately, the answer is so simple, even a primate can comprehend it. The Committee, in their infinite wisdom, have decided to test out a new feature this cycle to see how it resonates with our audience. I'll give you three guesses as to what that is but the first two don't count.

"How the fuck is this supposed to be a surprise? We already knew this asshole was a boss!"

I was barely even aware I'd said it aloud, until Drega added, **That's a good question!**

Wait, it is?

Hold on. Had Drega just answered me directly or had he simply guessed the most probable reaction when recording this?

I wasn't sure I wanted to know the answer.

You see, a surprise boss will still show as a boss on your map. That's not the surprise part. If it was, we'd probably all be looking for new jobs by now. The surprise comes in not being given any information about them until combat commences. Then and only then do you find out.

"How the fuck is that fair?"

Here's where the fun happens. They might be stronger than you imagined or they might be weaker. Hell, they might not even be a boss at all – just some poser trying to look cool. But if so, that's fine. Kick their ass and you'll still get some boss-level loot.

Well, okay, I can't say that wouldn't be a nice surprise.

So what happens if you manage to talk your way out of a fight with one? Not a damned thing other than your continued ignorance. You might walk away from an easy win or you may have just escaped certain death at the hands of a godlike entity. The bottom line is you'll never know.

Time Chaser

Fortunately for us, though, that last point is moot since, unsurprisingly, you managed to fuck that up.

With that last bit of snark out of the way, Wan's info became available to us.

Come on, fake boss, fake boss...

Protector Wan – level 22

Centennial Boss

A centennial boss?! "Fuck!"

So much for Drega's claim that a surprise boss might be weaker than expected. Although, he was apparently ready for that too.

Come now. You didn't expect to get *that* lucky on your first try, did you?

74

MEET THE NEW BOSS, WORSE THAN THE OLD BOSS

Protector Wan – level 22
Centennial Boss
Xu Wan, known as Zhu Wen in some realities, was a warlord and general in ninth century China who rose through the ranks to become the power behind the imperial throne. At least until he grew tired of that game and killed the fuck out of the existing emperor, proclaiming himself Great Protector of the Realm.

You can't say this guy didn't have ambition.

What you *can* say is he was equal parts paranoid and horny as fuck – assassinating his rivals and playing his nobles against one another, all while vigorously banging their wives and daughters on the side.

Dude was a serious playa!

And don't even get me started on the freaky shit he would do with those *concubines* of his. Let's just say I hope you used plenty of hand sanitizer before touching them.

On the upside, at least now you know why it's good to be the king.

You know what else it's good to be?

A fucking dragon, because that's exactly what he was

Time Chaser

back on Earth 31919 which is where we plucked this guy from.

What, you didn't think that whole fire breathing stunt from earlier was a parlor trick, did you?

Anyway, have fun with that knowledge for the three seconds it's gonna take for this badass to end you with extreme prejudice.

A dragon? Oh, that didn't sound good.

Don't get me wrong, I'm not sure how knowing any of this ahead of time would have helped. It's not like it would have changed my tune when it came to sacrificing Boog.

Although, had we known what we were up against, I could've simply taken a pot shot at the guy and committed us right away to this course of action. At least in that case the Vultures would've had no choice but to join the fight.

As much of a reprehensible dick as Friedrich had proven to be, I couldn't lie and pretend I wouldn't have accepted the help.

Alas, wishes were neither horses nor chasers, meaning we had no one but ourselves to rely on here as Wan bared his teeth at us.

On the upside, those dragon statues outside suddenly made a lot more sense.

Speaking of statues, from behind us there came the sound of steel grating against stone. I dared a glance back and immediately regretted it.

Those titanic stone soldiers guarding the door had once again animated – now standing at attention with their weapons at the ready.

Much as I was hoping they were there for show and nothing more, my HUD was singing a different tune.

Why now? No idea.

Maybe they were somehow connected to this surprise boss bullshit they'd sprung on us. Or maybe the producers were just having too much fun fucking us up the ass. Either way, Drega was mum on that part even as he expounded upon the rest.

Granite Guardian – level 14

Guardians are inanimate constructs enchanted with high level magic. Under most circumstances, they are indistinguishable from normal statues since they mostly stand around doing nothing.

What sets them apart is that each is given a specific trigger, either an action or a command word. Run afoul of that trigger and the guardian will instantly animate with only one goal in mind – to fucking annihilate whoever violated its parameters.

Think of it like a ten ton guard dog that never needs to eat, sleep, or take a crap on the rug.

As for beating them, good luck. They possess strength that is commensurate with both their size and the substance they're made of.

So hey, if the one you're fighting is made of straw and the size of an ant, then you've probably got a chance. If not, now would probably be a good time to discover religion.

Well, that settled it. We were screwed.

"No," Wan hissed. For a moment, I thought he was disagreeing with me for some reason, but then I realized he was talking to those guardians, his voice becoming deeper as it echoed through the chamber. "*They are mine.*"

The guardians neither hesitated nor questioned. They simply went back to the pose they'd been in when we'd first entered. However, their HUD description remained, telling me they were still active if needed.

I couldn't say whether that was a good thing, but it did speak to the fact that Wan was confident in his ability to squash us like bugs.

"Run!" Pixel cried.

Sound advice if ever I'd heard it. I glanced back toward the door we'd come in through, now unbarred.

"Not that way," Pixel said. "Get to the ascension ring! If we can reach it before they make this official, we might be able to..."

"GET READY FOR A THROWDOWN IN THE THRONE ROOM, CHASERS! YOU ARE THE LUCKY PARTICIPANTS IN A ... CENTENNIAL BOSS BATTLE!"

And just like that, all hope for an easy escape was erased as my HUD flashed with *Boss Battle Initiated*.

⌛⌛⌛⌛ ⋅⋛⋅⋛⋅⋛⋅ ⌛⌛⌛⌛

Pixel wasted no time launching an acid ball at Wan's face. His health bar appeared as the spell struck home, but if he suffered any real damage I couldn't see it. The FAST might as well have hit him with a handful of glitter.

Wan growled, more in annoyance than pain, as he casually wiped the acidic gunk from his face.

Call me crazy but I had a feeling attacking this guy with no game plan wasn't a winning strategy. So, I took advantage of Pixel's distraction to do what I should've done before we'd even walked in here – take quick stock of my inventory to see how things looked.

Let's just say I was suddenly feeling buyer's remorse over the fact that I'd wasted a good chunk of my healing potions on the party who'd fucked us over mere minutes earlier. No good deed...

Still, with eleven left, I hopefully had enough to survive for at least a little while. Ditto with mana potions. Between them and my existing points, that gave me ten shots between my two spells – possibly more if either Pixel or Boog had any to spare as the fight commenced.

Of course, the big question was whether they'd be enough.

If not, my Spell Hammer ability, now part of my racket, had fortunately reset at some point, as had my shield – both welcome bits of good news. Sadly, Vectorman still had another 9 hours to go. That meant I'd need to use up a Fortuitous Encore scroll if I needed it.

Probably a bridge best crossed only in an emergency.

Perhaps most disappointing was being out of those bronze warheads that had proven so effective against Apu. That left me two gunpowder jugs, about a dozen yaoguai tusks, and a decent stash of wolf teeth to use as ammo.

After that, I'd have to get up close and personal in this fight.

"Boog, take him out at the legs!" Pixel cried. "Once he's down, keep him down, Tim. I'm gonna try something crazy."

Or maybe there'd be no waiting on getting my hands dirty. Either way, I hoped whatever Pixel had planned was worth the risk of getting within arm's length of this boss.

Boog looked anything but happy that we were *all* now committed to what was, in all likelihood, a nigh unwinnable battle, but she quickly got with the program. A moment later Wan was knocked out of his chair and onto his back as surely as if the rug had been pulled out from under him.

Score one for Telekinesis.

I was already on the move, keeping my pace limited to a brisk walk lest I faceplant at the worst time imaginable. I got to the dais and took a leap of faith, quite literally, using my recently augmented strength to jump up onto it.

Though I managed not to trip, I just barely cleared the flames in front of it – wincing as my feet and ankles were singed in the process. That alone knocked maybe five percent off my already reduced health but I couldn't spare the time to worry about it.

Wan was in the process of rolling backward onto his shoulders, preparing to kip back up to his feet – a move no doubt meant to intimidate us.

Too bad for him I was a hair faster.

I brought my upgraded racket down in the same instant he tried to come up, saying a silent prayer that now wasn't the time my ten percent miss chance decided to fuck me in the ass.

Crunch!

Damage Buff: 1%.

Yes! Wan's health didn't drop by a lot but at least it was noticeable.

Now all I had to do was repeat this a hundred more times and we'd be set. Mind you, if I kept adding to that damage buff it was possible we'd get there a bit sooner.

Now was not the time to pop the cork on that champagne, though. I lifted my racket to try again, even as Wan locked eyes on me.

I swear, if looks could kill...

Maybe they couldn't but that didn't mean his fear aura wasn't capable of screwing me over. It activated, causing my bowels to almost release from the sheer terror which instantly flooded every fiber of my being.

Debuff – You are Fearful.

Ya think?

I didn't need to actually get closer to hit him again, yet I found myself fighting my own body nonetheless as I tried to bring the proverbial hammer down. Finally, I shut my eyes, gritted my teeth, and forced myself to take the swing.

Clonk!

Only to hit nothing but the floor.

Fuck! Not only did I have a miss chance from being fatigued but the Fearful debuff stacked another ten percent onto that. That gave me a twenty percent chance to hit nothing but air, even if Wan decided to give me a free shot. Still, that didn't mean I was giving up. Even though I wanted to do nothing less than turn and run for my life, I still...

Almost fell on my ass as the floor began to shake from beneath me.

What the hell?

Before I could shit a brick at the terrifying implications of this power, I realized the look on Wan's face had changed from anger to one of surprise. Whatever had caused this micro-quake, it wasn't his doing.

But if he wasn't responsible then who...?

"Now would be a really good time to move, Tim!"

The dais shook again, driving me to one knee this time and leaving me in prime position for Wan to simply throttle my tired ass. However, before he could make a move, a shadow fell over us both.

Despite being way too close to a boss who was leagues beyond anything we'd faced before, I dared a look over my shoulder.

Holy fucking shit.

Don't get me wrong, Wan was intimidating as fuck, true, but he was still person-sized.

His guardian statues on the other hand...

While one still stood guard at the door, the other had closed in on us. It held its massive spear over its head – big enough to harpoon Moby Dick – as it no doubt prepared to cleave me in two.

But then why the surprise on Wan's face? Had the statue somehow managed to ignore its orders and join the fray anyway?

Was that even possible?

I mean, sure, it's not like I was an expert on magical statues, but maybe these things had some kind of failsafe built into them. But if so, then why was only one of them moving?

"Jesus Christ, Tim, get your fucking ass out of there!"

"Run, Macmac!"

That's when it hit me – realization, not its spear. Pixel's newest psionic ability, *Everyone Hates You*. It allowed them to temporarily turn foe against foe. This had to be their doing, which meant I really needed to get out of the way.

I turned and tried to leap out of the way, knowing instinctively I was going to trip because there was no way Fatigued was going to let me get that lucky.

Time Chaser

The Granite Guardian's attack struck just as I felt my feet start to fumble – the blow so intense that it caused a miniature shockwave which sent me flying instead.

Same result I'd been going for, just somewhat less ... controlled.

Fuuuuck!

I pinwheeled through the air, activating my collapsible shield at the last second – slamming down shoulder-first into it just as it hit the floor, the sound of metal against stone echoing in my ears as I skidded to a stop.

Ow! Suffice to say, it was a bit less easy than *Captain America* made it look.

"Macmac!"

"D-don't worry about me," I grunted, pushing myself up and collapsing my shield. "I'm okay."

It wasn't too big a lie. My landing had erased a chunk of health but probably not nearly as much as if I'd broken the fall with my face. Even better, the Fearful debuff was now gone. Guess that guardian had managed to get Wan's full attention.

Whatever the case, I'd walked away from round one in better shape than expected. Still, it was best to not look a gift horse in the mouth.

"Use whatever potions you need to get back to full," I said to the others. "Because as cool as that last attack was, I have a feeling it's not going to be nearly enough."

75

DRAGON MY BUTT

"It *was* pretty cool, wasn't it?" Pixel said as I dusted myself off.

"Focus now, bend over backwards to kiss your own digital ass later," I replied, pulling a gunpowder jug from inventory and activating Aim Assist.

I turned back toward where I'd last seen Wan, noting that the dais was now a twisted and broken wreck. Though I couldn't see him thanks to the cloud of dust raised by the Guardian's attack, the boss's health bar was still visible within my HUD.

Amazingly enough, the stone guardian had done far more damage than any of us had managed so far, no doubt due to its size and level, but that still only translated to maybe six or seven percent of Wan's health.

"Move it, slowpoke," Pixel shouted at the statue. "The clock's ticking, so that means no dragging those granite feet."

"Quick thinking with that power," I said, swapping my racket for a torch so I could ignite that boom jug at a moment's notice.

"Lucky too," they replied. "It probably shouldn't have worked considering our level discrepancy, but it would seem statues don't have shit in the way of PSI resistance."

Pixel: *Lucky, but not a guess. Chalk one more up to those ill-gotten memories of mine.*

Way to go, Pixel! I couldn't say it out loud and right then I was incapable of chatting for shit, but I threw them a knowing nod nonetheless – even more so as another PSI-based idea began to form. "Boog, do you think your Telekinesis can maybe give that thing's next shot a little more oomph?"

"An excellent suggestion, my mate," she said turning its way. "I shall endeavor to try."

Ahead of us, the Guardian once again lifted its spear, now cracked and with the tip missing. From the look of things, the weapon maybe had one more big hit left in it but every shot counted.

Too bad Wan apparently realized this too.

PWOOOOSH!

Before the Guardian could attack again, a bolt of golden flame exploded out from the dust cloud and struck the statue dead center. The heat was nothing short of incredible, forcing both Pixel and I to turn away lest our eyebrows start smoking.

Well, mine anyway.

"No!"

Boog was the only one of us with fire resistance, thus she was able to bear witness to whatever was going on, although I was willing to bet it wasn't in our favor.

"Oh crap," Pixel cried. "Tim, your hand!"

Huh? I looked down just as a sizzling sound registered in my ears.

My eyes opened wide in terror as I realized Wan's attack had been hot enough to prematurely ignite the fuse on my jug.

Shit! I turned to throw it away, only to fumble it in my hands. *Son of a...* Talk about the absolute worst time for Fatigued to fuck me over.

Even as I struggled to regain control of the primitive bomb, I realized it wasn't going to be in time to avoid...

Or maybe not.

The jug abruptly flew from my hands, as surely as if someone had swatted it away. *What the?*

Pixel's TK Hand, it had to be.

Whatever the case, their quick thinking had probably saved both our lives. Pity that didn't mean it saved our asses too, at least not completely. The jug exploded, still way too close for comfort – catching both me and Pixel in the blast wave and sending us tumbling backward.

My health bar cratered, turning an angry red, and a dull ringing sounded in my ears as I hit the hard floor once again.

Debuff – You are Shellshocked: severity low.

My HUD helpfully informed me that this severity of Shellshocked rendered me deaf for the next minute and brought with it a twenty percent chance of unconsciousness – which I apparently overcame since I was still able to read the description. Less good, however, was learning that it also included a thirty second *Paralysis* debuff.

That can't be good.

I tried to sit up but found myself unable to move. Hell, I couldn't even turn my head to see how Pixel had fared.

Thirty seconds, Tim. It's only for thirty seconds.

Feeling panic starting to take hold, I tried to focus less on what I couldn't do and more on what was left.

Sadly, that didn't leave much.

Far as I could tell, the only things I could do were blink, breathe, and interact with my HUD.

Hold on...

Hoping that last part was a positive in my favor, especially with my health bar still blinking an angry red, I focused on one of my healing potions and activated it.

Gah!

Pungent medicinal flavor filled my mouth in the second before my airway was cut off, as the liquid began to drain down my throat. *Fuck!* I probably should've tested whether I could still swallow.

The upside was the potion did the trick as my health instantly rocketed back up. The downside was that ingesting it straight into my fucking lungs left me choking and completely unable to breathe.

Debuff – You are Drowning.

Oh for fuck's sake!

The floor rumbled beneath me again, vaguely making me wonder what was going on. Too bad I was currently preoccupied with trying not to drown on dry land.

My HUD *helpfully* filled in the details, letting me know that whilst Drowning I had one minute of consciousness per every 50 points of constitution. After that, I'd pass out and it would presumably only get worse from there.

With my Ruination Racket currently sitting in inventory, thus depriving me of its CON bonus, that gave me less than three minutes. Thankfully, the paralysis would wear off in only a few more...

And just like that I could move again.

Much as I wanted to see what was going on around me, I had no choice but to roll over and cough foul-tasting potion out of my lungs, choking as I desperately tried to replace the fluid with air. I'd still had plenty of time to spare but it sure as hell didn't feel like it.

I made a mental note to not do anything like that again, not unless my health was so far gone that I had no choice.

Goddamn, talk about a stupid way to die.

It wasn't like I was out of danger either. As I knelt there waiting for my hearing to return, the ambient heat from Wan's last attack caused my health to start slowly ticking down again.

I finally dared a glance over my shoulder only to see the exact opposite of good. The top half of the guardian statue was gone, completely melted, and the resulting molten rock was in the process of spreading out across the floor.

"Come on, Pixel," I said, my voice nothing but a dull echo to my ears. "We need to..."

Shit! The words died in my mouth as I saw the FAST on the ground, smoldering and inert. Pixel's health bar was yellow and my HUD thankfully confirmed they hadn't died again, but they too were *Shellshocked*. That told me all I needed to know. I hadn't been knocked out, but Pixel wasn't nearly so lucky.

"I need you to buy me a few seconds, Boog!" I shouted, just as all sound came rushing back to me, a disconcerting sensation if ever there was one.

"I shall endeavor to do my best, my mate," she called back.

"Your best? You will find it not nearly enough!"

At the sound of Wan's echoing voice, a small part of me wished that deafness had stretched on a bit longer. There was zero doubt we'd pissed him off.

I spied movement back where the dust was starting to settle, but I needed to focus on getting Pixel somewhere ... not safe, but maybe saf*er*. First things first, though. It was hotter than Hell over where the guardian statue was almost done melting. So, with Aim Assist still going, I pulled my last gunpowder jug from inventory and threw it that way.

I didn't bother to watch where it landed. Any damage it did was icing on the cake but it was mostly meant as a distraction so Boog could do whatever she needed to keep Wan off my back.

I scooped up Pixel and ... immediately screamed in pain.

Fuck!

However, the sound was lost as the jug exploded somewhere behind me.

The little ghost light was nearly too hot to hold. Goddamn, maybe I needed to use Loom o' Doom to craft a pair of magical oven mitts instead.

Oh well, I could deal with a singed palm. Fortunately, I had the perfect solution as I made my way to the far side of the throne room. I pulled a healing potion from inventory and proceeded to dump it out onto the FAST.

The effect was twofold. Their health returned to full and the liquid cooled them off enough so it didn't feel like I was juggling a hot potato.

Moments later, green light began to emit from the dormant FAST unit – growing stronger until they floated out of my grasp of their own accord.

"Uh, what happened?" they asked.

"You got knocked out saving my butt."

"Oh. You're welcome by the way."

"We'll square up later. For now, take a second and get your bearings. I need to go help..."

Pixel: *Holy shit, Tim. It happened again.*

Tim, JUST FUCKING TIM: *Wh...t d...?*

Goddamn it! "What did?" I asked aloud.

Pixel: *Try being less subtle why don't you? I'm talking about my recovered memories. They just shot up to thirteen percent. I might need to get knocked out more often.*

"Fine. We'll discuss that later too."

That was all well and good, but until they pulled something else out of those memories that could maybe help us win this fight, it wasn't worth wasting time...

Heat blasted against my backside, like someone had just turned on a furnace close by. Had I not been wearing my demon sweater, my skin would probably be blistering.

I spun back, expecting to see Wan trying to tag Boog with another flame attack. Instead, my eyes nearly fell out of my skull at what I saw.

Wan was on his hands and knees, although that was the least weird part about whatever was going on. His robes were stretched to the limit and starting to pop their seams as his body grew larger within – already twice his normal size and still going.

The fuck?

Sadly, I had a sinking feeling I knew what was going on, thanks to Drega's description still being fresh in my mind.

Wan's mouth was open at least three times wider than it should've been capable of. Even as his body continued to grow, a stream of yellow flame poured forth from it, but it wasn't aimed at my teammate. Wan was using it to melt down the remaining guardian statue, no doubt having grown wise to our tricks. So much for a repeat performance.

All the while, Boog was hammering him from afar with her jawbone axe. She'd hit him and the axe would return, only for her to immediately use her Telekinesis to send it out again for another volley.

As painful as the hits appeared, however, Wan ignored both her and the meager damage she was inflicting as he continued to reduce the statue to a molten puddle.

His robes ripped apart, falling from him as he continued to grow – now as least fifteen feet long and getting larger by the second. A tail sprouted from his backside as his skin became scaly and took on a golden hue.

"Are you seeing this?" I asked numbly.

"Really wish I wasn't," Pixel said.

I felt the same way, especially as Wan's head began to distort, growing longer and heavier while his teeth sharpened into wicked looking fangs.

Despite his head, body, and tail continuing to enlarge, his arms and legs stayed the same size, becoming stubby claws that were way too small for the rest of him.

By the time he was finished, he was fifty feet long if he was an inch, resembling nothing less than a dragon pulled straight from Chinese folklore.

The fact that Drega had already mentioned this meant Wan's transformation shouldn't have been a surprise.

Nonetheless, it was one thing to be told something, quite another to witness it happen with my own eyes.

Seeing Wan become an actual dragon somehow made it horrifyingly real.

Time Chaser

In that instant, it was like whatever hope I might've held onto when it came to winning this battle had just gone up in flames.

76

BEATEN AND KINDA BROKEN

"*Rejoice, insects and your fool. Not many are honored to behold my true form before they perish.*"

"Honored is one word for it," I remarked, pulling a handful of teeth from inventory.

The three of us were spread out along the perimeter of the vast throne room, trying to keep our distance from Wan without giving him the opportunity to blast us all with one shot.

His sheer size wasn't making it easy. Fortunately, we had a bit of extra room to maneuver as the weight of his dragon form crushed what was left of the dais upon which his throne had sat, likewise extinguishing the flames bisecting the room.

The downside was the ascension ring was now in clear view. Needless to say, it was proving distracting as fuck. Alas, there wasn't anything we could do about that now that we were committed to this boss battle.

So close, yet so fucking far.

I wasn't sure if it was a plus in our favor or not, but rather than try and finish us off quickly, which I had no doubt he could, Wan seemed to be playing cat and mouse with us. I guess that was to be expected from a boss with high intelligence and even higher arrogance. A mindless monster would've just steamrolled us and been done with it, but Wan seemed intent on drawing this out.

The upside was every second we continued to draw breath was another second in which we could conceivably figure out a way to win this, in theory anyway.

Whatever our chances, Pixel was at least determined to try – hashing out a hasty strategy via party chat as Wan finished his grotesque transformation.

Fortunately for me, their plan also included a few suggestions to make up for the fact that my ability to chat was basically fucked.

Pixel: *You ready for this, Tim?*
Tim, JUST FUCKING TIM: *

That was our code for right now. One asterisk for yes, two for no, and three for pay the fuck attention because something bad is about to happen.

And no, I'm not exaggerating with that last one.

It was crude at best, like communicating via Ouija board instead of a mind-powered chat, but it enabled us to strategize without Wan eavesdropping.

In truth, I wanted nothing more than to reply with two asterisks. Pixel's hastily thought out plan was ... not my favorite idea ever. Sadly, I was the only one with a chance in hell of pulling it off.

Boog: *Are you certain of this, Pissel?*
Pixel: *No, of course I'm not fucking certain, but desperate times... Anyway, enough with the small talk and grossly misspelled names. How are your PSI points looking?*
Boog: *I just utilized a potion, so they are at their maximum.*
Pixel: *Good to hear. Try to stick to small bursts to enhance your axe throws. That should keep you going for a while. Save the big stuff for either an emergency or a clear opening.*
Boog: *Thank you, but there is no need to state the obvious. I would suggest you focus instead on managing your own mana pool.*

Pixel: *Yes, mom.*

Boog wasn't finished yet, though.

Boog: *There is still time to change your mind, my mate.*

Much as I wanted to agree with her, fighting defensively wasn't going to win this. It was either go big or go ... well, dead.

Tim, JUST FUCKING TIM: **

Pixel: *That's settled then. Just don't forget that Foresight potion. If it tells you shit's about to go south, abort. Better to regroup and try again than end up a greasy smear on the floor.*

Gotta love the FAST's way with words. Regardless, they didn't need to tell me twice. Good thing, too, since it seemed the time for chat was over.

"*I see fear has stilled your tongues.*" Wan reared back his crocodile-like head, no doubt preparing to turn up the heat. "*Now the rest shall follow.*"

Pixel: *That's our cue. Let's do this!*

Here goes nothing.

I tossed a handful of wolf teeth into the air and swung for the fences. A shrill scream of sound penetrated the air – considerably more ear-splitting than before my racket's upgrade. Sadly, only one of the teeth went rocketing away from me as the rest clattered to the floor, the sound like that of spilled marbles.

"Shit!"

As for the lone tooth I'd managed to connect with, it missed by a mile.

Wan let out a rumbling laugh as his gaze settled upon me. "*A fool too frightened to fight is a fool that has grown tired of living.*"

There was no doubt I had his attention. Now for the next part.

I downed my last Foresight potion even as flames could be seen gathering in the back of Wan's throat.

Bleccch! I tried to ignore the taste as twinkling lights obscured my vision, swirling and growing ever thicker until a vision coalesced before me — a pile of broken, jagged metal shards, like the aftermath of a horrific car crash. The fuck?

Goddamn what a useless potion.

With my foresight providing zero insight, I decided to stick to the plan and do what needed to be done.

Too bad what I *needed* to do was in direct conflict with what I *wanted* to do, which was scream my head off as Wan prepared to launch a fiery bolt of death my way.

⌛⌛⌛⌛ ·❖·❖·❖·❖· ⌛⌛⌛⌛

"Run!" Pixel cried as they and Boog scattered.

Wish I could've done the same. On paper, I only had a twenty-five percent chance of tripping, yet it seemed that every single time I tried to hustle I ended up eating floor instead.

I wouldn't have doubted for a second that there was someone up in the broadcast room with their finger over a "Trip Tim" button, for no other reason than comedic value.

Well, this time either I'd have the last laugh or I'd never have to worry about such things ever again.

A win-win in my book.

"Macmac!"

"Tim!"

The raw heat coming from Wan's open mouth was enough to singe my nose hairs even as the panicked cries of my teammates reached my ears. There was no doubt Wan heard them too, judging by the slight grin coming from his toothy maw.

Their performance was a convincing one, probably because the danger to me was all too real. Hopefully, it would be worth the risk.

Come on, you son of a bitch!

Though the flames continued to crackle inside Wan's mouth, he didn't shoot. Instead he cocked his massive head to the side and asked, *"Do you truly think me that gullible?"*

Uh oh.

Time Chaser

Instead of blasting me, as we'd counted on, Wan spun his massive body, moving way faster than I'd have thought possible. Rather than unleash his hellfire, he lashed out with his whiplike tail, its sheer length enough to make up for the distance between us.

Goddamn it all!

With no hope of dodging, I activated my collapsible shield and ducked down beneath it, hoping it was enough to absorb the attack.

It wasn't.

There came a crack of thunder, nearly deafening, as Wan's tail struck.

In the next second I was sent flying as my shield literally shattered into pieces.

Oh, so that's what my foresight was trying to tell me.

It was a surprisingly banal thought to have as my health more than halved from the sheer force of the attack, right before I slammed into the wall, erasing nearly all the rest.

Fuuuuuuck.

Not only had my shield been obliterated by a single attack but, as I laid there in a heap trying to draw breath, my HUD flared with an angry red warning notification. I mentally clicked on it, only to be presented with a detailed list of my grievous injuries, including: a broken arm, a concussion, three broken ribs...

Huh. You'd think there would be more pain.

...and a fractured spine.

Oh. I guess that explained it.

I tried to sit up but found myself unable to move, except this time there were no debuffs to blame.

Uh oh.

In truth, I should've been absolutely horrified, but I guess that concussion had scrambled my brain real good. Oddly enough, I found the numbness a welcome alternative to my nerve endings firing off like an air raid siren.

Time Chaser

The weird things we think when we're about to die.
Pixel: *Heal and get the hell out of there, Tim. Trust me on this!*
"*Now burn!*"

Even if Pixel's frantic advice didn't cut through the brain fog, Wan's voice did. It made me realize I had a choice. I could either do something or kiss goodbye any chance at ever seeing Jeremy again.

I wasn't ready for that. Not yet.

Focusing best I could, I activated a healing potion, trying not to gag as the liquid filled my mouth. I managed to swallow, instantly turning my body into a rapid-fire symphony of agony.

It figured. Rather than reset my broken bones and lacerations upfront, the first thing the potion fixed was my spinal cord, reconnecting my disrupted nerve endings.

There was no time to lie there and scream, though, not if I'd heard Wan correctly. So instead I bit my tongue, causing a small sliver of health to disappear from my once again full health bar.

Shit on toast!

Whatever. My head cleared and along with it my body became responsive once again. So, rather than waste time I didn't have, I rolled over and prepared to scramble out of the way, hoping to hell that my trip percentage didn't count when it came to crab walking.

"Pissel!"

The sheer panic in Boog's cry caused me to look up, only to realize that Wan's threat hadn't been directed at me after all.

Oh no!

It was only then that I realized it made all the sense in the world. Why bother to finish me off when, far as Wan was concerned anyway, I'd been left a broken pile of meat?

Instead, the centennial boss was now directing his full rage at Pixel, no doubt intent on cutting off the proverbial head of our party's leader.

Shit!

The FAST fired off a trio of acid balls, one after another, just as Wan let loose with his flames. The first spell hit the dragon, doing minor damage at best. The remaining two balls were seemingly swallowed up by Wan's golden fire as the attack overcame them and closed in on his intended target.

"Get out of here, Boog!" Pixel cried.

She ignored them, though, racing in at full speed. Boog launched herself at the FAST, grabbing hold and shielding Pixel with her body as the fire engulfed them both.

Oh God!

Boog was the only one among us with any sort of fire resistance but, much as I wanted to believe otherwise, resistance wasn't the same thing as being fireproof.

She screamed from within the hellish corona of flame. Though I couldn't see her through the inferno, I was able to clearly track her health via my HUD. The smell of burnt hair hit my nose as her health bar plummeted and turned red, only to rocket back up again before it could fully disappear.

Wan continued to pour it on, though, not letting up even as the entire room grew uncomfortably hot. Then, a scant moment later, it happened again. Boog's health nearly zeroed out, only to quickly rise back up.

Even as she continued to scream in pain, I realized what was happening. Between her fire resistance and existing stash of health potions, she was doing her damnedest to hold the attack at bay.

Sadly, her supply of potions was limited whereas Wan didn't seem to be in any danger of tiring.

I needed to draw his attention to me once more.

I'd lost hold of my racket during Wan's tail attack, but a quick look around revealed it had landed close by. I quickly scooped it back up, eating some damage as the shaft was almost too hot to handle. Then I called forth a bunch of yaoguai tusks from inventory.

They were bigger and sharper than the wolf teeth, meaning they were almost certainly a lot harder to ignore. Hopefully

Boog's supply of potions could hold out long enough for one last bit of icing on this cake.

I cast Crackling Cannonball on the tusks.

Warning: the spell Crackling Cannonball has failed.

Motherfucker!

Rather than waste time grousing, I activated a mana potion instead, quickly swallowing the syrupy sweet liquid.

My insides gurgled as the potion hit my stomach, probably a result of this being the most I'd ever downed in a short period of time. Any pit stops would have to wait, though.

Move your ass, Tim!

I tried casting it again and this time the spell mercifully took hold. Thank goodness!

Sadly, at first level the spell only empowered a single projectile, but it was the best I could manage. At this point every little bit counted.

I dropped the tusks and swung my racket, hoping that, at the very least, the gods of entertainment value were smiling upon me.

A shrill scream rose up in the throne room as half a dozen miniature cannonballs went shooting in every direction imaginable.

God-fucking-damnit!

I quickly realized, however, that, while most of them had done nothing but gouge holes in the walls, one had actually flown true.

And it was the one that counted.

Wan's left eyeball exploded in a shower of lightning-lanced gore as his health dropped by almost the same amount as it had from that guardian's attack. He reared back his head, cutting off his flames, and let out a high-pitched screech.

There was no denying that sound – pain. It was the first such hint we'd gotten that our attacks were doing anything more than merely annoying him.

It was music to my ears.

Well, okay, not really. In actuality, it was about as annoying as those fucking guinea pigs. Unlike them, though, this didn't last long. The cry of pain quickly stopped and so too did Wan. His head remained raised toward the ceiling, while the rest of him stood there quivering but otherwise unmoving.

It took me a second to realize what was happening, but then it hit me. I'd somehow managed to stun the bastard with my Screaming Shot attack.

Sadly, I couldn't capitalize on what had been the luckiest of all lucky shots.

Instead, I turned my attention toward my companions. As the flames and smoke cleared, I finally made out Boog ... or what was left of her.

She was hunched over, hairless and with skin that was blackened and bubbling.

No! "Boog!"

In the next instant, though, her wounds healed and her fur grew back. Whole again, she staggered as she stood up straight, leaning backward until the weight of her head seemed to overbalance her body, causing her to fall onto her butt.

In the next moment, Pixel floated up out of her grasp. The FAST's health bar was yellow in color and they seemed to be dripping wet for some reason, but otherwise they appeared functional.

Boog, on the other hand, continued to merely sit there with a dazed look upon her face.

My HUD was quick to fill me in on the details. In addition to being Fatigued, she'd picked up a new debuff: *Overdosed: severity level 2.*

There was no time to listen to Drega's overblown explanation, so I skimmed to the important parts and tuned out the rest. Sure enough, she'd managed to use the game's mechanics in her favor, but not without suffering the consequences.

As my own stomach had hinted, there was a limit to how

many potions one could guzzle within a short span without suffering any ill effects.

According to the description, the limit was based on a chaser's constitution – one potion per minute for every 30 points of CON a chaser possessed. With most of us hovering around the 150 point mark, that was a threshold we hadn't come close to hitting, at least before now.

The problem was twofold. Not only were we facing an enemy unlike any we'd faced prior to this, but Boog was in her mutated smart form, meaning her constitution was barely a third of what it was normally.

Her rapid consumption of heals had saved her and Pixel, but had also inadvertently blown way past her personal limit. There simply had been no choice in the matter.

All of that said, a one-minute nausea debuff was imposed upon the victim at severity level one. Guess that explained why Pixel was all wet.

Ewww.

Reaching severity level two, however, involved doubling the number of potions to reach that first level – meaning Boog kept downing them even as she was barfing all over Pixel.

Amusing as that might've been in any other situation, the penalties in this case were more severe. In addition to nausea, she was now stunned for thirty seconds – leaving her unable to run, attack, or use spells. More importantly, if she ingested any more potions within the next thirty minutes, she had a fifty percent chance of becoming *poisoned*.

That wasn't good, not at all. We'd managed to injure Wan, but nothing that put us anywhere within reach of ending this battle. And now she was stuck there, a sitting duck.

I had no way of knowing how long Wan would remain stunned, but it seemed a fair bet it wouldn't be for long. If he woke up before she did, it would be all over for her.

That settled it. I didn't think about anything else, I simply turned and raced toward my friends.

On the upside, I made it a good fifteen feet before pinwheeling my arms and winding up back on the floor.

The downside was the roar of rage that followed, shaking the throne room enough to almost make me glad I was already lying flat. Whatever momentary reprieve we'd been given was over.

Sadly, Boog's stun was not. With her unable to run or fight, she'd be...

"*Fool.*"

Okay, at least for a moment or two, as the growl that issued from Wan's throat told me I'd almost certainly managed to get his attention.

Now it was apparently my turn again, not that I could really blame the guy.

I turned my head his way just in time to see the burning hatred etched upon his wounded face.

Sadly, that wasn't the kind of burning that worried me as he let loose with another bolt of golden flame – this one no doubt intended to reduce me to nothing more than a pile of bones and smoldering ash.

77

A PARTY TO DIE FOR

I was not in a good place – lying on the floor, with no chance of dodging much less outrunning Wan's attack.

Lucky for me, this also happened to be the exact same situation I'd been hoping for just minutes earlier, before Wan had done his best to fry my friends.

Mind you, I would've felt a bit more confident back on my feet and with a still working shield, but at this point beggars couldn't be choosers.

Please let this work... Spell Hammer!

As Pixel had explained via chat before everything went to hell, Wan's ability to breathe fire counted as a magical attack – or at least so they thought. That made sense to a point. After all, it's not like breathing fire was something normally found in nature. No, that was the sort of voodoo reserved for sword and sorcery movies, and maybe *Godzilla* too, but I was willing to bet Wan had been born too early to have been the victim of nuclear fallout.

Hopefully, the FAST was right because if this didn't work then I was done for. Lacking Boog's fire resistance, I had a feeling there was zero chance of me downing health potions fast enough to survive for more than a second or two.

Either way, it was too late to back out now.

Shiiiiiit!

For one painful moment my hands began to blister and my health started dropping at a perilous rate, making me certain I'd chosen poorly. But then the flames touched the strings of my racket and immediately reversed course.

Fuck yeah!

Now I just had to hope Spell Hammer didn't fail its redirection check, mostly because every other target here was on my team.

Fate, or perhaps a member of the production crew, was apparently smiling upon me, though, as the blast of fire slammed back into the body of the boss beast.

As the attack engulfed Wan, I got a notification from my HUD that my Spell Hammer ability had risen to level two. That brought its recharge time down to eighteen hours and its failure chance down to forty percent, both welcome bits of news.

Less good, however, was the fact that Wan's health barely took a hit as he was consumed in a sea of roaring flames.

Goddamn it! I should've guessed that a dragon would be resistant to its own attacks.

Still, it was a temporary reprieve, hopefully long enough for Boog to regain her mobility.

Pixel: *You okay, Tim?*

Tim, JUST FUCKING TIM: *

Pixel: *Glad to hear it. Now let's light this fucker up! I owe him big time for all the Boog puke I'm wearing.*

That was about as much altruism as Pixel was seemingly capable of, but oddly enough I was okay with that.

I pushed myself back to my feet, or attempted to anyway. My body was suddenly moving way too sluggishly, as if it were fighting against the very idea. Maybe using Spell Hammer had a side effect I wasn't...

yawn

A wave of weariness washed over me, making me wonder if I

was perhaps still suffering the residual effects from my earlier concussion. Then a notification popped into my HUD, dispelling any such *good* news.

Debuff – You are Fatigued: severity level 4.

Crap. That wasn't good. Not only was the weariness starting to overcome whatever adrenalin was coursing through my body, but all my level one and two penalties were now doubled. I was almost done for. One more level of Fatigued and I'd drop like a fucking rock.

That meant we needed to find a way to finish this before my body simply gave out. But how?

A short ways off, Pixel fired another Acid Ball toward the towering *Wan*ferno. As much as I appreciated their effort, I didn't expect much to come of it. However, right before it reached its target, the ball of corrosive goo split apart – becoming five globs of acid that grew in size until they more than matched the original.

What the?

Still partially engulfed in flame, Wan roared in rage as the acid struck him, this time doing enough damage to be noticeable.

Pixel: *Fuck yeah! Did you see that?*

I wasn't sure what I'd just witnessed but fortunately the party menu clued me in.

Pixel's spell had once again leveled up, this time to fifth, but that wasn't the biggest news.

Spell: Acid Ball has been upgraded to Spell: Acid Barrage.

Holy Pokémon evolution, Batman! It was just like Pixel had told me. Fifth level was apparently a big one where spells were concerned.

Pixel: *Someone upstairs must like us because this shit couldn't have come at a better time.*

That was putting it mildly.

Tim, JUST FUCKING TIM: *

Pixel: *You truly have a way with words, Tim. Anyway, I was* *hoping to get it to fifth sometime early during the next stage, but I sure as hell won't say no to an early Christmas present.*

Boog: *The more I hear of this Christmas, the more I like it.*

Boog? I turned her way, only to find her finally getting back to her feet. "Are you okay?"

"The concept of *okay* is a subjective one, my mate, but I appear to once again be nominally functional."

"Then let's make it a point to keep you that way," Pixel replied. "But in order to do that, we need to hit this fucker with everything we have left. We're talking damage, more damage, and maybe hoping for a few crits along the way."

"I am forced to admit," Boog replied, looking somewhat embarrassed, "that I find myself open to suggestion in that regard."

Pixel: *Ask and ye shall receive, sister. You and me are going to keep fuckface there busy. You with your axe, while I spam his ugly ass with acid. But first I need you to use a little PSI to get Tim over to Wan's throne.*

Tim, JUST FUCKING TIM: *???*

It wasn't part of our code, but it was a *key* I could still type reliably. Good thing too, because I had no idea what Pixel was getting at. Was there some secret there I'd missed, like maybe the throne was the source of Wan's power?

Pixel: *I was getting to that. Take a look over there. Wan busted up his chair pretty good when he kaiju'd out on us. The good news is that Jade ain't exactly Styrofoam if you catch my drift. So you're gonna get your butt over there and grab as many big chunks as you can. Then, while we distract him, you're gonna feed them to this asshole until he finally drops.*

I wasn't sure I liked our odds of this plan, since Wan still had over half his health left, but it was better than anything I could currently come up with. Even if we ultimately stood no chance, I was willing to bet we could at least give Wan reason to think twice before messing with the next group of *invaders* who crossed his path.

Fuck it.

I threw them a thumbs up to let them know I was in. A moment later, I was lifted off the ground by Boog's Telekinesis. Guess there was no time like the present.

It was as if a giant invisible hand had scooped me up. It carried me past my teammates, toward the back of the shattered dais where the remains of Wan's throne lay.

It wasn't a moment too soon. In the next instant, Wan undulated his serpentine body, shaking off the last of the flames which had been covering him.

My friends were ready for that, though, slapping him with flying axe attacks and acid blobs. I wasn't sure how long they could keep it up, so I had to move quickly. Pixel might've been good to go with mana potions, but Boog couldn't risk downing any of hers. Not good because she'd probably expended more than half her available PSI pool just to move me where I needed to be. She'd need to use the rest judiciously until such time as they naturally recovered.

Not that it was a bad call on Pixel's part. Thanks to the telekinetic lift, I'd made it to the ruined platform far faster than it would've taken me to safely walk.

While they were doing their part, keeping Wan busy, I started combing through the debris for *ammo* – aiming for chunks that were between three and ten pounds in weight. My Ruination Racket might've been able to handle more, but there was no point in pressing my luck.

It was the space of less than a minute for me to shunt four sizable pieces into inventory. Good thing too because it seemed I was already sorely needed.

"Aim for his ugly mug," Pixel told Boog. "I need a second to…"

"No, Pixel of Tim Chasers. You have been given time enough. No more shall you have!"

Wan was on the move even as he spoke, shaking off the effects of their combined barrage and launching himself forward. In less than two seconds, faster than I could hope to respond, he was within striking distance of my friends, lashing out once more with that lethal tail of his.

CRACK!

Thunder echoed in the throne room as Pixel took a direct hit.

No!

The FAST went flying like a cannonball, gouging a chunk out of the wall before clattering to the floor. Pixel's normal green light began to flash ominously as their health was reduced to a tiny sliver of red.

"Pixel!"

Wan threw me the barest of glances, raising the sides of his maw-like mouth in a contemptuous grin. In that moment I understood. He'd been playing possum, letting us think we stood a chance against him, while waiting for the perfect moment to shatter that illusion in the most painful way possible.

"I've got you," Boog cried, turning and using her Telekinesis to pluck the FAST's battered body from the floor.

"I think not, thick-skulled insect."

As quickly as Boog had responded, Wan was already closing in for the kill. He plucked Pixel from the air with his teeth then lifted his head for us to see.

"Now all that remains is a fool and a follower," Wan declared as he chomped down, his massive jaws utterly erasing Pixel's already depleted health bar.

78

GLITCH IN THE MATRIX

FAST: Pixel – Undisclosed – Level 7 – XX – EXPIRED
All I could do was stand there in stunned silence, staring as Wan spat out my friend's lifeless chassis while my HUD confirmed the worst.

Pixel was gone.

It wasn't for good, I knew that much. But in that moment it was hard not to succumb to anguish at seeing my friend and partner killed. Not only that, but Pixel had been the one responsible for mostly holding things together in this final leg of Stage One, especially once I became Fatigued.

Being betrayed by the Vultures had been a kick to the gut but it was nothing compared to this. It was like watching as the light at the end of this tunnel was extinguished, leaving us with no path forward save darkness and death.

No.

I couldn't think that way. That was what Drega and the Committee wanted us to believe. They wanted us to give in to the hopelessness, for no other reason than to laugh at our fate during one of their fucking live updates.

Jeremy. I had to keep picturing his face. He needed me and I absolutely, positively could not fail him. That simply wasn't an option.

But oh god I was tired, so tired.

And this monster standing over Pixel's still sparking body was so far beyond us.

"Pissel!" Boog let out a keening wail. It was one-hundred percent despair, as if every single emotion her smart form had kept bottled up came out in one tidal wave of anguish.

Wan in return let out a cruel chuckle as he turned her way, contemptuously kicking Pixel's remains in my direction as if to remind me of my failure.

Even if Jeremy hadn't been a factor, I needed to remember I wasn't the only one still here. More importantly, bad off as I was, Boog was in even worse shape. Any attempt to heal or recharge her powers could end with her being poisoned. And that wasn't the end of it either. According to my HUD, her Fatigued severity level was now at two, having apparently *leveled up* at some point in the past few minutes.

If there was any way this could get worse, I didn't know...

I stopped myself from completing that thought. It felt like tempting fate to even go there.

Instead, I tried to take stock of anything I had in my favor – knowing I had to do something to take Wan's focus away from the last person I had left in this living Hell.

Fortunately, I'd been stocking up for that very purpose.

First things first, though. I couldn't leave Pixel just lying on the ground, not when they were only a few steps away. I wasn't sure how long it would take the FAST to revive, but I wouldn't risk leaving them behind if, by some miracle, Boog and I managed to beat Wan and gain access to that ascension ring.

That's it. Keep thinking positive. Look past this fight as if it's a given.

Heh. If that wasn't thinking outside the box for me, especially considering the last month of my life, I didn't know what was.

Time Chaser

So I took a couple of long strides, hoping that didn't set off my debuff, and scooped up Pixel before shunting them into inventory.

I'd been warned that the inventory system wasn't meant for living creatures, but the FAST was technically dead right then so hopefully it wouldn't fuck things up even worse than they were.

An achievement popped up in my HUD, but I dismissed it without hesitation. Drega's bullshit could wait.

That done, I pulled my racket back out of inventory along with the largest of the jade pieces. At this point, it was go big or go home.

Wan's back was to me, having dismissed me to focus on my teammate, leaving him wide open.

Sadly, he was still a moving target, spinning and taking a potshot at Boog with his tail.

She launched herself out of the way at the last second, using up more of her precious PSI points.

Crack!

Wan's tail slammed into the floor where she'd been, gouging heavy chunks from it.

While he was distracted, I quickly recharged my mana, not caring how long it had been since my last potion. We were now in the endgame. Nausea was the least of my worries.

I cast Crackling Cannonball on the projectile, holding my breath until the spell took hold. Then I activated Aim Assist. Much as it sucked to give up the damage, no way did I want to miss. Sure, Wan's backside was practically at point blank range for me, but I knew how these things went.

Back in the real world, I would've needed to be both blind and drunk to miss something of that size. But this wasn't my world. The rules I'd grown up with didn't apply here. There were no sure things in this game. Believing otherwise was a fool's errand.

If the rules said I had a twenty percent chance to miss, then

I needed to respect that while doing everything I could to compensate.

Again Wan lashed out at Boog, once more just barely missing. Her Telekinesis allowed her to respond with the speed of thought itself, giving her an advantage the rest of us didn't have. But it came at a cost.

I quickly checked her character sheet in my HUD and sure enough her latest dodge had nearly depleted her PSI. She might've had one more dodge action in her, but I doubted it.

So did she from the look on her face.

"Leave her alone, asshole," I shouted, hoping to split Wan's attention as I lined up my shot.

I might as well have been talking to myself. As consolation for being ignored, I dropped the chunk of jade and swung. Where a heavy piece of ammunition such as this had made me nervous with my Banshee Racket, this new Ruination Racket was far sturdier. I had few worries about the strings snapping.

Sadly, missing my target completely was the far bigger worry. A shrill whine filled the air, only for the projectile to go sailing past Wan, not even close enough for the extra spell damage to affect him.

Fuck!

The only acknowledgement I got from the beast was a quick utterance of, "*Fool*," and then his full attention was back on Boog once more.

"All right, now you're just being insulting."

I sucked down another mana potion and grabbed the next largest hunk of jade from inventory.

Boog, fortunately, wasn't standing idle either. Whatever her shock over Pixel's death, she seemed to be coming around to the fact that we'd be next unless we did something.

She flung her axe at the boss, sending it spinning through the air at the great beast, where it gouged a small divot from the dragon's side.

"You have fire, insect," Wan said, staring her down, *"but so do I. Let us see how you fare against my flames a second time."*

Oh crap. "Run, Boog! Get out of there!"

She looked around even as Wan raised his head once more. Then, having chosen a direction, she took off and ... promptly tripped and fell on her face.

⌛⌛⌛⌛ ·:·¦·§·¦¦·§·¦·:· ⌛⌛⌛⌛

Goddamned Fatigued debuff!

She was a sitting duck and Wan knew it, letting out another chuckle even as fire gathered in his mouth.

Too bad for him she wasn't the only easy target in the room.

C'mon. Don't fuck me over a second time.

I let fly with the heavy rock, sending it screaming toward the boss.

It was like the world held its collective breath as the attack raced toward him, or maybe that was just me as...

Bingo!

The hunk of jade slammed into Wan's head like a green meteorite. Not only did it slice a sliver of health off his bar, but it ruined his aim, jolting him forward even as he loosed his flame. The attack went low, hitting the floor well short of Boog, and buying her the time to skitter out of the way.

All right. That was one. Time for another before he could ... *oof!*

Wan spun, fast as lightning. In one smooth move he lashed out, grabbed me around the waist with his claws, and hoisted me fifteen feet off the ground where he glared at me with his remaining eye.

"You cease to be amusing, fool."

"That's ... okay," I choked, just barely able to draw breath. "You're still a royal pain in the ass."

I cast *Burning Beatdown*.

My racket was instantly sheathed in a corona of flame. I

knew fire didn't exactly bother this guy, but I figured every little bit counted as I raised the spiked shaft over my head and then drove it down into the clawed hand holding me.

⌛︎⌛︎⌛︎⌛︎ ⋅∗⋅∗⋅∗⋅∗⋅ ⌛︎⌛︎⌛︎⌛︎

Wan screamed in pain, music to my ears. Less good was him flinging me away like yesterday's garbage.

I tried to hold onto my racket, now stuck six inches deep in Wan's flesh. Unfortunately, my grip slipped and I once more found myself airborne before slamming into the ground, hard enough to erase nearly all the meager health I had left.

I wasted no time healing myself, trying and failing to keep count of how many potions I was up to. Hell, it was all I could do to focus on this fight. I had a feeling it was only a matter of time before Fatigued notched up to its max.

That time wasn't yet, though.

First, though, I needed to get my damned weapon back. Without it, I...

ARGH!

Much to my dismay, Wan decided to bring my racket to me instead – undulating over to where I'd landed and slamming his clawed fist down onto me.

Once more my health cratered, prompting me to quickly chug another healing potion.

Wan wasn't finished, though, not by a longshot. He plucked my racket from his skin with his other claw, drawing a trickle of blood.

"*I believe this is yours, fool.*"

I saw what was coming a mile away, but was helpless to stop it. In the next second, Wan drove the spiked tip of my racket through my midsection, impaling me to the floor. I let out a gurgled scream as it punctured my backside – pinning me like the photos in Deb's scrapbooks.

My health plummeted, forcing me to heal again. My stock

of health potions was starting to run perilously low but that wasn't the worst of it.

No, that would be the regeneration brought on by the healing as it tried to push the racket's shaft out – dislodging it just enough to hurt like a motherfucker, but not enough to free it from either my body or the rocky floor.

Needless to say, my health bar, full for maybe a second or two, immediately started ticking down again.

Wan was obviously enjoying the show. He craned his neck and threw a quick bolt of flame at Boog but it seemed more to keep her on the defensive than finish her off. He then turned back to watch as I continued bleeding out courtesy of my own weapon.

"I am curious to see how long you can keep this up. Do struggle, fool, for this is most entertaining."

I flipped him the bird, unsure if he even knew what that meant. But then it was back to the task at hand, grabbing hold of my racket and...

And screaming my head off as even the slightest bit of movement sent waves of agony coursing through my punctured organs.

I had no choice but to down yet another of my rapidly diminishing stock of potions.

Debuff – You are Overdosed: severity level 1.

Debuff – You are Nauseous.

Nice as it was to see my health rise again, it was immediately offset by me puking out what felt like a gallon of blood, nearly choking in the process.

"Ah. Now this is more like it."

Once again, the potion's regeneration had tried to free me from my impalement and once again it had failed. The weapon was stuck fast.

This was it.

I was down to my final three healing potions. That wasn't

enough to push me over into the second stage of Overdosed, but this first one was already more than I could handle.

Judging by how my health was once again dropping, I had a few minutes left at most. I could use up the rest of my heals but what for? Much as I missed my son, did I really want to prolong my suffering?

There was no point. I was done, out of options. The only thing I had left was my Amulet of Spite. It would share whatever damage I took with Wan. I doubted that would be enough to finish him but maybe it would give Boog a shot.

Speaking of having a shot...

I pulled Pixel back out of inventory, setting their still sparking body down next to me. It probably wouldn't make much of a difference in the end, but at least I could die knowing Boog might have a chance of picking the FAST up before escaping.

That was something – one tiny bit of hope as my life flickered out for good. There were worse ways to die.

With any luck, I'd be dead when they finally shunted me back to that bus. At least that way there would be no pain. Although, knowing my luck, it was probably best not to count on that.

I turned my focus toward my health bar, watching as it once again ticked down into the red zone. This time I let it go with no intention of stopping it.

Little by little my vision began to grow dark around the edges. I turned my head a bit, not wanting Wan's ugly mug to be the last thing I saw. Instead, I tried to picture Jeremy's face.

Yeah. That was a good memory to hold onto as I...

Nadok: *Shall I assume, chaser, that you no longer have any interest in the assistance I have offered?*

Huh?

79

CHEATER, CHEATER

That Nadok clown was back. But why, and more importantly why *now* of all times?

Tim, JUST FUCKING TIM: L...ave m... ...lone.

Nadok: *Take a deep breath and focus, chaser. The penalties for debuffs tend to be relaxed the closer one's lifeforce is to being extinguished. The overmind has found that such things can add a bit of unexpected drama to the proceedings. I suggest you use that to your advantage.*

Take a deep breath? Did this moron not realize I was currently impaled?

Tim, JUST FUCKING TIM: *I ... sa..d, leave me ... wait. I can type again!*

Nadok: *As I just informed you, chaser. Now, I would suggest we dispense with the pleasantries as your time grows increasingly short.*

Tim, JUST FUCKING TIM: *Pleasantries? Fine. What do you want? Or are you here to throw more nonsense words at me before I die?*

Nadok: *Nonsense words? I did no such thing, chaser. What I did was give you the answer you had been seeking, the very key to changing destiny itself.*

Tim, JUST FUCKING TIM: *Okay, now you've lost me. What the fuck are you talking about?*

There wasn't time for this garbage. My HUD was currently blinking an angry red again. I was almost tempted to hang up on this asshole and check on my injuries instead. Too bad I had a feeling that would do nothing but depress me in my final seconds.

All I'd wanted was a peaceful death with Jeremy's face in my mind's eye, but instead I was dealing with this bullshit.

Nadok: *Penark Queeg, of course.*

Tim, JUST FUCKING TIM: *All right, enough of this shit. Listen up, whoever you think you are. I don't know what stupid boogeyman agenda you're following and honestly I don't care. Hell, for all I know, you're just some production assistant trying to stir up ratings.*

Nadok: *I can assure you, chaser, I am not.*

Tim, JUST FUCKING TIM: *And I suppose I should just take your word for it, huh? Hard pass. Besides, in case you hadn't noticed, I'm busy dying here. No offense, but that doesn't leave me many options when it comes to changing destiny. Now, if you'll excuse me, I'd like to envision my son's face one more time before the end.*

Nadok: *It's not your son you should be worried about, chaser, but his sons, and their sons, and so forth.*

Tim, JUST FUCKING TIM: *Seriously, what the fuck does that even mean?*

Nadok: *I am quite obviously speaking of the year 2541. I was led to believe you had a vested interest in the events of that time period.*

2541? What the hell was this guy talking about?

That's when I remembered its significance. That was the year it supposedly all ended for humanity. But why bring it up now?

I mean, sure, I'd been curious as to what was going to happen, had even bugged the shit out of Pixel about it, but I'm not sure that counted as a vested interest. I responded to Nadok telling them as much.

Nadok: *Quite the contrary in fact. Of all the chasers present, only two have shown any concern at all for humanity's inglorious end. And since the other came here already fully cognizant of this fact, that makes you unique. Ten thousand chasers, but only one who has dared to look beyond their current situation. That is why I have imparted upon you this precious information.*

I had no idea how to make sense out of that word salad. And goddamn, why did it seem to be taking so long for me to fucking die? You'd think Wan would be tired of waiting by now and would've simply decided to step on me like a bug and be done with it.

Maybe this cortexing thing fucked with my perception of time or something. Whatever the case, this dipshit had picked the wrong time to butt-dial me again.

Tim, JUST FUCKING TIM: *And why exactly should I care about this so-called* precious information*?*

Nadok: *Because I believe it is possible to change these events. More importantly, I believe doing so could conceivably have a ripple effect that could reach far beyond your small corner of the space-time continuum. Alas, that is all you need concern yourself with, for now anyway.*

Tim, JUST FUCKING TIM: *Fine, be that way. Even assuming any of this shit makes sense, which it doesn't, we're still talking the year 2541. That's five hundred years in my future. How the fuck am I supposed to do anything that could affect that?*

Nadok: *The answer should be quite obvious, chaser. You are in a void between dimensions, chosen for a competition that has and will continue to routinely violate the laws of time and space. All you need do is be mindful of the game's mechanics, including those that have yet to be introduced.*

Ask a stupid question...

Tim, JUST FUCKING TIM: *In case you hadn't noticed,*

jackass, the only thing I'm busy being mindful of is the fact that I'm dying.

Nadok: *A mere hurdle upon a long road. Your survival is likewise contingent on those same game mechanics. You simply need to utilize them to your advantage.*

Tim, JUST FUCKING TIM: *And how, pray tell, would I do that?*

Nadok: *By remembering a phrase I believe you are already familiar with.* Think outside the box.

Tim, JUST FUCKING TIM: *Wait. How would you even know that?*

Nadok: *How does one know anything, chaser? Observation, of course. Now, we can either continue this discourse until you expire or you can set those wheels in motion. The choice is yours.*

Tim, JUST FUCKING TIM: *Again, how?*

My health bar or lack thereof caught my eye before Nadok could answer me, the frantic red blinking informing me I had one tick left and then that was it.

Shit!

Despite having accepted my fate, I chugged another health potion – filling my health again, only to taste bloody, mint-flavored vomit mere moments later. The potion had come back up again as quickly as it had gone down, causing me to cough it all out lest I choke.

Regardless, it bought me at least another minute.

"*Such will to live from a fool,*" Wan growled from above me, seemingly enjoying the show as Boog took another ineffective whack at his massive form with her axe. "*It would almost be worthy of respect if not for its futility.*"

Fucking asshole.

Tim, JUST FUCKING TIM: *Al..ight, N...dok, h...w?*

I guess by healing I'd inadvertently reengaged those debuffs. Regardless, I waited for a response as my health continued to trickle down once more.

Tim, JUST FUCKING TIM: *H...llo?*

Time Chaser

And just like that, the fucker was gone again. All I'd been left with were two clues – think outside the box and use the game's mechanics. No offense to Nadok, whoever the fuck they were, but things like that were so much easier to figure out when my guts weren't being punctured by my own fucking weapon. I...

"Macmac, you need to get out of there!"

How? I was skewered fast, like a bug on a...

An odd sizzling sound caught my ear. With nothing better to do, I craned my neck to try and take a look.

The fuck?

A part of me was sure I must be hallucinating in these final moments as I watched a heavy glob of molten rock rise up into the air from the still liquified remains of that Granite Guardian. The steaming blob hovered there for a moment, then shot upward ... right into Wan's face.

"ARGHHHHH!!"

Holy shit!

But how...?

That became obvious a scant moment later, thanks to the retching sound that followed as well as my HUD informing me that Boog was now *Poisoned*.

She must've downed one of her PSI potions in a desperate bid to save me. Sadly, in doing so, she'd poisoned herself. I turned my head to find her on her knees coughing as her own health bar trickled down.

Above me, Wan roared in rage, desperately clawing at the burning lava covering his face. Guess even his fire resistance had limits. His health dropped a bit in response, albeit not nearly enough.

"M...move, Macmac. Puh-please!"

Sound advice as dripping hunks of lava began to rain down from above, sizzling wherever they hit the floor. Too bad there wasn't much I could do about it stuck fast as I was. All I could do was accept my fate with grace and...

No!

I couldn't just give up, not now. Boog had done the unthinkable. She'd sacrificed her own health to give me another chance, hitting Wan with a crazy attack that was the epitome of thinking outside the box.

Could I truly do any less?

Knowing it was likely fruitless, I called up my inventory and started desperately scrolling through it for something, *anything*, I could use to...

Wait ... my inventory!

But would that even work?

Fuck it, there was only one way to find out. I grabbed hold of my racket, still perforating my guts, and focused on it.

A moment later it disappeared, shunted into inventory and leaving me free to ... mostly bleed out.

Gah!

The pain was nearly as bad as when I'd first gotten stabbed, except now there was nothing to keep my innards from spilling out onto the floor around me.

I reached back into inventory, prepared to use one of my two remaining healing potions when my eyes fell upon another of my equipped items.

Goddamn, I am such an idiot.

Now to hope it didn't count toward making me even more Overdosed.

I activated my scroll of *Party On*.

A litany of strange words and phrases, nearly unintelligible, echoed through my brain like a stereo with the volume turned to eleven, and then...

Fuuuuuuuck!

For a second or two, I got to experience the *wondrous* sensation of my wounds knitting themselves shut. When it was all finished, though, my health was back to full and no longer falling.

Yes!

Better yet, Party On was a mass healing spell. I sat up to find Boog had been crawling her way slowly toward me as Wan continued to scream and claw at his face. She must've gotten within range just as I'd cast it. Her health was now replenished, although she was still poisoned – meaning it immediately started ticking down again, albeit at a much slower rate than mine had done while impaled. It would have to be enough for...

"Zzzzttttt..."

What the...?

I glanced over toward where the muffled crackling noise had come from, only for my eyes to open wide as saucers. Pixel was still a mess but the damage to their body appeared considerably less than it had been just moments earlier.

More importantly, the word *Expired* in their status was now flashing on and off. Thinking quickly, I pulled a health potion from inventory – leaving me with only one – and dumped it out onto the FAST.

Nothing changed, though. Maybe it was because the scroll was second level with a more powerful heal, or perhaps Pixel needed to come the rest of the way back on their own.

Whatever the case, I couldn't sit there and wait for it.

I grabbed the FAST, stood up, and began slowly making my way toward Boog. Nearby, far too close for comfort, Wan slammed into the wall, still trying to scrape the rapidly solidifying rock from his face.

We had mere moments before he came after us again. To do what, I wasn't sure, but maybe saying goodbye was enough.

"Are you okay, Boog?"

She managed to clamber to her feet with some help, looking way too green around the gills for my liking. "I wuh...will be, Macmac. Although, if you would be so kind as to spare an antivenom potion, perhaps I can..."

"Let's save that until we have no other choice," I warned, reminding her that, so long as she remained Overdosed, antivenom had a fifty-fifty shot of becoming poison itself.

She didn't look happy about that but nodded her agreement.

"By the way, thanks for the save back there," I told her. "That was a hell of a move."

"Anything for you, my mate," she replied, as we slowly put some distance between ourselves and Wan.

I wasn't sure why we even bothered. We'd managed to save our butts with a little quick thinking but all we'd done was delay the inevitable.

"What do we do now?" she asked.

Hopefully that was a rhetorical question because I didn't have an answer. Instead, I steered us toward where the ascension ring stood. Maybe it was the fatigue but I found its light comforting. Even if we couldn't step through and save ourselves, meeting our end knowing we'd reached it still felt like poetic justice.

Not to mention it would probably make for a super dramatic highlight during the next live update. One last curtain call to mark our...

"Uhh ... wuh...wha...?"

I looked down upon hearing the faint sound of Pixel's voice. The FAST was still banged up, but little by little bits of green light were beginning to become visible along their surface.

Likewise, *Expired* was now blinking much more slowly, turning off for seconds at a time before reappearing. There was no doubt to be had. Pixel was snapping out of it.

That was good. At least this way we'd all be together at the end.

"Wuh-what's ... happening?" the FAST croaked, sounding all tinny and staticky.

"I have you, buddy."

"W-where?"

"Yuh-you are with us, my friend," Boog said as we neared the ring. "As you should be."

Its light wasn't warm or anything, but being this close to it made me feel a bit better nonetheless.

Time Chaser

"*LOATHSOME INSECTS!*"

That was good, because I had a feeling we were all about to feel a hell of a lot worse.

"R...ring?" Pixel crackled. "A-ascension ring? Nuh-no! Can't. Boss fight. W-we'll be ... penalized."

"I know," I said to them. "I..."

All at once, Nadok's words repeated themselves in my mind.

Your survival is likewise contingent on those same game mechanics. You simply need to utilize them to your advantage.

To my advantage?

Think outside the box.

This was a boss fight, and the resulting penalty if we dared try to run was... Holy shit! That was it! But again, the question was whether it would work or ultimately screw us in the end.

Halfway across the throne room from us, Wan scraped the last of the molten rock off his scarred and pitted face – the once regal scales adorning it now charred and melted. He let out a roar of rage then opened his mouth wide, golden flames once more gathering at the back of his throat.

Fuck it. There was only one way to find out, and it's not like we had much to lose.

With Pixel still in one hand, I grabbed hold of Boog's arm with the other.

"Thank you, my mate. Dying alongside you shall be..."

"Fuck that noise," I interrupted. "I want to live to see tomorrow. How about you?"

"Yes, but..."

"Good. Then you're coming with me. Both of you are."

As the air around us heated up from the incoming blast, I turned and leapt into the ring's light, dragging my two companions in my wake toward whatever fate awaited us inside.

80

THE TIRED-ASS EPILOGUE

STAGE ONE EXPIRATION: 21 HOURS, 39 MINUTES

WARNING! YOU HAVE BEEN PENALIZED UNTIL THE END OF THIS STAGE!

The dire message within my HUD was quickly followed by: *CONGRATULATIONS, YOU HAVE SUCCESSFULLY ASCENDED!*

Then...

Penalty Negated.

Holy crap, it had worked. It had actually worked!

As if acknowledging our win, another achievement flashed in my HUD, but I ignored it. Drega could wait.

"We made it, Boog."

"Yes, I ... can see that, my mate, but how?"

"Y-yeah," Pixel crackled still in my grasp. "How?"

Rather than explain, I took a moment to catch my breath. There would hopefully be plenty of time now that we were safe.

The three of us appeared to be in a campground, although it was unlike the others I'd seen. There were no walls around us, just a large clearing full of tents surrounded by forest on all sides.

The only giveaway that this wasn't a normal Earth campground were the massive projection screens hovering in the air at regular intervals, all of them displaying scenes from the Chase. I had no idea whether it was a live feed or merely highlights, and quite frankly right at that moment I didn't care either way.

More important was the fact that this place appeared much smaller than I expected it to be, with relatively few chasers milling around. Forget the nearly six-thousand survivors we'd been told about, I could barely make out six dozen. Had Drega lied to us about the number of...?

You have been assigned to the Campground of Incalculable Suffering, Heartache, and Pain.

"The campground of what now?" I replied in response to this new notification from my HUD.

Almost as if answering my question, the air in front of us shimmered followed by a familiar hulking form suddenly appearing.

"Virto!"

The guild master stared at the three of us, astonishment etched on his reptilian face, for a moment anyway before being replaced by a big grin.

"TJFT? Holy shit, you actually managed to pop your Stage One cherry? Well, call me a flekn'oh and smack my pod-mother. No offense, kid, but of all the plongos I expected to see here, you are by far the biggest surprise."

"None taken," I replied, more than a little confused. "So ... what's going on here? I thought the space between stages was..."

"One giant cattle pen to hold all you Earthers?" he finished. "Yeah, that's how it was originally supposed to be. This here is a last minute change by order of the overmind. Go figure, but it seems you Earth slugs can't get along with each other for shit. Even with campground rules in effect, there's been no shortage of insults, slap fights, chasers setting each other's tents on fire, crap like that."

"That ... actually doesn't surprise me very much."

"Tell me about it," he said with a heavy sigh. "Now, normally nobody would care, but it was becoming a distraction.

Seems the audience was starting to focus more on the out-of-game drama than what was going on in the field. So, the Committee made an executive decision to separate you all by guild, meaning it's now on me to bust your ass if you step out of line. But hey, what's a little unpaid overtime?"

I considered this for a moment before raising my eyebrow and gesturing Boog's way.

"Relax, TJFT. They don't like to break up parties, at least not this early. I just listed her as your plus one." He turned toward Boog and gave her an appreciative glance. "But that also means the same rules apply to you. No starting trouble, otherwise I may have to swat that sweet little behind of yours."

"I would highly prefer you refrained," she replied.

Virto shrugged before throwing a dismissive nod Pixel's way. "Hey, speck, glad to see you made it too." The pleasantries finished, he then got to the meat of the matter. "All right, so here's how this works. Normal campground rules apply. That means no PVP. Doubly so since we're talking about your guildmates. All lethal debuffs, curses, mutations, et cetera, aka anything that would result in your deaths are hereby expunged from your character sheets. Likewise, all penalties have been reset, but I'm guessing you already figured that one out."

He smirked knowingly but didn't say anything further on our *solution* to that unwinnable boss fight.

"Anyway, consider that your reward for completing Stage One. Aside from that, all other status effects, buffs, and debuffs continue to function normally. So deal with that shit as you will."

"Wait, is that it?" I asked.

That seemed pretty lame for all we'd been through, basically *congratulations, you didn't die*. Hell, far as I could tell we hadn't even gotten any experience from our battle with Wan either. Sure, we ended up running from that battle, but you'd think there'd be something for all we'd done beforehand. Bunch of XP cheapskates if you asked me.

"You looking for a medal or a monument?" Virto replied. "This was just Stage One, kid. You survive a cake walk, you get shitty cake in return. That's how it works."

I wasn't sure I'd call it a cake walk but I had no strength left to argue so I merely shrugged.

"Any other questions?" Virto continued. "No? Good. Then I'm gonna shunt my ass back to the playing field because there's plenty of chasers still out there. As for the rest, help yourself to any food and drink, check out the live feed if you want to scope out the competition, but otherwise make it a point to stay out of trouble. Understood?"

I nodded.

"That's what I like to hear. Hells yeah!"

One shimmer of the air later and Virto disappeared again, leaving us to head into the campground proper.

"So, back to what we were talking about earlier," Pixel said, floating free of my grasp. They weren't quite back to full yet, but I was happy to see their resurrection well underway. "How'd you know that would work? I mean, getting us out of there unpenalized while Wan was still kicking our asses?"

I debated telling them the whole story, about how Nadok had once again reached out, followed by me slowly putting two and two together. But then I remembered such things were best not said aloud. Besides, that could wait for later when I was able to properly chat again. For now we were safe. That was what mattered.

"It just hit me in those final moments," I said as we passed the first row of tents, all of them with their flaps closed. "Running from a boss battle is an instant penalty until the end of a stage. The thing is, we were literally already at the end of the stage, so what did it really matter?" I shrugged. "I guess you could say I thought outside the box."

"More like exploited a loophole," the FAST replied. "One I have a feeling they're not gonna let us get away with twice."

"Probably, but that's a worry for another day."

"Indeed it is," Boog replied. "An excellent deduction nevertheless, my mate."

"That's an understatement," Pixel said, flitting in front of me. "Look at you, figuring shit out."

"And with only an 80 intelligence no less," I replied.

The FAST let out a laugh. "What's that phrase from your world? It's not the size that matters, it's how you use it."

"I don't think that's quite the context it's meant for but I'll take the compliment anyway."

"All right, so what now?" Pixel asked as we came upon the next row of tents. "You two want to eat? Maybe we can check out that live feed, see what sort of sad sacks are still out there."

"The only sack I'm interested in," I replied, spying a trio of unoccupied tents, "is the one I'm about to hit. We can figure out the rest later."

"I concur, Macmac," Boog said, suddenly sounding as tired as I felt. Big surprise. She was still Fatigued and Overdosed, not to mention under the effect of both a curse and a mutation. But at least her life was no longer in any danger. None of ours were. "I will sleep well knowing my friends are near."

"Fuck it," Pixel said, slowly floating over to the third tent. "It's gonna take at least another half hour before all these glitches work their way out of my subsystems. I might as well enjoy a little non-forced shutdown until then."

I stepped to my own tent but then paused before entering. "We did it, all of us."

"We did, didn't we," Pixel replied. "The question is, can we do it again?"

I took a moment to picture Jeremy's smiling face, finding it more motivating than ever. "I honestly don't know, but I'm willing to try if you are."

"Every stage finished is another stage closer to being free. So I guess what I'm saying, Tim, is you can count on me."

"Me too, my mate."

"Well then," I replied, "let's get some well-earned sleep then see what tomorrow brings."

With that, I stepped into my tent, closed the flap behind me, and approached the bed inside. Oddly enough, despite the interior once again reminding me of the motel room that had become my home back on Earth, it didn't bother me. If anything, it simply made me feel like I was one step closer to getting back to my boy.

That was a thought worth holding onto, at least until curiosity got the better of me and I decided to check out my new achievements, including the one that had popped up just as we'd arrived here.

Achievement unlocked! Snoozefest!

I couldn't help but chuckle. However, before Drega could read either the description or reward, my HUD began to glitch out, displaying one last notification before it turned off entirely.

Debuff – You are Fatigued: severity level 5.

Heh. If that wasn't perfect *timing* then I didn't know what was.

With that thought I collapsed, falling into a merciful and much welcomed darkness before my head even hit the pillow.

THE END

Tim, Pixel, & Boog will return...

If you liked this book, want to stay up to date on new releases, and would enjoy some free stories from each of my main series, then please consider joining my newsletter at: https://rickgualtieri.com/newsletter/.

R. GUALTIERI

TIME CHASER

Time is NOT on his side

AUTHOR'S NOTE

Finally! After years of people asking if I was ever going to write a LitRPG book, I've gone and done it.

You would think it would be a natural fit for me, after all, my *Tome of Bill* series is effectively reverse-LitRPG, if you will, involving a tale of a gamer who discovers monsters exist in the *real world*.

Obviously, a lot of that series comes from the heart, being a gamer myself, so why did it take me so long to turn my attention toward a genre that should come to me as easily as rolling up my next character.

The answer, ultimately, isn't a particularly complex one. Before Time Chaser I simply didn't have a story idea I liked. That's the way I've always written. I don't *chase* genres for the sake of writing in them. I write when inspiration strikes, and before this current year that inspiration simply wasn't there.

In truth, *Bill The Vampire* almost started life as a LitRPG tale before I switched gears and decided it made better sense if it were set in his version of the real world instead. But aside from that, I've toyed with a few ideas but never found one I liked enough to pursue.

That all changed once I read Matt Dinniman's excellent

Author's Note

Dungeon Crawler Carl books, because not only are they great reads but I found within them a take on the genre I hadn't seen before. Better yet, it purposely eschewed a few of the genre's tropes I wasn't particularly fond of, focusing instead on telling a compelling, yet brutal story of survival.

Won't lie, there's elements of Time Chaser that are a direct homage to Matt's stories. However, whereas there are certainly familiar story structure ideas to be found between the two, my goal with Time Chaser was to have it go in its own unique direction. Hopefully I succeeded enough to avoid any accusations of it merely being a rip-off.

And if not, then I hope you at least found it to be an *entertaining* rip-off.

Either way, I very much enjoyed bringing Tim, Pixel, and Boog to life, as well as their interesting, if not always productive dynamic with each other.

I know Tim isn't the typical hero of a story such as this. He isn't some kick-ass warrior who the ladies fawn over. He's a beaten down guy with a boring career who's trying to survive an ugly breakup, only to end up in *way* over his head. In short, he's just the sort of underdog I personally love to write – not a wannabe caped crusader with a solution to every problem, but someone I think many of us can relate to.

Whatever the case, I hope you enjoyed Time Chaser as much as I did writing it. With any luck, we'll catch up again with Tim and his friends as they set forth to tackle the next stage of the Chase. Until then...

- Rick G

ABOUT THE AUTHOR

Rick Gualtieri lives alone in central New Jersey with only his wife, three kids, and countless pets to both keep him company and constantly plot against him. When he's not busy monkey-clicking words, he can typically be found jealously guarding his collection of vintage Transformers from all who would seek to defile them.

Defilers beware!

Also by Rick Gualtieri
THE TOME OF BILL
Bill the Vampire
Scary Dead Things
The Mourning Woods
Holier Than Thou
Sunset Strip
Goddamned Freaky Monsters
Half A Prayer
The Wicked Dead
Shining Fury
The Last Coven

BILL OF THE DEAD
Strange Days
Everyday Horrors
Carnage À Trois
The Liching Hour

FALSE ICONS
Second String Savior
Wannabe Wizard
Halfhearted Hunter
Deviant Dark Dryads

HIGH MOON
The Girl Who Punches Werewolves
The Girl Who Fights Witches
The Girl Who Hunts Fairies
The Girl Who Defies Fate

Made in the USA
Middletown, DE
05 February 2025